'The Wrong Life'

by

August Smith

Copyright © 2015 August Smith

KINDLE Edition

All rights reserved, including the right to reproduce this book, or portions thereof in any form. No part of this text may be reproduced, transmitted, downloaded, decompiled, reverse engineered, or stored, in any form or introduced into any information storage and retrieval system, in any form or by any means, whether electronic or mechanical without the express written permission of the author.

This is a work of fiction. Names and characters are the product of the author's imagination and any resemblance to actual persons, living or dead, is entirely coincidental.

PublishNation, London

www.publishnation.co.uk

CHAPTER ONE

Wren listened but no words came from her newly stolen mother. She strained with anxious curiosity hoping to catch the sound of her mother's voice but she heard only wood-pigeons, crackling twigs and a throaty call of a cock pheasant as it took to the sky in fright.

No further clue as to this place on earth. All she knew was that it was the year 1947. She could feel her host's emotions. It was impossible not to be wrapped in the same dank climate of savage ignorance as the female whose body she had entered. That body moved. The noise of the mother's living seemed deafening at first. It had been a while since she listened to a strong heartbeat, coursing blood and the gurgling absurdity of food digestion. This body was shivering with cold, a nasty part of life that Wren had forgotten. She would have to strain to hear above the automatic systems of human life but it would become easier to listen to the voice of her host mother and those around her. It would need to. She had a lot of information to gather. Never had she thought to feel such a state of being again

Where was he?

'There are those who will stop you Wren. You cannot get away with it.'

Those parting words banged and clanged but she could not see where they came from. Silence fell with the realisation that she was now alone. Terrified. Lost.

It was warm and dark and familiar. She'd be here for nine months. Only she didn't actually know where she was. All she knew was that she had to find Allesandro. She did not know where he was either.

'If yu' tell yer dad, yer dead!' A male snarled.

'And don't forget; nobody crosses the Weighman!'

What was that? A coarse threat from a voice outside the body she was now inside of. A horrible, cruel voice accented of northern England? Maybe, but she would have to hear more.

There came a snivel then a shaking from racking sobs!

She felt anxious running up hill by the mother, short sharp breaths and the kind of lung pain that comes from frost sharpened air now tightened by shame and misery.

Hard shoes on harder concrete? Why did man have to spoil beautiful Earth with such ugly building materials? Was that the clunk of a heavy door latch, creaking hinges? Now a flood of warmth, heavy with scents of burning coal and cheap pungent soap, enclosed the senses, relaxing the shivering body but nothing came for emotional relief.

'Where've yu' been girl?' The shock of a loud voice so close.

Bullets of words shot towards her. 'For heaven's sake, late again!'

Annoyance spiked from a hard woman, sharp with internal fury.

'How many times have I told yu' not to dawdle about after school?'

Wren felt the body she was in shrink and shrivel like a salted snail.

School? This was a young girl. Oh no! It was always so much more difficult with a young mother, they had to be making so much effort on their own lives as well coping with a new-born. She would never have chosen this... but stolen things had less of a choice about them. It would have to be, the main point was to find Alessandro not to be bothered with maternal relationships. She would be off as soon as she was physically able anyway. This body she was in was innocent of the act which had just happened to it and innocent of the fact that it was pregnant.

All that would have to change.

Wren felt the cells of her being spread out and divide, thousands of new cells every second, on what seemed such an aggressive attack on the place she would call home for nine months. This body, only just starting to grow, would be the one she used to find him, to please him, to love him again as she always had. Now she was a secret to the awareness of this child mother but soon her presence would became a torment.

Loneliness saturated Wren; this nagging feeling was the opposite of why she had acted this way.

A combination of desperation and determination so common in the lovesick, oozed through her like cold porridge. Here she was, trapped in time yet hauntingly aware of timelessness.

She had taken a life that was not hers in a panic of need, now she was here, in the place another soul should be. It was like a crash, a blind fall, a sudden avalanche. Soaked in a jumble of fear, longing and strategy she tried to work out her physical being. She had only just started to grow the temporary outfit of flesh. Another's flesh.

How had they thought she could be without him? Waiting? No way! They had told her it was best to stay this time but she was crushingly miserable. They would not grant her a life to be with him. It was all about free will wasn't it?

Even this.

Especially this.

Well it was too late now anyway.

Spurt and it was done. It was so sudden. Had she not wandered in her misery onto that loving group of spirits who were saying goodbye to one of their cluster who was about to enter the energy for a life they had chosen and prepared for, she would never have done this. Why did they look so furtively at her? Why did she think she heard his name whispered so secretly? It seemed too tempting when the departing spirit turned at the last moment for one last goodbye hug, leaving the energy open, not to slip into the exquisitely sensitive vibration. Now she was here, in another's place. She had stolen this life she had just begun all hidden and secret even from the mother. This one felt young and lost in angst.

Those hormones are …what? Yes; fear. She knew it well from many lives. This conception had been a rape but not violent. No, no struggle but great fear and just bearing what had to happen in order to save someone. Not herself no, someone she loved?

Wren's heightened senses could be excruciating in awareness and empathy.

How she missed him!

His favourite saying was always. 'The most powerful force in the body and spirit is longing.'

Well she was longing now, longing for him to be her other half again. It had to work, didn't it?

It was a bit silly of her to barge into a life that was not hers just because it was the same time-frame as his and she thought she'd heard his name whispered. This planet looked little until you got here and then it looked enormous. He could be anywhere on Earth. Anywhere. And she was here in... where was she? Not a clue not a sniff....wait...there was a sniff coming from her host mother and a shiver. Yes cold. Just her luck to be in a cold country when Italy, Africa and anywhere near the Equator had plenty of need for fresh souls to torture into another life.

She had no connection with anyone here but it was up to the soul to find the best and most gracious way of dealing with others. Only Wren wouldn't be taking part in any of it; this wasn't her life. It wouldn't suit her high spirit. It wasn't hers. She'd have to live it differently.

For her, it was the wrong life.

CHAPTER TWO

Oh! The smell of food; the harsh voiced woman could cook. Nice; something to look forward to after all that milk sucking and toothless tasting. It was awful feeling that human desire to eat all the time. In all her lives, Wren could not wait until her teeth pushed through with agonizing certainty. Wailing, biting down on hard hot gums and red cheeked agony was always slowly rewarded with tastes savoury and sweet. She hoped the time zoomed until her taste buds remembered this kind of human blessing. Food! Food! Food!

'Look sharp girl!'

That was the voice outside the host body. The accent was northern too, a soft roundness of words that went up in pitch at the end of a sentence. It was abrupt and irritated.

The pervading aroma of cooking comforted but that was all. What was missing here was a welcome feeling of love. She felt a swell in her mother's chest and a hope that the tears wouldn't rise up to her eyes to betray her.

Wren still hadn't heard the voice of her mother but the word 'school' had frightened her. These were austere times, not good for unmarried mothers but life was valued yet mysterious.

If only they all knew that life is a bubble. You enter it forgetting how much else there is out there. But not Wren.

The host mother's shivering had been soothed by the fire which Wren felt glow right through to her.

'Whatever is wrong with you girl? Get on! Eat y'tea! Quick, and then I need help!'

Wren heard the scrape of a chair against stone and felt her mother sit down. Still no words had been uttered. Hot liquid filled the stomach but no food entered.

'Where's your appetite? Gone to the cat with yer tongue no doubt. Well get a move on, Useless! Dad will be home in a minute and the bath water isn't even warm yet.'

Her host breathed too shallow, unable to think and further hammered by words

There was the same heavy metal clunk of a door catch and then a cheery, 'Yoo hoo!'

'Ivy! I'm home!'

'Tot, thank God, I hate that filthy mine.' The stern voice had softened.

Wren felt a flood of pleasure and then anxiety as her mother rushed towards the male voice.

There was a rapid scattering of little toe nails and a stoop to pick up something warm, Wren sensed an animal of great emotion, a little dog? Yes, licking and the perfume of dog hair. Her host laughed, joy and love dissolving only the edge of murky misery.

'Oh oh; the second wet welcome of a thousand kisses.' A warm deep voice oozing with cheerful love. 'Jan was waitin' again at the pit head for me. They told me Fox Terriers were loyal when I got her but by Jove that 'ns got something special and her not even a year old yet!'

There was an intense long forgotten smell, a kissing sound then. 'Eee mind, watch your cardigan pet, 'am all black with pit muck. Good job I spit-licked the end of me nose clean or I wouldn't be gettin' that kiss I've been waiting all shift for.'

Here was love, not only fatherly but deep spiritual love.

There still hadn't been a sound uttered from the person Wren was now inside but she felt a start of a giggle which faded before the pleasure could increase. There was sadness weighing down on everything else but it was hidden from this man.

Wren was lulled by intense activity; lifting, then a metal clattering and much bending.

There was the searing heat of an open fire and repeated splashing of water.

'Dad! The bath's full. Howay, it's not ower hot anyway.' She could not say more past the fist in her throat.

Wren caught the words and held them. The voice was so young, a child of tenderness and caring and yet an urgency of pain that was being held in check with great courage.

'All right, all right am coming man, me tea's nearly finished.'

Wren heard the thunk of a heavy mug as it hit the scrubbed surface of a table.

The scrape of the chair was heavier and that smell again, sweet, damp muck. It was coal dust mixed with honest sweat.

'Give us a shout the second you've finished mind Dad, it's cold in that bedroom.'

'Bring some towels to warm on the range lass!' the sharp voice shot from further away.

There was a rush, another metal door sneck, a hit of cold air and then a bending to hear a drawer unwillingly dragged open. Towels found, the warmth returned to and then was left. Wren felt the girl's body get into bed and the shock of cold sheets which made the skin shrink. She knew the shivering would subside as the air around the body warmed. But it was fear not warmth that wrapped itself around this immature young female.

It seemed that it was winter in the North east of England and she had entered the womb of a schoolgirl of a mining family. This wasn't a town but somewhere near woods. In the other room, faint sounds of bathing could be heard and them some protesting giggling. This seemed like a tight family unit even with the barely hidden resentment oozing from the mother of the girl, but it wasn't the only deep sadness in her host's body. Wren couldn't give too much thought to another soul's problems, she had a big enough load as it was, and a deep sadness of her own.

She yearned for the soul she sought but all it brought her were memories of the first and most violent of their lives together.

It had been early for Earth; few souls had wanted to come as the struggle for survival was intense. She had been a female who had got through twelve years of starvation and feasts as the only living child of a small group of gatherers. The feared ones, the killers who lived in caves and branch shelters and kept wild pigs tied to stakes to drink their blood, had stumbled over her weak, defenceless group as they had slept, worn down by their search to end winter starvation with the fish river. The stinking hairy men had killed three males and two old ladies of thirty but had been fascinated by the pubescent hips and swelling breasts of the young female. Her stench had a strange effect on them as they dragged her back to the fly infested cave.

She had been tied by the neck with twisted stems and glared at as the killers roasted and ate the only other living souls she had seen. The meat smelled good to her starving senses and as scowling faces, glistening with the juices of her family, came near to offer her a torn lump of flesh she tried to grab it. It was snatched away and laughter tore into her ears as she was teased. Again the meat was offered and her hunger made her lunge forward onto her knees. As she stuffed and sucked the meat she felt rough hands grab her from behind. Searing pain, as she was poked with something repeatedly, only momentarily stopped her from swallowing. Fourteen men came into her view with poor scraps from their own feast which they offered before leaving her view to grab and poke crudely before shuddering from behind. It hurt and the rough grabbing and grunting seared her senses but it did not matter. She was fed.

Only one of their tribe, a bigger man cradling a new born in his arms, stayed where he was at the darkest part of the cave. He did not eat but she saw, when the fire flickered with spitting fat that he watched. He had a light in his eyes that the others lacked. She did not recognize that his face was drawn with grief but next morning when the men had poked her again she was led out into the spring sunshine to see him covering the body of a young female with rocks before wailing his agony to the sky.

She saw another cave, smaller and less sheltered, from where heavy faced females brought well sucked bones of her tribe to pile on top of other bones. They stopped when they saw her then stared and spat on her, disgusted with her wet, glistening female parts and thighs.

They were ordered to make a small branch covering which they did with resentment and sly glances at the nubile form who took their men from them. After she was tied, still by the neck in the shelter, she was left alone all day until nightfall when the morsels were offered to her by the males before they went behind her as she ate.

She saw the sad man twice a day as he passed the opening to take the infant to a female with pendulous breasts and a small baby of her own. He never hunted but his hands were stained with the coloured earths and plant juices he used to paint life onto the cave walls. She waited every night to see him as he took the baby back in his arms to the male cave, longing for those soft eyes to fall on her even once.

The tether round her neck stretched a little each day and frayed with the strain of the men as they jerked her about. Just before dawn on the day she would have been there two round moons, she woke to find the twisted stems so weak than she could pull herself free. Shocked with her freedom she sat a while before realising she could run. No one was around so she crept then darted towards the thunder of the river which had tempted her and her long ago eaten tribe to this place. The water frightened her but she drank greedily and realized it tasted the same as the drink which the men left in the stone with the dent in beside her every night, if she drank before the women spat into it. As she splashed away some of her filth four stinking hands coarsely lifted her up and hoisted her back to the shelter. There she was hit repeatedly in the face and forced onto her stomach before one man came into the shelter with a sharpened stone and sliced at her hamstrings behind her knees so that she could never run again.

The pain left as slowly as her belly grew. She had no defence but crawling so that young men came in from hunting to slake their male cruelty inside her before they ate. The older men still fed and poked after their feasting.

She gave birth alone after one pair of cruel youths had held her legs wide apart to allow the others deeper penetration inside her enormous body. They had not been happy with her swollen state or the blood that spurted onto their proud manhood so they stamped on her arm laughing at the crack and had used their angry fists to burst her lips and blacken her eyes which had swollen shut so that when the baby had slid between her useless thighs she had not been able to see it.

Instinct had lifted on her one good arm, the scrawny infant to her bruised breasts where it suckled until morning. She was woken by the mewing of her new born and found one eye slit just enough to be able to gaze at the blood covered tiny being. The doorway darkened and she saw the man with the baby on his way back from the female cave where he had left his son to be suckled. He stared down on the terrible sight before him and a new look that she did not know was compassion, blanketed around her. She drank in the only love she had ever seen in this place. Blood was covering the hard sandy floor, it was her strength and her hope wasted.

She heard the voices of the youths who had used her face and body for their evilness the night before as they approached to rid themselves of their distracting hardness before they went out hunting for the day.

The big man held them back with one look before he put one hand to his belt of twisted lizard skin and the other tenderly to her swollen head. The sharpness of the stone arrow head as it slit her throat made the job quick. As she felt her soul leave the broken useless body, the baby was lifted tenderly from her and she saw, just before her welcome return to the light, the love that was in this man's eyes. She knew then that the one who had dispatched her from her misery was her soul mate. Only when he came to spirit a few years later with both souls of those infants, sent back by disease new to the tribe, did she know he was Alessandro and that would be the first of many incarnations in which they would help each other grow.

There was a call from the other room and Wren felt the body rise, goose pimples shot up on the mother's arms as she tidied the bed, and then subsided as she entered the kitchen. Wren was becoming attuned to the mother's thoughts and emotions so felt a strong feeling of affection as one of the other people spoke.

'Come on Chicken.' The softness of love in this man's voice sheathed her pet name in downy comfort. 'Sorry you have to go into that tiny, cold bedroom. Let me warm you up!'

'See; all clean, even me teeth.'

Her host body laughed.

'You know pet it's only the happy miners who have black teeth when they leave the coal face. It's just those miserable buggers who come home with white teeth. An' I've got plenty to be happy about with a lovely lass like your mam to come home to and a tickly little chicken like my June for a daughter. Come on; come to your Cuddly Corner.' He pulled her close with the crook of his arm. His laughter welcomed and enclosed her, soothing all but the iron core of her misery. Wren stopped short, it was the first time she had heard her host's name.

She felt giggling as the girl was tickled and lifted before being swung around in joy. Excited yapping joined the exhilarated noise of a bouncing dog. The coal smell had been replaced with a rosy carbolic pungency. Clean strength eased June's mind, lifting some of her misery until her newly forming breasts rubbed against the neck of her father.

The laughter stopped suddenly and June was returned to the floor.

'Eee pet! You're getting too big for that now.' There was fluster in the voice and a sad realisation that his daughter was becoming a woman.

'Now I'll help your mam empty the tin bath from in front of the fire while you set the table, the smell of that corned beef and tattie pie is driving me mad.'

Knives and forks went from the girl's hands to the tablecloth but her eyes kept on the strong back of her father. How she wished she could tell him about the horrible Colin. Her daddy always fixed everything; this strength was nailed into his body. Dad would know how to deal with the hurt; he always said, 'Problems were for solving not avoiding.' He told her that when he was in the pit if something needed sorting but he couldn't think how, he'd imagine it all wrapped up in brown paper and string. In his mind he'd put this problem parcel on a high shelf ready to be dealt with when he had the brain time. June wondered if she'd ever have the brain time.

Wren was woken by the gurgling of food as it was digested in the stomach above her. She realised with heaviness that she hadn't been anywhere in their joint sleep. Before, when she'd been at the beginning of the lives of her own, she'd travelled far from the womb whilst leaving the very essence of her human side behind. Was this the start of her punishment? They could snatch her back to The Light in that other consciousness humans called Heaven after what she'd done and anyway there was nothing to discuss, no plans to fine tune, no advice offered or gratefully received. How could there be? There was no idea at all in Wren what this incarnation was for and therefore how was she to achieve anything on that level?

All her energy and power would be spent on finding Alessandro in whatever form he had taken.

He could be in the depths of the rainforest or right next door. Maybe he was sucking sun-warmed mango stones in the Philippines or chewing whale blubber in the frozen north. What was it he was sent to do? Who was it for? Where was he?

She just wanted to be alive; together.

Every human she met would be scrutinised on a spiritual level and if all Wren's hard won analytical powers were with her she'd know when Alessandro appeared in his physical form. No chance would be missed, she had the power... she could feel it. That had not been lost in her act of treachery. At this moment she was alone.

There would be no relief from the wait to be born.

If she was allowed to be born.

CHAPTER THREE

June's body rose with jerky movements from her miserable dozing, making Wren take note. The heartbeat quickened as the cold tightened every muscle. Clothes were hurriedly thrown on and then there was a lull where Wren sensed awe of beauty. A scraping sound and the huffing of air quickly expelled from the body followed.

'Come on June, you haven't got time for taking frost off windows! You'll miss that bus.'

'Look mam; it's so beautiful, like leaves, feathers and ferns from heaven. Jack Frost came last night to decorate the windows and I never even noticed. This is his message to me. He is showing me that more beauty exists than I know or understand.'

Wren felt a slight awakening of June's spirit but it was chopped down.

'Well if you've got time to shiver and drivel all day I haven't, your dad's on back shift and I have no jam for his bait. I have to get to the Co-op! Come on! Breakfast!'

June was tied to this woman and her prickled atmosphere by the invisible strings of kin and clan. Where was the maternal love?

As the hard cold shoes hit the cobbled street the sharpness of the sun smoothed the tension from June's brow. The sense of being a child with the whole day to enjoy filled Wren. She longed to feel the sun again and to see the person who was to be her mother for that might give her some clue as to her own soon to be physical appearance. She would have to stay close enough not to risk any contact from the Light. It was easy for such a highly evolved soul to hover in front of this human but courage was needed this time. She knew they were alone. The right moment was essential.

There seemed no better time than now!

Wren felt the frost and the delight of cutting winter sun. The skeleton fingers of winter trees poked a shining blue sky with exquisite sharpness. It was lovely here despite the snapping of bitter cold. Round shouldered hills gave in to white sparkled woods and wore them with pride.

Humans did not realise that when they felt this sense of awe in beauty they were looking at some tiny bit of reflected heaven, just a small amount but big enough to keep them here on Earth. Never enough to make them want to return before their chosen lessons and tasks were completed though.

These sensations filled her with long forgotten emotions for her last few lifetimes had not been in the Northern European part of this planet. There was beauty on all parts of Earth, some more than others and some already spoiled forever by man. She allowed her soul to soak in the exquisiteness. But the pleasure was soon snatched from her when she took her first look at her host body. The shock stopped her dead so that June passed straight through her. The girl walked downhill pulling at her woollen hat. The knitted mittens dangling from string were unevenly hanging at the sleeves of her thick dark green coat. Perhaps it was a trick of the light; sun shining right onto something could change the perception. Wren watched the winter dulled blonde hair that stuck beneath the hat from the back. She had to keep up. In front again she took another more careful look at the child's face. The mouth was generous and puffing vapour into the morning but it was the eyes that had to be seen to be believed. Wren hadn't made a mistake about those.

June was pretty enough but different, this would make things even harder. If Wren inherited those eyes she would stand out in her life and that was the last thing she had wanted. She needed to be discreet and unremarkable, her search for Alessandro quietly taking priority over anything else. This was a big blow. She needed to be ordinary. How could she be with eyes that shone and attracted curious attention? Nobody could go un-noticed when one of their eyes was bright blue and the other bright green.

Wren went back to the womb where the division of cells was at least familiar. She felt the vibration of the stones beneath young feet and heard gurgling calls of wood pigeons but her energy was concentrated into the future. This would be harder than she thought. She was so alone.

She so needed to feel his radiance.

Wren was too lost in her own searching to pay much attention to the rest of June's day but when fear hormones flooded she was flung from her own deep needs to those of the body she was in. The steps slowed and an outside voice compounded the terror.

'Thought you'd get away with it the night, did yu'?' It was unmistakable as the despicable voice she'd first heard from her stolen place in the womb. The voice of her biological father came menacing and rough. Oh dear, she had his genes. Wren rose from her host body to assess the frightening situation from the invisibility of spirit. It was dusk, sharp with bone searing frost; the soft path of pine needles on which June had stopped led a few yards down to where a youth of about twenty three stood blocking the path. He was only the same height as June but the lumping stockiness of his body and huge hands, nicotine stained with nails bitten to the quick, promised anything but gentleness. He wore a white muffler which he was now loosening from around his prominent Adam's apple. He tossed it to the ground before the rough hands started unbuttoning his trousers.

Wren looked back at June who was shaking as short white puffs of breath left her open mouth in quick bursts of fear.

'Get into the trees freak!' he growled.

CHAPTER FOUR

'No Colin! Leave me alone!'

Wren swirled in the terror generated by June and she felt her agony deepen as the atmosphere was blackened with bullying lust. The man's dark eyes protruded furiously as they raked over the girlish body.

'Do you want the back of me hand an' all!'

June's terror gushed into a near faint, as her body swayed there was a loud, quick rustling of dried bracken growing closer as it repeated over and over again. Colin fastened his buttons and retrieved his scarf in two swift movements just as a large black dog bounded from the winter crisped woodland flora.

'Towser! HEEL BOY!'

The steam puffing dog was collared by the welcome figure of Mr Farraige who lifted his head from fastening the lead to see who had attracted his faithful friend away from him. The winter evening dropped around them. His eyes swept over June and then Colin. It was obvious to Wren that the man had sensed the fear in the air and although he wasn't sure of the details knew his protection was needed for this neighbour's child he'd known since birth.

'Cold even for November.' The words puffed from below his red nose and greying ginger moustache as he played for more time to assess just what he'd interrupted.

The silent embarrassment was palpable, lying as still and thick as autumn mist.

'Well it's time for Towser's supper. Shall I walk back with you June?'

Although he addressed his words to the girl his eyes fixed to those of Colin in a stare of male dominance that forced the younger man to walk away too quickly to be guilt free.

June fell into silent step beside the dog, too nervous to solicit conversation to the man who had her unspoken gratitude.

He turned stiffly in his bundle of clothing; lifting and re-sighting the peaked cap June knew protected his balding head. His right eye, slightly narrowed by a boxing injury in his youth watered a little with the cold.

'That lad bothering you was he?'

June was torn between the longed for relief of telling of her misery at the hands of the only human being she had ever hated and trying to laugh to indicate it to be a schoolgirl flirtation. But that wasn't true and anyway laughter was the last thing she could solicit from her shaking body. But she couldn't allow herself the luxury of the truth. Not when it could affect her dad and his job. She could just imagine him coming up from the work face to the colliery office to be told there had been too much stone in his coal tubs and it had been tipped there and then, no payment for ten tons of back break and even lower wages. It was too bad that Colin was Weighman and the one who could say if a man was paid for his sweat or not. As he so often told June; her dad's living depended on her being nice to him.

She kept her head towards the ground as if checking for icy patches.

'Who Colin? No. He just stopped to tie his shoelace.'

There was a silence that neither had the words to end and it carried them down the street to the bottom step of the half brick, half-timber ducket house the colliery rented to the Stoker family to live in.

'There you are pet; safe and sound. It's a pity that bus from the village stops so far away from Woodland Terrace. It's too dark for a young lass like you to be walking home alone. Your mam should be out seeking you.'

June managed a little forced smile as she cupped both of Towser's ears in her mitten covered hands, rubbing gently as his reward for saving her.

'It's only for a few weeks in November and December when it gets dark so soon Mr Farraige. Mam has scrubbing and the tea to see to and I'm enough bother as it is.'

Wren had been so caught up in the drama that she had stayed outside June's body far too long.

As she re-entered it was hard to shake off the images she had been silent witness to but she must. Her rule was to have no emotional tie to her host mother; she had enough worry of her own. Perhaps it was a mistake to hover around; she should stay here in the womb...and plan.

That night in bed as June covered her head with the sheets in order to save the precious heat from her breath, Wren knew there would be no sleep for her.

Time dragged and sapped her strength. It wasn't the strenuous physical growth activity of a three week old foetus which was by now the shape of a long column, the foundation of her nervous system and brain that bothered her. There was a strong feeling of apprehension marinating into her being. She knew her instinct was never wrong. Something was going to happen. Wren didn't wait long.

The contact she had dreaded flooded around her. The white- silver brilliance of a different consciousness shrank her to where she knew she belonged. She was small and backward compared to the energy that now joined her in this physical womb where she didn't belong. The wrongness of what she had done made her feel even smaller.

In her other incarnations it had always been something to look forward to, these loving coaching visits of encouragement from the source. It had made the soul feel connected and secure to know that wisdom and courage could be topped up at will. Wren knew there could only be one reason for this visit.

'Have you come to take me back?' They talked in energies a thousand times more eloquent than any inadequate language on Earth.

'Is that what you want Wren? Saving from your wrong doing?'

'I DON'T WANT SAVING. I want help!'

'What about help for the disanointed soul whose life you stole. Should I help them?'

This feeling was new to Wren instead of the infinite love always poured into her during these visits; she felt annoyance hovering around her like a fog restricting all thoughts but how to survive in this envelope of shame.

'I will make it up to them when this life is over and I return with what I want.'

'What is it that you want Wren that you should commit such an act of selfishness making a mockery of many lifetimes you have lived to leave egocentrics behind?'

'I don't expect you to understand.'

The presence of the great one grew indignant and Wren's spirit felt suitably disgraced.

'I want to be with Alessandro.'

'You were told to wait. It is within your highly evolved awareness.'

'I thought so too but I found otherwise. I cannot bear to be without him.'

For a tiny split second Wren felt the compassion she knew would be there for her but it was smothered like a maggot that might infest the whole apple if left alive.

'But if it is not in the destiny of the soul whose life you stole to meet with the personality Alessandro is becoming, what have you gained?'

'I will change that destiny.'

The spirit stayed silent but a broth of unprojected incredulity oozed to clog the space of life between them.

'You cannot do that.'

'I can try. I haven't taken any preconceptions. I have to make my own.'

'Earth is a big place with billions of souls learning lessons. How will you find him in all this? Your chances are almost zero. You would have been better off staying in spirit and learning something while he was away. That is what he thinks you are doing and so would not recognise you here in your stolen garb even if your paths did cross.'

'But I will know him, I am in him. How can I fail when it is the only reason I am here. I will give every fibre of my being both physical and spiritual.'

The feeling between them thickened.

'I will feel his radiance and the air will be purer wherever he is.'

'I cannot help you Wren, no-one can. You took this without authorisation, without love and without knowledge. What kind of life do you think you will give this body by doing such a terrible thing?'

'I will take care of this body that is now being made and make it my own without any blemishes or affect.'

'You are wrong Wren. This body will bear the stigma for all who are wise enough to know.'

A new heaviness dulled Wren even further; her punishment was to start now.

'No! No! Don't make it deformed I need all the physical strength I can get for my search. Don't hinder me. I beg you.'

'You must take the consequences of your actions Wren. You took this body and life from another. You did not check to see if it would be perfect and I can't tell you if it will be. But I know it cannot escape at least some mark of your crime.'

Memories flushed dread and hated knowledge into Wren; hard lives with deformities too grim to want again even with all the lessons learned. She didn't want that now she had humility, compassion and self-sufficiency. She'd suffered lifetimes of it in the early incarnations. Leprosy was the worst.

The Great One knew her thoughts even when she didn't project them.

'What of the companion spirits chosen and arranged by the spirit you have robbed? They know of your act Wren and they will not look kindly upon you at all. You need all the kindness you can get in the circumstances. Where will it come from?'

Wren knew there would be none so she kept silent.

'You must take the physical form of what was already designed for the life you stole. That cannot be altered. You know how you were punished for theft in one early life but I will not tell you what to expect.'

'Does that mean....'

'Yes, I will not take you back although we both know I have the power to do so. But I will be watching with interest how this never before act will unfold.'

'You will help me?'

'You put me through a terrible seven days search on Earth Wren, and yet...'

'Seven days? But I have been here three weeks.'

'Yes but...well...never mind. It is so peculiar that you chose this place. Was it premeditated?'

'No; why? What do you mean?'

'Nothing, I have said too much. Do not forget; there are two ways of entering these lives only one of them is through the female body. I am telling you no more. I will give you one hope.'

She felt the familiar compassion straining through from the spirit but it was harnessed before it could reach her then returned to the source. Cold facts filled the space.

'There may come a chance, only once, when you can retrieve at least some of the grace you have so thoughtlessly thrown away. It will be at great cost to you, painful in the extreme. It is up to you to recognise that chance and grab it. If not....'

'Remember; only once!'

'I will hope this soul's guardian spirits will be strong enough.'

'What guardian spirits? They stayed behind with the soul you robbed. They are needed more to deal with that situation than anything the soul could learn in its incarnation?'

Fear sat upon her like a newly discovered set of chains.

'I am on my own?'

'You are on your own Wren. You will look at life in a way no-one has before. Good luck. Remember, silent communication is the way to the very core of self.'

The great-spirit was gone. In its place was a new fear and hopelessness.

This was something Wren had never considered. Panic filled her energies. How could she go on? How could she live a whole incarnation without the protection and wisdom of her guardians to help her through the tortures of life?

It couldn't be done. It was hard enough with all the help and without the near impossible task of finding a soul mate who wasn't aware he was being sought. Wren was forced to think again. What she had thought possible with monumental effort had now become totally impossible. She would be prey to all evil and have only her own karmic experience to live by.

How could she have been so stupid?

It couldn't be done. Fear and hopelessness were all there was. There had to be another way.

She would have to return, sort it from there.

But how could she?

Locked into her own despair, Wren cut herself off completely. The hormones responsible for the love bond had not been activated. The girl would experience only a short time of pain. Wren had to leave. This was too great a task to be carried out on her own.

Finding Alessandro seemed a million lifetimes away. She'd just have to return to suffer the wait and the consequences of her theft.

It was almost as monumental a task to return as to stay, both ways she would be struggling but The Light was safer than Earth even though Alessandro would not be there. She could try go through the right channels and get to know where and who he is then come down with blessings and help. Yes that is what she would do; return.

Leaving the womb for home had been something she had done many times before. To one host mother she had been impregnated three times in one year and each time the baby miscarried because of problems with the companion souls who had not yet left the light. It had been a year before the mother was strong enough to carry the body she was to inhabit but by then she had learned she was to have a twin. The spirit who had been chosen had not left its previous incarnation in time for the earlier conceptions. That had been a good life worth waiting for with an understanding friend always with her from leaving the light. They stayed close even after she had found Alessandro.

From her stolen place Wren sent out the request to return. This was new to her because every miscarriage previously had been arranged at source. She waited for the familiar hormones to kick in and the pain and bleeding to begin in her mother.

Nothing happened. She waited more, praying and begging.

No contractions squeezed, no foetus loosened and no light came for her.

Wren tried again.

Nothing.

Wren had never before felt such isolation. She was really on her own. She would have to stay.

It was her own fault, she should have thought things out but the pain of not having Alessandro constantly with her had chased all reason away. At least she knew where she was in this stolen lifetime. She was at the very beginning with no plan or help. Only one thing she knew for certain, every atom of her energy would go into finding Alessandro.

CHAPTER FIVE

'You're getting a bit too fat our June.'

Her mother pulled a face that meant once again June wasn't living life as she hoped any daughter of hers would. Looking the pale girl in the face she shook her head and tutted with her tongue behind her teeth so that the sharp noise of disapproval pierced June's already depressed state of mind.

'None of these clothes will do you again this year. It's the same every April, you grow too fast. You'll be taller than me next spring.' she poked her hands on her hips as she shook her head with hopelessness, the tight expression burning into June,

'Bigger, but never cleverer than me. I can see everything. I know more than you will ever notice. Remember that.'

Mrs Stoker pulled herself up from one knee where she'd been examining the hem on every cotton dress which June had obediently pulled over her head in a vain effort to find something that would fasten around the waist or do up at the back.

'Well at least I'm spared the pain of letting the hems down. Get that frock off, we'll have to pass them on to Jesse's kids though' we'll get nowt in return from that'n.'

June pushed her fists into wash-matted wool sleeves that covered her arms but not her wrists before she tugged the shrunken neck of the knitted jumper over her head, compressing the skin on her forehead and then the flesh at her cheekbones so that her eyes were pulled open from the bottom. The ghoulish look added to the flattened fair hair, caused another click of her mother's tongue to signal her hopelessness once again. June felt bad just for growing. She had no control over it and it looked very much as if she was going to be broad in the beam and belly like her father's sisters. After all, she had their dirty dishwater hair colour. Her mother would hate that.

June sunk even heavier into her hopelessness, weighed down by the thick pall of maternal expectation.

Wren was used to the feelings of hopelessness that her host mother had felt for these last four and a half months. She still didn't realise she was pregnant and that realisation would bring a new meaning to disgust in this house. She had gathered so much information during her time outside the growing foetus and June's childish body. This was definitely not a household she would have chosen to be born into. Oh there was love from the father but it was restricted by the ever disapproving eye of the mother, Wren still hadn't discovered why. Nothing was ever said but actions were constant in their effect of cowing this girl who was doing Wren the unknown great service of bringing her onto the Earth. But no energy could be wasted in feelings for any of this family. She had not met any-one of them previously in The Light as they were not of her spirit grouping.

Of course she had great respect for them as fellow souls on a hard journey doing what every soul does: it's very best. But she couldn't get involved. Their issues were not her issues and she had too much on her mind to even consider what their incarnations were about. Anyway they were lucky enough to have their own guardians around them although Wren had not felt any as yet. Crisis would definitely bring them. There would be plenty chances to meet and talk then.

The little dog who had been sleeping on the rag mat beside June as she endured the torture of being too big for her small amount of clothes, suddenly woke and ran to the back door.

'Lord is it that time already. Our Jan is better at being a clock than she is at being a dog.'

June hated any good deflected from the pet her dad had carried home inside his overcoat one snowy night. He'd had a hard job persuading his wife that the pup could add to their family life and had only won a week's trial from the woman who argued that it would be her that had to clean up after the mucky thing. After a few days when she saw that any love given to the pup was not given to this demanding child, she thought it could only do good in teaching her too confident daughter that she wasn't the only creature her da could lavish affection on. Besides, a dog's very presence cut down on the number of mice she had to hold by the tail as she released them from the traps to toss into the morning fire.

Jan was rocket fast, both in her legs and her learning ability. She demonstrated equally those skills now as she did at this time every working day. Even though her dad worked shifts his adoring dog knew exactly when to wake, scrat at the door and then tear the mile and a half to greet her master as he emerged black and tired from the pit head.

Since she had been steady on her legs Tot had never walked home alone. Even without her highly developed sensory skills Wren could see that this was some special dog. Once when she was out of the womb she met with the spirit of the dog and discovered that there was a bond to its master that went back several lifetimes even to a time when the position was reversed. Tot was being repaid with all the love he'd shown then to this soul who had been his mistress.

It was strange, Wren mused, that the dog was the only spirit who knew she was there. For four months now she had been around this family day and night and knew every habit and nuance of this post war hardship way of living.

Wren was capable of analysing all this from June's perception of the situation but saw that the girl's awareness didn't stretch that far. June thought that the only creature her mother loved was her dad and she was pleased with that at least and had long accepted that she would never feel any of that love. June had no idea of the reason her mother resented her and indeed she sought none as she, in her childishness, thought that she was simply unlovable. She felt her father's efforts were to compensate for her pain and she was ever grateful for the adoration of the family pet even if, as her mother told her often, dogs loved any-one no matter how ugly or hopeless.

Wren, although in the privileged position to see all this and analyse every relationship was not able to help or comfort the girl who was to bring her into this world once more. There was spiritual love and support for the early soul of June and Wren often saw the vivid blue energy coming into her aura to give strength and reminder at a soul level of her karmic reasons. June of course was unaware but no doubt benefited immensely. Wren, in the past, had known much new strength and a renewed determination to grow from all adversity. She hoped the guardians would show their worth when the family discovered June's pregnancy. Shame could be a killer.

Wren woke in the womb and felt shivering from her host. She came out to find out why that cold was mixed with strain. It was dark although a small paraffin lamp at June's feet gave a little light over a cracked concrete floor.

The girl was sitting on the outside toilet worrying why she had to push so hard for no results. It was horrible enough having to wake so often for a wee but this feeling of being blocked up was getting her down and her stomach was swelling too. Wren watched as the girl huddled inside an unbuttoned coat, her untied shoes, hard and cold, allowed freezing feet to slip in and out at the slightest movement. Checking for spiders was the first thing June did on entering the cold, draughty netty. Her eyes were skilled at scanning first the whitewashed walls, then the edges top and bottom before straining her eyes into the dark corners. She checked again, perhaps the fright of seeing a round body unwrap into a darting horror on black legs would be just the fright her bowels needed to get a move on. She pulled a square of torn newspaper from the string hanging beside the toilet. Even as she felt the inky hardness she knew she wouldn't need its services. As she fingered and turned the five inch square lavatory paper she could tell her mam had made up this batch. It was neat and even. Her dad's efforts were rough and given no thought for tidiness. Sometimes, if he'd been doing the job on a Sunday he had off from work, June would find little dolly tear outs and sometimes a cat or dog. If there was real time to spare, a newspaper pit pony would appear. Those were her da's real masterpieces, he knew all about pit ponies. There were no animal tear outs here, only neat squares of births, deaths, and marriages and blurry photos of headless men. June had to go to the next sheet to find out if the face fitted the suit.

She wouldn't be using the piece in her hands, after she'd read half a story of some war widow's rights demand it was flushed down the pan unshaped and unused. Wasted. Mam would hate that.

As June ran through the scary dark back to the house across the late frost covered cobbles, her flapping shoes slipping outside and in, she wished her dad was magic as he so often pretended to be. He had promised one day to magic for her a lav that was in the house, warm, and insect free and just beside her bed. June knew he never would as her mother had berated him saying there would never be such a thing as it was too unhygienic and the smell of dirty printer's ink on newspaper would keep folks awake as well as the smell of unmentionables. The flies in the house would be terrible. The health minister would never allow indoor lavs. No, if dad had never been able to magic a pony of her own to ride through the Durham countryside or a bridal doll as big as she was when she was six then inside toilets would never exist either. No chance.

Wren was so caught up in this little human drama it could be easy to allow herself to enjoy the life of this girl's child. She found it natural with all her experience to see ways to comfort and prepare the spirit of the body she now lay in, to bond with her. But no; what was she thinking of? Finding Alessandro was all she was here for and although the time had to be passed somehow; interest must not go beyond a mild state.

Her job was to grow. Linked to her umbilical life line that was all there was to do now.

The warmth came slowly from stiff sheets and thin blankets weighed down by a slippery, lumpy eiderdown which never stayed on the bed all night so that frequent wakings were all part of the night spent alone by June. It was interesting to feel the anguish that twirled around the mind of this child. Fear and excitement bound together like sawdust and treacle half stirred in a bowl that was only ever meant to hold warm milk. They could never be separated in this lifetime and the mixture was about to be agitated into an even more unpalatable concoction that would spew out and stick cancerously to the lives of the others in this house.

June did not understand what Colin had done to her when he'd caught her on the path home from school just where the bracken thickened and the hazel bushes were closer to each other in a curtain of seclusion. She only knew it was bad, her dad would kill him and that she could never tell anyone. How could she when she hadn't the words to describe the pain. She remembered the first time she had passed him in September, just back at school after a summer of hastily prepared picnics of fish paste sandwiches and a bottle of tap water gleefully shared with her father when the morning had presented itself with a flourish of sun and birdsong impossible to resist by two lovers of nature. Her mother had been pleased to see the back of them for what did silly joys of stumbling across a pool of tiddlers or a patch of wild garlic have compared to giving the carpets a good beating or scrubbing the front step. Mam had called their joyous days 'racing the roads' and never understood that they always avoided any road as much as possible only crossing any quiet path as a means to reaching even deeper woods or more fascinating winding stream. When the summer threw a few hot days at them they made their way to the river Derwent which split the woods. This is where Tot secretly taught June to swim, in a rocky pool he had mastered when he was a boy. He would dry her on his shirt and wear it home damp, hoping they both looked dry enough to have never gone near the river that Ivy thought dangerous and dirty.

The row of colliery houses set at the edge of a great wood with a yellow-cream brick cobbled path dividing the back yards from the outside lavatory fronted long gardens had been enough for June when she was little. But as soon as her two year old body could be slung onto dad's labour broadened shoulders and she'd understood not to hold on to his slick Brylcreemed hair for balance she'd been shown the real joy of life; nature. It was that richness of spirit that Wren was enjoying in the shared memory as sleep was sought hopelessly but when the sawdust remembrance of Colin clung to the sweet treacle of good thoughts it was just as interesting.

June, the only child in the hamlet who was old enough to take the bus to the secondary school three miles away, was ever aware of who she met and at first threw a cheery hello from smiling lips at the youth who came from Woodland Terrace as she went to it. They had passed and June continued a few steps when she stopped to pick up a tuft of fox hair that had blown into the grass edging the sandy, stony mud of the track up to home. As she'd bent her eye was caught again by Colin who had stopped a few yards away to turn and watch her. The look had disturbed her but when he stooped to tie his shoelace she allowed herself to become engrossed in identifying the age of the cub whose fur had been caught on the brambles. The next evening she had thought the youth was waiting for her as his step seemed short and just to have begun instead of a steady stride. He had stopped when he'd reached her.

'What's yer name?'

The childish politeness had offered up her vulnerability to a delighted predator.

'June Stoker and I go to Spen School.'

'You Tot Stoker's lass then?'

'Yes.' Lack of social awareness had kept June on the spot until her elder had dismissed her from his presence.

'You'd better gan then.' But just as June set off again. 'Do you always walk home alone?'

She turned and felt more than saw something that set a novel fear twist in her stomach.

'Yes. Why not?'

'Oh nowt. Just that these woods might be full of tigers and dinosaurs to a pretty little girl like you.'

He looked slyly from her laced up shoes to the blue ribbon now escaping from the tight bow of that morning to slide down her pale silky hair. 'Only you're not so little are you?'

June hadn't felt the usual inevitability she normally did when someone commented on her growing fast, she felt alarm and distaste and a strong hope that she wouldn't see him again as her quickened step had carried her home.

That night as dad had come into her bedroom for a goodnight kiss she had voiced her fears that had kept her quiet all teatime.

'Dad?'

'Aye, me poppet?'

'We haven't seen any animals in the woods big enough to eat us have we?'

'Like what pet?' He neatened the eiderdown and tucked the sheets much too tightly around her shoulders.

'Like dinosaurs or tigers.'

He looked serious for a moment before the twinkle she loved so much escaped into his eyes.

'Nah, no dinosaurs or tigers. The giant alligators have eaten them all.'

His laugh relaxed her enough to allow her to giggle when he tickled her beneath the ears.

'As if I would allow any monsters to harm a hair on the head of my precious little chicken.'

He kissed her on the forehead and put out the gas light. As she lay hoping for sleep to calm her mind she knew that there were monsters out in that wood she loved so much.

New unseen monsters.

CHAPTER SIX

The nights were getting lighter towards Easter, an experience June enjoyed almost as much as her new walking home companion. He didn't know it but he chased away monsters. Mr. Farraige had become a joy to listen to as he knew so much about nature, almost as much as Dad, but not quite. He knew different things and told her about how the wild daffodils came out almost a fortnight sooner in Devon where he'd grown up as a boy.

June thought that must have been a long time ago judging by the grey of his hair lining the back edge of his trilby, it seemed impossible to belong to someone with such a ginger moustache. She tried hard never to look at the watering eye.

Wren allowed herself to be out of June's body and her own growing foetus more now that spring was in the air. She saw at once that Mr. Farraige was a good soul using his daily dog walk to protect a young girl from a predatory youth.

The night after that first evening when Towser had disturbed Colin and his horrible intentions, June had been feeling the first twists of anguish as the cracking of twigs warned her that her fears were coming out of the wood. More terror lunged at her insides as a stick had landed halfway between the youth and herself as she shuffled pebbles in overpowering dread. Towser had bounded to grab the stick in bared teeth before dropping it at June's feet for a replay. Mr. Farraige followed on in a march he'd used to immense advantage in the Great War. Wren knew that he was fearless, that his reputation as a sergeant major brought cowardice to Colin's heart as he passed by his prey without even lifting his head.

That teatime, as they had rounded the climbing path to the top of Woodland Terrace June could see mam halfway down the street with the big homemade clippie mat hanging over their yard wall as she beat every bit of dirt and dog hair from its multi-coloured rag loops. Jan had scattered out of the concrete yard to sniff at Towser whose black tummy she could only dream of reaching. Mr. Farraige touched the front of his hat. 'Good afternoon Mrs. Stoker, here's your daughter safe from school and charming company she was all the way from the bus I must say.'

It was obvious to Wren that mam thought the man a gentleman as he didn't live in the pit houses of half brick and half wood. He rented, along with his ancient mother, a stone cottage behind the Methodist Church. Dad said he wouldn't know the inside of a mine if he saw one and meant it as an insult to his manhood but mam knew he was a cut above.

'Well thank you, but why wouldn't she be safe? She knows these woods better than most and has a good pair of running legs on her.' She'd stopped producing clouds of dust in honour of her refined caller.

'Quite so, Mrs. Stoker. Quite so!' Mr. Farraige left with another respectful tug at the brim of his hat and mam took up the beating with a new fury.

'You've not been bothering him with questions about badgers' setts ah hope.'

'No mam, just throwing the stick for Towser. He's a big boy but you know I bet he still couldn't outrun our Jan.' The terrier was wiggling its way out of June's arms up her chest to lick desperate kisses all over her face.

'Not on the mouth! How many times have I told you?'

'Oh but mam she's only kissing me and I love it.'

'Aye well she kisses her bum an' all and you wouldn't want that all ower yer face.'

Mam grabbed the dog from its happiness in June's arms and thrust it onto the yard where Jan knew to lie on the torn woollen blanket in her corner. June, knowing that was the end of any play she would have that evening, did as she was ordered and took one end of the big mat then helped mam re-lay it in front of the fire. They each took two corners of the heavy table to set it back in place then put the chairs straight.

Wren, affected by the stress, wondered how long this domestic habit and childish obedience would last. When the secret of her being came out everything would change. It didn't seem that this resentful woman would be too sympathetic towards a daughter who was to bring shame and disgrace on their family. What made her so aggrieved towards her own child? In Wren's spiritual state she could feel empathy with all she was to be born into but it wouldn't be her business once she was physical. Her only concern was to find Alessandro.

Wren was resting in the womb when she was woken by a sudden stitch and breathlessness in June's body.

She emerged into a concrete school yard to watch the school netball team gather around June lying on the rough concrete ground and the PE teacher ordering every-one back including June's best friend Rosemary.

Miss. Harbottle helped June onto her feet then walked her slowly back into the chalky, book smelling classroom where she pulled out a chair.

'I have noticed you've been a bit slow lately June.' She said taking off the pink cardigan she'd had hanging from her shoulders and laying it over those of her pupil. This got her close enough so that June could see the knitting of a worried forehead and globs of red lipstick in the corners of her teacher's pursed mouth. She smelled of powdery perfume and newly washed hair.

'Have you started your periods yet dear?'

June was feeling weak but didn't want any fuss so forced herself to her feet where she saw the teacher's gaze fall onto her thickening waist.

'My what?'

'Never mind.' she said looking at her watch. 'It's nearly lunch time; I'm taking you to see Doctor Kelly before his surgery finishes.' She stepped back out into the yard and blew the whistle which seemed a permanent feature hanging over huge bosoms.

June didn't object. She had been a little worried about her health herself but didn't dare tell mam about being sick every morning across the cobbles in the cold toilet because she was sure she'd get a blasting about wasting good food.

Heads turned and some-one missed the ball as wobbling legs followed Miss Harbottle across the yard where the game had resumed under the stern eye of a keen to impress prefect. June knew that her face was drained as she wove her way from the door beneath the heavy stone carved 'GIRLS', then up the leafy road to the part of the doctor's house he used as a surgery.

Wren, never more than a foot away was keen to see what she knew was going to change this poor girl's life and throw upon her tiny world shame, trouble and anger. She was unable to cut off her feelings now. It was almost too much to bear to watch the young slump of innocence try to warm up the leather of a worn out chair that had once graced the doctor's fireside but was now tatty enough to be used by the throng of patients who were lucky to ever sit on such a graceful chair. Wren could have entered the other room from where mutterings could be heard but she wanted to give this girl some loving energies in this difficult part of her human journey, some strength, some help. Any help.

The sudden crack that meant the door was opening sent adrenaline coursing through June's shivering body. Dr. Kelly's middle aged face did not wear the smile June was used to when he passed her cycling on his house-call rounds.

'Come in June.' he ordered in his soft Irish brogue, stepping back to allow the girl who was already bent by his uncustomary sternness to enter the surgery. Her eyes went to the examination table where a fresh white sheet had been laid. It looked cold, crisp and not at all welcoming. She knew it had been put there especially and that frightened her. The scrape of a chair pulled out from the doctor's desk further twanged her nerves. She shot a hopeful look at the teacher who had been so kind when June had fallen in the school yard. There was no comfort there just a cool, wide-eyed disbelief.

There was something seriously wrong with her and they both knew what it was. June thought she was dying.

Sitting, Dr. Kelly was the same height as June who's eyes widened in an effort to search for clues to what she was about to die from. When he spoke it was on the out breath of a great heaved in sigh.

'June, June, June, June. What on earth have you been doing girl?'

Wren watched as June's mind searched for some unusual happening in the last few weeks that could have given her a fatal illness and caused sickness, fainting and such a terrible day as this.

She hadn't even paddled in the river never mind swam, she'd always washed her hands before she ate, mam saw to that. She'd only eaten fresh eggs and never even handled one of the magpies she'd set free from the awful traps in the woods. Maybe it was because she couldn't pass any waste lately. That would be it. She was dying from constipation! Weeks of mam's dumplings were clogging her to death!

When her voice came it was cracked and thick from a throat dried out from such never before known tension.

'Nothing Doctor. I haven't done nothing.'

'Have you had a period lately June?'

Wren could have cried for the girl's innocence, but she must only be an observer in this awful scene.

'A what, Doctor?'

He was used to this lack of knowledge in young girls; it was nothing for married women to come to him with such ignorance about the workings of their bodies.

'Have you been bleeding June?'

Relief sped the withheld air from June's body and a little smile to her face. They'd got it wrong! They thought she was bleeding to death. They were mistaken. She'd never bled since that scrape on her knee last summer when she'd come down from peering into a deserted bird's nest faster than she'd ever left a tree before.

'Oh no! You've made a mistake Doctor! I'm not bleeding, just a bit sick and dizzy and a lot more tired than usual.'

For some reason her words made his face show more concern not less.

'Have you got a boyfriend June. Some-one special who you spend time alone with?'

He took her hands as if to encourage her to tell him everything but there was nothing to tell.

'No. I'm too young for that and anyway me mam says she'll kill me if I ever have anything to do with lads.'

June absorbed the look shot between the two concerned adults but she didn't understand it.

'I need to examine you June, could you get up onto the couch for me?'

New fear came on the stern stares of both people she had learned to respect and she hesitated.

'Miss. Harbottle will stay in the room. There's nothing to fear.'

The time it took to unlace her shoes seemed to stretch to the end of the week before June felt the crispness of the sheet as she lay much higher up than her own bed. She tensed even more.

The Doctor rubbed his hands briskly to warm them but it didn't work for she jumped as his fingers parted her blouse from the elasticated waistband of her skirt to touch bare flesh.

'I haven't been able to poo for three weeks.' she blurted as she realized he was feeling around her growing tummy.

'I'm afraid there's much more than poo in there June.' he said as he turned to take a trumpet like instrument which he used first to shock her with it's cold metal and then to listen to what was going on in her stomach.

As his fingers went into the waistband of her knickers to ease them down June heard a scream.

It was a blast that carried terror, pain and fear from where it had been suppressed for months now. It threw images of the wood, the startled pheasants and the rough Colin into her mind and she knew. She knew now that this was something to do with that nasty youth who had thrown her to the ground and kept her there as he'd lain on top of her suffocating her, frightening her and hurting her.

She knew it had been horrible and she knew it had been wrong otherwise why would he have threatened her with what would happen to her dad if she told any-one. What she hadn't known was that what Colin had done had given her a terrible disease that she was now going to die from.

She felt the arms of her teacher around her when the screaming stopped and she saw the Doctor washing at a tiny sink. He came towards her drying his hands on a little towel.

'Who has taken your knickers off June?'

His eyes fixed to hers. He would not miss one tiny word or signal that June gave. She gave none.

No-one would ever know who had given her this disease because if she breathed a word her dad would suffer. If she was dying anyway why make things worse.

Miss. Harbottle stroked June's hair which was now damp and cool.

'We need to know who and when pet.'

Eyes wide open but seeing only Colin gave the girl's face a ghostly, empty look which was shaken from her by her teacher.

'June! Is it a boy at school?'

Wren hovered above the scene and it was obvious that her host mother had gone into shock as she turned her glazed stare onto the doctor.

'When will I die?'

The sympathy which came from the old Irishman was visible to anyone with spiritual advancement to see. He took her hand, rubbing it as if she had just come in from the snow.

'June; you aren't going to die. You're going to have a baby.'

The fourteen year old girl with damp hair, wet face and shaking legs slumped to the floor. Two arms cradled her and her teacher searched the palest of faces for hope.

'But Miss I can't be having a baby....I'm not married.'

June drank the tea some-one had placed in her shaking hands without even noticing that her teacher had popped back to school to clear having the rest of the day off. Doctor Kelly took the rattling cup and saucer from hands that were too weak to object.

'Are you up to walking to the bus stop June?'

He looked at his watch and June stared at the dark glossy hairs on his wrist sneaking out from a clean white cuff that must have stopped them going as grey as the hair that didn't quite cover the Doctor's head.

Although Wren could not return to the shocked body she still knew every thought, every emotion and she was sad that June was in so much pain but at the same time knew that she had chosen this situation in order to discover if she had the strengths and abilities to see her through. Before June herself had been born into this body she had chosen her lessons and her soul group. She would ascend with this pain. She would grow spiritually and be strong enough to take more tests. It was the reason every human was here on Earth; Soul growing.

At this moment though she was suffering and Wren knew it was only the start.

Just as the three silent people turned the bend on the village road the yellow Venture bus threw out a cloud of black smoke and pulled away from them. Miss Harbottle had added her costume coat to the calf length turquoise woollen skirt and she loosened the tight buttons from around her breasts before allowing herself a word beneath her breath.

'Damn! What time is the next one Doctor?'

'Not until four and all the children will be taking that one home from school.' he turned his face to June who hadn't heard or thought of anything since she had left the surgery.

'Are you up to walking June? June?'

He turned to the teacher. 'Are you?'

'We both are.' she said taking June's hand and giving her the guidance she needed to walk the three miles past the church, through the winding rough road with the fields and woods June knew so well and loved every glance of. Only now she saw not one leaf, not one branch, even the violets she'd been willing to open enough to throw their scent into the air were crushed underfoot as she plodded onto the grass allowing her elders their space on the road.

June knew all the short cuts from school to home and Wren knew why she had shown her escorts none of them. The girl herself was not fully in her body. Shock had allowed a slight separation of body and spirit and it was just as well. As Wren moved her own spirit she saw the essence that was June travelling just three feet in front of her forehead. The light had a certain beauty but was dull with pain for only it knew of what was to come; only it knew this is what it had chosen.

Wren tried to offer the spirit of June some comfort but it had no awareness in its misery that she was there at all.

Although a near separation had occurred it was watching nothing but June and the agony this body was enduring and she had to respect that. With all her advancement she could have grown so bright and mingled her aura with this young soul but it didn't seem the time for introductions or distractions. Wren would stay close by and be ready if she was needed.

The downhill country lane soon levelled out to where the drift mine entrance showed in the small clearing of the trees. No-one was about. The children were at school, the men were down the mine and the early afternoon bus passengers had long wound their way home. Three pairs of feet tread the path of dry sandy soil, three pairs of feet scattered pebbles to the edging grass and three good souls dreaded what was to come. Soft spring sunshine failed to warm June's back or lift her heart and a bubbling sob left her mouth as she saw how near the dark wall of the fir trees that formed the boundary of both the forest and the end of the hamlet was. For in front of them all with just the rise of a stony path was the line of houses where June would have to change her parents' lives forever.

As the absorbed and resigned band rounded the corner at the first house which began the working class street, the hardness of the brick cobbles brought each one out of their thoughts. Wren watched the energy of June enter her body once more, she felt sad that she had lost her chance to communicate and help. All she could do was watch and care and store any information for her future.

The yard of June's home was the cleanest they had passed so far, the tin bath that hung on the wall the shiniest. June knew that inside the house the rooms would be the cleanest and the heart of the mother she was about to devastate the hardest.

The first thought June had as she opened the door which led straight into the room they used for cooking, eating and sitting was how furious her mother would be that she had taken company home when she had the brown velvet cushions off the horsehair stuffed hide couch. She had her back to the door as she kneeled to retrieve old Daily Heralds from where dad would not stop pushing them when he'd only half read the newspaper.

'Mam.'

The first look on the woman's face was surprise. June never came in until her tea was good and ready. Her features then showed curiosity at her daughter's companions and then embarrassment. She shot June a look that said she'd never be forgiven for bringing people when the place was upside down in a cleaning flurry.

Before she spoke she pulled the dog-eared journal from the jaws of the couch back and then replaced the cushions. The paper was thrown to the fire where it roared up lighting the woman who was smoothing her pinny with one hand and stray hair from its scarf covering with the other.

'Now then. Dr. Kelly what is this? Bringing my June home in the middle of the afternoon.'

The keen eyes raked over the woman she'd never met before and then around the room to check on its immaculate state. 'And me with a mess like Stageybank Fair!'

Wren noticed that the mother never glanced at June.

'And who's this?' she asked taking in the fading red lipstick that seemed to go not at all with the dusty shoes and escaping hair.

'Mrs. Stoker, this is Miss Harbottle one of the teachers at Spen school. She noticed that June was not well and brought her to me.'

A furious glance was thrown to June.

'She looks all right. A bit pale maybe but she's always complaining about something. Do you want tea? June fill the kettle.'

'Mrs. Stoker, we don't want tea. We want to talk. Is your husband around?'

June could see mam was more annoyed at her daughter not rushing into the scullery with the kettle than she was concerned for her health.

'No he's on back shift. I can deal with anything he can. Sit down.'

Even now, June thought, even now she is watching to see how creased her satin cushions will be, how wrinkled her lace antimacassars.

Mam remained standing with her back to the easy chair. June pulled out a wooden chair from beneath the table and for once ignored the glance that showed displeasure at the spoiled symmetry.

The teacher, who could have done with some tea, felt even sorrier for her pupil. There'd be no easing of her hard path by this woman.

At last mam seemed at enough peace with her surroundings to pay attention to the concerns of the unexpected guests.

'So; what is it that you think is wrong with my daughter Dr. Kelly?' Impatience was pulled back into herself on a tight, noisy breath.

The doctor, now being even more aware of this girl's family life, found his task grow suddenly harder than he had dreaded whilst his reluctant feet had some-how brought him here.

He turned to June whose face seemed frozen in fright and wondered how her mother could not see how her daughter was feeling.

It was then that the room became even more crowded for two spirits manifested. One, an advanced and beautiful energy hovered over June and the second a more solid and masculine guardian angel threw a protective wave around the mother. No-one noticed except Wren who had been expecting them.

'There is nothing wrong with June Mrs. Stoker.' He paused, feeling darkness congeal around his message, aware that his next words would change the lives of every-one in this house for ever. 'She is pregnant.'

The shoulders stiffened even more beneath the floral apron and the defensive thrust of the upper body put strain on the red bias binding that edged the crisp cotton pinny. The woman's stare left the doctor, settled on the teacher for a moment and then bore into her daughter.

There was a silence of sound but not of emotion. Nobody in the room had ever endured such feelings before and never wanted to again.

Wren, being a spirit of great sensitivity, could hardy bear to stay. But she had no choice, if she wanted to be born in this child's baby she had to stay close by or lose this chance she'd staked so much on. She watched as all eyes bound themselves to the woman who now knew she was to be her grandmother. She seemed to be only about thirty five herself but hard work, not a touch of feminine pampering and hair screwed tight beneath a turban- tied scarf did her youth no favours. The light lines around her eyes and narrow lips were not from smiling.

She said nothing but Wren did not have only human empathy with which to read this contained explosion of emotions, she knew exactly what horrors were unleashing themselves. It was so obvious why no soft understanding had ever been lavished upon the daughter she would now resent even more. Wren was shocked. Had she taken more notice of this family she was about to be born into instead of dwelling on Alessandro and how she would conduct her worldwide search, she would have known the secrets behind this woman's sternness.

Why hadn't she read her mind sooner? It was blindingly obvious. Wren had not been interested enough but really, what good would it have done June?

The karmic arrangements had to take place. Wren had the power but not the right to intervene.

She knew exactly what Mrs. Stoker would do before she actually stood up silently from the chair.

Dr. Kelly and Miss Harbottle seemed rooted to their own seats. They had taken their own involuntary action in a situation thrust upon them from their professional closeness in this mining community and their shared kindness. They could do no more. It was now a family matter.

They both followed the mother's stare to her daughter and read accurately the projection of disgust, disgrace and jealousy which stoked the anger to a roaring blaze.

So fast were the two steps, the arm going back and the crack that rent the air from the force of her open hand on June's cheek that the observers wondered how it had happened. They were forced to their feet when Mrs. Stoker pushed June so suddenly back in the chair that it hit the floor with a scuffling thud. The attack of blows, strangulation and hair pulling seemed impossible to end. Three adults shouted. One girl screamed again and again.

Only Wren heard the urgent scrabbling at the door and saw the rush of the little dog as it went straight for Mrs. Stoker's ankle. Teeth bared and holding, tearing and gripping created another scream this time from the predatory mother who seemed to want to kill her daughter.

'Get the bitch off me!'

'Off JAN! Off!'

The terrier obeyed the gasping girl it had learned to love for her affection and companionship.

Wren watched the mother scramble up; heaving back breath she'd spent in her vicious attack.

'Get out! Get out you whore! You evil cow! And take that animal with you! I'll have neither of you bitches in my house again. Get out! NOW!'

Limping towards the bedroom door she turned one last time, her whole body taking part in her anger, she hurled repulsion to the adults who were both kneeling to comfort the shaking girl. 'Take that away. I hate her!'

The door opened then closed behind her with uncustomary softness.

To June, the room seemed empty of everything except cold shock.

The dog whimpered but the girl was silent as snow. She didn't understand any of this. How was it that she was going to have a baby? Why had her mother attacked her in such a way?

Dr. Kelly silently felt over June's limbs for any serious damage then eased her to the settee.

Miss. Harbottle, who always thought that great distress should be discreet, was herself wide-eyed with shock as she kneeled beside June and picked up her limp hand.

'Are you ok dear ...any pains in your tummy... anywhere?'

She took the lack of response to mean that physically anyway, the girl was not suffering.

'What time does her father get in Doctor? We can't leave her alone with that mad woman.'

'She isn't mad Miss Harbottle. I've known Ivy all her life. Sad though it is; she has reason for such an outburst.'

Suddenly Wren was aware of something she'd never expected to happen. The mental agony and severe shock of what had happened to June was separating her spirit from her body, completely this time. A bright energy tinged with sad pewter floated from the heart chakra. Now for the first time Wren could communicate with the real essence of her future mother.

'Am I dead?' She asked as soon as she noticed the vivid blueness that was Wren.

Wren followed her to the top of the room from where they both looked down into the kitchen of the little terraced colliery house and the three bodies all exuding auras of extreme strain.

Only the terrier's head turned towards them. Only the dog could see.

Dr. Kelly was lifting open the eyelid of his patient to quell his fears they seemed to share.

Between both spirits there eased a new spectrum of communication.

'No. Not dead, only a stress induced out of body experience.'

'Yes of course. The suddenness has me a bit confused.'

The spirit of June was now a soft white glow with blue and pink tints flowing attractively around the edges. The dullness of the physical had cleared. Wren knew it was a good but early soul who was learning fast.

The two glowed together in an empathizing that June had forgotten existed. Free from the restrictions of inadequate language and the misunderstandings, intentional or not, of other physical beings.

'I can tell you are a very advanced soul. Who are you? Have you brought the spirit of my unborn baby? Can I meet with it again, now? I have things to add to the last time we communicated. It will need more help than first thought.'

Wren was glad of the distraction below them as the doctor tried to revive June from what he thought was a deep faint.

She had to somehow explain to this mothering soul that the spirit she had agreed and planned with in her spirit grouping before she was born into the physical had been robbed and that the thief was the one she saw before her.

'Elia should be here by now. My body is five months pregnant!'

The sound of the name stung Wren. It gave new awareness of the pain she had caused and so single-mindedly left behind. Before she had just stolen a life of some anonymous spirit and that was bad enough but now!

'Elia won't be coming.'

June's spirit expanded with a new shock and a sadness that hurt Wren even more.

'But we agreed. Am I to lose the baby? It can't be born without a soul it would be impossible as well as pointless. I don't understand. Why this change of plan?'

Wren watched as confusion coloured the light energy before her with little smokes of black.

'You know I don't have long? I must have this spirit, so much depends on it.'

This was worse than Wren thought.

'What is your spirit name?' she asked with love.

'I'm Sundia. I have had twenty two lifetimes and Elia has been with me in the last four. This time I was to do her the great service of birthing her into an incarnation where she'd learn much from hard times and relationships. She is to meet for the first time the one who will be her forever soul mate. But if she's not here then I cannot fulfil either of our destinies. This incarnation will have been wasted. I don't understand. She must come!'

Wren knew that the only way to explain was gently.

'I am Wren; the spirit of your unborn child Sundia my dearest.'

Sundia vibrated with confusion.

'But you can't be. Look at you; you are too far advanced for me ever to have met with you never mind agreed a mutual life. What could I help you with? You must have had hundreds more life times than me. This baby is surely not for you.'

'I have been with the baby since conception and know you and your family.'

'But where is Elia? Is she safe?'

'She's safe and well although I'm sure she won't be too happy with me for I stole her incarnation just as she was leaving to come to you. I am so sorry.'

'But you couldn't have. It's not possible.'

'I would have thought so too but just as I watched her planned departure she turned to give love to those she was leaving and I threw myself into the energy that was bringing her to you. It was so sudden that even I was surprised.'

Sundia oscillated with concern but no aggression came from her spirit to Wren.

'I have never heard of such a thing happening. Have the Greatlights not tried to get you back?'

'I have had one visit but have been allowed to stay.'

'Aren't you worried of what your punishment might be? I mean, what they could take from you?'

'No. It will all be worth it.'

'How? What could an early life give to some-one who has long passed the tests and lessons offered to this incoming soul?'

Wren was pleasantly surprised that this spirit would understand so much and be so generous in her emotions. She would ascend greatly through this even though Wren didn't deserve any acceptance at all for robbing her spirit friend.

'I have a soul mate Alessandro, the love of my very existence; we were ready to ascend beyond the first spirit level from which we would choose to be given physical lives. Alessandro was always slightly above me but because of our association it was always overlooked and assumed that he would help me catch up by teaching me the things I had missed. There would be no more incarnations, we had earned the right to stay in spirit and ascend. We were joyous and ecstatic that we would pass to a new awareness together; together as we had been in five hundred lives and every spirit rest and assessments.

'So why would you wish to leave him?'

Wren glowed at such an innocent question. 'I didn't leave him. I couldn't bear to be away from him for one second. He left me.'

'Didn't he feel the same?'

Wren didn't answer this early soul for quite a while, she was unable to. Feelings of such intensity flooded all her being and she remembered with bitter keenness just how splendid her love with Alessandro had been and was. How could she be expected to live without this for a whole lifetime?

So much had happened since she had last been with him, felt his adoration, his protection, his very essence when they merged in true and intense love.

She didn't feel the same now, alone.

'He felt the same certainly and still does, I know. But you see, so great was his awareness, so beautiful his soul that he alone could have carried out this task he has been sent on. It is an honour actually and at first I was happy for him and was prepared to take a secondary role as unimportant as it had to be, but it was not allowed. I even offered to be a series of his animals I would have been cats, dogs or even a horse just as long as I could have been with him in this world. Even that was turned down. I was devastated and bereft without him.'

More pink was edging the soul light of her listener. 'But we all have to allow freedom to our soul mates. I have entered this short life alone but I contact Jerrad my mate every time I need to either in my sleep or when I daydream. Could you not have been content with that?'

'Even that was denied this is what drove me. I became a thief. I not only robbed Elia, I robbed you. How could I have been so selfish? I never gave myself time to even consider what mayhem and pain I caused; I just saw my chance and took it. Can you ever forgive me?'

Wren knew by the softness of the other spirit that she bore no malice and that would go a long way in her growth.

'How could I refuse when you are in such desperate need of Alessandro? I wish you well and hope you don't have to wait too long to find the one who guides your longing in the life of this as yet unborn child.'

'It is so very generous of you Sundia. You are growing quickly and remind me of myself at that spirit age. I hope you soon become as ascended as I have, or had till this.'

There was a pause when no thought passed between them only love and understanding and it was like balm to Wren. Both were energies she missed and had not enjoyed since she arrived in June's body.

The communication they both allowed resumed.

'Wren.'

'Yes Sundia.'

'You know my life as June is to be short. Will you do me the honour of giving the father who gives me such love some comfort? Try to make up for my absence?'

Wren had not intended anything. She had given no thought as yet to any needs but her own but as she felt the desperate need of this fellow spirit, she knew now that she had to.

'I will love him as Elia would have, only I have no idea of the karmic link but love I know about and it will be given freely as needed.'

'Thank you.'

'And to the mother who resents me. Will you give her love too? You will understand that she needs it more as she gives my incarnation even greater lessons than we agreed when we were in spirit. She has such pain to deal with herself. You know what that is don't you Wren. I know too on this spirit level but as June I only understand the pain and lack of affection. Give her the most love even though it will be the hardest, will you?'

Sundia swirled in bright knowledge. 'And there will be others resenting you Wren.'

The swell of energy as both spirits agreed to give help where needed expanded in glorious colour and merged at the sensitive edges. Both took a bit of the other to love and nurture. They were bonded now. Strangely, it was Wren who felt she had taken the most.

When they drew gently apart Sundia gave one last thought which touched Wren so deeply that she knew this early soul would soar when she returned to spirit.

'Wren! That is my favourite Earth bird you know. They sing so sweetly. I will talk with the spirit whose life you took and give my understanding of you and your unique actions. I hope for much empathy for you.'

Together they descended to the physical. Together they hovered over the thin and pale body they both belonged to for such a short time. Sundia sent love energy to Wren and it was returned a thousand fold for they both knew that this would be the first and last time they'd meet.

Wren watched as the spirit of June entered through the crown chakra and took a moment to settle before allowing the body to gasp a signal that it was awake.

Wren remained above the heads of the three distressed people who only wished this day was over. She knew the foetus physically was doing well and the shock was leaving it too. June's head was a confusion of anxieties. The early battle scars would never heal but there was room left on her innocence for many more.

No-one noticed that the little dog had stopped tilting her head to the ceiling to turn eyes deep in love to the girl she adored.

'Oh June, June.' Miss. Harbottle almost sobbed in relief.

Some colour flushed the re-awakened tight face as the doctor took her pulse. He pushed her shoulders down to the settee as she rose slightly to see if the bedroom door was still shut.

'She won't be coming out me darlin'. What time will your father be in?'

June sped sore eyes to the mantle clock and was shocked to read a quarter past five.

'In an hour.' The words sounded slow and deep as the misery from which they were dragged. 'You'll know when it's time because the dog will ask to be out …to run to meet da. She has never missed. When she hears the jingle of the bridle on the pit ponies she knows he's finished his shift.' She slumped deeper into the velvet cushions and sobbed.

'Dad loves Jan and he always will. But he won't love me ever again.'

There were several presences in that gloom. Several energies supporting and encouraging.

Love loomed large from every one of them but not one human being could see.

Not one could know.

But all could feel.

CHAPTER SEVEN

The sobbing didn't seem as loud as the ticking of the large black clock on the mantelpiece.

Miss. Harbottle tried to solicit a response from June but soon gave up. The bedroom door could have been locked, bolted and battened for all its accessibility. Not even Irish charm could have depressed the sneck. The young teacher was terrified of unleashing more horrors which in her shocked and fertile mind grew second by second until she could stand no more.

'Tea?' The word seemed too loud, too high and too unimportant but she made her way into the scullery anyway for fear of dying of thirst. It was reassuring to find that the shaking legs still held her and to them she was grateful for taking her from the dull air of hopelessness to where her search took up some of the dense decelerated time. As she searched for cups, tea caddy and milk bottle she hoped the kettle would boil more slowly on the struggling fire to take up more of this unbearable waiting, for she suspected that even when the father came home she'd have to stay on in this pungent agony.

She found a tin of biscuits but it seemed too like theft to take any, tea was lifesaving, a universal right and anyway hadn't she been offered a cup when she first arrived. This didn't stop her drinking three cups to the doctor's one. June didn't even pick her cup and saucer up from the floor and it was still there, cold and milk skinned when the little dog's ears lifted with its chin and she was off.

The mildness of the early spring day left as the clear sky allowed the nip of light frost to enter an already cool house. The fire had gone out. There was no supper for a working man. No hot water to bathe away black dust and sweat and no welcome for a good man who had lain on his back all day in a dank twelve inch seam of coal, hewing for all he was worth, so that he could feed his family and have the basic comforts that were denied to him this evening.

Wren stayed around in the room watching everything. Would these people feature in her own life when it finally arrived? The doctor right at the beginning no doubt. He had no idea that the baby he would deliver already knew him and was grateful for his kindness. The teacher who was now smoothing her skirt and wiping fingers to the corners of her stretched open mouth, exuded anxiety that was well founded. Doctor Kelly blankly held June's hand. June lay still, as crumpled as the cushions and with continued vacancy.

Wren had experienced many of these homecomings and the joy that the man of the house had survived another day in the dangerous hole but was this the first time she would see anger in the man who'd be her grandfather?

The clunk of metal segs in the bottom of heavy pit boots that gave grip to working feet now gave grip to fear in two hearts. And they had reason to fear. The tension was extended by a shuffle Wren knew was of pit muck caked trousers as Tot sat on the step to heave off his boots and dirty outer jacket.

The door, still off its catch, pushed open.

'Yoo-hoo!'

Jan who had lost her scrambling enthusiasm to aching sensitivity, walked in slowly with ears down to heave back onto June's knee as if to show her master that she still loved his daughter and he could too. Embarrassment clanged and clattered around faces he never expected to see in his home this evening. The smile that contrasted with the blackened face soon closed as he saw and felt the dismal room he'd entered.

Wren knew what his first thoughts would be.

'Ivy! What's happened to Ivy? Where is she?'

A slosh of apprehension slackened his jaw.

No-one answered. No-one could.

The sneck clacked on the bedroom door whipping all heads to see a white face flush suddenly flush to red. Dad took a relieved step towards his wife. One step is all it took because she rushed up to meet him bringing her knee up with such force to his groin. When he hit the floor she clawed and tore at her husband with great frenzy. Surprise gave way to defence as he gathered his attacker's hands together behind her back allowing a minute for the temper to subside, the nostrils to stop flaring and the terrible words to cease gushing and lie around them like a pool of filth. Awkwardly, Tot got up from the floor. He proffered a shaking hand to his menacing wife who hit it aside before trying to scrabble up with pride.

She failed.

The pinafore that had earlier that afternoon been clean and crisp was now crumpled and dirty. The cleaning turban had come loose revealing pinned up hair that was now escaping and wild.

All dignity had left the room that seemed no longer to be a home. The air was as quiet and as thick as cotton wool.

Sinews stood out on a strong neck then rushed along arms to clenched fists that had never harmed a living thing. He had not handled his wife so roughly before, shame sent his eyes to the floor.

Silence.

Breathing.

Sobbing.

Tot, panting and scratched, flicked a glance to the strained strangers in his house. His wife was one of them. His daughter seemed gone from him. The only stare he understood was from his dog. Paleness was only just visible beneath his coal dust covered face.

Everything was different and no-one was telling him why.

'What's this about?' The sound from the dryness of his throat was deep and lifeless. He had no control over how he spoke just as he had no control over anything anymore.

'You bastard.' Ivy hurled the words at her husband on a vortex of hate.

'Come, come now Ivy'. Dr. Kelly bravely left June's hand to take the elbow of the woman who could at any moment attack him. 'It isn't Tot's fault. You've had a shock now. I think you should go back to bed.'

Miss. Harbottle held her breath and judgment that her colleague would be safe. But as she watched his head turn to one side she saw intelligence and compassion born of living that gave him understanding of the subtleties of this tortured mind. He didn't enter the bedroom but guided the woman through the door and then pulled it to.

His eyes went first to June and then to the dirt covered man. He had to reach up to lay an arm around his shoulder and he knew the pit grime would ruin his clothes for ever but he did it anyway.

Big green eyes were wide with trauma and as the head turned to the balding Irishman it was almost childlike in its questioning ignorance.

'Tot I'm afraid, June will be having a baby in August.'

For a moment the meaning seemed not to reveal itself but realization dawned when the eyes sought out the pitiful fourteen year old girl, her arms wrapped around herself to hold what was left together as she tried to melt with her misery into the couch.

It had to be true.

This big man whose strength was admired throughout the colliery hardly had legs strong enough to carry him the few steps to where the love of his life needed him so badly. For the first time that afternoon Jan's tail wagged furiously as she read the situation. She licked the hands with gratitude as they gently lifted her to the floor before going beneath the girl to pull her into his arms.

He wanted to save her from the iron claws of her sorrow but he knew he couldn't.

Tears flooded from father and daughter.

A visible waft of emotion left him to settle in her soul.

'Come to Cuddle Corner. I'll look after you chicken, don't you ever worry about that.'

There came new sobs on a vibration different to any the reluctant listeners had endured that day.

'Daddy! My Daddy.'

'Aye, and together we'll look after your bairn an' all.' he whispered into her tight shoulder.

To witness such a bond seemed an honour not to be spoiled with weak goodbyes and as the cool fresh air fell to the bodies of the doctor and Miss. Harbottle they breathed deeply at their welcome freedom. They ached together with the certainty that they were terrified by other peoples' tragedies because they pointed to the fragility of everything.

The silent but brisk walk home warmed them as did the certain knowledge that they had done their best.

Both knew it was never going to be enough.

Neither, dared to speak of the questions raised in their minds by Ivy's anger towards her husband.

As he gently laid his sobbing daughter into her bed Tot felt a hateful presence behind him.

'I ought to kill you.'

The words were even more frightening for their tight coolness, like newly starched sheets on a cold midwinter night.

'Nature studies my arse. Now we know the real reason you took your daughter to the woods.'

June sniffed in, trying to stifle noisy breath to hear.

She watched her dad's face go whiter through the tear cleaned smudges as his jaw dropped. As he turned to the wife he no longer seemed to know, his back stiffened with a terrible new awareness.

'You can't possibly think that.'

'Can't I?'

'Ivy I am not your father!' The words were flat.

'All men are the same. No wonder you wanted to teach her all you know. Wild flowers and the seasons. Pah! Wild animals and the rotten birds and the bees more like! I'll make sure you join that other bastard in jail!'

As she turned on her heel Tot grabbed at her wrist which pulled her back to where he could urgently search her eyes.

Her fearless anger burned into him. 'Go on then! Bash me an' all! I got it all from him and now you! Punch me! Strangle me! Throw me to the ground! Suffocate me with your greedy body!'

'Ivy, put your bitterness back in its cage! I am not going to lay a finger on you.'

'Oh aye, pity you didn't think the same about your daughter.'

Tot, used to the steady thump of criticism, had hardened himself to pained attacks from his wife but this was different.

'This is not my doing. I love June. I would never harm her....or you.'

There seemed to be a slight easing of accusation as if this was all she wanted to hear but she still wouldn't give up. Her memory wouldn't allow it.

'Oh aye. Prove it can you?'

Tot turned to his daughter in spite of his wife's grunt of scepticism. Smoothing pale hair across his child's hot forehead, he gently but earnestly encouraged her.

'You have to tell us who did this to you June. We have to know.'

The discomfort of looking at her dad's pain faded from her mind as she saw even more for his future if she told. She could see him working even harder on stony seams and picking up short pay packets. She knew that tubs of coal he had heaved from the darkness would be ticketed to some-one else. He would lose the regard of the men who saw him as the best hewer in the colliery. He would lose his pride. He would lose himself.

'I don't know dad. I don't know.'

She watched as her mother shook her head and snorted out the belief that she was right.

'But you must know chicken.' His face was scored with so much misery, 'And you must tell me.'

June couldn't bear the begging pouring from his eyes, but still she couldn't tell. She turned her head to the pillow and wept.

The strong hand smoothed her hair. 'We will get through this Chicken, pain feeds our awareness and makes us better people. We will be together in this hurt.'

June didn't go to school next morning although she would have gone anywhere to avoid the hate sodden atmosphere. Wren knew that the family would have to work this out and painful though it was, it had to happen. She had seen all this agony before in different places, in different people, but the same strain and the same slow painful lessons. The advancement of soul is so subtle it can hardly be observed in the course of one human life. But there were those who saw it all. This was life and good God how she wanted it.

June lay in a sleep-starved murk.

Only a tiny piece of her seemed real and that was too deep inside her mind to feel. She felt her whole awareness to be encased in metal. A little window opened to allow any movement that the body which seemed not to belong to her, to conduct day to day necessities.

There had been no further words between her parents. She rose and shuffled dully to her half opened bedroom door where she stopped, not wanting to enter this new land of cold bareness that used to be her family's warm kitchen. There was no hot water for tea, no breakfast and no bait.

Tot left silently for his 10am shift without food, conversation or love. The fire was not lit, Ivy used her abrasive anger to clean and polish the black iron range which was the very centre of the household.

Barefooted and with an out of shape yellow cardie over a crumpled nightdress, June crept from the bedroom to stand on the multi-coloured mat behind her mother. Watching; shivering, trying not to absorb the agony which emanated from the tortured body before her.

The back of the woman who had brought her into the world was rigid with pain and hopelessness, the movements furious.

June's face still hurt, her hair stung where some of it had been pulled out from its roots by the woman she so much wanted love from. It was hard to haul words from where they had no understanding but she had to say something or die of isolation.

'Dad didn't do this to me mam.'

Ivy's back lifted. If only she could believe these words she desperately needed to hear.

'If you go to the police we won't have him.' Her words seemed stilted and inadequate.

The woman flung herself around to project cold anger at the daughter she wanted to strike, to hate, to take revenge from.

'Him, him, him! That's all you care about isn't it? You know that thing in your belly will be born with two heads and be as stupid as a pig don't you?'

Wren willed June to give a response that would raise her in spirit, demonstrate her growth and it came. It left the mouth of a fourteen year old in torment. All June cared about was her dad.

'My baby won't be a monster mam. Dad is the best dad in the world and he would never hurt me just as he would never hurt you. He loves us both.... in the proper way.'

Ivy's searing eyes scanned the face before her, it was pale and bruised, its only emotion earnest honesty.

For a valuable split second it seemed that relief might throw a mother into a daughter's arms but it hung between them then passed unused.

But something was altered, softly and hidden; but there.

'You know you can't go out.' she turned her back and smeared more black lead to the metal. This time the rubbing was more even, less aggressive.

'We'll have to go away, to your Aunty Harriett's in Cramlington. If she can bear to have us.'

She threw a disdainful look at June's thick waist. 'Before that gets big enough for folks to notice. Before I die of shame!' There was a soft sniff, the ridged back shuddered a little.

'We'll tell people the bairns mine when we come back, though God only knows how I could ever love a child whose father I don't even know the name of!'

June tightened her lips as if to physically hold in the name that might at any second splurge unsought from the depths of her bleakness.

'When we find out who's been messing with you, your dad'll kill him.'

The relief that her daddy was no longer suspected allowed tiredness to overcome June's body and silently she slunk to bed, this time to sleep.

Two days later she woke to find the precipice still yawning at her feet.

Aunty Harriet could bear the shame even less than her sister it seemed. When the letter arrived telling them that she would not have them it was a relief to Tot and his daughter but it threw Ivy into a new fury.

'Bloody families. I would be there if she needed me! Too busy flirting with every widower on Tyneside and swilling gin to help her sister!' The letter went onto the fire and with it the whole relationship.

The next few weeks were like the three tormented people had never known. A hard suppression of normal family life pushed sunken eyes even further into June's head. Coldness clung to everything, light could not enter the home nor the heart.

Only necessary words were uttered, the speaker never looking at the person the bleak short words were thrown to.

Not going out into the nature she craved drove June into a melancholy madness.

She never returned to school. The spring and all she loved were denied to her, half in punishment half in effort to retain a desperate respectability Ivy had worked hard at since the terrible ordeal of giving evidence against her drunken father in Newcastle Crown Court and her sudden removal to the country at sixteen. There was one little chink of happiness. Worried about fresh air and pale cheeks, her mother or father escorted her out for a quick walk in the dark every night. The timing was worked out exactly. The times of the buses with ten minutes either side were avoided; especially the ones that spilled couples and families from the picture house chattering about what they'd just enjoyed, viewers came in a dream from a world June didn't know. She always felt out of it when the girls at school swooned over David Niven or combed their hair like Greta Garbo. June had never seen a film, mostly because the nickname for the cinema was the local flea pit. That was all it took for her mother to declare the pictures strictly out of bounds.

The family and their shame were never seen. Ivy took to wearing looser clothing. She washed and pressed the maternity smocks she'd worn almost fifteen years ago. One was worn by herself whenever she had to go out to a delivery man and the other, a floral smock of a loosely woven material, was tossed onto the bed beside June when she was dressing one morning.

The April dawn came earlier and earlier. It became impossible for June to resist the budding bluebells, the opening forget-me-nots and the nodding white of patches of wood anemones that she knew would be urging her forest towards summer. Carefully timed visits to the outside lavatory just as it was getting light, gave her precious half hours to visit dew covered curls of unfurling bracken and the fat leaves of foxgloves which she knew would soon push up pink spikes to tower above everything else on the woodland floor. With the little dog snuffling behind her it almost seemed like last year. Only it wasn't and never could be again. She went to the beginning of the pine and it's massed, scary darkness. This edging of greening deciduous trees were where the treasures were in spring and she loved each one of them. This was her wood. Her dad had given it to her when she was only little. He had carried her on his shoulders from where she had screamed with delight, to a sandy patch of grass that she'd thought was covered in jewels. When he'd seen the glow on his daughter's face he knew she was of his mind. He'd taken great delight in gently picking up white, purple and pale yellow flowers so that they held their sparkle of dew long enough to enchant his curly haired infant. He'd taught her the names and smells. Violet had the strongest perfume and white Bird's Eye the least but the primrose was shy in offering a soft fragrance that had to be drawn in from the very depths of its centre and she had loved this flower the best. As she picked chubby fists full of wildflowers Tot saw this tiny child had a natural empathy with beauty and that is when he had given her this wood.

'Knowledge and caring allow ownership June. I will teach you everything I know about this wood and all it holds to give you happiness. It is your wood little June. I give it to you.'

That had taken every season and every spare moment they were together but by the time June was nine she knew the wood truly belonged to her.

It seemed so long ago now not only in time but in happiness. Everything was different. There was another life inside of her and there was nothing she could do about it. She had brought disharmony into her family. Her mother hardly spoke to her but her looks of distain shrank any tiny rise of comfort in her daughter. Tot tried a few times to speak to his wife but when he did his legs were slashed from under him by the sharpened tongue of a woman in agony.

Her father went into quiet sadness. He could not be reached.

June would have loved to pick a tiny posy to have in a washed out fish-paste jar by her bed or to take a circle of primrose leaves presenting a mound of freshly picked primroses to her mother, but she would be discovered, the doors would be locked, the flowers thrown to the fire and Temper! Temper! Temper!

Wren, aroused by the slight rise in the spirit of June would allow herself to leave the womb for a little while to enjoy the beauty herself. She knew from experience that without the coldness of winter this sunshine she was enjoying would not have a chance to encourage the loveliness this child was about to bring her into. She watched her mother who had pulled up her nightdress to avoid a telling damp patch, sitting on a spread of wood sorrel, smelling the morning and she knew.

They would never come here as mother and child.

Sockless feet in hastily pulled on Wellingtons rushed back through the allotments, over the fence to dad's newly dug earth. She helped create this garden, planted many of the vegetables and blooms now sparse because of the 'dig for victory' war campaign but it was the wild flowers and trees she loved best with their admired disorder. June flung her dew soaked body into the coldness of the lavatory. She clanked the chain just in case some-one else was up and ran across the cobbled road into the house, ordered Jan back to her basket and found her own miserable safety in her bed.

It was only a minute before she heard some-one rise, the poker rattle in between the fire bars and the kettle clank to its rest. Dad was on night shift. He hadn't got into his bed until two thirty this morning but she knew it was him. She heard the water being splashed into the sink in the scullery and knew he was wincing at the sting of his new facial cuts and scrapes. Fresh agonies caused by herself.

Dad's wounds would heal but the sadness and pain of how he came by them was never to mend in June.

CHAPTER EIGHT

It had been a warm afternoon for the end of April but June's only connection with the day she longed to join was through a window yanked open by the angry and resentful hands of a tight lipped mother.

Isolation poured gnawing boredom into the tiny bedroom. So heavy was the depression that it seeped into the very bones of a young body made for running through springtime. Bed clung to June's back with a hopeless dragging of the spirit.

The months she loved best were taken from her with her innocence by her thickening waist and the awful knowledge that without knowing how she had slammed into the ground every smile this house had ever held.

It seemed too much effort even to turn her head on the pillow to follow the fat body of a bumble bee that buzzed it's way on tiny wings round and round her sunless prison. Gone was the desire and energy to grab a jar to capture, only for a moment, that wonder of God so that she could examine curiously jointed legs heavy with pollen sacks, look into the strange face of one of the garden's more lovable insects and wonder how such weight could ever be borne on such out of proportion flying aids. She lost sight of the bee for a moment but knew from the little whirring that it was on the floor crawling a marathon across the oil-cloth to her bedside mat. It was almost four o'clock and June knew that if her mother came in to thrust tea and a sharp word the bee would lose its life in a thump of a slipper powered by a foot and mind that believed every insect was out to sting the whole human race.

Wren had been sleeping in the womb but was woken by the first movement for hours and the sudden surge of urgent fear hormone that reached her through the umbilical cord. Unseen, she left June just in time to watch gentle scooping in still childish hands of a thrashing striped and furry body which dashed thankfully off into warm air towards freedom. June folded her arms onto the windowsill. It was almost too beautiful to bear. But there was a sadness in the unfurling bracken fronds that clothed the steep slope beneath her window. It was as if true beauty could not exist unless it was appreciated. She knew that soon the ferny bracts would hide the spreading arms of speedwells that covered the ground like sapphire studded octopus. The wild garlic compensated for its pungent offerings with a brilliant white halo of flowers too smelly to pick but it was that fragrance that hit nose and lungs now on a breath of longing and fear. She pulled nature into her lungs but it failed in its very purpose of causing a heart to soar. Instead it twisted in mission to be expelled on a cry of despair and longing that knew it would never see another day such as this.

The cry and the sobbing that would have followed were halted by the sudden and demanding knock on the front door. June dashed to her bedroom door where she angled her head to gather every infiltrating mumble that would identify the caller forbidden to her. She heard a muttered 'Damn', from her mother as she clunked the table with the dough filled mixing bowl she had worked out some of her frustration on. The outer door had been left half open to the sunshine and half shut to the flies so that it was easily pushed back by the caller who sounded as if he had met her mother half way.

'Please forgive me calling Mrs. Stoker but I just had to find out how June was.'

June's little surge of pleasure at the recognition of Mr. Farraige's boom of a voice was quickly sat upon by the realization that she would not be allowed to see him.

'She is quite poorly. I will tell her you called.' She barked in a voice meant to wither enthusiasm so that it plopped to the ground.

'Can't I see her? Only for a moment.'

The defence in the mother's voice made it rise two octaves.

'She is too infectious for any visitors Mr. Farraige and she is not to be excited.'

There was a small gap in which June imagined the man to be debating whether or not to use the strength of his personality to persuade the hardness before him to soften.

'Not too infectious to a woman in your condition I hope.'

No one ever got past mam; June didn't even bother to wish. She knew that eyes would be glaring in a successful attempt to wither the man's hope and confidence.

'Well then could you give her these Lily of the Valley and tell her me and Towser picked them this morning from the bottom of the wood, she'll know the spot. Fresh with dew they were. Oh and these books. I told her about them one time, she will love 'The Garden of Ignorance',

Marion Cran, the author had the same love of nature and animals as your daughter and she'll learn much from....'

'Yes, yes, yes, I'm sure she will. Now if you don't mind my bread will be rising before I have kneaded it.'

Sensitivity led the caller away. June waited for the flowers with her favourite scent and the books that might nibble the edges of her boredom. They never came.

Not feeling up to the bone carving shouting that would surely erupt if she took the few steps to the kitchen table to pick up the books, June was left to marinade in her tedium. She lay covered with just a sheet staring at the curtains which fluttered now and again like floral sails which could take you off to an island far away. The clusters of full blown roses and rose buds tied with gay ribbons and surrounded by trellis had seemed ordinary enough when she'd been taken to the co-op to help chose the material. But now? Now they showed her what they were really made of. Like looking at the clouds, shapes formed pictures.

Princesses in crowns, fat faced gnomes in grottos and puppies snuggling together beneath petals and leaves. These curtains held a whole world she'd been too busy to notice and as they lifted and fell to the walls in the breeze they dispersed the images already delighted in to present whole new characters, especially if June allowed her eyes to go out of focus slightly.

This vivid display of imagination was cut off suddenly by excited yelping from Jan as dad pushed into the house turning everything back to wretched reality but at least with some comfort. June swallowed away the dryness of her study and felt her face lift with a smile as the little dog snuffled around the tiny gap at the bottom of her door.

'Jan no! That dog is filthy, don't let her in!'

'Oh Ivy, she's clean enough, the soil is dry and she's just been sleeping on a pile of weeds in the wheelbarrow.'

This interchange sounded almost normal as if the speakers had forgotten what hell life had thrown at them.

'I got six rows of peas planted and pricked out all me leeks.'

There was a clank of kettle to the range.

'Is the bairn still in bed? It's not good for her you know Ivy, she needs fresh air.'

Dad's voice faded as he went into the scullery to wash his hands beneath the solitary cold tap; Mam's was extra loud to be heard over the running water.

'Oh yeah, you would have her showing her belly to all the gardeners, they'd really get their yakking gobs together on this one wouldn't they.'

June could imagine her dad walking back into the kitchen wiping his arms and hands with the striped towel which he would throw over the back of a chair prompting mam to dash to the rescue of her immaculate room by returning it to its rightful hook for life.

'I'll take her some tea.' Dad said clinking cups. 'Any coconut haystacks?

'In the cake tin on the table.'

'Oh what are these?'

'Humph; just some daft books from Mr. Farraige for June.'

'And the flowers, who brought them?'

'The same.'

'Arthur Farraige bringing our June flowers.... what for?'

'Don't ask me, said they were from the bottom of the wood and she'd know where.'

'Oh aye; and what's a man of his age doing down the wood with fourteen year old girl eh!'

'He walks her home from school on the dark nights.....'

Heavy silence was displaced by the hard opening of the bedroom door. Jan scrambled up onto the bed washing June's face with watery tongue.

'Jan basket!'

Dad's tone had the dog to its place in no time, leaving June to puzzle at this and his rigid face.

'Come out here June.' he ordered before stepping back towards the table.

The only welcome in the room was from the flattened clippie mat to her bare feet.

She saw the books on the table and the Lily of the Valley lying beside them wilting for want of a drink and she knew they would die for being in this house instead of the wood where they belonged. Those little pale flowers could be her. She knew their pain.

Both June's parents stared at her and she dropped her shoulders to allow the thin white material of her nightdress to further hide her growing abdomen.

'June, how well do you know Mr. Farraige?'

The girl glanced at both earnest faces fixed onto hers.

'Come on girl answer your father!'

'Leave this to me Ivy!'

'Come on now pet, it's an easy enough question.'

June knew he was right but this was no help in how she should reply because she knew exactly what was being sought here and it frightened her. Wren, jolted by fear hormones whooshed to her through the umbilical cord, came out to her mother's shoulder. It was pitiful to see and she would have done anything to ease the pinched look on June's face.

'He's nice dad. He loves all the things we love and Towser loves Jan and big as he is can't even catch a stick before her.'

'When do you throw sticks for the dogs June?'

'When we go for walks in my wood dad. Mr. Farraige says he never knew the wood belonged to me but now he sees it could never belong to any-one else.'

'And he's walked you home from school has he?'

'Yes,' June replied remembering the dark nights and the even darker threats. 'He looks after me dad.'

This didn't seem to please him.

'Was it him June, was it? Was it Mr. Farraige who hurt you? Did he give you this baby June. Answer me!'

'Dad! No! No! No! He loves me dad, he always says he'd never do anything to hurt me.'

'Oh aye! Oh aye! Well maybe he thinks it doesn't hurt for a bachelor of his age to be down the woods with my daughter but I sure as hell do!'

He grabbed at the books and was out of the door before June could say anymore.

'Get back in there!'

Her mother flung the words at her before picking up a cloth to lift the urgently steaming kettle off the heat. June's heart went out to the little dog whose eyes showed the hurt at being left behind when she could clearly hear outside boots being hastily pulled on. It made the same hopeless journey to the flagging stalks of fragrant cream bells ignored despite heart aching beauty, and to Mr. Farraige.

Especially to Mr. Farraige.

She fell to the bed and saw the curtains still hanging at her sunny window, still wafting in the breeze but no longer showing her the delights of a child's mind. What images clung to floral folds she could not tell, her eyes no longer saw anything good for there was nothing but pain. Everything else had gone. Her mind was full.

Wren withdrew in silent love, she knew this anguish was important to the soul of June and there was no way through it but to hurt. That hurt would bring strength and understanding.

It seemed an eternity before excited yelps from Jan told of Dad's return. There was a gasp from his wife and then indistinguishable mumbling. The sneck echoed through the murk of her worry and her dad stood before her. His top lip was twice its normal size on one side of his face and the other side was grazed and cut with blood smeared across a white cheek where skinned knuckles had investigated the damage.

'I got the bugger.'

June flung herself to his arms, he winced at the contact to his chest but he cuddled her anyway.

They both cried. Tot because he felt he had avenged a terrible hurt to his daughter. June because she knew he'd got it so very wrong.

That had been the pain of yesterday.

It didn't help her get through today.

With new agonies pushing June into the bed she became even more slack-jawed and staring. The need for the wood was buried beneath misery as it congealed around her, day layered on hopeless day. Meals came into the room and left untouched. Wren felt the foetus that would have to carry her weakening from constant misery and lack of food.

It was of paramount importance that this human vehicle she had stolen was strong and healthy. She would need no hold backs in her search. A sickly body was not helpful in utilizing the strength of such an advanced spirit. When first she'd entered this girl's body she had been determined not to have any involvement at all. Any vigour given was taken away from her purpose. She could have no distractions; use none of her highly evolved advantages. Now it was different, she needed to use powers to quicken this girl's heart. She needed nourishment and she wanted the baby she was to become to know and feel happiness but the hormones passed to her were all negative. She knew that a growing baby was parasitic to its mother but too much was being drained from this girl's brain and bones. She could become too weak to carry the growing weight and then too depleted to feed and love her child when it was born.

That is when June started to eat again. Only bread and dripping at first but it gave physical strength to the mind Wren had quickened with mental images of baby rabbits nibbling at new grass shoots and dandelion leaves and a slight unexplained feeling that something special would happen if only she could get out of this misery sodden house.

Wren hadn't needed to furnish any more energy for the food and the images had been enough to give daring to June's desires. That is when she had ventured into chilly dawns to await the warmth and magic of the sun in her wood.

She had managed to give her parents enough doubt of Mr. Farraige's guilt for them not to call the police. During gentle questioning by her father, she saw that he believed her and was aware of his embarrassment that he had attacked a man much older than himself. That he had been given as good as he got added to his mortification. June knew that to mention Mr. Farraige's bare fisted boxing awards from his army days would have given salve to his male pride but she dared not mention the man except to deny that he had ever hurt her.

Having failed breaking his daughter's silence as to who was the father of her shame, Dad stopped vocalizing his questioning guesses which left his mind to agitate torturously over boys at school and passing gypsies. It never occurred to him that he handed his coal tickets twice a week to the very person he wanted to kill.

May threw its glory over hawthorn hedges and cow parsley edged lanes. Creamy perfume from creamy blossom brushed past the growing body of the escapee from the shame shackled prison.

Without these daring dawn excursions June felt her soul would surely die. The sun was rising earlier each morning and this act seemed to exist simply to give her more time in her own bit of heaven. It was May the twentieth a date she would remember forever because of two things.

It was about six am when girl and dog sat back against a broad beech trunk staring up at fresh green leaves not yet tarnished or torn by heavy rain or north winds. Little glimpses of blue sky showed even brighter through the massed green when she heard a warning rapid cackling that she knew was the danger call from a wren. Jan flicked her head to the exact place in the hazel bush beside them where the agitated noise was coming from. A firm hand went to the dog's collar and Jan knew from much experience that she was to 'stay'. The stillness and quiet relaxed the little bird so it began to sing. Beauty pierced the air in clear and long heart lifting song that June herself rose to the sky upon. Wren felt the sheer joy in her womb and left its safety to be part of this exhilaration over the very creatures she had taken her name from but when she did she saw much more than June could see with her human eyes.

The song stopped and was replaced by gentle rustles only loud enough to be heard by canine ears at first. June followed the keen eyes of her dog to deeper into the hazel twigs and that is when she thought she might die of joy.

Four tiny fledglings were hopping wide-eyed and precariously closer to their mother who wanted to show them how to take the world before it took them.

June drank in the beauty and wonder but even this great understanding and appreciation was nothing compared to what Wren could see. June saw only the physical, miniature birds braving the might of the very nature which bore them. She had never seen such young birds out of the nest and she gave them the admiration they were due because she knew that despite their diminutive appearance they were fiercer than wolves when called upon to defend their young and mightier than the eagle in resourcefulness.

She couldn't see that these were really spiritual parts of her own soul family. Wren saw the blue glow of energy that emanated from the brown feathers and perpendicular tail. They had come to give love and support from a place June had left fifteen years ago. Their incandescence went with them as they darted from twig to twig, their weight not even enough to bend soft new shoot tips.

June's wonder and fascination did her justice. She was so taken with these birds because of her love of nature but it went even deeper, she didn't understand; but she felt it. There was a strange longing to be up there four feet above her head, side by side with these presences that kept her wide eyed and enthralled. Wren could see the beauty of these visitors from the light. They were part of June's spirit group. Sundia, the spirit of June, had spent her time with them when she wasn't incarnated and they were keen to give her love and energy now at this most difficult time of her life. They wanted to be seen by June so that they could touch her soul with their beauty and allow her to remember the love and guidance they would always give her. June felt it so strongly that as they left, dashing through bright green leaves to dense ivy clothing the trunk of a neighbouring ash, she rose as if to take flight herself to follow them. Her disappointment when she realized she was still earthbound crushed her soaring soul. Wren knew that was how it had to be and it wouldn't be too long before she followed the wrens.

Jan's tail was wagging furiously at the sight she'd shared with Wren. Her gaze was directed at her now and a great love passed between them. It was a love for each other because of the great appreciation of each other's souls and it was a bond in love for June. Wren, who came to this incarnation wanting to keep all her emotions for the gigantic task of finding Alessandro, realized at that moment that it was impossible not to care for these lovely energies she was about to share the world with.

'What is it Jan? What have you seen?'

June turned her head in the direction of the dog's stare hoping to see more birds, she saw nothing but felt an inexplicable love and understanding of what everything was about. In that split second she knew it all. The universe, God, the meaning of life, total love. As quick as it came it left, leaving a sense that it hadn't really been. But she felt different, elevated, and stronger.

Her legs seemed to be holding her up for no reason and it was without thought that she sat amongst dry leaf mould with her back against the green beech trunk. She was lost in euphoria, a feeling known to her throughout her visits here but not at this high-level. It was almost sheer ecstasy, a drug, a high of the mind from which she never wanted to descend.

Jan had snuffled off on a nose to ground search for rabbits leaving robin, blackbird and thrush songs the confidence to start up again. This was background to June's rejoicing, an addition rather than a thing on its own, an edging not an individual joy. Wren herself swelled with the sweet contamination of such joy and when a woodpigeon calling for its mate tossed bubbling, throaty poetry across the treetops, she watched a smile break onto June's face. The eyes, closed in efficiency of experience, opened into the sun and Wren saw just how beautiful the green and blue which shone from different eyes really was.

It was an exceptional moment for Wren.

June, seeing how high the sun was rising and realizing her escape time was up, reluctantly brought her mind and body into line. Wren returned to her foetus growing in the womb so that she might hold onto this most spiritual of earthly emotions a little longer. After the freedom of the woods it felt cramped, the baby was growing, the buds were now arms and legs and the body was catching up to the head in size. It was becoming harder to turn she noticed as she pushed weak legs against amniotic fluid and felt the boundary of the womb. She was aware of a little gasp from her mother and felt a hand go to the other side of the belly.

This was a revelation to the girl who was yet to turn fifteen. Until that moment her baby had been a terrible burden of shock and shame, the thief of all she had known and the destroyer of family security. She had been whacked into darkness by ignorance and pain. The baby had not existed as a real thing. It was only agony. Now, with its very first kick, it had announced it was a reality. This was a baby moving inside her. It was not a disgrace, something to be hidden or a terrible memory of dark afternoons in November. It was part of her and it was alive. A new kind of love seemed to spread from the deep core of her brain through the emotional roadways in her neck, down her back and then into her heart where she knew there was plenty of room for this new feeling to grow not just in size but in complexity. It pushed the old dread away with its brightness leaving just a little black edging of dread but it was not June's; it was her own mother's . It was Ivy's.

The experience had kept her out late and she now panicked a little as she read the sun again. It felt like seven o'clock but the mornings seemed to be racing ahead in their desire to experience summer once again. How she wished she was lucky enough to have a watch. The house held hard time in the clock above the fire and dad's pocket watch, still in the velvet case it languished in when it had belonged to his grandfather. These were things of beauty, cherished and admired not like the enamel alarm clock which ticked and rang its irritating life through every day and night turning her father out on freezing dark mornings to slave in an even darker pit. These were people's time keepers the real movements of morning were in the sky and feel of the air.

The dog reached the back door first leaving June's long stride to catch up to the scatter of little paws. She was just in the gate. A short expanse of cracked concrete, weedless and dustless, was all there was between the soft opening of the door, the fall to the bed and the pretence of never having left it. A loud crack spoiled the sequence she breathlessly carried herself through each dry morning. The door opened to produce an image which threw June's newly risen heart to her throat with fright. Her mother was coming out wrapped in a pale candlewick dressing gown that used to be pink. In her hand was a potty of adult capacity and design, its little sprigs of green flowers failing to pretty its real reason for being pulled from beneath the bed because of too much tea before bedtime. Mam stopped, her alarm at seeing another person in her yard so early turning quickly to annoyance.

'What are you doing out here. It's light for goodness sake!' Her eyes darted left and right in search of any early passer-by who might catch a glimpse of her daughter looking so round and herself looking so slim. 'Get into that house!'

'I was only at the netty.' She hated the lie as it left her lips but she would have hated the results of the truth even more.

'Why didn't you to use the po' under the bed, it is what they were invented for?'

Suspicion searched the face of her daughter but fear of being seen by neighbours was the stronger.

'Get in! Both of you!'

Her slipper went beneath the tummy of the dog to roughly encourage a hasty entrance into the kitchen before closing the door to imprison the two nuisances of her life.

A few minutes later she burst into the scullery where June was standing in front of a bowl of cold water having a hasty strip wash. Even from the back her mother could see the body was thickening and the sight fuelled her anger.

'Jan's tummy is wet!'

Fear sloshed through June's body as loudly as the water on it.

'Look at me girl.'

June, pulling the towel to her front turned to face the fear of discovery.

'Is it?'

She knew she'd been careful not to walk on any damp grass herself because the leather of her lace up shoes always showed darker for the rest of the day as it dried out.

'She must have gone into the garden whilst I was on the netty.'

Mam digested the scene these words offered but no comfort of acceptance was projected to ease June's fear of exposure. A thousand reasons for a wet dog were flashed through a mind behind a set face but none were given words. Eyes held to June's in warning. If there was anything going on it would not get past this woman.

'Get your clothes on. I'm making porridge and I don't want to see you at the table in that nightie and cardie again. Make yourself look respectable for when your da comes in.... even though you aren't.' These last words thrown on a look of disgust seared with liquid wretchedness right to the very core of June. But something strange happened. It was reflected away, glanced off the brightness and greatness that was still inside her. She was too glowing to absorb insult. She seemed to have a shield that sent nastiness back to where it began. As she wondered at this new awareness she saw her mother wince as she stretched to the top shelf for the porridge pan.

'Ow! My blooming back!' The heavy pan thumped to the scrubbed wood of the draining board as she put both hands to her waist in order to stretch at her upper body. 'Oh hell! That's all I damn well need. You'll have to get dad's bath for when he gets in. Come on!'

As she dressed, June wondered if what she had seen and felt was real for if it was she was sorry. Even if she had sent Ivy's nastiness back to the sender, the woman was suffering enough and she deserved no more.

On Saturday evening, the fire low enough not to heat the room too much but hot enough to have cooked a delicious supper which June had eaten voraciously, mam rose from her chair and pile of wash stiffened socks she was darning to go into the big bedroom. Dad and June looked up from an old book on baby mammals that dad had bought from the chapel jumble sale last weekend. There was a shuffling of drawers and their contents before mam reappeared with an old candy striped sheet. She snipped one of the edges with the scissors and then tore foot wide strips right down the length until the sheet which had covered the marital bed for seven years was no more.

'What on earth are you doing woman?'

'It was worn in the middle; I was going to make pillowcases and dusters out of it anyway. Now it will serve me well in chapel tomorrow. It's time we went back. Can't pretend that girl is infectious forever.'

There was a silence whilst the minds of the onlookers tried to work out how a worn out sheet would add anything to mam's singing or praying. There seemed no sane answer and when dad asked for one he was told to wait and see in an expression that did not promote anything worth waiting for.

June was ushered off to bed.

CHAPTER NINE

Sundays were usually days full of good clothes, chapel and roast beef with the crispiest Yorkshire Puddings known to the North East. Winter saw the afternoons around the fire giving burning fronts and freezing backs as the Stoker family tried to digest their huge dinners eaten at midday, in time to dive at a laden tea table that wouldn't shame the king. Spring and summer took willing backs and arms to work in the vegetable garden to try to work off too many roast potatoes and to earth up the swelling new potatoes of future Sunday dinners. Today there would be no chapel for June, food would be served without chatter and eaten with a heavy heart. It was five thirty when the sun first shone into her east facing window between curtains kept open for just such a joy to wake her.

She had missed going to chapel and the singing but as much as she loved the red brick Methodist building and all the people who worshipped there, she knew that God and Jesus were everywhere. Today she would make the trees her altar.

As she passed the gardens the dawn chorus was thickening, each new bird song seemed to push another into competition until beaked joy blended into a wall of sound and gladness. June believed that this Sunday bird song was for Jesus and she felt a huge surge of need to add her praise and understanding to the jubilation that was the wood in springtime. It had to be her favourite hymn and her very best voice as she would be the only worshipper in these woods who knew this tune. As soon as she felt far enough away from any house and human she spun around, head back to soar her way to the bulbous white clouds that hung in the fresh blue above her. To these she sang, hoping in some childish way that they were near enough to God and his son to nudge them into listening.

'Jesus wants me for a sunbeam to shine for him each day

Jesus wants me to be loving and kind in every way.

A sunbeam, a sunbeam, Jesus wants me for a sunbeam.

A sunbeam a sunbeam, I'll be a sunbeam for him.'

Jan had thrown back her head to howl tunelessly with June and she thought that this was why every bird had gone quiet. Wren knew the real reason. The sensitivity of the birds was high because of their short repeat lives bringing them into regular contact with the one who made them so they were aware of true beauty when they heard it. Their silence was out of inadequacy. Each bird in Garsefield wood knew it could never better the sound of that innocent voice.

This girl would be a loss to them.

Determined to return well before the seven o'clock alarm woke her parents June rushed through dew covered grass strewn with buttercups and daisies. Her hair brushed at the tips of hawthorn and birch leaves as she skipped through her wood. She threw herself into the lavatory where she hurriedly changed wet Wellingtons for dry shoes, rubbed vigorously at Jan's tummy and paws with four squares of newspaper from the string on the wall and pulled the chain.

Her bare feet were quieter than the snores and she made it into bed with minutes to spare.

She was breathless. Her growing weight and fattening tummy were for the first time making a difference to her movements. As she laid flat palms across her baby she willed it to move again as it did every so often for it was then that she would talk to it. She wanted it to feel love even before it was born, hoped it would identify with her voice when she had to pretend to be its sister. She knew from experience that being the child of Ivy wouldn't be easy even with dad and herself to ease the tension.

She told her baby to be good and secretly hoped that Colin would have very little of his personality passed onto the child he would never know he had fathered.

She would love the life growing inside of her towards being her own little sunbeam.

When the rudeness of the alarm broke into her thoughts June waited until her parents reached the kitchen and she heard the sneck of the back door as dad went to the netty first as he always did on Sundays when they were both at the table for breakfast. She allowed enough time for mam to stoke up the fire, put the kettle to boil and wash her whole body with the flannel as she did every day of her life. On hearing dad's return June pulled on her baggy yellow cardi' and went to the scullery to wash. Dad was just drying up to his elbows; his face glowed with the stimulation of cold water and carbolic soap. His dark hair fluffed by drying coal dust and sleep had yet to be sleeked with his dab of Brylcreem. She tipped his greyed water from the little bowl sitting in the white sink and ran some fresh. As she took the already lathered bright pink soap into her hands she felt a little kiss to the back of her head and then dad's fingers lightly in her hair.

'How are you today chicken? Enjoy your morning trip to the woods?' he whispered.

Eyes wide with unexpected discovery, June spun round, warming in those quick eyes and ready smile.

'The May blossom loves you so much it came home with you.' He held three tiny cream flowers in his big palm.

Mam returned and dad tossed the May into the sink then tipped June's water after them. They were both relieved to hear her go into the bedroom to dress.

'I dried your wellies an' all. Think on June, if you are caught she will make sure you never get out again.'

'Oh dad, you won't say?'

'Of course not. You are like a tree in chains pet. Nothing could stop you growing and reaching for the sky.'

June hugged her dad for his understanding and she knew that it would be hell for him if Mam knew he hadn't stopped her.

'You're getting to show ower much to be seen darlin'. Be careful. It won't be long now, in August it will all be over and you can go back to school in September.'

'But dad I'll be fifteen next week. I don't need to go back. I want to look after my baby.'

He took the towel from her hands and held them both firmly.

'You mustn't say that. It isn't your baby; its mam's and mine. Your brother or sister.'

His soft eyes searched the pain in hers. 'You are starting to love it aren't you?'

She looked down at her swelling waist and nodded.

'Is that because you love the father?'

June looked to his face with shock.

'Is this why you go to the woods...to meet him?'

'No dad! No!'

'I wish you would tell me who it is pet, I'll skin his bloody arse for him!'

The opening crack of the bedroom door made the two pick up plates and cutlery in unison before heading into the kitchen to lay the breakfast table.

Mam stayed at the door waiting to be noticed, embarrassment mixing with expected approval of her ingenuity.

'What the....?' Dad raked his eyes up the full length of her.

June held knives half way to the tablecloth as she took in the look of her mother as she had never seen her before. She wore her usual dress for chapel but now it was tight around her middle, a middle the same size exactly as June's.

'All right! All right! Don't stare!' she hurled her discomfort at the shocked and fascinated pair. 'Does it work?'

Tot absorbed in the curiousness of any man looking at his wife and daughter in exactly the same stage of pregnancy faltered. 'Yes....but how?'

'That's all right then. It's the strips of sheeting, folded into my pants and vest.'

'But mam, it's too warm for a vest.'

The withering look informed June that she would have been better not voicing her thoughts.

'Aye well, just another of the ways we all have to suffer for your behaviour.'

She walked to the table and began straightening the cloth.

'Well come on then. Breakfast won't jump onto the table itself.'

When they'd eaten, dad whistled Jan to his side then went out to his garden across the narrow street and behind the double brick block of lavatories. He returned just as June came out of her room with her hair neatly brushed and plaited onto one side.

Tot looked at the face on full show now the hair was pulled off it. It was a child's face, pale and tight, too young to have to go through this. She looked at him and smiled.

'He passed her the metal vegetable bucket, half full with potatoes which had lying on top of them tiny bright carrots with ferny tops still vigorous from a warm sunny morning's growing.

He washed his hands. 'Mam not out yet?'

'No, she's making sure she looks just right…just like me.' She looked away embarrassed.

'Well, I'd better not make her angry by being late. I'll go and shoehorn meself into me Sunday best and not complain about it. I've filled the coal scuttle, shined me shoes and walked the dog. Hope there's nowt left that I can get wrong for.' He laughed as he went towards the bedroom.

June cleared away crumbs and jammy knives, too soft butter and the remains of mam's home baked loaf.

At the door stood dad in his dark suit looking uncomfortable pulling around the tight starched shirt collar and mam with the cardigan she knitted in January draped over her shoulders, they turned.

June went towards them and dad stepped forward.

'Bye pet. We'll say a prayer for you.'

'Come on Tot. Me shoes are already too tight and we've the cobbles to cover before I can get a sit down.'

He opened the door and mam began to walk through.

'Set that table and have the veg on. Meat goes in at eleven and watch it! I don't want cinders on me plate as well as in me mouth.' Ivy threw the words on a disapproving glance.

Dad kissed June on the forehead and gave a conspiratorial wink that said she wasn't to listen.

June, glad to have a release from the terrible boredom of her bedroom and enjoying the peace of the house to herself, set about her work with relish.

When she'd washed up in the tiny sink and swilled cold water to chase away the Sunlight soap, she tossed the first of dad's early new potatoes into the bowl and covered them with more cold water.

The skins hardly needed scraping on the just dug tiny balls. She ran the carrots beneath the tap and watched the sandy soil wash down the plug hole. Dad had pulled too many and she knew the reason as one after the other, the two- bite size vegetables crunched between her teeth.

She had two pans waiting to go onto the range when she realized dad hadn't picked any spring cabbage. She knew where it was, hadn't she helped prick out the tiny seedlings into rows last October, but the garden might have been in China for all the accessibility she was allowed to it.

She looked at the clock. Half past ten, everyone respectable would be in chapel right now and there was nobody in this street of twenty houses who didn't want to appear respectable.

She went through a mental list; four couples were almost ready for retirement. The Thompson had two girls working at the Co-op and they were still being dragged out to family worship.

The toddlers at number eleven and fourteen would be by now running around the aisles causing mayhem. Every-one else had grown up offspring who had already made them grandparents.

There would almost certainly be no-one about. Did she dare?

She could still run and Jan would warn her of any-one in adjoining gardens who had escaped the colliery street's Sunday rituals.

Before she could have any doubt she pulled on her shoes and darted across the road, pushed the gate held shut with string and made straight for the rows of dark green leaves warming themselves in the sun. June pulled at one with not too much caterpillar damage, broke off the root with an experienced twist and then tossed it with a couple of yellowing bottom leaves onto the compost heap. Urgency sped her through the back door with a little squeal of released tension.

After leaving the cabbage to soak in salted water to flush out any clinging caterpillars June was suddenly hit by a desperate need to lie down. Her back was aching with too much standing at the low sink on stone flooring.

She flung open the windows of her little bedroom and dropped onto her newly made bed.

It seemed part of her dream when she heard her name being called and so she didn't get up.

It wasn't until Jan who was taking a nap of her own on the bottom of June's bed, started a low throaty growl that June realized some-one was outside her window.

'June! June! Are you there?'

Even in her sleepy state June knew it was a voice she'd not heard for quite a few weeks.

She got up slowly and pulled a pillow in front of her to disguise what would be obvious to anyone by now. When she got to the window she saw Mr. Farraige wobbling and slipping his way through thick bracken and gorse that clothed the steep bank falling away from the single storied ducket houses. Towser bounced excitedly when he saw June and the tips of Jan's ears as she stretched to see her friends.

Wren, woken from the deep sleep so necessary to the growth of a six month foetus by a strange mixture of fear and pleasure, rose to her viewing point above June's right shoulder.

Poor Mr. Farraige; his eyebrow had been deeply cut and the congealed scab forming over it made his forehead look too bulbous to be real. There was an almost healed graze beneath the mouth smiling his welcome. It struck June to her heart to know it was her dad who gave this good man his injuries. If he knew what he'd saved her from he would have thanked him heartily.

June felt her face flush. What if he saw how large her stomach had become? She tried to stoop into the pillow hoping that from his position he would only be able to see above her waist.

'Oh June, dearest, how have you been?'

'I'm still infectious. Don't come too near.' She faltered over the words and knew they had not one iota of a ring of truth.

His eyes held hers in truth. 'There's no need to pretend with me dear. Aren't I a good enough friend not to lie to?'

The pull of his honest scrutiny locked her to his soft gaze. She wanted to protest, to spin the prepared story but she knew it would only make her look like a liar.

She said nothing.

'I saw you pulling the cabbage June. Towser couldn't help his ears pricking up as he smelled his friends and remembered happy times. It was all I could do to snap the lead onto his eager body.'

'Oh, I....'

'It was Colin who did this to you wasn't it? Why don't you tell the truth? You'd have saved me an awful beating from that fierce dad of yours.' He laughed a little but June knew it was only to ease her discomfort. 'There had to be a reason why he came looking for me. But even with all his anger I gave as good as I got. He is a strong man June, but I have the training and the discipline.'

'I'm sorry. He knows now it wasn't you who hurt me. I managed to convince them both.'

'Colin mustn't get away with this June. Tell your parents.'

'I can't. He can alter dad's wages. He knows how to make them short, change the tickets to someone else. He has the power to tip all the coal dad has hewed by saying it is too much stone.'

A look of distaste tightened his mouth. 'Blackmailer too is he? If I get my hands on him....'

'No! Please. Just leave it.'

Mr. Farraige had the look of some-one who was pretending to agree but would not push this issue to the back of his mind. June read this but had neither the strength nor the skills to persuade him otherwise.

Wren knew he would not leave it. He hadn't worked out yet how he would deal with Colin but deal with him he would.

He looked down to a brown shopping bag hanging heavily in his hand.

'Oh! I brought you these.' He smiled as he lifted three dark green cloth covered books towards her. Their spines were broken, the stains where mud had been wiped from their hard backs told a story all of their own.'

'Did dad do this?'

'Yes,' he snorted. 'He threw them at me at the end of our lane. But don't worry, the words inside will still captivate you, muck or no muck.'

'I'm sorry.'

'Don't be sorry; enjoy.'

June dropped the pillow and with it her defence. She took the books, ruffled Towser's ears and then picked up her own dog so that she could come nose to nose with another wiggling body and furiously wagging tail.

'Is this the only time you're alone June.'

She nodded, feeling the hopelessness of her shame imprisonment.

'Well, as I'm the only one whose religion is books, I'll see you next week.' He glanced at his watch.

'Same time?'

June, flushed with the joy of having a friend who understood and the deliciousness of boredom slaying books, nodded.

When she was alone she slumped to the bed to dip into the pages of promised pleasure. The first book had a few black and white plates of a thirties garden, old fashioned girls in cotton bonnets, a long haired dog named Bouncer and a dovecot. With chapters entitled 'Cats,' 'The Autumn Garden' and 'The Children's Garden', June was thrust into a world too captivating to leave.

She stayed in her release until Jan's ears lifted in sleep to the sound of her parents return.

Shock threw June up from the bed and the world her reading had taken her to. She thrust the three books beneath her mattress then rushed to the door to allow the dog to leap in joy at dad's ankles.

She emerged to her mother's tight face as it sniffed the air. The tension spread as she pulled open the heavy black door of the big oven and found it empty. The silence enlarged the angry click of her shoes on the stone floor of the scullery where she found vegetables in pans of water and Yorkshire pudding mix still in the bowl in which she had left it to prove last night.

There was no lunch. No smell of roasting beef, no bubble of salted potatoes and the fire was all but out.

'Can't you do anything right girl?' The words were spat out, changing the Sunday peace to the hopeless gloom of everyday. 'I paid 2/6 for that beef bone and it sits rotting in the pantry! Don't you know some food is still rationed?'

'Now Ivy, the bairn must have fallen asleep. She is growing a baby in that body of hers, its tiring work.'

'Tiring work! Tiring work! Not half as tiring as smiling at people who congratulate you in chapel on a baby that is nowt but a pile of rags!'

She stomped to the bedroom leaving dad to take in the misery before him that was his daughter.

'Come on chicken; I'll build up the fire. We'll have a paste sandwich while the oven heats and look forward to our dinner at suppertime. It's too warm for a roast now anyway, I prefer it that way. I'll get some digging done in the garden as I am not weighed down with roast potatoes.'

Ivy came out wearing everyday clothes that clung to her thin bones proving her confidence that unlike the rest of the gossipy street where they wasted precious cleaning time by running in and out of each other's houses, no-one would dare call here without being invited.

She sat to grimly eat bread and paste and then took a pile of plates and knives to the scullery sink. When she returned seconds later she was carrying a pan which she thrust in front of her daughter's nose. 'What's this?'

'Cabbage.'

'Yes cabbage! Your dad was saying on the way home that he'd forgot to get it from the garden and he'd have to nip out whilst the Yorkshires were doing. So how come we've got a pan full of cabbage?'

The three froze waiting for the answer they already knew and the trouble that would follow.

'I got it.' June felt herself tumble into the thorny ditch of her mother's anger.

'You mean girl…that you went outside where every gossip monger in the street could see you just to get a cabbage.'

'There was no-one out, they were all at chapel like you.'

'You disobeyed my orders. Your stupidity could have spoiled our plans. Do you want everyone to know you for the whore you are?'

'Ivy stop…..' Dad's words were snowflakes falling on mam's burning fury.

'Get into that room and stay there until the brat comes.'

The forced inactivity was almost unendurable for June and as she grew bigger her early morning dashes to her wood grew less and less frequent. The door was locked on Sundays and the key went to chapel along with the ever growing girth of Ivy. If it hadn't been for the regular appearances of Mr. Farraige and Towser, June would have seen no-outsider but Dr. Kelly for two months. They came through July heat and downpour mud with the brown shopping bag hiding the only release from the boredom that June could look forward to when her dad was at work. Mr. Farraige's library soon ran out of books he thought would interest a girl who had just turned fifteen but June devoured each classic or military strategy book with voraciousness for it was her only relief. To help soften the blow he began pressing between the pages of dense text, wild flowers that had just opened to the summer. June smelled and kissed these surprise offerings which she used as bookmarks and began looking forward to them as much as the books.

One Sunday in early August there was something different, Mr. Farraige had handed over the brown paper package with his eyes to the ground but June could still see the blush to his neck. She untied the string bow, peeled away the stiff paper to find a book that smelled different to anything she'd ever read before. The book was clean and fresh; no other fingers had dipped into these pages or fanned their edges beneath grubby thumbs. This was a new book, shop bought from Newcastle. June turned the volume to its front, keen to read the title.

The cover was smart grey with a red medical cross both above and below one word written discretely with a certain importance.

'CHILDBIRTH'.

For some reason this book seemed more of a secret than any of the others and its very presence in June's hands made her unsteady. Her heart beat as she opened the pages at random and found horrible yet compelling drawings in black and red ink. Only a flash of a curled up baby held tight by a cross-sectioned womb and joined by a twisted cord entered her brain before the book slammed shut.

This couldn't be inside her now.

Her embarrassment drowned his own.

'You need to know what is happening to your body June. I'll pick the book up next week'. He would have done anything not to have caused this droop to her smile. 'Fancy me being the only bachelor in the North with a book on pregnancy on my shelves.'

It worked. June pushed out a little laugh on withheld breath.

'Thank you.' She hugged the book to her chest, polished Towser's head with a nervous hand and smiled her goodbyes to a man hoping he'd done the right thing.

June was dragged from the awful informative pages by the key in the lock. Jumping up, she pushed the book deeper beneath the mattress than any book had gone before, vainly trying to rid her features of the guilt she knew they portrayed by forcing a weak smile.

Mam didn't look at her anyway but pulling her pinny across the padded stomach went straight to the oven to pull a sizzling tin from the heat. She basted the little roll of pork and turned the potatoes in the fat before roughly shoving everything back for the last half hour.

'I'm tired Tot, I'll have a lie down before I put the Yorkshires in. Keep an eye on it will you?'

When she'd gone Dad pulled June toward his white shirted chest.

'Every-one was asking about you as usual and send their best wishes. I said you were picking up.

They asked if you were looking forward to having a new brother or sister.'

'Oh daddy.'

She clung to him as the roasted aromas of the just opened oven floated like greasy dust unseen onto them. How she wished she could feel like his little girl again.

Next day dad had left for back shift and mam had to appear pregnant by ten o'clock because this was the morning the paraffin oil man came to the street. When the horse and cart rattled to the yard entrance she became her outside self, the one who was expecting a baby at the end of August. June no longer had to be warned to keep back and she sat behind the open door until the can mam had taken out was returned filled and smelly. She heard neighbours who had long since learned Ivy didn't want to be friendly, but unable to curb their feminine concern, make stiff enquiries into her health.

'I'm fine thank you. Baby's fine an all.' Ivy's stiff reply cooled the group.

'Must be hard having to wait hand and foot on your lass and carry that belly in front of you.'

June knew this remark was meant with sympathy but mam took away it's dignity by making no reply and as she opened the door further, a wave of muttering flowed behind her and a clear 'She's a queer 'un that one', rose like broken foam into the clear air.

She put the can into the stick cupboard with the newspapers waiting to be rolled into paper kindling to light the fire next morning then went to wash her hands.

'You ready for Doctor Kelly? He'll be here in half an hour.'

June went to her room to make sure it was tidy and fresh. She would have loved some wild flowers on the table beside her bed but was grateful at least for the single pink rose dad had picked from the fence that surrounded his vegetable plot and the white petunia he'd potted up for her birthday.

By the time the doctor rapped his fingers to the door before opening it June had been dozing for several minutes.

'Getting tired June?' he said feeling her tummy and listening with the now familiar stethoscope and trumpet. 'It won't be long now.'

She sat up and offered her arm to the black band of the blood pressure machine.

'Doctor.'

'Yes.'

She paused, trying to gather strength as the rubber inflator gasped beneath his fingers.

'Where will the baby come out?'

He didn't look at her but scribbled tiny notes into his book.

'Same place it went in June. Hasn't your mother told you yet?'

He packed his bag then looked at her fondly. She felt the bed go down as he hitched himself beside her, taking one of her hands in both of his. He was sitting just above the book she had not dared to believe.

'The midwife will be coming at the end of this week June, I'll ask her to give you a women's talk. But don't worry, females are built for this and it will be all right, you're a strong girl.'

He went into the kitchen leaving June with the sinking confirmation that what she'd read was true. It was horribly, horribly true.

He stayed longer than usual and June was glad when the back door clunked into place so that she could finish hand washing the underwear she'd left soaking. Before she could reach the bedroom door it opened and mam stood with every bit of colour drained from her face where resentment had been ousted by hopelessness.

For a moment silence seemed to breath around them.

She seemed incapable of venom but the softness in her voice was even more terrifying.

'It's all gone wrong girl. I don't know how we'll get through now.'

CHAPTER TEN

'But Dr Kelly said everything would be all right!'

'Oh aye, everything will be all right ...with you! You'll have the brat, get on with your life and leave me and yu' dad to clear up your mess! But for once it's not you we're talking about is it?'

Barriers thickened between them, scathing bricks of derision stacking steadily.

'You just don't get it do you?' She breathed in a voice intended to scathe.

'Are you ill mam?'

'Ha! Ill? I wish I bloody well was. I wish I was dying! It's the only way out of this.'

Her flashing eyes darkened then narrowed as they fired at the target of her fury.

'You; you my girl, have ruined this family!'

The words were left hanging in the air as she punishingly relinquished them to her daughter, sinking her further into dread. The familiar slam of a door left June alone with new agony, unknown. Unbearable.

June spent the rest of the day wandering between her bedroom and the kitchen trying hopelessly to fill the time till dad came in from work. She let Jan in from the yard but could not return the dog's enthusiastic affection. After much whiny demanding, she blankly lifted the little body to just above her swelling stomach, holding and hugging so tight that the stiff claws scratched across her neck and chin. Nothing was to go right today. She trudged into the scullery to vacantly splash cold water on the bleeding marks.

What could the doctor have said? A thousand possibilities raced through her mind, all of them terrifying, each one unfinished through fear and ignorance. The images bled into one another, fused, matted and became terrifying clumps of despair.

In her agitated state she could not read, nor did she want to. The only book she had was as wretched as she was. It would only crush her further.

The fear chemicals woke Wren who was sleeping more and more in the baby that was now developed enough to be born safely. She left both bodies to see the physical manifestation of the dolour she already felt. Her mother flopped into a hide chair, despondent. There were no tears, only a girl sunk in misery. Wren didn't need her mind reading abilities to know who the cause of this melancholy was. Ivy was usually zipping about the house making sure there was a good meal for the man she undoubtedly loved after the layers of criticism and hardness were allowed a defensive display.

Wren, confident enough of her imminent birth, took her energy to Ivy who was lying on the bed curled up with eyes wide open. It was easy to read her racing mind and that was shock enough but there was something even greater here. Some-one she hoped never to meet. Wren had never expected this. Things were going to be very different to how she had imagined.

As she returned to June she wished so much that she could explain away her misery but she would know soon enough. Right now there was nothing for her in the outside world she'd soon be seen in. It was uncomfortable re-entering her little body with the depressing shared supply of blood and emotions, but she did. She needed time to mentally digest what she had just learned and plan how to use the awful knowledge to her advantage.

CHAPTER ELEVEN

The mood brightened a little when Jan scrabbled at the door. June rose clumsily to allow the little dog its freedom. In ten minutes her dad would be back.

He arrived to an ungainly daughter flinging herself into his arms with relief.

'What the....?' he raised her from his chest to search a pale face for information.

'Who scratched your neck like that?'

But June, amok with hormones and fear, was sobbing, unable to answer through forlorn tears.

Dad gave her a reassuring squeeze before loosening her arms from around his coal dust and sweat covered body. He led her gently to the chair she'd just left then padded in black pit socks to where the loud sneck clattered beneath his dirt stained hands.

'Ivy! Have you been at the bairn again?'

June, appalled at the injustice, used the chair arm to push herself up. Mam was lying on the bed, tear stained and limp.

'I cuddled Jan too hard dad, her claws caught me.'

Tot's eyes raked over them both, trying to work out why the atmosphere was darker than the place deep beneath the earth that he'd just left.

'What is it then?'

Ivy swallowed hard as she flicked accusing eyes at both the anxious faces.

'You won't like it.'

'For goodness sake woman, tell me what's wrong!'

'I'm pregnant Tot, three months.'

The words hung in the heavy summer air like an axe waiting to fall on what remained of this family's bond. It was then that the new foetus showed itself spiritually.

Dad, who flushed with all the emotions of the discovery of their first pregnancy, felt a surge of joy, cried. 'But that's wonderful Ivy!'

'Wonderful! Wonderful! It's a disaster you idiot; don't you see.'

Tot sat on the bed and put dirty but loving arms around his stiff, angry wife.

'How can I have a baby five months after I am supposed to have given birth? Every-one will know the truth; that I'm a bloody liar!'

'Oh Ivy, let them know. It's time we were honest. People will understand.'

'Aye, aye! They'll understand all right! They'll understand that I padded me belly and paraded meself in Chapel accepting the kind concerns of all the good folk wishing me well with a baby that's nowt but a pile o' rags!'

June stared at her parents and knew that this was all her fault. A new brother or sister should have been wonderful news. Her mother, terror ridden, looked suddenly so vulnerable that she wanted to rush into her arms and...what? She had nothing to offer; only a deepened sense of shame and an overwhelming wish that she'd never been born.

Dad was trying to comfort his ashen faced wife, smoothing back damp hair. Little streaks of pit muck trailed across her forehead.

'I can't have this baby Tot. I'll go to see old Ma Cooper tomorrow.'

Dad pulled away dropping the hand he had been holding.

'Knitting needle Cooper! You bloody won't! If I have to tie you to the bed till the bairn is born I will do! Make no mistake Ivy; if you so much as talk to that butchering woman it'll be the end of us.'

Ivy's eyes fell to the knees in front of her. She wanted her husband to make it all right but he couldn't. He stood up, expelled a breath of understanding blended with confidence then half turned.

'I'll have me bath and then we'll talk, sensible like. Nowt daft mind. You can get all that out o' your head.'

June had kept the fire going and watched dad bring in the tin bath from the yard wall to fill it himself. She was too lumbering to help but fetched the towels and soap as she had done since she was three. It was her way of showing love for she couldn't speak of her hopelessness.

As she lay on the bed half listening to the familiar splashing and saddening further at the lack of singing and chatter, she felt her baby kick then stick out an elbow or foot so that it made a little pointed mound in her belly. She stroked it gently.

'I will love you baby when you come and I will never let you suffer such misery as this. I promise.'

Wren felt the pureness of the emotions and heard the words but knew that this little girl to whom she would owe so much for eternity would never be allowed to keep her promise.

The house sank deeper into gloom and alienated itself to June so that every second seemed too slow. She was enormous or so mam nastily told her every time she passed. Beached whale! Bouncing bomb and Two Ton Tessie all hit their biting mark. June hadn't been out of the little colliery house for three weeks now. She was too tired for the walks in darkness and felt it was too risky to make any early morning trips to see what summer had clothed her wood with. She had missed the dragonflies on the lily pads and the moorhens that flicked in and out of the reeds at the end of the dewpond. She imagined the tiny, almost transparent baby newts growing strong and solid enough to leave the water with no-one but themselves to marvel at their achievement.

The sun was a hammer taking life out of the soft foliage beneath her window. June had studied and stared at the bramble stems chasing their way across the slope as long as her legs would stand her weight. Her stomach was stretched until she knew it would stretch no more. She had never seen a beached whale but she was sure she fitted exactly this description mam threw at her. It hurt no longer. Her mind was filled with plans for her baby. She would have to think of a way not to return to school. Mam would give her baby food and keep it clean...too clean sometimes; but this baby needed love and understanding. Dad would do his best, he was a wonderful father but the bond June already felt for the little one inside her was too strong to ignore.

Mam had stopped going to chapel unable to cope with the lie she had started with her padded belly and the truth that was starting to show in front of her. Dad had to do all the shopping taking the three bags and one basket on the bus to the Co-op every week according to his shifts. He was the only man at the fruit and veg cart and worked out a system with the bread man and butcher.

The tin bath, usually hanging from the wall was left upturned to protect deliveries from the sun.

Doctor Kelly and Nurse Sweeny began calling twice a week and became trained to enter the house bearing whatever food had been left in response to the little scribbles left on the back of used envelopes in the same hiding place.

The gossip started. A terrible disease? A deformity that had spread from daughter to mother?

A heavily pregnant Ivy with legs swollen to twice her body size?

All were curious. None dared ask.

'You have to get a little exercise June, you don't want blood clots in your legs.' Dr Kelly pulled the cool sheet across the mound he'd just been checking. 'It won't be long now. Don't forget; any pain and you send dad for me or Nurse Sweeny.'

Alone, June hoisted herself onto her side and listened to the mumblings that came through the wall as mam was checked. It was funny to think of two babies growing in this little house.

Dad was at work when June was woken by a dragging pain at half past ten that night. She wasn't sure of what she had felt in her half sleeping state but ten minutes later there was no doubt; the agony that squeezed her very being meant that her baby was about to be born.

She rolled to the edge of the bed and wearily pushed her arm beneath the mattress to bring out the book she had studied so much in the last few weeks. She knew every word and quickly found the page where she'd turned down the corner.

This was it. Her baby was coming. The book said it would be hours and dad's shift finished at two in the morning so he would be here.

She laid the book face down on the little pile of baby clothes dad had brought back from the drapers on one of his visits to the Spen. He had returned with a parcel wrapped in stiff brown paper tied with white string. They had opened it together and June fingered the tiny vests and nighties that seemed too small for any human being. Another time dad lifted a bundle of terry towelling nappies onto the kitchen table and they had laughed as he tried to show her how he had put them on her when she'd first being born. He stuck his thumb with the large nappy pin and declared his hands too big. Now she opened the drawer where she'd carefully folded the nappies alongside the slightly worn but still good knitted leggings and jumpers given to dad by another miner.

He'd been touched when he'd returned with the little garments.

'Jack Trainer said 'Wor lass has finished wi' these now, thought your lass could do wi' em.' Bless them.'

Mam had gingerly picked up the faded white clothes between finger and thumb and washed them right there and then. As they'd dried on the wooden clothes horse in front of the fire June had gazed at the rising steam finding it impossible to imagine what her baby might look like wearing them.

Soon she would know.

Excitement mixed with the pain, making sleep impossible. June carefully placed the rubber sheet brought by the midwife onto the bed. Over this she folded three old towels and sat on them with her back to a pile of pillows. If her waters broke she didn't want her bed ruined. Her hands went to her little breasts and she wondered how even in their slightly enlarged state they could feed a hungry baby. She picked up the book and gazed at the pictures demonstrating breast feeding. The drawings were of a large breast with a cross section showing bud like milk ducts and reservoirs. Surely her breasts could not look like this inside. Sometimes she wished Mr. Farraige had never given her the book or at least returned to pick it up. He would have watched for the sight of mam and dad disappearing into the chapel and realised they had not gone. What he must think she had no idea but in a few weeks when she joined the world again she would find him and explain it all.

Wren felt the pain too and the great surge of hormones that meant she was soon to enter the world again. That would be the first hurdle jumped in her desperate search for Allesandro. She wondered where he was now. She didn't even know if he had been born himself for when they had parted he had gone for briefing. He could be a one year old in the next village or a twenty year old in India. The spiritual dimension she had come from did not have the illusion of time that was necessary for Earth. As far as she knew he might be an old man or even a woman about to give birth like June. He could be any person anywhere but Wren knew with time earned awareness that she would find him. Her search was about to start.

Wren stayed inside the mind of the little body preparing for birth. She gave strength and healing to June and hoped she could cope with the ordeal she was about to endure.

June, feeling a sudden loneliness, struggled to the door trying to open it softly enough for her mother not to hear but loud enough to bring Jan scurrying into her room. As she held a finger to her lips the little dog licked at her toes and she bent awkwardly to lift her. Half way to the floor a labour pain gripped her so fiercely that she crumpled down to the mat. Jan whined then began running to and fro from June to the back door asking to be let out.

'It is too soon Jan. Dad has another three hours to work.' But the animal didn't understand the words only the urgency and the desperate need to bring her master home.

Deep breathing allowed enough strength for June to reach the kitchen door to free herself from the fear of the whining waking mam and the dog to its determination.

Picking up a glass of water from the scullery she returned to the bed only stopping to fling open the windows to find enough air for the gulping need she suddenly felt. Within the body, Wren was preparing herself to be born. It would need guidance and strength. The brain was still not fully developed, an inadequacy she always felt frustrated at but if human babies stayed in the womb until this happened it would take another twelve months and the head would be too big for the birth passage. It was a tight squeeze as it was. Her body felt the trauma as the muscles that had held her for months now had to expand to let her go into the world. Waves of hot muscle action swept across June's stomach in the agony most needed for life. It would take hour after hour of the walls of the uterus pressing upon the baby in powerful, regular contraction. At this moment the contractions were not moving the baby, their first purpose was to force open the neck of the womb. The cervix that had held her closely for nine months was now preparing to let her go. Wren felt such excitement. Such hope. Her freedom was near.

She felt her mother heave and throw her head back. She was sweating, afraid and exhilarated.

A cry, muffled by June's body reached the baby's ears and it was the loudest yet. The door burst open and Wren heard the suppressed voice of Tot.

'Oh darlin'! Is it time?'

June was never more pleased to see her dad and the grip she gave to both his offered hands could have broken the bones of a lesser man. Behind the work blackened, slightly panicked figure Ivy appeared still pushing balled fists into her old dressing gown sleeves.

'What the....?'

Tot turned, his face slack with urgent thinking.

'Look after the bairn Ivy! I'll have to get to the phone box quick. Have you got some pennies?'

'In me purse.'

Ivy looked at her writhing daughter and panicked for her safety. She felt confusion at the never before felt female bond.

'And run Tot!'

'I can't run in me pit boots...I'll take Joe Mullin's bike. He always leaves it in the yard. He'll never know!'

Mam, not able to find the words needed, left June's side to stoke up the fire and pour as much water into the boiler as it would hold. Then she came back to her bedroom and took out the big pile of old but immaculate towels folded neatly in the bottom of the dark wood wardrobe. A severe contraction caused June to cry out as she slid down the bed. She dashed to her.

'Come on now June! Don't go on like this. It's what all women have to bear. I've done it... aye an' I will again. I don't make such a fuss. You only have yourself to blame. If you'd given us the name of the dirty bugger who did this to you you'd not be so guilty and your pain would be less!'

June heard the clatter of a dropped bicycle through the open doors and dad clumped urgently into her room.

'He said he'll be about half an hour and he'll ring the midwife who'll be here as quick as she can pedal.'

June was resting now, panting. Jan leapt to the bed and began licking her face. Ivy abruptly lifted her down.

'How come you are here, you have another two hours of your shift Tot?'

'Jan came to the pit head and made such a fuss barking, two lads had just come up for more carbine for their lamps and ran down the drift to fetch me. They all know her at the pit head and how well behaved she usually is.'

To feel the brow of the daughter he loved so much he extended the back of his hand and realized how dirty it was.

'Listen chicken. I'm going for a wash but I'll be straight back.'

When he returned his hands and arms were clean like his face but a dark ring around his hairline showed how hurriedly he had soaped himself. His clothes were changed to the ones he wore for gardening that mam had washed and ironed that morning. He sat on the bed and nervously felt every pain with his little girl. Hopelessly mopping her forehead with a dampened cloth, he knew anything he did would not ease the pain of bringing a child into the world. If only he could do this for her.

They heard the clatter of bikes fall to the concrete yard before Dr. Kelly strode confidently into the bedroom he knew so well. Nurse Sweeny pulled off her blue Burberry Mac then opened her bag with an air of practised ease. She laid various instruments across the dressing table mam had cleared for just this purpose and pushed waterproof sleeves over her lower arms.

Wren could only hear and feel but she buzzed with excitement.

'Oh Dr. Kelly it hurts so much!' June cried as he held a stethoscope to her active belly.

'I know me darlin' but it will all be worth it. It's only your womb, it has to go from tight shut to wide open and that is a painful thing to do.'

June knew only too well, the book had been studied constantly. Perhaps she knew too much.

Wren listened to the filtered voices and tried to rest. Every birth she had experienced flooded through her memory now, all were tiring, each one exhilarating. There was always the strangeness of a tiny human baby seeming to know so little in its new born state and yet remembering everything. Each child was born with full soul remembrance, the whole knowledge of the dimension they had recently left and the accumulated qualities of previous lives and spirit rests. It was a valuable time just after birth to think and plan whilst the physical body needed so much sleep to grow. It was also unbearably thrilling to meet again on this plane the spirits of loved ones who had agreed just such a birth before they left. It was all gradually lost of course to the five sensory awareness and yet...and yet... always there was something, some place in the brain that held it all but seemed closed except for tiny, lightening quick chinks of knowledge that were recognised more in some than in others. Even for those who denied all soul awareness and swore that they had only one life and when you're dead you're dead, the end; even for these remained the love and recognition of spirit group members. Wren would have none of this. Those re-joining's belonged to Elia, the soul she had robbed. Wren would have to face each person in this life without the deep soul knowledge of who they were and what they had agreed to give to one another. This would be a huge disadvantage in every relationship. She'd had nine months to consider this and substitute her own plans, but now with what she had learned a few weeks ago, there was going to be even more struggle than she ever could have bargained for.

Wren had thought that there was nothing in her search for Allesandro that she wasn't capable of, in fact she was certain, but now there was to be a new unknown force. It was following close on her heels. She'd have to be even cleverer than she'd ever been before.

But that was later; right now she had a birth to prepare for. She wanted everything to be perfect and hoped to cause as little trouble to her mother as possible.

The labour pains were every three to four minutes now and the cervix was completely open, soon the squeezing would move her into the birth canal, her exit route was clear. Wren felt her head being used as a battering ram as it forged a way for the rest of the body she now felt part of. It was a difficult manoeuvre. As she entered the pelvis her head turned round to face June's spine bending her head and neck right back to a ninety degree angle.

Wren could hear her heart beat slowly, intermittently but she'd known this before. She tried to concentrate on the strained voices of the world she was about to become part of. Dr. Kelly firm but reassuring, the midwife almost shouting orders to June whose bellowing sounded even louder from inside.

'Push June, push!'

'I can't!'

'Yes you can, you have to, your baby's almost here. Good girl! Push!'

'Now pant June, not too fast.'

Wren felt the squeeze to her head as the soft bones pushed together in the birth canal. She was out, her head felt free and strangely cool. June cried out involuntarily, it was the first sound Wren had heard with these human ears. Then there was another push and she felt her body slither on a rush of fluid. She was here. In the world, the same world as Allesandro. It felt wonderful.

She was born carrying nothing but her future with her.

CHAPTER TWELVE

'It's a girl.' Doctor Kelly was the first one to hold the physical body of Wren.

He checked over the little body and Wren felt a tiny hesitation which kept his gaze on her a second too long. Wren already knew what he looked like and wasn't in a hurry to open her scrunched up eyes to be shot with the light from the gas lamps on the wall. The feel of another human touching her felt strange but it confirmed that she was at last what she had so wanted to be. The cord was cut and she was free! A separate human being once again.

Wren danced in the spirit of birth. She felt herself held up by the ankles and a sudden smack to her newly born bottom that forced a great cry from her throat. It was the first time she had used the voice she would have to train to communicate so inadequately for the rest of this life. Why couldn't humans use the mind power they all had? Wren was capable of conveying such advanced knowledge with her mind yet all she could bring her vocal cords to convey was 'Whaaaaa!'

This was already frustrating and even as mucus was wiped from her eyes and nose and a tube was pushed down her throat to suck out fluid, she was happy to feel the first physical sensations of this life. As she was washed and towelled dry she was aware with every wave of her tight fist of the slow and heavy vibration of the physical. This is what she had wanted and yet it was so restrictive. Like a humming bird trying to fly through mud.

This was life.

She felt herself placed against the body of her mother and enjoyed the snuggling and kissing warmth.

'Come on June,' Nurse Sweeny interrupted, her voice harsher than it had seemed from the womb 'one more push to deliver the afterbirth. We have other ladies, married ones, in need of our help right now, get a move on!'

Dr. Kelly rolled down his sleeves after drying his hands and came towards June.

'She is wonderful and you did so well, young bodies cope easily with childbirth.'

He smoothed the baby's cheek then took the same fingers to June's chin.

'There is something very special about your baby June. She's been here before that one.'

June laughed as she looked down into the scrunched up face and saw her baby blink with half open watery eyes. She saw it too.

'I will see you tomorrow. Nurse Sweeny will get you organised, show you how to feed your baby and then make you presentable so that those parents of yours straining at the door can come and see how beautiful you both are.'

'The swooning will have to wait Doctor.' The nurse shot an impatient glance. 'I haven't got all day!'

Wren couldn't help feeling glad that she wouldn't have to meet with this brusque woman again both because of her attitude right now and for something, some deep secret she had hidden well which had yet to show itself to the world.

When dad finally was allowed into the room the baby was facing the entrance in her mother's wondrous gaze. Awe captured his heart, he loved June even more for bearing this.

The little dog who had being scratting to get in rushed and stood blinking at the strange bundle stirring in June's gentle grip.

Everything was blurred to the newly born eyes but as the man walked in awe towards them Wren saw the love for both in the face and aura of her Granddad. He kissed his daughter and then, with his little finger, traced the baby's features before running it softly over her tiny fist. Through instinct the baby grasped the finger. It was big and rough but it felt wonderful.

'Well done chicken. She is beautiful' He tried to pull his hand away but the baby held tight for she needed every bit of love coming her way and she felt this was an inexhaustible source. 'Aren't her tiny fingers like little caterpillars?'

He searched the baby's eyes, heavy with all the secrets of the universe.

'Such big blue eyes just like yours were when you were born. This downy stuff she uses for hair will all come out and then we'll see if she takes after you or.....'

He quickly turned to Ivy. 'Come and see your grandchild. She's so lovely.'

His dancing, searching eyes that couldn't leave this wonder for long again caressed the little head.

'Have you thought of a name pet?'

'No not yet, although....well Wren would be nice.'

'Wren? Wren?'

This was the first time mam had spoken from her place at the door. 'Where on Earth did you get that from? Sounds more like a silly bird than a baby. Don't be stupid. What about Valerie or Pauline? Pamela is a nice name; you don't want to make a child different.'

She remained leaning against the door from where she dispatched her waves of disapproval.

'I've never heard such daftness.'

Dad tried to take the sting out of the comments. 'It's a nice name sweetheart, where did you hear that?'

'Don't know dad. It is my favourite bird, the smallness and that sweet song.'

'I know, like it comes straight from heaven. Your mam is right though. We don't want a name that'll be laughed at do we. What about Sarah after your grandma or Elizabeth Margaret after the little princesses, they've grown into fine young women?'

It was all sensed through a blur of infant's murk.

June didn't answer. For some reason she was stuck on the name even though she hadn't ever heard of a child being called after any other bird than a robin.

Nurse Sweeny bustled away Tot and Ivy with a mixture of annoyance and urgency.

'June your baby will need to suckle to get her stomach lined with colostrum. It's important that she has that first milk and I won't be hearing any nonsense about bottle feeding so I am going to show you once. You had better be a quick learner girl.'

June's breasts, although engorged with milk, were still adolescent but when she lifted Wren to them it was a unique ecstasy for them both. For that moment mother and baby were even closer than when one body had been inside the other. Wren would never forget that gentle intimacy. Dr Kelly came in draining the last from his tea cup, he was dressed for his bike.

'You look so tired. Get some sleep now.' The doctor smiled. 'You have to stay in bed for ten days mind, Here, I'll take the bairn. You'll have plenty of time with her, the rest of your life.'

Wren was lifted by firm hands and arms. The security and gentle strength lulled her deeper into sleepiness so that she never felt herself being eased into the blanket padded drawer which had been placed on two kitchen chairs beside the bed.

When Wren woke it was to the smell of wood oil and mothballs. She felt the pangs of hunger not experienced for so long but the need to cry out in demand was taken from her by a brightness in the room. Wren, knowing exactly what this meant, left the warm body of the little being she now was to watch the departing spirit of June.

The room was filled with peace. Wren looked down at her own little body to which she was attached by a silver cord of energy then across at the now empty body of June.

All was well; this was how it was to be only now the floodgates of grief on the physical level would have to be opened. Nothing could stop the rush of gnawing heartache.

In her physical state Wren was too immature to give comfort to the parents who were now sleeping so well in the next room with the spirit of June above them giving love and strength. Her body was hungry but if she stayed out a little longer she would not cry.

At six thirty dad slowly opened the door to peep in on his daughter and her new-born baby. Wren saw him tip-toe to June then pull the covers over her shoulders. As he turned to look at his grandchild in the drawer Wren re-entered the baby she had now become and opened her eyes. She felt hands beneath her and was held close as she was taken into the kitchen.

'This is where you will grow up Baby, in my arms, we call it Cuddle Corner. This is the range for cooking and this is the table with all your stuff on it.' He smudged loud kisses to baby cheeks. 'Mmm..aa. Mmm..aa!'

Holding his precious bundle in one arm he lifted the kettle, shook it and deeming it to have enough water for at least one cup of tea placed it on the extended iron holder which he pushed above the red ashes with the poker.

As he sat on the low stool beside the fire he clutched the baby to his chest. He was drunk with love.

'Eee! I nursed your mammy on this very cracket you know. She was a lovely baby. She'll love you too but from today we are to call her your sister.' He looked into the eyes which were struggling to focus. 'Yes, yes you are! You'll always know she is special and love her as much as I do, won't you baby.'

The dullness of the fire was slow to boil the kettle but Tot, caught in the spell of all new grandparents, did not notice.

The rush of Ivy entering the room popped the enchantment high into the air where it would hover until Tot and his new love were alone again.

'Am I not getting any tea this morning?'

'Oh sorry love. I got wrapped up in this little one.'

'For goodness sake Tot the fire isn't even red anymore. Am I to do everything around here?' She took the poker and tried to rattle the fire into life.

'Here Ivy, take the bairn and I'll sort it.'

'No, no. You look too dopey to do owt but stare at that'n. What about her mother? She's the one who should be looking after her. We are not starting that!'

'Oh Ivy, she's exhausted, sleeping as deep as the sea and twice as peaceful.'

When the fire was blazing again and Tot's arms felt cramped he took the baby and his own body, soft with adoration, back into June's bedroom.

'She's still asleep Ivy. Hardly moved.'

Ivy was throwing bacon into a greased pan and left it to go into the scullery. When she returned with eggs in a bowl and a newly baked loaf she put them onto the table as Tot took up bunches of cutlery to lay by the side of the two plates.

'She'll be awake as soon as that baby finds its full lungs and empty belly.'

'Do her some breakfast Ivy and I'll take it in to her, put it in the oven to keep warm till she wakes.'

As the table was cleared Dr. Kelly tapped on the door and entered carrying his bag.

'And how's the happy family this morning?' he said looking at tired figures through his own bleary eyes.

'You're up early Doctor.' Tot said as he shook the tea pot. 'Want some? I have to make fresh for June.'

'Oh how welcome. Haven't been home yet. Old Mr. Jackson is having an awful time, not long for this world.'

He made for the scullery where Tot followed him with a clean towel.

'How are the new mother and baby?' he asked splashing water.

'Baby's fine, as good as gold Doctor but June hasn't woken yet, poor bairn.'

'Well I need to take a look at them before I get myself home to bed.'

'I'll take her tea and get her up. Sit down. Want some toast? Ivy…'

Wren, hovering above her infant body watched as the door opened. She watched too as Tot put the cup and saucer on the table beside June and then leaned right over her.

'Come on chicken, you have a baby to feed and change and Dr. Kelly is here for you.'

His hand on her shoulder pulled back to his chest as the feel and sight his brain was trying to access sunk into his awareness.

'Doctor!'

The panic and loudness of the call made the man who had just helped Wren into the world dash to her side. The wide eyes and shocked face told Tot this was worse than he feared.

'Take the baby and wait in the kitchen Tot.'

'Now!'

Tot did as he was told but it was automatic, his brain seemed to have sunk beneath an avalanche of terror.

'What is it Tot?'

'The bairn...the bairn.....'

The house seemed to drop out of time. The baby was still. Ivy, frightened by the look on her husband's face, strode to the bedroom but was met by the doctor coming out.

His face was grey and lined, his chin shook with emotion.

'I'm sorry. It was postpartum haemorrhage. The uterine arteries haven't closed down. June has bled to death.'

Cold burning pain.

Tot held the baby but was not aware of anything but his agony. He felt himself whoosh through a dark tunnel of grief from which he would never return. The soft walls of sorrow closed behind him, there was no way out. Words left his brain, his mouth. His brows dropped heavy to his eyes and he felt muscles at the corners of his mouth drag. He no longer existed. And yet if that were true who made that cry of agony like a wolf howling for it's young. It came again and again. It filled the room, the house, the world but Tot didn't realise for he was inside himself, just him and his grief locked in total oneness.

His stricken face and inert body prompted Doctor Kelly to gently take the baby from him then lay her on the settee.

'Tot.....'

He heard nothing but seemed to glide to the bedroom door where he stood looking at the pale face of his much loved daughter. She couldn't be dead. Gone. He loved her too much. He could love her back surely! His love was strong enough for that. Death was not for June.

Sunshine, woods and flowers...they were for his little girl...not death. Not cold, still death.

He strode dumbly to her side. There was some mistake. This stillness before him was a trick. Soon she would sniff and stir, do a little laugh and complain that she was hungry. Yes that is what would happen. He took her hand. There was no grip of affection no pull of him towards her for a kiss. There was nothing.

There was death.

He was separate from everything around him. There was no bed, no wife no doctor. There was only inscape. That was all he knew and it was horrible and yet a sweet horror for somewhere inside of him was June. She was mixed into this lead-like heart and soft clamp of the solitude of suffering.

Wren knew he would always heft this sack of everlasting sorrow around.

He gazed down at the limp body. It looked like June only paler, smoother. But it was not June she wasn't in there. Where was she? He wanted her. He wanted her!

A small smudge of red had absorbed itself to the covers from the pool of blood that his daughter lay in. He had seen this blood before. It had oozed from childhood cuts and tumbling grazes.

Then he had stemmed the flow with a hanky or suck of his own mouth. What could he do now?

Nothing.

Nothing.

Nothing.

He heard mumblings from the next room. Words of comfort to a mother whose child had left and then reality.

'Ivy, certain practicalities have to be taken. That baby needs feeding and if we don't see to it soon it will yell the place down.'

Ivy, a strange mix of shock, relief and guilt occupying every cell in her brain, didn't move. Doctor Kelly guided her to the settee where she sat beside her new-born granddaughter but she neither looked at her nor touched her. He opened his bag and took out a sample tin of Ostermilk which he made up in a little jug then poured into the crescent shaped feeding bottle with a rubber teat on each end. He shook several drops to the back of his hand then Wren felt herself lifted into the crook of his arm before the rubber pressed gently against her lips. Her mouth opened and she took the teat, sucking as all new born babies do. It was warm and powdery, not as good or as comforting as being at her mother's breast but it was life giving and well overdue.

'Are you all right Ivy?' The doctor, used to death and used to birth, tried to keep his mind on what these poor folk seemed incapable of. He put the baby over his shoulder and rubbed gently at her back.

Wren, unable to focus newly born eyes could see only a blur in the bedroom beyond. Even when she was carted towards the little pile of nappies and came within two feet of Tot she couldn't see him properly. She was aware of Dr Kelly's hand going to the shoulder as it slumped over the vacant body of his daughter. It was so frustrating to her that when she was laid on the kitchen table to have her long overdue change of nappy she felt she could leave her body to automation.

In spiritual form she saw everything; it was a beautiful sight and feel.

Sundia, the spirit of June was standing at Tot's shoulder with her head resting on his. She was magnificent white energy edged with blue for she was giving healing to a good man in despair.

He couldn't see her but his head turned slightly as if....no, silly.

A peace filled the room and she was gone. Wren knew that she wouldn't go far yet so that she could be close to those who loved her but it was with surprise that she saw her only in the next room

close to the mother who had made June's life so difficult. She gave healing here too for she knew that there was great suffering to be borne. As she watched, Wren felt Sundia call upon the spirit of the baby Ivy was carrying and this made her slightly nervous for she was not yet ready for confrontation so she entered her own little body.

It felt good to be full of milk and clean and dry. This was two thirds of her needs fulfilled but it looked as if the love she needed to flourish might be hard to find.

Doctor Kelly lifted the chairs and drawers for the baby into the kitchen.

'Ivy, can you manage? You have to take care of yourself and this little soul who God knows didn't ask to be here. I'll bring some more tins of milk tomorrow.'

He left her still sitting motionless, giving no attention to the baby; he hoped that nature would take its course.

As he left, Jan ran through the door from the yard but instead of wagging an enthusiastic tail towards Tot, slunk to her stomach and whined. When she reached June's bedside she knew.

She half scrabbled, half jumped into the lap of the man gazing distraught at the bed before him.

His arms went around her and she knew his pain. She felt it too.

The house marinated in heartbreak. Wren moved her spiritual form from person to person to dog but only the little terrier was aware. As she left the bedroom to return to her baby body Jan leapt from Tot's knee and saw the brilliance enter the seven pound human form. She scrabbled into the drawer and began to lick the tiny face. From that moment she knew she was to dedicate all her being and protection to the new child in her life.

'Get down Jan!'

Ivy's push was sudden, the first move from her guilt ridden grief.

'Alaa. Alaaa. Alaaa.!'

The demanding cry of a new baby filled the house. It reached the ceiling in its constant demands. It reached the scullery and the bedrooms but it couldn't reach its target of Tot's heart.

'Tot! The baby needs you!'

Ivy looked to her side, her hands unable to move from her lap.

'Tot!'

The two cries tore at the edges of the impenetrable grief. He didn't want to be disturbed. Somewhere in this torment was June. Racked with distress he turned in what seemed to be the clinging treacle of his awareness to life. What was happening outside of him wasn't real. Nothing should be allowed to take his mind from thoughts of June. If he didn't hold his being fully onto the love it would go and she really would be lost to him.

The new-born need continued, louder and louder.

'Tot!'

He rose, his body a machine taking him away from the closeness of June.

When he reached the settee his eyes met those of his pregnant wife, she didn't seem to belong to him. The baby wailed on. It was alien, not part of his awareness.

'Tot! For God's sake see to that baby will you, before I do something I regret.'

A slow tumble of his eyes brought him the sight of a red faced, stiff limbed baby. He did nothing.

'How can I even touch the very thing that took our June from me?' His voice was dull and flat. Heavy feet shuffled him back to his daughter. He shut the door.

Wren knew that she might die of starvation if she could not get a caring response from these adults. Nothing came, she was new-born and alone, they were lost in grief.

The crying became louder, the face redder. Wailing became a permanent background to desolation. Weak with hunger and abandonment, the infant fell into exhausted sleep. Was it all to end so soon?

Cramps in her tiny stomach brought forth such screaming it might wake the dead. If only it could. The new born throat was growing raw with strain, but it would not stop.

Wren came out of her body and stirred the air around the lost woman she needed so much.

She sent every bit of awareness to this maternal instinct she knew was embedded in every female on Earth.

A huge sigh seemed to free Ivy's body from the ties of torment and she turned to pick up the baby she had never really accepted.

The feel in her hands was warm and soft. She remembered that sensation. Wren, playing this woman for her very survival, stopped crying and opened her eyes to throw vulnerability into the space between them. She felt the first positive emotion ever from this woman.

'There, there. Shhh now. What's the matter then, mmm?'

Even in this woman it was easy to kick start the protective urge babies bring with them to bestow on all who gaze on their helpless form. As Ivy tightened her soft grip around the baby she was flooded with long ago feelings. This little needy bundle looked exactly like the baby she had fifteen years earlier loved and protected. Where that love had gone to she could never understand. She had felt such an outsider to the bond between father and daughter. It had seemed as unnatural as the love her own father had shown her when she was twelve. She couldn't understand. She could only feel.

When she'd settled the baby enough to lay quiet she carefully measured out the milk powder so that it would last until the doctor returned. Active with being needed, she filled an enamel bucket with cold water for the soiled nappies and stoked up the fire.

Wren slept, happy that the knack all babies held wasn't forgotten. She should have being enjoying the sheltered simplicity of the first few days of a new-born but there was just too much to deal with.

Ivy was bustling now and it was with this attitude that she entered June's room. Her husband looked dreadful. His grey face turned towards her, she had never seen him look so old. He had arranged June's hair to spread out across the pillow and laid her hands together across her chest.

The years of resentment flooded before her adding to her pain. This was her daughter lying dead. It was her husband who sat sick at heart before her. She slid an arm around his shoulder and was surprised at the ferocity with which he grabbed it. He used her strength to pull himself up and for the first time in his life threw himself into her arms.

Weeping filled the room and Ivy's tight heart. This man deserved better than she had ever given him. She owed it to him to be strong now.

But what was in her that could comfort him?

CHAPTER THIRTEEN

With the visits of the Co-op funeral directors and the Methodist minister, gossip started.

The first speculation was that Ivy had died in early childbirth leaving her man with a sick child and a newly born bairn. Feelings were mixed, the woman had hardly made herself likable but oh that poor hardworking man; how would he cope?

When the minister had been pumped for information by some of his flock in the street he'd not been able to lie. It was that lovely little lass who had died. That; however, was all the truth he was prepared to give. The details were not his to make free with. New sympathies rose in the little community of miners. Fancy, what a terrible coincidence that your daughter should die on the same day your wife gave birth to a second child. It was too awful.

Ivy couldn't stop the stream of visitors who respected Tot. Those who he hewed coal with shook his hand and their own heads unable to say much of any help. The gardeners, those men who had given seed to three year old June and later showed her all the ways to keep pests off their 'Dig for Victory' crops, shared their memories and fondness with her grief-stricken father.

Ivy saw no-one. She was always busy with the baby in the bedroom and people respected that along with the mysteries that surrounded the female species when they'd just given birth.

Wren saw. She felt. She was.

She pulled a stream of healing energy from the universe and directed it to these two people in agony. She knew when Sundia was at their side and felt her grief at leaving the parents who had given her a chance to be on this Earth for one short but valuable life. If only she could remind them of what they already knew. At their soul level they would rejoice for her because the death of June meant she had accomplished all she had chosen to do. Earth was the hard bit. The working part of everyone's journey to better understanding. Limited understanding had been lifted with her death and she gave them strength. She wanted to communicate this to her father but his grief was too thick, too dense for the thoughts from her to enter his mind.

The day before he was to bury his daughter Tot had stared numbly out of the window that June had spent so much time at, he saw something that made him put down the hairbrush he had been holding to his cheek in desperate need to feel his daughter. Sundia had taken that part of her she knew he'd notice and sent two tiny wrens to flutter onto the window sill just long enough to catch his attention. Tot, startled from his longing, had followed their nipping flight to a group of gorse bushes from where he drank in their song. It had lifted his heart just enough for Sundia to get close to him. His vibration rose and he saw...or did he...something...nothing...a little light...a blue flash...stupid. He must be over tired, overwrought with the bringing of the coffin and the cleaning of the bed. And yet...why did he feel a sudden tiny bubble of joy in his dark oily sea. He looked at the bed on which his lovely daughter had left him. It was clean now. No sign of birth or death of which it knew so much. He slowly laid himself there longing to feel her energy. He crossed his hands across his chest just as hers had been placed and he tried to imagine how she felt lying there with all that agony of separation, of death. Many kisses came to him. The kisses he had given over the years. Many cuddles. Many hugs. In that tiny instance he felt all the love he had given so freely returned a thousand fold. It was sent by the daughter of whom he had nothing left except a body in a coffin lying in the kitchen and a baby he could not bring himself to look at.

Ivy and Tot had asked no-one to the funeral. When they'd completed the heart-breaking mile walk behind the hearse and taken their haggard cheeks and mouths after the coffin into the chapel, a sea of faces turned to sympathise with them. June was loved for her sunny personality and the days she'd spent amusing the gardeners first with her ignorance and then with her knowledge for one so young. Tot was respected for his hard work and generosity of his time and plant advice. There wasn't a man in Garesfield whose fence wasn't covered in the pink climbing rose Tot so generously grew from cuttings. The wives who had stood beside Ivy at the horse and carts selling fruit or in the long lines in the dark days of food rationing, gave gentle nods to the woman they knew to be of few words.

Their grief blanked faces gave no reaction except to the three who knew the truth Ivy had worked so hard to suppress. Two rows from the back Doctor Kelly stood with Miss Ridley and he gently took her arm as the red lips quivered at the sight of the child's coffin and the aching hearts following. Love came from the minister who ushered the woman he knew to be pregnant and carrying a week old baby, into the front seats.

The service was simple. The hymn 'All Things Bright and Beautiful' seemed to mean so much when those singing it remembered the shine from the different coloured eyes and the gleam from the blond hair as June had stood at this very altar reciting her anniversary piece.

The minister spoke of love, thankfulness and truth. His words bore into Ivy's brain, repeating themselves over and over again. She hadn't had much experience of the first two and lately none of the last but now it was time to be honest.

Wren, held low across Ivy's body to disguise the pregnant swell, felt the woman's rise in courage and nurtured it until it knew no bounds. Suddenly, in a pause the minister gave between praising June and giving thanks, Ivy rose.

Everyone stiffened, then angled and bent heads and bodies, craned necks to see just what the horror of a mother at the funeral of her child was about to succumb to. They saw a woman with no tears but with a face so stricken with grief that some cried out in empathy. Every mother's heart begged silently to God that this would never happen to them. Ivy's eyes landed on them all as a mass and then fleetingly on each and every face that was waiting. She held the baby close to her breast, and then, with the power she felt suddenly, inexplicitly she thrust the baby towards them and turned its tiny face from left to right so that none could miss its vulnerability.

The minister made a concerned step towards her but something stopped him.

'This baby,' Ivy cleared a strangled throat. 'This baby has not come from my womb. The baby I am to have will not be born until January. This is June's baby.'

The intake of breath was almost simultaneous with shock from everyone in the little chapel for it had been the furthest thought from their minds. Only a doctor, a teacher and a minister were not astonished by the news. Their surprise was in the actions of a woman they knew to be hard.

'Aye. You may all gasp. If anyone has a stone to cast, cast it now!'

Tot, as surprised as anyone when his wife left his side pushed his dejected body from the hardness of the pew and put his arm around the woman for whom his great admiration had just swelled to an overwhelming flood. He took the baby from her and kissed it. This allowed a muffled mumbling from the congregation as Ivy's swollen belly was revealed.

Every-one heard the words every-one saw the family group. To them they appeared to be alone. But there were others who could have been seen by any-one who understood. The greatness of the moment had called forth much help and support for Ivy and Tot. Both their major guardian energies glowed protectively behind them and to the side the bright presence of both Sundia and the spirit of Ivy's unborn child. Wren was just above the forehead of her baby body.

Only one person narrowed his eyes in his pushed up searching head in hope of seeing what the greatness he could feel, but he was at the back, a latecomer. One who had loved this dead child and tried to protect her. He had not been able to bear to come. But at the last minute he could not bear not to. If anyone had been able to see and feel the great light that had been June they would have seen it leave this group at the altar and go to him, sink into him and leave something that would go with him forever.

Only Wren knew.

It was Tot who carried Wren to her mother's grave side, tightening his shaking grip on her as he leaned over to toss the fragrant white rose June had adored onto her lonely coffin. The same strong arms cradled his granddaughter protectively up the narrow cobbled street to the single storied mean and damp house built in a hurry by a Coal Board wanting the new pit to pay quickly.

Bleakness was feeling hope at its barrier.

There was a new energy between them now, it was weak and buried beneath the layered numbness of Tot's shock but it was there. Wren hung onto what she felt coming from this man and worked on it in desperate need for survival. When he opened the door Jan didn't scatter her paws to get to him as she usually did. The little canine instinct could sense how important this bonding was. She was also the only one to know that the spirit of June had entered the kitchen with them. Sundia poured love onto the family she still very much belonged to and then left. But the dog was not concerned as she knew with the certainty of all she was that the one she loved was always there, simply in another dimension. It all seemed perfectly normal.

Tot, still clinging to the baby, sat beside the table then pulled at the tightness of the tie around his neck. He struggled to loosen the stud on the stiff collar then rearranged the little body so that one hand cradled the head and the other the bottom.

He gazed into the face which was so painfully like the one he longed for, the one he had left in the cold lonely ground.

Wren opened her eyes and sent strong bonding energies into the man she already loved.

Tears that had not yet being allowed their journey came with sobs and wails, wracking the bent body. Ivy who had taken off her tight shoes and cloying hat covered the back of her husband as closely as her growing stomach would allow.

She knew this man needed her and she would try with all she was worth to be softer, more understanding with the children she was responsible for. It would be a fight.

Over the next few weeks Wren spent most of her time with her body as so much energy was needed for the development of the brain. There was nothing physical she could do to continue her search for Alessandro, it was enough that it had begun.

The days cooled into September, the roses in the vase on the table were replaced by Tot's dahlias then chrysanthemums. Tot went back to work but his output was low, he was weak and lost for motivation. The men patted his back, gave looks of understanding that Tot knew meant well but none could really know. None of the faces sank into his awareness; all were just a blur outside the heaviness of his pain so that he failed to notice that one was different.

Ivy, free of pretence and fear of scandal, began to be the obsessive housewife she had always been. She stood alone in the little gaggle of women who were waiting at the veg cart in their pinnies and working turbans which served to at least suggest that they were hard at work behind their doors and not, as Ivy suspected by the dirty colour of their front steps, reading cheap romance novels with a fag in their gob. She wanted no part of their female lazy and gossipy conversations

Her step remained scrubbed and swilled with the soapy water from her poss tub every Monday. Six months pregnant didn't stop her home being the cleanest in the street. It didn't stop her pushing the second hand pram three miles up hill to the Co-op for her groceries either, or holding onto the handle as the big wheels aided in their desire to get down the slope by a week's food and a baby, dragged at her arms and pulled her feet into an involuntary totter.

Wren, determined not to add to the strain, made every effort to be a good baby. She lay in her pram in the yard bundled up to make sure she stayed snug whilst breathing in enough fresh air to make her grow healthy and give her an appetite. Often she watched Tot sitting on that doorstep chiselling with the potato knife at pit muck stuck between the segs of his pit boots. His thoughts dragging at the memory of his daughter.

Sometimes, out of boredom, she would follow her grandmother in spirit. She wanted to get to know the social structure of the community she'd landed herself in, see who might be useful to her later when her body had grown and she was able to communicate in the way they understood.

It was on one of these trips that she thought she might have to face the spirit of the soul she had robbed.

CHAPTER FOURTEEN

She was above the horse who, blinkered to all but what was in front of him, was driven to chew the oats left at the bottom of his nosebag. She watched Ivy take the corners of her pinny and hold it towards the greengrocer as he tipped precious oranges, bananas and the first cooking apples of the season from his metal weighing cradle into it. As she turned back into the waiting women who all wondered but dare not ask who the father of June's baby was, one woman stepped out of the loose line.

'Hey, Ivy!' She grinned to show unruly teeth fighting for space in her wide mouth. 'A've just found out that 'am having a bairn in March.'

Nora Henderson beamed as she took one arm from the pair folded beneath her bosoms to tap in camaraderie at Ivy's shoulder.

The other women smiled and chattered light congratulations but Ivy remained silent. The significance of the enthusiastic declaration lost on her.

'Well they'll be playmates won't they? It's what this street needs, bairns. New life.'

In spite of Ivy's blank look she clattered on.

'It'll be nice to have more little 'ns at the chapel. Have you thought of a name for that baby yet? It'll be the christening soon.'

'No, I haven't.' Ivy took her pinny full of fruit to the house and left the women looking after her.

'Eeh! She's just the same. Poor Tot, that's what I say. Well at least you tried Nora.'

Wren stayed with the gossiping group for there was something important to find out before she re-entered her sleeping body.

As the pregnant woman stood back in her place Wren called to the spirit who had newly entered her. Nothing appeared. Was it fear or anger that kept it from her? Feeling that this must be an early soul with no idea that it can leave the foetus and womb, she concentrated more direction of energy.

'Please meet with me.' Wren focused welcoming goodness towards Nora's tummy.

A weak orange light appeared just above the woman's flesh. Wren felt unsureness, then as the orange deepened with brown, a new dread.

The energy felt Wren and shimmered. Communication without the need for the inadequate words of Earth was natural to them both.

'Oh no! My embryo is aborting. I have waited so long for this incarnation.'

There was no recognition.

Wren, keen to reassure the frightened presence expanded to a great blue brilliance. The orange energy cowed.

'Have you come to take me back?'

'No, I am the same as you, here in a new born baby.'

'But...but you can't be, you are too bright. Too special.'

'It is important for me to be here.'

The early spirit looked down. 'Is that my host mother?'

'Yes. Haven't you been out to view her before?'

'No. I didn't know it was possible.'

The energy looked around mentally gulping in the details of the place and people it was about to be born to. 'Poor woman, I owe her so much. I chose her because she was my son in her last incarnation and I beat her...him. I have tortured the minds of my children as well as their bodies. I have such a long journey to grace.'

Wren, easy with relief, sent warmth.

'I wish you well with it.'

'Thank you. I will need all good wishes; it will be a hard life for me. These people look poor, so different from my last life of riches. I had accumulated great wealth during the Russian Revolution with black market goods, had everything a person could wish for, now look where I am.'

'The physical things you acquired mattered only in the lessons they brought to you. You can achieve much with awareness in poverty.'

'I wish I could forget my past lives and the pain.'

'But' Wren brightened. 'If your soul could not remember yesterday how would it know how to live today?'

The orange dulled as it surveyed the place and people into which it would soon be born. A cold wind lifted the coats slung quickly round the shoulders of the woman and they shuddered.

'I feel insecure now. Can I go back?'

Of course you can. You must do exactly as you wish. No-one is your keeper, remember that.'

As the young energy returned to the body and safety Wren hoped he would absorb her last comment and use it when they were both physical for she knew with the experience of a thousand lifetimes that he would need to.

Wren was startled by a shout from her own back door.

'Jan! Get in here!'

She hadn't noticed that the little dog had stayed with her in the street and she laughed in fondness as it followed her back to the high black pram then lay down beside it, guarding the spirit it already loved so much.

Ivy cared for the baby with deft but abrupt skills; she also cared for her grieving husband feeding his every need except the one she was hopeless to cope with. He didn't rush home anymore and although he was caring and kind towards his pregnant wife and held the baby with cherishing love, he seemed vacant. Tot went to the pit and came back to his fireside, he spent autumn days in his garden and yet he seemed never to really be in any of those places.

He wanted only to be with June, she drenched his head and saturated his heart. His need for her sucked everything he was into a vacuum and kept it from him and anyone around him.

It was on a sharp, bright day in November that Wren knew it had gone on long enough; she had to help. It had seemed that in the beginning, when she had first succeeded in stealing this life that she would keep all her energy for her own task of finding Alessandro. She had vowed not to get involved with these people who were to be merely hosts to her spirit. Now, she had to admit that she loved this man as much as if he was one of her spirit group. He was a good man and a good spirit who was growing fast seeming to be at the end of one dimension of spiritual growth and ready to ascend to the next with flying colours. She was useless in her three month old body to do much except analyse everyone who looked into her pram hood. That was not going to find Alessandro. She had skills to use, well-earned skills, why not use them to help this man who so needed to move on from the grief that was totally absorbing him. It was obvious what he needed.

This was something she could not do alone.

The time had to be exactly right and that is why she waited until she had been given her ten o'clock bottle, had her wind brought up over the shoulder of Ivy and a disgusting nappy changed. This is when she would sleep; she would be able to free herself enough from the physical to go to Sundia. Just a heartbeat away, yet unseen and unfelt by most people, the spirit of June was found. She would often be here near the earthbound spirits of those who grieved for her until she could spend more and more time in the higher level where she was to elevate to meet with the fullness of her soul. Her time on Earth wasn't done until Tot didn't need her anymore.

Wren felt the warmth and absorbed the brightness of the colours around her. It was so lovely here it was a wonder any spirit wanted to return to body. Sundia was sitting with her back to a tree just as she had when she was carrying her baby on Earth. Awareness lifted her head from her book.

'Wren!'

'Sundia. How are you doing?' The words came unspoken.

'Good. I'm glad you are here; it is easier to communicate on this energy level. You helped me a lot Wren, I'm grateful. You have my parents now, they love you but they are not able to move on much, stuck in grief aren't they.'

'That is why I have come here. I need your help.'

'Oh please, show me how I can help the man and woman who gave me so much when I was June.'

'I was aware of the kindness you did for Mr. Farraige in the chapel at your funeral.'

'Yes, well he had such thoughts of revenge towards Colin that he would set himself back spiritually if he was to do what was in his mind whilst he looked at the coffin of the child he had become so very fond of. I couldn't let him feel like that.'

'That did you credit.'

'It was easy, I found the only bit of malice he held in his heart.'

'You were close to him weren't you?'

'Yes, and he holds me dear now. I go to him, feel his pain, and try to ease it.'

'We must use this to help Tot and Ivy.'

'Oh I will do anything, but I was lost, hoping for your help. What can we do?'

'Tot is in the garden right now pulling up frost attacked dahlias and cutting down raspberry canes.'

Sundia glowed. 'Oh how I loved that job, seeing the compost heap grow. And how I hated the cold and the short days.'

Wren shuddered, knowing she had many years of winters to get through.

'Where is Mr. Farraige?' she asked.

'I have just seen him at home, peeling potatoes.'

Then we must act now, while his mind is on Beta waves.

Sundia glowed at the idea and was amazed at how easy it was to influence Mr. Farraige to act as the two spirits planned. It would have been impossible to make him do anything against his basic character but this took little effort.

Together, the two spirits watched.

They saw Mr. Farraige put aside the little pan of potatoes, pull his outdoor shoes on and take a surprised but delighted Towser out for a second walk that morning. They went with him as he rounded the Methodist Chapel and felt his heart swell as he turned his head to see June's grave glowing in the sun with the last of Tot's bronze chrysanthemums. His step quickened, pulling a leadless dog from powerful smells at the track side and up the cobbled street to where the climb evened off. At first he passed the garden where Tot's body used up the energy he couldn't stop producing just because it was his day off. He had noticed, just in the corner of his eye how slack the man's jaw was and how dull the garden seemed with no whistling, no chattering to a helpful daughter or mischievous dog.

Jan, drawn first by the presence of her two much loved spirits and then by the smell of the dog she'd not seen in months, scattered damp top leaves from her compost heap bed and ran to the gate.

Tot, pulled from his reverie by the sudden action lifted his head, added his flattened palm to the brim of his flat cap and looked into the sun. This wasn't enough but he knew from Jan's tail that it was a friend who bent over the gate to tickle her ears. His boots crunched the cinder path in steady pace, stopping before the final four steps when he saw who it was straightening up to greet him.

'Tot.'

'Arthur.'

'What you...?'

Both men spoke at once then went silent as they appreciated each other's unease.

Tension pushed between them like an over-inflated balloon. Last time they met it was with flying fists.

'That book, it's yours is it?' Tot surprised himself as well as his visitor.

'On childbirth? Yes. I hope you didn't mind.'

'I didn't know...well not till after...you know.'

'Yes. I hope you don't......'

'No, no no! I'm grateful, only sorry I didn't think of it myself. Should have.'

Tot opened the gate allowing Jan to rush to Towser so that they could both dash about the cobbles showing off.

The two men, left alone in their embarrassment allowed avoiding eyes to meet.

'Do you want a seat for a moment Arthur, just while our dogs have their daft half hour?' He drew aside and Mr. Farraige stepped into the garden he often passed but never entered. His eyes filled as he followed the gardener, his coat sweeping browning hydrangea flowers on bushes he knew June had propagated and nurtured. He'd laughed when she told him her dad had brought horseshoes home from the pit to bury beneath them hoping their iron content would change the pink blooms to blue. It was hard to see if this had worked as all the colour had gone anyway along with the spirit of the lovely girl.

Had he been able to raise his vibrational awareness just a little he would have seen that very spirit he longed for watching him, loving him.

Tot stopped when he reached a seat he had made from sawn off pit props and an old railway sleeper. Either side was guarded by tall round heads of the Opium poppy he was saving for seed, their leaves were withered and brittle but the beige balls with their hard frill stood erect and waiting, long since ripe but neglected. He sat at one end and gestured to Mr. Farraige to sit at the other. Both men turned, pushed their bodies into the corners to make more distance and at the same time get a better look at the man they wanted to know. The uneasiness between them hung heavily but their mutual need built up, charging at their throats like bulls seeing a fertile cow.

Wren and Sundia watched knowing that their pain was the space between how it was and how they wanted it.

Both men swallowed. Mr. Farraige spoke the first words in what they knew on some level was a mutual quest.

'How are you doing Tot?'

Tot gulped at the tears he felt rise first in his throat and then in his eyes. Yesterday he'd been able to stop them but today, no. He knew they had spilled but pretended they hadn't.

'Oh, you know, as well as can be expected.'

'She was a lovely girl your June.'

'Yes.' It was a whisper, all he would allow out of his memory of his daughter, as if a loud acknowledgement would somehow diminish all he had left of her.

He cleared his throat but it was not enough to push down the pain. He tried again.

'Erm, I feel I should thank you.'

'For what?'

'You made my daughter's life happier her last few months, taught her things even I didn't know about nature. She soaked it all up you know.'

'Yes. She was a delight.'

They both humphed out a smile and shook their heads at their private memories of her enchantment with nature and their enchantment with her.

'I'm sure she's in a better place Tot, a place where no evil bastard can get his hands on her.'

Tot grabbed his eyes from their study of his boots and fixed them onto the other man's face.

'What do you know about this evil bastard who hurt June?'

Mr. Farraige became aware of his face blanche. He felt Tot's sharpened rod of need poke his mind and understood it, but he had to be careful, any man who had lost his child like this was capable of murder. Tot was a strong man, he had first-hand...and fist knowledge of that, he couldn't let him go down that road, the same road he'd been down so many times in his own mind.

'I wasn't sure Tot, not at first.'

'Tell me man! Tell me!' Tot's eyes burned bright with horrible hope.

Mr. Farraige swallowed back his instinct to blurt out the name of the youth he now knew without a shadow of a doubt raped June. He took a deep breath and shuffled, lifted his trilby, pushed back what hair was left of his fast growing baldness. When he'd run out of things to give him time for his desperate mind to think he bit his lip as he allowed his eyes to be locked by the brightness of Tot's.

'I...'

Oh God! Why had he come here? Why had he stopped at the gate? He wanted to be at home boiling up his dinner, cutting slices from the cold joint of the day before.

Wren and Sundia knew why he was here and gave him the words and the strength to carry out the desperate healing of them both.

'I started walking June back from school one night when I saw her talking to some-one I felt she was afraid of.'

'Who?'

'He was acting strange and I...'

'Who was it man! Tell me!'

'I...I couldn't quite see.'

Tot flung himself to his feet, towered over the man he so desperately wanted the truth from.

'Divvent be so bloody daft man! Who was it?'

Anger glowed from his eyes, flooded red to his tight face and still had energy enough to ball big fists to his sides.

Mr. Farraige could never allow that fury to find its target. Tot would be had up for murder. No jury would understand, there was no proof enough for law. What would happen to Ivy and the two little bairns with a father hanged? No there was enough pain in this family; he would deal with Colin himself. After all, if he was tried and hung who would suffer, his mother was past recognising him now and his bones only had a few years left in them…only Towser would miss him.

'Tot, Tot, I only saw some-one rush into the woods that's all. I knew June was frightened but I didn't know any more till I saw her in the garden... pregnant.'

'You should have come to me then!'

'I'd already felt the power of your anger Tot and what could I say. June was the one to tell you.'

'Aye, well she never did and it's too bloody late now isn't it.'

The space between them widened making room for doubt. Tot coldly studied the face of the man before him. He was a clever man who was bound to have something up his sleeve. He would have to be watched that's all. He turned silent in seeing, in reading every tiny giveaway of the features that had now closed to him with a stare at feet. With the antennae of desperation he noted everything.

There was something.

'What shift 'r you on Tot?'

'Why?'

'Oh nothing, just a nice day for gardening that's all. Shame to spend it under the ground.'

The men parted in their quiet dissatisfaction of each other, called their dogs to their sides to go home to two different houses and two different dinners. Two different agonies.

Tot returned to the sterility of clamour. Ivy was stirring a pan of ham and leek broth with one hand and holding the baby onto her swollen belly with the other. She turned slightly, returned the lid to the bubbling pan and smiled tightly. It was the best she could do.

Some inner worm gnawed at anything brighter, but Tot was grateful even for this for it meant she was glad to see him in her own way.

'Tot! Boots!'

In his thoughts he was still with the man who could give him some sort of peace.

'Oh sorry pet.' he said before going back into the yard to push his toes at the back of his worn leather pit boots assigned to gardening. He had one foot wriggling in its freedom when he noticed Jan's nose twitch, her ears and neck lifted to take a clearer reading on something of extreme interest. When her face relaxed and her legs looked like they might dart off, Tot grabbed her and took her behind the door closing it all but three inches. It was all he would need.

He was right. Jan only reacted like this to another dog. It had to be Towser.

Mr. Farraige dashed past hoping against hope that Tot was well into his mid-day meal by now.

'Ivy, I've forgotten something.' he turned to see her ladle in hand at the range. 'Put that broth back in the pan will you? And don't let Jan out!'

'But where....?' Ivy's words were lost on him.

By the time Tot heaved on his boot and reached the street Mr. Farraige was just disappearing at the top of the hill where the cobbles gave out to the sandy mud softened by autumn rain. When he reached this point himself he stopped. Farraige had Towser on the lead and was beetling away towards the pit head. Tot waited. Whatever was going to happen had to be allowed time to get underway before he arrived. No point stopping something before it started. He made his way through the hazel bushes behind the stables to approach the pit from the back. There was no sign of the man or dog he was following. They had not passed the pit. They had gone into it.

Tot opened the door to an empty stable from where he had a good view of the yard and the shamble of offices. He thought he was alone in the smell of straw and horse muck but he was not.

Wren and Sundia were just above his urgent brow, willing him to keep his temper.

They knew Mr. Farraige would be handling this in a peaceful way because Sundia had removed any need for revenge from him at her funeral. All their calming energies were directed at Tot.

They watched with him as he saw the man he'd followed emerge from the weighing office. He was followed immediately by Colin, the man who used to weigh his tubs up to a couple of months ago until they were put on different shifts. He hadn't seen this lad for a while; he never went to chapel but worshipped at the beery bar of the working man's club instead.

What did Mr. Farraige want with Colin? He could hear only mumblings, firm and low from the older man and higher pitch growing higher as he seemed to become indignant. It couldn't be Colin who had hurt June; he had known Tot since he started in the colliery offices at fifteen. He didn't like the young lad, he was a bit of a waster, but surely he wasn't capable of something as awful as this.

Tot's mind tried to fight its way through turmoil handicapped by withheld breath and rumbling hunger. He strained his ears and angled his head jerkily in his desperation to get a better sense of just what was going on.

The voices droned inaudibly until suddenly Colin, clenching his fists to his side, lifted one in an angry right hook that never found its target. Towser growled but he was not needed to defend his master for the punch was caught and twisted behind Colin's back. Mr. Farraige whispered something long and low through curled lips right into the ear of a thunderously angry young man. He was allowed to wrench himself loose then rubbed at his shoulder before taking a wide berth of the man standing squarely in front of him. He made an abrupt move towards the office door. But was stopped by the sergeant major growl.

'No! Now!'

Colin pressed wrathful eyes into the man and his growling dog then stomped towards the path that would take him to the bus stop.

It had to be Colin.

Tot felt his knees weaken as he tried not to visualise what this youth had done to his little girl.

Terrible thoughts of her pain, indignity and helplessness raged and swirled uncontrollably as they brought sweat to his brow. He was only just aware of the man and dog passing the stable towards the entrance of colliery land.

Colin was responsible for taking June from him. It was his actions that made her life a misery for the last months of her young life.

Wren and Sundia combined their energies to engulf Tot with love and calm. They knew what he had in his mind and he must not be allowed to feel this way. They sent him images of Ivy pregnant and dealing with a three month old baby but so great was his furious need for revenge that nothing could penetrate the swirling red and blackness of his heart. Grief, hatred and revenge enclosed him in impenetrable armour.

When he had pushed the shock from his muscles enough to move, Tot threw back the half door and strode after Colin. When he was halfway past the office the glazed door opened. Mr. Turnbull, the office manager looked keenly around the yard.

'Colin! What the hell you playing at lad; we've got tubs backing up here! Where the bloody.....?'

'Tot? What are you doing here? Have you seen Colin?'

Tot was only aware of what was boiling in his brain and scalding his heart. He walked blindly past the man leaving him to shake his head angrily and dash back into the office to try to clear the backlog.

Colin was leaning on the black and white stripped pole that served to tell of the hourly bus service. He was licking at the side of a cigarette paper thinly filled with shredded tobacco. When he heard boots hit the tarmac he looked up. Tot watched his face pale and the unlit fag drop from his hand scattering golden tobacco over the checked jacket.

CHAPTER FIFTEEN

This was the moment Wren and Sundia had their hardest work to do. Tot had free will; he could kill the lad if he wanted. Even a spirit as advanced as Wren could not affect the free will of another when they were physical. Yet she had to summon up something to stop this man becoming a murderer. She held no deep knowledge of his spirit as she would have had if she'd not stolen the life as his granddaughter. Sundia had. Together the spirits gave all the good energies they could summon and thrust images of Ivy and the baby Tot had left at home into his raging mind. Tot halted in the middle of the road just long enough for Colin's eyes to meet his.

He knew.

Fear mixed with guilt, a poisonous and clinging taste could not be swallowed away by the terrified youth. He straightened up edgily, not knowing how long he had left to live. A quick glance behind him showed him the path into the woods where he could surely outrun this older man in worn pit boots. Tot read his darting eyes and moved forward first, Colin took to the path. It was the only evidence and trial that Tot needed.

He would get him. By God he would get him.

The young body darted and leapt, cracked twigs and flattened brown bracken. It sweated with fear and effort. Then it stopped.

Tot didn't need to use his energy this way, he knew this part of the wood. He knew every tuft, every twig. This was June's wood. He had given this wood to his daughter through the knowledge he had acquired from his own love of it. He needed that wisdom more than ever now. He would avenge June in her own special place. He walked at a firm even pace, all the time sending strength to his arms, burning the fire of grief with the fuel of justice. There had never been such strength behind his fists.

He found Colin to the side of the little pond, cowering behind an autumn reddened Gelder Rose with his back to the rock face that had captured him. The sheer sand stone behind him was only ten feet tall but it kept him from freedom as it had kept the spring winds from Tot and his daughter every year they had fished here for tadpoles.

It was as easy as pulling a rabbit from a trap. Tot held the youth by the collar and grew disgusted by the whimpering. Colin's hands came up to protect his fear twisted face from the huge fist pulled back behind Tot's sinewed neck. With eyes screwed tight shut he didn't see the bulge of his aggressor's eyes nor the baring of the teeth. Neither did he see the punch fly but he heard the crack of knuckles. By some miracle he felt nothing. He slowly dropped his hands and peeped through screwed up eyes to see Tot shaking his own injured hand. Then he felt himself loosened from the ferocious grip.

'Get up!' Tot growled. 'And if I ever see you again I will kill you!'

Colin scrambled to his feet. The man was mad. He had hit the rock face instead of him.

Tot nodded in the direction of two ash trees clinging to the smaller rocks.

'Go between those and it will bring you out over the cliff to the top edge of the wood.'

Colin hesitated. It had to be a trick.

'Go!'

The youth scrambled away gratefully but when he reached the top of the rock which had previously held him prisoner he looked down. Tot was stooped in pain as he gingerly felt his injured hand.

Colin felt big up there, looking down at the man not brave enough to hit anything that might hit back.

'You're a coward Tot Stoker! A dirty rotten coward! I'm glad your daughter croaked it. The dead can't speak. You'll never prove a thing.'

This time Tot ran. He leaped and dashed on land he knew so well so that he caught the stumbling youth almost immediately. His voice bulldozed through all opposition.

'Coward! Coward! You surely know what a coward is!'

With a flick of his good wrist and a sudden knee to the back he sent Colin flying over the cliff.

Tot didn't look down or back.

His feet thudded their way back to the main road. On and on, thump after thump. Through leaf mould and dead wood, onto deadened grass then tarmac. All he could hear was pounding.

Pounding boots, pounding blood, pounding heart.

When he neared the colliery he only half noticed the office manager flapping about the gate.

'Tot! What's going on? Where's Colin? Tot! Tot!' his voice trailed behind the man who seemed to be in a trance. Only the sleeves torn away at the shoulder seams of the soil stained jacket and the blood on the knuckles of the hand that pulled it together replied to him.

Pounding, only pounding.

Wren and Sundia were proud of him. Now they could both move on. Sundia without Tot and Wren with him. She felt they both stood outside the bright house of life. She was glad to have him as a father figure who would nurture her and help her grow until she was big enough to do what she came to this life to do.

Find Alessandro.

CHAPTER SIXTEEN

Growing was a serious business.

The human need for food and its natural process came automatically but it did distract Wren from where she wanted to be; in her spirit. Bodily functions had to be endured of course; this is why she'd taken the dense, slow form, to be human enough to be the same as Alessandro.

She was able to look around quite a bit during the many hours her little body slumbered.

Ivy was enormous. Her back ached and she found it increasingly difficult to rise quickly enough to attend to the bellowing, seemingly urgent needs of a five month old baby. Luckily the garden didn't need much attention throughout the winter and now in February, Tot took the old pram up the cinder path, bumping around a well wrapped up baby as he heaved the sprung chariot over frost covered steps. The cold hit them like a fist but it didn't matter.

Wren loved this time with Tot, alone except for the ever present terrier that followed his every step. Sitting up swathed in hand knitted woollen garments from head to toe she could feel the healthy glow on her face, watching her surroundings now with clear blue eyes she knew were going to cause a stir in the next few weeks. She felt his heart swell as the senses took in crisp air, hungry squawking birds gobbling up the stale bread Tot scattered and the spirit of June.

This was where he cried. He longed for her. He tried to remember every second of his time with her but it was becoming increasingly difficult even to see her face. Sundia often came to him. He seemed not to register completely that she was there, wondering if the rattle in the dry leaves was her or his imagination. Never picking up the white feathers that seemed always to be in his path, but she placed them before him anyway. Always, he showed a lightening of mood after she had been close. At first she was sad to see him so low but as her bright love penetrated his soul he often expelled air on a head shaking sigh, wiped his eye on his sleeve and smiled. It was only then that Sundia would touch spirits with Wren and tell her of her progress.

'Wren, you are a lovely healthy baby. Had I lived I would have been proud to be your mother, shame or no shame. My guides have told me I did well as June. They were very complimentary on my dealings with Ivy and Colin. You have caused quite a stir Wren. Many great ones are waiting for you to create soul history. No-one knows what will happen to you either on this Earth or when you pass over. There are some that think your life should be short, that you should be taken to task sooner rather than later. Others say perhaps the life should be extended to the full term a body can last, but you know who will have the final decision on that don't you? You must take the chance to redeem yourself, it will come only once….please do not miss it.'

Tot noticed Jan's enthusiastic wiggling at these times but he never once realised it was because Jan loved the spirit who was there.

This was the dog's one spiritual friend. She knew it was June.

Wren took every bit of love from the only spirit who came to her in the early months of her life.

She thought of how a baby was usually given much companionship, love and guidance to ease it through initial strangeness of the family and new surroundings. After the first reunion with the souls of its chosen parents only the human interactions would appear to matter, even though every action was soul driven. Children, ravenous with need, were helped to take the hand of their own wishes. She knew that as physical demands pushed in; most new children became less and less aware until only the few spirit guides, chosen in the exciting time before reincarnation, stayed around for the life duration and the final return.

She had much strength and awareness and would have to exercise her powers vigorously to prevent physical demands taking over to smothering her cognizance.

'Well baby, now you can see around what do you think of my garden eh?' Tot thrust his head forward and set a smile on the face that came so close as he pushed the tiny hand back into the mitten that had somehow fallen to the ground. Wren watched his stiff oversized fingers fiddle with the delicate woollen cord as he fumbled to tie a bow around her wrist.

'Look at that mark darlin'! Your mitten has been too tight.' he rubbed at the red circle usually hidden in the baby's wrist crease. Wren knew it was nothing to do with woollen cords. Tot was not to know it was not of this life.

She took the care he so naturally offered and watched his breath puff out in front of him. He was so easy to love. In him she was lucky. She saw his delight as she wobbled her head in the direction of the rose-bed. It was only weedless soil and newly pruned bare wood, but she had seen it in all its summer glory and inhaled its perfume and so smiled at the knowledge of what it would soon become once more.

Suddenly the smile fell from her face and she felt the downturn of her mouth as she whimpered. This was the physical reaction to what she had just read mentally. Tot was needed at home.

'Oh what is it Diddums? You can't be hungry so soon.'

Wren allowed her emotions to come out in a wail so energetic that Tot saw for the first time a tiny white mark pushing out through her gums.

'Oh darlin'! You're teething! Does it hurt?' He put a hand tenderly to the bright red cheek.

Quickly, he bent towards the inflexible brake then began to push the pram back down the cinder path towards the house. Wren, soothed by the motion of the pram allowed the crying to subside. She tried to capture this special bond for she knew that as soon as he reached the house everything would change.

'Yoo hoo! Ivy! This bairn's teething... Ivy'

The warmth from the blazing fire was too much as Wren was jiggled into the kitchen.

'Where's your Mammy then?'

'Ivy!'

'Tot! Tot! Here, in the bedroom.'

Wren didn't need to be carried to the sight to know that Ivy was in labour.

There had been several offers to Tot of help whenever he needed it from both the men he worked with and their wives. None had dared approach Ivy for fear of the stoniest of looks that could wither the offerer for the rest of the day. It was to one of these sympathisers that Wren was wheeled. She knew exactly what was going on in her own house but took the opportunity to take in other ways people had of looking after homes. Edna and Bert had children but the only sign in the kitchen which was a handed replica of her own was an alarming array of photos of stiff children standing up straight for the novelty honour of being in front of a camera. Beside these were the wedding photos of the same children on the day they left this haven of clean clothes and home baking.

'Look at this bairn Bert, she's been here before. You'd think she was taking everything in.

She's a wise one.'

Edna's hands were unsteady at first until the deftness of ingrained motherhood had the matinee coat and knitted leggings in a pile on top of the pixie hat and mittens.

'Poor baby.' Edna shook her head as she took in the thin fair hair and bright red cheeks.

'She doesn't know that she killed her mother.'

Bert sat beside his wife and looked into the baby blue eyes.

'Careful now Edna, she looks like she understands everything.'

'Don't be daft! Our little Albert was ten month before he understood a word.'

'Mind but she's bright. I hope I have time to give her a bottle, it's been ages.'

Bert stood up and took his pipe from a holder on the mantelpiece. 'Women!'

Wren liked these people; they were good souls who had a hard life now made more comfortable by just being the two of them again. Wren was padded into the corner of the settee with cushions and a tea towel beneath her chin.

'Tot should have sent in a bib.'

'Oh Edna, not in the state he was in. Poor man must be in agonies of suffering in case the same thing happens to his wife as did to his daughter.'

'But it's not Ivy's first bairn is it? And she's not only fifteen. Another thing Bert, they'll not be having that midwife anywhere near her. There was definitely neglect there I don't care what they say.'

'Careful love, we have no proof.'

'No, we don't. That poor bairn. June was so lovely, not a bad bone in her body. That rotten Colin got all Tot gave him.'

'Aye well, maybe Tot gave him more than we thought for his Mam's not seen hide nor hair of him since. She came to the pit to ask if anyone knew anything but not a word passed any man's lips.'

'You don't think....'

'Well if I did I'd not be alone. There's not a man in that pit who'd split on Tot, some even respect him for it. Why should the bastard who did that to a young lass be left to live?'

These people admired Tot for what they thought was the truth and Wren loved him for what she knew it to be.

Edna got her wish. As Wren lay back enjoying the warm milk and the soft bosom of this older lady she sent love and healing to Ivy but she did not go to her for she knew that her guardian spirits were with her helping to deliver the body of a soul she already knew and dreaded.

Her mind was brought back into the arms of the neighbour when the vibration of her voice called out to her husband.

'Do you know Bert this little'n still hasn't been given a name; isn't that awful? Her five months and not yet christened!'

'Aye well, if I'd had all the trouble Tot's had I'd not have time to think of names either. They could have called her June.'

'Don't be so insensitive man. It would be a reminder every time they used it.'

Wren felt herself passed nearer the fire to the man who held her whilst Edna cleared a space on the table to change her nappy. When it was done she felt overcome by sleep. She always welcomed deep satisfying sleep because this was when, free from the consciousness of being a baby, she could be herself.

She left her rounded body as it flooded with growth hormones safe in the arms of this delighted woman. Wren went first to the sideboard where the display of photos stood well-spaced and gleaming. She had to check, it was ridiculous of course to expect one of these offspring to be Alessandro, it would be too easy. But she had to look. How awful it would be to live her life searching for him and to have missed him right at the beginning. She felt nothing. The little hope was smothered when her instinct told her that she had never met any of the souls beaming out from the bodies dressed in Sunday best.

She went to her home. Dad was standing at the fire holding a new born baby. The spirit was an early one; it was easy for Wren to see the dullness of it. He would be an irritant she could have done without, especially when he realised what she'd done to one of his group. No-one saw her except Jan who was at Tot's feet not very sure of what to feel. Her tail wagged furiously when she greeted Wren.

'Hey Jan. You are pleased to have a new little baby to love aren't you?'

Only Wren knew that Jan was not at all pleased for she knew that in this child was a spirit who had not yet learned sensitivity towards animals. There would be no natural empathy for her there.

Ivy was worn out. She was still in bed ten days after she'd given birth and Tot had to go back to work on Monday. Ivy had refused every offer from the women Tot thought were kind and she thought were intrusive. He had taken over the care of two babies brilliantly and was glad that at least Paul was breast fed.

Wren still hadn't met with the spirit of the noisy ten pound baby boy whose main purpose in life so far seemed to be to have all the attention of both parents. Jan spent as much time with Wren as she could even guarding the pram in cold March winds and clinging fogs.

Ivy eventually got out of bed on Sunday evening after Nurse Bridges had said she could. Tot had put the eiderdown from June's bed over her legs as she fed Paul.

'We'll get both the bairns christened together as soon as you're up to it pet.' Tot said as he rolled up his sleeve so that he could shake a few drops of milk from the teat onto the crook of his arm.

Satisfied with the temperature he gathered up his grandchild who fed greedily.

'Can we agree on a name for this little'n Ivy? We can't keep on telling folk we haven't thought of one.'

'I've told you Tot. Sylvia is my choice and I don't know why you insist on sticking out for that stupid name you seem not to be able to get out of your head.'

'It's not stupid! June wanted it.'

'June was just a bairn herself. She might have come up with anything.'

'But she didn't, she came up with Wren and I must say I rather like it. Sounds a bit exotic, a bit different. Close to nature, like she is……was.'

'Aye, that's exactly what a child growing up in a mining community needs Tot, an exotic name. 'Make her different and she'll always be an outsider.'

Tot gazed at the little face gulping at the teat.

'But she is different Ivy, I can feel it. She won't always live in a pit house she won't.'

Ivy studied his adoring face as it took in the curl that the hair was now growing into.

'You haven't looked at Paul that way Tot. Don't you love him?'

Tot was shocked. 'Of course I love Paul, he's my son....how could you!'

A barrier dropped between them, created by Ivy but not approached by Tot. Then as only Ivy could do, she threw the words high and hard so that they passed over the obstruction to smack into the mind of the one she thought was hurting her.

'Call her what you like Tot. She is the child of a rapist anyway.'

There was always an excuse for his wife's harshness, hadn't she just given birth and lost her daughter only a few months apart. The matter was never discussed again. When they went to see the minister about the baptism Ivy had kept silent as he had asked the names of the two babies he was to bring into his church and God's kingdom together. Tot had hesitated so that the minister's hand hovered above his note book. He looked up feeling the tension but reading it as sadness for the other child of this family whom he had only just buried.

'Their names are Paul and Wren.'

'How do you spell that?'

Tot flinched as he felt Ivy's triumph and his voice deepened as he answered.

'W_R_E_N, like the bird with the sweetest song.'

'Well that's a new one. Foreign I suppose. The war has a lot to answer for.'

He felt Tot's discomfort and said. 'I mean in moving us forward, making us aware of the world out there.'

But it was too late, Tot knew that the name would make the baby who stirred in his arms different but he was pleased because he was the only one who had noticed just how different she was going to be.

It took Ivy a few days. The baby, who waited patiently in the corner of the settee for the wailing to be stopped at the breast before she had her own hunger appeased, was fixing her eyes firmly towards the window.

Tot always hung strips of suet on strings to enjoy the colours of the tits as they competed for food. The chirrups and movement drew Wren so that the early spring sun shone right onto her.

'Don't say you are going to have nowt in your head but nature an' all.' Ivy said as she laid the smaller, now quiet Paul beside her.

When she returned with the bottle and bent to push it into Wren's mouth the seven month old eyes were just caught by the bright light. There was no mistaking who this child had for her mother. One eye was changing. Instead of the blue it had been since birth it was now a soft green. This was the first step towards the brilliant emerald that had been her mother's right eye.

Wren read Ivy's mind and felt her worst fear. She had needed to be ordinary to blend into the background as she searched for Alessandro. Now her name and her eyes would mark her out for unwanted attention. Her only hope now was that she would not inherit her mother's beauty. She needed to be plain.

Wren had spent the months since Paul's birth at the bottom of the pram which had once been her own for a few peaceful months.

The small baby needed to lay flat. The March winds had whipped through the knitted bonnets without the protection of the pram hood so that Wren had one streaming cold after another. Part of Wren felt protective towards this tiny human being she shared every moment with but she knew that one day the dullness behind the eyes would clear through anger or passion and the spirit would know who she was.

When Ivy felt Paul was less fragile she would place the babies together at the top of the pram hoping Wren's brightness would somehow teach her son how to pay attention. When they were left alone outside the Co-op as Ivy waited her turn, Paul would flay jealous arms and kick at the older baby. He knew she was an intruder.

There was no escape and no comfort. When Wren had enough and let out a huge wail Paul would take over with greater weeping so that when a frustrated Ivy stomped from the store it would be Wren who took the smack to the bare leg. All summer beneath the fringed canopy which kept the sun from her children Ivy would pack the groceries around and beneath them so that the three mile push home was squashed and uncomfortable.

When Wren was ten months old Tot would lift her out of the pram so that she could feel her feet on the rough patch of grass he had sown over his dahlia bed. She had been crawling for a while now but when she pulled herself up at Tot's knee to bounce on unsteady bowed legs, he encouraged her to take a step holding her tiny fist in his big hands. She gripped his rough fingers and felt not only physical steadiness but an energy of love she so longed for.

In late July, just as Tot aimed the unfolded Penguin camera at the wobbling eleven month old baby, it happened. Wren took two faltering steps towards him and he pressed the silver button to capture the very moment his special love stood on her own two feet and took her first steps.

He was overjoyed. Tears burst from his heart. It had been so like the day his dear June had first walked from holding onto the tablecloth to grabbing the couch cushion. She had looked so overjoyed herself as he and Ivy had shouted their appreciation and clapped before sweeping her off her feet to cuddle the child with different coloured sparkling eyes.

He'd not had the camera then. There was no such photo. But his granddaughter was so like June that he could pretend. It eased the pain sometimes. Sometimes it intensified it to unbearable searing agony.

When the film had being processed at the chemist Ivy was at first pleased with the tiny black and white photos. When she had looked at all ten her face changed.

'Why is Paul only on one of these Tot?'

He took the shiny new snaps from her and searched through as if the very act itself would make his truculent son suddenly appear.

'No...I'm sure I took more.'

He searched in vain until Ivy took them from him and spread them one by one on the table.

'There; Wren splashing in the bath in the yard; Wren beside the delphiniums, Wren sitting on the step with Jan, Wren eating a scone at the back door and oh here it is, Wren with Paul...well isn't he lucky then! His one photo and he gets to share it with Wren. Will she mind do you think? After all she must believe that camera is solely for her own use by now!'

'Oh Ivy; it's just that Wren is more interesting.'

He saw his wife's mouth narrow and knew this close down of communication could last for days if he didn't stop it now.

'I mean she is doing eleven month old things and Paul is still mostly sleeping. It'll be the same when he is older.'

'No it won't....' She hesitated to say what she really thought. He was a good man maybe he would love his son as much when he could walk too. 'It will be the winter when he is at this stage. Too dark indoors for photographs.'

Tot lifted Paul from the corner of the chair into the crook of his arm.

'We'll think of something won't we son. We won't miss your special moments will we?'

Even as he said the words he felt nothing. This baby belonged to Ivy. He felt no connection, no bond. Ivy studied her husband and saw it all.

On Wren's first birthday on August 30th 1949 Paul was almost nine months old and not even showing signs of crawling yet. Wren grew ever more aware of the need not to alienate Ivy and so climbed up beside him as soon as Tot picked up the stiff leather case that she knew held the camera she'd had pointed at her so much. She knew he had wanted a picture of her on her own to put in a frame on the sideboard but for all their sakes she couldn't allow it. As she slipped her chubby arm around her Buddha shaped brother she despaired at the dullness behind his eyes. He turned slowly towards her so that she saw deep into him. His spirit was there of course but of such low awareness that she surrendered all hope of him ever fulfilling his karmic debts.

The photo was framed and it at least pleased Ivy but Tot was never happy with it. When he held it over the next few months he felt it shouldn't exist and yet he wouldn't allow the reasons for his dissatisfaction to surface. He told himself it was too shadowed even with the hot summer sun blasting through the open door. Wren's face was too light, Paul's too dark.

Ivy was happy that the two babies in her care sat together on the same photo but even she noticed the difference. As she dusted one morning when Tot had worked night shift she turned to him photo in hand. Her eyes lifted from the image to her family now sitting on the floor. Tot had a child under each arm and Jan snuggled into Wren. He was trying to calm their desire to go for the walk he had promised them before December winds had blown smoke back down the chimney and lashed rain to the newly cleaned windows. Wren was watching every expression on Tot's face as he made up a story of a magic teddy. Paul was staring dully into the fire.

'Tot. Do you think there is something wrong with Paul?'

He left his story mid-word.

'For heaven's sake! No! Babies develop at different rates that's all.'

'Yes but not our babies. June and Wren at that age...they shared the same quickness and a light shone from their smile, but with him...'

'There you go then; it's just girls, they are quicker. He'll catch up love, don't you worry.'

As he returned to his story he watched the head of his son. It didn't turn as he growled out the voice of the big bad brown bear, nor did it register any change as he tickled and hugged him at the bit where the magic teddy saved all the children. He knew he wasn't old enough to understand the story

but he despaired that he didn't smile or react at all to the physical contact. Wren squealed with glee as she wobbled up onto podgy legs and started to act out the teddy's walk through the wood peering into every bush.

She was only fifteen months and she seemed to understand everything. His only hope was that as Paul grew he would learn from the one he would think was his sister. Wren read his thoughts and was sad at what she knew but her Dad didn't.

In the room where she slept with Paul every night, the same tiny room where she was born, Wren worked with the mind of the baby she was physically and tried to make sure that her own self was strongest. She knew from experience that spiritual awareness dulled as human needs sharpened. This couldn't be allowed to happen to her. Things were already different to how she had planned when she had first arrived in her mother's womb. She was going to have no emotional ties and yet here she was adoring Tot, caring for Ivy and worrying about Paul. Her human side was stronger than she ever remembered it would be. Wren had to be zealous. She couldn't stop the emotions but she had only one purpose in being here in this cold room in a cold country.

A dread hit her stomach.

It was going to be harder than she ever thought possible.

CHAPTER SEVENTEEN

Ivy hadn't spoken to Tot for five days.

Every effort made by her husband to cajole Ivy out of her angry misery was shrugged off, wriggled out of or glared into icy hell. When he stopped trying and gave all his attention to the children she flew into such a rage that he thought her words might strangle her.

'Is that all you bloody care about? Bloody bairns! Is that why you have done this to me?'

Tot smoothed the hair of his frightened son then turned his eyes to Wren who once more looked as if she'd seen it all before. She had of course and she'd known for weeks that Ivy was carrying another baby and met with the spirit who had left her in no doubt of how it would affect her life.

'Ivy love; what have I done to you? Tell me pet.'

'Don't you pet me! That is what got me into this trouble in the first place.'

'What trouble Ivy? Do you mean you're pregnant again?'

He knew by her face that she was and when he stood up and used his strength to stop her running away she melted and allowed herself the comfort she had longed for all along.

'But hinny; that's wonderful.'

'No it's not! What's wonderful about squeezing another child into that tiny box room? We can hardly move as it is!'

Tot laughed in the way she had come to know meant that he knew a way and he'd take it.

'We'll ask the council for a house.'

'Oh no Tot! Not one of them dirty estates. What about the woods and your garden? You could never leave your garden.'

'Aye well; I'll get another garden Ivy and I can still visit the woods and June.'

The brightness left him for a second; he could still take the babies and Jan to the grave, only it wouldn't be every day.

'There's a new estate just being built at the bottom of Highcopse, the word is they're to have bathrooms and electric cookers.'

'Everybody wants those houses man! We'd never be so lucky Tot.'

'Luck has nowt to do with it.' His arms gave every comfort to the woman who so desperately needed it but his heart was secretly breaking at the thought of leaving this place.

'Just think what it would be like to have a bathroom. We're bound to be high up on the list wi' three bairns man.'

Ivy pulled away, angry at his useless dreaming.

'It's not bairns they count but bedrooms and we have two, one for us and one for the children. We don't stand a chance.'

At five the next morning he went to check on the sleeping children who depended on him so much. They lay head to tail in the wooden cot he'd bought and painted from another miner. Pushed right up against the high bed that had been June's, there was little room for him to squeeze between this and the dressing table. Tot opened the window and gazed into the darkness. All he could see was his dead daughter, pale and lifeless. Where was she? As his eyes adjusted to the darkness he began to see the stars. Was she there? Was there some other world? Some other way to be? He knew nothing. His heart clawed deeply at the wound his first born had left behind her so that a silent scream left for the sky.

Desolation could easily claim him.

Gradually, as a tiny gap in the clouds allowed orange red to show it was morning his spirit was lifted. Words came to him in June's voice and he grabbed at them whilst all the time knowing it was his own yearning mind playing tricks on him. And yet...?

'Daddy! My Daddy!' He squeezed his head in hands agonised by longing. 'You will not leave me behind in that grave. I am here in your heart whenever you want me.'

How he longed for those words to be real; how he wanted her. He struggled now to see her face, it took longer and longer. The feeling of her presence was probably just his memory and desperation. Whilst June gave him these gifts of love she knew she would never appear to him as he had known her in her human form, he would never be able to stand it. Instead she gently ruffled the hair at the crown of his head. It was sleep moulded and soft, free of any grease. His hand went to the place and smoothed first then rubbed and flicked vigorously. He looked behind him half expecting a spider or crane fly to have been brushed from its settlement. He turned his eyes to the window and hoped it might be June.

The rich orange sun glared half its mass over the horizon and he had to look away. When the dark spots cleared from his eyes he saw he was been studied by Wren. She was only two and yet she seemed to understand so much. He felt like the child. He wanted her to take care of him, show him the way. Take him from his grief.

A whimper which he knew from experience would lead to an irritatingly high pitched wail if not dealt with; left Paul's screwed up face. Tot lifted him before he could climb clumsily over his sister. He let down the side of the cot and Wren climbed out to follow Tot into the other bedroom where Ivy was just waking.

'You stay there pet. I'll bring you some tea.' He placed Paul into his mother's arms and Wren lifted her arms to him. He drank in the sleepy softness of her in his hold and tried not to show his ecstasy at her closeness. When she was sitting beneath the blankets in the place where Tot slept he went to the door.

'Are you going to the store the day Ivy?'

'Aye! I'm pregnant not ill Tot, and we still have to eat, three mile push or not. Have these bairns been on the potty?'

'So you'll be gone all morning will yu'?'

'Aye; why?'

'Oh nowt just thinking what I have to do on me day off. You'll be taking the bairns will you?'

Ivy looked suspiciously at her husband. She knew that look.

'Why don't you call at the council offices and see how long the list is for that new estate? It would be grand to have a bathroom, free us from potties, po-s and outside freezing lavs.'

As Ivy's time was taken up trying to calm a wriggling eighteen month boy she cursed at Tot's useless daydreaming. Hadn't she enough to do without wasting her time sitting with two bairns in some dusty council offices. She knew she wouldn't go.

Wren, sitting sucking her thumb on Tot's pillow, knew she would.

It was afternoon when Jan's ears pricked at the sound of pram wheels on cobbles Tot put down his spade and opened the garden gate to meet his wife at the bottom of the yard steps. As he bent to take the heavy end of a pram filled with children and groceries, the apprehension of Ivy's anger when she saw what he'd done stopped him swallowing.

'Yu' late, was the store busy?' he dared not ask the question that was burning in his mind.

'No; but the council office was.'

He tried not to appear too keen. 'So?'

'So nothing. I filled in a form that's all. Well half-filled it in.' He lifted two sleepy children out of the pram so they could toddle off to play with the dog who was nuzzling Wren and avoiding Paul.

'Half...why?' he tried to look casual as he lifted blue paper bags of sugar then tins of half pears from where they'd been packed around his offspring. Ivy followed him with the lighter basket.

Wren sensed Tot was anxious about something and knew as soon as she set foot in the house that the energies had changed. It didn't feel like her house.

Irritatingly for them both now, Ivy sent Tot out for the heavy shopping. His impatience was making him move even quicker. Ivy seemed to want everything put away before she talked. Tot wished she could do both at once but knew from years of experience that she had to have everything in order before his straining urgency could be satisfied. He put the kettle to boil and started to remove Wren's outdoor clothes. She searched his face.

'I swear baby, that you know everything I think.' He held her close and enjoyed the loveliness he didn't understand but was glad of anyway. He was drawn away by a yelp which meant he had to rescue Jan once more from Paul's uncaring clumsiness. The child cried at Tot's discipline which brought Ivy from the scullery.

'You're too rough with Paul Tot!'

'He has to learn not to mistreat animals Ivy.'

'You think more of that blooming dog than you do of your own child. How come Wren never gets a smack.'

'She treats Jan with respect.'

'Respect! What does a child of two know about respect?'

'She doesn't know Ivy, she just feels.'

Ivy, holding a sobbing boy, looked down at the rest of her family on the floor. It could have been fifteen years ago the scene was the same. It choked her to think how things were different and now another uncontrollable change.

'What happened at the council office Ivy?'

She put Paul on the floor and the dog scampered urgently outside.

'Huh! It was packed. I had to sit next to three other women and two of them was none too clean either. One lass, heavily pregnant got into conversation with me about our babies. She said it was best not to wait all afternoon with two hungry bairns and that I should take a form from the desk and fill it in. She said not to answer the bit on how many bedrooms as they wouldn't come out to investigate. Said they were used to ignorant folk not filling in the forms properly. When I said I wasn't ignorant and would be filling it in right she took it off me. Said, not if I wanted a house I wouldn't. She wrote 'Three children. No room.' right across the page and then put it in the box provided.'

Ivy's indignation made the relief Tot felt fire out on a tommy gun of laughter.

'It's not funny Tot! Some might not be bothered for folk to know they can hardly even spell their names but I am.'

Ivy pulled her coat from her shoulders and went to put it into her wardrobe. Tot steeled himself for fury.

'What the.....!'

'Tot! Why are the cot and other bed in our room?'

He didn't answer so she tapped towards him in hard outdoor shoes. 'Tot!'

'Billy Hargraves told me that he only got that house at The Folly because he had one bedroom and four bairns.'

'So?'

'So you want a new house don't you? Those inspectors just turn up you know.'

Wren climbed to her feet then fixed her vibrant eyes on her Grandmother. How she wished she could be softer. She sent her love.

Tot left the floor and gathered Paul into his arms for protection. 'Here Ivy' Tot said guiding her towards the children's' bedroom door which he flung open. Ivy's features were drawn into impatient puzzlement which quickly changed to belligerence.

'What the...?'

Wren toddled into her room to find it was now a cupboard.

'I pulled down the garden shed last week, before it fell down. Good supply of wood that, although I had a hard time making the wallpaper stick to it.'

Ivy put out a suspicious arm to feel the false wall.

'But Tot; that's dishonest.'

'Careful now, it won't stand any pressure, it was a quick job.'

'What's dishonest about wanting the best for your family eh? Tell me that!'

'But it could be ages before the inspector comes.'

'It might, but Billy said that the council had been given a lot of stick in the Chronicle for neglecting the needs of the miners in their hovels so I suspect it will be sooner rather than later.'

That night Wren practised astral travel for the first time in this life. She wanted to see where her new home would be; it could lead to meeting Alessandro. There would be new faces from all over the country. It was a long shot but he had just as much chance of being here as the rainforests of South America.

Her energies sped her to a building site. Four houses were finished and had their doors propped open to dry new plaster. Further along the row, two semi-detached homes were awaiting tiles to the roof. As she floated through the scaffold she knew that the sixth one would be where she would live. She checked the area outside. The garden would be smaller than Tot was used to but he expected that. A whole field had been cleared but at the edge of it a big dip held a narrow strip of woodland. It wasn't as dense or beautiful as June's wood but its proximity would offer her family the bird song to raise their spirits. The energies were not as healthy or as special as Woodland Terrace but life was about change and growth, she wasn't going to find Alessandro in that tiny community. It would be a start.

From that moment on Wren could sense the unsettled feelings of both these people she was encouraged to call Mammy and Daddy. Tot spent more time in his garden not knowing whether to plant winter cabbages or dig his many spring bulbs from where he had plunged them beneath the well nurtured soil many years ago. His emotions sprang between thrift and generosity, some-one else would be given this garden; it would be his gift to them. But what if they dug up the lot to lay to feeding themselves, then they would be wasted? Those bulbs would need dividing by now surely. Maybe he'd take half. He busied himself taking cuttings, four of everything and half a dozen of the rose he laid on June's coffin and the hydrangeas she grew herself. He had to be sure of those.

He was out when the inspector paid his surprise visit. It was the middle of September; the wallpaper paste had been drying for two weeks. Wren and Paul, making the most of this unexpected day of brazen blue, were playing with clothes pegs in the yard making huge efforts with pudgy arms to throw them far enough for Jan to run after. Ivy was engrossed in getting dirt from pit clothes by giving all her energy to the wooden poss tub and steaming water. She had to catch this warm breeze or the washing would be hanging around the house for days. Jan stopped wagging her tail then scattered her feet to the gate which was tied with rag to stop Paul dashing away in what was now his favourite game. Wren knew who it was even before Ivy looked up to the man's, 'Good morning!'

He was a wet seal of a man who was already licking his pencil to ensure it was as drenched and slippery as himself. Ivy flushed red when he said who he was then flustered as she encouraged him to go

into the house alone on the pretence of keeping the bairns out of his way during the examination of their need. She wanted no part in this deception and was furious with Tot for not being here. Thoughts of the horrors of being discovered to be a fraud pumped adrenaline through her veins and she yelled at the children who were doing nothing at all to annoy her.

It took only minutes for the man to emerge with an emotionless face that gave none of the relief Ivy so urgently needed. Her body would give her away and her face said what her tongue must not, she just knew it. He only had to look at her to know she was a fraudulent, a cheat, and a dishonest liar.

The man's watery eyes slopped a glance at his note book and took out the folded form which showed Ivy up as almost illiterate. She would kill Tot for being at work.

'It says here three children Mrs Stoker. I see only two."

It was all Ivy could do to lift her deceitful eyes to him. She patted her stomach self-consciously.

She just knew he was thinking how disgusting she was allowing her husband to get her pregnant whilst her two babies were in the same room. He was right. She was disgusting. She should have made Tot rip down that false wall the very day he put it up.

'When?'

'Early February.'

His eyes caught hers and she couldn't look away. This man was judge, jury and hangman and she deserved every agony he caused her. His fishy tongue met the lead of his pencil again to ensure he wrote the family's fate with deep sea precision. Ivy hoped it wouldn't have poisoned him before he reached his office. But if he had decided against them, she hoped it would. The man from the council, defined by his status. Did he have a real life, a wife, family? Slippers and a hand knitted jumper? Maybe, but right now he was the man from the council. Powerful.

He lifted his trilby from his shining head wiping sweat with a crumpled and caked handkerchief. He looked around the yard at the struggling domestic scene with the smug eyes of the well fed.

'I may have to make a second visit. Good day.'

He left without offering a clue to his thoughts or the secret little notes he'd made so solemnly, so importantly, so damningly.

She put her fury through the mangle with her clothes. Wren wished she could assure her that it would be all right.

'What are you staring at Wren?' she railed. 'Play with Paul before he starts to bubble and whine.'

When the basket was full of flattened clothes Ivy heaved it to her hip where it crackled with the urgency of all her housework. She flung open the gate and ushered the children before her.

'Come on! Stop dawdling.'

Wren knew her little legs would never move quickly enough for Ivy's fury but she tried anyway.

When they were safely across the street Ivy shot the bolt on the garden gate and strode ahead.

As Wren and Paul finally caught up to the rope line of flapping flags of family washing it was to see her weeping into dry sheets she had just taken from the line. She breathed in the pine fragrance all her clothes dried here absorbed from the trees. She would miss this. Wren sent her love and calm. Change always hurt but it made souls grow.

'Stop that gawking at me child for heaven's sake.'

There was a scream from behind her and she turned to see Paul had tumbled over the railway sleeper dad had edged the path with.

'You are supposed to look after him! You know he's just learned to walk!'

She slapped at Wren's legs before hauling a snivelling Paul to his feet. She seemed to forget that Wren was only five months older that her charge.

At tea time, Tot had no time to remove even his pit boots before Ivy let her tongue loose with what had held it prisoner all day. Her face was bleached with anxiety and tiredness. He patiently let her free herself of her frustration before asking.

'Did he say how long it would take to get to know?'

'Don't be daft! I told you he said nowt!' Shame fed her anger so that she spat out words to the only one she could.

'Aye but he knew plenty, I could tell! It was horrible! Horrible!'

Tot longed to comfort his angry wife but was beaten by the hammer of her disapproval.

When the babies were greeted, the pit muck washed away and the last smears of gravy from the tattie-pot mopped with home-made stotty, they sat together. Their thoughts were the same viscous phlegm of hope and dread, anticipation and root upheaval but they didn't share them with words.

When he woke next morning Tot felt the draw of the woods he feared might not surround him for much longer. He fed the children, wiped their faces and Paul's nose before taking a cup of tea to Ivy. Her eyes were shut but when he made to take away the cup and saucer she stirred.

'What time is it?'

'Just gone seven.' he said turning back to give the tea to his wife who was now heaving herself up and fingering squashed and ruffled hair. 'I thought I'd take the bairns out for a walk, give you a well-earned lie in.'

'No; Paul is starting a cold. Bring him in here with me.'

Tot dressed only Wren then snuggled Paul beside his mother where he was happiest anyway.

The little terrier hardly needed the tongue click from the eager man or the child who copied.

When Tot opened the door the bright autumn sun caught Wren's eyes, her excitement beamed back at him, she had caught the thread of this existence which had run through June.

The robins, hatched only that spring, were singing in the rose hedge as they past, he had Wren's tiny hand in his and the long forgotten feeling of fifteen years ago. The morning lit up her little being with such light it looked like the essence of God's grace shone through those beautiful odd eyes. He swung her into his arms and then onto his shoulders. It felt the same. It could be June. The love was the same and yet somehow achingly different for never again could he love without fear.

Wren knew that in spirit they could move each other swift as arrows and yet she merge with the softness this good soul who loved her so needed today.

The joy of being the only ones out on such a bright, sweet morning had the pair striding and giggling with one heart. Tot had to put Wren to the floor of the wood to avoid the whippy branches of hazel and beach. Suddenly she slipped from his grasp and ran to a sandy bank where rabbits had scratted to expose roots and smooth stones.

This was one of those rare perfect days and he wanted to lay it in Wren's hand like a new-laid egg.

'Pretty flowers!' Wren pointed but Tot saw only drying grass and the tall grey-brown of dried-out foxglove stalks which had shed billions of seeds along with their regal beauty.

'Where darling, where?' Tot looked closer thinking he had missed some hidden late bloom.

Wren toddled to one of the stalks which towered above her and stroked it with pudgy fingers.

'Foxgloves!' she cried with glee.

Tot was stunned. This child had never seen a Foxglove let alone heard its name, now she recognised the brown seedpods, empty and sad.

But further wonder was pulled from him as they both silenced to listen.

There was a cackling in the bushes and then clear beauty as two wrens decided to sing out their hearts. June was in every breath the wood took. The essence of his much loved daughter eased into his senses so that he turned his head to search. Where was she?

Only Wren knew exactly how close she was.

Wren was softened with relief that this very first walk into June's wood was a sign of healing in Tot. The thought made her comfortable but her spirit teemed with unrelenting thoughts. More children had created the need for bedrooms and some of the latest plumbing but his heart was here. His sacrifice was greater than any other human being would know, yet she was glad for she knew with all the intuition of her ascended spirit that others who would become important to them all were also trying to move to Highcopse.

New faces offered new hope.

One could be Alessandro.

CHAPTER EIGHTEEN

It was hard to keep up any excitement for the next two months.

Ivy's tension grew with her belly. Every letter was riven open then stuffed back into its envelope with her disappointment. Despair was masked by constant bickering.

'Bloody council! How can they leave people dangling like this?'

Paul picked up on the growing strain and whinged more often. Wren began to wonder at her advanced information. The house she felt they would get would have had time to be finished by now and could have been allocated to some-one else in need. She would astral travel there during her next sleep, although how a two year old could give these people the comfort they so desperately needed was beyond her.

After a lunch of banana sandwiches and milk the two children were put down to rest. They lay head to toe in the single bed where June had died and Wren was born. Keen to drift into the state where she could leave her body to travel to Highcopse Wren settled down immediately. Paul wasn't tired and started jumping off the bed, onto the big bed and back again.

'I'll give you two such a smack if you don't settle!'

Ivy's annoyance came through the door from where she was trying to get on with tasks made impossible with two toddlers under her feet.

Wren was glad when Paul, temporarily kept still on his parent's bed then started to trampoline merrily as he heard his mother's footsteps lead into the scullery. Wren used the rhythm to slow her breathing to enable her reach the vibration necessary to leave her body. She reached number six Ashfield Terrace in seconds, the three miles between them being only two as the crow flies over the leaf shedding woods and gorse strewn fields. What she saw disappointed her. The house was finished. It stood with its other half enclosed by a three foot brick wall capped with concrete slabs at the front and a rough pointed wood fence at the back so that gardens would be clearly marked. Surely if they were to have this house the council would have let them know by now. People had to pack and sort out oil cloth for the floors, scrub out the old house and arrange for curtains and lights. Her spirit went easily through the low vibration of the bricks so that she found herself within the pristine walls of a brand new 1950's house.

This was the most modern home she had been in on Earth. It was wonderful to see the advancements made by human beings since her last incarnation. This is where she'd spend quite a few years of her life and although poor by the standards of some of her other lives, rich compared to others, Wren knew it would be suitable. Why hadn't they got it? It felt like theirs already.

As she re-entered her body it was to hear self-pitying screaming from the wide open mouth of Paul who was rigid and purple on the floor with a gash on his forehead. Ivy bustled in to see Paul out of the bed and Wren still in it.

'You bad, bad girl!' she yelled as she smacked Wren across the head making her cheek bright red in an instance.

As Ivy took her sobbing boy to the fire where she cuddled his tears away Wren felt no injustice.

All she felt was horror. There was absolutely no doubt that her body deserved that hard slap for she knew with sad certainty that it had violently pushed Paul from the high bed onto the floor for no other reason than irritated spite.

She stung with that first shock of knowing. Without her total control this pretty, sweet child could be wicked. It was a sharp reminder that this wasn't her life but the life of the spirit she had robbed. Nature would out.

It was easy to stay in that room where Ivy thought the child was feeling shame. Wren needed this time alone to realise just what this new knowledge meant. Genetics had taken much from June and until now that had been all she had considered. Now with a horrible slap to her awareness that dwarfed the hand to her face, she had to accept that the loathsome Colin who Tot had dealt with in the woods had passed on genetic behaviour too. Wren had left this wickedness behind twenty incarnations ago. It could take over the entire life; stop her finding Alessandro or soak in to poison any relationship. She had to find how to control such badness.

Over the next few weeks Wren tried to make it up to Paul by offering every help she could. He took no comfort from her actions and merely spent his limited brain power trying to make her cry. From now on it was revenge that occupied his mind, a game he didn't realise the horrifying dangers of. Tot spent most of his time trying to teach the boy that aggression got him nowhere and he watched sadly as Wren seemed to let him get away with appalling behaviour. He was exhausted having had to get up to squabbling children at seven one morning after only getting to bed at three am sore from a backbreaking night shift. He was trying to take pressure off his pregnant wife who could get no sleep with the two children in the same room. It had been his fault. Such a stupid idea boarding up the other bedroom and where had it got him? Nowhere.

He would rip it out today.

Wren knew what he was thinking as she watched him dip bread into the bacon fat poured onto his bacon and eggs. When he'd eaten, she drank milk and watched him open the door to the room where she was born. He pushed against his false wall that made it a cupboard. When Ivy took the bairns to the store for her groceries he could make a noise. She would return to the two bedroomed house she'd lived in since the day they were married. It just wasn't fair on her.

It was getting harder to push the big pram up the cobbled street. Ivy was growing at an alarming rate and both children were getting heavier and taller. Soon they would have to walk everywhere to make room for the new baby. Breathlessness forced Ivy to rest at the top of the hill before the daunting task of holding onto the pram on whilst negotiating the sandy slope towards the road. The baby moved in her womb.

It was colder this October and her breath became visible as it panted out in front of her. A whistling she knew so well gave her back the present. The postman was pushing his bike up the same track she was dreading.

'Morning Mrs Stoker, want your post?' He stood before her shuffling a handful of letters that were meant for the whole street. 'Here we are.'

He whistled his way to deliver the rest of his sack leaving Ivy with an envelope she didn't recognise.

After turning the pram sideways to safety her hands had the freedom to tear into what might or might not be her future. Her work tightened fingers were stiffened further with cold and anxiety. Her heart was too afraid to open the envelope but she had to. At first the words meant nothing, unable to find their way from her eyes to her fear strangled brain. She read them again, stuffed the page and it's envelope under the blanket that covered the children then turned the pram around towards home.

CHAPTER NINETEEN

Ivy pushed the pram straight into the house with, for once, no regard for dirt.

Tot had his back to her and was just about to swing a hammer at the pristine wall he'd so carefully crafted only months ago. His muscles were paralysed by the startle of Ivy's tearful voice then he turned to have the letter pushed into his hand from where she had taken the heavy tool. He read twice before his eyes lifted to hers. They said nothing in their joint shock. Ivy put both her hands to the long clumsy handle of the hammer and swung towards the wall before her. It was the first hit to happiness. It didn't matter how small this bedroom was. She'd be leaving it in three short weeks.

New excitement and strength found Ivy's limbs so that she reached the Co-op quicker than ever before.

As she passed the large glass doors she felt the dull interest of the women listening half-heartedly to the gossip between shop girl and customer as they waited for their sugar to be weighed and their bacon to be sliced. The council offices would take only another few minutes. Excitement fumbled at the pram brakes, Paul was sleeping but Wren wanted to savour every moment of her family's good fortune. Ivy lifted her to the ground and abruptly grabbed the little hand in hers. When they reached the stairs she thudded the pram brake then clamped the toddler into her arms so that she might reach her destination quicker. Wren was still in her grip when she reached the desk. Behind the glass panel was a woman of about thirty who, in spite of her well cut hair and Newcastle bought clothes couldn't disguise a sad look of envy. She took the letter from Ivy but her eyes welded to the child in her care.

'Such a lovely little thing.' She dreamily put the back of her index finger to Wren's cheek. 'Who'd have thought it would only take seven days.'

'What? Seven days! What for? I waited more than that, I can tell you!' Ivy barked.

'I.... Did I say that? I don't know what possessed me. I'll get your file.'

Wren allowed an exchange of energies from this pleasant stranger and instantly understood her sadness. She turned to open a drawer and picked up an envelope which she handed to Ivy.

'Can I give the bairn a treat?'

Ivy, temporarily so good humoured, would have agreed to anything and nodded slightly as she took the pen to sign the form pinned to the top of the envelope. She had to put Wren to the floor. The clerk came round from a side door holding out a stick of liquorish. Wren knew immediately that this melancholy lady was pregnant but it was too early for her to know herself.

'She's a wise one Mrs Stoker and no mistake. Me and Mick, we've given up hoping for bairns but looking at her sets me off again.' As she gazed envious love to Wren the spirit of the three week old embryo showed itself. It was to be a boy who would cause as much heartache in later life as it would pleasure in the next few years. This woman was about to pay back a huge karmic debt.

The delay she and her husband experienced in conceiving was because this soul was still in a former life. It had been only a year since his death as this woman's irritating old uncle. She'd never know that the son she longed of her doing all his washing and having him to Sunday dinner throughout the war. He never brought anything from his rations but gobbled up the best of theirs.

As the grown-ups talked Wren stuck the black stick into her mouth. It was sweet and hard and she began to chew and suck. When they reached the pram again Ivy checked on Paul. Attracted to a dull silver metal of wide spaced bars on the barrier at the top of the steps, Wren added to her sweet ecstasy by swinging and climbing. As she turned upside down she felt the cold air hit her stomach where the flesh showed between her liberty bodice and her knickers. The moment of true childhood was savoured but short.

'Stop being so revolting child!'

Ivy pulled her sharply from her acrobatics and tore the remainder of the liquorish from her hand before throwing it with disgust to the road.

'Such a thing to give a child!' she said rubbing violently at Wren's mouth with a spit moistened handkerchief. Wren felt a fury build in her stomach, a primitive urge to kill spiralled to her brain. Thank God she was impotent in this small bundle. As the relief hit her so did the speed of her actions. She grabbed the liquorish now covered in dust and saliva then stuck it firmly to the bottom of Ivy's swagger coat. The spiteful action went unnoticed as she was lifted to her place at the end of the pram.

'Look at your hands!' Ivy tutted, furiously spitting again on the now filthy hanky.

'Doesn't deserve children that one! Stupid woman!'

Ivy was the only one who didn't notice the stick of black liquorish as it attended her to the Co-op, the three mile push home and then the bump up the steps into the house. These jerking movements and the state of the dried saliva loosened the grip so the liquorish fell into the yard where Jan who was waiting patiently for her very late dinner gobbled it up and then wished she hadn't.

Tot had left for back shift. It would be seven hours of torture before she could share her joy. Ivy lifted the children from where they had slept amongst half a pound of Sunlight soap, ha'penny Reckitt's Blue bags, Co-op '99' tea and the dark blue bag of sugar which had shed some of its crystals to irritate Paul's skin. He was already grisly but even his yowling and getting in her way as she unpacked her groceries couldn't spoil Ivy's pleasure as she deliberately left the special little package until last.

The envelope almost tingled in her fingers so magical was its effect on her life. Not only did it hold string tied keys and labels but it held hot running water, an indoor toilet and freedom from mouse traps hidden in damp bedrooms. The need to dash down to number six Ashfield Terrace made her heart bash into her chest but there was nothing she could do. It would take an hour to push the pram into Highcopse. The children needed feeding and Ivy herself was weary with the growing baby inside her. Wren watched her face as she toddled around after her; she had never seen such a glow. That she deserved better living conditions was not in doubt but how could she measure the effect the move would have on Tot.

When Jan scraped at the door at 6pm to be let out for her end of shift dash to the pit and the man she adored, Ivy began to set the table. When she heard Tot removing his boots she lifted the pan of bacon hock broth to the side of the range but set out the plate with different contents.

'Yoo Hoo!' he came in carrying the tin bath which he laid down in front of the fire. Never had Ivy seen the shabbiness of the inadequately small bath as she saw it right now. In a few weeks they would be free of this demeaning and backbreaking method of cleaning themselves. Tot kissed his wife, ruffled Paul's hair and stroked beneath Wren's chin before kissing her upturned nose. She beamed excitement and ran to where the table was laid for his supper. It was then that he saw in his big soup dish six shiny brass keys. Wren squealed with delight as his jaw dropped.

'That's a fine supper to give your man in from the pit mind! Six keys however will I eat them all? Not even any gravy to help them down to a hungry man's belly." Wren giggled as he took the keys in his coal dust engrained hands.

'Oh Tot! Isn't it wonderful? Two keys for the front door, two for the back and the others are for the wash house and coal house. Imagine! A place just for washing! Whoever deserved such luxury? I can't wait to get away from this place and all its memories.'

She didn't notice the drop of smile from his eyes.

It was a frosty Saturday morning when Tot rose to stoke the fire and take Ivy her tea. Today they would view their new house.

'You take the bus down Ivy and I'll push the bairns, meet you at the chip shop.' he said as he turned the toasting fork from the glowing embers to view how brown the bread had become.

The smell was mouth-watering. Sadness hit him, another of his pleasures disappearing.

He started out unnecessarily early and Wren knew why. They didn't take the steep and rutted path down through the woods, past the pit and onto the road. Tot turned the pram the other way down the cobbled street towards the chapel and June.

The grave had no expensive headstone but Tot knew it from so many similar plots because of the jam jar he had laid there on his last visit. The once proud chrysanthemums were now frost blackened and broken. There was no replacement in his winter garden. Instead he kissed his fingers and laid them to the tufts of uneven grass that covered his daughter's body. He did this several times as he imagined her forehead, her shoulders and her slim feet. His eyes brimmed, then overflowed, wetting his slackened mouth and chin. Wren, snuggled in blankets beside Paul in the pram, wished she could tell Tot that his beloved June was not there.

If only she could let him out of his grief by showing him how happy she was now planning another incarnation into a country where she would never be cold. Paul began to wail, dragging Tot out of a place he so needed to be. Stiff, work ingrained hands took the pram handle again and began the three mile push to where he would turn a new house into a home. Hopefully.

As he waited for the bus carrying Ivy to arrive, Tot asked a group of people where the new estate was. Every-one knew and looked at him with great envy. Ivy walked with her family for the last few hundred yards towards her new life. Everywhere was hard mud but the sixth house of the planned seven hundred stood out from the unmade road like a golden palace. Wren watched the faces of these simple people as they took the keys and tried them in the front door. Paint smells hit their lungs as newness hit every other sense. It was clean and light, newly plastered and modern. A door of bumpy glass separated the sitting room from the little dining area and the kitchen opened off from that. Here yellow painted cupboards gripped a new cooker between them and the pantry. A second door led to the stairs and three airy bedrooms but it was the last door they flung open that had Tot and Ivy speechless. Here a white enamel bath shone out to them. Ivy bent to caress the chrome taps which bore a simple 'C' and 'H'. This was how she would fill her bath in the future. She cried with relief so Tot held her shaking body, not allowing his hurt to spoil her joy. There was one more untried door which Tot flung open before calling Ivy to his side. It was a tiny room just big enough for a black seated lavatory that would never see anyone wearing Wellingtons or a coat over their nightclothes. He ushered every-one out onto the landing whilst he made sure he was the first one to try the only indoor toilet he had ever seen. He caught up with Ivy as she examined the tiny beige tiled fireplaces in two of the bedrooms then went downstairs to check how the tiled sitting room fire would so miraculously heat the water unseen and with no work. Little footsteps echoed across new floors and tripped again into every room. Wren and Paul who had never seen house stairs began heaving themselves up and down before a concerned Ivy ushered them into the concrete covered path which held an outside lav and her much dreamed of wash house. The garden, front and back was small and as yet just subsoil and rubble. As Tot allowed his gaze to settle he saw in his future a little lawn and roses with snapdragons coming after the forget-me-nots and wallflowers. As he moved to the back he could smell the washing blowing over rows of cabbages and well earthed up potatoes. This was heaven on earth and his family deserved it.

Wren was in no physical position to warn him of what she could clearly see

.

Back in the home they had lived all their married life everything suddenly looked worn, tired and ridiculously out-dated. In spite of Ivy's expanding girth she looked forward to scrubbing out the palace where her growing family would thrive.

'It's clean muck Tot, not like shovelling other peoples laziness out of the door as when we first got this house is it? Aye an' I'll not have to hump every drop of water from the boiler either. Imagine Tot; it just comes out of the tap hot! There's nowt left for them clever dicks to invent now, folk have it all.'

Wren knew he was hiding the pain of leaving his woods and the closeness of June, but she also knew he was a good man who was prepared to sacrifice everything for those who depended on him.

The day of the move excited Wren beyond belief. It wasn't the new house or the ultimate in modernity that made her blood race, for she had lived in truly magnificent houses in her past lives as well as hovels, but the thought of who she might meet. That there was an important energy coming towards her she was in no doubt, just how important she was yet to find out.

It was two weeks before Christmas when Wren found herself looking at a brand new ceiling. Ivy and Tot, exhausted by moving their lives along had put the children to bed early in their new rooms where they were alone for the first time in their short lives. Paul grizzled on as Wren went through a day filled with short tempers and reluctant excitement. Modern rooms and more of them showed her family's furniture as pitifully inadequate. The big van that came to take all their worldly goods to a new life had most of its floor taken up with pots and newspaper rolls full of Tot's dug up plants and cuttings. The garden of his past would have to brave the winter beneath the kitchen window as they waited for horse muck to combine with Tot's strength and enthusiasm to give them a hope of survival.

Wren thought of the soul who should have been lying here in the bed where she had been born and her mother had died. Was she watching her now? There was no feeling of it nor had June come along with them. It was over two years now which would mean that although June would visit her earthly family occasionally, mostly she had her progression to attend to.

It took until Christmas for Tot and Ivy to master the small fire encased in cream and beige tiles. Unlike the lead blackened open range they had left behind, it heated the water secretly and gave no help to unfamiliar cooking which Ivy had to face on electric rings and a soulless precision oven. She declared it useless as she presented flat Yorkshire Puddings, cakes that sank in the middle and tough stews to her family. This stress along with her growing belly far outweighed the convenience of hot running water and freedom from mice. Their first load of coal, delivered as part of Tot's wage, blocked the pavement and had to be barrowed up planks on three steps so that the whole job took twice as long as shovelling it into their old coal hole. She secretly longed for her black leaded range and cheap cuts of meat cooked to tenderness for hours on the free heat.

Wren knew Tot missed the background call of the winter puffed up woodpigeons and the crisp walks which reddened their cheeks to match chilblained feet. The hard rattle of a cold bus did nothing to make going to the mine more enjoyable. Jan became more of a house dog and sorely missed her dash to the pit head to escort Tot home. It was change and change was growth. But it still hurt.

'Kissy doggy.' Wren rubbed her little fingers towards the downcast terrier. Jan brushed past Paul who was tearing up newspapers on the mat in front of the fire. He grabbed dog hair when she past and as Jan struggled to get free, scratched his arm. The now common screams rent the smoke filled air. When Ivy didn't appear immediately, Paul pulled himself up on wet clothes covering the clothes-horse in front of the wind attacked fireplace. Fury and fear sent Ivy down the stairs so quickly that she slid on the bare wood crashing her body into the newel post. When she recovered her balance it was to see a mess of paper, clean washing all over the floor and Paul screaming as he lashed out at Wren who with Jan, huddled together in the corner of one of the brown hide chairs. Paul was picked up, Wren's legs were slapped and Jan was thrown out into the wind and rain.

Tot was the calming influence. When he was home every-one was cuddled and smiled at.

One morning as he tried to master his old toasting fork on his new fire he pointed out all the caves and dragons in the red glow of the coal he had laid on his back in water to hew from the dark.

His children were fascinated as he spun tales of another world. It was now that he told them about Santa Clause. Paul was too young to understand but when Tot asked Wren what special present she would ask Santa to bring her on Christmas Day she surprised herself with the strength and speed of her desire.

'A dolly daddy! A black dolly!'

He cuddled her then as he lifted her to his knee to eat the crispy toast dripping in butter. It wasn't bad. Not as good as the old range toast but it would do.

'A black dolly? Like your daddy when he comes in from the pit?'

'No not like daddy; like my baby. Like Suzi.'

Tot watched her. 'But you haven't got a baby, pet. You are just a baby yourself.'

Ivy bustled in with hot tea spoiling the moment. Wren started to cry.

'What's wrong with her? She never cries. Is she sickening for something do you think? Maybe she hasn't had her sleep out. Put her back to bed Tot.'

Wren wanted privacy. She needed the memories of a past life to flood to her. Suddenly she craved to recall Suzi and the special relationship with a husband who had been chosen for her but she had loved for his pride and need to care for her. Famished for understanding, she needed to feel Kenya and the hot sun. But what she didn't want to remember was how Suzi was taken from her.

As she lay shivering in the new bedroom of a council house in the north of England it was not as a small child. This was not a memory of the physical body she had stolen. It was part of her own long and painful past. The question was why? Why this one? What energy was near to cause such a potent flood of memory?

Cold was the main enemy towards Christmas. Ivy felt it was unsafe to light the bedroom fires and so frost opaqued the windows and sent bare feet scurrying each morning to the living room blaze.

This is where the children dressed and stayed most of the day. One crisp morning Tot brought in a tree he had cut on his way back from work. It was bliss to be in the winter sun walking upright on God's earth instead of bent awkwardly on his side beneath it. It had meant he had to walk the three miles after his eight hour shift but it was for his family. He fought the bones of winter for them.

After his bath and bacon Tot showed Wren and Paul how to hang the shabby scuffed globes and paper chains on the fragrant fir branches. The coal bucket filled with cold soil was wrapped in red crepe paper then stood on the floor boards just at the end of the mat to hold their Christmas tree.

It was Saturday morning when Tot took the bus to Newcastle. He never went anywhere alone except for work. So Wren feeling abandoned, spent most of the day pushing against the window frame hoping to catch a glimpse of his early return.

When it came darkness had fallen. Ivy was in the kitchen to greet him and Wren heard her voice rise.

'I thought we agreed only one thing each! We can't afford it Tot. The new baby needs things; everything is worn out! You'll have to take it back!'

'No Ivy, I won't.....' the words stopped as Wren ran to him and flung herself at the cold trousers which had absorbed the horrid smell of other people's cigarettes on the bus he had just left.

On Christmas morning Wren and Paul were brought into a room already warm. Tot was beaming.

'Santa Clause has been while you were asleep. Look what he has left for you bairns.'

Paul dashed towards a wooden train with three different trucks but Wren stood beside her father looking from his encouraging smile to the little pram beneath the tree.

'Go on chicken. Go see what Santa has brought you.' He led her by the hand to look into the closed eyes of a beautiful black baby doll lying on a tiny pillow.

'I hope she knows it will take us all year to pay for it!'

'Ivy!'

Wren tenderly turned back the apron of the pram to lift the baby to her chest. Her eyes closed with all the years of longing. The doll was no longer cold and hard with a red checked, puff sleeved dress. It was a sun warmed naked baby, soft and clinging, nuzzling at her breast left moist by satisfied guzzling.

'Just look at her Ivy, she'll be a natural mother when she's old enough.'

'Aye well let's hope it's not before like her mother! You have remembered you have a son haven't you?'

Paul was chuffing his present around the cold floor with one hand and clinging onto the lumpy stocking he had found at the bottom of his bed.

'It's a bright morning. I'll get the bairns dressed and out from under your feet whilst you make the dinner.'

As Tot was shoving reluctant, wiggling feet into Paul's shoes Wren, already in her coat and pixie hat went upstairs. When she came down she had a bath towel tied over her shoulder to form a sling which she laid her new doll into. Tot only noticed her when he raised his head from tying laces.

'Whatever are you doing pet?'

'Taking Suzi for water.'

'For water? No darlin', we are going for a walk with Suzi in her pram. She doesn't need a towel.'

He stared into her eyes, worrying that she seemed so far away as he removed the towel a folded it onto a chair.

Wren was pleased to be brought back to the reality of the life she was meant to be living. This was a pot doll bought from a shop and she was a toddler going for a walk in the frost with her brother and the man she called father.

Jan sniffed around outside hoping to find any new smells that may have arrived overnight. The path was slabbed with new concrete. Mud which would soon be spread with tarmac was hard and pale with little ice lakes between the inch high mountainous ruts. Through the vapour puffing from their mouths they saw other children at the far end of the street whooping from beneath new cowboy hats as they fired caps from silver guns. Tot lifted the doll's pram carefully down the steps painstakingly delivering its charge to Wren's nurturing hands in brown mittens. Paul was carried, train secure within chubby arms in danger only from two thick green candles of mucus sliding from his nose as they always did. The progress was slow. Tot, permanently bent with wary parenting, had to keep freeing wooden wheels from uneven paving slabs that tipped the trucks making unsatisfying progress. Wren was ahead thinking only of her new charge and the consuming responsibility she now had for it. When Tot made up the space between them to check on her he was dragged back to Paul who had fallen to his knees and new misery. The scream rent the Christmas morning air as Tot grabbed him under one arm, the toy in the other to jog back home, leaving his little dog to protect his daughter for a few moments.

The noise had drawn the attention of the other children who stopped banging their rolls of gunpowder caps to run towards Wren.

'Who are you?' demanded a rough boy of about five with brilliant red hair edging from a black fringed cowboy hat.

'Wren.' she murmured struggling to see in spite of the low winter sun.

'Stupid name! Stupid eyes!' he sneered.

He moved menacingly close to her and put the nose of the gun at her throat.

'You don't belong here. I will have to kill you!'

She could only meet one of his eyes which seemed enormous and too protruding behind round brown spectacles for the other was blocked out with dirty pink sticking plaster across the lens.

'What you got in that pram then?' he growled.

'My baby.'

Flanked by his posse, who seemed to be his brothers because of the common hair and Christmas outfits, he yanked at the pram cover laying bare to the cold the black doll wearing only its thin cotton frock.

'Got lost down the pit did it?' he guffawed meanly at his own joke. Wren shrank in fear for she knew what would happen next. The scabby, winter whitened fist that came towards Suzi was dirt engrained with warts and filthy nails but it was not what Wren saw. The hand that grabbed her child was long and lean and glistening black. Suzi was not thrown to concrete but to a hot hard mud path. It was not a toy gun and caps that ended her life but a spear which went straight through her heart. Jan barked fiercely and jumped up at the boy who brought the back of his hand across her jaw. Wren heard footsteps behind her and knew it was the men of her tribe come to chase away the hunter from the other side of the mountain. They ran straight past her and into the thick undergrowth. Blood soaked into the rain starved earth as Wren fell to the limp body of her new-born child. Yelling seemed to be far away as the pain engulfed her. She heard the scream as the warrior was murdered for his crime against her tribe and the men returned with blood on their knives.

It might have been the father of her baby who avenged its death. Who could know? All women were used by all men.

'Get out of it!' Tot's angry voice bellowed towards the bullies.

The boys ran but Alan's childish shout rammed into her ears as he turned.

'I'll get you Wren...when your dad is not there, that is when I'll get you!'

'Don't worry sweetheart; daddy will mend it.' He puffed on visible breath.

Tot lifted the two halves of the dolls head from the ice-cold pavement into the pram and then picked up its one armed body.

Wren climbed into his arms but didn't notice the strained position of his body as he bent to push her precious Christmas present home.

'This bairns in some sort of trance.' Tot said as he eased her into the corner of the fireside chair.

Ivy, clutching a sleepy Paul across her big stomach peered at Wren.

'It looks like shock. What on earth happened?'

'Those Taylor boys from the rough end of Scotswood Road, can't bear anybody having anything nice.' He nodded towards the pram as he eased Wren's arms from the stiff coat.

Wren stared into the fire and saw the cauldron spitting lime leaf and antelope broth into the wood embers. Tot rubbed at her limp little hands.

'Come on pet. You're safe now. Into cuddle corner, come on.'

Through her former life his words found her so that she shuddered to the present. As she clung to him the back door took a banging, screeching found its way through the steam of the Christmas vegetables. Jan barked defensively.

Ivy opened the door allowing an angry woman burst into the kitchen.

'Where's that man of yours? I'll bloody well teach him to clip my kid's ears!'

The words spat out of one corner of her mouth as she closed her eyes to the cigarette dangling there.

The yelling got louder as she reached the front room.

'You yu' bastard! Is this the snivelling little brat who set the dog on my Alan?'

'Calm down woman!'

'I'll bloody calm down after I see you flat on the floor when my Bill gets home from the pub! A grown man bashing an innocent little kid! He'll bloody flatten yu' and that dangerous dog of yours.'

'I did not bash any-one woman. I told him off for smashing my daughter's doll.'

'That's not what he says. It was broken already when you came out of the house. He's fair bubbling his eyes out back there! You'll not get away with this! An' I'll have that vicious dog of yours put to sleep an' all.'

As she turned on her heels she saw Ivy holding open the back door for her.

'Well, well, well. If it isn't Ivy Johnson as was. Fancy the council allowing the likes of you in this estate, it's meant to be a clean place you know. Respectable like!' She pulled the wet, nicotine stained cigarette end from her lips and flicked it to Ivy's spotless passage floor.

'Is yu' father coming for his Christmas dinner? Oh no, sorry. He's still locked up I suppose. I'd better warn the neighbours about having one of the Johnsons around. Wouldn't do to have their bairns contaminated with your filthy antics would it now?'

Satisfied that she had caused much more pain than any amount of ear clipping ever could have done, Verna Taylor left with a smile on her face and gossip on her lips.

She slammed out, replaced by a cold blast of wind.

Ivy was pale as Tot led her to the fireside chair. She had spent her whole life holding her fists up against the family scandal.

'You know that dreadful woman?'

'Aye, she lived in the next terrace when I was fourteen. She enjoyed every minute of the gossip when da was put away. She was one of that crowd who said I must have led him on and I should have gone to jail with him.'

'Oh Ivy; I'd never have come here if I'd known you'd be reminded of the past.'

The noise that came from Ivy's mouth seemed more physical in its forcing open of her throat. Her dream house was contaminated, like everything else in her life, by her criminal father.

Through it all Paul had climbed up beside Wren and the two children watched their parents suffering. Only Wren saw a third presence, a beautiful soul who had come from spirit to comfort them all. It hovered over Ivy and then re-entered her so that it would come into the world early, clothed in the softness of a new born baby. The groaning was the start of a sudden labour. Tot had no time to call any-one, this baby was arriving now.

He delivered his daughter alone on the clippie mat in front of the fire and would come to believe that is why she would always be so special to him. Wren knew the real reason but would never discuss it with any-one except if approached first by the soul who had just joined her family. This at least, was a good soul.

Three children in the house, two of them needing nappies meant that winter became a steam of drying clothes hiding the cheer of the fire from every-one badly needing some comfort. Tot was heavy eyed from sleep interrupted every two hours by gentle cries and snuffling. As Ivy pulled baby Noelene to her breast Tot would get all the things ready to clean and make comfortable the baby he had helped into the world. He'd be back on shifts soon; he'd have to give Ivy all the help he could now.

Wren heard through the thin walls the latest member of the family she'd stolen into, snuffling and mewing. She lay awake staring at nothing but thinking of all. Thank goodness this baby was easy.

The feel in the room had changed. Something momentous was creeping through the curtains. Secretive and pale, soft and quiet Wren knew exactly what had happened. It had snowed whilst she slept. She kneeled on her bed to part the thin curtains. Snow clouds were drifting away leaving the moon, almost full, to give glitter to the new fresh landscape. She would enjoy nature's gift in the morning. In this part of the world it was a treat, not like the harsh snows of Russia which could sap the very will to live.

Tot, as excited as the children, stirred sticky porridge for his family to keep the cold out. When they had eaten he took tea up to Ivy nursing her new infant in bed and came down with extra socks and jumpers which he struggled onto the bodies of two children becoming high with frustration. They had wanted to run out into the clean snow the moment it was light, hating every passing moment when the laughter of other children meant the freshness was being used up.

Bodies stiff with too many clothes felt the first soft compression beneath their Wellingtons. Still warm from indoors and oats the sun hit their eyes and bounced off the glitter to zing a million happiness to their little hearts.

Theirs were the first footprints on their narrow path. They stomped up and down making patterns, squealing with glee as Tot steadied them when they slipped. Quiet study fell as the children noticed bird's hopping marks then peered down at Jan's little paw prints and scrapes where her belly didn't quite make it over the snow. He took them out onto the unmade road which looked prettier than it had a right to. Other footprints had compacted some of the weather's gift so that bits of mud were starting to show through. At the end of the street children were just putting the rough, globular head of a snowman onto an uneven lumpy body. Tot noticed they were struggling with the weight so called towards them.

'Just a mo' lads! I'll help you with that'

As the boys stepped back to allow the welcome help Wren and Paul stood behind their daddy. Jan sat protectively in front of her charges. There was great cheer as the icy, out of proportion head met the too short body. It looked only remotely human. They didn't care; excitement glowed red to their cheeks as they patted the join to seal the personified snow. A carrot nose was stuck above a line of little coal nuggets forming an uneven smile but beneath two larger black lumps for eyes. Wren, her attention robbed by the discomfort of being watched, turned. She saw a stiff, dark coat stuck with bits of clinging snow hiding the boy who was studying her. But it couldn't hide the feelings.

The red hair sticking out of the balaclava gave a clue as to why Wren felt such hatred emanating towards her child's body. The grey wool of the hand knitted balaclava hat covered the mean mouth and pointed nose but the glasses were unmistakable. One eye met hers and she knew the need for revenge went back centuries. This boy didn't understand his hatred of Wren himself, his past lives were lost to him whilst he was in this incarnation; but his soul recognised her. He knew she should not be here in this body, in this family on this snow covered council estate. He felt only disgust and an overwhelming need to cause this little girl to suffer. Wren knew he would be struggling with his feelings as he had not planned any of this before he was born. He was not expecting to meet with her; she was in the wrong life.

She knew with the clarity of her awareness that she owed him no Karmic debt. He had died on that hot mud path as a result of his own actions. Killing her baby had been avenged by other members of her tribe. In all her subsequent lives she had never met him, there had been no need. Now he was confused. He glared into her very soul, tried to recognise her and couldn't. Yet there was something, he was too young to wrestle with his overpowering emotions.

There was some other reason why he was so determined to hurt her. Wren put up an energy shield so that all his hatred and aggression reflected off it back to him. Doubled with pain Alan's feet skidded beneath him so that the snow took his whole body. Tot turned.

'Careful lad.' He pulled him to his feet dusting snow from him. To Tot this was not the son of the spiteful woman who was spoiling his wife's peace of mind or the lad who'd broken his daughter's doll but a child who'd hurt himself.

'Come along you two.' Tot put out his hands to his children. 'There'll be unspoiled snow in our back garden; we'll make a little snow man of our own.'

As they toddled beside him Tot bent to carry Paul up the steps and continued round the corner of the house where he deposited him safely. It was only seconds before he returned to do the same for Wren but that was all it took. A hard snowball crashed into the back of her head forcing her little body to hit the snow. She didn't feel her front teeth go through her lip as she hit the step, it was too cold. But she did feel all the venom of a warrior who felt he'd lost his life because of her.

'See what a good shot I am?' said a little ginger Geordie boy. 'I'll get you... and your babies. I'll kill anyone who looks after you. One day I'll get you!'

He was off before the snow absorbed the red spots.

'There's lots ..... Wren!'

Tot picked her up from the ground.

'I shouldn't have left you! It's too slippery pet.'

In front of the fire the swollen lip prevented even a sip of the warm milky tea reaching her stomach where she needed it so much. But the physical wasn't important at that moment. She hadn't expected any of her former life situations to surface in this one, it was clear that Alan had a connection with the one who should be here in this little body too. What right had she to expect anything? This would get in the way of her freedom to search for Alessandro. If she always had to be looking over her shoulder for Alan she wouldn't be able to concentrate. He was a small boy now but his hatred and vengeance were enormous, they could only grow with him.

Wren hoped that she would deal with this through the knowledge of her spirit not the untamed anger of the body she had stolen. It wasn't until her child's body was put to bed that the peace she needed dropped realisation of just who else was at the deaths of both her baby and the warrior who was now Alan.

A new understanding of his hatred kept her from sleep.

CHAPTER TWENTY

There were two snowmen that winter but no peace.

Wren watched the parents of the child she was supposed to be struggle into 1951 with emotions dragging them apart. Ivy was worn out. Her milk was drying up. The house was clatteringly busier; Paul was developing the irritating character Wren knew him to be. She spent valuable energies repelling his teasing and spite. He would only become worse.

The spring was filled with ground-breaking and plant nurturing with backbreaking digging for Tot and helpful seed planting and eager learning from Wren. Their rewarding summer passed with the surprise and joy of plants having survived the move of garden to bloom beside a pram often left out to air the new baby.

In the longer days Tot was a little later home from work as he visited June's grave. He would tell Ivy of Forget-me-nots that smothered the whole plot and spread towards others where no-one visited. That pleased him. He felt that even now June was sharing and making the world a better place for it. Ivy tossed her head and changed the subject; she never visited the grave.

It was becoming too much to get the children to their church so she took to singing hymns on Sunday mornings as she slogged her way through the build-up of tasks.

Tot kept his bairns by him in the garden or in front of the fire gathering them all into Cuddle Corner when he would read the precious books he'd read to June. Paul wiggled and picked his nose and warts, relishing being able to cry when he drew blood from either of them. Noelene delighted Tot in her concentration but he never knew that Wren used this quiet time on greater tasks. Ivy discouraged all estate children who came knocking. Any-one from out there was a threat from her past. It was the only way to protect her family and herself from Alan and his noisy vindictive family.

The new estate grew so that by 1953 its streets and blocks added more people to avoid. If Verna Taylor spread the gossip of how Ivy's father was jailed, she didn't know. But she did know that scandal spread through a community like bad smells. It had before. That shame would always be part of her life. As she waited for the bus or sat by other mothers at the clinic waiting for her National Health baby milk and orange juice, Ivy kept her eyes on her shoes. If she had the children she fussed blindly, talking only to them. She'd never had friends since the day her father was hauled away shouting his revenge on expletives so vile that her own mother blamed her and never spoken to her again. She could live without others. Paul spent his time pulling legs off spiders and flies or trapping bees in jam jars to see how long they could live on the enclosed air. He was raucous and disobedient, growing worse as he saw that Noelene delighted every-one lucky enough to set eyes on her.

By that the end of May there was something to peak new temper in the house.

'Don't I have enough to do? He's expecting too much Tot! We're scraping along as it is.

The muffled words, mixed with much dragging, shoving and vigorous sweeping sounds, struggled through the ceiling above.

Wren, playing with Suzi who she loved even more because of the wire and black plastic electricians tape holding her cracked head to her body and the bridal doll Santa had left her last year, was trying to keep Paul from lighting rolled up newspaper in the fire. The baby, who at eighteen months was the only one not to have absorbed the tension, slept in her pram behind the increasingly worn sofa. The little fox terrier guarded her as she had guarded each baby. She had known this soul before.

Ivy thundered down the stairs half hidden by a bundle of exhausted sheets and cream wool utility blankets too thin to keep winter from the bodies that depended on them. Tot followed with the bucket and mop.

'George isn't a bad lad. He just needs a start. It's the least I can do for my brother.'

The voices continued into the kitchen. 'Oh aye! And where was he all through the war? Living it up in France with no sign of action! And since? He'd not be here now if his little Mademoiselle hadn't up and left him for another soldier daft enough to stay in a foreign country.'

Tot returned to the children, leaving Ivy angrily filling the boiler in the wash house.

'Let's allow the summer in and that coal smoke out!' he said urgently stretching to open the window. He gathered Paul to him and sat in the big chair patting his knee for Wren to join him but she felt his agitation as she snuggled beneath his arm.

'Shall we take Jan for a walk in the woods?' he beamed, deliberately cheery before any-one had a chance to settle.

After pushing the pram to where Ivy could watch Noelene out of the wash house window Tot took the willing hands of Paul and Wren. It was only a little wood but it had to do and maybe the wood anemone would be out in the grassy patch beneath the scrub oaks.

Jan trotted eagerly ahead, sniffing everything as they caught up. The pavement felt hot through the tired soles of Wren's worn sandshoes. When they reached the last four houses the dog's paws silenced their clicking as she turned her head and waited nervously for her humans. There was oozing dread here but it took someone advanced to feel it. Wren sensed overpowering malevolence coming somewhere from her left, to find it she had only to follow Jan's alert stare. She became suddenly aware of the thinness of her blue dress and the absurdity of the big bow tied at her back. Her delicate arms hanging from the puff sleeves rose in goose pimples despite the sun's warmth. All the comfort she felt from the energies of her natural mother who had worn this dress fifteen years before her faded.

Her gaze followed Jan's across the cracked concrete that topped the little wall and a lawn worn to dust and scrub by the feet of out of control boys. She blinked through the sun she'd waited all day to have on her face but she was robbed of the soft pleasure.

The joy of summer offered from the blackbird's song failed to reach her senses through the viscous flow of loathing. She focussed on grubby glass to be transfixed by the cock-eyed face and carrot red hair of the boy she often watched from the security of her home as he passed on his way to school. He had his mouth pressed up to the living room window so that it was distorted and pale like two slugs guarding slimy uneven teeth. As their eyes caught, Alan stuck out a slimy tongue to lick the glass as he moved his lips around turning his mouth even more downward so that he looked like the gargoyles Wren had seen on the old church.

She stumbled a little before her turned head caught up with her feet but Tot's strong arm merely raised her from the ground and replaced her a second later on two feet. Wren did not notice the purple tufted vetch that curled above the grass bordering the little wood nor the Red Admiral butterflies that took their nectar. All she could see was the hideous face of Alan as she analysed and re-analysed his vindictiveness. Jan trotted the worn path beside her, seeking and giving assurance. Tot stopped every now and then to show his children tiny Scarlet Pimpernels and sapphire Speedwells jewelling the grass before it became dominated by the bracken. This gift from nature was usually the song of her heart but today Wren saw none of it. The truth was dancing at the very edge of her awareness; she had only to concentrate on raising her vibration so that she was on the level where all Karmic debt was plain to see. It was there, just there! Why couldn't she grasp it?

'The rain has done so much good.' Tot said as he surveyed the fat juicy stems of the sturdy growing popping balsam.

'I hate rain daddy, we can't go out. It makes me feel squashed in the house.' Wren was too small to take his view of the burgeoning woodland.

'I would make it rain all the time if I could.' Paul needed little effort to be negative. 'Your dresses would always be wet then Wren, and your shoes squelchy.'

Tot ignored him. 'But rain is nature's drink. It would die if not for rain.'

A rapid tapping passed above their heads and silenced them.

'Listen, that's a woodpecker!'

'It sounds so near Daddy.' Wren beamed when she stopped holding her breath.

Paul kicked at stones deliberately scaring birds into silence. 'I'm going to cut heads off all Woodpeckers when I'm big!' he spat spitefully.

Wren watched his frown as he flicked his eyes towards Tot for his reaction. None came.

Tot walked on allowing Paul to swing on low branches and Wren to amble three steps behind deep in her thoughts of Alan.

'...and this is Sour Docken which we would also eat if we were not civilised.'

Tot was teaching his charges which plants were herbs or edible and which were dangerous or poisonous. He pushed some green into his mouth then offered a young tender leaf to Wren.

'Are you listening Chicken? This is important if you don't want people to die from eating the wrong plants.' She obediently chewed, releasing the sour astringent yet pleasant juices to her mouth. She had eaten this many times in many lives.

Suddenly, through the overwhelming sting of Alan's hate a blinding realisation reached her.

Tot had touched the truth without knowing anything about it. Alan's hatred became clear; but it was not the jubilation she would have wished for.

She'd been wrong about his motives. Now she knew with frightening clarity that his Karmic debt was stretching nearer, hot breathed to being paid.

The walk passed without one word of Tot's teachings reaching her brain. Paul's disobedient darts into the brambles or stamping on insects passed her by. Even the smacks to the little boy's legs didn't bring her from her search to understand every nuance of Alan's energies. Jan sniffed out rabbits and ran after sticks thrown far away by a strong miner's muscles but it was all happening outside Wren's awareness.

The only way she was brought back to the present was as Tot's arms gathered her to him as he saved her from walking straight into a huge patch of fresh nettles near the exit to the woods.

'Careful chicken! You don't seem to have been with us. Are you feeling unwell?'

He saw how the summer lay on her back with heart-breaking loveliness yet she seemed lost to it. He tried to catch the leaked imaginings shooting from her young mind.

'Come on, home; baking day today. Milk and a coconut haystack will put you right.'

He was spot on. She wasn't with them; she hung hopelessly in somewhere too dark to bear.

The excited talk over tea was about the Coronation Mug that every child in the country was to receive. Even Noelene who was only eighteen months old had been allocated this treasure to keep as an heirloom. The letter said the children were to report the next day to the school a mile away to receive their celebratory china. Wren tried to concentrate on this treat that meant so much to the real child. But to the soul she truly was there was only danger. Even so her nightmares were interspersed with a golden coach the diamond encrusted princess would ride in on her way to become the Queen of England. She wanted the mug and knew Noelene would treasure hers in the future.

Tot came in at ten thirty from a hard first shift exhausted and slept longer than usual. He'd had several interruptions to his much needed sleep with Paul yelling and screaming setting the baby off. He had beaten out quite a din with wooden spoons on biscuit tins before his mother had wrested them from his clamped fists. Ivy had taken them all out into the back garden hoping the warmth would tire them. Wren eased her toddler sister onto the low wall where she taught her to scent her bare feet by swinging them into the thick lavender bushes that lined the grass. After lettuce sandwiches and home-made ginger beer on the lawn Ivy took Paul in to the toilet leaving the two girls to hug with the joy of fragrant life and the goodness they sensed in each other.

After leaving mugs and plates on the kitchen table Wren trailed up the stairs behind them.

'What time is it mammy?' Wren whispered, anxious that Tot was up in time to take her and Paul down to the school to collect their mugs and the extra surprises the school governors had arranged.

'Shhhhh!' Ivy replied with a finger to her lips.

She ushered the children downstairs where she glanced at the clock.

'It's quarter to two.'

'But we have to be at the school at two to get our Coronation treasures!'

'Well that's just too bad! Don't mither me Wren. Daddy needs his sleep. It's only a mug after all, too fancy to use, only be gathering dust all over the house.'

'Can you take us mammy?'

The pleading green and blue eyes burned into Ivy, dragging her back to painful memories she did not want.

'What? Haven't I enough to do with one line of washing too dry to iron and another waiting to be hung out before I peel the tatties. Go and read a book or something! I don't want to hear about those ruddy mugs again! Do you hear?'

Wren had cleared a space on her windowsill for her Coronation Mug, dreaming that the Princesses had maybe drunk their tea on the palace lawn out of hers. She had to have those mugs!

Wren had never been in the school but on a walk Tot had shown her the huge red brick building with its long windows surrounded by a hard yard. It would be busy now with all the excited children queuing up for their Coronation Treats. Isolated by Ivy's fear, she knew none of them by name but she wanted to be with them, to feel the group exhilaration. Ivy was struggling with the mangle trying to put heavy pit clothes through the tight rubber rollers with Paul hanging onto her damp apron. Wren studied her actions to see if there was any hope that she'd finish in time. It was plain to see that Ivy's mind was only on children and washing. There was only one hope.

Upstairs, she pushed open the door to see if Tot was anywhere near awake. Jan, who had sneaked in to enjoy the coolness of the dark room lifted her head but immediately settled again when Wren put a finger to her silent lips. Through the dim stuffiness, she could hear soft breathing. In fact she knew immediately that he wasn't even there. He had left his body in sleep to go astrally wherever he was needed. This was no time to wake him even if she had the heart.

There was only one way to get her family's mugs.

The gate glinted in the sun. When it squealed its opening Wren held her breath. She was still alone a minute later proving that no-one heard her crossing the boundary she'd been warned against. She turned right to walk alone, for the first time, on the path out of the estate to the main road, down the hill to where her treasures lay. The drop of her feet competed with the fearful yet excited heartbeat. Before she reached the last house she sensed it. Momentarily she stopped but the force coming towards her didn't. She heard, from the narrow cut careless footsteps approach before two red haired boys clutching their mugs and sucking juicily on toffees appeared.

'Hey! Where d'yu think you're ganning? They divvent let the likes of you get in our school yu' kna!'

Alan stood square and intimidating before her, claiming the path to be his own.

'Come on Alan! I want to show mam me mug!' the smaller brother urged, not feeling the same need for vengeance.

'What and miss the fun with this odd eyed freak? No fear. You go on yu' cissy. Bugger off.'

Thrusting his mug into his brother's spare hand, he barked out the order with only his voice because his gaze remained firmly fixed on Wren's fear.

They might have been the only people in the whole world because everything faded away but the sinister bond between them. The paralysing magnetic attraction was nothing to do with two children living four doors away from each other on a council estate. Neither was it to do with Suzi. It was everything to do with ...with what? Something on the very edge of her awareness refused to be reined in for it was not in her soul memory.

'We don't want girls on our estate! Girls are shit!' He flung the words at Wren in the hope of some reaction. When none came he twisted his mouth so that it curiously took on the line of his crushed and crooked national health glasses. Wren stared at the filthy sticking plaster hiding his right eye. It only added repulsion to imagine what horrors might be beneath.

'Especially girls with stupid odd eyes! Freak girls are worst.'

Pulling every bit of her mind reading ability to the fore Wren bore into his skull but this skill was weakened by the body she had stolen. She saw the hate and the revenge but the motive remained hidden from her.

Her physical body locked frozen whilst Wren vigorously searched with her soul memory. That is why she didn't see it coming.

Maddened by her lack of response, Alan twisted his warty fist into the material at the front of her dress. She was inches from his stinking mouth as he started to haul her light frame along the path. Her white plimsolls dragged alternately along the paving stones at the toe and she felt the already worn canvas give in to a hole. His breath smelled of sugar and dental decay. Little globules of toffee spit had gathered in the corners of his mouth. He rolled his only visible eye in well-practised intimidation.

Trepidation and fear stiffened Wren's legs as they were pulled along after her body towards the wood. Leaf mould, rotting after a recent shower, filled her nostrils as she was rough handled past the first whippy hazel branches just off the road. Here he thought no one would see him as he brought his free hand, clenched except for the first two fingers, stiff and stocky as they aimed for her fear widened eyes. She was only four years old, he was seven and driven by evil of a past that haunted him uncontrollably.

She scrunched up her face and tried to turn but evasion was not needed as all the evilness and strength from her genetic father bubbled up. Perhaps she couldn't have done it if the boy had any weight on him or she hadn't ripped the glasses from the evil contorted face. But as she bent and jerked and he stumbled over her shoulder and into the patch of nettles she enjoyed the knowledge that they were at their very peak of stinging power.

The yells multiplied along with the stings as the squinting boy flayed to his feet. Menace left his body, forced out by alarm and terror delivered on the biggest shock of his life.

'What's going on?'

A man's voice, different to any round here.

'You OK little girl?'

Alan sniffled and yowled in pain as he felt around for his glasses which he shoved to his face. Agony stiffened fingers fumbled to curl the wires around his ears but gave up after one so the lopsided spectacles gave no aid to his vision.

'I'll get you for this! And I'll fucking get you for everything else an 'all!'

Masculine pride wouldn't allow him to look at the man who had seen him beaten by a girl.

Swearing, he rushed his red, blotchy body and face past the stranger. But he need not have bothered for the new eyes were riveted to Wren.

Wren felt her heart leap. For just an infinitesimal part of a second it was brilliantly clear that they knew each other. On a level that definitely was not childlike she knew a deeply disturbing desire for this man. The searing connection that skittered between them left just as quickly. Wren had never seen this man but she recognised what lay behind those dark lashed slits. She knew this soul, knew it well.

'I'm talking to you pet.' Gentle concern came from green eyes beneath brown brows darker than his hair.

Wren had to obey the knowledge and actions of the body she now was and which didn't know who stood before her.

'Yes mister.'

The timeless union, so precious and exquisite, disappeared into the present. Wren began to weep.

'Shall I take you home pet?' he jerked his thumb towards a van with writing on its side and a driver impatiently running the engine. 'Where do you live?'

The heavy sniff led shuddering to her chest. The mug! The one the princess had drunk from! It was vital to get to the school.

'No, no.'

'Are you sure? You look too little to be out on your own.'

When she nodded, the man jumped into the van then bent his head to a map as the peevish driver chugged away.

The shocking pulse of awareness on one level helped her feet fly the mile to the school. Two energies drove at different levels. Who was he that she knew him so well? She wanted him with an ancient hunger. If she'd been in her own incarnation it would have been clearer. This was further proof that the older she was becoming the more this body's path interfered with her clarity. It was becoming harder to expand and contract her energies.

He was not local; she should have grabbed at the contact. Why didn't she let him take her home so that at least he would know how to find her if any awareness broke in him? She might never see that man again. She was too impotent in her childish body to do anything about it.

Wren was almost at the school before her mind returned to what only an hour ago seemed like the most important thing in her young world.

Every child seemed to be going in the other direction clutching their precious mugs. Perhaps she was too late. When she finally found the echoing hall where trestle tables were being cleared she noticed, on the floor, three Coronation mugs each with a toothbrush wedged firmly into a handful of brightly wrapped Quality Street chocolates.

'Oh thank God!' A clear voice shot into the high room from a woman whose feet seemed to be made for clicking across the shiny wood floor. 'You must be Wren Stoker! Please say you are so we can get rid of these last three mugs and go home. It's meant to be a holiday for us all you know.'

She shoved one mug beneath the child's arm and thrust the handles of the others into her little hands.

'Mind you don't trip now!' she ordered before ticking off three names on her satisfyingly complete list.

On the walk home Wren wasn't tempted by the smell of chocolate emanating from the rustling wrappers. Now she had her prize she could think only one thought, feel only one emotion.

Need.

The cool feel of the porcelain warmed in her clutches but the thrill of her success disappeared. This life faded. Once again, only her search beyond mattered, even more than that desperate moment when she stole this body she found so inadequate. How could she, not yet five, look for a man who had just passed through her life so briefly and yet so devastatingly? He could be Alessandro presented to her fleetingly, hopelessly. She was tantalised by the unmistakable love awareness between them.

Wren followed a bluebottle as it buzzed its lazy way through the open kitchen door. No-one was about but she could hear drumming voices in the sitting room. As she edged the mugs across the red Formica table top to sit beside a huge pile of worn but brilliantly white nappies the fly lighted on one of the sweets. Her knees locked her into stillness allowing her eyes to focus on the glistening wings but her mind was helping her spirit to search, deep, so very deep.

Had she been with her body she would have heard Ivy's quick steps approach the kitchen then the rattle of the round knob as it obeyed her hand before the door pushed open.

'Where on earth have you been?'

Ivy took the dishcloth from the sink and wiped vigorously at Wren's face and hands.

'Have I not got enough to worry about without you buggering off? I was just about to tell your da but he's got more to deal with than selfish little girls disappearing when they've been told not to!' She shook the kettle, added more water and put it on to boil.

Ivy's eyes shot angrily towards the mugs. 'I might have known you couldn't resist! Now get dried and come through. Mind you leave that towel tidy; we've got surprise company.'

In the sitting room all backs were to the door, all bodies angled in the same corner and all eyes riveted to something Wren had never seen before.

Instantly it returned, that searing awareness of presence. He was here; in her house.

'Hello chicken. Come and see what we have.' Tot put out his arm excitedly. Wren felt her face suffuse with colour, her breath lock, her pulse race.

'Uncle George has brought us a television.'

CHAPTER TWENTY ONE

Uncle George? Television?

'This is our Wren, George.' Tot turned his mind back to twiddling knobs at the back of the new box.

As the man turned so did a thousand memories, but they passed through her mind urgently to leave room for what was happening now.

'Bonjour jolie mademoiselle. But we have met before.' He shot her a smile she had always known and the sheer power of his presence weakened her. Was he referring to an hour ago or thousands of years? Surely he must feel this too.

'If I had known you lived in the very house I was searching for I'd have been here a lot sooner.'

Outwardly he seemed only to be amused by the present but something was there in that fraction of a second too long that he held her gaze.

Her weakness changed slowly into enough strength to look away from him, she was able to see the cardboard box discarded in favour of its contents. In the corner, beside the family's bounced on, tatty hide chair, just off the carpet so that it stood on the oilcloth, was a wooden box with a square of greenish grey glass. Tot was wiggling and angling a strange wire thing.

'It was working when the man from the shop fixed it up, but we're buggered if...'

Wren watched her dad and his brother bright with reunion joy and shared goal. She burst into tears.

'Oh chicken. We'll have it working for the Coronation, don't fret.' As his arms went round her she let him think that the reason his little girl was crying was there before them for any-one with any sense to see. That was the trouble, Tot, like everyone else around, only used five of his senses but she saw in the flicker of a look George gave her as she was carried out of the door to bed that he was like her, multi-sensory.

'Here give her this!' Ivy said appearing round the bedroom door. 'She's been out in that sun.' Wren drank the water and it served to ground her as well as slake her thirst.

'Trust that brother of yours!' Ivy hissed as she pulled the thin curtains.

'What?'

'Wasting money on a television! We have a perfectly good radio. You can listen to that whilst you're working. I for one haven't time to sit around watching God knows what. It'll never catch on! People are only getting them for the Coronation, then there will be nothing to watch. Waste of time.'

'Aye well; maybe you're right. He just wanted to give the bairns something nice.'

'Huh! Shoes would be nice! Dresses without the hems taken down three times would be nice! But a wooden box which is no more than a passing phase that we'll be putting on the bonfire when it all fizzles out? Aye he's got money to burn all right 'cos that's all a television is good for.'

'Shh! Ivy. Just enjoy his visit.'

He ushered her out of the narrow gap left between Wren's bed and the bedding on the floor moved in for Paul. George was to have Paul's room until he got on his feet and found somewhere to live and work. His money made from property in France would not last for ever, especially in the hands of one so generous.

Wren was glad of the peace to search her truth. It was becoming harder to lose her present life to tune in to her real self. The Karmic patterns of this stolen incarnation were stronger than she ever thought they would be. They had never really been tested but she was determined they wouldn't win. She mustn't allow any physical impostors to interfere with the true reason she was here. As she closed her eyes a wave of desperation seemed to flood every corner of her mind. That George was of monumental importance was blindingly clear. Who was he? She should be able to tell. If he was Alessandro why was she not certain? If he was not she should also know. And yet.....

Her intense searching left her body to sleep so that when the door creaked with uncustomary speed she woke.

'Wren.'

It was him!

'Would you like to see Children's Hour? The television is working. I don't want you to miss out.'

She pulled herself up from groggy unrest to see Uncle George offer a wobbling cup of tea.

That's all he was. Uncle George. The man she had heard her dad speak of fondly but who had not returned after he was drafted to fight for his country.

'Your mam made this. I've been drinking coffee all that time in France so I'll have to get the knack back with tea.' The mattress went down as he sat beside her.

She drank silently, eyes wide and fixed on his face, using all her energy to search his aura.

'You're a strange, lovely little girl. Yet I already feel I know you so well.'

The milky tea left her mouth to fall back into the cup.

'Careful! You are so like me aren't you? Different.'

She felt his search of her eyes. 'Those eyes are very beautiful you know, just wait until you grow up, every male in the land will be knocked out by them.'

He stood up to open the curtains on the late afternoon.

'But I forgot. You don't like boys, if that horrible little runt I saved you from is any guide. If he hadn't fallen into those nettles I'd have beat him black and blue.'

He snorted pushing the air out of his lungs. His hair turned upward at the front just like Tot's. His laugh was just the same too.

'I recognise his type. Always seeking some kind of revenge for his pain on those weaker than himself. If only they realised the influence of their souls.'

It was a strange thing to say to a four year old child and yet Wren understood his point precisely.

He turned. 'Well I'm not weaker. I'm twice his size and army javelin champion.'

He hooked his arms upward as he clenched his fists to emphasize his muscles.

'These arms are as strong as your dad's and I've never been down the pit'. Just like Tot, he took great pride in his masculine strength, they were brothers all right. 'But I'm strong in other ways too, ways I sense you understand even though you are just little. You're a funny little one and no mistake. I like you!'

He took her cup from her then perched on the bed arching his back as he patted his shoulder.

'Come on; piggyback to the picture show.'

As she clambered aboard Wren knew it was the most natural thing in the world to be so close to this man.

She only wished she knew why.

CHAPTER TWENTY TWO

Princess Elizabeth was due to arrive at Westminster Abbey at eleven in the morning.

Tuesday 2nd of June was a dull day but nothing stopped Tot saving his brassicas from vicious cabbage white caterpillars and his nurtured lettuces from sly slugs. As he plopped his catch onto the bird table his meditational mood was spoiled.

'Come on. Looks like rain.' Ivy called her husband and the children in from across the garden. 'I've cleared away breakfast and made a fresh pot. It's almost time.'

Wren had been pulling new born weeds from around the pea plants just as Tot had shown her. Paul and Noelene were using their fingers to shoot each other and judge the best death fall. Noelene let Paul win every time, why not? It seemed important to him, kept him in a good mood for a bit.

Ivy despaired of children watching television during the day. Andy Pandy and Rag Tag and Bobtail certainly captivated her children's attention but calling those programmes 'Watch with Mother' was ridiculous. Who had the time? But this would be the exception; the BBC would not usually allow programmes whilst it was light surely. Today even Ivy was caught up in the sense of awe. Fancy having the Royal Family in her sitting room! It didn't bear thinking about.

The children had their best clothes on. Uncle George and Tot had tried in vain to flatten their flicked up hair with Tapoline and both were wearing a tie. Ivy had pressed her pale hair into stiff waves and clipped them tight to her head. She never had need to make her best hair-do and it showed. She pushed all her children onto floor cushions and tutted at their creased clothes ironed only this morning. Tot, Ivy and George sat up smartly on the old hide suite.

Every-one watched in wonder as the colourless screen warmed up, flickered into life then slipped away repeatedly. George fiddled with knobs then banged the top and suddenly magic was there on a tiny screen. Crowds filled the streets of London cheering at a golden carriage pulled by magnificent horses. Soldiers in wonderfully pretty outfits rode alongside on beautiful steeds of their own. It was hazy and they had to squint as Ivy would not let the children as near to the screen as they wanted in case they went blind, but it was still magnificent.

The grave voice of Richard Dimbleby told how crowds of well-wishers had slept out on the route from Buckingham Palace all night just to be there.

The family watched as ladies held their powder compact mirrors above the crowd in an effort to see over the heads of others as the royal carriages passed by, the atmosphere was electric with good energies.

Every-one in the room was silent and when the young Elizabeth sat on a throne to have a sparkling crown slowly lowered onto her head Wren thought her heart would burst with excitement. To hear that clear sweet voice promise to serve the commonwealth and know it was the new Queen of England was awe inspiring. Back out in the streets the carriage pulled through the throngs again. In the heavy rain the cameras showed Queen Salote of Tonga, leaving her carriage open so that every-one along the route could see her magnificent pink robe and headdress of red feathers. To the little family sitting in their council house in the North East of England the picture was snowy, the colours invisible but other pictures came into Wren's soul memory with hues so vivid they seared the back of her memory; it seemed she was there again.

It was then that Wren turned from her cushion on the floor to see Uncle George's eyes meet hers. The mention of Tonga meant something deep to both of them. She saw him not as a Brylcreemed uncle sitting patting Noelene on his knee but as some-one else.

Ivy disturbed the spell by getting up to bring little dishes and forks to feed her family. On the radio last week she'd heard a recipe for cold chicken, sultanas and a mild curried mayonnaise sauce, invented it was said, for eating whilst watching the Queen being crowned. She'd never used curry powder before but the store had suddenly been full of the stuff. With the very generous money George gave her for his keep she had splashed out guiltily. Well, she'd saved on the lettuce hadn't she? It was a secret pleasure that her family were eating Coronation Chicken in front of television and not just the radio as she had expected.

When the Royal family appeared on the balcony to wave Wren noticed the little Princess Anne and Prince Charles. He was about the same age as her and somehow she felt great empathy in his pride of his regal mother. She'd never heard such cheering or knew that there were so many people in this country. Yet it all felt so familiar. She had known such crowds cheering for her and Alessandro on a stone balcony in the hot sun centuries before today. Was George there too? Were they the same?

How she deplored the great reduction the soul had to undertake to take physical form, it robbed her of so much clarity. She did not envy the spiritual battles this Royal family would have to play out in full glare of critics all their lives. They would be judged on the apparent reasons for their actions not the real, deeper motivations. It was hard being Royal. She was glad she'd never have to be again.

'Wren!' George's voice came through her far away feelings. She turned to see Noelene sleeping in the crook of his arm. 'Come here.' he patted his spare knee.

Every time she touched him she knew something. And yet she knew nothing. It felt like home here on his lap, his strong arm easing her back to relax against his clean white shirt. She could feel the glossy dark hairs through the thin material and then the power of his very being.

Why couldn't she tell if this was Alessandro? Why didn't thunder clap in their hearts and tender golden threads bind their souls together? Was he not recognising her because his soul wasn't expecting her? Had he been stopped from recognizing her by the powers she'd crossed?

She felt such a strong connection with the soul of her grandfather's brother. The little chinks from where recognition and clarity beamed were not enough.

She would not let this rest.

CHAPTER TWENTY THREE

How strange it should be the first day at school when Wren felt a glimmer of something that would lead her to a greater realisation about Uncle George.

The moment she had nervously edged herself onto the tiny seat of the infant's desk in the front row she knew. Some-one other than herself in that echoing classroom was multi-sensory. It was a sensation that lifted her to new hope.

Tingling with exhilaration yet not daring to turn her head, she listened to the strict, upright figure of Mrs Biggins as she outlined the rules of the school which she emphasised started here in the baby class and continued until the day they left for the school the Eleven Plus had pointed them to.

Wren would have an ally, some-one who understood. The energy was good, there was no doubt. It would take several exchanges to understand just how old this soul was and just how they were connected but for now the excitement speeded her own energies.

She had dreaded school. It always annoyed her that every time a soul was re-born they had to learn everything again. It had seemed a waste at the end of a life, to have such an accumulation of knowledge and only retain the lessons of character and empathy, behaviour and goodness. Of course she realised that it was because sometimes a soul was born into different cultures, countries and languages. And time; that changed a lot. The physical brain had to grow to allow the spirit to carry out its karmic debts and become ever more whole so that it never needs to come to Earth school again. Why couldn't she have been an exception like Mozart who retained his composing skills from one quick incarnation to the next? Here she was having to learn to read and write more than her name which Tot had made sure she could. She'd felt the usual pain of separation and fear of the unknown as Tot, with blinked back tears in his eyes had left her at the classroom door. Already Wren realised that the brain of the body she had taken was merely average in intelligence.

She gave this brain up to the teacher but her spiritual intelligence began to search the room behind her. There were twenty eight children here; only one emanated awareness on her level.

Her white satin ribbon which Ivy had trimmed of all the frayed ends slipped down her sun lightened hair as she turned to look in the direction she felt drawn to. Her eyes never found the child she sought for a sharp pain wracked across her knuckles. As she shoved her hands into her armpits her search shot through the glass of round brown spectacles into the fierce eyes of a teacher who had seen it all before and dealt with everything in the same way.

'Stand up!'

Mrs Biggins was a tall icicle of a woman melting at the nose with a perpetual cold which sprayed over Wren as she towered above her.

'This, boys and girls,' she dripped, 'is a disobedient child. Children like this will not be tolerated in my class and so can leave now unless they promise never to annoy me again.'

The hush of fear was for themselves as the class watched their example shudder before them.

'What's your name girl?'

'Wren Stoker.'

'Wren Stoker what?'

Silence.

'Every time you address me girl, you add Mrs Biggins to your answer. Understand!'

She walked beside Wren viewing her from every angle as if examining her for dissection at the butchers.

'Yes Mrs Biggins.'

A bony hand nudged the thin ruler beneath Wren's chin forcing her head back until she thought she might topple.

'So!'

'Wren Stoker, Mrs Biggins.'

'This class,' she barked then sniffed back escaping mucus. 'This is what happens to disobedient children, Hold out your hands!'

This was how Wren became the example, burned into five year old brains forever, of how to respect teachers.

The little knuckles stung from six sharp raps. How sad, Wren thought, that this class of babies would be frightened away from learning instead of loved into it.

Never daring to turn, Wren took the blue exercise book in stinging fingers then obediently and painstakingly wrote her name on the dotted line provided. Mrs Biggins glanced, silent in her surprise as she passed on her way to other pupils who hadn't even handled a pencil until that moment. When another teacher came in to dump a crate of little bottles of milk on the teacher's desk it was Wren's turn to use the unfamiliar. Made to wait till last, she watched as metallic milk tops where first pressed in then removed to allow the paper straws to enter. The milk was sun warmed and slightly off but she dared do nothing but drink down to the very bottom.

At play time Wren excitedly searched the playground for the light and energy she knew abided in one of her classmates. The whiff of recognition was all she had to go on. It was exciting when she recognised the magnetic quality of a person, place or tune. Here was another who knew there was more to life than time and matter.

No-one dared to speak to the child who had been marked as a trouble maker during the first hour of school. Wren stood alone, her back to the brick wall robbed of its iron railings to make ammunition during the war. The newness of the school and people made play hesitant for babies only used to their mothers' love. Bigger children looked down on the baby class, easily forgetting how terrified they themselves had felt such a short time ago. Loud, heavy shoes of lofty strangers clattered past startling the five year old senses of those who had known only home and family.

Two of the girls who would sit their eleven plus that year exercised their maternal instincts and crouched down onto their hunkers to talk to a crying boy. Wren watched as later they took the hands of two little girls who had wet themselves rather than ask where the lavatories were. None of these children had bright enough souls to have affected her so strongly. Had she been mistaken? Maybe the soul was great enough to have recognised her as a thief of life and decided not to show themselves. Perhaps this was a soul sent by the Source to thwart her, allowed one brief moment of their own spiritual greatness to be able to recognise the one they sought before reverting to just their physical awareness. Maybe it was the very one she sort. Whoever it was, Wren needed to find this advanced soul.

A group of older boys charged past waving imaginary swords which they stuck into one another to judge best falls and most gruesome deaths. They were too busy to notice Alan's slight turn of head as he passed the little girl who had humiliated him. All summer he'd swelled with frustration as she'd remained in the protection of the one who'd saved her that day in the woods. He was subtle enough not to be seen taking any notice of the baby class. Only Wren felt the glance of hatred which she reflected back to him so that his involuntary fall won him Death of the Day.

Back in the vast classroom Wren sent her mind in search of what she had felt just a few short hours ago. All she heard was the little brown and cream Snakeshead cowne shells as they chinked together to teach these little ones how to count. She swept searching energies behind her.

There was nothing.

It was Uncle George who was waiting at the school gates holding an excited dog on a tight leash, as Tot had left for his ten o'clock back shift and wouldn't be back until almost an hour after it finished at six.

'Bet you were the cleverest girl in the whole school!' he laughed taking her sore five year old hand from flopping ears and licking tongue into his. He noticed how insular she was, how she alone had walked out with no cheery friend pulling at her elbow.

'Always remember you have something that no-one else in that school has.'

'What?'

He tucked his chin into his chest and turned his head down towards her.

'You know. I know. Just let's keep it to ourselves shall we, Cherie?'

As he swung her onto his shoulders she caught just a glimpse of the intensity of his eyes. It was too brief to find Alessandro in there but she saw something. How elusive it all was when cloaked in the human form.

In spite of the autumn winds Ivy wasn't pleased when George offered to take Wren to the Co-op to try on the Burberry macs he'd seen the other children skip to school in. Wren felt her hopes of being like the other children fall to the ground with her eyes as Ivy made her mood known.

'You've been here nearly five months George, your money will be running out soon.'

'I've got a couple of deals going in Newcastle Ivy and if they pay off I'll be out of your hair in no time.'

'I didn't mean that. Mind, I never thought I'd say this, but I like having you here. You take a lot of the bairn's weight off me." She spoke quickly, realising she had got used to the extra money he gave her every week for his keep.

When George returned from the store with not only the brown Mac but strong shoes of a most expensive type she said nothing.

Wren was glad to be released from the stern air when he handed Ivy the bag containing shoes one size larger than the shoes Paul and Noelene left by the kitchen door each night. The strain softened.

'Here Wren, show mammy how smart you look.'

He pulled the school coat from the tissue paper and held it against Wren's chest.

His voice dropped to a whisper as he leaned close enough to show how much growth he'd allowed in the arms.

'It should be gold silk I am dressing you in Môn amour.'

It was infinitesimal, a tiny strike of lightening remembrance when Wren knew everything. She tried to close the matter in her brain around it, to swaddle it, to hold it in order to expand the joy and clear knowledge but it was snuffed out by the sudden reality of this life.

'Mind, little girls who are so lucky have to take care of such clothes, do you here!'

Ivy snapped out the words she hoped would prevent this strange child who had been thrust into her life, from being spoilt.

It was gone.

Why, oh why wasn't the human mind more perceptive? Here she was at the peak of her multi-sensory abilities and awareness foiled by the very human side she had so desperately sought.

The excited chatter of the children as they tried on their shoes was only background to her. She hardly noticed the Swizzle lolly she began to suck after it was thrust into her hand by her uncle but she did notice the ugly grunt that came out of her mouth as a thank you. It was deep throaty and almost aggressive.

She saw every-one's stare of amazement fuelled by disgust. Except for Uncle George, he understood. As the slap from Ivy came to her legs and the pink and green lolly was ripped from her grasp, she knew.

She knew it all.

It was without a shadow of a doubt.

'You ungrateful little girl!'

'No Ivy; don't!'

'George you are too kind to this one and all she can do is be rude.'

She turned flashing eyes to Wren. 'Now get up them stairs!'

Clattering of feet on bare stair boards suddenly seemed strange. Nothing belonged in the world where Wren and George were. Not even the closeness of Jan when she urged a comforting nose beneath the automatic stroke of the little hand. As she felt the thin blankets warm beneath her Wren knew that the grunt of thanks she had given to the offerer of food came from a time before raiments of gold, royal processions or a hundred other lives. It was primitive. It came from her very first time on Earth and it had been given to George then. He understood it now.

Her mind swirled and sought, scouring the depths of her soul memory, licking out ancient vessels of past knowledges.

Who was he?

She had never been more desperate to find Alessandro.

There came a different, more puzzling look between them now. Uncle George started to go out in the evenings and sometimes didn't come home to his bed. Wren fought with her body's rolling jealousy. Spiritually she was way beyond that and it was an unpleasant emotion to feel again.

Wren went through the early days of school learning as she must and even played schoolyard games with the other children, gradually making friends as she'd never being allowed to do in her street. Alan, restricted by a stern teacher who whistled and barked at every misdemeanour his beady eye alighted on in the playground, had to make do with oily looks he hoped were threatening whenever he came near Wren. This unsettled her and she remained depressed by the unfruitful search of the soul who had raised her hopes on the very first day.

Towards the end of October she experienced her usual disappointment when Ivy impatiently waited at the school gates instead of George or Tot. It was always a rush home past looks from other mothers who may or may not have been friendly. Ivy never sought to find out. She rushed past smiles and words of greeting equally, turning them all to looks of 'who does she think she is'.

There was something different in the street as Ivy turned the push chair into it. Paul, complaining of his legs being tired was squashed in beside Noelene. Wren held on to the cold metal trying to keep up, her curious gaze focussed ahead. They hadn't been so close to any motorcar before never mind a brand new one.

Two men were sitting in the front seats with heads bent as they fiddled with the controls.

Wren took in the large black bonnet with a badge on its nose just above a grill which dropped to a piece of smooth metal going across the bottom of a car from where hung some writing.

She had learned enough to spell out the letters on the plate but 'VUU 334' spelled nothing to her. A horn honked making them all start and notice behind the windscreen the two beaming faces that belonged to Tot and George. Wren loosened her grip on the pushchair as Ivy turned backwards to bump the wheels up the steps to the house.

'Stay there with those two if you want.' she called from the back door. 'If I hear one more word about horse-power and cylinder heads I'll put my head in the oven. They've been at it all afternoon.'

Two round headlamps stared at Wren making her feel the car could see her. A rod attached above the front window burst into her wonder as it swished across the windscreen. The men laughed at her fright. A shiny door opened onto the pavement. Uncle George always looked happy but never this happy. He grinned at her as he pushed the seat forward and ushered her onto the cold leather of the back seat. As she moved his hand shot to his forehead in his very best army salute.

'Mademoiselle!'

The seat was too hard, too shiny for her Burberry covered bottom to get a grip but an engulfing sense of awe held her still. She was in a car.

That's where she was when the other children rattled along the street keen to eat their bread and jam before running wild in the woods until dark. She knew the rowdy procession and the warning feeling she always felt when Alan passed her house before she started school. Now she felt something change as he stopped in awe with just metal and glass dividing them. He couldn't see her sitting so low in the back, too taken was he with the shine and swank of a brand new car in his street. Wren saw his good eye reach the driver and his passenger who grinned before the horn blasted loud and long right beside his ear. He jumped back in fright.

'Shit car!' He spat the words at the two men he resented before running home screaming at his brother to follow.

The men's laughter scared Wren.

Uncle George turned to look at her.

'See this switch? If you look out of your window you'll see the trafficator appear from the side of the car. That tells other drivers that I am turning right or left. There's one at each side.'

He demonstrated enthusiastically and Wren turned her head to see the orange warning of intention flick in and out as she hoped it was never too dark or too foggy for others to notice.

'We are going for a spin after tea. I'm going to teach your dad how to drive. A couple of hours and he'll be as good as me. That's all I had in the army, the rest I picked up as I went along.'

Both men left the car to excitedly change places. Tot's comment as, hand on wheel, he turned to his little girl behind him seemed to go unheeded by the men in their element. But the novelty of the Ford

Popular faded as Wren ran his words again and again through her five year old brain and her much older awareness.

'It'll make a change me driving you chicken!'

Wren lived the next few days searching her awareness for the meaning of Tot's words.

'Wren! Do you hear me?' Ivy's voice stung through the centuries of past lives.

'Are you day dreaming again! I've told you about that! Now get off that settee and watch the bairns for me whilst I get that washing in before that sky drops its threat.'

As she wandered to the table where Paul and Noelene where wielding worn down pencils to draw faces on a saved up pile of flattened out envelopes, it hit her. Tot was more than she had ever realised.

Tot was the key to what she sought about his brother.

After two family trips around the stunning Durham countryside and a whizz along Scotswood Road which were all cut short by Paul's whingeing and Noelene's car sickness, the car was considered a grown up toy.

'You are the only one who's no bother you know.' George smiled at Wren as she watched him dry off his wheel spokes after a 'business trip'. Wren never asked why he tapped the side of his nose and said 'bloke's business' or 'went to see a man about a dog', when she enquired about where he'd been. But she longed to know.

'What've you got planned this fine Saturday afternoon then?' He tossed his head towards the sky. Looks like the rain has stopped for the day.'

'I'd like to look at the Enid Blyton book you brought until it's time for 'The Clearing in the Forest.' I was wanting you to help me with the hard words under the pictures.'

'You can't be watching television every tea time. Anyway that clever little dog of yours hasn't had a walk all day. I'll take you out.'

George put his head through to the kitchen where Ivy was beating sugar into marge at the start of her big bake.

'All right with you if I take Wren and Jan out?'

'Yes go on, get away with you but the other bairns are napping so you can't take them!'

'Oh dear!' he said winking at Wren.

'I'll get my old shoes on.' Wren moved towards the door.

'No don't. You get to look your best. And take your hat. November doesn't offer sun without slapping your ears with cold.'

Wren had grown used to being stared at. Now it was because she was the only child around who rode in a car. Jan knew to lie still on the old towel on the back seat but Wren wanted to be with her in case she was scared. It meant she didn't get to see out of the front window but as she had to strain her neck anyway it was better to hold onto her dog so that no scratches appeared on George's pride and joy that was plush leather seats.

She was talking softly to Jan when the car stopped after only a short bumpy ride.

A stretched body pushed up her nose to see that they had pulled up at the new playing fields the council had been pressured into providing for all the children it had brought into the area. She never thought she'd be allowed to come here. Ivy would never allow it.

'You won't say?' George opened the door to allow Jan to scramble out eager to sniff somewhere new.

Wren shook her head but her eyes were pulled to what she thought she'd only ever hear about from the children in her school. There were only a few people about. Three boys and a bigger girl flung their legs out in front of them and then pulled them back with such force that the swings beneath them seemed they would at any moment go over the top of the metal bars in full circle.

A father was holding the hand of a toddler as she jerkily reached the bottom of a shiny banana slide. As they watched they heard the clang of a see-saw hit the ground with its uneven weight of a mother and her daughter. The roundabout was free. Uncle George lifted Wren onto the cold wooden seat where she grasped uncertainly onto the freezing metal bar. Jan ran underneath as he began to push, gently at first then, carefully watching Wren's face, harder and harder until the force drew back her lips from her teeth to show her pleasure. He expertly flung himself besides her laughing in shared exhilaration. His foot went to the ground time and time again to keep the momentum. Spinning, spinning, dizzy.

George saw her face change and so allowed the roundabout to slow in its natural circle.

He lifted her down and held her for a few moments until the dizziness had left. Wren, flushed with the excitement of being a child, felt only her uncle. This man was taking care of her just as her daddy did and the warm pleasure was shared.

George pulled back to check her face. She felt the colour was restored and laughed.

'Good girl! Do you think you could cope with any more excitement?'

Wren looked over the rest of the grass playground. The sun had gone and with it most of the people. Only the see-saw clunked and squealed through the grey of late afternoon.

The banana slide had little steps which Wren made for but George caught her hand.

'No, this way; I have some-one I want you to meet.'

He pulled her towards the see-saw. Every step increased her silent curiosity. The mother and her daughter stopped the movement as they watched them approach. It was then that Wren felt it.

A joy rose in her, bubbling at her throat. It was like coming home.

The woman was in the hot flush of life and brilliant at twinkling her dark eyes, smiled as she took the hand George offered. Her gaze bathed all three of them in warm affection. She was soft and well covered with mounded cheeks that increased to pink apples as she eased back a generous lipsticked mouth. Her free hand went to push a clip back into her brown curled hair before winding around the shoulder of the girl Wren was riveted to.

'This is Wren my favourite niece and very special girl. Betty and Joyce have been dying to meet you.' George's voice seemed sparkling with something new.

Aware of the electricity between the smiling lady and her uncle Wren managed to smile back but it was hard to take her gaze away from the girl with plaits the same colour as her mother's hair and the immature promise of the same beauty and what was activating around her.

'Joyce is in your class at school, or at least she should be.'

'She goes back on Monday.' The lady tilted her head. 'Perhaps you two could be friends.'

In the stare that was hard to move Wren knew that they had been more than friends so many times before. There was a recognition from them both that matched only the feeling Wren experienced when she met Uncle George. And yet... a small hurriedly hidden resentment.

There was no need for the two girls to open their mouths to speak.

George laughed at their obvious mutual pleasure.

'Joyce started school but was whisked away at her very first playtime when a teacher recognised the red blotches just starting on her face. A chicken pox epidemic was the last thing that school wanted.'

Betty laughed. 'And then the shingles. Joyce has been quite ill. I thought we'd never be free to try out this new playground. But I'm glad we did.' She beamed an understanding to George. He absorbed and welcomed he soft feminine energy. Wren had never known such a woman.

'I asked Betty for directions just as she was finding out where this place was herself.'

'When the infectious stage was over the doctor told me to get Joyce to take fresh air and exercise. As a change from walking, this place is a Godsend.'

That was why the guardian lights were around Joyce. They were healing energies.

The sheer beauty and strength gave a pang of home sickness to Wren.

These were the first powers from the Light Wren had seen since her birth mother June had died. They had been constantly with Tot and Ivy for over a year but never with her. Looking at Joyce now made her so very sad that she was alone on this Earth. But nothing could spoil the excitement that this spirit before her was bright enough to be Alessandro.

'Here,' Betty pulled a packet of fruit gums from her pocket. 'Share these.'

The girl, muffled up against further infection, was lost in succinct computed analysis of Wren. She remained still and to those with them she appeared rude and quiet but Wren knew exactly what was going on.

'Say hello pet!' Betty nudged the tube of sweets into her daughter's hand. 'It'll be nice to know some-one at school now won't it?'

For a moment silence seemed to breath around them.

'Joyce!' The note of embarrassment lifted Betty's voice.

'Hello.'

Betty bent to see the face of her child, to her she looked awestruck.

'Well; I've never seen you like this before. I think you two will be great friends. Now take these sweets before we gobble them up for you.'

On the back seat Wren breathed in the soapy, ferny smell surrounding the woman in front of her as the car warmed. It was scent, not household cleaners; this was how she wanted to smell when she grew up. As they drove towards the house the way Uncle George seemed to know so well, both girls, parted only by Jan, and examined every clue to the other's existence. Wren knew that her intuitive skills matched those of this spirit but that there was a tiny bit she could not read. There was one enormous similarity in their incarnations. Joyce could be her best friend. She was perfect in every way. They thought the same, had reached almost the same level of awareness to ascend and yet they were both here suffering the same dense vibrations of Earth when they didn't need to be. Why was Joyce physical? There had to be a reason.

Alessandro had been her best friend before. And yet... she had these feelings about George -too. Only confusion rose from so many similarities in what was charging between them.

Alessandro had also been her Uncle, her adversary and her dog. There were countless lives and relationships. Always she'd recognised their spiritual partnership. But then she'd always been herself on Earth.

Wren had never been in these stone terraced houses before. They had seemed too posh not being council or pit owned. She had seen them down the hill but as they were past the school this was the first time she had been this close never mind in one

It was obvious by the way George shook the kettle before he filled it from the kitchen tap that he felt at home here.

Betty peeled the layers from both girls then set them, with Jan, before a fire encouraged into life by a poke and a shovelful of coal from an ornate coal caddy. As the lid fell back to its resting place the enamelled painting of Durham Cathedral, matched exactly the colours on the soft moquette three piece suite unscarred by signs of wear. There was no bucket by the fire, no squashed and scuffed settee. Everything felt different here. This house felt warmer. The carpet was fitted so that no cold oilcloth shocked the toes during a game of tag. Plump cushions and lace antimacassars were angled with flair on the chairs, pictures with gilded frames hung over pretty wall paper. There was only one similarity to home. In the corner, supporting a display of flowers not picked from any garden, was exactly the same television Wren watched every tea time.

From the kitchen, Wren heard soft murmuring stilled to a silence and then a female giggle.

Joyce tossed herself from the chair to a thick rug. Her angled arm supported her head for further scrutiny. Joyce recognised non-physical dynamics at work between them but for some reason refused to utilise them.

It was clear that Uncle George's relationship with this girl's mother was totally accepted. He had another life she had known nothing about. Wren wanted to know more about this girl whose glistening eyes seemed never to want to leave hers.

'Where's your daddy?' Wren asked pointedly.

'Same place as yours.'

'What down the pit?'

'No. Gone away.'

'But my daddy hasn't gone away. He's on back shift.'

'No that's Tot, he's your granddad.'

On her real level Wren knew that. But on the level of the little soul many lives less experienced than her she was confused.

'Tot is my daddy, I don't have a granddad.' Even as the words left her mouth she felt her throat tighten, the tears back up.

'It's a secret of course, like what he did to your real dad.' Joyce said flatly.

Wren could do nothing to stop the agony of the process meant for the little girl she was.

'Tea and cake?'

Usually George's entrance brightened Wren but as he lifted the tray to a small pouffe it was as an intruder.

'Shop bought cake Wren, there's a treat.'

Betty stood behind him, her lipstick had gone and the buttons on her blouse were done up wrong.

'You girls getting to know each other?'

She kneeled as she poured then handed Wren a plate. 'Battenberg?'

In response Wren had burst into tears.

Over the rest of the weekend Wren had been sickly. George had to admit to the shop bought cake to a furious Ivy who was happy to have something to blame for what she couldn't deal with.

Even Tot's Donald Duck impressions failed to raise a smile. Play seemed to belong to the other children. She wanted to be alone; bed was the only place for that.

It was so awful for Wren to know everything and still feel the physical and emotional suffering of the child in a quandary.

Did Joyce know every secret that Wren the child fought so hard to keep in her aching chest?

She had wanted to stay in bed and in her thoughts on Monday morning but Ivy had piles of washing to do and wasn't going to have another child under her feet all day. As she dragged Wren along to school beside her quick feet and the pushchair she didn't notice how reluctant the small child was.

Joyce would be in class today.

CHAPTER TWENTY FOUR

Tot had picked her up from school with a smile on his lips but not his eyes. He had held her hand firmly in the position ready to swing her up as she skipped beside the little dog but there was no skip in her and he didn't notice. His thoughts were captured by his own pain.

Ivy sat the children around a table offering freshly baked stotty-cake and Co-op jam but didn't eat. When George came down from the bathroom unrolling damp sleeves Wren could smell the carbolic soap. No-one jumped onto his knee or begged to sit next to him; no-one teasingly fought him for the bread roll with the brownest crust.

'Come on! Tea'll be cold! Ivy, the bairns have no milk in their cups.'

Tot couldn't look at his brother as he spoke; he had to pour his own tea.

Wren burst into tears.

'Now then; it's not that bad.' Tot put his arms around her but no-one told her what wasn't that bad.

George sent his eyes to her and with them the truth.

He was going away.

'I'll be back Wren. I have to make a living; the company in Spain has offered me a job because I speak two languages.'

'Two?' Ivy started buttering freshly torn stotties. Even the captivating yeasty aroma couldn't make Wren hungry.

'Aye, French and English.'

'But not Spanish!'

'No, not Spanish. But I'll pick it up as quickly as I did French. I'll just have to. Just think Wren while you are learning to read English I will be just as hard at work with reading something new too.'

'Oh aye, it'll be Senoritas instead of Mademoiselles will it?' Immediately Ivy was ashamed of her comment and aware of the jealousy it rode on.

George took bread and then the jam jar.

'I have a relationship here Ivy; I won't do anything to jeopardize that. I love both Betty and

Joyce. I am going to make money, real money not thirty bob a week for breaking my back underground.'

His words hung across the steam from his cup.

'Sorry Tot I...'

'It's all right lad. You are right to go, get on in the world. It's just that... we'll miss you.' He tried to swallow but the bread stayed in his mouth so he chewed it again. Knives and tea cup clatter seemed a poor substitute to the laughter that usually rose from the tea table when Tot was on night shift.

Noelene slid from the cushion which always tried but failed to bring her up to table height. She passed her daddy's knee and lifted fat arms to George who put his strong hands under them to get her to his lap. Wren stared at the squared fingers so different to hers. She would miss those hands and the way the damp hairs curled over his watch strap.

'Wren did you play with Joyce at school today?' George asked, being careful not to spill hot tea over the little girl clinging to his chest.

'Yes.' she lied.

He knew.

The shiny black car caused quite a stir at the school gates at home time on the last day she would have him. As George took Wren's hand to lead her through the gawping children she saw him search for Joyce in the stream of children behind her.

'Hasn't she spoken to you yet?' he asked before sounding the horn to clear the way.

'Oh dear. It's my fault, I shouldn't have pushed you two together. I just thought you'd be friends that's all.'

Wren stared at the book she'd been allowed to bring home until her embarrassment faded with the crowd.

'I thought she was different in the same way that we are. Eh, do you feel it? I don't know what it is Wren but it's there, happen she's just upset.' Wren knew he felt her misery.

'Your dad let me pick you up so as I could talk. He knows how close we are, that I love you as much as he does.'

Wren kept quiet, desperate for any words that may ease the longing she was already feeling for him. She wanted to feast her eyes on him, absorb every atom of his being whilst he was still in her sight but she couldn't lift her eyes from her lap.

He parked beside the little wood but the November dusk and winds kept them in the car.

As he turned she trembled, fighting for her heart not to break for want of looking at this special man. He could be the reason she was on the earth and yet he was going before she had time to find out.

'Wren, you are only five and you have only known me five months. Be as you were before I came. I will see you again and you can come to visit me in Spain.' His expression was dark and intense.

It was impossible to vocalise her feelings as a five year old girl but he picked up on her thoughts without realising it and answered as if she'd spoken.

He was looking so deeply into her eyes that her face was suffused with colour.

'You should realise by how often we've been apart in our past that love will bring us together again. I have my path to walk and as always you are part of it but just now I have to take a track into the hidden jungle but it leads back to our joint way. Have you forgotten? Shared life always leads us back.'

This was not Uncle George talking it was his soul.

'Always remember little girl, that a conscious lifetime is a great gift.'

How could he know that in this case it was a great theft?

After he had gone it grew colder.

The frost found not only the bedrooms and bathroom but the school yard and Joyce's heart. Wren saw the same sadness in her that occupied her own thoughts, yet what longings that should have brought them closer seemed to drive them further apart. She seemed to find some satisfaction in ignoring Wren as if jealous of her heartbreak. But as Joyce played with her new friends Wren always caught the sideward glance towards her huddling alone with a book in the corner made by the meeting of two walls of flaking bricks.

Different was a crime here. No-one wanted to play with the girl with odd eyes, especially one with a car in the family. The most resentment had come when Wren was asked questions in class and always knew the answer even if she had been staring out of the window all morning. The bullies had long been put off by her strange look and the way they felt unaccountably bad every time they approached Wren. They could not know that it was their own venom reflected back at them by the shield of energy Wren created around her so that she could stay in her deep, deep thoughts. Even Alan passed her by with a grimace and pain in his heart.

Next morning a strange anticipatory pleasure overlaid with pain seemed to fill the classroom; Wren wondered how they could not all feel it. At nine fifteen Joyce was brought out to the front of the class and even brushed the sleeve of Wren's cardigan as she reached the front row.

'Joyce Chambers is how I want you all to be.' Mrs Biggins took hold of her new pupil around the waist to lift her to her desk. 'Joyce has been ill but not idle. Unlike the rest of you she listens when she is being taught how to count and spell.'

She took her threatening look to Joyce where it changed to triumph.

'Spell your name Joyce.'

The voice came loud and clear but Joyce kept embarrassed eyes to the ceiling as she spoke.

'And can you count the children in this room?'

As Joyce's glance took in the little wooden desks each number was precise and correct until she reached Wren.

A thousand memories silenced her.

'Thirty two! Joyce! What comes after thirty two?'

'Thirty three Mrs Biggins'.

'Good girl.' the teacher smiled as she helped her down to the floor and ushered her to her seat in the second off back row.

'And that children, is how I want you to be by the end of this week. Now take out your counting shells. We are going to learn to count up to thirty three.'

It was playtime before Joyce came into Wren's view again. She was surrounded by three girls who were asking her to play skippy as they pulled on their coats in the cloakroom.

Her eyes caught Wren's but flicked away to the girl holding half a washing line to skip with before smiling her agreement.

The child that Wren was hurt, and continued to hurt over the next three weeks during which Joyce played with every girl in the class except her. On her spiritual level Wren knew Joyce had her own blueprint to work on and that didn't include any spirit as bright as hers who only offered confusion and awareness that she could well do without.

As Joyce proved herself cleverer than the others time and time again resentment began to grow amongst the boys whose only thoughts in the classroom were how long before they could get out of there to play fighter planes or football.

On the Thursday before Christmas the whole of the baby class queued, holding thick white plates to their chests as they shuffled along for their school dinner. Two of the boys displaying classical signs of an early soul blueprint were finding things to annoy every-one. The dinner ladies, not as strict as the teachers, had much to occupy them with hot metal trays of Shepherd's Pie and churns of steaming gravy. Whenever a teacher left the hall for a moment two boys would crawl along beneath the counter to wait unseen their chance to tip the newly gravied plate down the front of the child they most hated. About seven children in front of her Wren could see that their victim today was Clever Clogs Joyce. She longed to warn her but the crime of talking in the dinner queue was punishable by no food that day. Wren was starving and anyway knew that although the scene unfolding seemed small enough it could actually be an important link in the karma of Joyce's reasons for being here.

The duty teacher came back only seconds after the boy who was responsible for Joyce's hot sodden cardigan and dress returned to his place in the queue. She kept quiet as did every-one else who had learned not to interrupt the flow of food in that very tight hour.

Afterwards, in the play yard as sympathetic girls were offering neatly pressed and embroidered handkerchiefs to Joyce with which to clean her dress they didn't notice a group of boys whispering as they gathered around.

'Hey! Clever clogs! You're not so clever at holding a dinner plate are yu'!'

Nervous masculine guffaws were elbowed out of each other.

'Go away!'

'Oh; go away! La de dah.' They mimicked Joyce's voice high with fear as they pulled out their trouser bottoms to imitate a skirt. Group excitement made them dance around her singing and mocking!

'Nah, na na na na nah! Nah, na na na na nah!' Joyce has got a brai-ain; Joyce is a big pai-ian!'

Wren watched as one boy pulled Joyce's hair and then another. Other children stopped their games to gather round. The bigger boys, always on the scent of trouble, were there like a shot. Alan pushed aside some girls from his class who were shouting unlistened to orders to stop to the boys.

'What's this?' He demanded to every-one who knew he was the king of intimidation.

'This one thinks she is the cleverest in the school just because her mother taught her how to count.'

'Oh she does does she? And does she know what we give such show-offs?'

Awe silenced the boys as quickly as dread quietened the girls.

'So pig face; how many can you count up to then?'

'One hundred; four eyed rat face!'

Alan had never been insulted before, that it was a girl who had dared talk back to him in front of his friends added to his mortification and therefore his anger.

'Yeah! Well I can't count past ten an' it's never done me any harm; watch!'

As he lurched towards his five year old victim Wren could bear it no more. Each of the seven steps she took towards the mob grew in their importance, something great was motivating her. As she reached Alan's back she sent formidable energy out with her voice which boomed across the crowd of children to his ears.

'No!'

His elbow jutted back but held the fist behind his ear. Every-one froze. Alan was being bossed by a girl. She was a foot smaller than him and had no friends yet she had stopped the most hated thug in the school. She knew it, the spectators knew it and worst of all Alan knew it. Humiliation fed his mortification so that his face reddened as it contorted. There was a punch and fury to deal with. Alan had his hard earned reputation to maintain. The scene seemed frozen for every-one and Alan saw it as his eyes flicked to read those staring hard at him.

Waiting.

Waiting.

Waiting.

He dropped the lapels of Joyce's coat but not his clenched fist. All his reputation of the last three years was at stake. His brother would carry this tale home to his dad and he'd be belted for being a coward. He'd have to re-fight or intimidate every boy in the school.

All the girls would think they could boss him. The punch had to be spent. He looked at his original target; she seemed to be as annoying as Wren in her refusal to take his hatred.

'Al-an! Al-an! Al-an!' a chant broke out from his gang and he knew this would bring a teacher wielding a cane to further humiliate him.

His fury had to go somewhere and it was already aimed at Joyce so it hit its target right between her eyes. But as she fell to the ground he turned faster than lightening to give the same place on Wren's face a second blow from his warty knuckles.

Whatever happened next in that freezing play yard was gone to Joyce and Wren as they met in unconsciousness.

The spirit of Joyce was magnificent but although Wren knew she had known her before she couldn't find it in her to recognise. It was glorious to be in her blue brilliant light energy and to feel the beauty of Joyce beside her but it was only for an instant before both were taken in their consummate mutual search of each other to the very first time they were together.

Now there was instant recognition and understanding but the greatest shock came as they looked about them.

They weren't the only ones from this lifetime sitting around the fading fire.

They saw the spirits first and then heavy jawed heads above the dirty bent bodies. The cave stank of rotting animal flesh and human excrement. Fur skins half cleaned of the fat were being held in the mouths of the woman as they scraped with a stone flint to clean the pelt. The men only distinguishable by their larger size tossed matted hair off their bulbous brows as they tied sharpened flints to straight branches to make spears.

Firelight licked the rough walls. Some throats grunted in crude language but they knew each other's needs instinctively.

Wren could see what she couldn't have known then. One stone-age caveman was the spirit of Joyce. Alan and George sat right across from them.

The spirit of Alessandro was somewhere, of that there was no doubt. But which one was he?

Together Wren and Joyce watched the clan rise as they gathered the meagre belongings. They had exhausted the game and berries, winter was nearing. They had to move on.

The Neanderthal that held the spirit of Alan was old, at least thirty four. Old men were valuable as teachers to the young but when their physical strength faded there was no need to waste food on them.

The little clan journeyed on wind torn hills and plains, over rock and swamp in a land Wren knew was now Southern France.

The bodies of Wren and Joyce both suckled babies as they followed the strong lead of their joint mate she now knew as George. The old man fell more and more behind. When he caught up with the clan at dark there was no food left. The next day he stumbled. This was how he acquired his strange gait as he dragged his sprained ankle behind him. He sank exhausted to the ground. The others turned. He wasn't worth saving. They pushed heavy faces forward and walked away leaving him behind. The wolves would be pleased with their easy prey that night.

No wonder Alan hated them and all who were stronger. When he was young he'd let children stand on his back to gather bird's eggs, taught them how to cross rivers and kill game. This is how he was repaid. No need to search for the reason he wanted to be the toughest. His hatred of the clan had kept him in spirit so that he had missed other lives. His revenge with his act on Suzi was his next life, the first time he had reincarnated. He was only in his twenties when he died. Poor Alan; he'd had it so hard.

Still, in spite of all her insight Wren found it impossible to quell the compelling genetic need to kill him. There was no pushing down of this desire. Why? Why? Why?

The familiar sound of hand bell sent feet rushing away from the girls who lay on the freezing tarmac. To those around them their eyes had been shut for only a few seconds before normal school life had resumed. No-one knew how far away they had been.

With Alan detained in the headmaster's office for the rest of the day the school returned to normal. Children's eyes examined the two girls for signs of the assault through the brown iodine stain as they walked to the table to choose a book for the lesson called library reading even though most of the children could only look at the pictures. Two months of reading 'Janet and John' and, 'I see the kitty, the kitty sees me,' had not given them skills with any other book. Wren tried to concentrate. She always picked books with the boldest pictures so that she could read what was written beneath them and work out the big words that way. Today she chose 'Flowers of the Countryside.'

She sent a frequent hand to the growing lump on the back of her head.

At first she forced herself to become involved in finding the name of a little yellow flower that Tot had found growing in the hedgerow late that summer. It had reminded them of a strawberry flower but was too late to bear fruit. It was as she turned the page to 'Wayside Herbs', that she felt it. A new energy reached her. An energy that had been there all along but had only now been allowed through its hard shell of jealousy. This was an hour when no-one was allowed to speak so that the air was filled with squeaks and scuffles of feet beneath desks and loud disgusting snorts of mucus taken back up the noses of children too poor to have handkerchiefs.

The air began to smell of sleepy yawns.

Wren felt the thoughts of Joyce and welcomed them into her own energies. Joyce knew more now than she had allowed herself to recognise. Yet still she hung back.

When the school gate was opened Wren ran towards Tot keen to show him her wild flower book. He wasn't looking across the heads of the other children as he usually did; he was talking to some-one. She tried to single out the woman who was huddling the large red collar of her swagger coat across her throat as she stamped the frost from her bootees. It was Betty.

They both saw Wren at the same time and beamed their welcome. Joyce whose coat hook was at the back of the cloakroom was last out.

'Hello Wren. How nice to see you again.' She had to raise her voice a little to be heard over the excited whines and scrabble of Jan's greeting. 'What have you done to your face?'

Wren smiled. 'A rough game of rounders.'

Joyce caught up. Her coat was flapping allowing her mittens to trail to the ground dangling past cold stiff hands. Betty bent to fasten her daughter's buttons pulling off her own right hand glove with her teeth which she then dangled between lipsticked lips.

'There.' she said pushing her hand back into the warmth. 'Oh! You too! What have you done to your forehead? And look at your dress! Looks like your whole dinner went down it!'

'It's all right! Mam, can Wren come for tea to ours?'

'Well... what do you think Tot?'

'Oh I don't know, it's too cold and dark these afternoons.'

'Ahhh dad!'

'But I suppose Jan will be pleased if I have another walk in a couple of hours. Half past six all right with you Betty?'

He took the book from Wren, pulled his white handkerchief from his overcoat pocket, licked the bit stretched over his index finger and wiped around Wren's face. She tried not to wince.

'Is that a bruise under the iodine?'

'We bumped into each other.' Wren heard her childish voice and what it said was true, only she didn't say that it was during a game of rounders or that it was thousands of years ago. Both girls smiled in their shared knowledge.

'There you go!' he said loudly before whispering expertly in her ear. 'And no shop bought cake mind.'

The girls ate quickly in fear of the fire drying out the fish paste sandwiches before they finished.

It was so lovely to sit on cushions using the pouffe as a little table. Wren wondered at the luxury of not having to put up with horrible brothers or tearful baby sisters. Betty came back to exchange the tea tray with a box of Tiddlywinks. Wren saw at once that the little counters didn't fire half so far on carpet as they did on their own oilcloth at home but she was happy just to have a friend.

'Have you had a letter from George yet?' Joyce asked not raising her head from the container at which she was aiming her last Tiddlywink.

'No. Have you?'

'No.'

The bewildered feeling bonded them, relighting flames that had never really been doused. Flames of lasting friendship.

Joyce tidied the game into its dog-eared box. She trawled the words from where the hurt was fading.

'I thought it was your fault he'd gone away.'

'Mine?'

'He said it was to make life better for the special people in his life. That's you isn't it?'

'I thought it was you, he loves your mam too. He said he'd never lose her or you.'

There was a silence between them in which raged a million soul noises.

'We must never leave each other Wren.' Joyce's eyes locked hers. 'Now that we know.'

It was a strange thing for a five year old to say yet they both understood with a wisdom that went back lifetimes.

It was up to Wren to discover just how close they were.

It wasn't for quite a while that she met some-one who frenzied her mind to doubt that Alessandro had already entered her life.

CHAPTER TWENTY FIVE

With legs lengthened by spurts of growth just before she sat her eleven plus, Wren ran into the person who spun her out of control.

Jeremy Foggin arrived with such a brown skin that one could be mistaken to think he was a native of India instead of just born there of English parents.

He arrived in March when pale English skins were most starved of light. He seemed to bring the sunshine with him and every-one, including the boys, fell in love with him. That he was different was in his favour. Never before had the children of this school met some-one who had been on an aeroplane. Not one lad wanted to break his elegant nose or test his smooth artistic fingers in defence. Wren, used to boys in grey flannel short trousers held up by overstretched braces or carelessly twisted elastic belts with snake clasps, was fascinated by brown corduroy well cut enough to grip around the waist without cheap paraphernalia. His crisp white collar showing above the fine wool of a plain jumper seemed to stay sparkling all day. His hair seemed cut by superior scissors so that it fell into place no matter what speed the wind attacked it from the Pennines. Wren was riveted.

Was India the place where Alessandro had been incarnated? He had always adored the country and its religions. This person she was, held stationary by childhood, could never have travelled until much later in life. It was just possible that he was brought to her. Some twist arranged by those who needed to clear his path to allow him to get on with his work. She had learned over and over again not to be surprised by coincidence; there was no such thing. Coincidence was just God's way of staying anonymous.

But this was suspiciously easy.

Jeremy had a well-practised way of talking to others in a superior yet compelling manner so that each child wanted to be near him. They knew nothing of spiritual energies or why they couldn't take their eyes off him. He had knowledge of another part of the world they had only seen as a pink shape on the tin globe of Earth they weren't even allowed to touch.

He had his choice of new best friend. Every girl wanted to be his. Had to be.

That Jeremy was delivered to school in a car driven by an aloof mother in glamorous clothes and painted fingernails was expected. It added to his enigmatic air along with the rumour that their big house in the clearing beside the pit, was cleaned by an Indian woman wearing a sari.

Wren had passed the pit manager's house often when she lived at Woodland Terrace. Its mystery was almost hidden by clipped conifers. She had never known anyone who lived there, never cared.

But now.

'New pit owner arrived this week Ivy.' Tot looked up from teaching Noelene how to tie a double knot in her shoelace. 'He's from diamond mines in India. Wanted to meet the lads before our shift. He's so suntanned you'd think he was foreign but his family are related to the Northumberland Armstrongs'.

Ivy was washing down the tiles around the fireplace, wringing out the cloth with soap reddened hands.

'I don't care who he is related to as long as he gives the men a fairer wage than that last bugger.'

'He's got a son in your school hasn't he Wren?'

The book on her knee had failed to hold her attention but she pretended not to have been gripped by every word spoken.

'Mmm?' she managed to sound vague in spite of her thumping heart.

'New lad; in your class? Mind you I think it's only till they can arrange a boarding school.' The print grabbed Wren's eyes but not her mind as Tot spilled out every bit of gossip gleaned from the main topic amongst the miners. Her heart clattered to panic. She had only a short time to find out if Jeremy was Alessandro. But how could she even get into his range of vision when every child in the school vied for his attention?

The now monthly letter from George, fat with black and white snaps and a letter to Wren in a separate envelope, arrived just as Wren was leaving for school.

'Don't you want to take it to show Joyce then?' Tot looked up from his Daily Herald and second mug of strong Co-op '99' tea.

'No I'll be late, got to run as it is!'

It wasn't of George that she thought as her sandals were aimed to avoid the bad luck cracks in the pavement; it was Jeremy's ten year old face that hung before her mind's eye. He'd been near her for two weeks but hadn't even cast a glance in her direction. How could that be when energies vibrated from her every pore whenever he was anywhere near her?

How could he get past the heady experience of curious mass-admiration? How could she get him to look into her eyes and see?

That he preferred playing rough with the boys and even taught them a loose idea of Polo using imaginary horses and sticks only added to the desire backing up in the hearts of every girl. She was one of many but it didn't bother Wren. If this was Alessandro he'd find her; he always did. Only he'd better be quick.

'Damn!' The word she knew she'd get smacked for at home spat from her lips as her foot planted hard onto a gap in the path large enough to nurse fresh green spring weeds. She checked. Only Shepherd's Purse; no need to hold herself up any longer. That wrong foot would mean bad luck, another day would go by without a word from him in her direction.

At playtime out in the play yard, more peaceful now that Alan was facing older boys in the secondary modern school, Joyce produced from her pocket a letter bearing Spanish stamps. Wren wished now that she'd brought hers, if only to stop the waft of one-upmanship that Joyce tried to keep from her face.

'Didn't you get one yet?'

'It came this morning, no rush.'

She knew that every letter had been the highlight of their month before her mind had been stolen by the new boy. She let Joyce enjoy her triumph; after all she had to endure the annual scandal of George's fortnight staying with a woman to whom he was not married.

'Ours came yesterday.' She kept her dark eyes on the writing not wanting to enjoy the moment too much. Betty's personal letter had been removed before Joyce was handed the strange and foreign envelope with the Spanish address on the back.

'He's moved, see. Shall I read it to you?'

'You can if you want but ours will say the same probably.'

'Oh well; if you don't want to hear about our invitation.'

Invitation! George had promised to whisk the girls away to Granada every time he visited but Wren never thought he meant it.

'What's this? Foreign stamps.'

The voice both girls listened to with admiration was for the first time aimed at them.

'May I see?'

There was no grab or teasing from Jeremy only a smile that Wren thought might melt her whole body into a puddle of butter on the ground. She had been mesmerised by that smile before. Many times in many lives. She had loved this spirit so well.

His enquiry was to Joyce who seemed incapable of lifting her arms. Jeremy took the letter gently. Wren stared hungrily at the elegant, golden hands as they respected the envelope.

'Oh! I haven't got these. Would it be possible to have them? I save stamps you see. My European album would truly benefit from what you hold in your hands.'

Wren stared as she felt her inner state lurch from hopelessness to one of delirious euphoria. The radiant masculinity she had already enjoyed in him was there in all its ancient totality.

Joyce would have given him her heaving piggy bank, her new camel coat, her life or her unconsidered virginity but all she seemed to manage was a weak nod. Both girls, used to boys like scruffy wild puppies with rough salted hair, snapping talk and grabbing manners, gazed at this worldly silken prince.

'I say, thank you so very much.' He gave a lilt of gentle unselfconscious laughter which showed teeth whiter and more even than they knew existed. Both girls were too stricken to make the most of their chance. As he left, studying the torn envelope and its treasure, Wren hoped her face wasn't quite as red as Joyce's but she feared it was. There had to be freedom from this childish crush. If he was Alessandro she would know how to handle him for heaven sake. Her spiritual skills were already weakening, this was a good chance to exercise them and see if she could stop everything she had worked for disappearing into a mere biological machine.

'How does Mrs Joyce Foggin sound?' Joyce asked dreamily.

'Terrible.' Wren laughed.

'Well it's better than Wren Foggin!' Joyce stormed off and for once Wren didn't mind. She desperately wanted to search her cell memories from former lives. She found her corner where she had spent so much time alone before Joyce had become her best friend and given her the passport to other girls. She snuggled between the crumbling walls, trying not to mind the cold seeping from the tarmac through to her bottom.

In her heightened state she could feel the spirit she longed for near her. He was on the other side of the wall. It surprised them both just how quickly she stood up.

'I've got millions of foreign stamps!' Her words seemed shrill even to her. His initial surprise was smoothed by good manners and excitement.

He leapt the wall elegantly to stand in front of her. He wore his expensive clothes with nonchalance as if unaware of their worth.

'Millions?'

Her stomach was alive with tension.

'Well, lots. My uncle went to live in Spain, he writes every month.'

'Oh', he seemed disappointed and took a couple of steps back enabling her to notice how polished his heavy brogues were.

'Then they'll mostly be the same.'

'Well yes but you could swop them!' she tried to keep desperation from her words.

That didn't seem to impress him.

'Actually he travels...to Tunisia and Morocco.' She watched his head lift and the light grow.

'And he's off to Germany soon.'

'Oh I'd love to have any North African stamps. Could you bring them to school?'

His caramel coloured face was even more enticing when it held enthusiasm. He flicked at the dark fringe which flopped happily into keen eyes.

'Yes...well no.'

She couldn't bear to see the illumination leave his face.

'I could pay you for them.'

'Oh no! Never. It's not that.'

'Well what is it. Do you collect stamps yourself? Another philatelist?' At that moment she thought she might begin.

'A what? No it's just that he hasn't written to me from any of those places....but I could ask him to start!'

He laughed then and she knew it was with fondness. Everyone else had tried to impress him with their toughness or cleverness and she knew that he had taken her into his heart because of her charming hopelessness. Happiness swelled high and sweet in her soul

'Would you do that for me...em? Sorry, I don't know your name.'

'Wren, my name is Wren Stoker. Of course I will.'

At that moment she knew she was lavishly and embarrassingly in love. She tried to swallow down the passion she knew he would find ridiculous in their tender years.

He smiled just for her, to show his appreciation but she could feel spiritual energies at work and something crossed his face. Could he see past her outer childish clumsiness?

'Do you know that your name that of a special tiny bird; how did you come by it?'

'It's a spiritual name just like yours.'

'Mine? How do you know what my name means, got a hot line to Heaven Miss?'

He looked into her deeply, dragging up to his own soul things she wanted for herself. She looked away as if to close off his channel of free flowing knowledge.

'I don't have to tell you how I know anything.'

'No but you will.' His strength excited her immeasurably.

'Come on; what does my name mean?'

She turned to him squarely and sent waves of familiarity he would have to recognise.

'It means defender of men and you have always been that haven't you Alessandro.'

There was nothing new in him.

'You've not been listening have you? My name is Jeremy which is an Anglicized form of Jeremiah from the Hebrew 'appointed by God'. My parents are English and I am very special or hadn't you noticed.' His languid confidence boiled up her already heaving desires.

'I noticed how cheeky you are, that's all!'

'And I noticed how lovely you are.' There was a pause in his voice in which the irritant of a truth was tossed and coated again and again by beautiful memories too long ago to ever reveal anything but the vague sense. It was then that he saw the pearl made between them.

'We already know each other, don't we?'

There! It came from his own lips. This had to be him.

'Don't you remember?' Wren was still wrapped in the spell that kept them from the cold and the high pitched voices of the other children who flurried around them but she saw on his face that he had returned.

'You're daft! Don't even remember names when you've heard them a hundred times.'

He turned towards a ball carelessly kicked in his direction, aimed his foot and scored a goal with the same magic he did everything.

'Don't use those mystic eyes on me again.' He glanced back at her but not thoroughly enough to see the seeds of tears she'd been holding in her chest reach the eyes that so bothered him.

He ran to the coats dropped to the ground for a makeshift goal. She watched the other boys jumping as they punched triumphant fists into the air completely ignoring the fact that Jeremy hadn't been on their team. He could be on any-one's team and the admiration on every other players face as he expertly dribbled the ball told him that.

Wren was left to deal with the hectic clamour of her pulses so that when Joyce came towards her she forgot about their upset.

'Going to read me your letter then?' she asked trying to return to the day and place her body had to be in.

'You only want to know about when we are going to Spain.'

'We?'

'Yes he has asked my mam to take us both after we sit the scholarship. He's sending the money for fares. We get two weeks out of school!'

The hope she'd been living on for years meant nothing when it came to fruition. Had she heard this news minutes before her exchange with Jeremy she'd have jumped for joy, swung Joyce around the yard and whooped to the sky, but now she couldn't go. She couldn't leave Jeremy. It was impossible.

She had accepted Ivy's ruling that she was too young to go gallivanting to heathen countries. Tot's defence of Spain and the adults who wanted to take Wren there fell flat when no pleading, whining or foot stamping added to his case. The struggles he'd had to get her a passport were wasted. He kept his surprise at Wren's lack of enthusiasm to himself along with his secret relief that he would not have to give up his baccy allowance to provide her with spending money.

George, feeling guilty and wondering why his invitation had been refused, started sending letters and cards from every country, town and village he passed through. The stamps gave Wren her only opportunity to approach Jeremy. He was a lad not taking any direction from the right side of his brain where he would have found everything Wren needed him to know. He was polite and grateful but only took enough time off from ball kicking and impressing other lads to stuff the stamps neatly into his pocket as he devastated her desire with his hurried smile of gratitude.

Joyce returned from Spain to a letter telling her she'd passed the Eleven Plus which she brought along with photos of hot days and beaming faces. She held these out to Wren with brown hands which she then used to tuck sun-bleached hair behind her ears.

'So we are both going to the grammar school. Mam is buying me a bike for passing. What did you get?'

'Two bob.'

'Two shillings! For passing the scholarship!'

Wren knew where the bike money would be coming from.

'It's two shillings more than they can afford.' She knew there was acid in her voice and it wasn't all from the defence of her family.

There was a newly constructed barrier between them which Joyce made attempts to dissolve.

'We missed you in Spain. Here see, this is where George lives. He has a balcony overlooking olive trees.'

Wren smiled at the wellbeing of her uncle as he beamed almost tangible pleasure at having his arm around Betty again.

'Here we are at Alhambra, it's a Moorish palace with fantastic gardens. See the fountains?'

Wren's heart thrilled at the sight of George and she immediately regretted not taking what Tot had described as the chance of a lifetime. Especially as he'd gone to such lengths to get her a passport. His smile hit her heart with longing. She'd only had brief contact with Jeremy while Joyce was away. She realised now that George fostered exactly the same familiarities as Jeremy. She should have gone.

It came as a shock on the first day at Grammar school that Jeremy wasn't there.

Wren had seen him twice during the school holidays at the playing fields where she was now allowed to go to as long as it was with Joyce. He took only enough time off being leader of boys to politely thank her for the raggedly torn envelopes bearing his treasures. Nothing she longed for reached his eyes or smile. She spent miserable summer weeks thinking only of seeing him every day in a new class or watching him whoop about the large new playing fields.

Even the discomfort of her new school uniform bought two sizes too big for lasting, couldn't keep her mind from him. She worried that he was ill and even thought of going to his house to ask but the stories of how superior his parents were put her off.

When she returned home after the long walk Ivy made her take off the green blazer and skirt she had scrimped so hard to afford. But she was hungry and wanted to eat.

'Don't complain Wren.' Tot watched with obvious pride as he tried to keep the keen, bouncing dog off the new clothes. 'At least you can take off your uniform and curl up on your own sofa not like that poor lad belonging to pit owner.'

Wren's widened eyes pleaded for an explanation.

'Boarding school they say! Fancy, having bairns and then sending them off to the care of others. Make's me glad I don't have money if that's how hard it makes you.'

Wren took the stiff leather satchel up to her room where she began emptying books. Boarding school! How could she get through the time he was away? He already occupied her mind to the detriment of all else and now she wasn't to see him for months at a time. He'd have forgotten her. She felt the unyielding leg irons of her environment and youth. She threw herself on the bed when she had changed and hung the unfamiliar clothes on the picture rail to look down from the wall on her threateningly until morning.

Melancholy saturated her. Wet, heavy and cloying.

Why should he even give her a thought except when he looked at his stamp albums which probably he hadn't even taken with him.

The cloying pit of misery stopped her from doing homework so that when the shout came up the stairs for tea she had done nothing.

'Have we any wallpaper mam?'

Ivy was adjusting the wings on her angel cakes which Paul had stuck grubby fingers into after Noelene had iced them.

'I have to back these books by tomorrow.'

'There's brown wrapping off that parcel George sent last Christmas and a half roll of the dining room paper, some scraps of others but no Sellotape.'

After tea Wren sat at the kitchen table cutting up bits of her bedroom wallpaper Ivy had kept for patching. This was the most pretty paper and not as stiff as the embossed paleness of the rest of the house.

She had to write a composition entitled 'My first day at Hookerbank Grammar School.'

She could have filled several pages with longing and spiritual loneliness. Poured out her heart and frustrations or told the truth about how and why she was here. Her tale of a girl sitting in an itchy green uniform on a hard chair with a different spirit to the one God intended, would have her out of that school and into a lunatic asylum in no time. Instead she wrote of her walk to the gates, her shock at seeing so many children bus-ed in from outlying areas and the strangeness of teachers wearing black scholarly gowns over their normal clothes. Her comfort of knowing Joyce. Normal. That is what she had to seem. It was not easy.

A week later she was suddenly threatened by the loss of the seclusion of her own bedroom and was moved into the box room. Paul was too old to be in his parents' space and she was grateful when Noelene offered to share with him. She knew Wren would get no peace to read or study if she shared, she was a thoughtful soul. Everything was changing. She had no Jeremy and no George. How could the helpless child of eleven she was search for Alessandro in them when they were both so far away.

She raked the energy of every child in her new school but none gave off anything that hooked her spirit into hopeful joy. Joyce made new friends and tried to include Wren but with little success.

Jeremy didn't go to the playing fields during his holidays. The stories came from the pitmen of a tiger safari or winter break to Ayer's Rock, skiing for Easter and trips to Washington where the family had their picture taken outside The White House.

Not once did Wren feel him near. The pile of stamps grew. She re-arranged them often, not for the tidiness but to enter a feeling of closeness with the only tool she had. She longed to see his mouth, his overlong hair and his eyes. How she longed for those eyes to rest on her own.

There came a sense of waste. Why did the ones she thought, in her lessened state of humanness, to be Alessandro have to go away. There was only Joyce. She spent the next few years in the barren incarnation that wasn't hers and with no hope, no freedom from the drudge that was school.

George was finding it harder and harder to find the time from his successful business to come to England. Instead, ever more frequent trips were made by Betty and Joyce to Spain. His letters became less frequent, the newness of his adventure had long since been commented on and he had only the minutiae of life to report. He was doing well, working hard and missing them all. Wren's aching heart grew heavier every day.

On one last trip home George missed them no longer. Betty and Joyce were whisked away to a new life. Wren was on her own.

School went on, so did loneliness, frustration and yearning.

It was in the April before her fifteenth birthday when she felt such a surge of his energy that she knew Alessandro must be close.

CHAPTER TWENTY SIX

Every day of the Easter holidays Wren visited the playing fields in the grinding hope of finding him. Jan was aging but still lost no opportunity to run alongside the girl she loved to give a mixture of fun and protection. Smaller children who were not even born when Wren moved to the council estate seemed to own the play areas now but in her willowy, tall body Wren became the fastest turner of the metal and wood roundabout, the highest swinger of heavy chained swings and held the record for the most slidies in a day. Her bottom became sore, her legs scraped and aching with tiredness. But the punishment of her body was nothing to that of her need.

Jeremy never came.

Perhaps her reading had been wrong. It was still there but strangely muffled and yet she felt such an awareness of impending important events that he had to be near.

In the more advanced of former lives, when she had all her accumulated knowledge and spiritual awareness she'd have astral travelled to wherever he was. But now the strengths clinging to her spirit were weakening. This, worryingly, was allowing other traits to develop, traits she didn't want.

It was becoming increasingly difficult to push away the psychopathic thoughts. Paul irritated her, Noelene and Jan beyond belief so that when Wren finally lost her temper and told him to stop it or she'd kill him, she meant it. Wren was more shocked by her words and emotions than Paul. It took super human strength to smother any sign of her lethal side.

There was only one way to find Jeremy and that was physical. The certainty of what she must do sickened her. It was easy for her greater self to remember that privilege was only a setting in which the spirits set their assignments. Could she push this shy working class body to where it would never be accepted?

If she found the strength to walk through that imposing gate and into the hidden world of money and privilege then was caught and chased she would only be derided by people of her own class who felt it was their duty to keep the privileged secure.

But it was all there was.

She had to go to his house.

As always Jan's ears pricked up when she caught Wren's thoughts of woods and walking. The dog been on her bed all night, sneaked up for love and stroking not moving from the old red cardigan Wren put there to keep hairs from the bedding and Ivy's harsh eyes and tongue.

'You can't come this time Jan. I have to do this on my own.' She explained as she ruffled first a black ear then the white one, noticing for the first time how grey hairs had taken over the black just around that welcoming mouth. 'Come on out for your wee.'

Wren only had to say once for that dog would have followed her to the ends of the earth from the day she was born. When Jan came back from the garden she gobbled the plate of left-overs from last night's dinner. There was never anything left on Noelene's plate but it had been one of Paul's awkward nights when he sulkily protested that he hated anything put in front of him. This had freed Wren to eat everything, there was no need to leave special tasty bits for her four legged passion because she had lost the 'grab and gobble anything' appetite of her youth. Early morning sun tempted girl and dog out where they enjoyed the garden together entering the promise of a new morning and how much the day could hold. The soil was almost warm enough to plant the first potatoes she noticed as she opened the cold frame where her seed trays took their protection from any frost. But their reverie didn't last.

The open window threw at them the information that the kitchen was filled with urgent clattering and irritating squabbling. Wren knew she couldn't stay out any longer.

'Is that ruddy garden all you think about?' Ivy dolloped porridge into the children's bowls.

Jan, now older and less able to take shouting, slunk into her cardboard box behind Tot's chair. She knew this mood well and how to wait it out until the end of Tot's shift.

Wren felt her morning joy evaporate as she washed her hands.

'It is bed stripping day and I want you to get started as soon as you've cleared up here.'

Ivy sat only half on her chair ready to spring into clearing up mode the second her family put down their spoons.

'And you two! I want no fratching; if you want to fight do it outside away from me!'

Paul and Noelene knew the best thing was to eat quietly and go out to play for as long as their stomachs would let them. Wren had learned not to protest that she had urgent matters of her own. How could she explain? Ivy understood nothing, how could she.

Wren's obedient arms and legs stripped every sheet and pillowcase from where it had rested only a week from Ivy's relentless cleaning. She knew better than to interfere with a good drying day and Ivy's single mindedness. The little dog followed her and whined.

'No Jan you can't walk with me today. I have important things to do.'

The terrier scattered her claws in a dance of persuasion she'd used to great effect in the past. She wanted to be with Wren, to protect her from Alan's threatening glares and give her highly charged sense of perception to the person she loved most after Tot. This was exactly what Wren wanted to avoid.

She had to wait until Ivy took the last mangle flattened wash to the rope line near the cabbage patch before she encouraged Jan upstairs to her bedroom where she shut her in. Tot would be in off first shift for an early dinner, he would take her into the garden then. Wren would have to miss the corned beef hash and rice pudding she'd helped get into the oven. The smell was already pulling at her stomach but missing a midday meal was a small price to pay to get out unnoticed.

Tot would be horrified if he knew she was even contemplating going anywhere near the home of the owner of his pit. The miners had many grievances and daily gripes during secret meetings. Safety and wages were too low. Mr Foggin was playing a dangerous game with dangerous men. He didn't know it. Blindly he ruled with his 'us and them attitude' sharpened by obvious wealth. No-one knew how he would deal with a miner's daughter caught within his very impressive and strictly private gardens.

But it had to be done. Jeremy would not come to her. It was clear that he didn't feel the need. He had shown no recognition of her spirit since that first day. And yet?

She knew these woods first before she was born. It was the very first place on Earth she had come to in this incarnation. She knew the exact spot where her brutal conception took place but had always passed it by without a flicker on her face as Tot and the children followed Jan to her favourite scooting and sniffing areas. Paul and Noelene did not feel the magic of nature and Tot acted on his disappointment by no longer asking them if they wanted to walk. They found the constant stops to peer at tiny flowers or owl pellets annoying in the extreme so that their boredom manifested itself by swinging on and snapping immature branches or kicking over ant hills. Noelene was taking too much of a lead from her older brother. When they were disciplined by Tot they began picking on each other so that wild life was frightened away and the spell was broken.

If Jan knew she was missing a trip to here she'd be devastated. Anyway, she was getting too slow in her dotage to keep up. Wren had to push the terrier out of her mind in case she picked up on her thoughts. She urgently created a mental image of the playing field, hoping she wouldn't be too disappointed.

The thick covering of cowslips for once remained unpicked as she passed by Bullerwell's meadows. As the earth became sandier the hazel and hornbeam's unfurling leaves created a fresh green haze across the young bushes. She remained so sincerely alive to colour. It smelled like spring and this added to the excitement of love she felt in her young heart. She wouldn't take the road. Even in her quest she was unable to stop herself passing the top wood badger set to see if the tell-tale cobwebs had gone to indicate that the badgers had returned. From there it was only a few yards to the steep incline from where she viewed the colliery spread below.

The green paint of the offices stood out. Anxiety had grabbed her beneath those shining slate roofs many a Friday watching Ivy count the money from her husband's buff pay packet. It never was wrong but Ivy was always ready for a fight, just in case. Quite a way beyond, mostly hidden by exotic trees brought back by Victorian plant hunters, were the double chimneys of Kadiemuir Gables where Jeremy lived. The path to that grandeur was winding and tough to both the feet and the mind. It would take only minutes to pass the four big oaks that surrounded the disused ventilation shaft where Tot had said June used to admire the wall clinging ferns growing in the dampness. His daughter would shout down into the dark and hidden depths hoping he would hear her as he worked in the mine. It wasn't until she was eight that he told her no-one ever worked that exhausted coal seam any more.

The spell that held Wren's eyes to the four big chimneys sent her hasty toes behind tree roots instead of over them so that she stumbled. But determination and certainty made her climb to her feet to study the house she could only dream of ever entering.

He was there, she could feel it. As she stared trance like at the grand home that held the one she sought, she became lost in uncertainty and fear.

'Good view, eh?'

Wren spun around to see who had sneaked into her space whilst she was sunk in her deep need.

The man leered as his attention was drawn by the silhouette of her long legs through the thin cotton. The sun behind her lit his face well. His stocky body was covered in clothes she'd only seen on television, no-one round here knew where to buy a shirt with a frill down the centre, hipster trousers or have their hair cut and styled in such a purposeful way.

'By you're a bonny lass and no mistake!'

The lecherous eyes raked her body as the man's pink tongue curled out of the side of his mouth glistening wet and slimy like his eyes which moved from her flat chest to her face. Arrogance fed by success and raw strength moulded his pock marked face.

She knew exactly who he was.

CHAPTER TWENTY SEVEN

A cloudburst of nervous cautions soaked Wren in seconds.

When he recognised her terror it obviously pleased him and he laughed waving his podgy fist gripping a fat cigar long gone out for want of attention. This he tossed to the ground in order to free his manicured hand to trace her cheek. She winced and stepped back.

'Don't be like that pet. I can be very generous when I like a lass. You know there are girls in London who'll do anything I ask for a fraction of what I've got in here.' He pulled open his jacket to reveal an expensive wallet bulging with notes poking from the pocket in luxurious lining.

Her eyes glued to his posturing body.

'Oh you like the suit do yu'?' This is Saville Row; real good stuff. The shirt's Carnaby Street. Don't see the likes of this around here do yu', eh? Miners'll never make enough money to buy this class.'

Her nerves were drawing sickeningly at the base of her stomach.

Wren tried not to allow her thoughts into the energy between them. He was sharp but she knew instinctively some of the secrets of his personality.

'By, I could show you some other things you'd like an all bonnie lass.' He rubbed his spare hand up and down the front of his trousers, 'Starting with this.'

Wren knew her eyes had widened in shock and terror but on a higher level she knew that this man was just on his spiritual path as every other soul. She should help him. She held wisdom with which to council his every evil, and yet?

'Would you like to feel what I have here pet?'

She held her silence, trying to haul up deep understanding from her soul but instead came the evil she had tried so hard to suppress and she knew now exactly where it came from. It was in her genes, the same genes as this disgusting man before her.

All her sweetness and caring dissipated into the air, swallowed by the hatred fuelled cruelty she had spent fourteen years trying to correct. Suddenly it didn't matter that her hundreds of lifetimes had taught her how to help lost and evil souls. The voice coming from this leering man before her was the first voice she had heard on Earth in this incarnation. Hate overtook everything giving her the strength to do what she hadn't done in centuries

Her heart fired like a weapon, discharging strength through her body.

This was the feeling she had been dreading coming to fruition. Wren was horrified but could do nothing to prevent responses she had worked many lifetimes to eradicate coming to the surface.

He was truly revolting.

As he wound his arm around her waist she smelled the stale tobacco, the overpowering aftershave failing to mask day old sweat. She yanked away wincing at the burn his grip made on her wrist but he forced her back against the first of the great oaks. He twisted her completely so that she was facing into the sun. She saw his shock of recognition as it lit up her eyes. This momentary switch of power was all she needed to harness the potency of her own evil. She thrust her knee up to where she knew it would hurt him most, he bellowed in shock and agony. This fuelled his fury so that her next move was surprisingly simple. She slumped against the decaying wall of the well-like shaft top then laughed at him.

He was so predictable, her timing so accurate. As his anger propelled him towards her, all she had to do was duck. At first only the top of the wall crumbled but as he hung over the shaft struggling and cursing she knew how simple it was.

'Pull me up you whore! You stupid stinking bitch!'

They were engulfed by the same ribbon of evil genetics. Wren had no power to prevent what she knew would happen next. She offered her hand and he grabbed it. It would be all in the judgement. As she pulled him up the split second came when he was relying on her strength completely. Powdery cement and flaking bricks were sent by his flaying feet into the depths of black water accumulated in the years of neglect.

She bent slightly towards him as if to help him further but instead she said only five words.

'This is for my mother.'

Her ragged nails in fists of fury tore across his wrist so that the shock opened his hand.

The splash was followed by a thud. The water wasn't so deep after all Wren thought as she rebuilt as best she could the wall that had so assisted her. Her hands, as they sought the old pale bricks, were careful not to damage the new unfurling shoots of the bracken rising from the dried carpet of last year's fronds. He had trampled many in his evil pursuit of her and probably throughout the wood. He was thoughtless and spiteful even towards nature.

As she stepped back her heel was caught by a low hoop of a racing bramble shoot eager to cover as much ground as possible before it flowered and fruited.

Shock threw Wren's hands under her side to save herself. But there was something beneath them that was not from nature.

Her racing mind first thought it was a stone but it took only seconds for her senses to realize the surface was too soft. She turned to see his stuffed wallet. The grey leather was forced to bulge out by the sheer volume of notes. The wallet alone would have cost more than any honest man would make in a week Wren thought as she picked the weight from the ground. Nothing could persuade her to open the straining press stud. This was evil money and could only produce further badness. Yet if it was found it would start an early search. Colin was not yet dead, she was certain of that because his spirit had not risen. It was easy for Wren to hide anything in this wood for she knew every rock and hole. It was only a short walk to the sandy rabbit warren long ago abandoned by the rabbits who had so painstakingly dug it, but she strode on legs of conquest. Grass was starting to grow in front of the round entrances and softly vibrating spiders barred off some in the centre of their newly spun webs. She chose a rabbit hole she knew had early twists and turns from many hours playing here with Jan. Lying flat in order to stretch her body and arms, she wiggled her hands expertly so that the wallet disappeared easily into the tunnel as it twisted back on itself. It had saved many a rabbit from a fox and now it would hold this secret for ever for nothing would induce her to ever touch his filthy money again.

It was this thought that made Wren realise that she was now returning to her greater spirit from total surrender to the spirit of the life she had stolen. Now she would do anything to save a life so that it could travel along the path it had chosen so carefully. But what was Colin's path? Her first urge was to dash back to the shaft to save Colin. She knew she would never be left in peace again and yet she must.

She broke into an urgent run towards the four oaks but was stopped in her tracks by a strange force.

It was then that she saw the luminous rainbow iridescent light energies enter the hole and take only seconds before they emerged with a dull grey light she recognised immediately as Colin's soul. This was his Karmic debt repaid. It was too late to save his life but these gentle energies would now work with him on the other side of life to progress his awareness. There was a split second when the bright colours realised they were perceived but there was no time to investigate further, they had a job to do. The personality Wren had stolen into was born to commit this murder. She couldn't have stopped it. It was quick and thorough in the way of all things meant to be.

How could she go on with her plan now? It must never be known that she was in the woods today. Any link to this could seriously hold up her valuable life. Chains of guilt dropped onto her shoulders, curled around her limbs and dragged behind her. She was no longer an innocent young girl. She was a murderer.

As she hurried along the same path which had brought her here she stopped in surprise to see Jan sniffing a pile of moss covered stones in the shade.

'Jan! Here girl! Who let you out...?

Her words tailed off as she realised that she would need a different energy to communicate with her dog for this was not fur and paws but spirit.

The little animal soul was visiting the place and person she loved before she left the Earth. Wren knew she'd already have been to Tot. He'd been dreading this, he'd often said Jan was very old for a dog. It was as if he accepted her leaving soon but Wren knew he kept his emotions under hammered floorboards so that others around him would not be too sad.

June felt her heart leap first in sadness and then in pleasure as she watched delightful pink energies waft towards her.

The two spirits met in understanding. Jan glowed as she thanked Wren for all her love and kindness. Wren had a lot to praise the dog for. She'd known her all her life and enjoyed total devotion. There was nothing to stay for now. Jan faded from her awareness. Wren was happy the little soul would be joining June and others who loved her in her true spiritual home.

She was half way home when she found the little body she knew had died of a heart attack as it had rushed to find her. The fur was sun warmed in her arms, the head and paws floppy as they had been so many times in sleep. She had tried not to notice her dog growing old but now she could see how fragile the little frame had become. She lowered her head to breath in the smell she would miss so much. Grief pulled tears from her loss.

Tot would never get over it.

CHAPTER TWENTY EIGHT

She woke at two am convinced it was a dream, prayed for it. But no-one would listen to her prayer, she knew. It took only seconds for the terrible sadness to engulf her. The misery of Tot seeped through the walls. How much more would there be if he had to grieve not only for his treasured dog but also for his murderous daughter. How she wished that with the sadness of death came an excitement. It was wonderful that a soul had completed its chosen tasks and would now meet others who loved them. Raw emotion trapped her in wakefulness until she heard Tot shuffle heavily down stairs to dig the grave of his adored friend.

She watched from the window as he held the fifteen year old dog to his breast and sobbed. Where there had been depth of personality, loyalty, deep devotion now there was only surface. Bones and hair. Adoring eyes could not sparkle through ever closed lids. Ears that twitched and turned with intelligent curiosity were forever still. His closest friend had gone. Tot laid the empty body gently on the ground, wrapped it in the old sheet he had slept in for years then began to dig.

In her own misery she thought of another body, only she knew lay broken and lifeless. The only way Wren could digest the thought that she was responsible for murder at only fourteen, was to repeat over and over again that it was the plan for the life she had stolen. It was clear that this girl's Karma was too set to stop. How much would cloud her purpose was hard to tell. She'd just have to deal with the two, sometimes never knowing which was which. But this, this was definitely not Wren's. Every quiet night of the following weeks she had to fight away the image of Colin and what she had done. It had been several lifetimes since she had learned not to harm a living thing so that it came hard to know what she had done. This surely would have been the main horror of the young spirit whose incarnation was taken from her. Wren wondered if she had actually been there. Often she felt energies around her but had long since stopped asking them to come forward to make themselves known.

In August 1962 three things happened. Wren turned fourteen, Marilyn Monroe was found dead and so was Colin.

Tot, still suffering from the loss of his dog, had come in for a ride of disappointment from the pitmen who all thought he'd killed Colin years ago after the rape and death of his daughter. The admiration from some faded but from others it grew. Talk was that he might be involved now but when the police had checked every miner's alibi it was proven that he was on his back in a wet coal seam three foot high hewing with the rest of them. The time of the murder was ascertained by the fact that Colin's mother had been expecting him off a certain bus after the train from London to Newcastle. He had promised her that he would take her to buy a car with more money than she had ever seen. She knew her son's dishonesty and thought that he simply had changed his mind. Disappointed and furious she had cut him out of her thoughts leaving him to live his life of crime in London. The newspaper told how she had not even realised that he had been on that train and bus until a Pauline Everett who had been sharing Colin's flat had found herself pregnant. Angry at his lengthy stay in Newcastle with not even a phone call she had written to Colin at his mother's. The police had launched a search for him only when Pauline told them his involvement in the club protection racket, prostitution and murder of two bar owners.

They also had a scared witness who had seen Colin on the bus but gone past his stop to avoid walking the path at the same time as the boy who had viciously bullied him at school. The search had taken them to Garesfield wood where they had found his body but not his wallet. The missing money swayed the police from the theory of accident to one of murder. The warm weather, rats and maggots had robbed the body of all flesh but it was found that his back was broken and his skull smashed on rocks.

The stir it caused locally came to an early end when the news was pushed off the front pages by the sudden death of Marilyn Monroe. Television showed a multitude of pictures of a beautiful woman who paid for her success with personal happiness. It was easy for Wren to see the sad soul who longed to go home through the eyes of the film star. Perhaps the truth of how she got there would never come out on

Earth. She knew how happy she would be now in her period of rest and reunion before the hard work of revision and choice of a new life.

Spiritually, Colin would have passed through his hard bit, made to feel the pain of every hurt he had inflicted both directly and indirectly. His reincarnation would be quick, his spirit urgently needed to grow and understand.

Wren was dreading the return to school for the final year. She had hated the grammar school Tot had been so proud to send her to. The girls in her class had grown into deodorant wearing women with breasts which had become the main topic of conversation amongst the boys. Wren was stick thin and still wearing ankle socks.

Jeremy had still not appeared. No gossip came through Tot or the other miners. Wren's dreams in sleep were the same right now as she stared through the windows of the classroom screening out the master's voice droning on about the maths she would never understand.

Uncle George was always somewhere in her mind. There was still the strong chance he could be Alessandro but as with Joyce and Jeremy she couldn't be sure. She was like a wasp caught in honey.

It was on such a daydreaming lesson that her mind was dragged back to the boring necessities of this life she had stolen.

'Wren! Wren! Pay attention! Do you want to sit the Civil Service exam or not?'

The English teacher was standing before her with a pile of application forms.

'There's nothing else around here you know unless you want to waste your years at Grammar School to work in a pub or a shop?'

'I want neither Mr. Milburn. I want to be a gardener.'

The class laughed.

'You can be a gardener if you wish Wren but how are you to make a living?'

Wren was as surprised as every-one else at her statement, it had obviously come from the original life plan.

'Don't know sir.'

'You girls think you don't need a career, all you want is a husband and babies, isn't it?'

The boys laughed and sneered and most of the girls wondered what was wrong with being a mother.

'Do you want a Civil Service application form Wren?'

'Yes sir, thank you sir.'

Tot and Ivy were thrilled with the idea of their offspring working for the government. Even Wren's explanation that even if she passed the entrance exam she would go in at the lowest grade possible didn't seem to dampen their pleasure that Wren wouldn't be working in a factory in Newcastle or have to go into domestic service as Ivy had done.

For them she sat and passed.

But her heart wasn't in it. All she wanted to do was grow things but who would pay her for this?

Dressed in the clothes Ivy had ordered from a mail order catalogue taken so she could pay weekly for the grown up facade needed to earn money, Wren went to work at the Ministry of Pensions and Social Security at Longbenton: two buses and fifteen miles away.

The spread out offices were hot and smoky. She was shown the job by a girl who knew what she was doing both with her pen and with every man who glanced at her. There was much excitement about a new computer block that would make their lives easier but at the moment it wasn't perfect and threw out reject sheets of handwriting even a spider would be ashamed of. It was Wren's job to decipher this writing and find the correct details from heavy dusty binders that seemed to have absorbed the smelly airless environment.

It was clear from the energies here that Alessandro was nowhere near the place. Day after day she searched her feelings as she came into contact with many of the thousands of people who worked in this enormous metal windowed sprawl.

She dreamed of fresh air. She longed to get back home to Tot's gardens or the woods and fields still surrounding the ever growing council estate. She missed Joyce miserably. But it was September and the nights were drawing in so that by the time she'd ridden home in cigarette fugged buses it was too late to clear the head stuffed with all the wrong things.

Tot was keen to hear of her new job and sympathised with her need to be outside amongst plants. He'd felt the same all his life but folk had to sacrifice to make a living. At least she had windows and daylight

Ivy growled that she would just have to stick in. They needed the money.

Every day was a torture of imprisonment to both soul and personality. She tried hard to be part of the giggling group of girls enjoying earning their first pay amongst so many keen young men, but she just couldn't connect. Wren was wasting the time she had stolen. She was trapped.

By the time the primroses started to bloom the following spring Wren was heartily sick of airless offices. The winter had bitten into her bones and her happiness. She went to work in the dark and came home to dreary dullness. Now at least the sky was lightening so that she felt part of this world again. The excited promise of spring lifted her mood so that it took her longer to walk to the bus every morning. There was much to see escaping into the sunshine from the winter flattened earth. It was hard to drag herself away from the burgeoning gardens. To give her mind more stimulation she started to go out of the Ministry offices at lunchtimes to walk around the surrounding houses. It was a feast to her mind to noticed new plants in different soil, and mentally redesigned those gardens with no plan or style.

Every second of the weekend was spent in Tot's garden. She had to be careful to leave some precious jobs for him when she began to notice disappointed looks instead of gratitude. His heavy work in the pit took more of his energy these days but he railed against taking the advice of his work mates who were also in their fifties to ease up on life and let the young'uns have their time.

'That rain won't let you into the garden today Wren.' Ivy said handing her a wobbling pile of cereal dishes from the cupboard. 'You can help me bottom the bedrooms if we can get those two up.'

Noelene and Paul had become sullen teenagers who felt bed was the place to be if they weren't at school.

When the rain stopped it felt good to crunch the cinder path as Wren and Tot checked the cabbage seedlings she had puddled in only last night. As she had poured tap water into the dibbed holes before she eased the long and delicate roots into the soil there had been no sign of rain.

Now it was too wet to even touch the garden.

'Go to the store for me will you Wren?' Ivy emerged into the weak sunshine with a purse and note scribbled on a torn envelope. Wren took the string bag, picked up her coat from the hook by the door and tried to feel glad that at least she was outside. It was good to be free of the threat of meeting Alan. He'd gone away. To the Army some said, others reported a youth detention centre. She didn't care as long as he was not walking the same paths as her.

Every garden on the way to the Co-op was checked for growth over the past week.

There was a queue in the store. People had been waiting for the rain to dry up before they got in a weekend's shopping. It would be ages before her turn, the light would fade. The gossip around her dulled as she began to read the notices stuck up on the counters and walls.

Broken biscuits were only 3d a pound, corned beef had a penny off and the Newcastle choir was giving a concert at the City Hall. Who cared!

Below the professionally printed notices there was a hand written note about a jumble sale in the Welfare Hall. Boredom began robbing her of her senses. The nagging wheel of questioning on which Jeremy, George and Joyce spun, reeled through her brain. It had to be stopped. She read the notice board one more time but again and again her eyes were drawn to the notice on the Jumble Sale. The gossip between the shop assistants and the customer doubled the time it would have taken if they had any idea of what efficiency was. The desire to break free was too much. Wren looked at the list in her hand. There was nothing fresh that the store would run out of if she came back later.

It was only a little detour to the hall. The draw of a jumble sale had always been the books but there was a feeling about this one. Perhaps there would be some-one she would meet.

She felt the pleasure of the two women behind her as she left her place in the queue enabling them to move up one place nearer the glass topped biscuit tins lining the serving counter.

It cost her tuppence to get into the Jumble sale. As soon as the stench of the second hand clothes hit her nostrils it was clear she had read too much into the compulsion to come here. Three woman volunteers were fussily tidying with deft hands as their self-important feet squeaked soles on polished wood. Chair leg rubber squealed about its involuntary grab towards two tired ladies clinging cast off clothes to them as they bent over the white elephant stall clattering cups and saucers in a vain hope that they might match. The echo seared even louder to her brain than the reeking poverty.

Wren watched one of them sit without breaking her concentration in finding the bargain of the year. The book bench had been picked over and the remains were being packed back into cardboard boxes. As Wren made her way over to the trestle table it was as if all the Beano annuals and dog eared encyclopaedias faded away because only one publication seemed visible to her. A dull green, hard book with black writing and edging drew her towards it. The energies emanating from this book were different to anything else in this Welfare Hall. 'The Garden of Ignorance' by Marion Cran was in her hands. It had been written in 1910. Black and white photos of old fashion gardens and girls in bonnets flicked over to pages entitled 'Herbs and the Sundial'. 'The Rose Garden' and 'Cats'. Some-one had scribbled '6d' in pencil on the leaf.

Trembling hands showed that there was more to her need for this find than gardening. Through her grip she felt the energies of every-one who had read this book. No-one but her knew that it was eyes of the same colours that last read these very pages. A painful, searing vision of Mr. Farraige and a shamefully pregnant girl talking nervously through an open window numbed her physical actions so that she paid for the book not hearing the glib comment from the jumble sale helper.

The queue had reduced so that Wren was home in the same time as if she'd wasted her life away waiting for bacon to be sliced and gossip to be repeated. Her thoughts never strayed from the book and now on her bed she began to feast on the reasons it meant so much to her.

Before she was half way through she knew exactly what she had to do.

CHAPTER TWENTY NINE

The book was devoured, re-read, examined and totally digested. It had to be.

This was the biggest clue she'd had so far in this wrong life. It sang to her!

The spell it cast on the mind of Wren so needing this direction, was delicious. It would lead her into a new life and she was oh so sure to new people, one of whom would be Alessandro.

This absolute certainty never left her for one word. It was right for two reasons. Both Wren and the life she had stolen would be fulfilled. She could feel the race ahead would be exciting, furious and dangerous. But this much she knew. She would find Alessandro. This direction would lead her to him whether or not she had already met him.

It was a strange feeling to be so certain. The book had put her on a new energy level where those she met would show their true spirit for love of nature, animals and people.

Everything Alessandro always was.

'It's a wonderful book pet.' Tot placed the weight back into her hands before he knocked his pipe out into the fire. It had taken him all week to read 'The Garden of Ignorance'. He had no clue that this book had been held and read just as deliciously by the first daughter he had loved and never mentioned. His mind was full of June when he was digging in the dark mine, when he was just about to sleep and as soon as he woke from searing dreams of her. He saw her in every flower bud and heard her in every birdsong. His heart broke anew every day but June was never talked about so that the myth of the Stoker family was kept. Tot and Ivy thought none of the children knew the truth about Wren's birth.

Each time Wren was in the house when he was at work she took out the torn bit of Daily Herald he used as a bookmark and savoured the bit he'd just read. How many times had he said she was his right hand girl in his little garden? She warmed at sharing these new ways with him in the sun.

'You two and your blooming books! You'd be better putting your time to use helping me clean me brasses!' Ivy, tight with holding it all together, snapped out the words.

'Everybody's different Ivy.' Tot took up a clean rag from the table spread with candlesticks, a brass bowl and two thin ash trays. These were Ivy's treasures. The pair of candlesticks had never seen wax nor the bowl fruit and no-one dared to put out a cigarette in something she had saved so hard to own. He hooked his rag covered finger round the many contours of a candlestick back and forth until it shone. Wren could see he was lost in the same world she was.

'Don't wear it away man!' Ivy glared at the blackening rag. 'And you, get those eggs scrambled and the toast on those two will be in soon shouting their hunger!'

As she broke eggs into an enamel pan Wren smiled out of the kitchen window. She could see the cold frame where she and Tot had started off their brassica seedlings and the newly dug rows for the potatoes that were chitting in the dark wash house. June's Forget-Me-Nots he'd sown on Jan's grave were vibrant. This garden was too small. There was a whole world to cultivate, a whole world in which to search for Alessandro. Now she had her key.

The fact that early sun lit her eyes as she walked to the bus stop at 7.15 the next Monday morning didn't make it any easier to head towards a stuffy office full of nice enough girls who talked only of Coty L'Amaint perfume, Max Factor panstick and whether they preferred mods' or rockers' style clothing. Wren owned none of these having saved most of her share of her wages spending only a little on seeds from catalogues showing varieties of peas, parsnips and annual flowers that Tot had never even heard of.

'Flamin' 'eck!' The sound came from a woman in the last garden she passed on the estate. She was finding it hard to bend over her cushion-like middle. 'Oops sorry! Didn't think many would be around this early to hear me swear. Bloody roses! Oh damn! I said Bloody!'

Wren laughed.

'Oh there I go again.' She widened tired brown eyes set in a considerate, busy face.

Wren looked at the woman's rag wrapped hands as she pulled at the base of a woody old rosebush.

'What are you trying to do?'

'This rose is past it. My Jim planted it when we first moved here and he was fit. But it hardly flowered last year and it's what he sees when he looks out of his window. He wheezes now instead of weeding.' she tapped her chest. 'Pneumoconiosis! Colliery won't give him a penny!'

'You need a spade and fork to loosen the roots.'

'I 'aven't got time for that. He'll be up later and I have to be off to me cleaning job. I wanted the new bush in so that he'd get a nice surprise when he was having his breakfast. He needs to 'ave something to look forward to all spring.'

'Well you definitely need a spade if you are planting and what about all these weeds. They'll smother the new rose just like they did the old one no matter how much feeding you do.'

'Feeding?'

Wren smiled knowingly. 'Would you like me to do it?'

'Would you? Oh I'm not a gardener. Jim said this plot were too small when we moved in here, now it seems like a whole country overgrown with things I don't understand and never will.'

'It's a tiny garden really.'

'Oh you must think old Lil a right 'nana. We do have tools but God knows how many spiders have spun webs around them by now.'

As Wren followed Lil she tried to keep her eyes off the wobbling bottom by watching even more greyish fair strands escaping from half a dozen hair clips failing their job. The coal house proved her right about the cobwebs.

She knew she'd have missed her bus by now. It felt wonderful.

As she chose the fork and spade she could feel the silkiness of the wood where many years of handling had worn it smooth. What a goldmine this garden was. Her eyes caught every

Over-grown shrub and each self-seeded annual. This garden had been laid with real love of nature but now needed weeks of work.

'Have you got time for this me dearie? Looks like you were off to catch a bus or summit.'

'Nowhere important!' her answer felt so right. Going to the Ministry of Social Security and Pensions was no longer important in her life.

'But you can't be ripping those lovely clean clothes now can you?'

Lil disappeared into the house leaving Wren to smile at a robin who had begun to sing in a mock orange blossom bush. He knew that a spade meant the turning of soil and plenty of worms for the taking.

Lil reappeared carrying an old cross-over pinafore and some old Wellingtons; Wren could see were two sizes too big for her.

'Are you sure you have the time for this? I must be off, Sir Saul will be wondering where I am. Don't worry about disturbing Jim.' she yanked a thumb at the drawn curtains of an upstairs window, 'He'll be dead to the world all morning, spent last night heaving his guts out poor lamb.'

Wren was alone with the robin. It took half an hour to dig out the vicious old rose and twenty minutes to rummage around the cobwebs for a damp box of bone meal she hoped would have enough energy to feed the roots of the new one. Whilst the pot of all Lil's dreams soaked in an enamel bucket Wren attacked the weeds, carefully digging and pulling around the struggling violets and spotted leaves of blue and pink Lungwort.

The new rose was only just shooting red tender leaves promising something spectacular this June. Right now it didn't give much to a spring garden especially one newly cleared leaving new shoots of perennials pale and shy to light. Wren was lost in horticultural ecstasy when a wheezy voice pierced her peace.

'By lass. I don't know who you are but you surely deserve this for all your efforts.'

The robin flew off leaving Wren turning to see a man with a pyjama cord tied tightly around his hollow chest. The striped and crumpled night wear seemed as if it had once fitted over a substantial girth and muscles.

He gave a cough filled with rattling phlegm and suffering. This grey, drawn man was holding out a mug of tea and a plate groaning beneath a doorstep of a bacon sandwich. Wren was too hungry to spend too much time thinking of how much wheezing and coughing the bread had been subjected to before it reached her.

Tomato sauce oozed onto her soil caked hands. 'Is this a late breakfast or an early dinner?' Her words struggled out through yielding white bread softened by eager saliva.

'Don't know! Don't care! I eat when I'm able and thank God that I can.' His breathing was laboured and unproductive. He disappeared indoors and came out with his own half loaf and quarter pig. He had been rounder, his baggy face said that, and his big mouth and goodness lit eyes that made him ugly-handsome. Now he looked as thin and frayed as old rope. Two people passed as Wren in pinafore and oversized wellies sat on the garden wall of the council house swilling tea with a pyjama clad man.

It struck Wren as ridiculous but she had never been happier.

Later, when green soap had removed all evidence that she had not spent the day at her desk, Wren found a telephone box and rang her Executive Officer at work to book a day's leave so that she wouldn't lose that day's pay.

Alone in her bedroom that night she knew her life had changed as she counted out her savings. This would take careful planning. When it was dark she hid her old clothes behind the brick pillar that held the gate that separated the Stoker family from the rest of the estate. Her heart thumped as she picked the damp bundle up next morning and headed straight for Jim and Lil's; she knew she'd never go back to work; ever. This was the only work she wanted to do now. It always had been. The fact that she didn't get paid was a small annoyance but one she hoped would solve itself with the sureness that being on the life's right path always did.

She knew it would lead to Allesandro.

Jim had let the back garden get into an even greater state than the front; Wren loved it. It took all week. On Thursday, from her envelope of savings hidden behind a pile of books in her room she took £3 to give to

Ivy for her board. She knew exactly how long this charade could continue.

'You look much more tired than usual these days pet.' Tot spoke his gentle concern as Wren woke from the sleep she hadn't known she was taking during 'Top of the Pops'.

'You missed those Beatles again, shaking their heads about and 'Yeah, Yeah-ing' all over the place. Its lack of fresh air probably making you so exhausted, you'll have to get into the garden more. I'll make you some Ovaltine and bring it up to you.'

Ivy looked up from her knitting to bore her eyes into Wren. The discomfort gave Wren the energy to push herself up from the chair. As she passed Ivy she felt a grab to her wrist.

'You've been eating more lately too.' She tightened her grip. 'You've not being seeing too much of any boys at that fancy office of yours have you?'

'No!' The shock of what lay behind her hissed suspicion made even this one word seem guilty.

'Cos it would kill your da'. You know that don't you?'

Tot came in then with a mug and a digestive biscuit on a tray. He understood both these women in his life so the heavy atmosphere didn't escape him. He followed Wren up stairs and put the tray onto the bedside cabinet.

'You reading this again?' He had to pick up 'The Garden of Ignorance.' to place the tray.

'It teaches me so much, dad.'

Determinedly he laid the book onto the bed and she felt her wrists taken for the second time that evening. This time the grip was gentle.

'You would come to me for help if anything bad was happening in your life wouldn't you chicken?'

His concerned eyes flicked backwards and forwards as they swept hers for truth.

'cos you know I can't fix anything that I don't know is happening.'

She knew what lay behind his anguished eyes and wish she could ease the pain he thought was a secret.

'There are no boys in my life dad. I'm very happy at the moment. You would be the first one I'd come to if I couldn't handle something. You always have been.'

He said goodnight then the door closed behind him. As his kiss faded from her forehead her confidence went with it.

She had only one more day's work at Jim's. After that she had nowhere to go.

The spring sunshine and exhilarating dawn chorus lifted her spirits as she picked up the parcel of gardening clothes from behind the toolbox in the coalhouse. She had made the right decision. She knew how her heart would sink if she had to get on a bus to spend the whole day amongst dusty binders and chain smokers.

Instead she would feel the sunshine on her back and the soil between her fingers. Every bird seemed to be singing its heart out in the ten minutes it took to reach Jim and Lil's. Her robin was already sitting on the big fork handle she'd left shoved into the last bit of neglected compost heap she was distributing.

The back door slammed in the April breeze?

'Damn and blast!'

Lil emerged still fastening her blouse. 'Ooh! Pardon me French, pet. I've not got a minute to spare. There's such a rush on at the big house. Sir Saul has a shooting party coming up, he wants all the curtains cleaned, the carpets changed an' I have to wash all the crystal.....'

Lil tried vainly to straighten the crumpled skirt she'd dropped to the floor in exhaustion the night before. As she turned the corner to the front path she threw words over her shoulder throwing more hair out of the grips.

'Oh an' he wants to see you an' all!'

'Me? What for?'

Lil lifted her shoulders and spread her hands in a 'search me' kind of way before allowing the metal to clang behind her.

It was five to twelve before Jim emerged with two mugs of tea and a plate of banana sandwiches.

She stretched her mouth around the familiar chunky cut bread and didn't speak until she felt her blood sugar rise enough.

'You look well today Jim.' she said trying to keep her eyes off the band of hair usually plastered across his bald pate but now flopping towards his shoulder in the breeze.

'Aye well, funnily enough the busier Lil is at the big house the more I have to do here and it makes me feel better.' He lifted his sandwich towards her. 'Don't you think me cookin's improving?'

They both laughed but he looked excited when he told her of the stew he'd done last night and the corned beef patties he was planning for tea tonight.

'Mind you I'm a bit restricted 'cos me lungs won't take me to the shops so I'm stuck with what's here. But that's part of the fun. I'm going for Yorkshire puddings on Sunday. She's been asked to work all weekend yu' know.'

'Yes, she said how busy she was.'

He clinked the empty mugs together; tossed the crumbs and too thick bits of crust onto the tiny square of grass he optimistically called a lawn.

'Oh you've seen her? She was off early; did she give you your message?'

'Well sort of. She said Sir Saul wanted to see me but that's all.'

'Bugger! She's in such a tizz what with those important folks coming from London and Leeds for the shoot. And it's not till October!'

'Shoot?'

'Oh aye. The best pheasant this side of Yorkshire Moors.'

'Ohh...I couldn't see any-one who breeds creatures to murder.'

Jim looked at her shocked face.

'It's a hard world you know and you can't always live by your principles. Keep your appointment, I have a feeling you won't be sorry.'

'Appointment? What appointment? What for?'

'Didn't Lil tell you? You have to be at Amblin Hall at two to meet 'is Lordship in the Orangery.'

'What Orangery? I don't even know where Amblin Hall is never mind what an Orangery is!'

He laughed and scraped towards the ground in an exaggerated bow.

'Well M'Lady I'm buggered if I know what them toffs do in an Orangery but I can tell you how to get to Amblin Hall, the quick way mind. Me and Lil did all w' courtin' round them woods hiding from gamekeepers and avoiding ant hills.'

Wren blushed. She knew exactly what he meant but the sixteen year old body she was in didn't.

The map Jim had drawn on the back of his football pools envelope took Wren into woods she could tell were managed. Piles of pine trunks awaited transport and she could see where they had been cut from rows and rows of trees planted for their wood not their beauty. It was incredible to her that she had never ventured here before. It seemed as if these woods had just sprung up suddenly when she had looked for them. But of course she had not known how to ignore the 'Trespassers will be prosecuted' signs if she'd not had Jim's map. Neither had she had a request to go here through the very dense coppiced willow and hazel. It must have been a long time ago that any courting went on here.

It was the voices that told her she was near the house. Newly sprouting bluebells kept her gaze to the ground; there was no way she could stand on any one of their hopes. The sun stung her gloom widened pupils just as she came to a barbed wire fence. Her hand went to her brow to shade enough of her face to see where she was. The Corinthian pillars which held up the front of the house also half hid two men talking as they held broken guns by their sides. Two spaniels and a golden retriever jerked their noses towards her. One of the spaniels yapped.

'All right, all right Chummy I know you are impatient! Come on we have an appointment.' The man who had spoken stepped back towards the circle of straggly, slug attacked pansies struggling through tired grass and weeds surrounding an enormous weeping ash still awaiting its leaves to clothe its gracious skeleton after winter. As he turned to rub the dogs ears between his fingers Wren felt her heart stop. She knew this man. Knew his energy well. His broad shoulders were covered by a well cut tweed jacket which toned beautifully with the long moleskin trousers tucked into riding boots. He was much taller than the other man who doffed his cap before clicking his tongue bringing one of the spaniels and the retriever to his side before they walked down the long chestnut lined drive.

The love shone from this man to his dogs who bounded to his side as he turned to blindly face Wren.

It was a beautiful face which held the same familiarity that Uncle George, Jeremy and Joyce had. Blood whacked into her ears and she swayed.

This Sir Saul was special. He could certainly be Alessandro. She felt her female body surge with what she knew was desire. It was the same desire that had embroiled her and Alessandro in passion time after time in many lives. She'd know that feeling anywhere.

As her knees weakened she watched the dogs dash off to the other side of the house and the man stride out his long legs to follow them.

She knew now why she was here. The request though, was still a mystery.

It took a few moments to gather her thoughts enough to look at the map which certainly hadn't taken her to the front of the biggest house she had ever seen. The back door was where she'd been guided.

She found the gate leading to what she knew must be the kitchen because of dishes rattling against a porcelain sink. She heard 'One enchanted evenin' you will see a stranger, you will see a stranger across a crowded room...' being sung by the none-too gentle creature who was washing up. She smiled as she approached who she knew for certain would be Lil.

'Not exactly Beatles or Stones is it.' Wren said to the back rounded over a large pan and Brillo pad.

'Oh! You made me jump!'

The shock fell to a smile as Lil dried her hands on a spotless tea towel.

'I was worried I hadn't given you that message properly this mornin'. I was in such a rush to do Sir's breakfast before he gets the grumps.'

Wren thought Sir Saul looked strong enough to get his own breakfast and it would serve him right to be grumpy if he didn't.

'Well you're here and he's looking forward to meeting you. You're just in time to go with me when I take his coffee in.' Lil jerked her thumb to a tray laid with beautiful delicate china and a lidless pot. She poured steaming water from the kettle onto the grounds releasing an aroma not at all like the coffee Tot drank from the store, replaced the lid then took a good look at Wren.

'Tidy your hair pet. He's a good looking man and likes others to try their best an' all. Although he's given up wi' me like!' She laughed as she picked up the tray.

'But why does he want to see me Lil?'

'Cos I told him how special you was!'

'What?'

Wren hadn't heard the delicate clunk of a silver lid being placed into such grandness before but the wonder couldn't cut through her absolute certainty about the true identity of the man she was just about to meet. Reckless need delivered unsustainable euphoria.

She was aware of Lil's arms stretching with the weight of the tray and smiling at how this same woman delivered a cheap cup and saucer with a biscuit on the side to her own man.

This man was special, a fact which was confirmed by the hit of energies as she opened the door for his housekeeper. Every one of Wren's senses wakened, shot around the room and sped back to her loaded with familiar awareness.

Two spaniels gave glad yelps of welcome but were ordered back to the heels of the man sitting hidden in the winged chair facing open French doors into a glass roofed conservatory filled with huge plants, some were dying and others were without hope.

'Your coffee Sir Saul.' said Lil in her poshest voice. 'And the young lass I told you about.'

Wren tried to rein in the excitement from her features so that Lil wouldn't know, but pride was the only emotion on Lil's face as she waved her hands to secretly tell Wren to stand by the huge paper strewn desk.

'Thank you Lillian. That will be all.'

Such a rich voice.

Wren worked furiously on holding in the emotions she knew would ooze from her soul the moment he turned to her. If this was Alessandro there could be such an energy surge that it could make them both ill.

'Come on then puppies let's get our visitor some refreshment.'

Well-polished boots met Indian rugs to lever up the man she had come to Earth to find.

The hair seemed fluffier than she had seen this morning and the body stiffer. As soon as the man turned she could see that it was not the one she had expected. Disappointment seared into her brain yet did nothing to dissipate the energies between these two people.

He felt it.

He pulled crisp blue cuffs out of the brown and black tweed jacket before straightening his silk tie with manicured fingers.

His warmly lined face held the smile he'd meant. Wonder and puzzlement crossed his features, narrowed his eyes. Then a better smile than he'd ever given any-one in his entire seventy six years lit his whole being.

'Have we met before?'

'No Sir, we haven't.'

But she knew they had.

CHAPTER THIRTY

It took all of the coffee ritual for Wren to find her voice.

As he poured, Sir Saul's eyes flicked intermittently on the shocked face of Wren. She could tell he was searching deep into his memory to find out why this girl with hair still pulled back into a pony tail when all others of her age were copying Twiggy or Dusty Springfield, was so familiar to him.

Wren knew.

She spluttered at the dark strong drink. This was strange coffee. So different to the milky pale stuff they had at home. He smiled at her.

'You're a tea person I suppose. Don't go in for them new-fangled coffee bars in Newcastle then; what?'

Their eyes locked in silent search. Only Wren could bring up the memory. She wondered if she would ever share with him the startling truth.

It was enough that he took to her; it was all his soul could deal with at this point in his life. Their past was not relevant to him now; it would only cloud his purpose.

As he drank, drawn by the sheer power of his feelings for her, Wren wondered who the younger man she thought to be Sir Saul really was. Perhaps some-one employed on the land. She could never ask about the man who had set her pulses racing. She was still hoarding the memory of his effect on her. Perhaps she'd see him around.

Wren thought how pretty the tinkle of his empty cup sounded when he replaced it in his saucer. She did the same but felt embarrassed about the cup being three quarters full.

He smiled. 'Did Lillian tell you why I wanted to see you?'

'No.' anything else would only prolong her agony.

'Rushing I suppose. Poor woman, always trying to appear so full of beans when really she is worn out with work and her sick husband.' It wasn't a smile that came to his face but a soft light of understanding that was close to admiration.

'She told me what a good gardener you were. I was so impressed at a young lady like you setting up her own business that I thought you could help me.'

'What?'

'You mean pardon?'

'Yes...pardon.'

'Not a secret is it? I know you young'uns like to be hip these days; all mods and rockers. None of them like to get their hands dirty I'll bet.'

She self-consciously tucked her fists into her arm pits.

'No need to be ashamed about the tools of the trade my dear. I respect some-one who makes a living from the land. No reason why gardening should only be for old men and rich ladies what!'

'But I ....'

He held up a hand to stop her.

'No need to explain. Digging for victory has taken a bit of the pleasure out of flowers for most of England but I admire you for helping to put it back.'

Wren was torn between stopping him right there to explain the misunderstanding and protecting Lil's integrity.

He pulled himself up from the desk to amble over to where the dogs had obediently stayed.

'Here.' He waved her over and the dogs' tails wagged so that nothing could stop her rubbing their ears and making soft sounds of greeting. The eye contact they made was like a sword to her heart. Soft brown pools of dog adoration bled a thousand memories from her. Jan, dear Jan how I miss you, she thought. The dogs read her mind and yelped closer to her pain, they wanted to help. All they could do was lick her hands and face but she knew they understood.

'Ah ha! An animal lover to boot eh! Bracken and Clover like you. Well you'll do for me.'

'Do what?'

'My garden and this.'

She looked where he spread his arms.

'This is the pride and joy of Amblin Hall or rather it was when my wife was alive. It needs love and knowledge of which I have neither.'

The dogs had sniffed almost all of Wren's shins as they reached the outside door of the Orangery.

'Have you restored an Orangery before?'

Wren gazed around in the extra warmth the glass gave the sun. 'I don't even know what an Orangery is!'

He laughed. 'Well I suppose your age is against you there but good for your CV what?'

Wren didn't know what a CV was either but had no doubt that life would show her. He picked up crisp leaves still hanging onto an almost dead spiky plant.

'I've rather lost the plot here also. It's been three years and I only just feel as if I have woken up to the world. I've organised a shooting party in October and I want the garden perfect by then.'

She followed his gaze outside.

Gravel was interrupted by patchy grass. Tired daffodils, most of them blind, pushed half-heartedly through scrubby perennials and long dried corpses of once vibrant annuals. Ancient oak, horse chestnut and elm spread out and along pointing the way to woodland and meadow.

'Can you do it Wren? Can you make the birds sing in my garden once more? Somehow I instinctively know you can.'

It would have been impossible for anyone not to feel his pain and longing for the time when his wife bloomed with his garden. Wren knew that the birds would sing even louder in an unkempt garden but that he had simply not heard them through his sorrow.

'But it's enormous!'

'Yes two hundred acres!' He watched her pale. 'But only four are garden.'

'Only four?'

Her irony showed in her voice.

'Well I only want a bit at a time; starting with the entrance circle and herbaceous avenues that my guests will see as they approach the house.'

He turned his gaze towards her so suddenly that she hoped she'd turned her look of fear to one of concentration.

'How many staff do you have?'

'Staff?'

'Well labourers I suppose you call them at your company, Garden Angel.'

This was quite enough. It was one thing Lil building her up to get work but creating a business with a name she'd never even heard.

'Sir Saul. I think you should know that there has been a slight misunderstanding. I have no staff, er..labourers.'

'His eye brows shot up. 'I say; you do all the work yourself? I'm even more impressed. Never mind Smith will help you, plenty of muscle going there. Not enough to do since I gave up the hunt. Do him good to bend his back.'

The old man, glowing, rubbed his hands together. 'Well now that's sorted...'

'I'm afraid it's not...'

'Ah ha! Good business brain as well as flair and experience eh? Money. How do you want it? Price for the job or hourly? What do you usually do?'

'I don't usually do anything I...'

'Ok then. Hourly it is 12/6 take it or leave it.'

'12/6!' she repeated thinking how long it took her to earn that much in an office.

'Oh all right. Lillian told me how hard you work and you are wonderfully creative and I suppose one must pay for expertise. 14/-!'

To prevent further discussion he put a hand to her back and steered her to the door.

'Just go and do what you want. All I ask is that my garden is as splendid as it can possibly be for my shoot.'

He took her hand and turned it over tracing his fingers over the blisters made by Lil and Jim's tools.

'I like you and trust you. Feel like I have known you forever and the dogs never get it wrong.' He put his left hand into his breast pocket and took out an envelope.

'As Lil so rightly pointed out you will need money for plants and stuff.'

He rang a little crystal bell from the table outside his study door and Lil came bustling up drying her hands on her apron. Nothing was said but Lil averted her eyes from Wren's.

'Did it work?' She said pouring freshly brewed tea from a china pot at the kitchen table.

'What?'

'My plan; did it work?'

'But Lil some of it wasn't true and I have this fat envelope of money…'

Lil looked a little disappointed. 'But you can do the job, I know you can, so he'll get what he wants and so what if I fibbed a bit...'

'A bit!'

'Yes ok, more than a bit but, well you are good.'

'Yes on council house size back gardens; but this!'

'You can do it and I know you must be getting short of money so...'

A sigh plunged Wren into a chair beside a steaming cup.

'You're right about that but 'Garden Angel!'

Lil laughed. 'It came to me in a flash and when I said it to him he liked it. Well that's surely what you've been to me an' Jim, and you do have a sort of angelic quality about you, you know. Don't you think it sounds grand?'

'Too grand but I suppose I'm stuck with it now.'

'Here,' she laughed pushing the cup towards Wren. 'Let's celebrate with a nice cup of tea, I knew you wouldn't like that tar the toffs call coffee.'

Left standing on stable yard cobbles at the open door of a huge barn, Wren waved her thanks to Lil who dashed off muttering about pastry and pie for supper.

She felt as if she'd been dropped into the sea from the air and she had to learn to swim; but in which direction?

'Oi!'

Wren turned towards the gruffness.

'Get out of it you!'

A man of about forty with weather whisked hair springing from a greasy cap waved a whip towards Wren. He had a face on which a sulk felt comfy.

'I beg your pardon.' she said as he trounced near enough to deepen his sneer.

'Who the bloody hell do you think you are wandering around here? Its private property you know. Bugger off!' He yanked a dirty fist and thumb towards the wood.

His angry closeness allowed Wren to see he had parted with his tooth brush at the same time as his manners. Perhaps he'd never had either.

'I know who I am and I have a perfect right to be here thank you.'

'Ohhh; uppity an'all! Well we'll see what perfect right you have when I escort you off Sir's land after I meet the new gardener. Bloody hell, where is he?'

'Here.' She smiled but he was too busy with his anger to see.

'What? Where?'

'Here! I'm the new gardener.'

He beat the side of his trousers rapidly with the leather whip.

'I'm not working with a flamin' female. You're nowt but a lass and a skinny one at that.'

'As far as you are concerned I am a gardener. Now I want to get on.'

'Not without me you don't.' he hated having to say that.

Dread sunk into her brain. Surely this is not the man Sir Saul said would help her.

'You're Smith?'

'Aye and I'm no flamin' gardener either. I'll dig your muck and wheel your barrows but I'm not getting' involved in pansies and gladioli so you can get that straight right now.'

'So you agree to work with me then?'

'So long as you remember it is 'with' not 'for'. Got no choice with a naggin' wife and a tied cottage 'ave I?'

Wren fought with the idea to turn down Sir Saul, there'd be no peace with this man around, but there'd be no money either and Ivy wouldn't take kindly to a cut of three pounds a week. 'I don't need you today Smith, I'm just at the thinking and planning stage.'

'Oh, ladi bloody dah! That's a good one! Getting paid for daydreaming are you!' he looked pleased to be released from her company but walked insultingly around her before leaving.

'You don't look strong enough to be a gardener. Nice arse though.'

He walked towards a bit of the estate he seemed so familiar with and Wren had yet to see. She needed him unfortunately. But she tried to put her fear behind her. If only he knew how she'd already dealt with someone even more revolting than him, he'd be as meek as a lamb.

A gift and a pain in one day. How life was cruel. But she accepted both willingly as she knew that joy and pain gave learning in equal measure. She realised the real reason she was here had been just a glimpse on her arrival. Alessandro had to be here somewhere.

Alessandro.

She wouldn't let the thought of Smith spoil today. It was early May and she had to get on to get this place looking splendid for October and the toffs in tweed.

Already running through her head were the things that would be out in October. Ice Plant and Dahlias if there hadn't been an early frost. She had to get plenty of Chrysanthemums and Michaelmas daisies.

Her heart sank. These well-known flowers were all very well for miners' and council house gardens where they stood caned and erect mirroring the fierce pride of the working man. She knew they were pitifully inadequate for a garden like this. Was there enough time to get some Nerine bulbs in? She'd get lots of early autumn colour in the herbaceous and follow on for spring. She'd not been asked to do more than lick this garden into shape for the shoot but nature would have to be helped along for after that too. She made a mental list of all the seeds she could gather from Tot's garden and now Jim and Lil's in September.

The caw of pheasants lifted from the surrounding woodlands to bring her back to reality. Crunchy gravel accompanied her on her inspection. This had been a great garden once. She peered and pushed back vigorously spreading weeds to identify hundreds of crowns and hefty buds that she could lift and would spread once they were set free from neglect. There were plants here that she'd never seen before. It would be a night pouring over Percy Thrower's books and 'The Practical Gardener'. There was a sense of disappointment that she couldn't share her excitement with Tot. But he'd be heartbroken that she'd given up years of security and the chance to dress nice for work bending her back and getting dirty which is exactly how he described his years in the pit. At least she'd not be in the dark. The sun came from behind a fat cloud then as if to encourage her. Wrens twittered their warning of danger as she approached the shrubbery. They were quiet when they recognised her and sang a sweet welcome to pledge their support and company.

It was later than usual when she collected her office clothes from Lil's coal house. After she'd changed she took three pounds from the plant money then shoved the rest back into the envelope which she rolled in the centre of her gardening clothes. It was always tense getting into the wash house to hide her bundle before any-one saw her. But Ivy was pouring fat from the grill pan into the chip pan to get the beef dripping to bulk out enough to fry the pile of chipped potatoes she had resting in a clean tea towel.

'Hello mam,' she said flatly 'here's my keep.' She put the three pound notes down on the bench above the drawer where Ivy kept her purse. The step taken to walk straight past and into the front room to where she could hear the telly blaring, was stopped by Ivy.

'Just a minute my girl.' She plunged the grill pan beneath soapy water in the sink.

'Have you got a lad?'

The words were said six inches from her face so that no nuance of the reply could escape.

'What?'

'Are you courtin'?' The words nipped out and bit into their target.

Wren was shocked by the question.

'No!'

'Well you are often late home and you look especially shifty tonight!' The words were tame compared to the deep search of Ivy's eyes. 'If you do anything to bring further pain to this family I will yark your arse so hard.....'

Tot came in from the garden and plunged his dirty hands into the sink.

'Ah! My favourite Civil Servant back from a hard day at the office.' he called offering his face over his shoulder for the kiss he got every time he saw her.

Ivy flung her fury towards him.

'You can wash that pan as you have now sullied the water with your muck! Did you think I had filled up the sink for you?'

Tot did as he was ordered; he wanted no mood making the children's and his favourite crispy, golden brown 'mammy's chips' stick in his throat

To elicit Tot's help and enthusiasm Wren asked if she could have a patch to make into an October garden. He fell upon the idea with enthusiasm and began sending for catalogues on Chrysanthemums and Dahlias.

Marion Cran's book 'The Garden of Ignorance' had a chapter on 'Lawns- the Autumn Garden', and reminded Wren of something she never thought she'd have to chance to achieve; a croquet lawn.

Oh this would impress house guests even if the weather did not allow them to play.

She took all of Tot's catalogues up to bed and wrote out an order putting Amblin Hall as the address. It felt wonderful, almost as if it was her address. She'd get the postal orders in the morning. It was then when she realised what a tangled web she was weaving. There was no way that Mrs Grahame at the post office would not ask why she was wanting such a large sum. There was even less chance that she wouldn't chatter about it to Ivy when she collected her family allowance.

Lil had set her up for this and she'd have to help out. She'd enjoy spinning a line to the post mistress who made it her business to know everything.

She fell into bed exhausted from excitement and apprehension. Sleep couldn't enter a brain full of seedlings, Orangeries and constant replays of a tall young man with a spaniel at his heels.

How long before the garden delivered him?

CHAPTER THIRTY ONE

When the letter came from Uncle George that Saturday it remained unopened for hours.

Usually the envelope was ripped open, the stamp carefully torn out and the contents devoured by a girl longing to find just one tiny clue that the man who had meant so much to her before he left for Spain was the reason Wren was here on Earth.

As she talked to Tot less and less about her work at the Ministry and more about gardening she knew he thought she wasn't happy there. Any thoughts Ivy seemed to have were alleviated each Thursday night when she had three pound notes left on the bench above the drawer where she secreted her purse.

With blood so full of spring and a mind taken over by nature such a distraction might have been tolerated but a new possibility of Alessandro had been thrown in her path of life. How she wished she had the clarity of recognition the hard work of many lives had given her. It was so frustrating! Even now at sixteen she was becoming more the life she had stolen.

When Wren had gone to work next morning wearing a pale pink lipstick and her hair scooped into a French pleat instead of swinging in its usual pony tail, Ivy knew she was up to something.

She had a lad. That would be stopped for certain.

The walk through the fields and woods sincerely alive with energy lifted her so high she felt she could reach out for her true home. The colours were surely borrowed from there. The sky turned from softly bruised purples through soft lavenders, rosy pinks then opal- turquoise. All the while the dawn chorus built as each bird tried to undo the last. Stunning blue that went on forever started the gentle fluttering of wings as the day's search for slugs, buds and insects started. Truly this was from God. How many saw, how many knew?

Wren started each day at Amblin Hall with a search of the energies. Had he been? Had she missed him? That young man certainly never went anywhere without leaving a tantalising whiff of his being. Her thoughts slid despairingly muddled, he was the only thing she wanted to think about. There was no feel of him whatsoever. Wren dared ask no-one about him. Embarrassment of what others might read into her enquiries sent a flare of dread over any opportunity. Lil would certainly rib her, reducing any interaction to giggles and gossip.

What if he never came back?

It was a promising late May morning when the peaceful energies of the garden stirred. She was standing in the centre of the driveway looking towards the house when the power of a presence she had been mildly aware of for weeks vibrated onto her own level. Smith had started to dig out the herbaceous border on the East. Wren was furious to see that along with the weeds he had dug up every tulip, daffodil and muscari bulb that had been the only colour on offer. Her instructions had been to lift every tired clump of plant and leave them to one side to be accessed, divided and replanted removing the couch grass and nettles as he did. This is what came of using some-one not sensitive to gardens and nature. Everything Smith did was begrudging. Each spade he thrust into the ground was callous, every action uncaring. This was a man who thought he was working beneath him and showed it; yet she could do nothing but accept what Sir Saul had intended to be a help. Early attempts at opening his sensitivities had proved that he hadn't any. He was doing this to keep his cottage and his wage. Nothing could persuade him that a girl with ideas above her station was worth engaging in conversation with. Sometimes she knew he hadn't even listened.

Wren's devastation on looking at the wasted life was palpable. The flowers and stems had wilted in the early morning sun. The daffodils cruelly robbed of their last few days and all replenishment the leaves would give for future years lay with tulips torn from the earth before they could show off their waxy colours.

Her pain and anger swelled to twice the capacity she was able to contain. As it oozed from her it was touched and she knew, she wasn't alone.

'I planted every-one of those early bulbs.'

These were not words that came to Wren's brain but to a level she was elated to exercise.

The light whitened allowing Wren to feel energy raised in spirit. Blues and purples oscillated into vibrant form as she thrilled to the beauty she missed so much. Beside her the essence of a beautiful soul struggled into the physical world. Wren still had enough power to recognise her.

'Are you Sir Saul's wife?'

'My dear you see me?'

'Of course, and feel you.'

'You seem more advanced than I first thought. I have been around this garden often in the years since my passing and have been saddened by the neglect. That is why I was so pleased when Sausage found you.'

Her light glowed when she allowed herself the pleasure of communicating about her husband.

'Sausage?'

'That was my special name for him. His for me was Lettuce Although I was christened Letitia. Sausage and Lettuce don't usually go together do they; but in this case....oh we were perfect?'

Such was the pleasure of being with spirit that Wren absorbed the moment in sheer ecstasy.

'I am so glad he is coming out of the fog of grief enough to get on with what is left of his life.

He is so stuck in his love for me that he can't see he needs more love whilst he is physical; he has a few more years yet. Often Saul feels me with him you know but he is so hard headed that he puts it down to wishful thinking. He believes the times we have met when his body has been asleep are delicious dreams. If only he knew how much effort I have to put in to be where he can find me.'

'He is still so sad.' Wren wished she hadn't communicated the thought as the spirit energy darkened and dulled.

'I'm sorry.'

'Then do something. Let him know I still exist and that he will be with me again. Help him change his vibration. Show him how; you of all souls Wren can do this. Tell him his dreams are astral travel to the edge of where I am continuing. Tell him the little signals he feels from me are not his longing imagination. Reassure him that the love he perceives from me is real.'

'If I can find a way....'

'Not if; when! Saul's only comfort is that I am with our son Simon. I hope you never find out what a cold hell it is to have your child die before you. He still suffers from that.'

Letitia sensed this frequency was hurting Wren.

'Anyway Wren I trust you with my garden. You will find a way to control Smith believe me. I will help. Just remember; sometimes things have to get worse before they get better.'

Letitia picked up a limp tulip stem caressing the tight green bud as it dangled despondently in its loss of seeing the sun.

'Give Saul this and say it is from me.'

As she placed the fat bulb and seemingly hopeless stem in Wren's hands she faded away.

Wren felt the loss of being with a higher vibration like lead in her shoes. The slowness of the Earth vibration dragged at her happiness and for the first time she felt depression. Why was she putting herself through this? It was then that she caught, just at the edge of her awareness, the last hint and sweetness of Letitia.

'The one you seek is very near. If I can help in return for your kindness I..'

She was gone. What did she know of Alessandro? Did every-one in spirit know of Wren's wrong life?

Surely not; if Letitia was often around the garden then she would have picked up many thoughts from Wren's longing. She knew how difficult Smith was being after all. Did she know who Alessandro was? She must!

Renewed by the encounter Wren strode to the part of the stable she'd discovered had been used as a potting shed carrying the limp tulip Letitia had placed in her hands. Rich new compost she'd tipped from the delivery yesterday heaped over the potting bench invitingly. She hadn't cleaned the clay pots spiders had claimed as their own private pile but it took only seconds to choose a deep 'A' line pot with the makers stamp indented near the bottom. Wren rubbed away the sticky dirt to see the illegible name and place of manufacture in a deep cockeyed splodge resembled a round smiling face. This was perfect.

She wet the compost at the bottom of the pot before carefully sifting more around the delicate roots she hoped would not be too damaged to start sucking up the moisture. The stem, leaves and hopeful flower bud hung over the side of the pot like the corpse she feared it now was. But she had to try and left the casualty in the cool dark to give it every chance.

There was no change in the floppy leaves and bud the next morning but Wren sensed there was still life. There had to be. To give Sir Saul a message so lifeless like how he thought his beloved wife was, would hardly raise his mood. That was the very least Wren could do for Letitia. She had fed her resolve, swelled her hope that soon she would find Alessandro. But what did she mean 'near'; nearby or near in time? Excitement gnawed at her hope. Perhaps both.

She had to give Sir Saul the heartening boost she had just received.

This gift needed to be showing strong continuation of life. It had been touched by Letitia's loving energies and Saul must feel them.

After three anxious days it was obvious that the tulip was in mild recovery. Before she went home that night Wren placed the pot outside so that it would take the gentle morning light. Perhaps the green bud would unfold enough to show what colour this special flower would offer to the world.

After two hours of spreading muck and helping Smith to dig it into the driveway borders, Wren turned to see Lil coming down the path holding her nose.

'Poo-ey! Now I know why I never rode horses.' She stopped a few yards away and waved Wren towards her.

'I hope you don't stink like that, Sir wants you to give him a progress report.'

'What; now?'

'Aye; with his morning coffee.'

Wren pulled a face.

'I know but I have managed to put a cup half full of hot milk on the tray for you hinny. He'll never notice.'

Lil turned but had a second thought which made her face Wren again.

'Oh by the way some-one called to see you. I told them you were in the garden but they just said they had to dash but to tell you it only took a week.'

'What? Who?'

Lil shrugged. 'Search me! These new-fangled hippies with their long hair and beads can't even tell if they are lads or lasses. It should be stopped!'

Wren, trying to work out who could have possibly called with such a silly message, cleaned up as best she could in the cold water from the potting shed then smoothed out the red notebook she'd kept a careful record of her expenditures.

She was rolling down her sleeves when her foot knocked something. It was the tulip pot. She picked it up disappointed to see the head still flopping slightly to one side. It was too early to look like the message it was. She took it to a shady spot against the wall but as she straightened up she was surprised to see a blush of colour at the base of the head and a small strip of purple showing at just one edge where the tight petals overlapped. It took two hands to contain the excitement she held. This was the most precious flower she had ever handled.

Lil, who thought the gift was no more than a sweet little token found a place for the pot on the coffee tray which Wren carried to the study door. It took one gentle, bare foot movement to push the heavy oak open.

'Aha! Coffee and my favourite gardener in one package. How blessed can one old gentleman get.' He called from the Orangery, turning from intently rubbing oily leaves between his fingers. 'How on earth did you find these fine specimens of lemon trees my dear?'

Wren pushed the tray onto his desk and joined him to smell the warm blossom.

'It wasn't easy.' she laughed remembering how much time she'd spent on his phone sourcing the best supplier in the country.

'Well I'm glad you managed and I see how much work you are doing in the garden. I have to remember that things sometimes have to get worse before they get better.'

'Did your wife used to tell you that?'

He jerked his head towards her, searching her eyes for a truth he sensed might be there.

'Why do you say that?'

'Oh just a feeling.' She smiled over her sadness that he couldn't know all she knew about how death was just a change of being.

He looked disappointed and took her hand as he had that first day.

'These are suffering aren't they?'

Wren smiled and gently squeezed the fingers around hers to show that she was glad to have such soil engrained nails and hard skin just where the spade offered most resistance.

He read her willingness and smiled warmly.

'I wanted you to give me a progress report before I go to Yorkshire.'

'Yorkshire?'

Yes, I have a little estate there; let it run down too much. Gave it to my Grandson Lintern but I fear he is too young. Something has to be made of it but I don't know what.'

He rubbed his hands gleefully. 'That rich aroma is driving me mad. Shall we drink?'

He moved towards the desk but paled and stopped before he reached his chair.

'What's this?'

'It's a present.'

'Where did you get that pot and that tulip?' There was no smile on his lips and Wren felt nerves creep into her voice.

'From the border and the potting shed, right at the back.'

'That is one of the funny face pots that my wife made me buy at Chelsea Flower Show one year. I thought they looked cheap but she said the stamps on the bottom looked like my smile.'

He turned his gaze from his sweet ache to Wren as if seeing her for the first time.

'She ordered the purple tulips that year too, couldn't wait to see them rise above the blue sea of forget-me-nots in her borders.'

'The gift isn't from me. It's from her.' She felt the words she meant to ease his pain only made it worse. His mouth hung open, suspended until he could make sense of what she was saying.

'I...I don't believe you. How could she...she's been dead three years.'

'Letitia will never be dead.'

Something like anger sprung to his eyes.

'How do you know her name?'

'She told me in the garden a few days ago.'

'Don't be so ridiculous! What are you playing at?'

'She told me that Sausage and Lettuce don't usually go together but in this case they did ...beautifully.'

Wren braced herself for apoplectic flailings or a barked order to get out but all that happened was a look of joy and wonder.

'So it was her.'

'When?' Wren asked gently.

'In the garden just before you came.' He found his seat and used the comfort to go deeper into his reverie.

'It was just a glimpse, a vague feeling that she was wandering around looking sad at the neglect. That was the instant I knew that what the garden needed was a woman's softness. Never thought I'd find one. It was only when I told Lil how the garden missed a woman's touch that she told me about Garden Angel.'

He looked up to her smile. 'And angel is what you truly are my dear. How I wish you could have known her, you'd have adored her.'

'I did! I do!'

They both laughed. There was so much more she could have told him but he didn't ask.

A new bond flourished as he drank his thick black coffee and Wren warmly held her milky drink close to her chest.

A silent, knowing bond.

Somehow this brought a strong, excited feeling of Alessandro.

In a hot flash of realisation she knew exactly why she had been led to this man before her.

CHAPTER THIRTY TWO

It gave a thrill to Wren each time she discovered something new in the vast garden that she knew had been touched by Letitia. She hoped that the feeling she had promoted with Saul had been enough. Perhaps Letitia would return to show her pleasure. Perhaps there would come a time when Wren could ask what she knew about Alessandro. She stretched her bent back and stood up to see where the crunching of angry steps was coming from.

'What the bloody hell is going on?'

Wren edged her hand to her brow in order to look into the sun just in time to see Smith spit onto the pile of wilting weeds she had yet to lift into the barrow.

She smelt last night's sweat grow ever nearer as the steel capped boots carelessly kicked gravel onto her neatly sieved borders.

'You've got 'im as daft as yoursel', bloody bonkers!'

'I beg your pardon.' Wren tried to sound contained.

'Sir; asking me if I seen Ma'am in the garden for God's sake. She's been rottin' in the ground long enough for him to 'ave noticed. He was just getting over it when you go putting daft ideas into his already puddled head!'

His uncombed hair and incredulous face blocked the low morning sun so that Wren could see him properly. It wasn't pleasant; usually she found jobs to keep him away from her until after he had his wash for lunch, the only one of his day.

'Don't you believe in life after death then?' She tried not to enter into his fury.

'What the hell.... you deranged or summat? When you're dead, you're dead! End of story!'

'Don't you acknowledge the existence of a Superior Intellect? Someone or thing responsible for the design and development of a brain-mind relationship and continuation of the soul? A God who loves us all?'

The scum that always joined his top lip to his bottom stretched with his incredulity.

'You obviously don't think that everything we see before us including each other had an intelligent beginning and therefore a continuation.'

He thought that last comment was really ridiculous, a point he demonstrated by taking his bare arm across his mouth in order to free his lips to spit again.

'What? Horse shit? Breaking my back every day and going home to a woman uglier than a badger's arse?'

'No; people, beauty and feelings. Love.'

He really thought she'd lost it and shook his head as he exhaled every foul breath held by his lungs in exasperation.

'Would I have to be a dogsbody to a weird Grammar School lass with odd eyes, shifting shit and hating every minute of it if some-one could offer me more?' He put his thumb up to pick at crusty gatherings around his mouth.

'You create your own surroundings and people.'

'Hah!' you really are mad!' he said striding straight past her to work as far away as possible.

'I'm not stopping here! You are seriously unhinged. Sir's got a load of wild boar piglets arriving today; got to settle them into their wood. I live a real life!'

Wren allowed herself a little laugh. She'd seen this many times in many lifetimes. Whether or not the seed would take root was another matter but there had been success on even rougher ground than Smith.

He looked more human when he'd eaten and combed his cold water splashed hair back off his face. She looked up as he rounded the stable corner.

'What you want me to do this afternoon then brainbox?'

Wren laughed, he'd obviously assigned her to another level of human being dwelling in a place he would never go.

She still found him grating to look at but she wanted him near enough to make it seem as if what she was going to ask him, what had been strumming in her head all day, was casual.

'Could you help me with this sieving?' She gave him the shovel she'd been using and took up the huge sieve to hold above the barrow. For a while there was only the noise of earth on wire mesh, stones tossed into a growing pile and buzzing bees searching ever closer to where they were sure there had been juicy clover yesterday.

'When is Sir Saul going to Yorkshire?' she said knowing full well it was the following morning.

'Don't know; don't care, just as long as he leaves me wages.'

Wren smiled inwardly at that for she knew and had seen it demonstrated many times that what Smith felt for the man who had employed him since he was fourteen was as close to love as he'd ever get.

'Staying with his grandson I believe?'

Smith obviously didn't feel this was worth taking his eyes away from where he was digging.

'Must love him a lot to give him so much.'

This hardly seemed worth opening his mouth for but Wren wouldn't give up. It might be her only chance.

'What does he look like?'

'Who?'

'Sir's grandson. Lintern isn't it?'

'What the buggerie does it matter what he looks like?'

'I thought I saw him, the day I arrived.'

'That young'un's never been here since Christmas.'

'Oh!'

'Disappointed you won't be able to save his soul an' all?'

He wasn't all wrong for her disappointment took the strength from her arms so that she dropped the sieve. She only half caught the exasperated look from Smith that said 'bloody women'.

How could she find out who it was she recognised on a soul level that first time she came here? It could be anybody, anywhere. She found it hard to lose the mental image as if the very memory would conjure up the one she thought might be Alessandro. Even the thought of this young man felt important. Perhaps the autumn and the shoot would bring more rewards than satisfaction with her work and the promised bonus.

Had she not being so deep in thought on her way home she'd have noticed some-one watching her that night from behind the hedge opposite Lil and Jim's.

Hot summer days followed the welcome warmth of spring so that a huge amount of time was spent watering her hopes for autumn. Smith was digging out and levelling the croquet lawn. As she passed his

bent figure, her arms pulled with a barrow load of sloshing watering cans on her way to where the hosepipe just wouldn't stretch, she wondered if it was him watching her in the woods sometimes.

Her secret pleasure in the knowledge that Lil got the bus to the bottom lane and then walked the few yards to the front gate of Amblin Hall had faded as her uneasiness increased. After changing at Lil and Jim's Wren relished the three mile walk through the back woods to her work. But now, though only sometimes, she heard a footfall that was not of deer, fox or rabbit. Smith had those wild boar piglets enclosed in wire fencing as much for their own protection until they were big enough to make the woods their own. The welcome blanket of bird song changed, becoming quiet and shy before growing hesitantly back to delivering joy to Wren's brain. Tot had taught her well, she knew when things weren't right in the woods. Even if she had never spent quiet hours with well-trained Jan at her side she'd have been able to read the energies. But it wasn't just her own safety she feared for. Whoever it was had no good intended. She shivered as she thought of what she had done to Colin. There was no way she could have overridden it at the time. Could it become a pattern?

The gratification Wren received from rounding the bend to see her ever developing work in front of her lifted her concerns. She was responsible for this garden. Well, her and God as well as Letitia's great start and Sir Saul's money. She felt pleasure in the realisation that her small part in this creation had achieved so much. She would never have known about sophisticated plants without the need to search for them and that wouldn't have come without money. There was something in this posh gardening.

Wren had unsuccessfully tried to keep the thought of money from her mind. The job would be complete soon and she'd have nowhere to go each day. Unable to face the fury of Ivy and the disappointment from Tot, she would have to stay out somewhere for the same hours, not easy in the cold and dark. She thought of the bundle of savings she had hidden in the coal house. That would soon deplete having to be the sole source of giving Ivy her keep.

The shooting season would start on the twelfth of October and with it would end her job here at Amblin Hall. There had been no sign of the one person she longed to meet.

'You'll be off soon then.' Smith said flatly not giving away any hint of whether or not he'd be pleased to see the back of her.

Wren stopped pulling at the entanglement of polyanthus roots she was dividing when he came into the potting shed. He looked dishevelled, sucked dry of all juices and reeked of last night's Newcastle Brown Ale.

'Yes I will. And you'll have nothing to do but annoy poor Mrs Smith all day.'

He burped loudly, patting his stomach with a fist to lengthen the noise he found so therapeutic.

'Oh she'll not have to double her nagging time just yet. Best beater Sir ever 'ad I am!'

'Beater?'

'Aye yu' know; beating the undergrowth to chase up the pheasants for them rich buggers to shoot.'

'How revolting.'

'No, it's not really. I love being in those woods and the banging of the guns really excites me, does every-one! They all come back with an appetite for Lil's cooking.'

The sour smell of the contents of his gut pervaded the whole area. She wanted to wretch and run but knew that being in his presence was the price she had to pay for information.

'Who's coming?' Her voice left on narrow breath as she tried to ration how much she expelled so that the revolting air was further from being inhaled.

'Oh the usual.' he began picking at the skin around his nails with putrid teeth.

'Who are they?' She tried to keep her eyes on the soft green leaves of the plants before her but he spat onto the floor.

'I dunno! Call them all sir and then they're happy. There's tips to be had for good beaters, that's what I'm after.'

Not able to stand his closeness for one more second she yanked at the tray of divided plants and carried them outside. He followed her out wincing at the low sun just shooting out from a bank of last night's rain clouds.

'Are they all local?'

'Dunno.' He shrugged. 'Do you want me to plant these in the spring garden?'

Hardly noticing his unprecedented initiative she found a new way to roundabout the question she shied from asking.

'Any-one coming from Lincolnshire or southerners, do they come?'

'Aye.'

'And Yorkshire?'

'For God's sake woman! Yes! And Cumbria and bloody Timbuktu for all I know.'

He picked up the tray and wandered off spitting out the phlegm from too many roll-ups.

The young man was certain to be coming and she wouldn't even be here. She could hide in the woods and hope to catch a glimpse. No, that was stupid. Apart from pheasants and dogs giving her away she'd be shot a thousand times. How was it that she recognised Sir Saul as some-one who had been important to both Alessandro and herself, yet had not introduced her to one person he might be. Why?

Why? Why?

She was leaving Saul now, there was no chance. Something would have to come up. She had to be here. If she imagined it strongly enough she would be. Creative visualisation usually worked. It had to.

'So, today is your last day here.' Lil shook the big spoon to dislodge creamy mashed potato onto a plate of waiting sausages.

'Oh don't. I'm already near tears.' Wren was sharing her last dinner time with her friend who she found herself wishing could have been her mother; a soft, round, jolly mother.

'How did your inspection tour go with Sir, pleased was he?' Lil sipped at the hot tea before dabbing mustard along a shiny sausage.

'Thrilled! Yes that's the word. Said he couldn't believe it. He asked Smith to hunt out the old croquet set and give it an oiling.'

'Oh no! That means Smith'll smell of linseed for days!' Lil gasped, opening her mouth at the unexpected strength of her mustard.

'A great improvement I'd say.' They both laughed.

'But it won't affect me will it? I'll be gone.'

Lil looked at Wren's untouched plate. 'It's a great place isn't it, Amblin.'

'I love every inch.'

'Well there is a chance you could stay a bit longer.'

'No. How? The garden couldn't stand another touch of my trowel.'

Lil put her fork down and held the white teacup in front of her face tantalising the contents awaiting her sip.

'Sir hasn't told you of the Hidden Well Garden 'as he?'

'What?'

'No he wouldn't. 'is wife called it that because she found a long forgotten water well in there and you can't see the garden because of that old wall. Really well hidden it is. I'd better not say more, it's his business. Touchy subject! But I didn't mean gardening I meant cooking.'

'Cooking!'

'Do you know how much them blasted guns and beaters eat? I couldn't do it all myself. Usually Dottie Hall comes up for a fortnight but her joints is real bad just now.'

'So?'

'You could do it?'

'Me! I can't cook.'

'Didn't your mam teach you?'

Wren thought of how close proximity in Ivy's kitchen always meant short temper and yelling.

'Only peeling veg and scrambling eggs….and toast with the fork on the fire.'

'Oh.' She looked disappointed. 'Well it'll be a start.'

This was it. Her chance to meet the man who had never being out of her mind since her first day at Amblin. She should shut up and grab it with both hands.

'I could teach you. You're a clever lass." Lil said hopefully still thinking Wren had to be persuaded.

'I'll need some teaching mind.'

'No you won't hinny, a girl like you can turn her hand to anything.'

The sudden rush of joy released her hunger, she womped into the creamy mash. Lil smiled pleased to have her friend with her and happy her cooking was appreciated.

'Won't Sir mind?'

'He gives me the wages and eats the food. It's up to me who I employ.'

A moment passed when both women held their individual joy to them.

He would be there! She just knew it. This was her chance.

'Mind,' said Lil pointing her knife at Wren. 'You're coming on the bus wi' me. I won't have you walking through those woods now the nights are drawing in. The dogs have been going mad at something in there; the gamekeeper's been right worried about the pheasants.'

CHAPTER THIRTY THREE

Wren tried to shut out the banging that meant birds were being killed as she laid out a feast for the men who were doing it. The beat was uneven like her agitated heart.

Autumn gave misty mornings and this one promised rain. As soon as it was light enough she had searched the littered garden for flower arrangement material. The leaves she kicked through had lost their full-bellied summer gloss and sounded thin and near to crumbling into death and mould. Plums, decaying into mush exposing their stones, lay on the grass helpless against flies, she had left them for the butterflies who loved their sweetness, a few still plump and jewel like lay half covered by leaves. She gathered those the birds had not yet spotted.

Lil had made a hot lunch as the rain chased in with the north wind would have the men glowing but damp when they returned. The older woman had been brought up with old fashioned English cooking and in her hands nothing was stodgy, greasy or lumpy. Wren had been run off her feet labouring to a cook she now knew to be very creative, she loved it. The shock of the green and dark pink dining room decorated by heavy ceiling roses with garlands and cherubs had been an inspiration. As she picked up a fallen berry from the table decoration she'd amazed herself with, Wren was silent in admiration of such a lay out. How the crystal sparkled in the firelight, how the silver glowed. Twenty set places edged towards each other with knife after knife and fork after fork. All heads would face each other over the splendid dark red and green flower arrangement Wren had made from Ice Plant, Sweet Nutmeg and dark fruiting ivy. The firelight gave the flush of black elderberries she'd used around the base a new radiance. On the side table, presented from rosehips and hawthorn berries, huge maroon and pink chrysanthemums sprayed out like flags announcing that this was where the desperate would find the single malt Scotch, Irish and the best of Sir Saul's cellar.

Trepidation gnawed at her stomach.

He was bound to be here. She ran a mental picture of the first and only time she had seen him standing with the other man and dogs outside Amblin. She hadn't been very near, perhaps she'd not recognise him from his looks but certainly she'd feel the same frisson. She tried to calm the bashing of her untidy, desire torn, rag and bone heart.

When the guns stopped, Lil sweated. As she poured piping hot gammon and lentil broth into four tureens she made Wren go through the plan she had made whilst showing her how to set the table. They carried through the broth and freshly made stotties that smelled of yeast and would melt butter to run down chattering chins.

The noise moved into the house. Loud jokes, guffaws and sudden laughter dulling whilst the whisky was drunk and then lulling to allow hot nourishment to slide down cold stomachs only falsely warmed by liquor. The din added to the tension that had been growing for months. From the kitchen they heard the noise grow again; they were ready for the next course.

She was about to go in.

Heavy dishes stilled Wren's nervous hands as she entered the room full of brash bonhomie and masculine cacophony. She doubted if anyone even noticed the food never mind the garden. Why did Sir spend so much time and money on this party of wild life killers? Deep voices competed with each other in good natured banter but Wren needed all her concentration not to trip. She passed the table to lay a great game pie slopping with wine enriched gravy on the sideboard; Lil laid another then nodded for them to clear away empty dishes, crumbs and five already drained wine bottles. Some eyes fell on Wren's breasts and others on her black clad bottom escaping from a tightly wrapped white apron. One man wiped his mouth salaciously as she removed his soup dish and side plate.

'Well I know what I'd like for my next course!' He bellowed as he winked. The roar of laughter stung even more than the slap to her rump. She sought comfort or redress from the eyes of Sir Saul but he was looking the other way bending his head towards the man on his right as he waited for the punch line to his excited joke. She felt stroked all over her body by lurid male gazes. Several eyes followed her to the door. Then when she was out of sight a great roar filled the room then her ears. She had no doubt that the laughter was at her expense.

Her discomfort was compounded when she reached the kitchen to find Smith and the other beaters coming in from putting the dogs away, jamming up the table.

'Take those in, hinny!' Lil's high voice showed her stress as she ladled broth in front of the men who were already tearing at piles of stotties fresh from the oven.

'And take no notice of that lot; you'd think they'd never seen a pretty girl before.'

Wren's arms ached with the great wooden tray bearing dishes of creamed potatoes and jugs of gravy. She had to make another journey with the thyme roasted carrots, parsnips and cumin buttered cabbage. But each brave entrance into the rampant noise was a chance to search the faces for the special person her heart swelled for. Every embarrassed move she made needed total concentration so that only the leering faces she tried to avoid magnetised themselves to her eyes. It was when she was clearing away pudding bowls sticking with remains of blackberry pudding and custard that she saw two men younger than the rest. They were locked into emphasising differing points of view so that their faces were hidden from her as she cleared their plates. No frisson of recognition seared into her even when her arm brushed the coarse wool of one's jumper. Perhaps the energies were too laden with hearty masculine voices competing for superiority. Maybe it was the whisky, the wine, the heat!

Maybe he wasn't here.

Desperation reached every corner of her body. The sheer volume of noise had eased to a lull from overfull men soused in alcohol. Every man here was as English as Yorkshire pudding, some old school, some working class made good. Wren placed jugs of celery and plates of biscuits around the table as Lil eased a whole ripe Stilton in front of Sir Saul who scooped out some of the top before pouring vintage port into the hollow. Wren, used only to pale Cheshire and bright Cheddar from the Co-op wondered how any-one could face eating stinking mouldy cheese, but the eyes that weren't on her were on the delicacy.

Whilst preparing the coffee Wren and Lil heard some of the men trip or shamble over the polished wood floor to the lavatory.

'Be a right mess in there' an all.' Lil inclined her head towards the double cubical she'd scrubbed out the morning before.

Lil sallied ahead with tiny cups and the chocolate truffles she'd stayed up till midnight to make. Two silver coffee pots weighed down Wren's arms as she swung open the kitchen door and found herself facing the man who had slapped her bottom.

'Mmmm! The tastiest course yet.' He leered through drunken eyes and gravy stained moustache. His wide eyes sprung from a tornado of hair studded with food particles.

Wren stopped like a rabbit caught in headlights, her shoulders began to heave in an effort to retrieve her breath.

'You and I could make our own sport this afternoon. How about it? I'd prefer a nice cosy barn to drizzly woods and men too drunk to aim.'

Her protest dried to a mass in her throat as he began to stroke her hand nearest to him.

'Come on; I'll make it worth your while.'

The pot seemed to tip itself over his legs, too low down to hit the intended target, and as he yelled with pain Wren made her move towards the dining room.

'Bloody hell!' the swearing shot out on the same vigour with which he flicked hot coffee from his trousers. 'By God I like a girl with spirit! There'll be no stopping me now!' He yelled taking in his best view yet of her mini-skirted legs.

The whole lunch had been a nightmare. Even with the mellowness of a good meal and Blue Mountain coffee none of the men sent anything remotely spiritually aware to Wren. When the woods became blessed with fellows unable to remember their own dog's names never mind why they were holding a gun, Lil had even more work to do. The clearing away and washing up took until five. The whole table had to be set again for supper.

'Help me get this lot onto the table pet.' Lil dragged the words from an exhausted body the second she picked up on gravel crunching and dog commands. Wren's hands, still stiff from the cold water she washed piles of salad in worked as deftly as they could. The last bus was at eight.

Lil placed the half carved ham near the head of the table and made a few adjustments to the dishes of beetroot she knew would stain the white tablecloth she'd have to bleach in the morning. Imaginative salad platters lay between the wholemeal loaves and plates of smoked salmon which Wren had avoided touching after Lil had told her it was raw.

'These people with money eat some queer stuff!' Wren said as she piled moss covered logs onto the dying embers.

'Aye well, you'll be eatin' it yerself someday hinny. I don't think you realise how pretty you are. You could marry any one of a dozen men coming into this room tonight.'

'Urgh!' Wren tore her gaze away from sparks spluttering up the wide chimney. 'I couldn't think of anything worse Lil!'

'There's a wide world out there hinny. Don't tie yoursel' to a miner like I did. Don't get me wrong I love Jim with every bone in me body; but I had chances and I never took them.'

Wren's questions died on her lips as the front door cracked open spilling in first a bearded huggable bear of a man leading the burst of a raucous hungry throng.

'Howay lass! We'll miss that bus if we don't get a wiggle on and I need a bit of sleep at least before frying twenty breakfasts.'

Wren needed no encouragement to escape any further attention from the lecher. She was tired, oh so deeply tired.

At home she was too exhausted to think up an excuse for her lateness and so merely said she'd gone to a coffee bar with some friends from work.

'I hope you enjoyed yourself chicken.' Tot pulled her close to kiss her hair. 'You smell of wood smoke and gravy!'

She hated lying to him but her regret was dragged into fear when she saw the knowing look with which Ivy branded every inch of her. This ganged up with her devastating disappointment to keep sleep from her except in torrid patches where she dreamed of Alessandro and the lecher. She was too weary to stop them merging into one person.

With the anticipation of meeting the one she hoped was Alessandro dissipated, the work at Amblin became easier. Great dishes of sausages, kidneys and bacon edged their way between two platters of fried eggs edged with crispy fried bread on the wide sideboard. Lil had cleared out the cool ashes before giving new life to the dead fire and setting the table yet again. Wren came in when a man who had an explosion of red hair coming out of his ears and nostrils as if a firework had just gone off in his thick head, led the hung-over, overfed rabble into the breakfast room.

'You'll be doing this with your eyes shut by Sunday afternoon.' Weary words were dragged from her lips as the great pots of tea had been placed across the table. She made a last few vigorous pushes with the hand carpet sweeper just as the last bleary eyed men yawned their hungry way into their chairs.

The weekend passed in a blur of serving, cooking and cleaning. Tot wondered why Wren returned home from a day out in Newcastle shopping so exhausted without even one shop carrier bag but the incongruity only seemed to aggravate Ivy more. Tight lips zipped tighter.

It was on Monday morning when Amblin Hall accepted the quiet it needed that Lil opened the subject Wren had been pushing from her mind along with her disappointment.

'What will you do next week when we've finished this lot." she asked pulling crumpled sheets from the seventh bedroom they'd stripped that day.

'Don't know. Haven't had time to think.' Wren peeled down pillows from sweaty linen cases.

But it was all she thought about as they pushed more sheets into the round washing machine on their first leg of the race to join the steaming linen hanging from the dryer hoisted to the kitchen ceiling.

'Oh I hate these damp windless days, washin' needs a good blow, takes half the creases out. I can't see Sir Saul changing his crisp white cotton sheets for Bri-nylon from the Co-op can you?'

Wren laughed at the thought of purple and orange decor amongst the grace of Amblin.

'I could help you iron and get this lot back on the beds for a couple of days if you like.'

Lil ran the big poss stick through her hand to remove the glistening suds.

'There's no budget for any more help.'

'Doesn't matter.' Wren shrugged. 'I haven't spent a penny on bus fares all the time I've been pretending to be Garden Angels. Anyway I have nowhere else to go. If it was summer I could read in the woods but this mist doesn't even make walking pleasant.'

'I'm not 'aving you in them woods these dull days pet, you could keep Jim company. You might read to him, tear him away from his racing paper. He's been low lately with me putting in the hours here.'

With the week ahead of her filled, Wren felt happier. She planned weekend walks with Tot; he'd also been neglected only he was too happy for his daughter to be having a life to mention it.

When all the autumn tidying had been done in Lil and Jim's garden with only the progressively falling leaves to spoil her neatness, Lil dropped another one of her bombshells.

It was Friday morning; Wren had arrived seconds before Lil dashed out to catch her bus.

'Glad you caught me hinny, I was just about to leave you a note.'

She fastened the top button on her serviceable black woollen coat before pulling on the knitted mittens. Fashion would never catch Lil, it had given up chasing.

'Wren it's good news! Sir wants to see you.'

'What for?'

'Don't look so surprised! More gardening I think, probably the garden we're not allowed to mention. He's come out of himself since you arrived. He asked me if you had much work on, at first I said you were so snowed under what with you being in such demand and all. I thought he was just asking after you but he looked disappointed rather than pleased so I told him most of your contracts were for spring and you might have a little window soon.'

'Lil!'

'Well you won't let on will you? He asked if you'd call up as soon as you had a spare minute.'

'I've got nowt but!' She brightened. 'I'll come with you now if you like.'

'Righty-oh but you'd better change into your gardening clothes, look busy like.'

The two women thought that it might be prudent to wait until after lunch to approach Sir. Wren fancied she might wander around the gardens she now loved so much but she could see Smith sweeping up leaves around the Hall and she didn't want to spoil his day with the news she was coming back.

Lil knew Sir Saul well enough to know he'd appreciate the surprise as Wren took in his lunch.

When she'd laid the tray with Lil's wild mushroom soup and cheese and onion bread onto the little table in the study, he beckoned her over.

'My dear! Such an unexpected pleasure! These hands worked such magic here, I wonder if they have time to work some more?'

He squeezed her hands before letting them drop but Wren was flooded with energy and a scene lifetimes ago when he wasn't so keen to leave her physically. She knew then exactly what his karmic debt to her was.

'The garden drew many comments; they've all noticed the neglect. It was too damp to play croquet but the lawn interested many. No doubt I'll be having them bringing their wives back in summer.'

'I'm glad they were impressed.'

'Oh they were that all right but when I told them that the one responsible was the pretty girl who'd just served them supper they were flabbergasted.'

Wren laughed at the picture.

'More than one asked for your company phone number but I said I didn't have it or indeed know where your office is.'

'I don't have a phone or an office, in fact I don't have a company.'

'But...'

'Oh I know but Lil is the best promoter of all time. Yours was my first job. My only job.'

'Well I never. That makes you even cleverer.' He took time to think.

'You should have all these things Wren, you are so very good. I'm even more impressed than I already was. Good for you, making use of your natural talents.'

He went to his desk drawer and took out a sheet of paper.

'I trust you can get to use a public phone to ring this number. He's only at home evenings and Saturdays, so maybe tomorrow?'

Wren looked at the number and saw it was local.

'I picked that one first because I knew you hadn't a car. You really should learn to drive you know. You look disappointed was I being too presumptuous?'

'Oh no, no! I'm really grateful that you bothered, it's just that I was hoping you wanted me to work here.'

'Here? But you've done it all.'

'But what about...?' She could see how he wasn't about to acknowledge the secret walled garden and she had no wish to cause him pain, 'the clearing up, it can get quite messy at this time of year.'

'Yes and I have to keep Smith busy somehow. You are a very talented young lady and should be out there making money. I told this man your rate and he agreed. Now go on out and make Garden Angels the success it deserves to be before my soup gets too cold.'

It was mild and sunny on Saturday morning. Wren hoped Tot wouldn't make sandwiches and want to be out walking all day, she couldn't bear the nervousness of secretly dashing to the phone and finding out if her next job was imminent.

'I really miss Jan at times like this.' Tot said as they wound around the track rabbits had made at the foot of their warren.

'Get another dog Dad. Why not?'

'Well...no; too painful when they go.'

'Yes I know but that is the price of all those years love and we have to pay it. Get a dog from the rescue in Newcastle, they're longing for an owner like you.'

He shook his head cheerlessly. 'Your mam won't let me. I've broached the subject once or twice but she's right, she does have enough clearing up to do without muddy paw prints all winter.'

He looked resigned but the longing never left him.

'I can't eat a lamb chop without thinking how much Jan would love the bone; still can't help leaving more meat than I should.'

They both suffered their own thoughts before Tot felt he should change the mood.

'Anyway chicken, how's work going? Still fighting that fag faced old woman over opening the window to breathe?'

'No that problem's resolved dad.' she said not realising how long it had been since she'd thought of chain smokers, dusty binders and luncheon vouchers.'

She longed to tell him the truth but knew he'd be disappointed and that he would naturally tell Ivy, she couldn't stand the furore.

'Work is good Dad.'

She saw him beam. 'I'm glad you have lots of friends from the ministry pet, apart from Joyce you never seemed to bond with lasses of your own age and I used to fret about that.'

He stopped walking to face her, gently he pushed a strand of her hair from her eyes to behind her ear. 'This lovely hair suits you long, I hope you don't get it cut like the rest of those young lasses at work.'

'I won't dad…I promise.'

He smiled a smile of adoration. 'You would tell me if something was bothering you, wouldn't you?'

'I'm happy dad. Don't worry.'

Unable to enter into a tissue of lies with the man she truly loved with both personalities, Wren strode ahead into plans of how to get out on her own so that she could ring the number she'd hidden in her good shoes beneath the bed.

'This is Wren Stoker of Garden Angels speaking, are you the person who wants some garden renovated?' It wasn't until she'd pressed button 'A' and the deep voice answered that she realised Sir hadn't put the name above the number.

'Ah yes my dear that's me. Thank you for ringing. Can't wait to get you here!'

'Pardon?'

'Need you desperately! Got roses coming today; nowhere to put them except in a pile of horse manure.'

'No! Don't do that! You'll burn the roots with the acid.' Wren jumped to the defence of the plants.

'Well I could come on Monday; see what needs to be done. What's the address?'

She licked the tip of her pencil in readiness but it never met the reverse side of the paper in front of her.

As the heavy glass and red painted metal door groaned back on its resisting hinges, Wren stood shaking outside the box and fought to work out what life had put in front of her.

The address was Kademiur House. Shock and implication had burned into her brain as Jeremy's father gave explicit directions to his house not knowing that she could have found her way blindfold.

What was happening? She'd been thrown back into Jeremy's life when she had given up seeking it. Was it because he was Alessandro?

Her head hurt with the confusion. She hadn't even met the one she was so sure had been him at Amblin, maybe this was why? She had felt Sir Saul would lead her to him but now he had led her back to some-one she still longed for and wondered about. This was more than coincidence. It was fate. It was such a relief that thoughts of the young shooting man, of Uncle George and Joyce lost their once vivid importance.

Wren's sleep deprived eyes squinted in the attack by the harsh kitchen light. She made up two jam sandwiches and filled an old Tizer bottle with tap water. It was only 5 am, the October light was still hours away but she was unable to stop her mind buzzing with excitement. She couldn't get her gardening clothes from Lil's until 6.30 so there was no point in leaving the house until then. Pulling her coat over her she sat in Tot's seat in front of grey ashes sending up acrid smells as the spent and weakened coal fell onto itself.

She flicked through the rose catalogues from which Tot had chosen a new fragrant climber for the front of the house. He'd ordered only that. She imagined the company collecting the orders together, one rose for the council house; two hundred and forty four for the posh address.

She searched Percy Thrower's book for autumn and rose planting but as she read the words they failed to mean anything to her. There was only one thing on her mind.

It was a bile producing nightmare to pass the air shaft where she'd pushed Colin. Her heart caught on a fresh wave of pain at the memory of her act robed as destiny. How she wished she could have helped Colin with all she was instead of allowing the wrong life to take over.

The light was just reaching the top of the imported tree ferns in the sunken garden Wren had felt brave enough to enter. For the first time she had a right to be here. She was a little early perhaps, but if some-one challenged her they could hardly accuse her of not being keen.

There were plants here that she'd never seen or smelled. Everything was exotic, expensive and totally pampered. Her head was permanently tilted towards feathery fronds so that she tripped and fell flat onto something soft. In the path lay clean coal sacks cut open and stacked beside a huge ball of soft string.

'Oh ho! Just where I like a woman...on her back.'

Wren looked up to see a man wearing pyjamas and a dressing gown. The damp, still mildness of the morning had obviously encouraged him to bring his coffee into the fresh air. He indicated towards the group of tree ferns she'd been admiring ten minutes ago.

'You might have to save their lives if there's a frost forecast.' he said watching her scramble back to her feet and her dignity.

'Bloody annoying time for my gardener's wife to give birth! Chap has to look after the other five for a fortnight until she's back on her feet. Ought to stay there if you ask me. Only way not to get pregnant again, eh?'

He drained his cup and wiped his moustache. The growing light showed her it was the same moustache that had allowed leering and suggestive comments from behind it at Amblin.

'There's no chance of having coffee poured over my legs now is there? Silk doesn't like to let go of stains.'

Her heart sank, how could she work here? This man didn't want her for her gardening skills. There was only one reason he'd got her here and it was nothing to do with planting. How awful that he should be Jeremy's father.

'Well I never thought you'd be here to welcome me during my pre-breakfast wander but it's got my day off to a good start I must say.' He was obviously pleased with her young mouth as he studied what he thought was his game.

'Sir.'

A sari clad Indian lady appeared gracefully behind Mr. Foggin. She had a warm, superior air around her which Wren felt as she nodded a slight smile at her.

'Your breakfast sir.'

His eyes never left hers. 'You'll find the place I am making into a rose garden at the back of the house beyond the fountain. I'll join you there in an hour.'

The young seventeen year old girl that she was felt pulled towards the way she'd just come. It would be easy to retrace her steps home. That's all she had to do to be safe and sound. But she'd also be defeated, empty and penniless. Anyway she wasn't here because of the girl, she was here because of the spirit she was and the search she was compelled by. It was such a frustration that it was fogged by uncertainty. She would have found him by now if she had stolen the life of some-one more advanced. But she hadn't thought it through properly, made any plan. She had acted on impulse and this is where it had landed her.

No, there was no choice but to stay on this path and hope the evil genetics she held from her biological father stayed deep and un-prodded. For Mr. Foggin's sake, she hoped they would.

Excitement gave her energy. This was where she'd meet Jeremy again. Her search could be over soon. She picked up the knife left by a gardener in a hurry and used it to slash at the paper bags from Gandi's Roses to reveal bundles of dirty roots and heavily pruned thorny stems. This is where she had to be.

After walking around the large square divided by a nine inch high box hedge Wren's gardening and design mind took over. There would have to be some central point to give height to each part and perhaps some spring interest. The undergrowth swamped a hump of half - buried bricks in an igloo shape she thought must be an old ice-house, like the one she had read about, where the well-off Victorians stored ice in the cool underground. But if it had a door it was long ago hidden by brambles and covered over by rampant green and gold ivy. She would keep that in mind for flower arranging. She took in the rose beds from every angle and then sat on the stone scroll seat from where summer sitters would view the whole scene.

The dank coldness sank through her bottom, chilling her back to the present.

'Oh yes! I can just see you as lady of the manor peeping at the roses from beneath a parasol shading you not only from the sun but the almost unbearably seductive fragrance.'

Mr Foggin appeared in a classical suit, no sixties modern design for him. He had a mine to run not a fashion boutique.

'I'm not a lady I'm a gardener.' she quipped taking her eyes back to the dark bare earth.

'Oh but you could be much more if you were nice to me dear.'

In spite of his offensive suggestions Wren could discern a powerful sexuality that pushed any better judgement away from his life. There was reason he was like this but it still didn't mean he could get anywhere with her. She was, it amused her to think, in this life so far, a virgin. And that was how she intended to stay until she was sure she'd found Alessandro.

'Would there be room on this seat for two?' she asked, innocence deliberately setting her tone.

'Yes my dear of course, we'd have to squeeze up tight but that would be all the better.'

'I wasn't thinking of you but of your wife. She is the one who would sit here enjoying the garden her loving husband had made for her don't you think?'

'Oh I wouldn't let a little unimportance like a wife come between us.' He twinkled and laughed apparently egged on by her cheekiness.

'Well I would and so would she if I had a word with her.'

'There's no need for that now is there? Our feelings can remain a secret between us can't they?' His left eyebrow rose so that the silly seduction attempt and boyishness almost made her laugh.

Wren wondered what feelings he thought she had but only one thing was certain, they were entirely different to reality.

He fished into his breast pocket.

'Here's the plan I worked out for the rose colours.' He held the paper in front of him using it to beckon to her.

'Here! Take it.'

Wren wasn't a servant and knew too much about respect to allow this man to belittle her.

She turned her back to him, slitting more sacks to free the rose plants.

'Just leave it tucked in the hedge will you.'

He felt a little anger flare but soon reined it in to add to his fantasy of taming this unusually spirited girl. He did as he was told, never taking his eyes off her denim covered rear. This one was special. All the better for the taking.

Lil was home from Amblin after lunch so that by five when Wren came in to change her clothes she was bursting with questions. Was it as glorious as Sir Saul's place; was it true that there was a disused ice house buried in the rocky scrubby area behind the garden, had she seen any scarlet women draped around the house?

'It is only quarter the size and with a tenth of the grace of Amblin, Lil, and all I saw were rose roots, rose roots, and more rose roots.'

'Aye but did you see a mysterious foreign lady in foreign clothes? Dark as a warm night and just as beautiful they say.'

'Yes I did see an exotic lady in a sari, she had an inner beauty I don't think Mr. Foggin has even noticed yet but I could see he enjoyed her looks. But there is no mystery; she is his housekeeper.'

This seemed to worry Lil and Jim because the look they didn't mean to share with Wren concerned her.

'You be careful now. You know Mrs Foggin is in India staying with friends for a month and that pit owner has a certain reputation....you stay the good girl that you are and don't be wearing any of them miniskirts to work now!'

Wren thought of all the experience she'd had in former lives dealing with men just like this one and even one or two incarnations being one. She understood exactly how to handle him. He wasn't a problem; it was his son Lil should be worried about. It was Jeremy who would change her life.

The beauty that met Wren early next morning could not have been forged by man. A wet fog was lifting to leave heavily dewed spider-webs everywhere Wren looked. Brown and cream garden spiders had worked hard the day before and would again today mending their webs too drenched to catch any of last night's moths. Several water jewelled drapes honoured the wrought metal gate and others joined lamps to the brickwork of the pillars they stood on. Every shrub, bare branch and windowsill looked better for its autumn gift.

The sun glistened to give the tiny dew beads rainbows as if to remind them what was in heaven and tempt them to return. Wren wished she could go with them and longed for the lights in hues earth could never dream of. But all the peace and splendour there meant nothing without Alessandro. The sooner she found him the sooner she could copy the rainbows in the dew and return to where she was happiest.

The thought slowed her vibration. How long before Jeremy appeared at Kademuir? He was the sole purpose she was coming out in the dark, changing clothes at Lil's and walking the half hour here. She'd not been up in time to pack any bread for bait and had been in too much of a rush to ask Lil for anything. Care was so important at home because they still thought she was at the office enjoying the three course lunch with coffee, courtesy of luncheon vouchers. She'd soon lose that well fed look Lil's cooking had given her with this hard work and nothing to eat all day.

The soil had just started to cake on her hands when she noticed Mr Foggin go through his garden room door. He'd been drinking coffee walking around the garden as he said he did every morning but she had neither seen him nor heard him. She hadn't even taken the warning of the blackbird as it cackled and tripped across the gravel. This worried her. Normally her senses were so acute she knew when any-one was concentrating on her. He hadn't wanted to be seen this morning but he'd wanted to see her. The discomfort his actions gave her were only just passing to the back of her mind as she shovelled well-rotted manure into the tenth hole she'd dug, working up enough body heat to remove her jacket when she caught a glimpse of him looking at her through the full length upstairs window. He had a dreamy look of some-one in another world. Perhaps there was a karmic tie up here that he was determined to satisfy. Whether it was with her or the destiny of the spirit she had robbed she didn't know. But his thoughts would have no awareness of this link. He would merely act on it. This worried her more than she liked.

At one o'clock, just as she was coming out of the gardener's toilet some-one startled her.

'You have not stopped for food?'

The soft concern in the voice attracted Wren strongly to the spirit of the person before her.

'No I...'

'Come into the house, eat with Indira. Wash properly.'

Wren followed the flowing silk and grace of the Indian housekeeper and the deep memory dragging perfume that stayed behind her just a fraction of a second. She breathed in a cloud of the smell which strangely seemed to make her secure as the pair bent together around a neat row of slippers and discarded dirty boots.

The warmth of the kitchen made Wren's face seem taught. Fresh air and crisp cold never bothered her but it was good to feel the heat relax every aching muscle.

The whole room was absorbed in delicious spicy heaviness that was completely new to Wren in this life. But she knew every ingredient that had been toasted and ground to make the delicious garam masala used to flavour the vegetable and rice dish set on the table before her.

This house oozed with generous over-provision in everything that made a home.

'Here wash.' The smile was beauteous beyond words from the lady handing Wren a clean tea towel. The warm water and perfumed soap was a pleasure she could have fallen into for too long but she heard cutlery being cleared behind her and a casual question thrown through her enjoyment.

'Are you happy working for Mr Foggin?'

'Well I only started yesterday so I haven't seen him much. How long have you worked for him?'

'I was sold to him when I was thirteen, twenty years ago.'

'Sold!' Wren flung her eyes to the other woman's leaving the tap to waste its hot water in a steady stream.

'But you don't have to stay you...'

An elegant hand stopped her protestations and then the wasteful tap.

'My family are poor in money but not in honour. Sir is very generous and sends my wages to them every month, without him they'd die.'

'But what about you? Don't you get anything?'

'What could I want? He feeds me, clothes me and keeps me warm.'

'But surely..!

'He is a very unusual man and I must inform you...'

It was Wren's turn to interrupt.

'I know! I know you want to warn me but believe me I understand him.'

The shock on Indira's face was compelling.

'Warn you? Warn you? I don't want to warn you! I want to ask you not to take him from me again!'

'What?'

'He is everything to me. Oh yes his wife does know, it was she who encouraged it. It sets her free to do as she pleases which is exactly what she is doing now with a certain hotel owner in Jaipur.'

This was more than anything Wren could have ever envisaged. Strangely, there was something about this woman that she felt was very familiar.

'You must keep this secret and I know that you will because of what I discovered last night.'

'Last night?'

'Yes I will show you all but first you must eat.'

CHAPTER THIRTY FOUR

Tempting food slipped enthusiastically down to her empty stomach as quickly as Wren could instinctively use the flat bread to lift it to her mouth. Eating was a serious business here and no talking was allowed until every mouthful was swallowed and hands washed once more.

Strangely Wren accepted every vibration that passed between them warmly. There was information here but although it was being absorbed it would take quiet meditation to analyse and realise its true value.

'You like this? Your favourite lentil dish is it not?' Kind words but Wren knew she had never had this food before.

The quiet companionship she felt for this lady was reciprocated but there was a knot, something that should have been unravelled a long time ago.

When she spoke again, it was as if there was no gap in the conversation.

'Wren I ask you not to take him from me because you can and you have.'

'What?'

'I have seen him watching you and know how he has behaved since you have been here.'

'But this is ridiculous! I want nothing to do with him...'

'Yes I know. It is not him that you seek.' Kohl rimmed eyes burned with eons of knowledge.

This was too much awareness to take.

'What do you know of me?'

'Last night I meditated. Your presence here bothered me in two ways. Jealousy was the first and most easy to feel but there was something else; something much deeper.'

'With all respect you do not think I could want a middle aged man who lechers after every girl who comes within bottom pinching distance do you! For heaven's sake this is the sixties!'

She looked hurt then making Wren regretted her outburst.

'I know what he is. He tries to hide what he does from me but I know every time he slips out to the garden shed or stays away in Newcastle or London. I know him too well. He doesn't wish to hurt me.'

'Neither do I! Believe me he is safely yours I wouldn't want to take him away from you for one millisecond.'

'But you already have.'

'No! Any thoughts beyond doing that garden are entirely his.'

'Yes in this lifetime but it wasn't always the sixties; don't you remember little sister?'

The 'little sister' was so familiar to Wren that she responded immediately. Words bubbled up from another life spilling out unchecked.

'Well you should have kept him happy! It wasn't grace he was after... it was fire!'

'Yes I should have. And that is why I am doing so now in my second chance. I begged for this but I didn't know I would meet you in my second lifetime with him.'

Wren felt the wafting heat of India before the smells woke a billion awareness hits. Whose soul memory was this?

'You were so determined to have him in the build up to our marriage that you gave him what I couldn't, your virginity.'

That was all it took to release the pain of the last time she had met this lovely soul before her.

'That is why he is so disturbed by you and he doesn't know why.'

The pain was shared but Wren was so certain she didn't want him.

'You think that I am his slave because he has bought me. Don't you see that he is mine; my slave! He has to repay his debt to me and so must you.'

It was then that Wren pulled from the deepening confusion of her body's two histories the certainty that this was not her karma she was feeling so calmly but that of the life she stole. The reason she and Alessandro were ascending was because they had played out every karmic debt owing to and from them. They had learned each single painful and joyous lesson the earth school had to teach.

'I don't have time for this in my lifetime Indira, he is all yours.'

The new relief settled onto the beautiful Indian face, softening dark, kohl lined eyes.

The energies between them calmed, satisfying the woman who was terrified to lose the man she was presently unaware was her soul mate.

'But for your own sake you must clear this debt to me. How will you do it?'

Wren groaned inwardly. She hadn't bargained for this.

'Indira, there are complications you could never guess. I don't know. I simply don't know.'

Back in the garden the planting became automatic. Several times she had to check the name labels on the roses. There simply wasn't room for any more detail in her brain. It seemed impossible not to meet with karma that wasn't hers. First it had led her to murder and now what?

Perhaps she owed it to the spirit from whom she had taken the chance to work out this karma. Did she have the time?

It had been hard not to blurt out at least some of the truth each time Mr Foggin and his coffee cup wandered into the garden. His bedroom wear was now covered by an overcoat but his expensive leather slippers still strode out across the gravel. The lowering temperature had prompted him to get her to cover the tree ferns with sacking, a job for two really but she struggled on with the help of a step ladder and hastily tied knots.

He set her the job of dividing his clumps of herbaceous plants in the borders and had much comment and interference on how many new plants to get from each parent.

'Ah this is doing me good. I'm not getting enough fresh air stuck in that office all day.'

He glanced at her hair escaping from the hastily tied elastic band.

'You do me good too. Such skills and so pretty, the way your hair falls is tantalising.'

'I'm meant to be perking up your perennials not you!' she said not caring about her cheekiness.

He laughed and sloshed the end of his coffee into the neat hedge she had trimmed the day before.

'Oh I so envy your boyfriend; you are full of fire.'

His last comment burned through her allowing scenes of passion and desire that were not really hers to burst into her body. Had he touched her that second he would have the success he sought. Wren's assurances to Indira would have counted for nothing. She dragged herself from want, thankful that the need was not really hers.

Although Wren knew this situation did not belong there was no escape. Early on in her soul's journey on earth she had been in a similar situation. This had been in the Iron Age when she had taken every man who'd turned to her or offered food. The man who protected her and her offspring was driven mad with jealousy. He threw himself onto an open fire to quell his pain. Chaos and murder followed. She had been reborn immediately to rectify that and after feeling the pain of losing some-one she was so sure of, understood how her actions affected others. She was too immature to recognise Alessandro then. This was early on when not many souls were queuing up to come to Earth. The harshness was too uncomfortable but when others who had elected to go to other planets in other universes or different vibrations saw how quickly the earth cycle progressed, there was the great rush. Now, especially with the recent war creating foetal vacancies, it was much quicker to join the cycle.

Indira was a quick learner and way above the soul she thought Wren was. That is why she was aware of the situation and how she recognised the souls she was waiting for. Lucky her, Wren thought as his voice brought her back to her physical actions.

He'd taken her introspection to be today's rejection.

'Well if you aren't going to talk to me I might as well go. You are doing good work Wren. I'd like you to give me help with a croquet lawn. Can't have Sir Saul being one up on me can I?'

He'd never know how close he'd come to getting his way.

Next morning when Wren looked sadly at cold, drooping plants she heard his voice.

'You are costing me a fortune!' Mr Foggin, heralded by a visible puff of breath, came through the November air wearing a huge checked muffler over his pyjamas but under his coat.

Wren looked up from where she'd tried a fork in the frosted earth and took the opportunity to rub at chilled fingers.

'I assure you...'

He held up a hand stiffened by a huge Astrakhan and leather glove.

'No, no, no! You don't understand. Williamson is not coming back on Monday as planned, whole family has flu, him too. Don't want the bloody germs getting down here.'

He didn't stop talking as he moved his eyes across her flushed face and into the eyes he was so hungry for.

'You'll have to stay on. Is it too late to prune the wisterias and clematis? Oh what a situation!'

'Of course I'll stay on but I'm not thinking of putting my rate up.'

'No but I'll have to pay you both. Got my orders don't you know, if I want to eat.'

This was the first time he had alluded to his relationship with Indira and Wren would have thought it strange had she not been aware of things and come to love Indira during their quick but enjoyable lunches together.

He clapped his thick gloves together and laughed.

'Well my son is coming back from school in Scotland next week. Do you know him? He went to Highcopse school for a while when we first moved here. Is that where you went?'

Strangely, for all she knew that Jeremy was the very reason she was here the news that he would soon be within reach shook her, she hoped he didn't see her flush.

'What's his name?' She felt a fraud but did not want to destroy the status quo.

'Jeremy.'

'Well there was a new boy.'

'That might be him. Very dark and beautiful. Collects stamps... must have pestered the whole school to add to his collection.'

'Yes I think I did see him.'

'I hope he doesn't distract you, he has as much of an eye for a pretty girl as I do. Don't relish the competition.'

'As far as I'm concerned there is no competition.'

'Ouch! You know how to hurt a man gone all tender on you don't you?'

Wren laughed at him which seemed the only way she'd had any success in keeping him away from her.

The weekend Jeremy was due home Wren tried everything to take her mind away from the knowledge of his close proximity. Not one word from the book she had been reading reached her brain. Tot had to repeat himself each time he spoke to her and Paul delighted in calling her a nerd without redress. She could hardly wait for Monday when she'd be in the same place as Jeremy; the place to where fate had moved her.

Wren had never been so grateful to the dark mornings for they had robbed Mr. Foggin of his morning walk. Of course it meant she had to start a little later but this was better than trying to be normal when her whole heart was quivering with anticipation.

Cold bit at her nose when she tried to work outside. Blowing on her stiff fingertips on her way to the heated greenhouse, she noticed curtains at an upstairs window pulled shut. It had to be where Jeremy slept. It became her only thought; the whole morning was spent unable to concentrate. The curtains were still closed at twelve thirty when Indira called her in for the lunch they now both looked forward to. The older woman had come to love Wren and promised help when the time came for the debt between them to be repaid. They were both sure it would.

Wren relaxed a little as the warmth of the kitchen hit her but her spirits tumbled when she saw the table set only for two.

'It was to be a special lunch today Wren but we've been robbed by some-one's need to recover from an end of term celebration.' Indira frowned as pushed a bowl of scented lentils decorated with crisp garlic slices across the table.

'Oh?' Wren tried not to seem too interested but every antenna was bristled onto full alert.

'The joy of the whole house returned last night. Do you know Jeremy? He went to the village school for a while when we first returned from India?'

Before she answered Wren took a drink to try to make her voice not sound as if her heart were beating at her tonsils.

'Did he collect stamps? Is he the one? I gave him some of mine from letters my uncle sent me from Spain and other countries.'

'That would be him. I fear he has given up collecting stamps for collecting girls and beer bottles if the state of him when he arrived here last night is anything to go by.'

'And,' Indira said with mock crossness, 'I sent all the way to an importer's in Newcastle for these Okra just for his return and what does he do? Stays in bed with weak tea and toast.'

Did she know how deeply her disappointment was shared?

'This is his favourite but he'll just have to wait; like I have for his company.'

It was easy to see the love Indira had for the son of the house and feel the frustration that he had not shown for the special meal she had prepared for his return. Wren felt her excited heart sink to her stomach.

She wouldn't see him today.

The days were shortening before Christmas so that it was becoming later and later in the morning when Wren caught sight of the three tall chimneys that still gave her a thrill as she came down the woodland path to work. She had not slept last night knowing Jeremy was in the house and yet so far away from every longing need she had since she first telephoned Mr. Foggin. Every second of the last time she'd seen him ran through her mind again and again. It had to be today.

The curtains of his room were still shut every time she glanced up on her way from the conservatory to the pile of compost delivered yesterday to the back of the garages. She held his image so close to her chest to staunch the fast flowing yearning inside. The north wind had tossed snow flurries into the air yesterday so Wren had planned to re-pot the starving plants kept at a constant temperature. She'd share their luxury by spending the day indoors. Still she had to struggle with the heavy sacks as she brought them in to warm up to the same temperature as the soil she was replacing. It was on her last journey that she looked up from the wobbling barrow to see Jeremy's curtains had been flung untidily open.

Snow flurried around her eyes as it tried to fight the wind to blanket the earth. The gusts won. Tiny flakes, too weak to build into any idea of white beauty they might have left the heavens with, disappeared like the panicked breath shooting out in front of her.

Back in the warmth Wren teased her slightly damp hair from its elastic band and curled it up into a double pony tail. The lipstick she pulled from her jeans pocket was cold but it still melted to the mouth she hoped Jeremy would find attractive. The cream jumper had been washed by Lil and kept for yesterday. It was still clean and smelled slightly of the lavender laundry bags she'd helped to fill in August. She began to sweat. What was she doing? Preparing herself for perusal from a man. If he was Alessandro he'd be attracted to her no matter what.

She had half an hour to wait until she entered that kitchen where today he'd be having lunch.

She closed her eyes as desperation seemed to vibrate every inch of her body. Compost shook from her hands onto the marble floor. Plants fell from her shaking grasp. She abandoned all attempts to take her mind from the minute she would set eyes on Jeremy and just fell into her urgent hope.

When she opened the door to the kitchen she was alone. The table was set for three.

The sight of the place laid for Jeremy flushed blood to her face. When she pulled the towel from its hook to dry her hands she was still the only person in the room. Over held breath she heard voices in an echoing hall and then a door slam. Urgent footsteps were followed by a swift lift to a sneck and the door opened.

Indira was alone.

Years of waiting. Thousands of nights of wondering and still she was made to wait.

'I don't know what that boy has learned from school but he seems to have pushed his manners out of his brain.' She said bustling silk sari and embarrassment into the room.

Silence seemed to rush forward and surround the two women disappointed by the same person.

The torment of it had to be ended.

'Ah well. More food for us.' Indira sighed leaning into the oven to bring out two lidded dishes.

All Wren's hopelessness seemed to have wrenched out her appetite so that the fork went to her mouth loaded and came back to the plate the same way.

'Oh I'm sorry. I shouldn't let my crossness affect you. Just forget it. I had hoped Jeremy would be here to meet another person his own age. You could tell him where it's all happening, you know; discos and all those things you teenagers seem to have these days.'

It was then that Indira noticed Wren's lipstick and new hairdo.

'I see you were hoping to make an impression on him too. Sorry.'

Wren, devastated that she had been so shallow and obvious, forced herself to eat.

'Well the way he seems to be these days you might be better off not meeting him. He prefers to seek out his father at the office and get him to give him a driving lesson to the country club. He knows I don't approve of alcohol. Water is all he'd get here.'

'Such a shame you didn't meet him on your last day before Christmas.'

'My last day?' Wren hooked her glance.

'Yes; I'm sorry. I allowed my disappointed anger to swamp the good news I had for you.'

She pushed back her chair and took from the work bench, a Christmas card envelope.

'Mr Foggin left this for you. He is thrilled with your work but knows there is nothing left to do. He has given you a special bonus.'

When Wren made no move to take the card; it was placed on the table as flat as her hopes.

'Aren't you pleased? Mr Foggin fears he's been too greedy, he knows you have a backlog of work, Sir Saul told him this when he asked for your help.'

Intuition, first from the woman then from an advanced soul, searched Wren's energy through knowing and loving eyes.

'You must be sick of those cold walks through the woods every day.'

Wren slowly took the card.

Indira placed an understanding hand over hers enclosing in its grasp their ancient shared bond.

'I'm sorry. It must be hard leaving souls you have known from a previous life but you have proved to me that you have learned. I have grown to love you again. There hasn't been time to completely settle our karma. Maybe later...oh well. This was only part of your purpose this time. You must get on.'

Their eyes locked, slowly producing a special energy.

'I will miss you little sister.'

Both women were shot back to the last time those words were said. Red blood ran from the nose of the Hindu girl who had flung herself from the roof of the house she'd been left in alone after the man she'd stolen from her sister ran off with some-one prettier, younger and virginal. He only wanted virgins.

Indira thought it was the girl in front of her now and Wren took on a new understanding of the soul she'd robbed. She knew that one day she would have to repay her.

So deep was their reverie that they missed all noises of some-one entering the house until the kitchen door crashed open and hit the fridge behind it.

'Blast! Blast! Blast! Would you believe it? He doesn't want me to drive because of the snow! It's only a little flurry! Not even lying for heaven's sake.'

'You've been drinking never the less Jeremy.'

The soft grey polo neck sweater had dots of melted snow at the neck where it showed beneath a well cut Napa jacket which he peeled from his body. At the same time he pushed his toes into the back of expensive Chelsea boots to kick them off.

Indira rose quickly to shake and tidy up the discarded garments.

'Yes well; a seasonal nip isn't drinking. Father was giving his managers a festive scotch. It's nearly Christmas isn't it?'

Long fingers picked at saffron chicken in a dish on the Aga.

'I'll get you some hot.' Indira slapped at his hand before whisking the dish into the oven.

Wren, yanked from one sensation to another, pulled at her mouth so that it stopped hanging open.

He had grown to be taller than his father. The flush in his face from rushing in cold then the heat of the kitchen made a rosy glow through the colour Indian sun had blessed him with. His boyish charms had disappeared and allowed a stronger face and longer hair to present well cared for teeth to Wren on a surprised but delighted grin. Her breath came out raggedly and heat dampened her temples.

'Hello. Who's this?'

She wanted to deny his dark gaze but her heart had pumped her to a standstill.

'I told you I had some-one I wanted you to meet.'

He moved towards a chair and swinging it towards him lifted one long leg to sit astride backwards but facing Wren. His chin leaned on folded arms along the top. He narrowed his eyes touching every hypersensitive nerve as they glittered over Wren.

'You said it was the gardener not a babe.'

Need throbbed in the space between them as his eyes pulled in from her body and small breasts to her mouth and then welded to her own eyes.

'Good God! I know you.....don't I?'

Called upon to speak, Wren dragged her voice from some deep shock hidden location.

'Do Spanish stamps ring a bell?' her voice did not sound like her own but some feeble echo of it.

'Yes of course; but it's those eyes I remember. What happened to those ankle socks and flat chest?'

'Don't be so personal Jeremy.' Indira chided, pulling the chair so that he had to get up.

Automatically he went to wash. The tap splashed over the sheen on the stainless steel draining board as he turned to reaffirm his view. He took in the dead leaf caught in her hair just as it fell to her shoulders and the chunky knitted socks pulled over the bottom of her jeans.

'You the gardener then?'

Indira dried the mess he'd made before pushing the towel into his hands.

'Don't sound so surprised. Wren has her own business and is forging the way for women to do anything they want in any field.'

'She can do anything she wants in my field anytime.'

Indira shook her head then flicked him with the tea towel.

'You've gathered impertinence along with a tan on your last trip Jeremy but neither have any use in this house.'

There was a fondness between these two that was a pleasure to see but the dynamics of their relationship wasn't what was making Wren's heart thump and palms sweat.

He hardly looked at the food placed before him but kept his eyes on Wren.

She wanted to stay forever in his gaze for she knew with a certainty that it was where she belonged. It was the look from Indira which forced her to get up. It was a knowing and yet curious look. Wren wanted to escape before the query turned to triumph.

'I'd better get on. Tidy up before the light goes.'

Indira waited until Wren zipped up her grubby work coat before hugging her and kissing her cheek.

'I've had more pleasure from our lunches than you could ever know. And thank you for the greatest gift of all.'

Wren squeezed a kiss back to the woman she felt love for then looked out of the window.

'Good! The snow has stopped and there is enough blue sky to make a pair of trousers out of...but only for a mouse!'

Indira laughed. 'I'll miss your funny little country sayings; and I'll miss you. Goodbye my dear.'

As she left by the back door Jeremy's eyes never left her. He said no farewell. He raised no hand in parting.

He knew.

He really knew!

CHAPTER THIRTY FIVE

Wren tidied up every tool she'd used, cleaned all trace of use and hung them up exactly where she'd found them. There could be no criticism from the gardener when he returned. No jealousy. No reason to fear for his employment.

The work was done automatically because she needed all her mind to sift what had just happened. Every word from Jeremy, every glance, every deep penetrating search was played over and over in her heart and brain. She had never been more sure. The attraction between the two was palpable. It didn't seem to matter that he took after his father for his direct and seductive manner. Her blood sang in her veins, she felt capable of anything.

Wren had no doubt that she would be chased; but this time she wanted it.

Jeremy had no clue where she lived. Where she would work next or when he would see her again. He had to make his move sooner or later and Wren knew it would be sooner.

'I still have your stamps you know.'

His voice came from the back of the shed.

'You'll be telling me next that you've thought of me often since you went away.'

'Well...'

'Save it Jeremy. I know you had no interest in me what so ever.'

'Well you didn't look like this then.'

He took her elbow to spin her around. His touch was electric. He'd developed a disturbing masculinity. She knew she was a poor slave to her want for this disturbingly beautiful youth.

His eyes had darkened and his voice deepened. Wren had no doubt that his hormones had got him here. Of this she was pleased. Her own hormones had been awakened for the first time in this life. But there had to be more from him.

'I still have a pile of stamps for you do you want them?' she croaked.

He laughed, knowing she was playing the game they both wanted.

Gently, he took secateurs from her hands so that he could hold them both, pressing them to his thumping heart. She saw and felt his breath against her face tormenting them together.

'This is what I want.'

He captured her eyes so she couldn't move. His head tilted as he parted his lips slightly.

When his mouth met hers it was sweet and soft at first but gradually, inescapably sank into a passion that went back to the very beginning of both their souls.

His hands went to her waist to urge her body to his so that she felt everything he was and ever had been. Everything he was going to be again. She was lost.

Each touch of his kiss seemed forever, relighting flames that had never been doused. Her body took her mind to places she'd forgotten, all of them with the energy she was now willing to go anywhere with.

There was giggling outside. Reality dragged them both from what was charging between them.

Voices. One she recognised. One she didn't.

Jeremy whipped her out of the potting shed with one tug to her wrist. Two steps were all it took to hide behind the pulled back door just in time not to be seen by Mr Foggin and a large busted girl with her coat open to display her charms.

Totally engrossed in each other, they entered the place Wren and Jeremy had just shot out of and a male hand pulled shut the door behind them without noticing.

Left in the open by the disappearing hiding place, trying to stifle laughter and shock Jeremy steered Wren down an overgrown path and into the darkness of old pine trees.

When they felt it was safe to allow feelings their freedom they laughed half with nervousness and half with disappointment.

'Who was that?'

'It's father's latest secretary. Too full of Christmas booze to realise she'll have to face him in the New Year.'

'Oh! Poor thing.'

'Yes, he'll have to employ a new one. He never learns.'

'I didn't mean him.'

'Never mind. It's me and you I care about. Now where were we?'

But the sleaze of the situation had muddied her desire.

'We were nowhere. I was going home and you were looking for something you have no right to expect.'

Her terseness seemed not to dent his raw and burning passion which Wren sensed she had to stand back from or go up in flames.

'Right is the exact word I'd use but not in that context. I feel we belong together.'

He was correct of course but just now his masculine needs were what drove him.

She couldn't trust that kind of hot sexual pull. One that was new to her in this life.

'Perhaps we do but not here not in the cold and damp, not in the dark.'

He seemed to study her very energy, absorbing everything she was.

'You do want me? You've been searching for me haven't you?'

'Oh Alessandro...'

'What?' he laughed. 'How many men do you have on the go at the moment?'

Horrified with his response, her eyes raked his. Was he teasing? Did he not yet realise?

Whatever the motives for his comments he seemed even keener.

'Jeremy, Jeremy!'

Indira's anxious tone met them through the stillness of frost.

'Coming!'

The suddenness of his shout cut her free and she walked backwards towards the path and the back gate.

'Will you be all right in the dark? What time's your bus? Where do you live?'

The whisper was as loud as he dared make it but Wren put a finger to her lips before turning around to run the path she knew so well.

The snow had come to nothing. The zinging race home through early moonlit branches added to her glow of happiness. Nothing could stop her now. She had found him.

She had no work and yet still had to be out of the house for the office hours every-one still thought she worked. She could hear Paul irritating Noelene in the next bedroom. He was saying she shouldn't get two presents just because her birthday was on Christmas.

Wren resented the squabbling entering her thoughts. There was only one subject she wanted to feast her mind on. How could she possibly meet up with him again? She couldn't telephone the house as Indira would answer. She couldn't go back. Hadn't she been paid off handsomely?

Jeremy hadn't a clue where she lived and even if he supposed it was on this estate where would he start looking now that three thousand houses had cancelled out the fields. There had to be a way; she just couldn't think of it.

She spent the next two days sneaking about the trees outside Kademuir Gables. It was impossible to see anything without entering the gate she had grown so used to pushing open but was now forbidden to her. Jeremy never once appeared. He was either out or in bed. There was no sign of any-one, disappointment made the cold colder and the damp damper. Misery only deepened the fear that she could have been wrong. Alessandro would move heaven and earth to be with her once they had met. Could she doubt his feelings? They had been so strong. Right now she wouldn't have minded if it was only his hormones that drove him to her. At least he'd be here.

When a sniffle made her realise she might die of exposure if she continued her ridiculous hanging around, Wren knew she had to think of something else. As she made her way to Jim and Lil's she gathered berried holly and flowering ivy deliberately choosing whippy stems.

She was still teaching a clumsy Jim how to make a seasonal wreath for his front door when Lil came in puffing out icy breath and stamping frosty boots.

'What's this? Bringing the garden inside now its winter eh!'

Jim held up his attempt which immediately fell to pieces as he glowed with pride.

'Have another go Jim.' Lil encouraged when she examined the generous, full ring bursting with red berries on prickles and black berries on waxy ivy.

Jim sucked at a pricked finger.

'No bloody fear. Dangerous work that; best left to women.'

'You can have this one Lil, I made it for you.'

'Mind girl, you never cease to amaze me.' She held the Christmas wreath by the wire proffered to her. 'You know Sir Saul could do with his halls decked with boughs of holly an' all. Why don't you come up wi' me the morrow?'

'Oh I couldn't just turn up.'

'Get away with you! Sir loves you around and that Grandson of his is coming for Christmas, you could make the place look so welcoming for a young 'n.'

Wren glanced at her watch, cleared away the unused pieces and said absentmindedly.

'We'll see.'

She was on Lil's doorstep at seven thirty having spent a night weighing up her chances of seeing Jeremy at his gate, catching 'flu, against doing something useful that would at least allow fate to do its work.

Sir Saul was delighted to have Wren around the place again and once he'd seen the first of her wreaths he asked for table decorations and candle holders. He begged her to choose and decorate his tree.

She found plenty of things to be garnered from the garden and woods. Statuesque seed heads of teasel, dried lacy umbrellas of Sweet Cicely, spiky Musk thistle and majestic spoke like heads of the African

Agapanthus. Wren gathered a basket of acorns not yet split from their cups and a few handsome, spiked horse chestnuts. Whilst she was routing around for white paint and wire in the potting shed Wren came across a box with little packets of silver and gold dust neatly stacked beside ironed out ribbon and tired tinsel. She knew this forgotten box had been used by Letitia so it gave her even more pleasure to use.

With Smith's grumbling help she chose and brought in a majestic fir from a tree crowded slope at the back of the wood. The hall would look even grander with this and the garland swung across the fireplace.

'You bring this place to life you know Wren.' Sir Saul was heralded back from his walk by two spaniels glowing with exercise and pleasure at the sight of Wren.

'You love and understand this house and it seems to blossom when you are here. I hope you are still working on Christmas Eve when Lintern arrives.'

'Lintern?' Wren asked picking stray berries from the floor to add to the winter pot pourri needing some new zip in its bowl on the polished table.

'My Grandson; I told you.'

'I have enough of boys and their ways at home with my brother thank you very much.'

The phone rang and Sir strode into his study to silence the persistent peace breaker. He came out again really quickly startling Wren just as she reached the top of the step ladder to wire the golden star to the tree's pinnacle.

'That was Timothy Foggin asking me for lunch at the Country Club. I told him you had made my house a home again. Seemed rather jealous. He was really pleased with your work for him.'

'Damn!' The phone rang again. 'Oh excuse me! I'll never get out in time.'

Wren took the tidyings of her work into the kitchen where Lil had laid out a dish of Parsnip and Mushroom soup.

They sat down together enjoying the rest and deliciousness of a creative cook's imagination.

'Do you think Sir will like it?'

Before Wren could answer the man himself came abruptly into the kitchen wearing his boots and overcoat.

'I hope I haven't inconvenienced you Lillian but I've been asked out to lunch; sorry.'

'Of course not Sir. It'll keep.'

He looked at Wren. 'I'm afraid I'll be robbing you of your company too. Shot myself in the foot rather.'

'How's that then sir?' Lil looked disappointed to be plundered of her gossip and coffee with Wren.

'Told Foggin too enthusiastically about the skills of our dear decorator here. Had a call back to bring her with me.' He looked at the cheese and celery sandwich waiting for Wren to finish her soup.

'I do apologise my dear. Do you think you could bring that with you? Eat it on the way?'

The car swept into the driveway of Kadiemuir Gables with Wren and her sandwich intact. She had not dared eat in such a fine car which was the excuse she gave Sir instead of admitting to a stomach lurching with nervous excitement.

Mr Foggin was waiting on the front step for his lift and seemed rather surprised to see Wren.

'Hello my dear.'

'I'll pick you up later, drop you off home.' Sir Saul said leaning across the seat Wren had just vacated to allow the well turned out gentleman join his friend.

'Don't worry. There will only be a couple of hours decent light left for gathering, and then I'll have decorations to make. You'll be long gone by then.'

He waved his assent and Wren; sandwich in hand stood outside the house alone looking around for inspiration. It was hard to take anything through the thick blanket of excitement.

It took a few moments for the birds to sing after their garden had been intruded upon by such a noisy car. Wren could hardly hear them above her heart beat which threatened to choke her. She broke up the bread and cheese into small pieces and tossed them onto a bit of lawn.

He was around, she could feel it. But it would take quite a while before she could let him know she was here by taking things into the house. Fighting memories of the last time she was in the potting shed she took secateurs then made towards the trees and bushes looking for winter treasure.

She might have passed by a million suitable boughs and berries because she couldn't concentrate. There was nothing in her mind but Jeremy; nothing in her ears but a thumping heart and nothing in her body but raging desire.

From the pined area came a soft owl call. This at least penetrated her captured brain so that she looked up to try to see her favourite beige flash of barn owl.

'He's not up there, he's down here.'

Startled and lifted with sudden joy at hearing the voice she'd played over and over again in her thoughts, dreams and every waking moment she turned, flushed with hope.

'I can imitate any bird you ask.' he laughed jumping in front of her.

'I must say you look remarkably alive for the person I'd thought didn't exist!'

He was wearing a soft wine sweater over a blue shirt. His hair, damp at the ears looked newly washed and he smelled delicious. He was eight feet away but she felt as if he was pulling her towards him.

'What are you talking about?' It wasn't what she wanted to say but it was all she could manage.

'I have searched the world for you, well the world of Highcopse anyway. I came to the conclusion you didn't exist. Every driving lesson I took with Dad or the instructor was around the terrace and council houses. When they queried why I wanted to spend so much time there I told them I was looking for good places to practice three point turns and reversing around corners. They didn't think it was good as I didn't improve for my mind was elsewhere. I was looking for you.'

The pleasure of this confirmation that his desire was at least as great as hers flooded out into a smile.

'I also walked the woods, every inch. I've been in every pub and disco this side of Newcastle and quite a few in the city as well. Where have you been.....? Apart from in my heart?'

His expression remained dark and intense, his eyes locked to hers. He was serious.

The constant ache she felt for him grew to something she'd never known in this lifetime.

The masculinity of the hand that reached out to hers made her own shake as he moved near enough to take it.

His other arm went around her shoulder releasing days and nights of tension from her muscles and changing it to sheer physical electricity. She melted into a walk beside him not knowing where his steps and hers would lead, caring only for the warmth of his lips as they brushed her forehead.

She tensed slightly when they stopped at the ice house but he encouraged her by opening the old wooden door. Warmth hit her along with a soft glow of three dozen candles.

The old Aladdin paraffin stove seemed incongruous beside a shining silver bucket from which poked the neck of a Champagne bottle. A thick eiderdown lay on top of a ground sheet.

'Don't look so surprised. You said you wouldn't make love to me in the cold and damp.'

'But you didn't know I was coming.' She said wounded into a blush.

'Of course I did. I heard Father on the phone and rang back to say he wanted you here immediately. Saul, being the gentleman that he is said he'd oblige.'

'But that was only half an hour ago.'

'I've been preparing for days, almost gave up but I knew fate would help us.'

This echo of her own thoughts made her even more sure of who he was. Excitement teamed about them and spread out ahead of them.

'Champagne?'

He took the bottle and twisted it so that the cork popped, hitting the old stone ceiling.

'Oh I never have...'

'What never?' he laughed handing her a sparkling glass.

'To us...and love.' he said chinking his glass to hers. He took almost half the contents in one go and shook his head at her timid sip.

'Don't you like it?'

'Well it's not what I expected. I thought it would taste like pop.' she grimaced and he laughed again before downing the rest of his glass and refilling it as high as the effervescent bubbles would allow.

He gulped the froth from the top and put his glass on the tray beside the bucket. With his eyes never leaving hers he gently eased her fingers from the crystal flute, placing it alongside his.

He placed tender lips to each of her hands.

'What's this?' he asked moving his thumb over the mark around her wrist. 'Looks like you left an elastic band on too long.'

'No, I've had it since birth.'

'Then I love it.' He kissed it lingeringly, his mouth wandered softly over her arm drawing needs from her very core.

She came alive in a way that sent doubt flying.

Pulling her towards him he gently gave her lips the closeness she'd longed for. His hands went through her hair to pull the carelessly tied ribbon holding it from her face. He stood back taking only a little of the powerful static emanating between them with him. Dark eyes held her gaze as he urged her to the eiderdown; she went naturally.

Then she felt herself draw back.

'What is it?'

'Oh Jeremy. Champagne isn't the only thing I haven't tried.'

He cupped her face in his trembling hands. There was fate and something irresistible about them.

'But that's perfect my darling. Just perfect.'

The candles grew shorter and were often replaced during the next month.

They wrapped around each other alone in the ice-house, hands entwined, exquisite caresses and gentle kisses to her neck as he lay wrapped around her back like a secret.

Her body was loved into a radiant memory.

This had been the confirmation Wren had been waiting for. The closeness and passion that had developed between her and Jeremy left her in no doubt of whom he was.

Christmas had been a kind of deprived hell. Neither had been able to escape family Christmas so that when they met again for one glorious afternoon before New Year it was electric. After devouring each other in torrents of pent up need they'd made each other laugh with tales of how they'd suffered. Jeremy's mother had returned but not spoken to her husband for four days even when she'd taken his arm to accompany him to the Friendly

Ball. Wren had tales of how she and Ivy had spent hours preparing vegetables only for Paul to be sick over his dinner because of stealing Tot's liqueur chocolates.

That they were meant to be together neither doubted. How to be together for the rest of their lives baffled them both. Jeremy wanted this. He said so didn't he? And yet!

Each time they met Wren gently probed for something other than their passion to confirm the history she was so sure they shared.

Alone in her bed listening to the intrusive drone of TV's, 'In Town Tonight', through the floor boards she thought of Tot and how he needed television to help him relax. He seemed so tired lately, sitting more and more in the chair almost as worn as he was and she felt the guilt of not spending the time to encourage him out on their winter walks. He shared with her so much, the glorious, ever changing drama of a sunset, the uplifting joy of birdsong, so much beauty on Earth. Now he just stayed at home. She hoped he was all right.

But her mind soon dragged back to the only place it wanted to be. She analysed every murmur from Jeremy's mind, each silken touch, every climax that confirmed their love. She wondered what great task he would undertake later in his life that had warranted him returning to Earth when he should now have been enjoying another place. When thoughts came of how he'd entered her life so conveniently after he'd been born in India she marvelled at the manipulation of the patterns set before birth. And yet it was not in the plan for her to even be here. Was it the life of the soul she had robbed who would so need his help? Could she have been so lucky?

So much love; so much laughter.

The intricacies of the situation threatened to blow up her mind.

She was here in his life that was what she had wanted wasn't it? So what if he didn't recognise her. She wasn't meant to be here was she? There would come a time.

She only had to wait.

CHAPTER THIRTY SIX

The laughter stopped the same week as her period did.

Wren frantically thumbed at the pages of the diary where she so meticulously marked four days a month with a red dot. Perhaps she'd got it wrong, turned two pages at once. Maybe she'd misread the previous month. Counting the days again and again made no difference. She was three days late. She threw the dairy on the bed in disgust at her own stupidity.

Terrified that Ivy might notice and seek out confirmation of what she kept so rigorously in her head; Wren tucked the proof into the bottom of her bag then went to the airing cupboard to take a handful of sanitary towels from where they were hidden by Ivy from the men.

How she wish she needed them. How could she have been so reckless?

The afternoons with Jeremy increased. The paraffin smell welcomed her with warmth; the candles were reduced to only three and the champagne replaced by whisky. He didn't notice she had something on her mind and had long since given up offering her a drink before or after they made love.

That there was a fresh bottle to open every day even though Jeremy had alcohol on his breath when he arrived didn't seem to mean anything. It never cooled his ardour or gave him the 'brewer's droop' he so often laughed about.

His eyes glittered as he rolled from her to his bottle.

'I wish I could persuade you to take a nip. Give you a warm tummy to get back home on.'

She looked at his head as it tipped back the contents of the glass he refilled twice before turning his attention back to her.

'My tummy has plenty of warmth at the moment, thank you.'

This opening, so obvious, so God given was lost as he grabbed her to him.

'I know! And I intend to feel just how hot it is once more before I send you out into that February wind.'

Lost in whisky fumes and love, Wren gave up caring about anything but their mutual need. She had long since stopped asking him why he hadn't returned to school or India.

Trust, she told herself! He was here in this life for a reason. She didn't know what it was and it was obvious that he knew only on a soul level. She could deal with that. She was with him. That was all that mattered.

Her money was running out. She spent nothing on herself or fares. Her only outgoing was her keep which Ivy had increased to three pounds seven and six after realising that the Ministry would have given Wren a pay rise.

Things were coming to a head. If she were pregnant everything would change. Jeremy would have to be told and then their parents. There would be a wedding but a shotgun one. Wren realized a lot of people would be made miserable by her thoughtlessness but it was done now.

Life was about change. This was how people moved through their karmic maze.

Pain gave growth. She knew that. But still she couldn't separate it from dread.

Twice she had to wait for Jeremy. He arrived glowing saying he'd been testing his newly acquired driving licence in the busy streets of Newcastle. The turquoise Ford Anglia had threatened to take him away from her at first but he'd soon got over the novelty. Wren's enquiries into what he was using for money were met with the same vague mumblings about helping his father in business as when she asked him about his education. His eager mouth easily silenced hers. What did it matter? He'd fulfil his destiny.

Every morning Wren hoped for the period she thought might arrive. Maybe it was strain keeping her monthlies away. If she was pregnant maybe she'd miscarry! Perhaps she was ill! Not eating enough? Making love too vigorously?

Fear and a strange kind of hope had pushed out of her mind the most obvious way of finding out if a baby was inside her. When she remembered how easy it was the relief she could have enjoyed was weakened by the realisation that her original knowledge was becoming even more diluted.

It should have been the first thing she did!

If there was a baby she would accept it as fate. It would be dreadfully shaming of course but a sure way of gluing her to Jeremy so that although she certainly was not his purpose for this incarnation, she would be alongside him whilst he fulfilled his tasks. It would be wonderful to find out exactly what was so great that he should have left her behind.

She'd be right there beside him.

Maybe he'd come to recognise her true self.

The peace she needed seemed so elusive. Television, squabbling siblings and Ivy's frequent calls for help in the kitchen filled the time she spent at home. Taking Tot his plate of bread and jam and mug of tea whilst he was watching boxing on Grandstand, Wren was shocked at how grey he looked. Never taking his eyes from the possibility of a great right hook he thanked her by squeezing her hand. She felt her mouth turn down. How could she have allowed Jeremy to push everything else in her life to so little importance? Tot needed his week-ends in the fresh air. The soil was too wet for any work but she should have been walking with him. He had no motivation. He had lost his dog and now his daughter seemed to push him to second place.

Soon there would be violets and primroses for them to enjoy together. She would make time.

He needed her. Jeremy would have to miss one day. Even the thought of that crumpled her.

She needed complete peace to be able to meditate and bring forward the spirit of the life starting inside her. There would have been no need for this in normal circumstances. The spirits would have agreed before they became physical that they would be adopting the mother and child relationship. This was different. Wren had no clue as to who the spirit so newly left the glorious place of happiness with the Pure Lights could be. If there was a new life inside her she'd know this way.

It must have been guilt that muddied the blissful state she so needed. It was late when the tinny half chatter of radio Luxemburg or Caroline stopped irritating through the wall from Noelene and Paul's room. Even with the house so quiet in the strange two a.m. hush she was aware of energies gathering dreams to sort out the problems of the other people sleeping in this house. She felt she should have tuned in to some of them, particularly Tot's. Instead she gave him some healing energy and moved back to her desperate need.

It was no good.

Sparse sleep was all she could find that night.

Monday morning she knew she would make different. Clear blue skies fooled every-one into thinking there might be an early spring but nipped the hope out of them as soon as they left the warm side of the widow to smell the air.

This was exactly the sort of day Wren needed. After changing at Lil and Jim's she didn't hang around as she usually did tidying a kitchen she had become to know as well as her own or finding any tiny job outside that might fill her time until Jeremy had woken up enough to leave his bed.

There was a place she just had to go. Somewhere she hadn't been to since before she was born.

She hoped she'd find it.

It was strange to pass Kademuir Gables and enter the second wave of woodland her mother had frequented when she was carrying her. Eighteen years had passed and the brambles would be thicker, the trees taller and the path less defined. She was met by a wall of dry barked pines sticking close with bare twiggy branches until they made love to one another where their green tops met and wove together. Was it through here? Was it to the left behind the hillock? Was it not this wood at all but some other in her distant memory that no longer existed?

Disappointment started to dissolve the edges of her intentions. It could be anywhere over six square miles. Only Tot and June had ever visited this special place. Tot had not been able to drag himself anywhere near it since the death of his daughter, his wild¬-life companion.

The sun brought her so sincerely alive to colour.

A few rosehip haws still clung to their post not realizing they should have been eaten or set seed before new life overtook them. Nutrient and sun starved grass bent and shone glossy in its beigeness. The rich caramel litter of pine needles and their large cones bullied fir cones out of the way. It was clear that no-one had walked this path for years. Wren peered into the mass of dark trunks. It was not inviting, yet she knew that like life she had to travel through a dark place to reach the light and beauty.

The only feet that had tread here were cloven. Deer runs showed Wren the way to grassy glades and spring fed ponds but none felt right.

The wood had to thin to allow the beech to grow for Wren held in her mind a vivid picture of her mother leaning against a broad green trunk of an ancient beech. The sounds from underfoot changed first. Dried beechnut husks, robbed of their fruit by lucky squirrels, crunched and cracked. There was beech here and oak but nothing grand enough to lay your back on and not be seen from behind. It wasn't here. It must be further.

The litter on the floor of the wood began to show patches of morning frost, this excited Wren as she knew the canopy had to open to allow this. A few steps showed more sky. The birds had stopped their rejoicing of morning to weigh up what was disturbing their security. It was then that Wren heard it. A clear, open throated song that told her she was near. Hearty voice from a tiny bird that trusted and knew her. The wren darted about flexible new branches and guided her. This way and that, faster and faster. Running. Bending. Ducking. Panting.

It stopped.

Wren stopped.

It was here.

The tiny wren glowed with joy and its true being. It perched on a low branch to gaze at the one who had sought her help. That was when it changed from brown to blue. From solid to light. From bird to knowledge.

It had been May many years ago when she'd last been here, brought in the body of a mother so desperate. Jan had been here that day too. Darling, darling dog. She would have led Wren straight to the place she sought, no doubt about it for she too felt what was here.

The fledgling wrens who had shown June such love and understanding that day were long gone. Many descendants would not have survived the harshness of winter; others would be taken by the owls and sparrow hawks. But there would be some. They would carry the same spirituality.

These tiny wrens were often used to bring reassurance and help to those on Earth who needed spiritual help but could not accept much more than the physical. That they came to June here meant that there was a concentration of transfer energy. This was a special place.

The wren called up others and lifted Wren's joy to a new level. She almost burst with relief. This was the nearest she had ever been in this lifetime to any guidance from the spirit world she so loved.

She communicated with the birds not with sounds but with an understanding beyond words. Unique, economic and totally comprehending; they both knew that words were clumsy and insufficient. This was true mind reading. No questions needed to be asked.

The wrens knew why she was here. They knew how to help her.

They also knew they would not.

CHAPTER THIRTY SEVEN

'Why won't you tell me?'

She would have to sway them. She had before.

Wren felt the love. She wallowed in the relaxing, heavenly energies these wrens brought with them from a place she wished she'd never left.

These tiny spirit birds knew who she really was and empathised but this didn't persuade them to impart the knowledge Wren so desperately sought.

'But why? You do know if I am carrying a new physical life?'

'We can tell you that much.'

Wren felt a mixture of relief and dread slow her vibration for a second.

'So who is the spirit? I must know.'

'You would normally have a bond and agreement with this soul now within you. Who are we to change the way God works his special incarnations.'

'So it is special.'

'All incarnations are.'

'Yes but I feel this is especially so.'

'Do you?'

Wren knew the birds had all the information she wanted but not the reason they held it from her.

'Didn't you welcome in the soul on your highest level at the moment of conception?'

'No. I wasn't even sure I was pregnant until now.'

'We furnish you with love and energy to get through this Wren but we cannot give what is not ours to give.'

'Oh well at least I have Alessandro, he'll help me.'

'Alessandro! You have met Alessandro?'

'Don't you know? I thought you were watching over us. Alessandro is the father of the soul growing a physical body inside me.'

The wrens were silent.

'He is Alessandro isn't he? Wren was sending frantic energy of need towards the little helpers before her but no peace came back.

'Wren; we cannot interfere with this strange incarnation. You did steal life but there was no way you could steal the knowledge and karmic awareness of Elia you must proceed without it.

You do wish to proceed don't you?'

'Of course. I am not returning until Alessandro returns too.'

'How will you know?'

'What? I'll be there with him of course. I'll never leave his side.'

There was some fluttering in their thoughts that mirrored their wings.

'But he might leave yours.'

The wrens were frightening her now. They felt this and tried to calm her.

'Wren all we are saying is that we can't confirm who Alessandro is or if he will be with you when he leaves his physical to return. These are questions you can only answer for yourself.'

There had to be another way. This would take some careful handling.

The wrens led her with love back to the route she'd taken no notice of in her need. Jeremy must be the first to know they had made a physical body together. Perhaps he'd be able to meditate to meet with the soul starting its journey within her. The scramble of karma beaten with the whisk of her theft made it impossible to even guess at who might already be with them. The incoming soul would certainly have lessons and gifts for both mother and father as well as others involved in its early life. Later it might move on to even greater ties. Who knows? Only itself. There had to be a way to find out.

It was too early for Jeremy to come to the ice house and she had no way of telling him she was there. The sun had no warmth and in any case was shaded from the ice house by the trees first and then the damp earth and stones which was its roof. After her eyes adjusted to the gloom she felt around for the matches tossed carelessly aside when Jeremy had last lit the place.

The candles were mostly stubs and she had to struggle with the oil soaked wick of the stove to get the last inch of use from it. Huddling into her jumper and duffle coat offered no comfort. She meditated into the flickering flame of the candle nearest to her. Perhaps here calmness would bring the spirit of her unborn child to her consciousness. She remembered how easily she had watched her own mother but it only served to dull her hope when she remembered she never communicated with her until crisis.

Hopelessness filled the underground space. Wren tried to dissolve it by practising how she would tell Jeremy that they had made a child together. She would stroke back his hair and give him the news that would they would soon be able to show their love for each other with a beautiful baby. She would laugh at his joy and then tell him she hoped it would have his dark eyes and black silky hair.

Alessandro had always been a wonderful father whether she had been his wife or his child. She had admired him too when Wren had been grandmother to his children. Whatever their relationship he'd always loved and taught his children. This time it would be no different.

The oil stove was spluttering and only three candles had enough wax left to give any joy when the door creaked open.

'Well,' Jeremy raised his brows with unexpected pleasure. 'You are early. I didn't expect to find you here. Just came to sort these out.'

He raised an oil can and a bundle of candles towards her.

'The wicks were getting damp left here.' He kissed her as he freed his hands to shrug the coat from his shoulders.

He smelled of last night's whisky and sleepy clothes.

Her mood went unnoticed. His most urgent task was replacing the burnt out candles.

'Jeremy. Can you stop that please?'

He turned slightly but kept on digging wax out of the holders with a pen knife.

'Won't be long, then we'll get to see what we are doing as well as feeling it.'

'No! Stop now!'

This was a new tone of voice. He showed her he hated it by dropping his smile.

'Don't look at me like that Jeremy I have some important news.'

'Oh and what is it that you have to be so snappy?'

'I'm pregnant Jeremy.'

He looked at her for a few moments as if seeing her for the first time.

'But I thought you were on the pill.'

'I never said that.'

'No but all girls like you are these days, aren't they?'

She wondered what girls like her were and how many he knew.

'Whose is it?'

'What?'

'Who do you think is the father?' His eyes were steady, he was serious.

'Jeremy! You of course! Who else?'

'I don't know? I never felt the right to ask what you might be doing when you aren't here.'

She pulled her brows down with her confusion.

'But Jeremy, you know I was a virgin when we first came here. There has only ever been you?'

'Oh come on! You said that to excite me and it worked but you never thought I'd swallow it did you?'

'Swallow what. It's the truth! I love only you.'

'Who said anything about love?'

'Well no-one but it's what we both feel isn't it?'

'I love every woman I'm doing it with at the time.'

She stood up trembling with the effect of his callous comments.

'What do you mean?'

'Oh come on you don't honestly think you are the only one to ever fall for my charm do you.'

'You bring others here?'

'No, not here. Only girls like you would put up with this.'

Disgust wove itself into the air above them.

'Like what?'

'Gardeners, council house girls. Ones who'd rather lie on their backs than go to University. Girls who don't know any better.' She sucked in an angry breath and held onto it keeping her shame with it.

'Don't try to pin this on me Wren. You probably think I am the best bet because of my inheritance. Well think again girl because that's a long way off and I have no money yet. In fact quite the opposite.'

The words rang through Wren's ears but she couldn't believe them. She never knew he could be so cruel. She felt weak with impotent fury and disappointment.

She sank tortured, back to the eiderdown that had wrapped their passion and naked bodies in so much joy. Suddenly it looked weary and degrading, grubby with body fluids, floor dust and the beginnings of damp mould.

As she crumpled he studied her face. There was some of the old Alessandro peeping through. 'My God you are telling the truth aren't you?'

'Yes.'

'Oh no; you poor girl.' The tenderness when he took her hands pierced the pressure banking back her tears. She sobbed into his unwashed sweater. But he did not pull her in closer. He waited for a gap in the spasms that thrust through her and held her at arm's length.

'You'll have to get rid of it.'

'What do you mean?'

'Don't worry, I know a lady just over the Tyne Bridge but she costs. Do you have any money?'

Wren thought of the bundle she had hidden behind the brick in the coal house. All the notes had gone. Only two half-crowns weighted the old school shirt she'd so often wrapped her treasure in.

'Even if I were a millionaire I wouldn't commit such an act. We are in this together Jeremy. We have to think of a way.'

'With no money and a brat to bring up? Not us.'

She hoped this was a kind of test they were giving each other. Alessandro had been the father of her children before but only in the early incarnations had he been so cruel. Why wasn't he more caring, more understanding?

As if he'd read her feelings he pulled her to him but when his mouth sought hers it was not with comfort or understanding. Lust was pushing his head to hers, his hands to her breasts and his desire to the fore.

She pulled back.

'Oh come on. It's a shame to waste the paraffin.'

Is that all I am to you?'

'What?' he feared her disgust? 'Look. You are special to me of course you are. Actually I really enjoy our little bits of fun, more than any other.'

He didn't understand why she slapped him but when the shock wore off it excited him even more.

Unwillingly, she felt her anger turn to desire in the passion sent from his eyes to her needy heart. When he crashed his lips to her again she filled the throbbing space between them with her body. Whatever his dealings with this situation she knew they'd come through.

Together.

Dread filled her walk home and wrestled with Jeremy's last words to her. She had never been frightened during this journey in the dark. To her the trees and shrubs spoke a different language than in the light. Was it her strained state of mind that sensed something different this afternoon? She could see no-one and yet there was a strong sense of love walking with her just above her brow. That it was friendly and kind she had no doubt but there was also a slight sadness there.

Could it be the spirit of her unborn child at last? Maybe it was some help meant for Elia in her distress? Wren tried to communicate but the energy dashed off as if called away to something better.

'Damn this low awareness,' she said to herself. 'Damn everything!'

Tot and Ivy would be hurt. She would of course have to keep the deception of the last few months from them. Now too was the time to say she had left the safeness of a job with the civil service. There was no money to give Ivy for her keep. In some ways Ivy's rage would be easier to deal with than Tot's disappointment.

How would she tell them?

Together would be the best on them, the easiest on herself. Her groan ached in her chest.

It had to be done now; the torture of delay must be kept to a minimum.

Tot was on back shift which meant he finished at six pm but it would be nearer seven when he got in. She'd wait until he had eaten or she might rob him of his appetite as well as his happiness.

Paul and Noelene would be going to the church youth club that was certain, they'd never miss a night of end to end Beatles' music.

By the time Wren had changed, chatting to Jim as casually as she could, it was time to face her shame. She slung on the coat that hadn't been on a bus in ages, grabbed at the bag with its Ministry pencils and notepad and walked home as if from the bus stop.

The kitchen was filled with steam from a big broth pan. A ferociously boiled ham bone sat waiting to cool enough to be stripped of any remaining meat bits and clinging barley, split peas and lentils. The smell, usually so comforting and tempting brought retching to a stomach that had only had weak tea and half a biscuit from Lil's tin. Wren rushed to the sink only to be further nauseated by the smell of earth clinging to the peelings of swede, carrot and leeks piled up on a page of newspaper. She heard Ivy's footsteps on the stairs and then on the oilcloth floor behind her. She managed to take an upside down glass from the draining board and fill it with water which she drank with her back to the woman whom she would soon devastate.

When she turned she knew the colour had drained out of her.

Ivy studied her face and met her eyes with derision.

'Did I hear you being sick?'

'No, she said honestly. 'I just wanted a drink.'

'What have you been doing at work today?' the question was pointed, the glare sharp and damning.

'Oh the usual.'

'Was the bus crowded?' '

Mm? Well same as always.'

Ivy held her eyes.

'Any of your la-de-da friends lower themselves to get on the bus with you?'

Panic struck Wren. Ivy knew something which would surely put her at a disadvantage.

'I don't know what you are talking about.'

Ivy took two steps nearer imprisoning Wren against the sink.

'Oh I think you do! You haven't been near that Ministry in months have you?'

The shock was like a slap in the face but unlike physical action promised so much more to come.

'Do you think I'm soft in the head? I know when you are up to something. Bad blood will out!'

Wren, silenced by shock, didn't ask what she meant but waited to hear just how much Ivy would fling at her.

'Oh yes; I know who's been giving you money and what he's been giving you it for. Now we have the consequences don't we. Going to marry you is he? I bet he's not! He'll be casting you off for your own class to deal with I'll bet. He'll not care that his bastard child is brought up with miners on a council estate as long as he doesn't know about it.'

'No, it's not like that!'

'Don't bother with the lies! I know when a woman is carrying a bairn. Just like your stupid bloody mother aren't you! This'll kill your dad!'

Wren began to cry then. 'Dad will understand.'

'Oh you think so do you? Well just wait until he gets in. He knows all about Sir Saul and his taste in young girls!'

'Sir Saul?'

'Do you not think I'd get to know what you've been up to? At least my son is loyal to me!'

'Paul. He's been following me.'

'Oh aye! And some tales he's come back with an' all.' Disgust spewed out of Ivy.

'And he has been paying you for it an' all! That is where you get your money from isn't it?'

Wren couldn't bear that the fine man who she loved like a grandfather could be thought of in such a way.

'No! No! It's not like that.'

'Save your lies. Tot will have it all out of you when he comes in. He's had plenty time to think about it.'

'He knows?'

'I told him this morning. He didn't hear you being sick but I was just passing the bathroom door with his morning tea. It was just the confirmation I needed.'

This was terrible. Wren was so out of control. Everything she had planned to say was thrown to the floor.

'You have it wrong mam. I was going to tell you both tonight after supper.'

'Well tough luck my girl. Your dad won't be in until later. He isn't getting off the bus at Highcopse tonight. He's staying on till the stop nearest Amblin Hall. Sir Saul won't like a mucky pitman dirtying his carpet no doubt but it doesn't matter how dirty his pit muck is it couldn't be as filthy as that old man.'

'No!'

'You can't stop him now. He'll be there now, punching his posh lights out.'

'Ivy. It's all wrong! You must listen to me it's not...'

The banging on the door shot both women to look at it.

The intrusion came again, more urgently. Neither of them made to answer it.

They heard the handle rattle and then the door flung open.

'Ivy! Ivy! Oh Ivy.'

-The man who had been Tot's hewing partner, working alongside him for the last ten years had no smile on his coal blackened face.

A gully of fear cracked open inside Wren.

'Ivy. It's Tot.' he seemed incapable of forming the words they all dreaded. He had to deliver his message but his face said what his lips could not.

'Sit down lass, both of you.'

His words started to reach her through the spinning room.

'Never mind that.' Ivy's voice was flat. 'Just tell me.'

'He had a heart attack; a mile underground, couldn't get him out for ages.'

Wren tried to speak but found no air in her lungs. Leaden legs held her still then began to shake uncontrollably.

Ivy tore at the ties on her apron. 'Where is he? I must go to him.'

'He's at Cotely Bridge hospital.'

'Can you take me?'

'Ivy.' Billy's eyes shot from Wren to the wife of the man he loved too. 'There's no point. He's gone Ivy. He was carried out. No-one could save him.'

Ivy staggered against him.

His voice was distanced by a solid wall of agony holding Wren prisoner in her horror.

Heavy silence pushed in at her. Not her daddy. Not her daddy. How could she not have seen this coming?

Billy guided a numb Ivy to the sofa where she sat obediently, silently.

'Shall I make you some tea?' Billy asked feeling terrible that this was the only thing he could do to help.

Wren, aware he would be feeling harrowed himself after losing his friend and delivering the message he knew had just devastated this family, floundered for words. All warmth scythed by her heart, she offered him an icy cold hand

'Thank you Billy. You must want to get home to your own wife. I'll look after mam.'

Wren became aware of Tot watching them. It was a more beautiful presence than his earthly body could ever have projected. He was still in shock at his sudden death but happy to be in the place where he always knew he would be going. He stayed near his wife to send healing. Wren recognised the same feeling she had in the wood. She knew now exactly who it had been. How could she have been so insensitive? Her own needs had swallowed her up, coated her in impenetrable steel. The man she loved who had given her so much had visited her immediately after his passing and she had not been there for him. How could she be so lost in the physical?

Ivy, soaked in the heavy agony of new grief could not see or feel the husband she so depended on.

Wren communicated without the inadequacy of words.

'Oh Daddy. I am so sorry.'

'You know how much I love you Wren. I would have seen you through this.'

'The father is Jeremy Foggin dad not Sir Saul. It hasn't been how Ivy thinks it was.'

'I know chicken, I know. I am not so worried about you now I know the truth. Take care of Ivy for me, she is going to need you. I love it here already and you know how nice it is to come home after the hard knocks of life.'

'Oh daddy. I am so sorry. I robbed you of the spirit who was meant to be your real granddaughter...'

'Wren. I wouldn't have missed knowing you for the world.'

'And I you.'

'June met me you know. Oh the joy. She told me what you had done and that much interest was being taken in how you handle this wrong life.'

'Sometimes I wish I'd never done it.'

'Shush, all will be made clear. You are a wonderful spirit; I wish you well in your search.'

'It could be over. Do you know if Jeremy is my soul mate? Do you know who the spirit inside me is? I so need to know.'

'Steady on. I have only just got to the other dimension. You can be certain that you will find out exactly what you need to know when you need to know it. You of all people must be aware of that.'

'I am losing my advanced learning to the personality that was meant for this life.'

'No. You can still communicate with me can't you? Wren I must go, I am anxious to be with June and Jan. They are waiting along with the rest of my spirit group who are here. As well as the sadness of leaving you all I feel a strange excitement.'

'And Elia? Is she there too?'

'Yes. I love you all.'

The room dulled.

Wren was alone with Ivy who was staring into the hot embers she had encouraged to heat water for her husband's bath. All she could think about was that it would be wasted. Like his favourite bacon broth. Like the shirts she had ironed for him that day. Like the very reason she existed.

'Mam.' Wren knew her voice was not reaching. 'Mam.'

'Get out!' Terrible loss was scribbled all over her face.

Ivy's eyes never left the fire.

'Mam?'

Get out I said. Don't ever come back. Not for your clothes, not for your books and not for my husband's funeral.'

'He's my daddy.'

'He's not your daddy. Never was; never will be. Your daddy is an evil rapist who ended up gnawed by rats at the bottom of a mine shaft. Probably put there by others like him. You are detestable too. You were responsible for him losing his real daughter. He never loved any-one like her. Not even you. Now get out!'

'Mam you don't mean...'

Her head turned then shooting hatred to the target she despised.

'You killed him. I told him what I knew. Paul saw you. I'm glad he's dead so that he doesn't know just how rotten you are.'

CHAPTER THIRTY EIGHT

She had lain wide eyed all night in the cold box room at Lil and Jim's.

The stiff cotton sheets waiting for visitors who never came rubbed starch into her bare skin as she listened to rhythm after rhythm of Jim's snores repeatedly broken by gut wrenching coughing fits. How could she have got here? It had been the plan not to love any-one except Alessandro and here she was emotionally numb with grief over a man she was certain could not be him. The reality hit her like a steam train. Why? Tot could have been the one she sought and she could have missed him! He was certainly wonderful enough to be the one soul mate she searched for. She thought back over many of their past lives together. He hadn't always been good to her. Some of their most stressful incarnations had been the ones where they'd learned the most. She tried to call Tot's spirit. Nothing. He would be extremely busy reuniting with those he needed to meet. He would come, just as he would come to comfort Ivy, Noelene and Paul, but when he could and when he chose. There would be no more Cuddle Corner, no more Mr Fixit, no more warm arms of security; no more Tot for any of them. In the meantime she would think of him and speak so that her communications would be stored for him to access when he could.

She lay squinting at the unfamiliar blocks of shadow, watching them gradually become furniture as the light found its way through the curtains.

She pretended to be asleep when Lil brought a cup of tea at six thirty in the morning. There could be no words between them to muddy the thoughts she needed to keep with her. She was loaded down with grief, pregnancy and Alessandro. The grim comfort of life re-runs, hopes and needs had wandered around the room and her head all night. There was space for no more.

As soon as the back door closed behind Lil, Wren gulped at the tea, lukewarm and sickly. It was easy to get out into fresh air before Jim was rested enough to go downstairs.

Nature couldn't reach through her grief and need on her walk. The signs of spring she'd longed for all winter went unnoticed and unloved.

The ice house smelled of paraffin fumes and wax which seemed to welcome her though the man-made cave was bone achingly damp. Oil spilled over her hands as they unbendingly aimed the full can at the empty stove. Risking setting herself alight she struck match after match but it was no good. The wick was burnt out. The candles gave a little heat but it wasn't enough to reach through to her nourishment starved body or desolate soul.

Wren's legs stiffened as she hugged them to her. It would be hours before Jeremy would even check in here. She would have to communicate her need to him telepathically. She imagined his face, his dark exotic eyes and went past them to his soul.

'Come to me Jeremy I need you. I desperately need you.'

She waited.

Her limbs grew as stiff as her mind. She needed him so much. Where was he?

The reality of this lonely cold was brutal. The stone glowed with dampness, the air painful to breathe, stinging her throat and nose. She tried to swim up through her sodden grief to think but found her mind buried within her shrivelled self.

She waited.

Faint with hunger and misery she stumbled to her feet. She would have to go to the house. Indira and Mr Foggin would find out soon anyway that Wren and Jeremy had made a baby. Knowing this wasn't the way, that there would be anger, recriminations and misery wasn't enough to stop her. The birds sang in spite of her heartache as she made her way from the trees to the open garden from where she could see the house. The path guided her past the red pointed buds of the rose bushes she had planted last winter but she took no joy in noticing their success. When she trudged around the bend thick with rhododendrons she heard a car draw up at the gate. It couldn't be Jeremy he would have come around on the drive to leave his Anglia as near the front door as possible. There was a short quiet time then a door slammed. Jeremy entered the gate turned as he closed it and waved as he blew a kiss. He punched the air and made an imaginary jump and score of a netball goal. He had a grin on his face which left swiftly when he saw Wren to be replaced with shocked guilt. He glanced at his watch.

'What are you doing here so soon? God you look a mess.' He hissed with a stare that said she looked awful in some indefinable way that had lodged in her eyes and dragged at her mouth.

He made no move towards her so that when she fell to the litter of dead leaves and bark he was too far away to catch her.

'What the....?' He pulled her to him and she smelled Apple Blossom on his jacket.

'I have been urgently sending you thought Jeremy. Where have you been?' she mumbled pathetically.

'I've had lunch at the country club. I have been thinking of you really strongly too but I had no idea you'd be here this early.'

'Who dropped you off?' Her voice sounded flattened and hopeless.

'Never mind let's get you inside. There's no-one there dad has taken Indira to a meeting with a spice importer in Birmingham. They won't be back until late.'

The kitchen was warm with the Aga. Jeremy sat Wren at the table then took a casserole dish from the small oven.

'Here.' he said ladling some rich gravy and meat onto the dish already waiting on a beautifully laid out tray. 'It's not spicy. It's English, well French actually, Boeuf Bourguignon Indira tells me. Eat some. You look as if you need it.'

For the sake of the foetus inside her and to keep her from sinking into a glucose starved coma, Wren took some of the gravy and vegetables.

'See the colour is returning to your cheeks already.' He smoothed her hair lightly.

'What on earth have you been doing? It looks as if you haven't even combed your hair.'

She turned to him knowing her gauntness was repulsing him.

She saw a thousand things in his eyes as she tried to make the words that were scything through her brain.

'My dad died yesterday.'

'Oh Wren. I'm so sorry. How...?'

'He died in the pit. Didn't your father say anything?'

'No. He is usually so het up when there is an accident everybody in the house knows about it.

Costs him money you see.'

'He died of a heart attack.'

'I'm sorry. That's why.'

Wren thought of the end of Tot's life. It had devastated her and the rest of her family. What had it meant to the man who owned the mine in which he'd died? Nothing. It hadn't even stopped him taking his housekeeper away to find new spices for the Indian cooking he loved so much.

'I'm running you a hot bath and then you can rest in my bed. Eat some more whilst I sort it.'

Jeremy cuddled Wren to sleep holding her sobbing damp body to his naked flesh. This is all she wanted. To be taken care of by the being who held the soul of Alessandro. She knew by the way they melted together without passion for the first time that he would take care of her.

She woke alone to mumblings from downstairs in the hall. Pulling her jumper over her sleep softened body she padded to the landing. She longed to leave her misery in the bed behind her but it dragged at her very being. Jeremy was on the phone speaking quietly and urgently.

Attracted by the movement he glanced at her.

'Not now!' he mumbled into the black receiver as he turned his back to replace it.

He took the stairs two at a time.

'What are you doing up?' He looked flustered but guided her back to the room she'd taken no notice of in her misery.

Her bare feet felt the softness of the Indian rugs as he shook the blankets over the Damask sheets to straighten the bed before he put her back in it. Three pillows cushioned her back from the brass behind her.

'Jeremy we need to talk.'

'I'm going to make you some cocoa first.'

'I'm surprised you know how.'

'I don't but I can read packets.' he laughed weakly. 'Won't be long.'

Wren looked towards the window she'd stared at many times from the garden waiting for those curtains to be open. From outside they had looked dull and beige but she could see now that was only the lining. Heavy chenille had been woven into an intricate pattern that did not mirror but complemented the rich rugs. Ivy had never lined a pair of curtains as she made them. These were like the ones at Amblin, made to state wealth as well as comfort and dress.

There was a tallboy bearing model yachts arranged proudly beside a group of six glass wall cases displaying butterflies so enormous and colourful that they had to have come from a hot country rich in exotic flowers. Beside a polished walnut wardrobe stood a table with everything a stamp collector could ever need. She wondered if her stamps were in one of those albums or had been flung into the wicker basket beneath them. On a pile of envelopes waiting to be processed lay a heavy cream rock split open to reveal a little cave of glistening stalagmites and stalactites of quartz crystal. She would have struggled to hold it in her hands but the rock drew her into it. She could imagine herself small enough to live in there. She would sit in the middle accepting every reflected light and the knowledge it brought. She would know everything in there, if only she were an inch tall.

'Here. I hope it's not too weak. The tin said to add cocoa to taste.'

She took the mug from him and saw that the drink was so dark that she would have trouble getting it past her taste buds.

'Thanks, its perfect.' she said in case he disappeared again.

'Would you like some music?'

'Jeremy we don't need to dance we have to work out our lives.'

He looked surprised at that as if he had already worked out his.

He went over to a hi-fi. 'This isn't the Byrds or Stones you know. Mozart taps into your mind, makes you feel wonderful. At school they made us listen to it during study periods and exams. Don't know why but it makes you cleverer.'

He fingered a pile of L.Ps. 'Ah this is the one.'

He was right. As the music filled the air it penetrated every atom of her being. This music made something she could never describe take place in her. Tot would have loved it. She wondered if he ever heard Mozart. She'd never know now.

He sat on the bed to hold her. As she leaned into him her grief found a release first in bellowing then in sobs. He encouraged this noisy manifestation knowing it was what she needed.

He eased her away from him kissing her swollen eyes and wet cheeks.

'Ivy ordered me to keep away from Dad's funeral.' The thought brought thudding breaths through her chest to her mouth.

'She can't do that.'

'You don't know her Jeremy. She is very fierce.'

'He is your father. Nothing can change that. Just turn up.'

This wasn't the time to explain.

Later when they were married and bonded with the baby. Then she'd tell him.

'Will you come with me?'

He stood up then. 'Whoa.' he held his palms rigid towards her. 'That would really cause a stir. I don't want to get involved in that.'

'But you are involved. You are the father of my child.'

'Yes well; I want to talk to you about that.'

The ringing of the phone pierced through Mozart and her dread.

'Aren't you going to answer it?'

'No. Let it ring.' As he said the words she could feel that he was distracted and really wanted to talk to whoever it was refusing to put their receiver down.

'Jeremy'

'Mm?'

'Who was on the phone earlier?'

'When?'

'When I came to the landing.'

'Oh no-one.' He looked away then going over to his rack of records to choose another for when this one ended.

'Was it the person who dropped you off after lunch?'

'When...what?' He was being deliberately vague.

'Who was that?' With the antennae of a lover, she could feel him drifting away.

'Oh for heaven's sake. What does it matter? No-one important.'

'Important enough to blow a kiss to.'

'You were spying on me?'

He looked hard at her then, at her crumpled, tear stained face and swollen eyes. 'I'm sorry I know you were upset.'

'I wasn't spying Jeremy. I just happened to be there.'

'I know. It was just a friend of my mother's that's all. Sometimes she is at the Country Club and asks me to sit with her.' His fixed smile was already absent.

'How did you get to the Club?'

'For heaven's sake what's this, the Spanish Inquisition?' he flung at her.

She took a controlling breath. 'I just wondered why you left your car behind.'

'Alright; she rang me and asked me out to lunch. She knew I was on my own today.' He smirked in his hazy dazzle of social freedom he saw as his right.

'How old is she?' Wren hated herself for giving life to other suspicions.

'I don't know. Old. As old as my mother who asked her to take care of me whilst she is away.'

'How old is your mother?'

'For heaven's sake Wren. Leave it will you.'

Unsatisfied and resenting his tone, she felt she must do as he asked.

This had all turned out wrong. She had come to him to help in her grief and to sort out their lives. He had naturally done the first but seemed reluctant to go very far on the second.

She reached for the mug beside the bed and drank. The cocoa went down warmly seeming to seek the ache of her bereavement. The record ended leaving a painful silence which she fought valiantly to fill but no words came.

The inside sleeve of the LP rustled as it was forced from the record it was meant to protect.

The new notes haunted the air.

'Like it?' he asked turning to her for the first time after his anger. He had a glow of self-worth about him, it made her feel separate.

'Yes. Thank you.' She knew she was grabbing onto any tiny kindness that would dispel her doubts and fears.

'It's his concerto for flute and harp. You should get this for your home.'

'I no longer have a home. We will make a new one together.'

'Hah? Is that what you are after? How are we going to do that without any money?'

She was stung by the fact he thought she was 'after' anything.

'Surely your father will help.'

'Help! Help!' he flung the word high between them. 'He'll bloody kill me.'

'Jeremy. We will find a way.'

He came over to the bed. 'Oh yes and how are we going to do that. Money doesn't grow on trees you know. Perhaps you are hoping to find buried treasure when you are digging little holes for your plants.'

He saw her paleness, interpreting it as a result of his indignation, and was sorry.

He couldn't know that his words had brought back a memory too horrible to be anywhere but the very deepest part of Wren's brain.

CHAPTER THIRTY NINE

She had her answer.

How she was going to carry out the very act that could make sure Jeremy stayed by her side was beyond her. With her advanced experience not belonging to the life she had stolen, Wren had been able to shelve most of the horrors of the day she now must recall. The tangle of feelings, understanding and capabilities she'd created by her actions was now too knotted to deal with.

But she was 17, pregnant and within reach of her goal. Surely Jeremy would know on some level who he really was. She would guide him to realisation. They would have a lifetime together. He would help her get over Tot's death. She'd be there to help with his great Earthly task. When they passed back to their true home Alessandro would be delighted with her devotion and touched by just how much she'd gone through to prove it.

Right now they needed money. Her actions could provide exactly that but how much and where she would find the stomach to retrieve it remained to be seen.

'Get dressed, I'll take you home.' He smiled and his eyes gave her hope.

In his car hung a silence of thoughts, Wren hoped they were the same.

The dread of tomorrow was thickening round her heart.

She hardly remembered the journey as he drove her back to the only place that would have her.

After days and nights incapable of getting out of the bed Lil insisted she got into, Wren knew something wasn't right. She'd eaten the small bowls of soup and creamy, sugar drowned porridge only because Lil had taken so much care then stood over her refusing to go to Amblin or see to Jim before she'd finished. This strange detachment was something she had never felt before. Desperation grew that she hadn't seen Jeremy or got the money he so needed and yet she felt more and more exhausted, heavy with the pain of grief.

She wasn't sure how long she had been tossing sweatily around the sheets, out of the world. Tot's funeral could have come and gone. Ivy's pain injected words shot in and out of Wren's torment. Jeremy would be frantic with worry. Perhaps he'd been looking for her?

Everything in her ached for Tot and Jeremy. The wounds to her heart gaped wider as it shuddered with its burden.

When she woke it was getting light. She heard Lil rattling at the ash pan making sure Jim had plenty of hot water. A lighter feeling reached her giving her the urge to go down to see Lil and tell her she was feeling a little better. When her legs couldn't hold, flopping her back to the pillows, her spirit kept going. She had not had an involuntary out of body experience in this lifetime, but then she'd never been so ill.

Wren noticed the pictures of Bamborough Castle and Holy Island on the wall as she passed unseen over the stairs and into the kitchen. Lil, always dressed with great attention to comfort, wore threadbare slippers with flattened heels and an out of shape multi weave cardigan. She was concentrating on something at the table. Wren realised how much she loved this woman. She was a caretaker of people in need. She looked after Jim and Sir Saul with every atom of her being. Now Wren. How wonderful she would have been as a real mother.

Wren saw the tray with the small amount of porridge and the warm sweet tea. Lil, her broad back hiding her hands, scooped something she'd been crushing onto a tea spoon, sprinkled it onto the food and stirred vigorously. When she had picked up the tray and gone towards the stairs Wren examined the bottle left open where Lil had just been.

Sleeping pills! Wren knew exactly why she had lost days. In a split second she was back in her body forcing it to get to the bathroom before Lil opened the bedroom door.

'Wren?' She knocked. 'Are you all right?'

She had turned on the bath taps hard so that the gushing would reach through to the landing.

'I'm a little better thank you Lil, just had to get rid of this sweat and greasy hair.'

'It's still early days; mind you eat that porridge before it gets too cold.'

'Don't worry. I know what's best for me.'

Happy with the response Lil dashed out to catch her bus.

The water filled Wren's ears and covered her face until she needed breath.

Sleeping pills! Lil was only doing what she thought the girl she loved so needed. She couldn't know about the baby. Not blessed with any pregnancies herself she was not party to the detection instincts of mothers everywhere.

She took her tea downstairs to dry her hair in front of the fire. She needed strength in both her mind and body to do what was so urgently making her heart bang. One slice of toast was all she could manage on the porridge dampened glow of the fire. Lil's toasting fork was so like the one Tot had taught her to use with care when she was little. He made an art out of sniffing the air for just the right moment the bread would be golden brown enough to melt the butter so it would run down her chin and arms. This toast suffered neglect from her attention to memory but she ate it anyway except for the really burnt edges too bitter to be anything but cinders.

Dread thudded into her stomach.

What if she had missed Tot's funeral?

It was only as she was cleaning the black bits from her teeth that she managed to concentrate enough to formulate her plan.

February cold gnawed at her limp body as she propelled it to where it didn't want to go.

She hadn't been near the air shaft since that horrible day she'd been forced to defend herself but her tortured mind wouldn't let her forget the rabbit hole she so needed now.

Speeding wind nagged at her body and mind. She strode on reluctantly.

Bramble runners had become impenetrable mounds of thick stalks and thorns. Her wobbly legs tottered then lifted themselves to where her whole being dreaded. There had been a path here used by picnicking families and dog walkers, now it was gone. The sixties had become too exciting to waste time in the country. Television and cinemas, shopping centres and discos, pop groups and American imports. These had not tempted Wren away from her countryside.

She could not find the warren. Whippy hazel and sycamore had sprouted up to change the landscape. She knew it was east of the air shaft; she would have to make that her starting point.

The diluted strength she had gathered was leaving her legs as she sought the edge of the little hill which looked over onto the shaft opening. As if to race her own tolerance she pushed on, tearing through a screen of rampant birch saplings. Wild rose stems tore at her cheeks trying to slap her into defeat. Mental strain was not helping. She thought of the man to whom she believed she could shout down that shaft. Her childish mind had imagined Tot sitting just below the light merrily eating bread and jam and drinking cold tea. How she shuddered to think of the reality of all those years lying on his back in the wet dark hewing coal with all his strength.

She hoped his uncomplaining dedication to his work and family would earn him an easier life next time. Knowing him, he'd choose something equally as hard to hasten his progress.

The sick wave of love, loss and sadness weakened her further.

She had to get to the last place she ever wanted to go. One final push would have her over the crest of the hill; she must urge it from her exhaustion. Foot after foot trudged over hardened mud until the round wall surrounding the shaft came into view. She tried intensely not to stare at the place where she'd

ended some-one's life, pulling her eyes back to her task as she stopped to search out the easiest route that would take her to the rabbit hole she'd never wanted to see again. There was a rustle through the dry bracken that stunned her to a reluctant standstill. Forcing her breath to hold she allowed it out again at the sight of a fox swarming its way over to the very place she sought. She hoped against hope that he would be more disappointed than her. She cleared the wind whipped hair from her eyes. What should have taken her minutes had she been well, took almost half an hour. She needed to drag her body no more. Fifty abandoned holes faced her but it was burned into her memory which one held guilty treasure.

She watched the fox sniff around a few entrances then lift his leg to mark the place his own just in case tasty rabbits did return. After making a noise on purpose, she watched him nervously scramble off leaving it to her vital search through the pungent reek of fresh fox.

It was this one. Wasn't it? Third from the right? No the left. Suddenly they all looked the same. Her heart sank along with her strength. She stood back to get a better look, the gusts boxing her ears and stinging her cheeks.

No. She had to go with her first instinct.

As her hand went through the cobwebs then around the turn her heart stopped. It wasn't there. Her fingers scrabbled, making themselves longer in their desperate quest. Was it the right hole? She stood back to scan several. Some of them were blocked. There had been a fall. Sandy soil had spilled out of some of the mouths of the warren. She had no tools. Only grief weakened hands. The cold earth seemed to suck her body towards it as she lay on her stomach at the awkward angle most generous with her arm's length. Four times she had to scrabble back to remove the little piles of sand she'd scraped towards her. Twice her spirits had risen when she'd felt something solid. The first time a stone had fooled her, the second it was a cold white skull of a long dead rabbit. Wren thought she'd have to go all the way back to Lil's for a spade. The thought made her sob in desperation. Fine sand blew into her mouth and eyes. She hadn't the strength.

One last scrabble. She could force her sand stuffed nails around for that couldn't she? Taking back the last remains of her energy from her sobbing chest Wren thrust her arm up to her shoulder so that her damp cheeks allowed dirty grains to cling in a little tear river.

This could be another stone. Dear God! Please don't let it be another stone. It felt too soft even through her gritty fingers. Excitement twisted her round so that she could bring her sore hand within view.

It held the wallet.

'What's this?'

Jeremy swept a glimpse over her but was too interested in what she had thrust into his hand to ask why she was so dishevelled.

'Our future.'

'But I don't understand. Where did you get it?'

'I found it.'

Wren looked upon the face she so loved enjoying the relief almost childishly displayed there. He saw nothing in her. He was unaware of her last few days, her exhausting search even how she used her last energy to avoid the gardener as she made her way to the ice house then throw tiny stones at his window. It was enough that he had checked for her presence here twice a day. He didn't ask about her health or the scratches on her cheek or the sand in her hair but she loved him for reading the local paper so that he knew the funeral was in two days' time. He could hardly perceive her for staring at the grubby wallet.

'This morning? On your way here?' Jeremy turned over the dirt engrained leather.

'What luck when money is what I so need right now. How? Where?'

'I didn't find it this morning I found it three years ago.'

'Three years! But you could have done so much with this.'

'But it isn't mine Jeremy.'

'Oh it is now. Finders keepers is what I always say.' He pulled at the press-stud.

'Gosh!' Wren watched as he counted out the sand spilling notes, her eyes widened as she realised that only the first ten were pound notes. The rest were fifties and hundreds.

'Is there enough for a new start for us Jeremy?' Wren did not want to touch the money and connect with the dark vibes of the person who had last counted it out.

'Enough? Enough?' There's enough for ten new starts! And that new Mini I have my eye on. You clever girl.'

'I'm a long way off being clever Jeremy.'

She longed for his arms and fingers to hold her close enough to massage away the tired tension, but he was too absorbed in making little piles of thousand pounds.

'Who do you think it belonged to?' He kept his eyes on what delighted him most.

'Don't you know? The man who was found in the shaft?'

'When? What man?'

'It was in all the papers. About the same time Marilyn Monroe died.'

'I was at school in India then. Did the vile murderers mean to return for this do you think?'

'How should I know?' The snappiness in her voice startled Jeremy.

'I have to go. I'll see you after the funeral. Can you have worked out a plan for us by then?'

'Certainly. My mind is already racing. And I'll start with a slap up lunch!'

'What?'

'Only joking, but we do have to use it fast what with all this talk of decimalisation.'

'We will.' she said suddenly too weary to stand but she had to get back to Lil's and sink into her first proper sleep in days.

The following evening Wren demonstrated to Lil how much better she was feeling by making tattie-pot for supper. There could never be any mention that she knew about the sleeping pills. Lil and Jim tried their best to give her the love and support that she needed urging her to stay away from Tot's funeral in case there was a scene.

'No! I love that man and he loved me. I must go. I'll be as discreet as I can.' Even the words terrified her. This thought was all she could deal with. Telling Lil and Jim that she would be leaving to be with the one she loved, to marry and have their baby was the last thing needing her energy. It could wait until she knew the details.

'Do you want me to go with you pet?' Lil's pleading eyes watched Wren dress in the smallest coat Lil could dig out of her mothball wardrobe on the morning of the funeral. Still it swamped him.

'Thank you but I must do this on my own.'

It was the only love she'd be given today, and she was glad of it.

She held the feeling close to her as she reached the steps that would lead her into the Methodist Church Tot had so loved. Outside huddled a crowd of miners, some had seen Tot die, others had respected him since they started working with him at only fourteen, all of them once in a group of frightened schoolboys pushed into the mines by gnawing poverty. It was amongst these men that she waited. The church was already full but the searing wind didn't matter to any-one. They waited, listening to muffled strains of hymns. When silence fell it would be filled with a joint fond memory of Tot's hard work, generosity or creative solutions to work problems. Not able to bear the coffin carrying her daddy's body passing so close and not wanting to upset Ivy further, Wren made her way to a mound of earth piled beside a freshly dug grave.

This would be her daddy's last resting place.

As the procession wound its way towards her Wren moved back to where she could watch from behind a group of trees. The crowd around the grave swallowed the family from view but Wren felt sudden ice as Ivy's eyes settled on her. Paul followed his mother's gaze and flashed an ugly warning to Wren. When Noelene looked up she sent a plea to the sister she so needed and knew needed her.

Wren forgave them. They all had been disappointed on a soul level not to have met with Elia. It was too late now.

Ivy pulled both her children to her forcing Wren into dank awareness that she was alone once more.

If only they could see Tot beside them bolstered by the obvious good regard and yet sad at the grief. He sent a knowing smile to Wren as he bent to scoop his dog into his embrace. They were the only two here who were conscious of what happened when they died. If only the others could remember the place they had been to many times themselves and would go to again.

The minister gave his blessings and then began to read something that startled Wren into realising that perhaps some-one else did understand. As he began to read even the wind listened.

'What is dying?

A ship sails and I stand watching from the horizon and some-one at my side says, 'She is gone.'

Gone where? Gone from my side that is all. She is just as large as when I saw her.

The diminished size and total loss is in me, not her.

And just at the moment when some-one at my side says. 'She is gone.'

There are others watching her coming and other voices sending up a glad shout.

'Here she comes!'

And that is dying.'

The minister left a little time for his words to settle into the brains of the living who began to be uncomfortable about how many years they had left themselves.

As the mourners wandered off to commiserate and enjoy whatever spread Ivy would have proudly prepared for them at home Wren turned her back against a tree, closed her eyes and said goodbye to Tot and his dog Jan.

He left then and she envied the joy he was going to, but as he went his love was replaced by another. The feelings were so special that they could only have come from one source.

He wouldn't let her suffer alone. How like Alessandro to be here when she needed him. He hadn't cared that it might be awkward that their secret might be out. He had come to support her. Darling, darling Jeremy.

Wren opened her eyes and turned to see the face she would spend the rest of this life loving.

It was not Jeremy.

CHAPTER FORTY

Grief and the wind had obviously clouded her judgement. Instead of the tall body she so needed to lean on, a group of three moved from blocking the low sun to face it showing Wren love from a source she had not expected today.

'Uncle George!' she howled out on relief.

As she withdrew sobbing from the urgent, comforting hug she looked into the concerned faces of Joyce and her mother. They looked prosperous and well fed.

'I never thought you'd be here.' Her voice was clotted with crying. She hiccoughed trying to swallow tears she felt might never stop.

'It's only four hours. Planes fly to Newcastle now you know. Your painful gaze didn't find us at the grave but we saw you.'

Wren took the warm arms of the ones oozing concern; George bent a harrowed face to kiss her.

'Joyce. Look at you! You're gorgeous! And those legs. When did they get so long?'

But there was no answer because George, through a sad grey face, had more urgent questions.

'Where have you been Wren? We have been trying to find you...Ivy won't talk about you at all. What on earth is going on?'

George took both her hands but it didn't stop them trembling.

'Ivy won't even mention your name; we've had a hell of a time looking for you.'

'I'm all right; staying with some friends. I'll tell you all later, you must go back for the tea. Ivy needs the support.'

'Where shall we meet?' George asked anxiously, knowing she was right.

'I'll be right here. I want to be at my mother's grave and Tot's for a while.'

'I'll be back in two hours.' he kissed her reassuringly. His arms felt wonderful.

Wretched with grief and unable to watch the task the workers put to their shovels Wren turned her back and followed the song of two courting blackbirds. All these people now remembered only with a headstone as time had brought the ones who buried them to the same place. Old names, old times. It was as she pulled her head to see a darting wren that knew some-one important to her was buried near. The tiny bird perched on a plain stone. There was no doubt it wanted her to read what it had drawn her towards.

Her heart lurched as she peered close enough to read the simple inscription. This was a man she knew so much of yet had never met; the man who had been so kind to her mother.

Mr. Farraige. The dates showed he died only six months after June but it didn't show that June would have met him to thank him for the part he had played in her short life. Their bond they had arranged before either was born.

The fresh mound of soil over Tot's grave almost broke her heart. She knew he wasn't there of course but the fact that his body spent all his working life underground should have meant it was free, his ashes blown to the wind in the wood he had so loved. But on his physical level he would have wanted to be near June. The Forget-me-Nots were not yet out. Tot had been so pleased with how they had spread from his daughter's grave to others with their generous seeding and tough winter resistance. She'd be back here in summer to shake the seeds over him.

He would never be forgotten.

Wherever she was.

As she hauled herself towards the gate she saw Joyce sitting on the seat beside the composting heap of dead flowers taken from graves.

Joyce stood up and waved.

'I couldn't leave you but I knew you needed this time alone. The wind had died down so I just sat here, taking England back into my bones.'

Joyce pulled up a sleeve with manicured fingers to show a gold watch enhancing a tanned arm. She had a flattering shade of lipstick expertly applied and discreet eye make-up. Her hair was well cut and fell beautifully around her face. Wren felt grey and scruffy. Worn out.

'We have fifteen minutes before they come back for us. Do you want to talk?'

Through her grief Wren struggled to think of anything but Tot. She turned to her friend with eyes sandpapered with exhaustion.

'Oh Joyce so much has happened. I'm going away.'

'Where?'

'I'm not sure yet. Everything has taken a back seat to Tot.' she turned hardly daring to allow the smile reach her mouth. 'I'm madly in love.'

'Oh Wren.'

'I know. I'm too young...have my life in front of me...' the old familiarity was there but with the understanding of maturing young women.

'And is he handsome, this man who can put a glint in your eye even now?'

'Oh Joyce, I love him so much he is planning our future right now.'

'So where is he? Who is he?'

'You'll never guess.'

'Some-one we know?'

'A little.'

'From school?'

'Yes.' Wren was beaming through sadness, excited to be able to talk of her love of Jeremy for the first time.

'Clive Rushton!'

'Who? Yuk no. All those snots and scabs.'

The girls giggled. It was as if no time or space had come between them.

'Dennis Carruthers? He was always keen on you.'

'Ha! All that puppy fat. I'd easily have been able to catch him. He was lovely but no, not him.'

They were snatched from their excited game when two people entered the gate with fresh flowers. Watching them wander off to tidy the grave of their own loved one Wren and Joyce turned to a loud and sudden peep from the car rented by George at the airport.

'Where to madam?' George turned from the front seat beside Betty.

Wren told him where Lil lived and the girls snuggled into the back seat with their secret, dying for the privacy to continue when they were alone.

'Talking of people we know, guess who was staying in our hotel last night at the airport?'

'Oh I haven't a clue? Some-one famous?'

'No silly! I said some-one we knew. Or used to.'

'Give in.'

'Remember that boy who came to our school for a bit from India, you used to give him stamps. Couldn't remember his name then but never could forget those looks.'

'What? At the airport?'

'Yes but that's not all. He was with a right glamour puss. Old enough to be his mother I'd say. But you'd never kiss your mother like that, know what I mean.'

She winked and nudged at Wren hoping to get at least a little laugh to cheer her up. She put a hand over her mouth as she drew closer to whisper behind it.

'Flashing money around on champagne he was. They left after breakfast for an early plane. Still joined at the hip and looking like sleep wasn't what they went to bed for.'

A rod of blistering shock poked at her fear, searing into already highly strung nerves.

'Are you sure it was him?'

'Well the way she called his name when he went more than two foot away from her confirmed that. As soon as she said 'Jeremy', it all flooded back.'

'Yes but are you sure it was the same Jeremy we knew at school?'

'Positive.'

'Stop the car! She's fainted.'

She entered a far-off state, escaping a tattered mind, worn threadbare with two ripping griefs.

'It's all been too much for her.' Wren heard the distant voice of Uncle George as he followed Lil up the stairs. She felt her legs lifted onto the bed and water pressed to her lips. She knew her face was chalky and hideous with tears of betrayal and grief.

'I'll be back in the morning. Now rest.' He kissed the words to her brow then left.

The room was loud with the silence of fear.

'Is she well enough to fly?'

'All she has to do is sit there; we'll do the rest Joyce.'

Three days later, George put through the scant luggage he'd coaxed Noelene to rescue from the wash house and showed the unused passport to the official. He fastened her seat belt then urged her to his shoulder never disturbing her to take food or drink nor moving to stretch his legs as usual. Wren allowed thoughtless sleep to swallow her. She needed peace so desperately.

Somehow and moon slow, she was moved through the airport at Malaga all the time wondering why it was so warm. She could not access normal thought. Faces, kind words, tender guiding were they there?

Air reached her nostrils. It gave velvety fragrances which carried incessant insect noises making her look up to stars brighter than had been around her lately.

Lying back in an open topped car the stars swirled as they drove around and up bends, she flopped and was steadied. She gave herself up completely to these loving, whispering people.

She did not realise she was in a foreign country.

She only knew she had lost Alessandro.

Water was urged through her lips by some-one arriving unannounced but leaving on feet that smacked away on floor tiles. A doctor came and spoke a strange language. He left her to her pit of darkness. He returned and was followed by cool tomatoes sieved so that they would go down the throat she had forgotten was hers. People talked, people walked. They held her. They bathed her. Even the love couldn't get through the dense wrappings of her shock.

It was dark when she opened her eyes. The cool sheet and light blanket seemed new to her. The air whirred with noise she knew from former lives to be cicadas rubbing their back legs together. Where was she? Her feet didn't touch the thickness of Lil's clippie mat she'd made herself, nor did they find the square of off-cut carpet so long at her own bedside. The smoothness was cool but not cold. Her hand took shaky help from a chair beside her and found a light bedspread which she fumbled over her shoulders. The bedroom door was slightly ajar and she was aware that other people were in this house but who and where were beyond her. The house ticked with sleep and cracked with changing temperature. She felt air which she pulled her weakened body towards. There was no moon but crowds of stars nearer and more vibrant than she had ever seen before, gave silver light. A lizard's tail disappeared into a crack on the whitewashed balcony. Soft night opened as her eyes adjusted. The noise grew giving a veil of hope and relaxation.

She could not remember who she was.

Where she was at this moment seemed hidden from her. She was physical that was certain for there was a feeling of need and fear.

Most of all there was a deep well of desolation.

Wren jumped in shock when a cockerel crowed for it seemed only feet to her right. One songbird seemed to know the dark was lifting, then two. Gradually, as if noise would drag the sun from its hiding place, hundreds of birds coaxed light into the sky. This showed silhouettes of bushes and short contorted trees. Rocks led to bigger rocks down a slope she was surprised to see. When a red arch took her view she saw that it was a big sun rising over water a few miles away.

Warmth was the gift of the roundness in front of her. It also brought countryside and a winding road. On the balcony, over wrought iron, climbed papery pink flowers on sturdy stems.

The chair she sat on had five other companions all around a huge planked table with a flower filled pot in its centre. Bright red geraniums in terracotta pots were alternated with hanging lanterns. She realised the smell she'd taken in was from Jasmine and Honeysuckle which was now plain to see scrambling around wooden supports.

'Wren?' A voice she didn't know.

'She's up everybody!'

Other feet, other faces other proclamations of joy.

She knew none of them but smiled anyway.

CHAPTER FORTY ONE

The determination that she would be loved back to health was the only thing that Wren could grasp. These people, this place, all heaving with devotion. All she knew for certain was that her shock frozen brain held things she didn't care to know. She ate new fresh food. Salad was covered in oil and sweet smelling herbs her tongue didn't recognise. She supped cold pungent soup. Fish appeared at most meals without batter and even when it wasn't Friday. At first she spat out the olives decorating her oregano and red onion covered tomatoes but when she saw the little pile of stones in a dish after almost every meal she began adding to it. Soon olives of all different kinds were her favourite snack.

She secretly learned the names of the people around her so that they never knew she'd forgotten.

No-one else seemed to notice that there was some other presence around. Perhaps there wasn't. She was so weak it would be easy to feel someone was trying urgently to tell her something.

'You have grown up Wren. You don't call me Uncle George anymore.'

He was cooking outside on a hip high stone lined fire.

'He was her uncle?' She just smiled and accepted three little fish charcoaled with garlic.

'Come on eat your sardines.' He pushed knife and fork in her hands. 'Betty will be in with the omelettes in a second.' Through his caring smiles she could see etched grief but was so burdened herself that she couldn't ask why.

They brought her books to read. The ones she felt most wrapped in were the detailed and illustrated books of Southern European Flora and Fauna. Some of the drawings looked familiar but the stony soil and rocky terrain they were growing in appeared too mean to give up any goodness.

'See this plant Wren.' Joyce came behind her to check if her chair needed moving out of the late morning sun. She pointed a glossed finger nail down at the page to a rosette of fat leaves which ended in a vicious point. Beautiful women know how to use this to their advantage.'

'Well nobody would smell that if it was used as a button hole.'

Joyce swung round and squatted so that she could take full on the first smile she'd seen in ten days.

'Wren! You made a joke.' her delight spread between them so that Wren began laughing gently at first then spasm took her stomach and she lost control of her face and mind. She saw another face from years ago looking down at her beaming with the same delight.

'You clever girl! Ivy! The baby said 'Dadda'. She really did. All by herself.'

She knew she would never see that face again. The longing was too great so she closed down the memory and stared into the eyes raking hers for sense.

The noise caused the others to come running.

'What is it? Is she alright?' George had a pencil behind his ear and one in his mouth which he'd removed to speak. Betty held pungent onion stained hands in front of her.

'She made a joke.' Joyce had lost some of her joy to concern as she related the trigger to the outburst. Wren felt her thin wan expression give in to a smile.

Betty sniffed at her onion tears bringing the smell nearer so she could look at the page open on Wren's knee. 'Oh Aloe Vera. Yes the Spanish girls used it for years to soften their skin. It has antiseptic properties too. It makes short work of mosquito bites.'

'Mosquito?'

Her audience looked at her and she could see their disappointment.

She didn't know what mosquito was but she knew now that their teeth were to be avoided.

The taste was better than the smell and she said so. The others laughed as they took first bite of the dish Betty had set before them.

'It is goat's cheese roasted on red capsicums Wren and we felt exactly the same when we first had it. Here try this.'

He offered her an earthenware plate with burnt-ish pointed plants on it.

'This is chicory halved and roasted in olive oil and sea salt. You must wipe up every drop of the juices with your bread.'

'Why?'

'Taste and you'll know.'

At first the bitterness shocked her but as the natural juiciness exploded in her mouth she knew she could never wish for more succulence or flavour.

When the last shiny traces had been mopped into her mouth Wren beamed at Betty.

'Will you teach me to cook these?'

'I'd be delighted.' Wren didn't miss the look that went between the man and woman who seemed to love her.

George helped take the dishes from the patio to the kitchen where Wren had opened the fridge to search for things to cook.

'It's good to see you in here.' he said kissing her forehead. 'But I must be off to work.'

Wren fought with the feelings hooked out of her by past kisses with that same masculine smell. Her brain felt fuzzy, wrapped in cotton wool to stopping it working properly.

'So many oranges.' she said chirpily to Betty as she picked one from the string bag hanging on the back of the door.

'Where do you think we get that delicious orange juice you love so much?'

'What you squeeze them yourself?'

'It's the best way.'

Everything in the kitchen seemed alien to Wren but her mind surprised her with its next question.

'What does George do for work?'

'You may well ask!' Joyce came in to rinse out the cloth she'd used to wipe the table.

'This might come as a shock to you Wren but he doesn't work at all.' Betty took an apron from under the bag of oranges and hooked it over Wren's head.

'But all this?' She waved an arm to include every inch of the villa she hadn't yet left.'

'It is lovely isn't it, and the fifty hectares surrounding it?'

'So big? Then how....'

'Oh he used to work; hard. That is why he doesn't have to now.'

'But he just said...'

'I know. He is drawing rare plants he finds on his land. He is also breeding moths and butterflies of endangered species.'

'Breeding them! Can't they do that for themselves?'

'Not if their food is taken away from them and there is every chance it will.'

'Why?'

'George spent years making money out of property development, doing up tumbling down houses and restoring them to rent out, now he's fighting it.'

Joyce handed a tea towel to Wren then filled the sink with all the lunch dishes.

'Tourism.' she made the word as dirty as possible.

Betty beckoned Wren to the back door which opened up to a mountain at the back. Twenty steps took them to the most breath-taking view Wren hadn't even known was there.

'See this. George named the place 'Imagine,' he said it was one of your favourite words when you were little and something sparkled in your eyes, he knew you were awestruck. He felt that way the first time he saw this place, you can tell why. It's beautiful. It's warm and sunny and it takes only three or four hours to reach from sun starved Britain and Germany. People love it when they come here. They need hotels to stay in and the richer ones want to buy houses to use for the winter.'

'But there is so much of it.'

'Yes but in twenty years it will be all gobbled up by concrete and greedy developers who cram houses together for maximum profits.'

'And this. Our place?'

Betty was pleased with the slip of the tongue but Wren was concerned at what she had said.

'It's safe. George learned his lesson. He built new houses in Granada where there was a need for housing and some of the land was brown site...used before. But here; no. His heart is here.'

Wren knew hers wasn't, not quite, but she had no clue as to where it belonged. She felt again the heavy drag that pulled yearning from her to far away. The search for it was too heavy laden. This would do for now.

But not for ever.

Memory could be selective. Wren hadn't a clue why she was here, where she'd come from or what she would do next. Life was happening to her. She had food and shelter for her body and love for her spirit. What else could she want? Something. There was something.

At 2 am every morning Wren woke with a feeling of dread and longing. That was all it was for she knew not what to dread or long for.

At the same time her stomach churned and sleep was kept from her, she felt a need to do something. Achievement was missing. She didn't know why God had put her on this Earth but she knew it wasn't for eating and reading although she was sure he approved of both.

'Come with me to Spanish classes?' Joyce had suggested when the two were sharing their thoughts over fresh lemon juice and tonic water.

Wren watched the big foamy bubbles burst at the top of her glass as she popped another anchovy stuffed olive into her mouth.

'Oh I am sure you are too far advanced. I'd only hold you back and besides I feel an overwhelming need to be outdoors.'

'Well you'd better get that out of your system as soon it will be too hot to be out for long.'

Wren stood up and looked over the balcony to the sweep of sun whitened earth surprising every-one with tiny olive blossom.

'I don't think I will ever get nature out of my system Joyce. It seems to be me.'

Joyce, trying to stick to the family code of not discussing any of Wren's past unless she asked for information, waited.

'Oh I don't know!' Wren flopped back onto the cane chair sideways so her long legs lolled as if kicking from the past into the future.

'Write.' Joyce said suddenly trying not to suggest anything or anyone in particular. 'Write letters. I always find that in telling people how I'm feeling I tell myself my answer.'

She waited hoping this would gently bring back a need to let the one she'd been so excited about at the churchyard know where she was. Joyce was the only one who knew Wren was in love. It was a shared secret, except Wren didn't seem to be the one sharing it. Joyce had been plagued with thoughts of a boy on his knees with worry about where his girlfriend had disappeared to.

George had sent a letter to Lil and Jim to let them know she was all right. When they wrote back perhaps there would be some information. Maybe they had explained to him.

Whatever was happening with him Joyce wanted to have at least some information to give Wren when her memories returned.

George was glad that Wren seemed strong enough in body and spirit to make some of the trips with him on his field studies. He'd taken his three 'Gorgeous Geordie Girls' into Marbella to get new clothes for Wren. She couldn't wear Joyce's for ever.

The sun darkened her skin and lightened her shoulder length hair. Good food took the scrawniness from her limbs but seemed to be giving her a bit of trouble in the stomach department. George hoped the stress hadn't given her ulcers but she was bound to stop being sick when her stomach adjusted fully to the Mediterranean diet.

One late afternoon a month after Wren had first glimpsed the sun rise onto the mountain, George took her to his favourite place of all time.

'It's funny you know Wren. I love and adore Betty and Joyce but I have never ever brought them here.'

'Why? '

'It seems to hold something that only I can know. But strangely I feel you will understand.'

He was looking around enraptured but Wren kept her eyes from the scenery to the splendour in front of her. She was taken by the radiance he couldn't keep to himself. Euphoria gathered them and everything about them together. He was so much more than her uncle.

'I do. I don't know why I do but I feel part of this place. It must be wonderful to own such special land.'

'Oh I don't own it, not yet at least. I only found out it was for sale two weeks ago when I happened to glance into a real estate window. The agent told me there had been a sign up here for six months but I have never seen it.'

'Have you put an offer in? '

'Immediately. But Spanish law! Let's just say we won't hold our breath but I offered the full asking price and the owner accepted.'

'Do you need more land to be happy? '

He caught her eye and in it the real question she was asking. His large brown hand swept over clumps of wild thyme before taking the scent to his grateful nostrils.

'Need? No. Want, yes. I think this land need me actually. The sun hits this side of the slope differently, it's not much but it does make subtle changes to the flora. There are fruits here that attract different birds. Flowers with nectar so sweet that butterflies can't resist. They deserve to be saved.'

They both wallowed in the glory of nature, taking samples, pouring over books, analysing soil. Taking the place that would soon belong to George so completely into their souls.

They were happy with the place and with each other. Lost in a frenzy of excited learning and discovery, their closeness grew. To Wren it didn't feel fresh or novel. It went deeper than that. It was if they were renewing something. Gradually she gathered information about when she was little and George arrived at Highcopse. Each memory brought surprise but did not furnish her with new realisation. She had forgotten why she was here. How she got here.

Just finishing her orange juice after a breakfast of homemade bread and Spanish sausage, Wren was surprised by her uncle returning to the table.

'There.' George placed the small brown case in her hands.

'What is it? '

'I noticed how you hang dreamily over my shoulder when I am painting. It's time you drew your own. You have such an eye for colour that I have no doubt you will become even better than me at recording nature.'

'But...'

'No buts. Just do it. Take it out onto the hills so that you can catch the movement and live essence we can't capture with photos.'

Wren opened the proud new leather, breathing deeply to take in the rich smell. Water colour paints, fresh and new, lay beside ten different brushes and pencils. Paper she knew to be of the highest quality peeped out from a flap in the lid.

'But I can't accept this. It's so expensive.'

'Quality for quality Wren. All I ask is that you do it justice.' he kissed her hair. 'And I know you will. Now get out and prove it.'

She followed him to his study breathing in the leather and polished wood.

She watched him sit down in his swivel chair.

'I'll never let it out of my sight.' she clasped the gift card with words he'd written to her heart then kissed him before he took up his pen.

'Make sure you don't.'

'Aren't you coming? '

'No, I'm at a really crucial stage in what is proving to be my most important development yet. Go on. Enjoy yourself but take plenty of water. Betty will give you a sandwich and some sun cream. It's getting hotter this end of April. Here! '

He topped her head with a cream Panama hat. 'I got this in the tropics but it always was a bit small. Keep it on.' he laughed. 'You look so cool.'

Wren took her Panama hat, treasured painting case and a canvas bag with water and lunch out into a myriad of prods to every sense she possessed. Could she ever have hoped for such beauty? Towering mountains and hills with roots of green heightening to a sandy grey had their own majesty enriched by their differing sizes. The misshapen olive trees and carpets of wild flowers led away from Imagine. She turned to look back, her eyes taken with the vibrant high bushes of scented pelargoniums shouting out to the sky to be noticed amongst fragrant rosemary, feathery fennel and vivid blue borage. George deserved the beauty he surrounded himself with.

She tottered down one hillside searching the ground for some plant worthy of her virgin paints.

The land rose again but just as she looked up her eyes were caught by sapphire glass sea throwing fresh white foam gently to random rocks. Water diamonds scattered on the calmer surface. All that water scared her a little. She could never see herself enjoying water sports or sailing: she was afraid of the sea, too unknown. Not like her glorious land.

The richness of insect and plant life excited Wren each time she wandered around. She'd found little fossils and rocks so different that she had quite a little pile waiting in her room for identification.

The relentless rain of the last two days had forced the hills to display April flora with eager glory.

Pink lavatera, blue pimpernel and white daisied camomile smiled alongside a host of other delicate wild flowers. She could capture any one of them or she could paint them all.

Sitting in the middle of many different grasses all fighting for space and nourishment from the thin soil, she swigged greedily at her water. George was right, it was getting hotter. After finding a high rock which offered some shade she leaned against it to catch the view which seemed to have been waiting to be painted for centuries. She was glad George was buying this land. It needed to be preserved.

She wasn't proud of her first painting effort which she tucked away when it was dry. She had a vague memory of herself as a child, using a stick wound around with thread as it tried and failed to secure a snip of hair not suitable for painting because of its slight wave. This homemade paint brush was made by a man, the owner of the haircut, with love. That hopelessness made her give up art. Searing pain bit suddenly the edge of a memory, a smile and a voice threatened to come from where she had entombed it. She heaved great slabs of the present over it. It was gone.

After eating her bread and honey both made by Betty, Wren noticed the heat had faded leaving pleasant warmth and softer light. She carefully practised her art on several flowers but needed more time to become skilled at coming anywhere near a painting she could show any-one.

As the sun seemed to be dipping Wren decided to pack up. She had wandered further than ever. This unfamiliar area certainly wasn't the place to be lost in when darkness fell. As she swigged the last of her water then bent to put the bottle into the bag she noticed an orderly line of worker ants carrying honeyed crumbs from the tea towel her lunch had been wrapped in. Each tiny creature was disappearing laden with its precious load towards a crack in porous rock. How long the ants had mesmerised her she didn't know but she wouldn't have ended her fascination if it hadn't been for the sudden shadow across her study area.

Fear caused her to turn abruptly. Her sudden start toppled her backward. As sharp as the rocks hitting the soft palms she threw to steady her, deep dread pierced her awareness but would not allow the reason to surface. Her search was replaced as a deep familiarity touched her instincts.

'George?' She turned and dipped her head trying to recognise the man hiding the sinking sun from her view. He moved slightly, bending towards her, shooting out his hand. Before it reached her breast she hit it away and used the momentum to scramble to her feet.

'Don't you dare touch me!'

'Steady on Senorita. I try to help you!'

It was English spoken with an accent enhanced by a deep masculine voice. He held the flattened palms of large hands in front of him but bare muscular legs stood their ground.

'Don't you try to touch me either. That's quite a temper to show some-one who wonders are you OK.'

There was something about him somewhere deep, deep. A battering ram couldn't access her memory right now so she abandoned trying.

'Now as you must leave can I show way to you?' he stepped aside throwing his arm to indicate his preferred way down to the coast.

'Thank you but I will leave the way I choose when I choose.'

He smiled and allowed his appraisal of her limbs to be noticed. When his eyes fell to her chest she remembered that she had loosened the buttons to take advantage of a cooling breeze earlier. Wren hated the tiny ripple of female response that tingled through her body.

He laughed then, a slow derisory sound that made her dislike him at exactly the same moment as desire settled into her heart.

'Come!' he held out a powerful hand, tanned and desirable, she longed to put hers in it, to feel the thrill of its masculinity. What was she thinking?

'Get lost!' Her voice betrayed her in its huskiness.

'You English are so polite. It is you who are already lost. What is it that you do here?'

'I mind my own business.'

'No you mind mine!'

'What does that mean?' she flashed at him.

'You have the splendid eyes. Especially for an English.'

She struggled not to allow his own deep brown eyes to touch a place inside.

'I have every right to be here recording wild life every day if I want!'

'This, my exquisite lady, is my land. But as you add a certain beauty to the place, I give you leave to plunder its wild flowers anytime you like. Only you'd better be quick.'

His generous mouth and slight dark shadow of a day's beard growth made his even, strong teeth even more attractive. She tried not to care.

'This is not your land. It is up for sale and I happen to know who is buying it.'

'Really. I thought we had not met before this moment. If that is true then you must also know that as soon as I can get a road up here for my bulldozers I will begin building another high specification urbanization.'

To her mortification she felt herself redden with anger.

'...but that's absurd. You can't!'

He shrugged. 'I can and I will. It is what I do.' His words poked her in the ribs.

His tanned face showed the confidence of many successes. She scanned the lavish mouth which had taken on a hard line telling her this conversation was now over. He stood in front of her just waiting for her to leave. Flustered, she grabbed at everything around her and turned. She stomped out ten paces before he spoke.

'Hey! Senorita. Don't forget this expensive case. Your lover won't be pleased if you mislay his special gift.'

Embarrassed to have to retrace her steps she tried to snatch the case from his strong grip.

'I don't have a lover!' She was aware of the crassness of her words and regretted them.

'I'm very glad to hear it. Here!'

He took a small gold edged card from his pocket thrusting it into her case before buckling the flapping straps. The one last step she needed to take towards him seemed enormous but she forced her hand to take the proffered case.

'You may want to see me again.'

The words made her so angry that she hastily pulled one buckle to shove her hand into the stiff leather to retrieve the foreign body he had tainted it with. She flipped the card over her shoulder with distain.

He laughed. 'Please yourself.'

Every step she made away from him seemed awkward beneath his gaze and although she didn't turn she was sure his eyes never left her.

Wren couldn't tell George what she knew. To take that exuberant expectancy from his life was not in her. Yet he had to know. Maybe the Spanish man was bluffing, hoping to buy the land but finding out that a price had been agreed would give up. At supper nothing could possess her to say anything to fade the smile from her uncle's face. He'd had a good day and spread his enthusiasm around his family. There was no point in delivering her bombshell now when the agents were closed and he was impotent to act; it would only keep him awake. She would sleep on the information.

It was with some relief that George had left early for a meeting in Granada and wasn't sitting across from her at breakfast. She wouldn't go out today.

'Would you bring me back some flowers for this vase?' Betty touched her knife to the fading arrangement of days ago.

'When?'

'Today; when you go out recording and painting. How's it going by the way?'

Wren stood up as Joyce pushed back her chair. 'I wish I was out topping up my tan instead of gruelling over Spanish verbs in a hot classroom.'

'Then come with me Joyce.'

'Can't. Anyway there's a sweet young doctor, a Swede that would be as disappointed as me if our eyes didn't meet over conjunctions and tenses.'

'I might stay here.'

'Oh no you won't.' Betty stacked plates on top of each other and deftly gathered cutlery. I have the bridge ladies coming. How can we discuss our juicy gossip in front of a brooding teenager? Anyway, George is so looking forward to seeing your first painting.'

It seemed she had no choice but to go out, she didn't need to go anywhere near where she saw that awful man yesterday. Her heart quickened when his face flashed before her.

Noting which flowers to pick for Betty on her way back Wren took the path to where she'd seen ancient cork trees that might be easier to paint than delicate petals and fluttering wings. The air seemed to have lost the carefree attitude she'd taken for granted the day before. The light didn't seem as good as yesterday and she spent all her time pushing thoughts of an arrogant man from her mind. Who was he? She didn't even know his name.

If only she hadn't made such a gesture in throwing his card away. It had only made him laugh and perhaps the information could have been useful to George. Having persuaded herself that this was the reason other than the flutter her heart felt at the thought of his presence, she re-packed her case and took the route to where she would find the knowledge she so carelessly discarded last evening.

The sun was already hot on the top of her head as she climbed the unpathed hill. The bees droned into the smooth heat telling her that she was alone. A hefty sigh brought sanity to her. She really should get on with the task in hand and wait until she was armed with more facts before she spent another night turning and twisting in thoughts of wilful destruction and rape of this hillside.

Flora is what she should be scouting for not business cards. No matter how much she told her eyes to not look for what she'd thrown away she couldn't stop them. Triumph swelled her heart when a glint of gold edging pulled her eyes to where his card languished on a bed of delicate wild euphorbia.

Her hands did not go to it. Her left fingers gripped her right wrist as if to stop it entering a future she knew she couldn't avoid.

This was stupid. Standing here with sun baking her alive wasn't going to do anything.

As if reaching for fire she allowed her forefinger and thumb to reach out. When she brought the card towards her it felt normal and dull. She laughed out a single sigh of self-derision but was prevented from giving it a partner when she read the words before her.

'Warwick Theodores.

WT CONSTRUCTION

HALCYON HOMES IN SPAIN."

So it was true. The various telephone numbers faded from her sight. She wouldn't be using them but George might.

She tucked the card to the back of her paper realising with guilt that she hadn't drawn or painted anything yet. After a drink she'd march on, force herself to concentrate, produce a paper George would be proud of, instead of those embarrassing attempts tucked away in her case. As she looked about her to quench her thirst she realised she'd left her lunch basket at the villa gate when she'd stopped to tie her shoe lace.

'Damn! Damn! Damn!' the words echoed across the mountain. She could do without food but not water, not in this heat. She'd have to go back. It was just as she turned that the purple and pink fat spike caught her eye. Wild orchid! This was one of the treasures George had hoped to find on his dream land. She couldn't pick it and rob the land of any seed. If only she had a camera. She pushed her dry tongue to the top of her mouth. Maybe a little time, half an hour. Yes that would do it. She pulled out paper and pencil and sketched where she was in relation to the sea. Then with her decisive eye pulled out the colours she knows would reproduce exactly the tightly gathered petals before her. The little water jar sent hope to her heart. How much could she drink? As the cloudy water was held in front of her eyes she realised it was none. She should have washed the jar out to rid it of yesterday's painting. She glanced over the pages. Not even worth the effort.

The delicate intricacy of each tiny part crowding to cover the four inch orchid spike took some sketching. It was getting hotter and the sweat on her forehead caused the oversized hat to slip constantly forward over her eyes. In frustration she lifted it to allow a few moments for her hair and brow to dry off. Her mind pushed her fingers through sheer determination and need to prove she could do it. Perhaps she shouldn't have raised her head so suddenly to view the orchid from the top.

The sickly feeling came in waves.

The air clung to her like a hot rubber cap. It was imperative that she found shade. She stood up quickly, too quickly. Everything went black as she swayed on unsteady feet. It took only a few ghastly moments to ease. Groggily she stumbled towards an untidy group of immature pine. The shade was dappled but she'd have taken anything. Her relief was only slight as she slumped her back against one of the narrow trunks. The skin on her arms and legs was red and sore.

Nausea returned with a thudding headache to give her a weakness she'd never experienced before.

The bright day turned to deep red then black as the chatter of noisy sparrows failed to find her ears. She was lost in weakness.

Here there was someone.

Someone with harrowing words she wouldn't hear.

CHAPTER FORTY TWO

The next thing Wren heard was the tinkling of fine bone china cups in saucers. Intermittent and intrusive clicks of heels shot off hard marble floors to hammer against her brain. She heaved at eyelids reluctant to give her even the tiniest peep of where she was and who was torturing her with their feet. Tiny painful slits allowed her to groggily focus on the cool cotton sheet covering her almost to her nose. The heels clattered forward.

'Aha! You wake! Foolish English. No hat...no sense...no good! You like the tea?'

The seamed face that tipped inquiringly towards her was motherly and dark.

'Where am I?' The words left as the woman stepped back to allow Wren a view of a luxuriously furnished room.

'Ah! Where am I?' Tea was being poured by podgy middle aged hands. 'You see too many movies.' She laughed and turned towards the door. 'I tell him you waked'

The heels clicked her away allowing Wren to shakenly raise herself onto one arm from where it was possible to gingerly find the floor with leaden legs.

Sunlight knifed through softly billowing lace curtains drawn to cool and dim the room.

A tray of gold and white china lay on an ornate heavy table in front of her. Bergamot fragrant tea steamed up to her nose. She sipped then gorged, pouring the tea into both cups in front of her to allow it to cool quicker. She got through four cupful's, greedily replacing the liquid robbed from her by the deceptively ruthless sun. Air wafted over as a door opened from the outside behind her. It was warm and on it came an enticing scent of cologne and body heat. Some instinct made her draw an even deeper breath.

'So! The case lady lives.' The voice hit first at her feminine senses with its deepness and control but the second realisation came with the sight that cut through the treacle of her mind.

Warwick Theodores tried to keep triumph from his face along with a smile that started as he traced her long legs from the floor to where they disappeared beneath the sheet. She pulled them up quickly to join the rest of her body.

'You know we really should be grateful to that little brown case of yours.' He made his way over and sat above her on the arm of the sofa.

'We?'

He displayed magnificent teeth in a teasing grin then allowed full lips to cover them in mock seriousness.

'Yes we. I shall be ever indebted to it for bringing me the most persistent flower seeker and you...' He kept the words as a way of holding her attention. '...you as it just saved your life.'

She tried to concentrate on the words instead of the towering male presence above her.

'I don't understand.'

'We...that is Tim my surveyor and I...came across that precious case of yours on our way over the hill. It was just lying there, alone. Knowing how you guard it with your very life, I knew you wouldn't be far but we couldn't see you anywhere. I called out but when there was no reply I feared the worst. After a few minutes search we found you slumped beneath some trees. You were unconscious, suffering from sunstroke.'

'And you brought me here, to your house?'

He nodded as he displayed those teeth again, seeming to enjoy her discomfort.

He laughed. 'You are very red! You have no sun in England do you?'

The abrupt movement as she pulled the sheet off her was more wobbly than she would have liked but when her feet pressed the cool floor there was not enough strength to keep her up.

'Careful!' strong arms encircled her and pulled her to his chest. She became aware of him through every pore in her body. Feminine madness blanketed her brain.

But only for a moment. The flat of her hand pushed at the hard bones beneath his throat.

'Get off me!'

'It feels nice. I thought you liked that as much as I did.'

'How dare you?'

'No! How dare you!' he echoed.

'What?'

'Assume that my holding you was anything more than to save your skull splattering on my nice clean marble floor.'

He eased her back to the softness of the seat then went around to the other side of the coffee table.

'I see you drank my tea as well as your own; just like you want my land. What else do you want from me?'

'Nothing other than to see the back of you.'

He laughed but she could see his confidence was shaken.

'You know you should have been carrying water and sun screen in that little case of yours instead of prissy little paints and useless scribblings and clumsy paintings.'

'You have been in my case!' she shouted mortified that any-one had seen her inelegant early attempts at painting.

'That is private. The contents of my case are none of your business!'

Even as she threw the words at him she knew she was being harsh. He had just saved her life even if he was intent on destroying nature.

'Perhaps not but then I would not have known that you travelled all the way back to where we met yesterday just to retrieve my card.'

Embarrassment crippled her tongue then freed it with anger.

'You think so highly of yourself. I never gave you or your card a single thought. I hate litter that's all.'

'So yesterday you throw litter and today you nearly kill yourself to retrieve it. Sounds like a busy life. No?'

She knew he was baiting her so he spoke slowly and quietly.

'I was out there to paint and log wild flowers. It was just luck that I came across your card.'

'I'm glad to hear you think it lucky.'

'It is only litter.'

He softened as if not wanting to spar any more.

'I had to look in your case to see if there was an address of your hotel or finca. I could have done without the complication of bringing you all the way down here. I am a busy man you know.'

'Yes raping mountains must keep you very stretched.'

'People have to have somewhere to live Wren.'

It was a shock to find out he knew her name and a surprise to hear how softly he spoke it.

'There was a little card in your case. 'To darling Wren, to capture your dreams.' I haven't guessed your name in spite of the strange feeling that we have met before.'

He locked into her eyes and Wren knew it too.

'But no.' he shook his head. 'I would have remembered those beautiful eyes. They don't share colour but they share knowing and seeking."

She was pulled by his searching look, absorbing and enjoying the luxury of familiarity.

What was wrong with her? Did sunstroke weaken the mind as well as the body? She turned her head away from him and dizziness saved her from further intimacy.

Groggily, she allowed herself to be tucked under the sheet like a three year old.

'Just rest.' His touch to her shoulder was all too brief. She wanted his hands all over her; she needed his body pressed to hers and those lips seeking her mouth and throat.

'Get lost!'

Was that her voice that sounded so rude? Strange new feelings robbed her of much needed sleep and her pounding heart bullied every brain cell to consider only one subject. One man. One feeling.

How could she rest when something had been triggered inside her that she knew couldn't be allowed to grow? She'd had this feeling before. There was no way she could remember when.

A strong feeling of not belonging overpowered her. It wasn't just here in this opulent villa. There was more. It was as if she didn't even belong in the world.

'Senorita! Wake now. It late!'

The concerned smile of the Spanish housekeeper eased her to consciousness.

'You wish bathroom? I show.'

Her eyes peeled back just enough to see her panama hat perched on the sofa across the table from her. It took a while for the incongruity of the sight to explain itself to her brain.

Leaden legged; Wren followed the pumpkin shaped rear across a vast hall to a rosemary fragrant guestroom. The shower door was opened and the water set to lukewarm before she was left alone. She dismissed the mirror that showed how damp and creased her clothes had become, how sticky her hair. How bright red she was in unbecoming patches. He must be laughing at the sight of such a mess. Her longing for such an attractive, successful man must be making the universe laugh too. As she entered the stream lethargy was slaked from her but the sting to the sunburn on the back of her neck reminded her of her foolishness. Wrapped in a thick towel she sat at the dressing table. Sun had coloured her face tawny pink except where the hair, now wet and slicked back had edged it. Thank goodness she had put cream on that at least. She was glad she had not copied the 'Twiggy' style she had so wanted but not had the courage to seek.

That thought slapped her mind to force a harder stare at herself. That was her past. But where? When?

As she stepped into the hallway in search of her clothes she almost collided with Warwick. He had changed into brief shorts and a narrow sports vest clinging with perspiration. He pulled at a towel around his neck forcing her to look up to eyes sparkling with excess energy.

'Feeling better?' He took in the warm damp woman before him. 'You certainly look it.'

He stared at her with hot eyes then seemed to remember something.

'I've just had a work out in the gym. Now I take a swim to cool off before dinner. Care to watch.'

There was an embarrassment that she didn't understand about being in such close proximity to another hot almost naked human being, but the urge she felt was unmistakable.

'I...no. Dinner? What time is it?'

'Around six. Why? Will some-one be missing you? George perhaps?'

'You know him?'

'Only from his card writing. It's a pity he wasn't worried enough to stop you trundling around mountain sides making daisy chains without water...or sense.'

'Mr. Theodores; I was not making daisy chains! I was recording. And for your information, I take care of myself.'

She realised that wasn't true and yet it should be. It had been. Hadn't it? Once...?

Relief came via his good manners.

'OK I understand you are worried. I will drive you back to where you are staying. Is it far?'

'I don't know. Where am I?'

'Here.' His hand slid beautifully into hers and she had no desire to stop it. He led her outside onto a patio of steps leading from the white painted villa walls, through lush planting of trees and greenery to another paved area. Loungers were arranged with the same passion for exactness around the bluest water she had ever seen.

'You are in Heaven. Look at that view.'

Her eyes swept over groupings of palm trees set into lush lawns, down the red and speckled rooftops of a distanced village to the sparkle of evening sea.

This ecstasy joined with the way her legs felt as if they were not connected to her body singing with his closeness, whacked into her senses.

She gazed around, her pleasure seemed overloaded.

'It is beautiful, but where....?'

'You have the honour of standing in the Villa Heaven set in the hills just above the idyllic village of Lamas de Marbella. My Villa.'

She became lost in the way the blue-green of the sea met the keener blue of the sky and how the green lushness of the gardens meant so many people cared. There was a soft splash beside her and she turned to catch the water in the pool split by strong arms and legs as they forced the brown body powerfully along. Unable to drag her eyes from what had disturbed not only the water she watched him heave himself onto the side to stand dripping before her.

'Wow! That's better.' he wiped water from his eyes and mouth then breathed out hard. He knew he was magnificent. She knew she wanted him.

'I bet you couldn't do that in spring emerging from a cold northern English river. Your body wouldn't be quite so keen or brown then.'

'Keen no.' he laughed. 'But brown perhaps. My mother is English; my father gave me his Spaniard blood and skin. And although I was born here you could say I was made in England, conceived during a picnic in the grounds of the castle I am named after. Quite daring, my father!'

She had never heard of Warwick castle, he knew more about England than she did.

'And here? Is this his Villa?'

He pulled a towel from a pile on a table and wrapped it around his waist.

'Heaven? No. I built this as my first project when I took over the business at twenty one. Six years I have lived here working harder and harder to keep up the standard my father taught me.'

'It's very beautiful, no?'

There was a moment when neither of them spoke. Wren took pleasure in her surroundings all the time aware the magnificent man before her was taking pleasure in the sight of her.

'So are you Wren.'

The feeling Wren was trying to fight wasn't clear. It was plain enough to know that she desired the man who set her pulses racing. It was easy to know that he wanted to destroy all she held dear but there was another inference somewhere deep, somewhere hidden. Did she already feel this way about some other man?

'Will you take dinner with me?' His words broke into her thoughts.

'No.' she said harshly deliberately trying to break the mood. 'I'm late.'

'But you need to eat. I have asked Maria to make us a special supper.'

'Some-one else will have cooked for me. I can't let them worry.'

'Then ring them.'

She had no idea of telephone numbers, she had never taken notice of anything other than getting better and her beloved nature.

'No, I must go.'

Disappointment let go of his smile. 'I'll run you home then. Where are you staying?'

He began walking towards the villa extending an arm to guide her with him.

'I'm staying north of Mijas, at a small finca called Imagine.'

His turn was quick.

'You are staying with George Stoker?'

'Yes, he's my uncle.'

Coldness seemed to leap from the marble floor to his heart and then his eyes.

He pushed back his wet hair with suppressed savagery. His face darkened like a thunder cloud in the wake of a lightning bolt.

'Wait here.' He snapped.

She stood alone not understanding why everything had changed; embarrassed that she was impotent to leave. When Warwick returned he was not alone.

'Tim here will drive you home.'

Through her bewilderment Wren followed Tim but as she past Warwick he grabbed her arm.

'If you have any concern for your dear Uncle you won't mention anything about me; do you understand'

He thrust her newly pressed clothes into her towelled chest and followed it with her case.

'Not a word.' he added menacingly. 'It's for his own good.'

As the car wound upwards Wren knew she had to get over the embarrassment of the situation she had just escaped. But careful pumping of Tim didn't net a thing. He had only worked for WT Construction for two months and didn't have a clue to Warwick's behaviour either.

Anxious faces came first to the window and then the open door when the car tyres heralded their arrival. Wren was quick to dismiss Tim before he had to answer any questions. Inside Joyce, Betty and George all rushed at once with a little anger mixed with their relief.

'Where the hell have you been? We've been so worried. It is almost dark.'

Hugging silenced her.

'Who was that blond man?' George's voice was worried but Joyce made a look of excited approval.

Wren explained everything except the identity of the man who had rescued her. They assumed it was the man who drove her here and she let them.

'I can't believe you left your vital food and water at the gate. We found it around five and that really started us worrying. But your hat. Where's your hat?'

'Oh, I must have left it at the villa.'

'Well don't worry. I'll take you there tomorrow; it'll give me a chance to thank your young man properly.'

'No!'

She was upset by the hurt and puzzled look on his face.

'I mean I can't remember the way to the villa.'

Dinner had been dominated by Joyce teasing Wren about how pretending to faint in the sun never got her such a good looking man but that she would definitely try it one day.

'He could make you forget any Bonnie who lay over the ocean I hope Wren.'

There were no protests when she went to bed early; they knew she needed to sleep. But sleep was the last thing she could find.

Joyce's excited face was planted before her eyes. She had been silenced by a look from her mother but Wren scrutinised every word. She remembered when they were little together singing the song 'My Bonnie Lies Over the Ocean' and doing all the exaggerated hand movements but why had Joyce brought it up now?' A grey curtain hung between her memory and her heart. Trauma had made her want to forget everything in England but perhaps there was something she really should remember.

She could not bear the mental struggle; she merely gave up and so stayed in the current that had swept her along since she arrived in this country.

With a mind filled with questions, need and disappointment she urged back that strange feeling that she was not alone. There seemed to be someone always there beside her and yet she saw no-one; nothing. But whatever it was it would not be pushed away.

That there were some very important issues locked in her memory she had no doubt but she did not have the mental strength or desire to seek them. Whatever they were they could stay with the pain they were soaked in; buried deeply by the immediate need to survive.

CHAPTER FORTY THREE

'I'm not letting you out of my sight today Wren.'

George's eyes scrutinised her as they both gathered breakfast dishes to follow Betty and Joyce into the kitchen.

'I'm all right; really.'

He turned her camomile lotion covered arms gently over. 'You can stay here; indoors.'

'No. I need to be out. I'll wear long sleeves and six hats, promise.'

'Well there is no way I am allowing you out alone.' He gave a look on a sigh that said he couldn't denied those eyes anything

'I'm excited to see that Orchid you told me about, there could be others around. Would you be able to find it?'

The weight of three water bottles, one floppy flower-power hat from Joyce's wardrobe, a large umbrella and an over protective Uncle slowed their progress across the rough ground. When hot feet left George's land to tread amongst plants not yet his, Wren sang as she went 'In The Middle of Nowhere,' much louder than was necessary for pleasure. If there was any-one else around this place she wanted them to stay out of her way.

'Ah! Dusty Springfield eh? I love that song.' George chirruped before joining in with a few words he knew and lots of humming.

The little map she'd done of where the orchid was showed the bay beneath them and an outcrop of rock to have at the back of the searcher but as George took up that position further eye-lining wasn't needed.

'Hello! There's your hat; right beside the orchid. You must have left it there to mark the place.'

She watched George rush to pick up the hat he had loaned her then bend towards his floral treasure.

She was too shocked to join in his ecstasy.

That hat had not been left there last night; it was definitely at Villa Heaven when she was drinking her tea. Warwick had been here before them. He had known exactly where the orchid was without the benefit of her map.

Was he here now, watching them? Spying.

The camera clicked all morning stopping only when George had found seven more orchids, two species of butterfly he would have to look up and a handful of seeds with such hard shells that he suspected they would need fire to crack them open.

'You see nature provides for every eventuality. Dry summers heighten the risk of fires so that some trees have seeds that lie dormant until a fire allows them to burst into life. They are the insurance policy to regenerate the plant life.'

Wren, ordered to sit beneath the black umbrella, could only listen with one ear and gave so little concentration that George began to notice.

'Do you think I have the pink right.' he leaned over to show her his painting then noticed the blank page on her board.

'Your heart isn't in this is it? You are still suffering from your heat stroke yesterday.' He began packing away his paints. 'I should never have allowed you out, come on.'

Wren didn't protest when she was ushered along home. There was too much on her mind, her stomach ached and she was so very tired.

She had looked at but not taken in one page of the book on her lap when George strode out onto the balcony to join her in her shade.

'I've phoned the real estate about that land, those orchids have got me even more desperate to own it. They say there has been a little hiccough but I told them things will have to be sorted soon. Hope I didn't sound too keen.'

Wren closed her eyes not wanting to allow any of the information in her brain leak out to spoil his happiness.

'It is vital I get that land. It would be disastrous if a developer got their hands on it. Still the Officina at the Centro Comercial Plaza are so careless with their signs if I didn't see it no developer would. They'd want it cheap anyway, bargain the owner down.'

She stayed silent not wanting to say the wrong thing and searching her mind for a way to stop Warwick Theodores from ruining both land and dreams. George's next words seared through her like a hot barbeque skewer.

'Still I'd rather know if I had competition. A man doesn't need to run as fast if he's in a race by himself.'

He kissed her on the head. 'We have good times ahead together Wren. Nothing can stop us. It is me, you and nature!'

His misplaced confidence fed her determination.

She had to thwart Warwick.

The trouble was, she pondered all night, she didn't even want to set eyes on him ever again never mind work the impossible.

Next morning she told every-one she was going to walk the two miles into Mijas for shopping and to have her hair that had grown unmanageably long cut into shape.

She took the thousand pesetas George had given her on their trip to Marbella, perhaps she'd buy some new sandals. The crisp sunlight that promised the scorcher to come led her feet over sand and rocks to cobbles lining bright white streets hanging with singing caged birds, pink trailing pelargonium and vivid blue plumbago. Some doors were open to the street and Wren found it hard not to glance in to other people's lives.

One old lady dressed in black sitting with one arm resting on a tiled table smiled back with a toothless grin and a friendly wave of 'Hola!'

Betty's directions had been to head downwards until she came to the post office perched on magnificent steps. From there she'd see the street she'd come from and the ones she wanted. How she could have lived here and not come into town she never knew, it was so wonderful.

Unable to enjoy the holiday atmosphere that had the pavements sprinkled with tables and delicious coffee smells, Wren pushed on to the left. No wonder there was a demand for homes here. She questioned how long the charm would last when it was forced open to entice sun starved Northern Europeans. She stopped at a notice board and shuddered at the vivid illustration of a bullfight. The Spanish saw this as sport; the fighters as brave. Maybe that was how Warwick saw himself, as a hero of people with money, not seeing the cruelty to nature. Perhaps she wouldn't have to see him again. She could just talk to him on the phone. If, that was, she could fathom how Spanish telephones worked.

She had trotted through most of the town, often downward on steps paced out every five strides, before she saw a telephone booth. It stood shaded by a Laburnum tree in a gardened square lined with well-groomed and plumed horses pulling pink, wide smiling tourists in jingling ornate carts. She had no change and in fact had never even looked at Spanish money. As she edged towards the front of the square she saw leather goods displayed on the pavement beneath even more hanging down over held back doors.

'Finest handbags for Senorita. Good strong purses?' A dark lizardy man fastened his tiny eyes on her.

She knew she had neither bag nor purse but it was sandals she needed, and change.

Choosing the first pair that fit from the pungent pile she offered too many notes. Perhaps he would rob her, she didn't care.

'Telephone?' she asked pointing to the coins in her hands.

The mahogany fingers lifted a coin out of the weight they'd just put in her hand. Then he gave her more notes. She was glad to see honesty in action and returned his little bow of farewell.

After much fumbling and wishing she could read Spanish Wren managed to get a dialling tone and her money to drop. She checked each number on the card carefully not wanting to misdial wasting her coin and concentration.

The Spanish spoken into her ear meant nothing. 'English please?'

'WT Construction. Gillaine speaking.' The heavily accented female voice promised efficiency and no nonsense.

'Mr Theodores please.'

'Who is calling?' The secretary fell easily into English.

'I.... a client.'

'And does this client have a name?'

'Is he in please? I really need to speak to him.'

'Mr. Theodores is out to lunch but if you leave your details he will call you back.'

Wren returned the receiver to its cradle. All the adrenalin that sloshed through her veins was wasted, serving only to make her sweat in an already hot booth. Disappointment that her courage was failing sent her arm flying to the door which wasn't as heavy as she thought. When it hit a passer-by she was forced from her thoughts into a prolific apology.

'Well you have a habit of getting in my way don't you.'

Wren was so shocked to see the very person she sought that she couldn't speak.

'You have changed colour I see.' His eyes were soft on her body.

Words would not surface through the explosion of feeling inside her. He took her silence as aggression.

'Oh come on I'm not all that bad am I? I'm just trying to make a living and maybe have a little lunch with a colleague.'

He tipped his head to her silent face. 'Hello! Are you all right?'

'Yes...sorry. Where are you meeting him?' she said in an effort to sound normal.

'Here. He jerked a thumb over his back towards the top of the square. 'Won't you join me? I have reserved the table on the upstairs balcony. It has shade, the best view and delicious food.'

'I... won't your colleague mind?'

'No he won't mind because he won't be there I'll ring him, tell him something has come up; although I'll say it is urgent not beautiful.' He bent towards her ear allowing warm delicate scent into her breathing space. 'He might get jealous.'

He didn't wait for an answer but pulled open the door of the phone booth she'd just left.

She watched the broad back and soft curling hair on his neck as he took up the receiver she'd just held to call him. She'd not tell. It was to her advantage for him to chase her.

With white linen napkins spread across their knees and a jug of ice water in front of them Warwick spoke to the waiter in Spanish. His voice was even more beautiful. She did not recognise the words but the tune was one already in her heart.

'Hope you don't mind, I've ordered. I know what is excellent here.'

He dipped his forehead with polite enquiry, not allowing his eyes to leave hers. As if to escape she latched on to the sudden, hectic clamour of her pulses to look into the avenue below. All the time he watched her.

Almost immediately little dishes were placed before them. Wren recognised some of the food from Betty's cooking but the sardine slivers in olive oil, crushed garlic and sea salt was temptingly new.

'Do you like tapas? He asked dipping crisp bread into a green sauce.'

'I don't know. I've only been here a month, haven't eaten out much; in fact only once, in Marbella.'

He held his palm up to stop the waiter pouring wine.

'I am driving after this and I'm already dizzy with seeing you. You are much more intoxicating than even the very best of wines.'

His slow intake of breath seemed to touch the raw dread of her own deeply disturbing desire for this man.

'What's this?' she asked with burning cheeks.

'Calamari.'

She bit a little.

'Yuk! Feels like sliced rubber gloves.'

'You have strong opinions on all things Spanish considering you have been here such a short time.' he laughed.

'What does that mean?'

'Well first you tell me what to do with my land...'

'Nature belongs to every-one.' She was surprised at her outburst but felt it was worth riding on.

She put down her fork and grasped his mood.

'I want to ask you not to buy that parcel of land. My Uncle has its best interests at heart; you want only to destroy it.'

Her words hung in the air as the dishes were cleared and the crumbs wiped from the stiff cloth.

The way his eyes crinkled at the corners told her that he thought her concern was cute rather that threatening.

'Wren I do not want to destroy it, I want to develop it so that people can have a good place to live. You and your uncle are so greedy wanting to keep it to yourselves.'

'Greedy! Greedy is taking huge profits.'

'At least I intend to share the mountain. I have already lost land to that preservation control fanatic you call Uncle. I have sworn he will never out do me again!'

So that was it!

'Come on.' He smiled as sea bass and sauté potatoes went under their noses. 'Don't spoil good lunch.'

But it was spoiled.

She found it hard to eat with what was charging between them. He had no such restriction.

'You know you speak English differently to any other person I have met from your country. You have a very attractive accent.'

'Geordie.'

'What? You speak like your Uncle?'

'No. I come from near Newcastle in the north of England. The people there are Geordies.'

'Are they all so feisty so captivating?'

She knew it was line but she smiled. If only he knew how much she wanted him.

He was a man of disturbing masculinity which only served to coil her stomach so tightly that she put down her glass for fear of choking.

'Here.' He took her fork and lifted some fish to her mouth. 'You need all your strength.'

His caring comment took her away to some time when he'd said those words before. But how? She'd only met him twice; and yet.

The accidental brush of his darkly haired arm on her breast flared at feelings she knew were long ago lit but never doused. Confusion opened her mouth.

'There. Now, when that fish is nothing but bones, I would like to spend the afternoon with you. What would you like to do?'

His confidence astounded her but it was her chance to work on him.

'You've got a nerve! If I say yes, can I choose anything I like?'

'If it keeps you in my company, of course.' He stared hungrily at her.

'Let us go together to the land agent to tell them that you are not interested in that mountain.'

She heard his shocked breath leave on what she had no doubt was a Spanish swearword.

'You are serious aren't you?'

'You said anything.'

'Not that.'

He pushed his chair back and motioned for the bill. Silence hung as he paid. Then he picked up the bag with her new sandals; took her elbow in his firm grip and guided her out.

The dark stairs leading to the sun-baked cobbles heard their feet but not their voices.

As the sun wacked onto their bodies he slowly studied her, shaking his head, deep in consideration. Although they weren't even touching she felt as if he was pulling her towards him. He took a step back, his eyes holding her for one killing moment.

'If you are serious about this I will discuss it with you.'

The surprise shot energy to her brain.

'Meet me here tomorrow at nine in the morning.'

Not waiting for her reply he strode to his open topped Mercedes which he lurched away without even a wave. He still had her shoes.

'How pompous! How bloody arrogant.' She shouted after him but he was long gone.

She wouldn't go of course.

He was too dangerous. There must be other ways for George to get that land. She would have to tell him he had competition. The burden was too great for her to carry alone. And the mad attraction too overwhelming.

That evening Joyce brought three friends from the language school for supper. With their laughing voices they filled the patio, the kitchen and every moment of George's time. He showed them tricks with cards and matches that Wren knew she'd seen before. Her memory took her back to a colder place with hands positioning matches between cracked finger tips with coal engrained nails. It wasn't George's hands and yet she loved them too. Pain closed down that train of thought. Slammed the lid of forgetfulness tight shut.

She'd trailed into bed long before the laughing and singing had stopped. There had not been one moment to talk privately to George.

She was onto her second cup of morning tea when Betty padded into the kitchen yawning.

'Oh no? Is it eight already? George isn't even awake yet. Two am he fell into bed! I told him he wouldn't be able to get up in the morning. Still, it's not often.' She wandered back in to the bedroom with two cups on a tray leaving Wren to try to soften the beating of her heart brought about by her private thoughts. If she didn't go to meet

Warwick she could miss a valuable chance to be heard and at the same time risk irritating him. Maybe she would just ask for her shoes and leave.

She'd have to go.

After showering she hit the path with her hair drying in the sun, it was getting too long to handle. Pink lipstick and good cream kept rays from her skin as she walked the same path as yesterday holding her breath from what might be, from what she might feel at the first sight of him.

He wasn't there.

She swallowed at the horrid pill of dread; he was toying with her. She walked twice around the square then diagonally across it. The wild birds competed with the caged canaries for the sweetest song and lost. They had more to do than practice notes. There was food to find, mates to mate and shade to consider and they were enjoying every second of it, showing off to their sad captive competitors.

Wren took to one of the wooden seats not yet hot from the morning sun. As she watched the road either side of the phone box she felt a dreadful premonition swelling in the recesses of her mind. Everything here was beautiful. Air, flowers, trees the gently rising sound of the day unfolding to the locals. But there was one thing, one horrible, dreadful thing that she couldn't quite remember.

She looked at her watch. Twenty minutes past nine. He wasn't coming now.

Excitement faded from her body. All night she had practised things to say to him, searching for new ways to bury the longing her body felt despite her forbidding.

Everything was wasted. He was playing her for a fool. An older experienced man like him knew when a young foreign girl fluttered at the sight of him, no matter what she said. He had plenty of opportunity with all these wide eyed visitors seeking sun and fun far away from cold countries.

A man with his looks and success could have any-one he wanted, why should he do anything but play with a naive teenager. He'd be laughing now in his office with his capable secretary sharing the joke of how the little Geordie girl thought she could take on such a might.

A new thought rushed her to her feet. Perhaps he was making sure she was out of the way here so that he could be up to something on the mountain. She had to get there.

It was just as she passed the last horse, polished to perfection like the cart it pulled, that a familiar roar made her turn.

'Good morning pretty lady.' he smiled as he slowed the open topped car beside her. She kept on walking. Easily he cajoled the car to her pace lifting his sunglasses to the top of his head to take an even better look at her.

'Aren't you getting in? We have a date.'

'Do we? I don't remember.'

'Then why are you here? '

'Shopping... I ...we ran out of bread.' she said without turning.

'But we agreed to meet here at nine.'

She made an exaggerated look at her watch.

'Oh you British, so stuffy, so exact. It is the Spanish way to take your time; anyway I had to get the picnic.'

She stopped then and he copied, smiling his amusement at her surprise. Narrowed eyes touched every one of her hypersensitive nerve ends as they ran over her. He looked wonderful.

With pulses hammering out of control she managed to push out one word.

'Picnic? '

'Yes you don't think I agreed to meet you here so that I could follow those long legs from my car or watch the way the sun glows and moves with every tantalising sway of that long golden hair do you?'

He got out of the convertible, towering above her showing white teeth in a soft smile.

'Get in to the car I have something to show you.' His touch on her arm was like gentle fire.

'Please.'

She made no move, she was chained to a standstill by the sudden need of him.

'Wren? '

There was something about the soft way he said her name that melted her even further. That tiny hint of Spanish over excellent command of English only dual nationality parents could give.

As his mouth closed over his smile she had to pull her eyes away from it and the sheer desire to have it touch her own.

'How can I talk to you about Heaven Hills if I have to drive behind you like some servant on special duty? '

'Heaven Hills? '

'Yes do you like the name I have come up with for a new development? '

'It is nothing to do with me what you call your destruction of nature but you haven't got your own way yet.'

He saw that anger was rising in her.

'It is a nice name even if you and your uncle decide to selfishly keep it all to yourselves.'

'What? Do you mean...?'

'Wren, I have such lovely things to show you and food will go to waste if we don't eat it. Please come.' He pleaded.

Could she trust him?

'We have to talk…and I have your sandals.'

He walked around the car and opened the passenger door. She was the first to surrender the stare; then with a self-conscious shrug she got in.

He seemed to know these roads so well, easily taking sharp bends nerve bitingly near the edge of rocky ravines. They wound down towards the coast and then along it racing the sun behind them.

He said nothing but gave the odd approving glance at Wren. She noticed bigger buildings as they stopped at traffic lights in towns and when he turned left towards the coast again Wren opened her eyes to new sights.

'This is Puerto Banus; where the millionaires have their boats.'

The car bulled through thickening traffic and more people than Wren had seen in one place at one time. When they turned onto the harbour Wren's overwhelming feeling was how inadequate her clothes were. Plain khaki shorts and pink shirt tied to rabbit's ears at the waist like Joyce had shown her suddenly seemed so boring amongst flower-power flowing robes, swaying chains and hipster pants clinging to snake-like hips.

Suddenly a face came at hers.

'Peace man.' Long wavy hair matted and secured by a flower stuffed bandana across the brow followed fingers grasping a pungent, out of shape cigarette into the car space.

'Here, care for a draw on my joint.' The thin man's eyes were glazed and he seemed to be in some sort of ecstasy. Warwick spurted off scattering groups of people jingling finger bells and flicking back their flower strewn hair.

'Is it a festival?' Wren asked wondering how any-one could buy such clothes never mind wear them.

'What? Where have you been the last few months? This is 'Peace Man', 'Flower power'.

'But the clothes they are so ....patterned all swirling shapes and luminous colours.'

'It's psychedelic. I thought you liked flowers.'

A girl with eyes ringed in black and her mouth blotted out with thick make-up came writhing towards them waving two fingers from each hand as she smiled and leered.

'Is she all right?'

'Yes, seems normal these days. LSD created no doubt.'

'LSD? You mean money? Pounds shillings and pence? '

They edged ever more slowly towards the backdrop of large white aitches.

'Oh Wren. This North East of England, doesn't it have television? Young people? '

'I can't remember.'

He laughed thinking it was a joke not a statement.

'Haven't you heard of lysergic acid diethylamide?'

'No I never use poisons on God's earth. What is it?'

'Drugs. Half these people are on mind altering drugs and some of them much nicer for it. What they are doing to their brains however doesn't bear thinking about.'

Embarrassed by a couple writhing together as they locked lips, Wren turned her head away.

'Have you ever taken drugs Warwick?'

'No. Why should I. I get my highs from natural means.' He allowed his eyes to slide over her. 'Beauty! That is my high.'

'Mine too.' She smiled, missing his inference.

A small gap cleared as people rushed to the harbour's edge to look at some-one who had splashed into the sea. Warwick spurted through, parking just to the left of where the crowd had knotted.

'Aren't you going to help him?' Wren craned her neck.

'No. If I went to save some-one who thought they could walk on water every time they proved otherwise, I would be permanently in the harbour. Besides it is warm and clean-ish.'

He turned off the engine. 'Come on.'

Wren was so engrossed in the people she hadn't noticed she was alone in the car with him standing holding open the door.

Lines of white hulls glared before her, bobbing in water so clear that shoals of foot long fish could easily be seen nibbling at the harbour wall.

Warwick said some-thing to a man on a large imposing yacht who then tossed down a bunch of keys.

Expertly, Warwick stepped onto the front of a smaller boat where he stowed away the bags he'd taken from the car boot. Just as confidently he planted one foot on the harbour, straddling the gap easily. The boat bobbed dangerously Wren thought but Warwick adjusted with skill born of experience. He held out a hand.

'Coming?'

'What me! On there! I'm scared of the water. No.'

She felt herself tense as he waved brown fingers towards her.

'Wren stop joking. I told you about the picnic didn't I?'

The man who had provided the keys was looking down at her laughing and three or four hippies had stopped to watch. Fear of looking foolish seemed larger than fear of drowning so she took his hand which he immediately pulled forcing one foot after another onto the boat which rocked wildly.

'Just relax Wren. You'd think you'd never been on a boat before!' He guided her towards two seats and a steering wheel beside which the keys were now dangling.

'Do you want to sit here with me or lie there to sunbathe?' He splayed his palm towards a large cushioned area edged with more seats, taking in her widened eyes and open mouth.

'You'd better ride up here with me.'

'Ride? We aren't going out in this thing are we?'

'But of course. What's wrong; too small for you?'

'Small no...too... too ...wobbly.'

He laughed. 'Oh Wren you get funnier by the minute. What a tonic to be with. Any-one would think you'd never been on the sea charging along at speed.'

'Speed!' her voice sounded thin. 'I haven't.'

'Of course you have. How do you get out to water-ski.' He turned the key to fire a throbbing charge, the boat reversed into the wide gap of the marina and slowly out towards the sea.

Wren clung to the sides of the seat full of fear but at the same time enthralled by beautiful boats, colours and people. The sight of the land going away from her swirled feelings of wonder and insecurity.

'Ready?'

She glanced at his broad back. He was standing expertly balanced not turning in his careful concentration.

'We are clear now we can go!'

He pushed at the throttle and the boat lifted into a confident speed towards the open sea. The land and marina shrank away as they turned to follow the coast line from a distance.

A slight motion sickness hit her ears but she swallowed it back. He turned. 'You OK?'

'I can't stop thinking about all that water beneath me.'

'Isn't it great?'

'No! And the fish and tangle weed and all those jelly things that you can't see but sting you.'

'It's fine; great for swimming. Have you brought your costume?'

His hair was forced back by the wind they were riding into.

'I don't have a costume and if I did I certainly wouldn't have brought it on a meeting with some-one about land.'

He laughed. 'I guess you are right.'

He took time out of his obvious joy to point out landmarks. The Spanish hills rose unevenly and sharply, dotted with proud houses on stilts and slashes of razor cut roads to them.

'Is this what you wanted to show me?' she asked raising her voice above the noise.

'Isn't it enough?'

'It is captivating but you said you had something special to show me.' She shouted into the breeze.

'There's plenty time.'

He pushed further at the throttle, charging into a private masculine bliss of testosterone and speed. Wren picked a line on the mountains to the right of them and tried to think of how soon this trip would be over.

The boat turned into a tight figure eight and then scooted around jagged rocks before slowing to glide into a secluded bay with flat clean sand.

He turned to see her green tinged face and white knuckles. Turning off the ignition he took the few steps towards her rocking the boat wildly with his eagerness.

'Oh no! I am sorry. You weren't joking were you? Have you ever been in a speedboat before?'

'No.' She hated the way he glanced at the hands still gripping the side of the seats so she sent one to her pocket to find the elastic band to gather her wind whisked hair behind her neck.

When she stood up his arm went around her, she needed the support whilst her balance found itself. That citrus, musky smell again, she hated the way her body demanded she breathe it in.

'Here. See how shallow the water is. Take off your shoes and step over. We'll have lunch on the beach.' The very thought made Wren wretch.

'Oh lovely.'

He jumped easily over the side and took her hand. 'Come on now. You'll feel better once you can feel solid land between your toes.'

She fell onto him as he lifted her so that her feet never got wet. The gentle splashing of his legs tried to distract her from the warm aroma of him and failed. Wren felt at home in his arms. There was a sureness that she had belonged there before.

She watched him wade back to the speed boat and then return with the bags. After spreading a large thick towel in the shade of the rocks he poured a drink into a paper cup.

'You'll need water.'

'What are we doing here?' She said as steadiness returned with her courage.

'Two things; very important. First; I have broken off my engagement.'

'Engagement?'

'To Gillaine.'

'You are to marry your secretary?'

'Not now.'

'Why?'

'I have known Gillaine for four years. She is the best secretary on the Costa del Sol, she is funny, kind and beautiful.'

'So? Marry her.'

'I can't. Not since I have met you.'

'Me!'

'Oh I do love her. She makes my life easy and comfortable but I knew something was missing only I didn't know what.'

Wren fought to keep the jealousy from her face. 'I don't understand.'

He put his hand to the stray bits of hair the warm wind had torn from her band.

'The moment I saw this beautiful hair, the eyes like both the deep sea and sky in spring and most of all what lay behind them, I knew.'

His voice had dropped as he looked at her mouth then moved towards it. Softly, his slightly parted lips met hers drawn by the sheer need created by belonging. Something distant was relighted so that she returned his craving with ever increasing tantalising pressure. His hands went to the small of her back and pulled her body towards him. He urged his need swollen mouth to give greater closeness, more unbearable pleasure. Ecstasy was their bond. But only for a moment.

She pulled away embarrassed by her reaction and his awareness that she wanted the kiss as much as he did.

'I was right.'

She fought to recover. 'I... we mustn't.'

His hands went to her face only just touching as they cupped her cheeks in their strength.

'Why? Must the rain not find the earth, must the stars not find the night sky, and must love not find its destiny?'

'You are my enemy.' It sounded weak even to her as the husky voice betrayed its words.

With his questioning eyes gently raking every inch of her she turned away searching for a way to break the bond.

'Did you say something about food?' She asked.

She heard the exasperation leave his lungs. He went with her and opened a bag. The smell would have tempted an angel. Chicken spit roasted in herbs and sea salt was torn still warm, and then placed alongside wafer thin crisps, golden and fresh.

Wren ate, needing the strength to fight her longing for him. She refused the wine but gobbled the sweetest black grapes her fingers had ever held.

He absorbed her every move.

'They say a lady with a good appetite for food has a good appetite for love.'

She left her eyes on the cloth gathering the remains of their meal.

'You will never know Warwick.' She stood up, brushed her shorts with her wrists then took the few steps to rinse her hands in the sea.

'Can we go now?'

Silently, he shoved everything back then helped her to the boat. This time she didn't care that her sandals would get wet. She had more. When the electricity ran from his steadying arm to flood her body she pulled away too quickly.

'Please don't be like this; sit up here with me.' he turned with his hands on the key.

'Just take me home, as far away as possible from you.'

He studied her look, taking some of the harshness she immediately regretted. Anger seemed to mix with disappointment and hurt making him plunge the throttle to its extreme.

As the boat left the curl of the bay it found a wind that was churning the sea to sharp edged choppiness.

Wren was pushed back on her seat by a speed she had never experienced before. The boat confidently rode waves then slapped back onto the sea with a horrible sharpness. Up and down, forward and thudding. Banging and thrashing. Her head spun and fear thumped her heart in her chest. He was angry.

Suddenly the engine was cut. The boat curved and tipped to one side then stopped. The sea that had seemed to attack them in speed only tipped them gently from side to side.

He turned, not seeming to notice her fury. 'I said I had something to show you.'

He pointed towards the shore.

'This is the best view you'll ever get of Heaven Hills.' He saw the wonder soften her jaw so he moved towards her taking hold of her hand.

'We could look at it together forever or forever apart. The choice is yours.'

His eyes drew hers. 'What do you mean?'

He took her shoulders gently but with firm passion, and turned her to look deeply into her soul.

'I have been gripped by madness ever since I met you. There is something driving all that I am and have been. For the first time ever I feel out of control. I know you are mine. I feel I was born for you.'

Wren thought he was ridiculous and shrugged to get from his grip but he held even tighter.

'Marry me and I will give you the mountain.'

'What?'

'I mean it.'

'But we hardly know each other?'

'I feel as if I have known you for centuries Wren and I know you feel strongly for me. I never want to let those captivating eyes out of my sight.'

'But you destroy what I love!'

'It is totally and utterly inevitable that Spain will be highly developed. Now I can't buy up all the land but what I do I develop sympathetically with great effort on plant landscaping. This costs me a fortune and eats into my profits but I want what I build to be beautiful and to complement the area not destroy it.'

'But...'

'I will give you the hills for a wedding present. You may keep them as you like.'

Nausea wrapped itself around her confusion so that all she wanted was an escape. There was something bigger than her at work here, she felt smothered by it.

'Take me back!'

As gently as her thoughts he drove her back to the marina. The man who had handed her the keys leapt down from the big yacht to help them.

Warwick spoke in Spanish to the man who saluted and left.

'We need to talk Wren. Would you like to have tea on the yacht?'

She looked over to the shining, sleek luxury.

'Won't the owner mind?'

He laughed, shaking his head at the naivety he found so appealing. 'No, he'd positively encourage it.'

She stayed silent. Only the distant ting of halyards on masts reached her brain.

'Could you take me back to Mijas please?'

He looked defeated. 'What can I do to convince you?'

She walked towards his car glinting in the hot afternoon sun.

'There is nothing.'

He drove upwards and around bends with the same deftness he'd driven the boat, never looking at her. They passed through the white streets not stopping on a route he seemed to know well.

Dust filled the air as he stopped suddenly at the gates of 'Imagine'.

She didn't voice her surprise but merely stepped out of the car and turned.

'There seems a reason bigger than we know why we should be together. I will prove my feelings to you Wren. After that you have five days to accept my proposal or I will marry Gillaine as planned.'

The words stung her so unexpectedly that she stopped.

She wanted him, of that there was no doubt. He could make her happy as a woman and she could be in a position to mix conservation with Spain's inevitable development.

She made no turn.

He'd have to think of something pretty spectacular to convince her.

CHAPTER FORTY FOUR

'Wren.' George looked concerned, scared in fact. 'There is a letter. For you.'

They looked relieved as if they'd been waiting all day for her to return from Mijas.

In front of her were three searching faces. No letter.

'Who's it from?'

'We don't know.' Betty was looking as anxious as George.

'Wren.' his voice was low with trepidation. 'You are happy here aren't you.'

He was frightening her with his intensity. 'Yes.'

'I'm glad. We love having you here.' Leaving his eyes on her face he took one step towards her lifting her hands to his mouth to gently kiss them both.

'Do you remember anything about...about before?'

'Only what you've told me, when I was little and you came to England.'

Anxious faces searched each other as if looking for guidance none could give.

'Do you remember what happened just before you came to Spain, why you are here.'

A buzz shot from her brain to her stomach; surely they weren't going to send her back.

'I ...no; I don't want to.'

'Then you don't want the letter?'

'I don't know. Where is it?'

'We have put it away safely. You know that who-ever it is from it will bring back memories we are not sure if you are ready to deal with.'

They were really worrying her now.

Joyce has told us that she thinks you should have the letter. She says you told her you had a boyfriend in England.

'A boyfriend?'

He eagerly searched her eyes. 'You don't remember.'

'No.'

'Wren.' Joyce looked as if she had to announce World War Three. 'You were so excited about him. You became very ill and we brought you here. You told me he was a secret. I never would have said but today I had to make a decision.'

'Do you want the letter? George's voice was flat.

Before her shot the only life she knew and the people she loved. The taste of Warwick's kiss was still sweet on her lips.

She looked at them. Each one would have torn out their hearts to save her pain. In fact they looked like they already had.

Why were they so worried? Could this be from the one they said she knew, loved even?

She wished the letter had never come, that everything had stayed as it was fifteen minutes ago. But the letter existed. It couldn't be ignored, to fester away in the back of a drawer and her mind.

'Where is it?'

'Here.' George lifted up the fruit bowl. His hand reluctantly pushed the letter towards Wren.

She looked at it for a moment then looked at his worried face.

'Do you recognise the writing Wren?' Joyce's voice was strained. Why was she so worried?

'No...I.' Wren took the letter. No thunderbolt hit. No acid burned her skin.

The writing meant nothing to her. The faces still searched hers.

'We...would you like to open that in private Wren?'

'I think I would.'

'Well go to your bedroom. We will be right here. Just come out or call if you want us.'

The handwriting was neat but she didn't recognise it. The envelope was expensive and so was the paper she shakingly edged from it until it was open.

The first words could have come from any-one. 'My dearest, dearest Wren...' it sounded as if affection had been held. 'The last thing I wanted to do was write this letter....

Who? Who would this be from? She turned the first page and saw, half way down the second page, the signature. Indira.

Who was Indira?

'You must come home. Please ....'

Still the name, the words meant nothing to her. She read on.

'Jeremy...'

Jeremy? Jeremy? Jeremy who?

She lay on the bed not reading the rest of the words, knowing her memory was on a path they would soon crowd.

Eyes came to her. Deep searching eyes.

A tap on the door. 'Are you all right?' George sounded as if he wasn't.

'I'm OK.' She knew her voice told otherwise but what she needed now was time.

She closed her eyes. A deep cave lit with candles and laughter. And love. Yes love. Joyce had been right. The feeling was incredible, how could she have blocked it out of her memory. Why should she have?

Clarity slammed into her. She no longer wondered why God had put her here.

He hadn't.

She had forced herself into this life and had such a price to pay.

She could hear footsteps going about everyday business then come to her door a couple of times to stop as if the owner was listening. They would have heard nothing for deep searching of the mind was silent and incredibly painful.

It grew dark around her allowing little lights to shoot into her mind. There was a man. A kind and loving man who had left her life with pain and others; who?

Sleep closed down her brain. It was two o'clock when total recall slammed her awake.

Agony; abandonment; grief; hopelessness; resentment! A thick stew of pain she had to eat.

She remembered everything.

A deep longing hit her. For her father. For Jeremy. For Alessandro. My God!

How could she have forgotten Alessandro?

In an instant she knew what her bond was to Warwick.

The feeling of belonging was common to all the people who crowded her brain. She had felt like this before. Which one was Alessandro? How could she have been so silly as to think she could find him in this big world? Her powers were weakening as she was maturing.

What had she done?

Yes, grief. Need. Hopelessness. Murder! NO! That was all she had given herself. And what about the soul she had stolen an incarnation from? What had she done to them? It was too awful. She wished the letter had never arrived and then she'd have lived out the rest of her life here with Warwick not knowing it was the wrong life.

Pain gripped her belly. It was a squeezing, heaving pain that pushed a groan from her mouth.

It stayed with her gripping as it doubled her so that her head was near the floor, then something worse.

There was wetness between her legs. She sent down a hand. Blood.

With bare feet she half crept, half staggered to the bathroom. A second wave of pain pushed downward. She edged the bolt in the door trying not to wake any-one. When the next fierce grip dragged down she pushed her fist into her mouth so that the scream of agony stayed hers. Her legs went, sending her to the floor where she felt a warm glob leave her body. Quickly she pushed her fingers into her pants to feel the warm slimy lump. Shaking hands brought what she had found to her face to examine in the harsh electric light what had been forced from her body.

It looked like a small piece of liver attached by a cord to something. She straightened it out on her palm.

'No! No! No!'

It was a baby. A tiny under-formed curved baby in the early stages of development. Horrified she stared at the two bulges developing into a head, a long curved backbone and tiny buds for arms.

Dead but still clinging to the offal like life support system, it shook with her hands.

How could she have forgotten she was pregnant? She had been so ill, not eaten for days and then the sunstroke and all that gadding about.

She was not the only one looking down at the natural abortion.

She recognised the dull light that was the spirit of the miscarriage she'd just suffered.

'No. No. I have lost my chance.' Feelings shot from its wrenched hope.

Wren was unable to stop her revulsion.

'It was you! Inside of me all this time! No wonder I couldn't connect with you. How could you do this to me?'

The spirit should have departed the Earth by now but it glowed dimly in the corner of the bathroom holding desperately on to a thin thread of life force.

'I needed a quick incarnation. Do you think I want to be evil? I want to learn. I need to be physical and you owe me.'

'Owe you?'

'Of course. You robbed me of my life and lessons. You killed me Wren. It was only you who left me in that mineshaft.'

More memories slammed. This was a waking nightmare.

'Colin's karma was not with me but with another spirit; the spirit I stole this life from. Can't you see more now?'

'That is why I stayed quiet when you tried to communicate. I thought you would try to abort me but I had so many debts to repay, so many contracts. You can see I am quite an early spirit. Why could you not have given me the life I crave?'

For a moment great awareness returned. She remembered hundreds of lifetimes ago when she struggled just as the soul of Colin struggled now.

'You know that greater powers than both of us decide these things.

'Yes but the physical world has invented a pill which will stop millions of pregnancies. I had to take a chance I saw. The life you stole owed me that much.'

'You know you must join the light. There will be something else for you. Take my love and understanding with you. When you do find another mother remember when you cause her the pain you no doubt will that she is helping you. Carry a bit of awareness with you. You will learn more quickly that way.' Wren sensed others around them.

'Go now. The welcomers are waiting.'

The spirit looked up. 'I feel sorry for you and what you yet have to go through Wren.'

The beautiful light drowned him. For a moment Wren was jealous. She envied where he was going. She would welcome the love, peace and happiness that every-one on earth was searching for.

'I hope you find him.' That was the last thought the spirit that had been Colin sent her before the light took him home. She held his tiny kindness to her. He was learning.

He would be all right.

She flushed his physical remains down the toilet. There was nothing else she could do.

An anxious face came through the early morning light to join her on the patio.

'Joyce.'

Her dear friend searched the pale face for anything that might give her the hope she sought. Wren knew she couldn't smile away the truth but she tried anyway.

'You look so weak Wren. Go back to bed.'

She shook her head. She was exhausted from losing both sleep and blood but there was only one course she could take.

'You've remembered haven't you Wren?'

'Yes.'

'Why didn't you call for us?'

'There are some things we have to do alone.'

Joyce pulled up a chair, pushed sleep-angled hair from her face then took both Wren's hands.

'What did you remember?'

'Tot. Ivy.'

'Poor, poor you. Did you remember the boy you were so keen on? Was the letter from him?'

The letter was not from him, but it spoke of him.'

'So?'

'I need to go back to England. I have to do something. Put right a wrong I committed.'

Joyce screwed her face, and then took Wrens cold limp hands.

'That is what we were afraid of. We love you so much Wren.'

George had phoned for a seat on the eleven am flight to Newcastle. He only asked if she would be all right, would she be met at the airport and had she somewhere to stay. When he was satisfied with her answers he left her in private to phone Indira, pack and say her goodbyes through tears and hugs to Betty and Joyce. Just as the car reached the gates the postman, blocking the drive with his van, handed George a small bundle held with an elastic band.

'Oh bother. We haven't time to drop the mail back at the house.'

'Well take it with you.'

He smiled. 'There is always so much time to kill at airports. I'll read it there.'

Wren tried not to look lost as they entered the large departure hall but she was grateful for George's much travelled nonchalance. When they had checked in they sat over two untouched coffee cups.

'Have you remembered Tot?' It pained George to talk of his brother.

'I have. You must miss him so much yourself.' She murmured through the catch in her voice.

'Oh Wren, if you hadn't been so ill we'd have talked ourselves out of the grief. There are so many personal memories I'd like to have shared.'

'About when you were children?'

'Yes, and after. He was the one who taught me to be honest you know. We were playing football in the street when one of the older lads who were already working down the pit put his jacket down to mark the goal. I noticed that a sixpence had fallen from the pocket so I slyly picked it up. Tot saw me, gave me hell that evening, made me take it back and admit the theft next day. The pain made me think.'

'Yes, he always told me that if it wasn't mine I wasn't to touch it.'

His eyes filled with the cold grief she knew was in both their hearts.

'You know Wren, if you have inherited half Tot's greatness you will be a lovely person. I saw how to forgive through him. During the war there was a stone fall in the pit and four men were trapped for three days. Tot dug for all that time to save them. He wore himself to a frazzle with exhaustion.'

'I never knew this!'

'No well, then you don't know that when he was ordered home for some rest when they had pulled three of the men out, he could not sleep for worrying about the fourth that the management said was surely dead. He walked to the pit at midnight and started digging on his own, risking his life but he pulled out Frank White, almost dead.'

Wren was silent, imagining the scene and her daddy toiling away for others.

'This was during the austerity times of the war when meat was scarce. The man he save had a pig, all the villagers gave their vegetable peels and slops to feed this pig. When Frank was recovered a month after the rescue he killed the pig. Ivy was furious that he never even gave a sausage to the man who had saved his life. She was incensed with marching down there and giving him a piece of her mind and you know what Tot did?'

'No. What?'

'He just calmed her down and said, 'Leave it Ivy. He must need all the meat and black market money he would make. The rescue gave me its own reward.' He would not let her thunder down the street with a black heart.'

George sucked his lip in thought. 'He was generous too. We both applied for the services when the war broke out. Tot was made to stay in the pit as it was a reserved occupation but me, being in an office, got in the army. Whenever I was home on leave he'd give me ten shillings to enjoy myself. It wasn't until years later I realised he only got fifteen shillings pocket money from his wages. He went without for me.'

'That's why you are so kind to his family.'

Wren, still feeling weak, squeezed his hand. They so needed to talk of the man they both loved.

They sat awhile in their deep thoughts before she asked him to direct her to the lavatories.

'Here I got you a magazine.' He said as he met her outside the ladies. 'And here's some English money I had left.' He pushed against her protests. 'You'll need it Wren. Come on, let's sit down, it won't be long before they call your flight.'

It seemed wasteful to read about recipes and make-up when she had only a few precious moments left with this man who meant so much to her.

'Did you get yourself a paper?' she asked as they sat waiting.

'No I'll open my mail.'

He worked methodically. She watched him over her open pages taking in every last second of his presence. Suddenly his face brightened.

'Oh look. It's the papers for buying the mountain. They took their time. The letter says they had a better offer but that buyer withdrew yesterday afternoon.'

'What?'

As she took in his happiness through her shock the moment was broken by the fractured voice over the tannoy announcing her flight was boarding. He'd never know how near he came to disappointment.

They stood up together.

'Will you call the mountain 'Heaven Hills', for me?

He nodded in an 'anything for you' kind of way.

She fumbled in her little shoulder backpack for something she treasured beyond words then placed Tot's pipe she'd found that morning wrapped in her warm cardigan, into his surprised grip. He looked pleased to have his treasure back so soon.

'Keep that safe for me until we are together again.'

Tears wobbled his words.

'Come back safe pet. It will be a long few days. There is so much love here for you.'

She hugged him and then made her way to the line he guided her to. She'd have to do without his steadying hand on her back and in her life. For the next few days she was on her own. He didn't know just how much love she was walking away from.

Neither had she until now.

She'd be coming back to Warwick.

The flight taxied into greyness and Wren left the plane into damp hugged Britain.

She followed the other passengers and copied everything they did agreeing with the many groans about bloody English weather and why hadn't they stayed on the plane and gone right back to the sun. There was a depressed feeling here; it banged into you as soon as you left the plane. She watched a group of girls shivering but intent on displaying tanned legs with mini-skirts and shaking dangling plastic earrings. They swore they would live in Spain one day.

As she pushed through the doors to see the little huddles of people, some with name notices, her eyes fixed on the lined face of Indira. Her former peace was ravaged from her features. The relief when she saw Wren was pitiful. Below a face sunken with grief she was wearing European clothes with pearl earrings and necklace.

'Thank you. Thank you for coming. I owe you everything. We have not a moment to spare.'

She was ushered to the car she knew was Jeremy's.

'Is he here?'

'No.' she choked with her head to the ground.

There was no fumbling as Indira unlocked the boot and then held open the passenger door for Wren.

'You are driving?'

'There are lots of things you don't know about me Wren.'

The expertise with which her driver handled the car amazed Wren. Even though her mind was racing she knew the road they took was not towards Kademuir.

'Hey...that sign said Newcastle and the coast!'

'I know. I have a room prepared for you at Kademuir but first we have to go to the police station.'

'The police station?'

'My son is in Durham jail.'

'Jail? Your son? Jeremy is your son?'

'Had you not guessed?'

'No. Never. He didn't mention it.'

Indira looked shocked. 'Oh he doesn't know. He must never.'

'But...' The countryside met houses and they joined tea time traffic going into Newcastle.

'Why is he in jail?'

'He has been arrested and found guilty of murder.'

'Murder!'

'He is innocent of course but he says only you can prove it. He was confident that he would be found innocent as he swears he is. Only when he was given life imprisonment did he tell of your involvement.'

'Life? In prison? Jeremy?'

'Oh he was reluctant to implicate you at first; didn't want to involve you. He didn't know you had run away.'

'I didn't run away.'

'I don't know the ins and outs Wren. I just know you weren't here. You said nothing about leaving.'

'How did you find me then?'

'His stamp collection. You gave him some new Spanish stamps which luckily he hadn't sorted yet. One was still on the envelope. The address of the sender was on the back, torn but legible. It was all I could do to stop his father from flying out there that minute. But he is a broken man Wren. I fear for his health.'

Indira nosed the car into the police station car park and came to a stop beside a green Zodiac. A rounded man with a neat moustache stubbed out a cigarette when he saw them, then scrambled from his car to pull at their door.

'Is she willing.' he said to Indira.

'I don't know. I have left it to you.' She turned to Wren who had joined them between the two cars.

Wren this is Mr. Bryson- Brown the best criminal lawyer in the North East.'

The smell of cigarette smoke sickened Wren to the stomach when they all got into the Zodiac. It had to be done. The solicitor turned to her with urgency in his eyes.

'Did you or did you not give Jeremy Foggin a wallet stuffed with money on the 4th of February?'

'I did.'

The cry of relief from Indira turned her head.

'Where did you find said wallet?'

'In sand just inside a rabbit hole.'

'Thank God. Thank God.' Indira leaned forward and kissed her head.

The solicitor had no time for womanly ways and harshly pulled Wren's attention back to his task.

'Are you willing to swear to these facts and show police exactly where you found this wallet?'

'Of course. But who has Jeremy been accused of murdering?'

'The owner of the wallet of course; a right bad lot. He was already been sought by the Metropolitan Police in London over extortion. He was involved in protection rackets; the Met was on to him. The money was already marked and traced to an airline. It was easy to find him in the Cote D'Azure after that.'

There was no mention of the woman he was with, Wren kept the question to herself.

It took three days for the courts to free Jeremy but she was determined to miss his home coming.

She had rested in the exotic guest room of Kadiemuir recovering from her miscarriage and ordeal. There was pleasure to be had in seeing the red vigorous growth springing from the dormant roses she had planted last year. Nothing could make her go near the bottom of the garden where enthusiastic leaves now hid the ice house once more. She took natural healing from the April birdsong, Indira's nourishing food and constant love.

Jeremy's father was cool towards her. He mixed his thanks that she had returned with veiled accusations about why she had given him this money in the first place.

Wren said nothing about their love or the baby they had made together. Neither did she tell how his precious son had abandoned her when she needed him most.

Indira watched and knew. She had all the intuition of a woman enriched by advancement of spirit.

She was not surprised when Wren announced her plans.

CHAPTER FORTY FIVE

Indira pushed back the hair that had fallen over Wren's forehead in sleep then gently rattled the cup and saucer down on the bedside table.

'Oh...what time is it....have I overslept?' Wren slurred the words from a moss laden mouth.

'No, but I know you want to get off early.' She opened the wardrobe to take out Wren's bag.

'I understand that you don't want to see Jeremy. I have to pick him up at nine. I don't know what went on between you but I do know him to be his father's son.' She left her pointed look to walk to the window and pulled the curtains to reveal a red streaked sky splattered with a flock of noisy rooks leaving their roost to search for breakfast.

'You have my eternal gratitude for this Wren.' She turned, dragged both their stares from the black birds to each other. 'But the newspapers will have a field day. I don't want you to be involved in that. Your plane is not until two, how will you get to the airport? Will you go to your family?'

'I have plans.' It was all she said.

The bag Joyce had loaned her wasn't too heavy but it did slow her progress across the woodland she had loved so much. If only she could go straight to Lil's house, it would half her journey but she would be at Amblin now making lunch.

It was a joy to be in the English countryside in mid-April. Nature threw everything at the earth and expected humans to be able to stand the splendour of it. It was the edges of the woodland she had always become so inebriated by.

She tossed down her bag then lay back in cool grass blessed with silky buttercups and dainty daisies.

'You look like you've had six pints of beer.' Tot would laugh as she'd flopped amongst the soft new grass grasping a bunch of wildflowers and stopping Jan licking her face. He'd always tickle her then until she begged him to stop.

The memory tumbled from joy to despair. She thought of those strong hands now in his grave, a stone's throw from her mother. But she wouldn't go. He wasn't there. Only the vehicle that got him around for one incarnation was there, hidden from human eyes. If those same eyes could see the brilliance of the real Tot they'd be blinded. The truth of what spirits humans really were did not fit with any concept the brain was capable of. Some advanced people had an inkling but when on their deaths they were once again in that state of grace they would be amazed that they hadn't remembered what it was all about. Then they'd know the reason why.

Graves didn't mean anything to Wren. She knew the truth.

The past was gone. It was only eighteen years since she had stolen this life; it had been so rich and full of learning pains. She knew how valuable it would have been to the spirit who should have been living it. Would she have met the same people? Handled Ivy in the same way? She knew Colin was certainly in that spirit grouping with Tot and Noelene and Paul. But Jeremy? Joyce or George? Lil or Warwick? Her heart flipped over; the sooner she returned to Warwick the better.

There was just enough time to get to Amblin, show Lil and Sir Saul if he was there how well she was. They'd ring for a taxi to the airport. She couldn't wait to tell Lil about Warwick.

The way was full of blackbird courting calls, budding Hawthorne and star-like celandine. Spring soaked into her being but one sight stopped her short.

Soft whippy hazel saplings surrounded a pool of fresh spring grass glowing with wild forget-me-nots. Soft rays lighted the tiny brilliant faces of vibrant blue. It was as if Tot had placed them there before her to let her know he was with her. They could have been taken from her mother's grave. There was always a sign for those with eyes to see. How she wished she could have her painting case with her now but it was tucked neatly under her bed in Spain and in it the precious card bearing the telephone number she would ring the minute she returned to tell Warwick she accepted his proposal.

The unborn baby, Jeremy and the family she stole into would stay where they belonged, behind her. Warwick, George and Spain were her future.

Nothing would keep her from that.

She changed the bag from her aching left hand to her right. Only one more mile through the wood belonging to Sir Saul and she'd be surprising Lil from behind just as she was stirring some delicious, fragrant old English creation. Hunger sent saliva to her mouth.

She pushed on, not stopping, only changing pace as she swung the bag from one stretched arm to the next. There was an edge to the air now that the sun was kept from her by new green leaves then thicker pine.

The birds listened then continued their songs as she passed deciding either that they trusted her or they were so high up that what did a human matter anyway? She hoped it was the first, she sent them joyous love. It was then that all song stopped.

Wren knew from experience that this meant only one thing, danger. She felt it wasn't her gentle presence, but what?

As she flicked her eyes in a fear held head she saw nothing but felt everything. It was as if God had stopped the world so that her senses, reduced as they were, would notice what was here in the woods with her.

It was everything she sought. His feel, the one she had so often, was stronger than ever. Almost double the conviction she had felt before was here, silencing the woods and with it her heart. Had he followed her?

'Warwick?'

The name came from her lips in spite of her brain telling her it was impossible. He was the one she loved wasn't he. He would go to the ends of the earth he had said; why not Amblin Wood?

How ridiculous she thought taking back her breath and charge over her feet. It was longing that put the feeling here, her own heart and desire. Yet could that quiet the birds?

A fall of twigs snapped into the soft pine needled earth. It was behind her. No gentle hello or call of her name. Whatever it was didn't want her to know it was there. The wild boar! How big were they by now?

She dropped her bag and ran. Heavy feet or hooves matched hers fall for fall. Each drop into wood litter grew quicker than hers. She ran into whippy branches which stung her face. Her feet flung themselves at moss covered stones then thumped to brittle fallen branches. Her ankles gathered more and more moisture from new bracken and woodland balsam.

'Stop!' a man pointed his gun behind her. 'I'll get the bastard!'

As she ran to take shelter behind him she turned for the first time to see what had pursued her.

It was Jeremy.

The gun was aimed, the trigger squeezed. A death was certain.

'No!' she yelled as she leapt up to grab the barrel of the gun which already had power coming through it. She pulled it down out of harm's way. The hunter yelled and fell on top of her.

'Arrgh! My leg! My leg!'

The man was shot. Blood oozed from the torn calf, and then gushed.

'Help me Jeremy!'

A spaniel raced through the undergrowth towards the cries of agony which it added too with distressed whines.

'Who the hell is he?'

'It doesn't matter. He is bleeding to death!'

Frozen and helpless, they watched the blood pump as if it wanted to soak the whole pine-needle forest floor.

'Tear something!' Wren began pulling at her tie-dye top and denims.

'What?'

'Your shirt! He needs a tourniquet!'

'But it's a Saville Row! Anyway, he was going to shoot me!'

'What! Don't be an idiot!'

'It won't tear! What about your tee-shirt?'

'It's too short! For God's sake Jeremy we have to find something. If only we had a knife.'

Wren began patting the man's pockets. The dog growled but Wren gave it a reassuring look and made an effort at a heartening rub. It tried to lick healing into its master's face.

Wren sent desperate hands into two pockets then gave a little shriek as she pulled out a Swiss army knife. It bent her thumb nail to pull out the biggest blade but she still found nothing to cut.

Damn! If only she'd put a ribbon in her hair. Her hair!

Without another thought she sent the knife to her scalp and hacked off a strand thick enough. Jeremy looked horrified at the inch tuft it had left sticking out from her crown.

'Your hair! Your beautiful hair!'

'Who cares? This man might die!' As she bent to twist then tie her hair rope as tightly as the silkiness would allow around his leg just above the knee, she felt him lift a wobbly hand to take in the spoiled head. It was more than just gratitude in his closing eyes. He passed out then.

'Help me get him up to Amblin Jeremy!'

'Me? No way. He was trying to kill me.'

'Don't be so ridiculous. He was trying to protect me.'

'What from? A crocodile? These woods are not really infested with man eating dinosaurs are they?'

His uncaring attitude pulled something up in her. She felt that dangerous gene kicking in.

'Jeremy!'

'I ran after you to talk to you not drag a stupid, gun careless men through the woods.'

Jeremy grabbed at her wrist in an effort to pull him to her.

'He needs help! Ohhhhg! Stay here. Take care of him!'

She jerked away and started running.

'What about our baby? I want to know about our baby!'

His call was urgent and in it she heard a bit of why she'd loved him. He wasn't what was important now. It wasn't time for the injured man to leave his life. There was no sign of any energy to take him. He had to be saved.

Her legs were aided in their desperate flight by the need to escape her urge to kill.

With her heart pounding in her ears she saw the smoke from a bonfire and pelted towards it. Smith was dawdling along with a barrow load of weeds too green to burn.

'Smith!'

His grip dropped with his jaw as he took in Wren's blood soaked hands waving towards him.

'Bugger me! What the....?'

She ran up, tipped the contents of the barrow and turned with it.

'It's not me who's hurt! Come on!'

She half expected, hoped, Jeremy to be with the man comforting him, marking the place where he lay. But there was only silence and Wren's remarkable powers of observation to lead them to the wind damaged pine where the injured man lay. The dog hugged the earth close to its master but wagged its stumpy tail when it saw Smith.

'My God; it's young Lintern!'

Familiarity crowded her senses. She hadn't heard the name but there was something about him.

The realisation slammed into her. Could he be the reason she had felt Alessandro so strongly in the woods. No, that was Jeremy and yet...! How could she know? There was something in them all that told her they might be the one she had spent so many lifetimes with. Confusion clouded her reason. There was only one way to go and that was forward.

The future was urgent.

It was with an unconscious man in a wheelbarrow, his shotgun across his chest, that they entered the back way to Amblin as they shouted for help.

Lil came out drying her hands on her apron as she scanned the situation then shouted behind her. Sir Saul appeared, dropping the bread he was eating, to dash towards the urgent group.

When others took over, Wren was glad as she trembled with relief. The patient was bustled away leaving her to regain her strength and thoughts. She washed her hands before sitting at the table where the abandoned lunch for two steamed to coolness.

Lil bustled back.

'The doctor is coming. What? How? Where....oh come here lass and give us a cuddle!'

Wren began to shake as the stress was hugged out of her. Lil smelled of meat and vegetables.

'What a surprise. Where did you spring from? Saving lives and then nearly shocking me to death!'

'I was coming to see you before catching my plane back to Spain.'

'Oh pet; you aren't staying then? Do you love it there?'

'Yes Lil I love it and the place isn't the only reason I'm so keen to get back.'

'Well thank God you were in the woods when Sir Saul's grandson had his accident. I don't think Sir could take any more grief.'

'His grandson? I thought he was only a boy!'

'He is, only twenty four on the second of last month.'

'Oh Lil, that's an older man to me.'

Lil laughed. 'Seems only yesterday I was making birthday cakes for him with cowboys and Indians on 'em. I made him a Davy Crocket hat out of an old fur coat the dogs slept on once. Too sophisticated now.'

She pushed the dishes of hot-pot back into the Aga.

'You hungry? You look as if you've recovered your appetite as well as your colour.'

Wren nodded pulling towards her all the memories of the old fashioned country food she'd eaten here with this woman she loved.

'Well help me get table sorted and then I want to know everything about Spain. I had a letter from George. He told me how ill you were.'

'I lost my memory Lil.'

'Aye that can happen with trauma, but I don't have to ask how you are now lass, you positively glow. What's his name?'

Loud voices came from the hall just before the brass knob rattled. Sir Saul burst in then smiled at the anxious faces.

'He's fine! Five stitches and plenty of rest.'

He came towards Wren, taking her hands and kissing her cheek noisily.

'My dear, it could have been so different if you had not turned up or you hadn't been the generous person you are.'

'But…' she wanted to explain that nothing at all would have happened if she had not been in his wood, that it was in fact her fault, but he held up his hands.

'For a woman to sacrifice her hair...'

Wren sent up a hand to feel a strange spikiness near her crown.

'I will pay for the best coiffeur in Newcastle of course.'

'Don't think even they could make a better of this.' she smiled. 'Might start a new fashion.'

Sir Saul hugged her close. 'It is so good to have you in my house again. He wants to talk to you.'

'I'll make up a tray.' Lil bustled around in her element.

'Come in!'

He was lying with his flicked back hair catching the sun making it look more golden than the sandy she'd thought it in the wood, it was past his collar but not long. He'd wanted it modern but refined. He eased up using his wide shoulders and elbows and his brow took a flop of a loose wave to one side.

Wren edged towards him, wide eyes beneath a strange new hair-do, self-conscious of her bloody tee-shirt.

He laughed widening hazel eyes before they narrowed with mirth.

'You poor thing. You'll have to have it all cut short now.' She absorbed the words even though his even toothed smile captured her gaze.

She sent a hand to the sharpness of the tuft amongst the silkiness.

'Oh! I can't. I promised my dad.'

'He'll understand. As soon as he sees you, and knows why you did it, he'll not mind.'

She felt and heard her voice change to slow and halting.

'My dad died in February.'

There. She had said it out loud. It was real.

'Oh! I'm sorry. He'll be proud anyway.'

It was a knowing look, beautiful and centuries old.

'What do you mean?' She was searching for his feelings not his knowledge.

'You know as well as I do. You have talked to my Grandmother haven't you?'

She didn't need to answer, their stares communicated much more than words.

'If only people knew their loved ones have not gone but are right by in another reality.' He said.

'They'd not grieve but rejoice.' They said the words in perfect unison then laughed.

There was a pulling silence which melted away any strangeness.

'Who are you? I feel…' he said searching every atom of her being.

The door opened allowing Lil to carry the heavy tray towards the sofa.

'Can I leave you two to manage?' she said the words not wanting an answer but too obviously pleased with how well they were getting on.

'Soup?' Wren smiled moving the tray nearer to him.

'Yes please. I've grown up on Lil's famous broths for all ills. Do you know I was seventeen before I realised soup wasn't medicine.' His grin split his lovely face in half.

'Perhaps it is.' she smiled tucking a napkin into his neck.

Their closeness sang.

Two pairs of eyes raked the other then pulled away embarrassed by their knowing.

'Well it certainly cured everything.' The words tripped from the surface of his mind forcing back what he really wanted to say. 'Let's hope it works on my leg.'

Between feeding spoonful's to his eager mouth Wren managed to eat her own chicken, carrot and rice soup. He was beautiful, had she not already been in love.....

'Thank you. Although I could have managed you know. It is my leg that has been injured not my hands.' he said grinning at so much attention. 'I feel so cosy and sleepy now.' he said looking at his watch. 'Doc's drugs kicking in.'

'For crying out loud!' she stood up quickly. 'What time is it?'

'Almost two.'

'No! Oh no!'

He laughed. 'Why have you got a bus to catch?'

'No not a bus, a plane!'

'A plane?' he said not bothering to hide his disappointment. 'Where to?'

'Malaga. That's where I live; in Spain.'

'I wondered how you were so tanned. What were you doing in our woods?'

'Coming to see Lil and.... I've missed it. I've missed my plane home.'

He took her hand pulling him gently towards him. There'll be other planes. I'm glad. Maybe it will give me the chance to persuade you not to go back at all.'

'But I must. You don't understand.'

He read the look.

'I see. It's not just the country you are so keen to return to is it.'

Saul showed her how to phone Spain so that she could stop George leaving for the airport. If only she had brought Warwick's card with her. There was no way of finding his number without it. Thrilled as she was to hear George's delighted progress in his buying of Heaven Hills she couldn't do more than make the right noises.

George was right when he said she could get another plane in a few days and that she should enjoy seeing the people at Amblin she loved so much. But he was wrong when he said there was nothing spoiling.

'Some-one's loss is our gain.' Sir Saul tried to comfort her. 'Stay a few days with us. I could do with you ordering Smith around in the garden.'

Wren smiled. 'I'd love to but I have urgent business in Spain.'

'Why look so worried?'

'I need to ring some-one else but I don't have the number.'

'Directory enquiries?'

It's a Spanish number?'

Saul delighted Wren by showing her how to ring international enquiries then left her alone to secure her future. Excitement gave her careless fingers. What would she say to him? What could she say except that her future was with him?

Minutes of careful dialling didn't connect. She tried again, some-one spoke rapidly in French. It was a long number; she'd have to do it slowly. Anxiety crept to her breath not allowing it out. She had to talk to Warwick, tell him she wanted him.

She tried again watching the dial spin back to its base each time she took her finger from the numbered hole. There was a delay, a long ringing tone. Again and again. No-one answered.

'Sorted?' Saul came back into his study.

'No. They aren't there.'

'Well there's always tomorrow.'

Tomorrow would be too late.

He watched her replace the receiver.

'Don't look so sad. Lintern will cheer you up. He's looking forward to getting to know his heroine. You will stay the night won't you? Have you luggage?'

'My bag! I dropped in the woods.'

He laughed. 'Take Chummy he can sniff out anything at fifty yards and warn off the boars. He's with Lintern. He'll agree.'

The brown and white spaniel's ears pricked up when she entered the room but its head didn't lift from his sleeping master's chest. She took a sneaky look at Lintern's well-toned body in relaxation.

'Here boy, sweetie.' she clicked her tongue as quietly as possible but the dog stayed.

She gave the softest of whistles. Still nothing.

'Go boy.' the command was soft but obeyed immediately. Lintern kept his eyes closed.

'If you called me like that I'd be there in a shot, bad leg or no bad leg.' He spoke in a voice lined with laughter.

'I doubt you'd have the sniffing skills to find my bag in the woods.'

'Oh. That's why you want my dog. He's yours. He'll guard you from any wild boars. I will pledge him to you for life if you stay in England.' His eyes opened slightly and a grin spread over his sleepy face.

He watched Wren welcome Chummy to her and took in the natural empathy between them.

'He loves you, he sees your soul. I know how he feels; I've had a quick glimpse of it myself.'

No-one had ever said that to her but Alessandro. 'I see your soul.'

She stopped fur ruffling and stared.

'Come back soon.' His voice was languid and full of sincerity.

He was the second person to say that to her this week.

She left him there, eyes closed, a rug covering his bandaged leg. He looked so lengthy lying across the chaise longue. Strangely she wanted to come back.

Wren spent the rest of the afternoon with Lil. She found it hard to concentrate as they made up a spare bed together, prepared supper and caught up with all the news on Spain and Jim's health.

'He'd love to see you before you go. Will you have time?'

'Of course. I just need to re-book my flight and talk to some-one.'

'Hey, don't look so disturbed pet. He'll wait. If he knows you he'll know how much you are worth waiting for.'

Wren gave a little attempt at a smile but it was for Lil. Inside panic was tearing into her stomach.

With Saul's permission she rang Warwick's number three more times. Each time her pulses throbbed in her throat, the long tone rang out, no-one answered. Sickness flooded her.

It was strange to wake up at Amblin. The heavy curtains cut out the light but not the dawn chorus. Wren stepped from the high bed onto the Indian carpet. She'd known every time the clock downstairs had chimed a new hour. Her dreams, during snatches when her sleep hormones took over, were of dashing into a Spanish wedding to see all heads turn as she shouted the loudest 'NO!' ever screamed.

She was washed and outside just as the light was creating its magic on the cherry blossom. This garden was so different to last spring. When the sun finally peeped over the candle laden chestnuts Wren gasped. She knew she'd planted all these spring bulbs but forgotten where and just how many. Beneath the budding weeping ash a carpet of pink cyclamen looked up with backward petals that made them look as if they'd arrived on a motor bike.

The birdsong, the sight and energy of spring hit her senses so that she soared. Walking in the beauty she had helped to create raised her spirit so high that she became aware she was not alone. Another soul who loved the garden was here, waiting.

'Wren you have brought the love back to my spring garden…I am so grateful.'

Letitia drew her to a stretch of grass punctured with spearing daffodil buds.

'He needs you Wren.'

'I know but I can't ring him.'

'Wren I mean my Grandson, Lintern.'

'What do you mean?'

'Do you know the love a grandmother has for her grandchild? It is like no other. A desperate need to protect something so small that has come from you creates an overwhelming passion.'

'I have experienced it in former lives, you are right. It is very compelling.'

Letitia grew in love.

'That love enriches as the child grows. It was me who made you think of using your hair to save Lintern. Only you could have made the sacrifice.'

'You were there?'

'Of course. It was not his time to leave his physical. He has so much to achieve Wren. You can help him.'

'Me? No, I've done enough. I have to get back to Spain.'

'Wren you have nurtured my garden, given me back my tulips. Only a special person could have done that. I am also aware of the past life connection you have to my darling Saul. You have all the insight and qualities Lintern needs.'

'But you don't understand…'

'You have to find Alessandro.'

'Yes.'

'Then help my grandson.'

Wren watched the energy of Letitia fade. No further explanation would come.

CHAPTER FORTY SIX

'Have you still not got through to Spain?'

Saul looked concerned when he saw how down Wren looked when she brought his coffee into the Orangery. He was sitting with tail wagging dogs in a pool of sun just beside a huge palm Wren herself had potted.

'What seems to be the problem?'

'It just rings and rings, once I got some French person.'

'Have you checked the country dialling code? Sometimes there is only one digit different.'

He watched the new light glide into her eyes. 'Go on. Close the French doors, leave me to my coffee and try again.'

The relief when she compared the new number with the old was palpable. The dial seemed to spin slowly on purpose but when it rang it rang only once.

'WT Constructions, Gillaine speaking, how can I help you?'

'Is Warwick there please?'

There was a slight pause. 'Who is that please?'

'This is Wren Stoker I must speak to Warwick urgently!'

There was another pause then. 'My fiancée is out making wedding arrangements at the moment. You will not steal from me again.'

It was Wren's turn to pause. The words seemed to hit her brain and fly around it at the same time. Hopelessness vied with those dreaded urges of murder.

She put the receiver back and fled to seclusion.

Tears in the privacy of the potting shed could flow with her thoughts. Warwick had thought she didn't love him. He had made the ultimate sacrifice, done everything to win her, to make her realise her future was with him. Perhaps he thought she'd tricked him. He could be the very person she was seeking on this Earth and she had let him go. What had Gillaine meant about stealing from her? Was it the man she loved or......Wren looked down at the red mark she'd had around her wrist from birth, it tingled. As she rubbed the itch she knew it was all there in the past, but whose? Persian sun blazed down on her black hair which she was unable to push back from her face. She was male and being held by three others. An older man held a curved sword above the arm forced down on the stone of repayment. In the moment the hand was chopped from her wrist she met the eyes of her injurer. It was an incarnation of Gillaine; Wren had stolen his horse and tried to gallop away with his thirteen year old daughter. The theft was avenged; the mark forever on display.

Even now.

Chummy unexpectedly bound up to her lap and licked the tears. The sun was coming in through the door he'd pushed open just a little after he'd heard her distress.

'Chummy!' slowly the door opened wider courtesy of walking stick. 'Come on boy...'

It was Lintern hobbling after his dog. Even bent a little he must have been over six foot.

'Good heavens. He really likes you.' he pretended not to notice her red eyes and sniffs.

'How's the leg?' her voice was strangled.

'Oh sore, but it could have been much worse. I just had to get out of that bedroom Grandfather and Lillian seem to want to keep me in, as much for Chummy as me.'

Wren sniffed in a vain effort to take her mood back into herself lest it should be notice then pushed a smile to her eyes to greet them both.

'You been crying?' he bent his head towards her filling her nostrils with a light scent from his wet hair.

'No! It's Chummy; big wet tongues aren't the best way of cleaning your face.' she laughed lightly but he didn't even smile.

'You can have the baby here you know. We'll look after you.'

She stood up so quickly that the dog stumbled to the floor.

'Baby! What baby?'

'That man in the woods. The one I thought was the wild boar, he shouted after you when you went for help. Is he your lover?'

'No! He...he's no-one. You must have been delirious. I'm not pregnant. What a thought!'

'Oh goodness! I'm sorry if I've offended you. You're right. I did pass out after that. Got a good look at him though as he stood over me. He didn't seem to be no-one.'

Wren pulled at the door. 'I don't think you should be standing around on that leg. Come on I'll walk you back to the house.'

'Lead the way. I know what's good for me.' He smiled but his eyes told her he knew more than she wanted him to. He laid a hand on the back of her shoulder for support. It felt electric.

The close attention to the back of her head made Wren pleased when their slow pace reached the kitchen. Lil was making Macaroni cheese for lunch.

'Ah no; caught me with the mustard pot! Now you know the secret of the best Macaroni Cheese in county Durham.'

She used the words to try to hide her pleasure in seeing the two together but the redness in Wren's eyes didn't go unnoticed.

When Lintern had left to sit in the Orangery with Saul, Lil was able to reveal her real thoughts. Concern tipped her head to one side.

'What is it pet? Missing Spain and those who pull you back there?'

Wren expelled most of the tense air which had held her tight all day.

'Oh Lil why do things keep going against us?'

'It's called life darlin'. It's why we are here to find ways around, through or over obstacles. Make's us stronger.'

Wren knew this but she loved Lil more for reminding her.

'You know sometimes life has a way of giving us what we need in spite of ourselves.'

Encouraged by Wren's hopeful look she continued on her theme.

'When I met Jim I was engaged to somebody else.'

'No!' Wren said surprised that Lil had ever been young. 'You little devil.'

'Aye, I was that all right. But Jim was right for me and others could see it even if I couldn't.'

'What happened to the first man?'

'Harry? Oh he wasn't the first, mind he was the only one I promised to marry.'

'But he can't have been right for you or Jim would have seen that and left you to it.'

'Oh but he was right, that's the point. You see Jim knew I would be content with Harry and fought all the harder to win me. I would have been just as happy living with my big strong bus driver.'

'So?'

'Harry went to London on a course for advanced driving. While he was away Jim tempted me with a cycling weekend in Cumbria.'

'A cycling weekend!'

'Hey cheeky! I wasn't always so well padded in the derriere you know. Anyway, all that exercise and too many Cumberland sausages and I came back pregnant.'

'Pregnant! But you don't have any children.'

Lil looked down at the pile of cheese she had just grated. 'No. Lost the bairn didn't I, never got another chance. But it got me Jim and I'll tell you, there couldn't be a more loving man.'

'And Harry?'

'Oh he was so heartbroken he married my best friend. Has his own bus company in Southport. I get a Christmas card every year just so as they can boast about their five bedroomed house and four successful children.'

'Oh Lil.'

'Hey less of that. I love my life with Jim, sick as he is. And my girl, I would never have met you. The nearest thing I have to a daughter. No, I'm grateful all right.'

'But you have to work so hard.'

'Aye but it's good for the soul. I'm just saying, sometimes life manoeuvres you.'

Wren felt she was being manoeuvred but knew for certain it wasn't by the same guardian angels as Lil's.

George phoned the next day to see if Wren was all right.

'Well I'm glad you are with those lovely people. Why don't you stay a little while? You know it's getting rather hot here and I would be so worried about you…and your pale skin.'

The offer seemed so tempting, English spring could not be equalled.

'Well if you are sure, Saul has asked me to help with the garden again.'

'Of course Wren, take advantage of being there. Your ticket will always be open. Remember we love you.'

It hurt to put down the receiver on the land and people she loved so much. She fought not to admit that there seemed more reason than gardening to be hanging around here.

'Lintern has asked you to have a goodbye tea with him.'

Lil's words stung into her hopes.

'Goodbye? Doesn't he know I'm staying on a bit?'

'No, you've only just told me! But it isn't you whose leaving it's him.'

'Why? Where?'

'Oh Wren you know he doesn't live here. He has to get back to Yorkshire. There's so much work waiting for him.'

'With that leg?'

'Well he's been given the job of saving Troutbeck, Saul sees it as his initiation, his proof of manhood. He has lions to kill and he can't give up just because he has a sore leg.'

Wren wrinkled her brow. 'Who is Troutbeck, a lion he must wrestle?'

'May as well be, yes it is, sort of.' She laughed.

She poured boiling water onto tea leaves then placed the pot on the tray between cups, a plate of sandwiches and hot cheese scones.

'Go on. Many a young girl would dream of tea with a handsome land owner, even one with no money. Now go on before I take your place and get you to scrub this floor.'

Lintern was reading a report on growing trees for profit which he tossed onto the coffee table when she entered drawing room. The fire had been lit when the spring sun had left to make way for light showers and a stiff breeze.

'Ah my favourite!' he glowed, pushing himself up with strong arms.

'Are they? I don't know what is between the bread.'

'I wasn't referring to the tea.' His eyes held hers before they led his fingers to lift a corner of one sandwich. 'Ah but they are too. Marmite and cucumber! Yum!'

He ordered a disappointed Chummy to the thick fireside rug from where the dog followed every mouthful with begging eyes. He took the cucumber from one sandwich then tossed the remainder into an eager canine mouth.

'You don't mind having tea with me do you? After all we'll be in different countries by this weekend.'

She poured the tea. 'No, only different counties. I'm staying on a bit first.'

'Just to give your hair a chance to grow?' He laughed to cover the excited change in his voice.

Her hand went up to where she hadn't thought of since she'd shampooed that morning.

'I wish it was as simple as that.'

He tucked the saucer onto his chest and sipped at the hot tea, never taking his eyes off her. There was no doubt about it, he knew. He knew lots.

'Well I'm sure England will be all the happier for having your beauty to add to the merry month of May. Do you like bluebells?'

She felt a beam spread across her face. 'Like them? They are one of my favourites. The colour reminds me of home.'

'But not quite as vivid or ethereal eh?'

Strangely he knew it wasn't Durham she was referring to but her real home, the brilliant light of pure love. It was the one she should still be in, waiting for Alessandro.

'Saul has wonderful Bluebells here.' She said trying to get back to the reality they were both certain of.

'Oh indeed he has. I grew up with their fragrance. The house was always filled with great vases of them. Lillian used to make huge arrangements with fresh green beech only just popping their buds.'

Wren gushed. 'They look good with contorted willow and delicate white stitchwort; oh and cowslips, that fabulous yellow and blue bunch.'

They laughed together seeing how silly it was to have a competition on displaying bluebells.

'Saul's woods aren't as old as the ones around Troutbeck Lodge, the tumbled down place he is sending me to. There is real ancient woodland there. The bluebells are as thick as a sheep's fleece. I go every year at this time. You've never seen bluebells until you've been to Troutbeck on the edge of the Yorkshire moors.

He watched carefully from under his flop of hair to see if the temptation had found its target.

'Maybe I'll visit one day.'

'How about tomorrow?'

'Tomorrow!'

'Well I do need looking after.' He pulled the face of all men wanting sympathy from a woman.

'I'm not a nurse.' She laughed.

'No; but it's your fault I'm incapacitated. You owe me.'

They raked each other's eyes each skating through the implications of everything between them.

'After all,' he added seeing she needed a little more pushing. 'I've looked after you lots.'

She gathered her eyebrows downwards. 'When?'

'Other lives…other times.' His serious look seemed to lasso around her soul.

'Can you remember exactly?'

'No. I just recognise you. We've been close and I want that again.'

She knew he was right. If he was Alessandro why didn't he know it? Why hadn't she been hit with a bolt from the blue? Why hadn't they fallen into each other's arms? Would Alessandro have been born here and sent to Yorkshire to complete his great task? Why not? It seemed they had both lost the power and awareness they had when not physical.

There was only one way to find out if he was Alessandro.

'Spain gets so hot in summer and as there seems a very good reason why you should not return you might as well come to Troutbeck and think up some creative scheme to save it.'

She stood up and gave the last bite of her scone to Chummy.

'OK, OK don't oversell yourself!'

'You mean you'll come?'

'Might as well.'

He looked scared as well as pleased. Wren felt in tune with his every feeling.

'I can see you hope you've done the right thing.' she said. 'Aren't you sure?'

'I just don't know what I'm getting myself into Wren. I just know it's impossible to stop.'

CHAPTER FORTY SEVEN

Wren was lost in a world moving around her.

Had she no roots and no income during a lifetime where she wasn't aware of her spiritual motivation, she would be desperately insecure. What did it matter where she was now?

She could admit to no-one that it was not only the heat keeping her from Spain. Here at least she was too far from Gillaine and Warwick to carry out the murderous thoughts she wrestled and sweated with instead of sleeping.

It was safer to go with this man; around him she didn't need to suppress her father's genes. From her he drew protectiveness, consideration and care. He hadn't done anything to provoke the hideous side she fought to bury. Perhaps he never would.

Here she was, about to go with a man she'd only known a few days to a place she'd only heard of. Every-one around her was pleased and encouraging. They knew both people and seemed excited to see them as a possible couple. But Lintern and Wren didn't really know each other. Not in this lifetime at least.

Wren had visited Jim yesterday evening and picked up her gardening clothes. By the sound of Troutbeck she'd need them and was happy to work for her keep. It had been hard to visit the council estate she'd lived in since she was two. Lil and Jim's house was built only a year after the one she'd shared with Tot, Ivy, Paul and Noelene. The layout was the same but the feel was different. It was possible to feel relaxed here. As she'd sat by the window to admire the bursting Telstar Rose that had brought her into this river of life she turned her eyes to the crackling in the fireplace. Ivy and her children would be around the same tiles grieving for their husband and father, wondering if the coal they shovelled onto the dying embers was the same coal he'd hewed on his last day. She could have given them so much comfort. Noelene at least should have had her sister with her. How sad that Noelene had not enjoyed the sisterly closeness she deserved. Really, she was the children's Aunt. But she had robbed them of that at the same time she had stolen this life.

Saul had picked her up with her precious Gandy's rose catalogues, a few of her books and clean, pressed working clothes to add to the few she had in her bag. As he drove her back to Amblin Hall she wondered how she had got here. Was this the fate of Elia or her own energies? It was hard to tell. All that kept her going was the hope that she might yet find Alessandro; if she hadn't already.

'Can you drive all the way to North Yorkshire with that leg?'

'Well I can hardly go without it Lil.'

Saul and Lil stood beside the little red MG Midget kissing the two young people they loved and giving a goodbye ear ruffle to Chummy lying on the squab behind them.

Saul laughed. 'Don't worry, it's his clutch leg, the doctor said it would be alright as long as he didn't have the seat too far out. I wouldn't have let him go if I wasn't confident that Wren would look after him.'

He turned his twinkling eyes to her. 'You will my dear, won't you?'

Lil dabbed a 'what a lovely couple' tear from her cheek.

Sad in love for the people waving their goodbyes, they left Amblin behind but felt grateful to take the love with them. Even Smith gave a cheery wave as they passed though Wren did notice a gentle shake of his head.

Enclosed together for a long journey seemed daunting to Wren; if only it had been calm enough to have the hood folded down. He might be the very one she sought but she couldn't tell sitting beside him with his dog panting nervously in her ear. He drove confidently but his masculine interpretation of handling a car didn't give a comfortable ride for passengers. He sped up to junctions, tested his brakes at every stop sign and then pulled away with such urgency that she was jerked from right to left, front to back. It would be a long two and a half hours.

They turned off the A1 into even more winding roads; challenging for him, wearing for her.

It hit her that she had never seen so many pretty villages, but there was no sign of mines, only farming. They came to a sign which read 'York' but he turned off left to one that said Pickering and Scarborough.

The land became hilly and more beautiful. Spring seemed softer here, more advanced by a week judging by the flowers glowing in front of the stone cottages. Even the brick was mellower, the roofs easier on the eye and the light smell of smoke in the air came from wood not cloying coal.

'Welcome to the North Yorkshire moors; my home.' Lintern delivered the words from awe.

'I thought you were brought up in County Durham.'

'Yes I was born there, but I went to boarding school in York. When my father died I was only ten and my mother re-married and went to live in Harrogate. She loved Grandmother and Grandfather enough to let me spend the summers at Amblin and Troutbeck and it gave her time to grow a new family.'

'You have brothers and sisters?'

'Yes, but I am the only heir to Saul. I hope he lives a lot longer yet but he saw my need to be my own man and so gave me Troutbeck on condition I made it pay.'

'How lucky.'

'Well he didn't think so. It was and still is very run down, neglected for fifteen years.

An estate has to pay for itself.'

She tore her eyes from the pleasure of a bank dotted with huge clumps of primrose.

'Estate?'

'Yes Troutbeck is an estate but just a small one with a couple of shepherds' cottages, streams and fishing rights to a stretch of river. It's not as grand as Amblin.'

'It's not the kind of estate I'm used to.' she laughed.

Lintern obviously loved the way he had to negotiate climbing up through yellow gorse bushes, heather captured moors and unaware sheep. It seemed an empty place except for coarse grass, dun dead bracken and dull-eyed creatures willing to try to graze it. The wind blew the bleak beauty into her heart so that she was glad when they took a track down again into softening, kinder countryside.

The road narrowed to more rocks, pot-holes and clumps of established grass, thick and tangled so that Wren was hopeful when they stopped at a five bar gate shut right across their path.

'Oh you've taken the wrong road.'

Lintern only laughed.

'Haven't you seen a gated road before?'

'No.'

'It costs sixpence to have it opened for you.'

Wren looked at the deserted countryside, it was obvious there was no-one around for miles. Lintern grinned.

'Grandfather still held shooting parties here until I was ten. We used to bundle up with all we needed for a week-end of sheer bliss. There was always a race amongst the children of the various families to open the gate because there was sixpence in it for them.'

'I'll do it!' she said glad to stretch her legs in the fresh breeze. Chummy took advantage by scrambling out behind her to cock his leg to the post and sniff about. Opening the latch wasn't as easy as it looked. The whole lichen covered gate was wet and rotting. Dirty, frayed string blew around the fastener, stopped from true flight by many tired knots forged by hands long ago lost. One bossy new length of bailing twine displayed it's superiority by holding the rickety gate in place with a confident sheep-shank. Wren fiddled the gate free. She had to give it a hefty lift to clear the ground but the bottom plank fell off anyway just clinging on enough to drag disobediently across the rutted mud road. As he drove past her through the gate he gave a cheery wave. She followed him to where he had stopped, trying vainly to rub green slimy lichen stains from her hands.

'Hey! You can't get back in until you have closed the gate again!'

'What?'

'You don't get paid until the job's complete.'

'You can keep your rotten sixpence!'

'Don't be cheeky or I'll make you run to the Lodge.'

Wren took the few steps back to the gate and lugged its weight towards the gatepost where it didn't want to go, frustrated, she looped the temporary fastener over to hold it. As she turned to leave she felt a strong urge to kick the stupid, wooden planks but was stopped by an early dragonfly, newly emerged and drying its wings on the top rung, in hope of a good new life. There must be a pond nearby she thought with pleasure. She leaned gratefully on the lichen painted gate post. A sudden invasive peep of his car horn dragged her back to her task.

Back in the car she held her grubby palms towards him.

'Thanks very much.' she said.

'No, thank you very much.' They both laughed as he tossed a sixpenny piece into her lap.

Somehow that gate symbolised her entrance to a good new life for herself but as yet she didn't know what. She also felt dread, a knowingness that this place would be the end of her. She shook herself back to the now, there would be a time to face her dread but it wasn't yet. All she could think of was the ethereal sparkle on those oh so delicate dragonfly wings and hoped that here, she would fly as high as they would.

He jerked away again but this time for only a few hundred yards. The half hidden sun suddenly appeared as if to light the smoothness of the beech trees that lined the road but as the car reached the brow of the hill she saw what its real job was.

He turned to enjoy the awe he knew would be invading her face.

'Come on.' He opened the car door and she copied, her feet crunching dried leaves and beechnut cases emptied and discarded by many squirrels, only seconds after his.

'What do you think?' he asked knowing the beauty had caught her soul.

Wren couldn't leave the feeling suddenly swamping her to answer a question he already knew the answer to.

'This valley holds my heart in its hands.' He sighed.

She felt what he meant. It had enclosed her too. She wanted to gaze at this peace inspiring place forever.

The road led away from their stillness, tunnelling through thickening trees from which escaped the warm smell of a million bluebells and up to two high stone gateposts. More trees only just allowed a tall chimney above their budding grace.

He said nothing but when he stiffly eased his sore leg back into the car and turned on the engine she silently took her seat beside him. It was only tantalising seconds before they reached the gates. A sign, weathered and half loose read 'Troutbeck Lodge.' Wren wondered who had carved the little squirrel eating a nut alongside the letters. The peeling metal gates seemed permanently open so that the car had only to avoid the potholes as it passed the rough orchard lit with apple and pear blossom. How she drew in the fragrance with open nostrils and closed eyes.

They followed an overgrown beech hedge still grasping last year's brown leaves beside the new soft green, and then turned.

It was in front of them. Glorious, faded and peaceful. Woodpigeons cooed into the air and Wren knew this could be home.

What had she expected? Not this. Long sloping weedy lawns strewn with decaying leaves led up to a huge expanse of building only two stories high beneath a red tiled roof supporting five regal chimneys. White walls scurried about many windows gazing at the edge of the moor then pasture land and fields brown and furrowed. North and south facing slopes were prevented from meeting by a racing, tumbling river winding its way to the east coast. The whole lodge was surrounded by a wide wooden balcony shamefacedly showing flaking, yellowing paint. It had its own jungle clawing up and almost into the house whilst scratching at dusty windows. Two windows were swinging open. Poor guardians to emptiness.

'It's a mess isn't it?' Lintern matched her actions and got out of the car holding back the seat to set Chummy free to smell familiar smells. Wren traced the horizontal; trunk of a deformed willow, the wood was polished and worn smooth by many tired bottoms that used nature's seat to gaze at the views. She felt it for size and pulled the thin green leaves through her fingers.

'What's that noise?' She asked turning to strain an ear.

It's my lullaby,' he laughed 'the gentle fall of spring water over Yorkshire rock.'

'It's the most beautiful place I have ever seen.'

She could feel his emotion, his pleasure that she could love this place as much as him. Joy soared from them both so that the house felt them and pulled them towards it with great relief.

It was special and so was he.

It was a start. And yet? There was something, a pull starting in her stomach and twisting backwards to past fear.

The mustiness hit her nostrils along with old wood smoke absorbed by the planked floors and their rugs. Deep dark panelling covered the bottom half of the walls but left the top to paintings of pheasants, dogs, woodland animals and honoured photos of long ago shooting parties.

'Don't think badly of me.' he said dropping her bag at her feet. 'I know you don't approve of shooting.'

She noticed his slight limp as he went to open full length shutters at the French window. The rush of sun added to what the windows had already allowed in to highlight dust motes and his glowing face. She could see how he adored the place. As he turned he caught her look and read it correctly, much to her embarrassment.

'Could you get to call this place home do you think?'

She had no doubt that she'd lived in Yorkshire before and with this man…who was he? Hope lifted her heart.

Quick tapping toenails from an excited Chummy took their eyes to the floor.

'Now there's some-one who doesn't have to think of an answer.' he laughed forgetting his leg as he bent towards his dog.

'Ow!'

Wren pulled a chair towards him.

'Here, I am meant to be taking care of you.' she tutted. 'All that driving! I'll get the rest of the things from the car. Where's the kitchen?'

He pointed to the left, glad to be able to pull up his trouser leg to check the dressing before Chummy scrambled to his knee. Wren left them to ear rubbing and licking.

She lifted the boxes of food, fearful it might have got too warm on the journey. When she nudged open the door to the vast room spread before her she was reminded of Amblin. This kitchen had been built for serious cooking. She placed the boxes onto a once well-scrubbed wooden bench before her eyes reached a sight she thought had long gone from her life.

An iron range, like the one she was warmed in front of as a baby, spread three ovens and a vast grate before her.

'I'm starving!'

He had come in behind her carrying the shirts Lil had washed and ironed for him. She shot him a look of disapproval.

'I'm not going to let my leg get in the way. The doctor said to rest it not stay off it. I see you have found our only cooking joy!'

'It's impressive!'

'Impressive? It's a pain in the neck. A dinosaur. I haven't a clue how to use it which is why I bought this.' He pointed to a duty two ringed gas plate.

'That's no good for real cooking.'

'No but it heats tins of soup and beans brilliantly.' He opened one of the many oak door cupboards to display almost every tinned food known to man. The labels at least looked past it and faded. Another open door showed hoards of candles.

'But tonight we dine 'a la Lillian', thank God. Come on you can choose a room.'

One by one Lintern flung open the door to seven bedrooms most of them dusty, all had a large white wash basin and heavy mahogany furniture.

'Not very modern I'm afraid. Should chuck it out and buy some 'G-Plan', teak is easier on the eye.'

'Don't you dare! This will last longer than any sixties stuff.' She could tell he was pleased she approved of the old furnishings so that he was quite jolly when he opened the last door. Chummy rushed past both their legs and leapt to a rug strewn across the bottom of the bed.

'Your room I suppose.' she laughed.

'Yup. One man and his dog sleep here. I suppose you think that's a bit scruffy.'

'No. I think it is a bit wonderful! I think a bed is not a bed without feeling that comforting weight when you send your legs down on a cold night.'

'I'm glad you approve.' He studied her taking in the feel of the place.

'It's very tidy and the one room without too much dust.'

He pulled the door to, leaving just enough gap to allow a wet nose back through when its owner felt hungry.

They wandered through memories of the way a house holds all those lives and yet outlives them all.

She chose the room at the other end of the Lodge putting five bedrooms and three bathrooms between them; she felt safer that way. She hoped he was as honourable as Lil said he was.

'It's a long way from me.' he laughed 'what if you need me during the night?'

He was flirting with her.

'Oh, and why should I need you?'

'Oh I don't know, spider or something. The owls can sound quite eerie in darkness you know.'

'I find hooting owls a huge comfort to my wondering if I am still alive. And as for spiders; well there isn't one big enough not to be glad to be lifted out of the window when it is terrified by the sight of me.'

'So why have you chosen this room?'

'Oh I don't know. The curtains are so pretty and I like the fact it has two windows. It just feels right....special.'

He smiled. 'An interesting choice, in more ways that you think.'

He turned before she could ask him why but she didn't follow him. The room drew her in so that she sat on the stool to look at herself in the mirror.

Even in candle light she looked travel rumpled and tired. She was sorry she had reminded herself of the missing hair.

What would Warwick have thought? She tried to push his image from her mind because it never came alone now, there was always a beautiful Spanish woman laughing beside him.

It surprised her when she woke to the piercing morning sun that she was not the first up. The vast kitchen table had been set at one end with cereal bowls and tea cups. One set had been used.

'Good morning!' Lintern limped in after Chummy who stopped his panting long enough to show Wren how pleased he was she was still here. Lintern laid a huge handful of bluebells on the draining board then turned to find a big vase in a high cupboard.

'I thought you might have a lie in. It's only seven.' He turned as he filled the dog's water bowl.

'That was a lie in! I'm a lark; morning is the best bit of the day especially in spring.'

He looked absurdly pleased. 'Good! We agree on that. The light should tell us when to rise not the alarm clock.' He placed the just picked flowers in front of her cereal bowl and smiled.

'How's your leg? You haven't been trying to burst those stitches?' She asked smelling the divine perfume.

'Almost better. But you have plenty more hair if I do. Mind you, I felt it when I climbed over a stile. Mostly stick throwing this morning. Tea?'

She nodded wondering who was supposed to be looking after who. Lintern eased off his tweed jacket parting the top of his shirt he'd left unbuttoned. She looked away as her breath caught; he was a man of disturbing masculinity. Something he did not seem to realize. He pushed into the pantry.

'This place is cool but not like a fridge. The milk Lillian sent will only last a few days so make the most of it. I only like to go into York once a week.'

'She dug for Shredded Wheat noticing that he'd eaten well from the new packet they'd brought with them.'

'When do you need your leg checked?'

'Three days' time.'

'Is that what the doctor said?'

'No. But it's Friday when I usually make the big drive so it will have to do.'

He placed the hot tea pot on a mat in front of her and took a clean cup from the cupboard for himself.

'You can drive me in. You need to get to know the route, don't want to be beholding to me.'

'But I can't drive!'

'Really? Well I'll teach you. You don't need a provisional licence up here on private land.'

She felt excitement pushing at her fear.

'Won't you be too busy with work?'

He laughed. 'Chance would be a fine thing. I have enough money to last me...er us, for six months. I have to have Troutbeck working for me by then.'

She spooned the last of the milk from her cereal bowl into her mouth then asked.

'What will that involve?'

'Haven't a clue.'

'Aren't you going to open it as a shooting lodge?'

'Not enough money in that and anyway you wouldn't approve. All those cute little pheasants and cuddly partridges dying for sport.'

She was glad he had taken that on board.

'Well what qualifications did you get at University?'

'Trained to be a land agent, not much help in making this place pay.'

They became thoughtful together.

'Come on he said draining his cup. First driving lesson.'

He was a good teacher, not minding her seeming stupidity about gears and how far to turn the wheel. They laughed together when she drove the car off the track into heather and she loved the large hand covering hers to ease the gearstick into bumpy unfathomable fourth. Wren felt his eyes on her as her tongue eased out between her lips in peering, concentrated effort to steer a straight line.

'You know the morning sun really makes the most of those beautiful eyes of yours.'

There was huskiness to his voice that sent a thrill through her.

'Oh yeah? And which do you prefer, the green or the blue?'

They both lurched forward.

'Sorry.' she turned to see his reaction but he seemed in a trance of appreciation.

'I don't mind you stalling the car every five minutes as long as I can be here. You are wonderful company Wren, do you know that?'

It seemed that she was but it wasn't down to her that she was experiencing such joie de vivre. It was Lintern, he made her mind free in a way it had never been; in this lifetime at least.

He saw that she had joined him in the delicate current of his feelings. She welcomed his hand as it gently took the back of her neck but could not take her gaze from his which fell to her slightly parted lips.

'I'd love to kiss that sexy, pillow mouth Wren.'

It was impossible to speed up her mind enough to think up anything other than her true need.

'Why don't you then?'

When his face came close it seemed too long before the warmth of his mouth covered hers. Sweetness filled her. She felt a pull on that cord that awoke physical need. He moved gently across her face with desire softened lips. It was like being worshipped. It was like coming home.

When they parted enough to search each other's need he spoke softly through thumping a heart.

'Wren, you do something to me. You turn me into the person I always wanted to be.'

Her smile told him she was in it with him.

'I feel as if I have always known you, as if you belong in my house, in my heart.'

She was silent, searching for him in her other lives. If he was Alessandro why wasn't he alluding to it? She'd felt this near before but still wasn't sure of any-one. What was the reason? Should she allow him close?

There was some quality of caution in her silence and he sensed it.

He cleared his throat and with it the disappointment that she hadn't spoken the words he wanted.

'Anyway, you took your foot off the clutch too suddenly and out of gear. Try again.' he spoke hard words of dissatisfaction. But he stayed polite and caring though she could tell he felt rejected.

The moment was lost and she hated his loss almost as much as she hated hers.

They drove slowly and juddered towards Troutbeck Lodge to see Chummy dozing on a pile of logs.

'Cheeky dog. He waited whilst I chopped those, never lifted a paw to help, but loves to lie in front of them on a cold evening.'

Chummy, hearing the car, stretched and leapt to the ground where he shook himself clear of sleep.

'Can we have a fire tonight?' Wren tried to bring normality back into the space that had grown between them.

'Don't see why not. There's some coal too, keeps the logs burning slower.'

He made sure she'd turned off the engine then got out of the car to accept the overblown demonstration of pleasure his dog was showing at his return.

'I'll give him a drink then we'll sort that fire so we only have to put a match to it later.'

As he turned his back she could see the hurt in the droop of his shoulders.

It was good to stretch her legs after having them in never before tried positions on clutch and accelerator and that all too sensitive brake. She walked gently around the Lodge noticing things she hadn't seen in the excited sweep her eyes had given it on arrival. She pushed her way through secret branches of dripping rhododendrons. Spring was bursting out from earth and into her very being. Her feet longed to follow her eyes on the muddy paths winding their way into promising woods. For now she studied the sturdy building, admiring that long ago craftsmanship through the shabby tricks of time. When she reached the far end of the house she noticed a set of steps leading down. Her curiosity took her beneath the house to a small dark green door kept closed by a heavy metal bolt.

She tugged at the rusted fastening which jigged back but the door seemed swollen into its hole. Suddenly it cracked open courtesy of Lintern's size eleven foot.

'I see you've found the coal mine.' He said wincing at putting all his weight on his sore leg.

'The what?'

'Come on.' he pulled her into the cellar bending his tall frame.

'It's not a real coal mine, only a store but to us children in our summer holidays it was real. See how dark it is? We used to play coal miners.'

Their eyes were adjusting so that she saw him rub his fingers over the grimy wall and smudge dirt to her cheek.

'There, now you look the part!'

The coal dust felt and smelt just like Tot after his eight hour shift in deeper, dirtier, and wetter conditions than this.

'God it's cold. Just think of the poor miners who have to work in this all day.'

That's exactly what Wren was thinking of. Hard feelings of grief resurfaced to cut her with their spikes. He felt her sadness through the gloom.

'Come on; let's get you out of here. I'll get the coal later.'

When they reached the door he noticed her tears in sun squinted eyes.

'Oh my God I am sorry. It will wash off you know. We used to do it all the time.'

'It was in the mine that my daddy died a few months ago.'

He pulled her towards him not caring that the dirty cheek was pressed against the pale blue shirt Lil had washed and ironed for him only yesterday.

'Oh no, I'm sorry. Come into this cuddly corner of my arms. I can be so thoughtless. There now, cry all you want.' he passed her his handkerchief which she dabbed to her face, breathing in the essence she knew him to be.

Why did he say that? No-one but Tot knew about Cuddle Corner.

'You know when my father died I felt his body had gone to the ground and his soul to the next dimension but I know he left his heart with me.' His voice was soft.

'I miss him so much.' she sobbed pulling away slightly to look at his kind face.

'I know, but you know Wren, life is just a small part of our existence. We are here to experience who we are...kind, generous or cruel. If we know what we do is right we can enjoy it, if wrong change it. This is why giving feels good and badness awful for the doer. The very act of being born ensures that we will die and it's not so bad. Life is much better in the next dimension, less stress. We only come to Earth when we choose hard lessons.'

He was comforting her with his words she knew but trying to say much more with his mind.

Wren felt excitement at his displaying knowledge, he felt so much.

'What do you know about the next dimension?'

'Well I don't say too much because people think I'm strange but I know I have been there many times. It is my true home.'

'And?'

'You'll laugh.'

'No.' She hoped her expression conveyed her seriousness.

'Well, the separation from those you love on Earth is painful but as you pass through the thread of tunnel to the other dimension its light draws you. People's brains are not chemically equipped to deal with transcendental reality. It's like a birth and it's wonderful to meet all you love who have gone before you and those you left in the spiritual vibration to be physical.'

She glowed at the relief his knowledge gave her. He was so right, no-one in this life had ever talked like this.

'Have many died before you?'

'Yes, there's Father of course and my grandmother Letitia. Waiting to greet me will be the others in my spirit grouping who haven't been in this incarnation with me. It seemed so quick this time. They will have given me help and support whilst I am here though.'

'Any-one else?'

'Yes. The one some call God, true brilliance! God, the One...whatever people call him, is the one who puts us in this world so that we can find our way back to Him.' He beamed at this but she sensed he was holding some-thing back.

'And?'

'And what?' He smiled at her apparent knowing. 'Well there is my soul mate who usually accompanies my on every life but she had to stay for this one.'

Excitement gnawed at her heart as it began to thump.

'Why?'

'I don't know. I was just told that she had something to do that only she could. Really important. I only remember her sometimes, when my senses are heightened...like now.'

She knew her stunned look affected him.

'See I knew you wouldn't understand, you'll be laughing at me next.'

'Never.'

Gathering in her studied look he read every emotion before pulling her to his chest once more.

His words vibrated through his ribs to her ears.

'You know if I didn't know she was there waiting patiently for me I would have thought you were her.'

She tilted back her head so that she caught the wistful look in his eye.

'Maybe I am.' she said softly.

'I think I'd know, but...'

'But what? Go on.'

His reply was his lips touching hers. An act of relief mixed with love and sheer need from both of them. When she responded it was to a kiss of a thousand lifetimes.

She saw in his hazel eyes the clinging look she could only interpret as want. The same hungry, unhidden want that she must have been revealing. He pulled from her a need she had forgotten. The need of a woman for a man. Not since Jeremy had she so urgently grabbed at the physical closeness of a male.

His honeyed touches from determined yet soft hands and mouth lulled her dream-like into a cocoon of mutual love and pleasure.

She hardly noticed the slow, sensual soaked walk to his bed, only the bliss that he was able to lie above her still kissing, still adoring. His need was urgent, she felt that but his fingers traced over her body like a butterfly in slow motion, drunk on the passion of finding a nectar it always knew existed but never thought to find. His mouth hovered above hers then kissed the tip of his fingers before he touched them to her lips. He gazed at her as if hardly daring to believe she was real. As they joined in the deepened need for each other Wren's senses heightened. It was something to do with touch and ache and something to do with abandonment and a lot to do with finding oneself. But in that delirious knowledge she found that she wasn't sure. Even with all he had said and made her feel, there was something unfathomable.

It became lost in pure love….and yet….and yet….

FORTY EIGHT

Robins singing in the trees outside the window brought them out of their shared ecstasy to the soft afterglow of lovemaking at its most drowning sensitivity.

He sought her hand and enclosed it with more of the strength and gentleness he had just given her. She squeezed back with the reassurance he sought, both lost in the narcotic bliss of early love.

They had shared their bodies and with it their developed consciousness.

Like the brilliant blue of a diving kingfisher, he had entered her life with hardly a ripple.

That he belonged, she had no doubt, but in which life? Even with all they had just been she didn't know if this was Alessandro. But there was one way to find out.

Wren?' his voice was husky from exertion and further weakened by love.

'You OK?'

'More than OK?' She pulled her voice from the intoxicating vitality of new love.

'Me too.' They giggled together.

'They can say what they like about the swinging sixties with all that free love but it doesn't beat waiting for that special some-one.' Lintern seemed to waft the joyous words to her. 'Does this mean we are fuddy-duddies?'

'Don't care.' she laughed. 'Fads and fashions aren't where my needs are.'

'Wren you don't want to go back to Letitia's old room do you?'

She pushed up to one elbow. 'Letitia? Is that why you thought it was interesting I'd picked that room?'

'Yes. She slept there when Saul had to be up early for shoots. He always referred to it as the Queen's room. She was queen of the Lodge and its owner's heart. It seemed right; you are both too, to me.'

'You know,' Wren said softly, 'I have seen your Grandmother sitting, delicately wrapped in a thousand memories on the chaise longue in that room. There is a strange trace of her everywhere, soft, comforting and kind.'

'You feel it too? It is her benediction with all the mystery of death and love.'

Their kiss made more than words. He eased back, holding the nape of her neck in one hand so that he could fix her eyes to his. She saw his brilliant summer skies bursting with feathered blessings.

'I only dared hope you were as spiritually aware as I thought you might be. It's hard isn't it?' he whispered.

'What is?'

'Trying to live the life you have chosen aware that you are spiritual. Sometimes I envy the guy who is ignorant of what we really are and just lives for the physical.'

'Surely not? You'd be all grab and ambition, not caring who you hurt or crushed.'

'It seems impossible to live my life with this constant knowledge. Sometimes I just forget and act as a simply human.' He seemed sad at the words as if he'd only just realised.

'That's what we have to do.' She pulled him closer. 'But we must never forget that we are not physical beings having a spiritual experience, but spiritual beings having a physical experience. Experience is the physical wealth of our lives; our unfolding personal heritage. Let's get on with it.'

Wren wanted to be by his side now even more, she snuggled as close as she could but it could never be close enough.

'We have to make Troutbeck pay don't we? Its setting in this natural world transmits natural tranquillity humans so badly need. How I wish we could sell that.'

He turned to her. 'Perhaps we can and I like the 'we'! I never thought I'd find some-one so like me. You love the countryside, getting up early and animals. What more could a man want?'

'And you. I love you.'

'That's the greatest gift. Together we can do it! Any suggestions?'

It was hard to push the feelings of joy she felt out of her mind to allow business thoughts in so she didn't. She pulled the two together and was amazed at the wealth of thought she had.

'We have to gather to us what we have and what we were.' Wren spoke not knowing where the thoughts had been formed.

'Well I know what we have...but what we were?'

'Our former lives together.' she explained.

'You feel it too?'

'Yes.' She said hoping for the positive reaction she felt was in him. 'There must be some reason why we have met up again; all we have to do is find it.'

'And use it.' he said. 'But how, how do we remember?'

Wren knew the energies snuggling around them after such spell binding lovemaking were similar to those she needed. How she longed to capture, bottle and give to others such joy.

She spoke slowly, hoping he would co-operate.

'Close your eyes and find yourself at the top of a long staircase with this life at your back.'

'Uhuh.'

'Then take a few steps down until you feel me there and want to stop.'

His breathing deepened as she went down her own staircase and waited for him.

It seemed an age before he spoke.

'Do you remember our former life together in the late 1800s as homeless boys living in poverty and disadvantage? With others we used to sleep in wide roof guttering to avoid arrest on the streets. We were taken to Dr. Barnardo's home where we were de-loused and given new clothes.' He pulled his arms about him shivering with cold and want.

Wren was there with him remembering the desolation and the relief that they at least had each other.

'I'm there, I'm with you. I do, and how we had to get up at 5.25am for drilling by that ex-sergeant major before prayers. It was tough but it taught us application and we took all those lessons into manhood to start our own foundry.'

She let him take over.

'We had it easy near the end of our lives and made sure our own children would never be homeless.'

'I wish we had some of that money now.' Wren said.

'Yes. But we have something better. We have the experience. We know how to work hard.' His voice seemed different and then he was still and quiet.

'I wish we had the sun like our life as truffle hunters in Tuscany.' she said waiting for him to catch up.

'My God. Chummy was there! He was a truffle hound. He sniffed the floors of ivy clad woods on the Tuscan hills. I can see him now digging amongst the leaf litter beneath an oak tree when he knew there was a truffle a few inches beneath the soil.' He wallowed in the recognition of his dog but she had to move him on.

'Oh the smell of Tartufo Bianca! It became one of the world's greatest gastronomic luxuries. We didn't know it at the time but it only grew in a handful of locations around our beautiful village of Lucignano. It couldn't be cultivated, only unique ecological conditions allowed the fungus to come to fruition. I can breathe the delicious pungency in now.'

'Do you remember,' he laughed 'in the early days we'd fill a frying pan with eggs and flake our truffles over. When it was set we'd slice it up dabbing our rough bread into the yolk and truffle flavoured oil. Oh the smell was indescribable and the taste highly elusive like the gliding past of a beautiful woman who doesn't stop and you wonder if you really saw.'

'We often found truffles weighing up to 30 grammes, remember, but one day we found one at 860 grams. We became famous and so did the region unfortunately.

'I remember you were called Fabritzio and I Lido. That was a good life. After that fuss we sold our truffle but had two dogs poisoned by jealous poachers. I can feel our despair as we carried the bodies of our furry faithful workers home on our shoulders.'

She felt his pain as he realised one of those dogs was Chummy, who strangely pushed open the bedroom door with his wet nose and whimpered as he jumped up to be close to Lintern, so she pushed on.

'I can see you now combing olive trees in November to make the greenest olive oil ever. We sat amongst the olive nets eating cold spaghetti and drinking wine straight from our bottles. We used to cold press olives and then, oh that first taste soaked into home-made bread or drizzled onto warm haricot beans.'

'Yes, I can taste it now, the oil of Angels. So refined and pure.' His hand raked Chummy's ears and head.

'Oh the colours of Tuscany and the rhythm of the wind and the Tuscan nights of calm.' His reveries seemed to be part of her.

'What about all we learned when we worked together building the Salvadore Dahli curved building in Barcelona?'

'Oh,' she lilted. 'How much we learned of diverse style and aesthetics then?'

He huffed out a laugh at the memory. 'But we both married others in each of these lives. Were we soul mates do you think?'

Wren searched for that special feeling, the one she'd stolen a life to find, but it couldn't be caught.

'Some things we are not meant to remember.' If only she could find some proof, either way.

Alessandro might have been an adversary in these lives, teaching in the most dramatic way.

She turned in enveloping arms.

'These things are our strengths Lintern; we should learn from them and use these skills now in this lifetime.'

'What do you mean?'

'Well we don't have lice or regimented days, neither do we have truffle woods or olive trees but we started businesses and knew what was good to eat. We both know beauty when we see it and we should combine our strengths in these incarnations.'

He was quiet, then spoke as if in awe.

'I remember a life where we were married. I was a sword maker and you Wren; you were the cook in Scottish castle. God it was cold but you still managed to grow, against a south facing wall, herbs that made our meagre rations more palatable.'

She joined him in his fifteenth century memories but left when she recalled how her children were slaughtered by marauding clans.

'We have to take the lessons and work with them. We have to think.'

He pulled himself up on his elbow to look at her. Chummy left in bored disgust.

'There is something I haven't shown you yet.' he spoke gently as he lifted hair from her brow.

'There is something I haven't shown you either.' Wren pulled him towards her mouth with a special kiss she hadn't given him since they lay in the heather above a Highland castle. He remembered that soft play of her tongue and responded as he had then. It was lovemaking they had forgotten. It bonded them then and it bonded them now.

Chummy scratching at a door wafted closed to him woke them from their exhaustion.

'My God! We've had a lie in. It's ten o'clock.'

'But it's still dark!' Wren pushed herself up to check the clock.

'Ten at night! Chummy will be starving! We will be starving.' he turned to her laugh. 'We are aren't we?'

'I must say I hadn't noticed.'

Lintern got up naked to relieve his dog's anxiety. Wren saw the man she had just given her love to in all his glory. He was magnificent. Walking on the moors must tone every muscle. His only imperfection was the bruise and wound to his shin. The dressing had come off leaving the ends of black stitching marking the second they'd met.

'Stop watching me, you!'

'Never.'

'I hoped you'd say that.' he followed Chummy to the bed where he kissed her, responding to her welcome. 'Hey get off. I have the hungry to feed.' he pulled his dressing gown around him and disappeared towards the kitchen.

Wren dozed into her warm honeyed mind trying to push aside the one gnawing doubt that could spoil what life had given her. The thought hit that life had given her nothing. She had taken it.

Was this love for her or for Elia?

She heard the bath run and smelled pine when Lintern opened the door.

It's a big bath in here Wren; shame to waste all that water.'

The fragrance drew her almost as much as the man. She'd smelled it often before she was born, then it had meant flapping washing and vegetable picking. Now? Oh now…..

With just silky foam between them Wren lay back onto the chest of a very special person, the one she had just shared her body with and longed to do so again.

'I have a culinary feast awaiting your pleasure.' he said sponging warm water onto muscles he'd been making her use.

'Oh can't wait. What is it?'

'Beans and sausages from a tin with fried eggs on top.'

'Sounds demanding.'

'It's all I can manage without using that beast of a range glaring at me in the corner.'

The perfumed water sloshed as she sat up with her idea.

'It could be your biggest asset you know.'

'What? Biggest?' he smiled pulling her towards him so that she knew his mind had moved away from food.

'Well, second biggest.' she giggled and turned to grab him swilling the water onto tiles below.

He grabbed her wrists noticing for the first time the mark brightened by the hot water.

He had no need to ask. He knew how she'd been dealt with as a thief in an earlier life.

She saw his understanding and was glad. But how would her theft be dealt with in this life?

For now she would just enjoy the warmth of the water and the love whoever they belonged to.

In her starving need the food seemed delicious. They cleaned their plates with the last of Lil's stottie bread.

'Ambrosia.' He said raking his wet hair back into place.

He lifted the dishes to the sink.

'That's what we could cook here you know.'

He put the kettle to boil on the gas ring. 'Not on here we couldn't.'

'No, but on the range.'

'You must be joking!' His eyes followed hers to the black iron monster dominating the wall behind her.

'I haven't a clue how it works.'

'I do.'

'Really?'

'I often bathed in front of one like it and saw many a dinner cooked from scratch.'

'Now that I'd like to see.' He raised his eyebrows with his grin.

'What me cooking?'

'No the other bit.'

'Now don't get cheeky or I won't tell you my plan.'

'You have a plan? When did you make that? When I was guzzling extra eggs? I hope I come into it.'

'The plan is for you, for us if you like the idea.'

He brought his look of admiration nearer to her and cupped her chin in hands smelling of beans.

'I like the thought of us very much.'

She accepted his kiss still forming ideas in her racing mind.

'Troutbeck is perfect. And we can sell the tranquillity. We can offer holidays to stressed city workers in the Yorkshire moorland. You can teach them to walk to beauty and appreciate the nature and I can grow perfect flowers, herbs and vegetables which I will then cook into something special.'

'Like what? You can't cook….can you?'

'I can make every dish Lil has taught me and some old family recipes Ivy still prepared, she learned them from her family way back. These were passed from generation to generation and will be very old. The theme can be old English cooking. I'll do some research.'

'We could have an old Tuscan menu too by the sound of it.'

'If we can get the ingredients, why not? That's a brilliant idea!' She piped, loud with entrepreneurial enthusiasm.

'Glad to be of some help.' he said fascinated by her glowing eyes.

'It could happen but it will take lots of work.'

'I have enough energy to fuel a rocket.'

She laughed coyly.

'You've just demonstrated that.'

They laughed together in their first glory of love but Wren was now plugged into her vast creativity. It was a zone of overpowering ideas.

'We need to be different. We need a special draw.'

He laughed. 'Oh a country hotel on the moors with old English and Tuscan cooking isn't different enough? What else do we have to do?'

'We need a gimmick...no that doesn't sound classy enough. We need something to attract people with money as well as taste.'

'Yes like in the old days when people came from all over the country to see Grandfather's gun collection. It pulled Lords, Sirs, Colonels and aristocracy.'

'Sounds perfect. If only it were here now.'

'But it is.'

'What…where?'

'Remember I said I had something else to show you? Well that was it. Only I wondered if I should what with you hating killing.'

'Hunting for food is allowed. Could these guns be used for clay pigeon shooting?'

'Well, I suppose…some are much too valuable though.' He poured the boiling water into the tea pot, rattled the lid thoughtfully into its place then took her hand pulling her up to him.

'Judge for yourself.'

Stopping only to take a huge bunch of keys from a cupboard beneath the stairs Lintern led her into the hall. He took a long pole with which he pulled down a folding staircase leading to the attic hatch.

'I think my stitches will hold, only a slight twinge now.' He smiled testing his legs on steel rungs.

'Are you OK with ladders?' he spoke down from the top where he used two keys to unlock padlocks. She followed him up watching his legs disappear, then his face and arms reappeared to help her into the boarded out attic.

'Wow!'

'Wow indeed.'

Wren followed the lines of guns all padlocked, across three walls. Even to a gun hater she could see there was grace in this room. There was smell of gunpowder which she sucked into her nostrils.

'Lovely isn't it. Guns can be about beauty and art, not always killing.'

'I can see that.' but she still shivered. 'Are they worth anything?'

'Beyond words some of them. See these? A pair of Holland Ryalls too valuable to use. We could sell them to finance our venture.'

'Things can have more value than money.'

'Grandfather used to say that. See these hammer guns with the blue marbling. They are from G.E. Lewis in Birmingham, a specialist in wild fowling guns. Lovely!'

'I can see the attraction.'

'George the fifth used to say 'A gun without a hammer is like a spaniel without ears.'

Wren laughed. 'I expect things have moved on a bit since then.'

He unlocked a light gun and handed it to her.

'You could handle this small bore. It's tight and light, a nice little gun for a girl.'

'She pushed it back at him. No thank you, I prefer cooking.'

'It's serious stuff. They are all registered with the Proof House established in 1815 in Birmingham and London you know. I have Spanish guns from Barretta who've been making guns since 1526.'

Wren yawned exaggeratedly. 'Very interesting.'

Lintern didn't notice her message. He was lost in the dream of history and beauty.

'This is a cross over stock for somebody with a master left eye; see this strange twist in the barrel. It's Belgian, before the war.

'You don't say?'

She could see he was lost in enthusiasm and let him enjoy it.

'What's this?' she said holding up a long cylinder.

'Careful; that's a cartridge for a one bore. It takes five ounces of black powder.'

'Ouch!' she laughed.

He noticed her blank look.

'Sorry it's just such a fantastic collection. People would pay to see this.'

'That's all I wanted to know. Can we go now?'

'Oh but I haven't shown you the Westley Richards or my Thomas Bland single four bore.'

'You'll bore me into bed in a minute.'

'That's got to be worth it,' he said taking his hand from a rook rifle he was about to show her to follow her down the ladder.

Later, in front of a boisterous fire in the grate they started planning together. The kitchen table filled to overflowing with paper on which they scribbled their plans, rough at first, and then over a few days with much talking, thought and inspiration interrupted only with languid, bonding lovemaking, they were perfected.

'Do you think it will work?' he asked taking the Biro he was sucking from between his lip.

'There's only one way to find out.' Wren answered crossing her legs as well as her fingers.

It was mid-summer before they placed their first advertisements in Lady, Country Life and Shooting magazines. The summer had passed in a flurry of vegetable growing, driving lessons and heavy smartening of the neglected grounds. Up-market English country shooting lodge was what they aimed at, even they were surprised with the result. Bird feeders were put outside all the windows; it was her gift to Tot. Early morning walks were a mix of research and stick throwing, spotting curlews and watching skylarks. Everything of interest was noted.

'You don't have to note every mole hill do you?' Lintern asked when the walk was held up yet again with Wren's rough map drawing.

'We have to sell this place in a brochure Lintern. Selling is like loading a set of scales. Clients might be considering another hotel with which we are equally balanced. We don't know which little rose petal of information would tip the scales in our favour. It can be as close as that.'

The day Wren passed her driving test they celebrated by taking a picnic consisting of five new recipes onto the moors where they made love until the first drops of rain hit their naked bodies. The rolling clouds began to spit gently at first then spitefully.

'Come on chauffeuse.' Lintern said as he hopped on one now perfect leg trying to pull on passion discarded clothes. 'I don't expect my driver to lie naked on the moors getting wet.'

She deftly dressed then started to clear away the cloth and remains of their experimental feast.

'It is early. Let me show you those shepherds' cottages down by the stream, one day, with enough money, we can modernise them. 'Black Fleece Cottage' is roofless but 'Lambing Cottage' is not too bad. Maybe I can seduce you in there too.'

Wren threw the last sips of her Mateus Rose at him but he ducked. The rain was staring to wet them so she rushed.

She broke up the remainder of the oat bread she'd copied from a sixteenth century cookery book.

'Only the birds would want that.' Lintern pulled a face then grabbed at his throat as if he were poisoned.

'Very funny, but I agree, it is horrible. I won't be adding that to my menus.'

It was a relief to get under the cover of the Land Rover.

Lintern shook drops from his flop of hair and she squealed.

'Well you don't need me to drive you into York any more so you will be able to research at the library yourself.'

Next morning she left him polishing an old big bore Goose gun and talking about how he found it in an old box. He was cleaning an ornate carved double four bore with handless ejector action too and his day seemed full to bursting. Glad to get away from guns to window shop for new jeans she headed for York on her first solo drive. Still having to concentrate, she slowed down on the humped bridge to take in the stream gushing over coppery stained rocks to splash into shale lined pools. Such beauty had to be her home. She needed to soak in nature to be happy. To think, she could have missed all this because of a false lead in Spain.

The traffic thickened with her first visual thrill of York Minster so that nervousness made her extra cautious. It was hard to keep her eyes on the road as she came into Bootham Gate, the fascination of such regal buildings as she turned right past the Museum always thrilled her. Only now she wasn't a passenger she had to keep her eyes on the road. She'd spent three afternoons in that vast hall of books but still had much to see. Heading slightly out of the city she crossed Lendal Bridge over the River Ouse of which she'd heard such stories of flooding. The water was at a summer low now she was glad to have noticed when she passed Memorial Gardens into relaxing familiarity.

This city seemed flat after the hills where she lived. York was alive with the past and seemed unimpressed by the modern 1960s. She parked at the railway station where Lintern had taken her many times. She knew this wasn't the nearest to the shops but lack of experience made her stick to what she knew. This was a magical city, the history never failed to ooze into your bones. She felt eased into the past glory and terror.

The narrow streets were flowing with tourists and shoppers as she trotted towards the Library after she retraced her route on foot over the bridge and past the turrets and castellation's of Lendal Tower below. The bells welcomed her passing the Theatre Royal drawing her to their source in the tall towers of York Minster as she headed for Kings Square where street entertainers had drawn quite a crowd. Wren heard cheering and clapping as she turned into the Shambles she had first been in awe of when Lintern had shown her the narrowest medieval street. Here it was said occupants of upstairs rooms could lean out to shake hands with some-one in the beamed house across the street. It was easy to absorb the energies of the days when human waste ran down the gullies after it was thrown from the first floor. Wren knew the best views were above the tourists heads.

To grab the essence of the ancient buildings as the streets tempted her to cross back up Colliergate to Goodramgate, she looked up. She didn't know where she was going only that she was being pulled to this route. It was nowhere near the clothes shops; in fact it seemed she would leave York if she went much further towards the college but she couldn't help it. She peered up beneath Monk Bar, with its Richard 111 Museum she had yet to explore. It was hard to imagine the workers who built York's walls in the thirteenth and fourteenth centuries, but simple to be in their awe. She was surprised when she was drawn to a low doorway beside a window stuffed with old books. The feeling of pleasure reminded her of when she found Marion Cran's volume at the jumble sale.

After the tinkle of the doorbell, the smell of damp paper, mysterious book spores and other people's grime almost spun her on her heels. In fact if it hadn't been for the kind intelligence in the voice that preceded the balding head with sliding spectacles halfway down its nose, she might have left.

'Good morning dear heart.' he trilled pushing his glasses up nearer unravelling eyebrows. 'Any-one who enters here has a special need so what is yours?'

So taken was she by the old soul who looked as if he had been here when the first book arrived to capture him forever in the dusty bookshop never wanting to leave one tome unread, that she closed the door behind her.

'Old English cooking.' She said responding to his request.

'With social behaviour and drawings of table settings?'

'You have that?'

'Second case on the right, third shelf down, half way along. Green binding.'

He was right. Wren took the book from its tightly packed neighbours; she could never have imagined such treasure.

'Were you expecting me?'

He came out from behind the stacked and groaning counter fully then, unsuccessfully straightening the lopsided bow-tie he wore above a soup-stained waistcoat.

'My dearest I am always expecting special people to find me and the book they need. Indeed I firmly believe God smooths the way to my shop in the same way ice curlers smooth the way for their stones.'

'Sorry?'

'Canadian Winter Sports 1939'. Books from abroad, turn right, elbow height, to the left five along.'

He pushed his sliding glasses up in front of his eyes and she saw they were as crooked as his neckwear.

'Elizabethan cooking any good?' He asked fingering two gilded volumes with reverence.

'They are so beautiful. How much?'

'Twenty pounds each.'

Her heart sank.

'Oh. And this?' she held the first book towards him fearing it would never be hers.

'Make me an offer.'

'Half a crown?'

'Done!'

'Oh I got it right.'

'No. That's sixpence more than I was going to charge. Works every time!'

'I've been done.' she laughed.

'Yes you have but just to show I'm not all rogue you can take a little peep at the books you can't afford. What do you want them for?'

'My partner and I are opening a small country hotel on the moors specialising in Olde Worlde food.'

'Mmm,' he wrinkled his brow up in admiration.

'Well if I let you copy anything will I get a mention on your menu?'

'Of course. She laughed playing him at his own game. 'Just as long as you display a tasteful stack of our brochures.'

'This is business dear heart. Are you the cook?'

'Yes.'

'Then the food will be very sensitive. You can't fail. Fully booked are you?'

'Haven't even started yet.'

Pleased with her find in both the book and Martin Hampton, Wren left with a smile on her face ducking a head bumping beam into the street. As soon as she closed the door behind her the energies changed. Dread swam about her making the hairs on her arms prickle. There had been a foreboding presence here on the now empty street. One she recognised but couldn't place. From how long ago the evil settled she did not know, she only knew it made her shiver.

She hurried away clutching the brown paper wrapped book to her chest in search of the shops.

Between trying out recipes on the now mastered black range Wren and Lintern searched for all the linen and crockery used in the Lodge's heyday. Washing the fine china and heavy silver cutlery was easier than laundering weighty white sheets and pillowcases. Table linen suffering from years of game gravy and after-dinner port was too stained to be of use.

'We will have to send this out for laundering when we get going. Having no electricity is charming when used to captivate clients but it loses its appeal when lugging heavy wet sheets around.'

Lintern agreed. 'You'll have enough to do anyway. Although like the food suppliers we'll have to pay extra for delivery way up here.'

'We should charge them for the beauty.'

'I'm sure but they won't see it that way.'

Their first postal enquiry was quickly followed by a booking. Then another, then four and the next week fifteen clients sent deposits checks. Everything had to be done by letter. The August, September and October diary was full along with two Christmas bookings from couples hoping to be snowed in with candles, good food and roaring fires.

Wren and Lintern had their breath taken away by this early success so that the day the first guests arrived they were tense and terrified. After greeting five couples in middle age Wren had to produce ten teas with Lavender scones on the veranda. On that sultry day she had to keep the fire stoked for the baths hot water so that the kitchen could have cooked the venison and trout without the oven.

She watched Lintern talking to Major Glendinning-Jones and his wife beside the pewter jug of blowsy second cut green and foaming Lady's Mantle and pink roses on the polished oak table they used for a desk. He took from a basket some of the leaflets Wren had picked up from the tourist centre. He could have tempted them to York Castle and every medieval gem of churches without maps and illustrations, so well did he know the city he regarded as his own. He made them laugh about the grotesque faces and animals of the roof bosses on the Guildhall. He captivated them with descriptions of the Eye of York which showed a cobbled Victorian street and the prison cell of Highwayman Dick Turpin. The Major was more interested in York dungeon which Lintern told him brought more than 2000 years vividly back to life-and death, the plague, guy Fawkes and the Lost Roman Legion along with the horror of the witch trials.

First of course, he said, the guests would rest, eat and enjoy the moors before history and culture tempted them away from such a comfortable country house hotel.

The words thrilled Wren almost as much as the glow she saw on the face of the man she loved.

He had arranged his first gun viewing and booked two men into clay pigeon shoots.

He had found his niche.

There was a two day break between when their first guests left and their second batch arrived.

As Lintern counted the money from where he set aside his costs he tossed into the air every penny of their profit.

'It's raining money!' he cried rubbing pound notes into his face. 'We've done it Wren! We are a brilliant team. Just look at these comments.'

He pushed the guest book towards her.

'Such a wonderful cocoon of peace and sumptuous repast, we'll be back with our friends.'

'The most delicious holiday we have ever had. Such young proprietors give new life.'

'As good as Reid's in Madeira without the sea views.'

Wren glowed. 'Where is that?'

'Who knows but if it is so good I will take you there one day. I promise.'

He pulled her to his chest. 'You are a very special person Wren. We haven't had much private time these last few days have we. Come on I want to show you that bed isn't just for falling exhausted into.'

Next day they drove to York together. Lintern visited the vintner and Wren took a note pad to visit the book shop.

'Please call me Martin', Mr Hampton said clearing a little space amongst the clutter so that she could copy the Elizabethan recipes.

'I suppose I must give you tea to go with these delicious cinnamon buns you have baked for me.'

'Yes please. But I warn you, no one knows if they are delicious yet. You are my guinea pig.'

The treasure in the books outweighed their monetary value. Although not written in Elizabethan times they luckily captured forgotten recipes for roasted swan and creamed nettle. They also gave a great insight into the domestic growing of food.

Martin called Wren into his cramped office.

'Got to keep you away from those books with threats of splashes and crumbs.' he said pouring Earl grey from a fine china pot into delicate companion cups and saucers. He read her surprise.

'Thought I'd have chipped mugs and wet rings? It's all right if the paperwork seems in chaos but tea is a serious business. I hope you will be able to afford those volumes someday, it's best to own good books. They should be read in youth, again in maturity and once more in old age just like a fine building should be seen by morning light at noon and by moonlight.'

She laughed. 'That is as English as the art of spreading marmite onto hot buttered toast.'

'Wrong!' he laughed fondly. 'See why you ought to read more. It's Robertson Davies 1913, a Canadian novelist.'

He ummed his approval of her sweet buns then sipped at the too hot tea.

'There's a book in the window for you. I put it there hoping it would delight you when you came.'

'But you didn't know when I would come. Some-one could have bought it.' She stood up unable to wait.

'I placed it there not twenty minutes ago Wren. I just had this feeling.'

'Where?' She called backwards from peering into the window space.

'Dead centre…with the price tag of fifty pounds I placed on it to deter any would be interest.'

Wren's keen eyes swept across the display but didn't find the book. Her attention was drawn to a dirty person making a place to sit on the pavement by spreading a filthy, once shiny eiderdown.

Without even seeing a face Wren felt a shiver of dread. It had the same tinge as the feeling she had when she had last left this shop.

She came back without the book.

'Oh you are hopeless. I really thought you'd do whoops of joy when you saw what I had found for you.'

He put down his cake and pushed a stray crumb into his mouth with an arthritic finger.

She watched him stretch over his display to take a book which he gave a little wave with.

'Here it is. 'Medieval Mead and Manna.' Got it from a book fair in Bath.' He offered her the book but she took it blindly.

'There was a funny person outside Martin.'

'Funny? Who?' he looked back. 'Oh you mean our homeless person. I just waved to him. He's not funny, just sad' He read her face. 'You mustn't be afraid of him dear heart. He is down on his luck that's all.'

'But it feels.... he feels... dangerous.'

'Well I haven't spoken to him. My kindness is not to chase him away. He gets enough of that all day. He likes to sit outside my shop because of the bakery opposite. Some people buy him a sausage roll or give him coppers as they leave with their daily bread.'

He turned his attention to the book then but it was impossible for Wren to join him.

She didn't know how she copied six recipes from the books in front of her but she did. Martin's new find remained unexplored.

'Oh.' he said returning from his cellar with an empty tea chest which he put beside a pile of sorted tomes. 'You haven't even opened it.'

'No....too involved.'

He looked at her note pad. 'You are a slow writer aren't you? That's not much. Tell you what.'

He dabbed his finger onto the crumbs on his tea plate. 'You use me as guinea pig again and I'll trust you with that book.'

'What you mean I can take it home?'

'Yes, but do treasure it. I know you will.' She noticed how smeared his glasses were as they caught the light.

'Thank you; I know how expensive it is. I'll be very careful.'

Martin wrapped the book in two tea towels. 'Did you bring me some of your brochures?'

'Oh yes, thanks for reminding me, here.' She dived shaking hands into her basket.

'Looks lovely.' He peered at the photos of Troutbeck.

'Maybe you'll come up sometime when we are quiet. Sample my roast swan.'

He laughed. 'Pheasant will do for me, thank you.'

She left him to his pleasures but when the bell jingled her departure alarm grabbed every part of her mind. The homeless person was still there sitting with crossed legs and cupped hands.

Desperately Wren tried not to look at him but his eyes drew her to his and held her from her flight of panic.

The cruel smile that pleasured his lips told her he recognised her.

She turned and ran down the street not caring if it was the right way or not.

CHAPTER FORTY NINE

'You need help.' Lintern looked up from the female feet he was trying to rub exhaustion from. She looked so tired.

More bookings had flooded in. Two Sirs, a bunch of models and photographers who didn't get out of bed for two days and a self-made millionaire from Blackpool, showed another side of life to the moors and to Wren. She was worn out serving 'groovy chics' and 'with it' fashion snappers meals in their rooms, perfecting food and doing everything she'd promised to do to make Troutbeck Lodge the success it was becoming.

'And you Darling. You never stop either.'

'Granny Letitia always used to say 'If a job's worth doing, it's worth doing properly.' That really stuck with me.'

Wren changed feet on his lap. 'Oh oh oh, that is sheer heaven.'

He kissed her toes. 'Even Chummy is earning his living. There is never a walk taken he doesn't go on whether guests want his company or not.'

'They usually do.' she laughed. 'He shows them hidden waterfalls and great views. He even posed with some weird looking clothes from Carnaby Street. I wouldn't be surprised to see him in Vogue.'

'He's a hit, and my guns. I don't think I realised how much of a draw they would be.' Lintern gave tension relieving pressure to the insteps where experience told him she needed it most.

'Do you want some Horlicks or Ovaltine?'

Wren got up from the sofa, glad to have the Lodge to themselves for the first time in weeks.

'No, come on, I'll give you a back rub in bed.'

Morning rain gave them an excuse to take their tea back to bed where they made love appreciating and relishing each other more than ever.

Wren's ecstasy went from hopes that this had to be Alessandro to fear that he was meant for Elia. That she had robbed another soul of this beautiful and satisfying man drove nails into her heart. But if he was the soul mate she sought what was his relationship to the soul she had so wronged? The complications were endless.

'Right that's it!' Lintern said noticing her faraway look. 'We'll advertise for help. You are worn out.'

'No; it's not that. We don't need help. This is our place. I don't want any-one prodding our dream.'

Wren was happy to be left in solitude when Lintern drove to York to bank their takings and restock the plundered Babycham and lager. It was a while since she had listened to skylarks and searched for wildflowers. The last of the Bilberries would be hers for the taking as long as the grouse hadn't been too greedy. It was sheer pleasure to pluck the dark blue berries and hear them ting into the washed out Nescafe tin. The let up in the rain was only temporary, she was getting to know Yorkshire weather.

Soon the October rush would start and so would the mists, the wind and frosty mornings. Summer salads and puddings would give way to herb dumplings and steamed puddings. She wished now she had gone to York and Martin's bookshop to search for autumn recipes.

Chummy, happy to tag along tamely, suddenly made a dash into the heather.

'Come on Chummy!'

She glanced at the sky bruised by a storm to the east. Clouds were coming in from Scarborough she wanted to be home before they dropped their darkness onto her shoulders.

'Chummy!'

The spaniel, usually so obedient, refused to take his head from whatever it was making him wag his tail so furiously. Wren had to pull him back with his collar but immediately she saw the box she knew why he was so excited.

'Oh Chummy. You clever, clever boy!'

Concern made it seem a long way back to the lodge carrying the disintegrating cardboard box made even heavier with the blue cardigan she'd been wearing, one of the models had given it to her with pity in her eyes for the girl who was not at all 'with it'. Twenty pounds she had said that cost with its designer label and up to the minute styling. Only in London, Wren had thought, here it was just another bit of knitting that would shrink in the wash and bobble at the cuffs and hips. But it did a wonderful job in drying and warming up the weak and undernourished kittens some-one had cruelly abandoned to the elements. The King's Road could be proud.

Wren made a thin gruel of some dog food and warm water which the kittens refused to take. The tabby lay still, its dull eyes not even flickering when Wren warmed it in her palm and whispered words of love. She knew it would not live the night. She had to concentrate on the tiny tuxedo cat with shaking white whiskers and his sister with grateful eyes lighting her total blackness.

Using her little finger, Wren managed to get some of the nourishment into tiny mouths with sharp teeth she hadn't expected. It seemed they understood as dinky, soft pink pads with thin claws grabbed her fingers gratefully. They couldn't have been on this Earth even four or five weeks and already the cruelty had shown itself. As they dried off in front of the range true beauty came to their eyes as the warmth fluffed their fur.

Chummy seemed to think he was their uncle and lay watching their bodies take comfort and strength from their luck. Wren couldn't wait to see Lintern's face when he returned. She knew she had a new, maternal glow to her eyes and it felt wonderful.

When the door spun opened Lintern's glowing excitement peeped from behind parcels and boxes.

'Have I a surprise for you.' he said enthusiastically before spotting the beer crate lined with the London knitwear.

'Hello! What's this?'

'You aren't the only one with a surprise!'

She watched him peer over to see the kittens she was already starting to love.

'Oh goodness. They look unwell.'

'Only one. The others will make it.'

'But we can't keep them, Chummy will hate them and he'll be jealous.'

At the mention of his name the dog stopped bouncing his welcome and looked into the crate.

'It was Chummy who found them for you. He loves them. Thinks they are the babies he never had or something.' She laughed rubbing the dog with her fondness.

She told him her story as he touched the thin ears with his big fingers.

'They are so helpless.'

'I could kill whoever abandoned them!' Wren knew the words were common enough but she really meant it. She tried hard to swallow down the genetic murderous need. 'Driving up here with such cruel intentions. I mean, do they think they'd catch rats and birds or something like that to eat?'

'Probably.'

'At four weeks! With wobbling legs and milk teeth?'

'Hey steady on. It wasn't me. You really love to defend small things don't you? You'd make a wonderful mother.'

She knew the look he started but starved it of life by getting off her knees to rustle open the bags he'd dumped on the kitchen table.

'So; where's my surprise then?'

Lintern grinned as he pulled, from beneath bags of groceries, a tea towel wrapped flat parcel. Wren was too excited to untie the precise knot so pulled at the tight string.

'Oh but... no. Martin's let these out of his sight. He must really trust us.'

Wren reverently fingered the expensive gilded books.

'Well he trusted the money anyway.'

'What? You bought them? But we can't afford it.'

Lintern laughed. 'You deserve it. If I had to pay a person of your calibre they'd be able to afford these books easily. The money is ours to share. You never buy yourself anything.'

His warm enjoyment of giving flooded him as she hugged the books with happiness.

'That's not all. I have another surprise for you.'

Unable to take her eyes off the treasure in front of her, Wren jumped when a loud knock came to the door.

'That will be our new general help. I dropped him off at Lambing Cottage to see if he felt he was able to live there. I left him to walk up to assess the place.'

'But I said I didn't want any-one. Did you go to the job centre without discussing it with me?'

'No. It was fate. That's why I knew you'd approve.' He moved towards the door. 'And you'll feel at home. He has a very strong Geordie accent.'

'Come in.' Lintern stepped back allowing the man to enter. 'This is Wren.' he smiled.

She was too shocked to speak. Chummy rushed to the kittens and growled in their defence.

The man stepped nearer to lift a crate of 'Cherry B's' he'd picked up from the car on top of one of Babycham on the table. Wren couldn't speak, couldn't take her eyes off him.

Between them was complete silence with a thousand words beating behind it.

'I have promised Winger a bath and some of your great casserole. Is there plenty hot water?'

Lintern sensed the tense atmosphere and when she didn't reply turned to the man.

'What did you think of Lambing Cottage then? Not too many leaks?'

The man took his triumphant gaze away from Wren.

'Oh no, not at all like, dry as a bone you might say, but mind there's some cobwebs around that place.' His eyes flitted sharply around.

The voice did have strong Geordie accent, usually Wren adored its warmth and charm. This one she hated. It skewered her in the stomach.

'Well if you want to stay here we'll deal with that tomorrow, sort you out a bed and other things you'll need down there. Sorry about the outside lavatory.'

'Wey no man, I'm used t'that.'

Embarrassed by Wren's unusual silence Lintern led Winger away to the bathroom and her clean towels.

He was back in seconds but found Wren standing motionless exactly where she had been.

'Don't worry, he'll scrub up.'

'I don't want him here Lintern. He'll have to go.'

'What?' Now don't be silly. You of all people with your compassionate heart. You'd take in needy animals but not needy humans?'

'You don't understand.' She muttered, feeling like a new blossom flattened by a summer storm.

'Well tell me then.'

How could she explain the dread in her heart, the revulsion? The icy fear.

'I told you I don't need help.' They were the only words that would form.

'Well I do. I'm worn to a frazzle and so are you. We are victims of our own success.'

He moved the drinks to the door of the cellar, turning and grimacing to show how heavy they were.

'See he's already demonstrated how strong he is, and he needs a job.'

'Where did he find you?'

'You mean where did I find him?'

Wren didn't push her point.

'It just seemed as if it was meant to be. I went to the book shop and he was sitting outside begging. When I came out he was still there and I put my hand in my pocket to give him half a crown, then I thought 'No. He needs more than just money; he needs self-respect and some chance in life.'

'Well is he experienced?'

'No, but he is strong and he can drive. Spent time in the army. He's not afraid of hard work.'

'He's not us Lintern. He doesn't look creative or sympathetic to the place.'

'Oh Wren! He won't be greeting people or doing flower arrangements. He'll do anything that needs muscle and he can handle guns.'

Lintern's words, meant to reassure her, struck ice into her heart. The guns.

'Artillery, not antique fowl guns of great value to you!' she regretted the high pitched raise in her voice.

'Hey; hey! Now don't over react. He is here to do donkey work. I won't let him near the guns.'

Lintern tried to hug away her fears but Wren knew everything would change.

Left alone in the kitchen she tried to understand why everything suddenly felt unsettled as fate hurdled towards her.

Fear oozed into her very being and she did not know why.

'Nearest thing you got to a baby those black kittens eh. Your favourite colour is it?'

She was on her own when he emerged smelling of Lintern's Penhaligan Windsor cologne and glowing rosy red with too vigorous scrubbing.

His hair still needed cutting but her Stablonde shampoo had revealed red highlighted locks hanging down to powerful shoulders. He was naked except for one of her new towels knotted around his waist.

'What?' he said in reply to her look of disgust. 'I couldn't put my scruffy clothes back on could I? That ponce of yours said he'd fit me out with some of his toff's cast offs.'

'He's down the cellar. And don't talk of him like that. He is trying to help you.'

The space between them was loaded with her anger.

'Well. Never thought I'd see those odd eyes of yours again Wren. Didn't recognise me in York did you. Got mine fixed. Simple job in the end. Couldn't get in the army without it. Never have found out how good I was with guns then.'

'Still the same old Alan, vicious and sly.' She tugged at the words finding that she did not want to pull anything from her mind for this horrible man. 'I'll have Lintern take you back where you belong tomorrow.'

He moved towards her and she knew he could detect her shaking. Drips of water ran off the end of his hair to trickle down a well-muscled chest.

'Why should you be the only hard up one who benefits from being nice to the wealthy gentry eh?' he smiled slyly. 'I know how you get everything you want off him. I won't be trying that though. Don't be so greedy. He looks like he has enough for both of us to fleece him.'

'You are disgusting. You will leave in the morning!'

'You wouldn't want me to be chatting all the way to York would you? I could talk non-stop about your mam and her filthy father, that real mother of yours and just how much gossip there has been about that poor man down the air shaft and how his wallet was found.'

She saw in his face how much he was enjoying his power over her.

'You see Wren; I have learned how to control my violence. It is different tools that I use now. Much more effective.'

'Your low-life connections are impeccable.'

They both heard creaks and scrabbling dogs paws on the cellar steps. Alan made towards the bathroom moving the crate with the kittens just a little with his bare foot.

'You want to look after those kittens, very vulnerable they are being so small, light bones they have. Easily crushed I expect.'

He disappeared at the same moment Lintern's smiling face came up the last stair.

'Is he not out yet?'

'He is. Said you promised him some clothes.'

'Yes. I'd better sort that.' he kissed her cheek. 'Don't worry. He'll be alright. Just one night in the Lodge then we'll fix up the shepherd's cottage.'

He went happily to find some jeans and a shirt to give to the man who was about to change everything he loved.

CHAPTER FIFTY

Lintern agreed that the kittens could sleep in the bedroom with them but made it plain he didn't understand why.

'They might have fleas or something.'

She felt panic like bat's wings smashing around her head.

'Like Chummy who sleeps on our bed every night. Those kind of fleas do you mean?'

'Chummy is family, we know where he's been. If he has fleas they are our fleas, good and clean. Familial fleas of fine pedigree.'

Wren could not raise her usual laughter but picked up each tiny body to cradle in her palm where she blew into sleepy baby fur to examine them.

'Don't worry. I've checked my babies. Their mother looked after them well even if humans didn't.'

'Then will you stop acting agitated and come to bed.' he pulled back the covers.' What is the matter with you?'

'It's nothing to do with the kittens. It's because I had to share my dinner with a man I don't know and don't like. I had to watch him roll up the sleeves of your shirt I only just ironed for you this morning! Now he is sleeping in our home only feet away!' She spoke through the hazy tumble of the past.

'He's all right. What on earth is all this fuss?'

'He might have fleas!'

'Don't be ridiculous.'

'Why? We don't know where he's been sleeping or why he is homeless? And why do you call him Winger? His name is Alan!'

'Is it? He told me he got that name in the army, from the position he played in football.'

As she got into bed Wren, for the first time, noticed that his welcoming arm didn't go around her.

He leaned away to put the light out.

Wren couldn't get from her mind the thought of how pleased Alan would be if he could see he was already driving a wedge between them.

There was much banging and edging as the men angled a single bed from the store room. They leaned its iron heading against the wall before they splurged out a mattress rolled and tied with string.

'Well at least we didn't gouge the plaster off the walls Winger. We're a good team you and me!'

Wren watched them laugh together, glowing with exertion and camaraderie. She was the only one not laughing. Alan caught her eye holding it as he spoke to Lintern's back.

'I think you'll be pleased at just how good we'll work together Mr Hadleigh-Bridges'

Lintern turned from where he had unrolled the mattress onto the gravel to check its state.

'It's perfect, old but in good condition and please, call me Lintern.' He missed the glow of triumph in Alan's eye.

'OK Lintern it is. I don't know how I will ever repay you for all this.'

'You don't have to. Just be a good worker that's all I ask.'

'I intend to be. But I will pay you back one day. I always repay everything with interest.' Alan straightened his back to enable his every inch of his face to be seen by Wren. 'Good or bad.'

How she hated him. Why could Lintern not see what he was really like? Men are blind to so much.

Wren watched as the two men disappeared out of the gate towards the first shepherd's cottage that bore the least leaking roof. It would take some cleaning. She had checked them both one hot day with a view to converting them into holiday cottages. No way would she volunteer to help. If Lintern wanted some-one intruding into their lives he'd have to get on with it. He could wallow there on his grotty little ownsome. She had kittens to feed again and menus to decide upon for the shooting party arriving on the glorious twelfth. She was just glad to get Alan and his negative energies out of the house.

It was good to know that even some of the most historically ingrained shooting families were turning against killing although they still ate game from the butcher. It was easy for the London set to be anti-hunt especially when they had seen an exceptionally handsome fox disappearing into the woods. Many photographs had been taken of vibrant light playing on male pheasant finery. These next guests would not be languid or draping themselves artistically around Lintern's wall mounted stag horns and fireplaces like the last lot. They'd be up at the crack of dawn sending robust bodies into the crisp autumn air. Their food would have to be different.

Lintern returned to find her weeping.

When he eased up her face towards him he saw the lifeless body of the smallest kitten in her palm.

'Oh no.'

'He died just as I tried once again to ease milk into his mouth.'

'He was so weak Wren. He's better off now, you know that.'

'Yes but I am crying for his disappointment. He will have waited so long for his chance to be born. How can humans be so cruel to such a tiny helpless life?'

'He'll get another life, soon if he needs it. He met you, for that he will be grateful.'

She kissed the still head.

'I saw his life force leave his little body. It was so beautiful.'

Lintern stood up. 'Come on we'll bury him beneath the plum tree.' He bent over the crate where the two remaining kittens were rolling around biting each other's ears.

'You have these two robust kittens to think about now. What are you going to call them?'

'Well,' she sniffed 'I was thinking about dumplings and puddings when I found them so I suppose it will suit them.'

'That's great Dumpling and Pudding it is. They are both going to be quite roly-poly the way they gobble that food.'

Wren managed a little smile. 'I was going to call him Stew.'

'You still can. He deserves a name.'

The door opened abruptly.

'Do you have any Vim or Flash?'

Cool air wafted colder energy towards her.

Alan took in what was happening.

'Oh, a right goner that one looks.'

Wren shot him a look that told him her hatred of him had just grown.

'What? It's only a bloody kitten for heaven sake. I've put hundreds of them in a bucket of water with a brick on top before now.'

Lintern strode to a cupboard from where he thrust a box of cleaning materials into Alan's chest.

'Take the rest of the day. I'll be down later when I've sorted more furniture.' He shut the door behind him.

Wren hated having Alan around but she was pleased with the weight it took from Lintern's shoulders. They had more time together and grew closer. Dumpling and Pudding were great time wasters. Wren had not known how playful kittens were or how easily they became house trained. Lintern cut a hole in the back door for the cat flap he came home with and they all had much fun showing the two sisters how to get outside whenever they wanted.

The wobbling playmates soon found how to follow Chummy to his woodpile to make his life a misery chewing his ears and catching his tail. It seemed natural that when they were out Wren only had to think of them and in they trotted meowing as if to say 'What?'

It was quite a surprise when Lintern went into York one day in the MG and came home in a green Land Rover.

Wren had gone to the window to check the unfamiliar engine and tyre sounds. Lintern was in the passenger seat beside a beaming Alan.

The door opened when she went out.

'What's this?'

Lintern came to the front of the vehicle and put his arm around Wren's waist excitedly.

'Isn't it great? Winger suggested it. It was becoming impossible to get all our stuff into that sports car.'

'You didn't discuss it with me.'

'There wasn't time. We would have struggled with everything we had to bring to the Lodge. Winger is used to driving these things in the army. He suggested it over lunch, knew where the garage was and everything.'

The ginger hair glinted in the sun but did not detract from the grin he showed at her exquisite pain.

'What you bothering about Wren, he doesn't have to ask your permission, it is man's work. Nowt to do with women, cars like!'

'You took him for lunch?'

'Yes. Well, we both have to eat. We had quite a laugh actually. The tales he told me.'

'You'll be asking him to marry you next!' She flounced off into the house leaving Alan tinkering with his new toy. She was meant to hear the rye chuckle that flew to her ears and dumped furious tension on her shoulders.

'What's this about?' Lintern followed then tried to turn her but she resisted pulling her arm from his grasp.

'Wren, you can't be jealous of some-one we pay to take the pressure off us. I must admit it was nice to have some male company for a change! But your reaction?'

'You don't pay him to run your life. You loved that MG.'

'I did! I still do! But that was for the old bachelor me who gadded about the countryside with no real aim in life. Things have moved on, I have a different life style and you.'

Wren slammed shut the food book she'd been copying from. 'I'm glad you remember.'

The engine revved outside and a shower of gravel hit the door. Wren stormed out just as Alan practised another emergency stop a few feet from the step. She tore at the driver's door and pulled the keys from the ignition.

'Have you forgotten we have small animals around here?' she barked.

Alan looked shocked first then pleased that he had angered her.

'Oh, your precious 'Babies'! If they have anything about them they'd get out of the way quick enough.'

The anger thickened the air so that Wren couldn't draw breath.

'Get off to Lambing Cottage.'

'You mean 'Creaking Gate Cottage.' I've re-named it.'

'What did you say?'

'It's more apt and a bit more swinging don't you think?'

He stared at her realising she hated him more by the second.

'It's a joke, get it?'

'That cottage is not yours to re-name!'

'Oh for heaven's sake don't get your knickers in a twist. It's not yours either.'

'I never said it was. It belongs to my partner as well you know.'

'Oh your partner. I see, you think his nibs is your property is that it?'

She threw fury at him with a turn of her head.

'No. He's my partner, in more ways than one.'

'Oh just because you give him what he asks for in bed is it and are you sure about that?'

'What do you mean?'

'Nothing's forever Wren. He could be taken away from you, quite easily from what I've seen of him. The barmaid at the pub seems to light up when he comes in. What if some better meat were to come along, tempt him into the bushes eh? He is a man after all. What would you care about what cottages were called then?'

'You are even more disgusting than you look Alan. I don't want you here.'

He laughed then, a cruel, sinister laugh that she had heard from his mother that first Christmas when she was little.

'I know and I love it. Lintern wants me here though, thinks I'm quite a find actually. I'll probably be here long after he's got rid of you...and your babies! You won't be looking down your nose at me then will you?'

'I've never looked down my nose at you. You are on your path, I accept that. You just aren't nice to be around. In fact you are repulsive.'

'Really. Well some girls would disagree. In fact there are those who think I am very nice to be around especially when I'm using all my muscle power to give them a good time. You should try it sometime. I won't tell Lintern if you don't!'

'You are truly disgusting.'

Lintern came out then. 'What are you two mumbling about?'

He looked from face to face. 'What is going on?'

'Ask yer girlfriend.'

Wren strode into the house hating herself for being so angry and hating the laughter that came from two men jointly lost in the mysteries of motors.

Lintern approved of all the dishes she had tested that evening.

'Mmm. What's this? From here is it?'

He picked up the open book reading 'The Forme of Cury'.

'Yes, it's medieval Blanc-Mange from King Richard the second's reign. It has chicken, rice and almonds. I'll have to get some pomegranates for the garnish though.'

She thumbed through the books showing him some of the medieval spellings. They laughed at a recipe for Spring Soup calling for 'a mutchkin of young pease' and Fritters of Spinnedge calling for 'sinamon, currans and rowle them like a ball', before frying in a batter made of 'ale and flower'.

'Well I suppose cooks weren't scholars and it shows how language evolves.' He picked up a spoon dipping it into dishes before him.

'A bit heavy on thyme that one.' he said pointing to a vegetarian dish she had yet to think of a name for. 'You've made too much again, shall we give some to Alan, see what he thinks?'

'No! I do not care what he thinks, he does not belong here!'

'Oh Wren I wish you would at least try to tolerate him. He is a very hard worker.'

'More than that I would say.'

'What do you mean by that?'

'He has persuaded you to part with a car you loved. What else will he have power to influence you to lose?'

'What are you on about?'

'He told me of the barmaid where you have your cosy lunches, she is after you!'

'Oh you mean Sally! Yeah! Me and every other man in trousers she's so desperate. She has had every other man in York, sees me as fresh meat. Winger is just joking.'

'You know I want rid of him.'

'Now who's influencing me? It made sense to get a bigger vehicle and anyway Winger can go into York in that.'

'What; by himself you mean?'

'Why not? He suggested it when I went for the insurance. It will take the pressure off me.'

'Oh now I see. He was sitting in filthy clothes, begging, you pass him one day and suddenly he has a job, a cottage and now a car.'

'He works for it Wren.'

'Yes on you!'

'Don't you want me to help some-one who is down on their luck?'

'Not him.'

'Why not for heaven's sake?'

'He always smells of booze.'

'So he likes a drink.'

'Probably why he was homeless in the first place.'

'Yes. But I thought up here far away from the pubs....'

'Lintern you have put him just down the road from our wine cellar. He knows everything in there. He carries it in for heaven's sake.'

'Wren a person isn't bad because he had an addiction problem. Give the man a chance.'

'An addiction. What you mean he's an alcoholic?'

'Seems so, but he's fighting it. Got to respect the man."

'You knew this all along?'

'As soon as I saw him. Wren I felt I had to help him. My instinct told me to. I have this strange feeling that he will lead me...us... to something important.'

'Destruction you mean! He'll be the undoing of us Lintern. Don't give him the chance.'

'Only if we let him Wren and you seem to be doing quite a good job of that yourself.'

It was the first time he had abruptly left the table, the room. And her.

Wren felt bad about making her own inventory of all the alcohol when Lintern was in charge of that area of the Lodge. She had taken the opportunity to have on hour in the cellar whilst he was out with Chummy.

A knocking seemed to be coming from the kitchen door or was it the kittens playing with their Ping-Pong ball? It was unlikely to be a visitor all the way up here. No, it would just be the exuberance of those growing cats.

It was harder than she thought to list every bottle in the cellar, but when it was done Wren closed her note book and climbed the steps reaching the door just as the back door opened spilling Alan into the kitchen.

'Got any scran? I'm starved.' he said waving a beer can in the direction of the pantry. 'Not a thing to eat at the cottage.'

'But you went to York yesterday.'

'I know. Got this but food completely went out of my head.'

'Like you, you mean?'

'Ooh ho ho! That's a good one. Getting better at the verbal swipes aren't you?'

'You can starve to death for all I care.'

Chummy rattled in then, snuffling Dumpling and Pudding awake before joining them in front of the fire.

'Oh am I early or is lunch late?' Lintern swung his coat to the peg then tossed his cap after it.

Wren struggled to gather her growing need to murder this hateful man intruding upon her happiness. It showed in the hoarseness of her voice.

'Late, got lost in something I'm afraid.'

'Never mind, I'll rustle us up a bacon and egg sandwich.' he opened the pantry door. 'Winger do you want one as you are here.'

'Two would be better.' he grinned pulling a chair from beneath the table.

'With yolk and hot butter running down my chin.' He began fingering the book Wren had just written the wine and spirit figures in. She swiped it from him.

'He can have mine. I have things to do.'

Alan managed to speak despite his look of sheer triumph.

'Oh by the way, some-one called for you Wren.'

'Where?'

'At Creaking...Lambing Cottage.'

'What?'

'Oh they were coming from here, just noticed me fixing that stone wall.'

The smell and sizzling of bacon wafted between them.

'Who was it, a customer?'

'Don't know, just wanted to know if you were here.'

'Well was it a man or a woman?'

'Don't know. It's hard to tell these days with all that long hair.' Alan pulled out a chair at the table and plonked down before easing another towards him for his feet.

'Seemed a bit mad to me.'

'Mad?'

'Offered them a drink. Refused?'

'So that makes them mad does it?'

'Well it's a long way up here without a car.' He gave her a look that said she was stupid.

'Were they wearing walking gear?'

'No, hippy stuff, Jesus sandals and no socks. Had a little dog with them.'

'Which way did they go?'

'I don't know do I? They just left. Said to tell you it only took a week.' He leaned back with his hands behind his head, his face shut down, he'd had enough.

The shattered glass of his words sent shards into her memories.

'What did you say?'

'Told you they were bonkers.'

She yanked the chair from under his feet and pushed it back into its place. It was good to get away from him and the smell of frying and into fresh air.

Wren hadn't planned to work in the herb garden but it was the only thing she could think of to get away from Alan. Chummy, she knew, felt the same. Although she cut and tidied many plants there was only one thing looping through her brain.

'Who was it Chummy; could you smell anything strange?' She ruffled his ears and gazed at the bolting Sorrel and wind tattered Fennel fronds. But she could hardly see them, her mind was too hectic.

The October visitors were more active than the Christmas guests who spent much time downing spiced wine and peeling roast chestnuts which Wren had gathered in autumn from the sweet chestnut trees at the back of the lodge. They received many letters of praise of their hospitality and originality; every-one commented on her Champagne Sneeze dessert. Best of all, they were making money.

Alan had surprised her by staying for long periods in Lambing Cottage with a smoking chimney and his own cooking. He lived by the chip pan and ate every brand of sausage known to man.

Strangely her relief that he only came to the lodge when given a job to do soon turned into curiosity. In the run up to Easter she had refused all Lintern's offers and suggestions that Alan should help her prepare the soil for potato and vegetable planting. She could have done with some help but used the excuse that the last time she had left him alone he had dug up an entire asparagus bed that was only just reaching its best having been planted years ago. Lintern had defended him, laughing that the roots he had stacked in an untidy pile ready to burn looked like scruffy dead tarantulas anyway. She lived in hope that the precious roots were re-planted in time.

Lintern had gone up to Pickering to check out a new fencing to keep the deer and badgers from her spring bulbs. No doubt he would come back with tales of how he had to drag Alan away from the bar and recount a new joke that only men understood. Still she treasured the time she had alone and Lintern had become even more loving in the time they had together. They were a fantastic team, of that there was no doubt, but if he was Alessandro she had yet to find proof. He was happy and that pleased her immensely.

She often wondered how Alan was living. She had not visited Lambing Cottage once since he moved there. The top road passed by the slate roofed stone house where Alan lived but it was still two fields away. There was never any need or notion to allow her legs down that winding path to where her 'bête noir', lay.

'Come on Chummy!' The spaniel was glad to be called away from the indignity of losing both his favourite sleeping places on the veranda to two feline, fur licking girls.

Even to herself she pretended she didn't know where she was going. At first she allowed the daffodils to take her attention. She noted those she must have planted too shallow so that they grew blind. She could never improve on the self-sown primrose dotted banks but knew by the thick clumps of long snowdrop leaves that she should divide them now before the Easter guests kept her too busy. For now she would enjoy the softness of spring. Chummy sniffed around the gate which started the path to Alan's home. She watched the dog easily push his body through the post and rail fence and allowed him to smell out the route he must have taken so many times with Lintern. Her heart pounded. If she followed him she could pretend, if only to herself that she'd had to find him. Just this once. Alan and Lintern would be miles away filling the Land Rover with tools and interesting bits that only men could find compelling.

It surprised her to see as she neared the front door, two pots of primulas, pink mixed with blue and cream. The way the accompanying ivy trailed over the side seemed particularly artistic for the most coarse and irritating man on the planet. Her thoughts were drawn by a flapping noise so that when she followed it into the back garden she saw new jeans hanging on a washing line, water flicking from the flared bottoms. She felt guilty then that she had never suggested Alan put his clothes with theirs to the laundry. By the look of those they'd take three days to dry. Chummy's tail started to wag as he emitted a funny little noise. He hated Alan as much as she did so she took it as a sign that he was pleased to be here when Alan wasn't, a theory that evaporated when his ears pricked. The sound was coming from an open window at the end. Surely no-one would break in all the way out here. Perhaps a pigeon had flown in, or a squirrel. Squirrels were notorious thieves. The five steps towards the window were five she wished she had never taken.

CHAPTER FIFTY ONE

The room was small with the single bed pushed up with its head against the window. There was movement and a noise she had only ever heard from herself. Two bodies were writhing in great pleasurable effort to be closer to each other. The thin sheet and blanket were only half covering the buttocks of the man lying on top of a slight, dark haired woman. There was no mistaking that red hair. Mesmerised by the private sight she should never have seen Wren didn't know how to leave it. The couple were deep in a kiss that triggered a need in her. When it ended Alan raised himself to look passionately into the eyes of the woman he left no doubt he was enjoying. Wren's guilty gasp turned his head. At first shock threw anger to his face but almost immediately a new pleasure came to him. He locked Wren's eyes and began thrusting slowly at first, expertly building rhythm with pleasure. Wren froze. She didn't know what kept her legs from buckling with shame or fleeing with fear but she stayed mesmerised by the scene in spite of every atom of her body screaming at her to leave. Alan drove himself powerfully into the body of his unsuspecting lover and she vocally appreciated every stroke. His eyes never left Wren's. When at last the pleasure became too much for his woman he expertly enhanced her orgasm before driving wildly into his own shattering ecstasy. Still he locked Wren's gaze. Determinedly he kissed the woman before rising from the bed to walk naked to the window. He was still hard and smiled at the way Wren's eyes dropped to his groin.

'I'll shut the window Merle. I wouldn't want the breeze to slow our next fuck. We don't know what rubbish might blow by.' He eased the iron stay towards him and pulled the curtains to shut out the view that had burned into her brain forever.

She noticed nothing during the walk home. Over and over again Alan's deliberate display played itself to her defenceless brain. Why would he do such a thing? Why couldn't she stop the wanton response her body subjected her to?

Lintern opened the door full of smiles.

'You're early.' she kissed him trying to bury her thoughts at the back of her mind.

'Yes, had no lunch though, Winger didn't come, is there a sandwich?'

'Cucumber and marmite OK? Why?'

'Said he needed a day in bed. I hope nothing's ailing him, we're full for Easter. I need him to help me with the antique gun shooting trials.'

Wren emerged from the pantry without the food.

'What? You said you wouldn't let him near the guns, you promised!'

'Yes I did darling, but that was then, eons ago when we didn't know him. I trust him now.'

'Well I don't.'

'We can't give all the trials I booked without Winger. He keeps telling me what a good shot he is. I have booked two days simultaneous. He can handle the world war guns I bought last week at the Leeds auction.'

Wren couldn't think of a thing to say. All she felt was dread.

Lintern went to the pantry and came out with the things she had left behind.

'You should have taken on help too. How many cookery classes have you booked?'

'Too many.'

'See,' he said slicing cucumber fragrance into the air. 'I wish you would take on a girl.'

But Wren wasn't listening.

Over Easter Wren exhausted herself. She decorated a blossoming wild damson branch with painted egg shells and stood it in the entrance hall. The rooms welcomed with the heavy fragrance of hyacinths and her daffodil and forsythia arrangements. Spring was everywhere except in her heart. She hated watching Alan go up the attic stairs with clients to choose their guns. Every time he entered the Lodge she stopped what he was doing. A gun in his hands seemed lethal. It wasn't clay he wanted to shoot. She could see it in his pleasure as he waved his choice tauntingly in the air before he left the Lodge.

They were never alone so that the secret between them began to seem as if it were imagined. Only the slight lift of one side of Alan's mouth as he sent her a furtive look behind guests' backs, confirmed he was still enjoying the scene that could never be talked about.

They had two days off between guests but there seemed even more work to do.

Lintern clattered his empty tea cup into the saucer, and then wiped toast crumbs from licked lips.

'Come into York with me Wren. We'll have a nice lunch and a bit of a shop. You could do with new shoes and some nice jewellery. You look too plain beside our guests.'

'Plain? Plain? I am not on holiday like them. I don't have to compete with the size of diamond in my ring or the most expensive cashmere jumper. I am working.'

He moved towards her massaging the tense muscles of her shoulders and neck.

She stopped cutting the dried flower heads into the huge china bowl to make pot-pourri.

'Darling you are more beautiful than any other woman who enters through that door. I just want you to have nice things, that's all.'

'I have all the nice things I want. I have you, Troutbeck, Chummy and the cats. I have a sense of achievement and a challenge. What more is there?'

'It's wearing you out. We hardly ever get to make love any more. Please say you'll think about taking help.' The way he held her and smiled with his head to one side told her how much he cared.

'OK.'

'You will?'

'I said I'd think about it that's all. Now go on, get yourself to York. I have to perfume this then create a new menu.'

Alone, she turned to her books, took the pen from behind her ear and searched for inspiration.

The animals were asleep, piled into one heap in the overflowing dog bed, their gentle snoring lulled her deep into thought….into remembering long, long ago.

By the time he returned Wren had made a vague list of all the food she could remember from her life in Tuscany. She knew from experience that inspiration would come but whether or not she could source the ingredients was a different matter. Chummy rattled up at the sound of tyres on gravel.

'You're back! Get everything you wanted? Any mail?' she said stretching her back from the cramped position.

He dropped a wad of letters held tight by an elastic band. The stamp on the top letter was Spanish.

'Here.' From behind, he kissed her neck and massaged her shoulders gently in the way he knew she needed.

'Oh, oh. That is wonderful. I've hardly moved. Have you had lunch?'

He moved his thumbs gently into her hairline. 'Yes Winger and I had chicken in a basket, the chips were like cardboard. These pubs serve everything in a basket these days.'

'Even soup?'

They both laughed and realised they needed to do more together. Wren began to turn.

'No stay there. Promise not to move.'

She heard a fumble, the rustle of tissue and then a little creaking noise before the soft feel of something cool around her neck.

'There.' He came round to admire his decorative work which Wren sent her hand to.

'What?'

'Oh you need a mirror. Come into the bedroom.'

She allowed herself to be led childlike along the passage wondering what he'd placed so lovingly around her throat. When they reached the dressing table he stood behind her.

'There you are, pearls.'

'But...'

'No buts! You deserve every single one of them. They are real you know. Well, cultured.'

'But when would I wear them?'

'When guests are here. The women wear such classy jewellery and I want them to know you are worth everything they are.'

'Real you say?'

'Yes and these.' He produced two silky pearl studs. 'For those beautiful ears. I didn't know if you needed studs or clips so I brought both.'

'Both?'

'Oh don't worry; the jeweller said I could take them back. What is the difference? I didn't like to appear ignorant.'

She fingered the present lovingly. 'I think these are for pierced ears.'

'Yuk!'

'Well I haven't any little holes in my lobes so I guess I'll have to keep the clips.'

She placed the pearls on her ears and turned to him.

'I never thought you could be more beautiful Wren.' his voice deepened. Slow male fingers traced her cheek and throat with excited tenderness.

'I'd like to see you naked with just the pearls.'

He held her eyes so sensuously that she began to slowly peel off her clothes. When all that showed below the string of lustrous beads were her breasts he kissed her throat languidly before cupping them deliciously in his hands.

'I have always loved you Wren, and I always will.'

Her hands reached for his and with entwined fingers they leaned together with need.

As her softened mouth silenced his earnest words she gave way to a passion they had nurtured together. Nothing could be more wonderful that the intense, bonding closeness they would enjoy for the rest of the afternoon.

The only thing that spoiled it was the occasional glance towards the open window. It would be just like Alan to find revenge.

Chummy woke them when he'd been waiting for his supper longer than he was prepared to tolerate.

'My God! It's six o'clock!'

When Chummy was wolfing at his dog bowl, gentle growling at daring cats, they sat down to reheated broccoli and nutmeg cream soup that Wren had experimented with the day before.

'More?' she said, pushing her hand through tangled hair.

There came a sudden knock making Wren pull her robe more tightly around her.

'Who's that?'

Lintern got up and went to the door, glancing at his watch again.

'I have another surprise for you. Now don't get all precious on me, it's for your own good.'

She heard voices when the door opened then Lintern stood back to allow Alan to lead in a stunning dark girl with shiny black hair and eyes to match. Her hipster trousers showed a flat olive tummy below small curvaceous breasts. When she smiled her tongue came nervously between perfect teeth.'

'Wren.' Lintern beamed from behind them not seeming to notice that her appearance spoke loudly of what they'd just been doing. 'This is Mademoiselle Aupy, your helper.'

Painfully aware of this girls perfect grooming and neatness, Wren felt so disadvantage that she couldn't speak. Her eyes saw only eagerness to please and total acceptance of what was before her from this beauty but the man behind her was different. Alan, his usual 'toilet end of a rat's nest' hair was conditioned and soft, he almost looked groomed. He leered and raised his eyebrows in an approving way; no doubt he thought pearls went wonderfully with sweaty bodies. Wren could read his thoughts that the gift had bought Lintern an afternoon of what all men were after. She felt cheapened by his enjoyment of her discomfort.

Lintern did not notice but was keen to sell the qualities of the person he had brought in.

'This lady is very talented, worked in one of Paris's most famous restaurant.'

'As a chef?'

'No; but she was the girlfriend of the chef and learned much from him as she helped, even taking over when he was sick. No one noticed a difference in the food. She'll be ideal to take the pressure off you.'

Wren heard a dismissive snort from her own nose and knew her mouth had tightened.

'I can do all the cooking thank you. It's cleaning and preparing where I need help.'

The girl smiled understandingly. 'I he'v help bring up five younger infants. I don't want intrude you, just help. I need a job or I cannot be stay in England.'

The way her mouth moved, the slight language mistakes and the French accent was so captivating even to Wren; goodness knows what it did to men.

'You'll work hard won't you Merle?' Alan encouraged.

The name struck lightening to Wren's brain. Alan smirked at her shock. He saw her discomfort and wallowed in it.

'I'll think about it.' she clipped out the words before heading for the bedroom.

It was a few moments before Lintern joined her.

'I can't believe you were so rude. The girl was nervous to start with. What is the matter with you, she is perfect?'

'Where did you find her?'

'At the job centre of course.'

'Oh.' She turned pulling on her soft sweater then reaching for the hairbrush. 'Not through Alan?'

'Alan?'

'Sorry, you mean you placed a position with the job centre and she was interviewed by them?'

'Not exactly; Alan suggested it after lunch. Well he knew we wanted some-one and as soon as we got to the office there she was.'

'Just handy.'

'Yes; I went to the catering section just to see what wages were paid and she was there looking at the cards; asked me if I wanted a cook or cleaner. It saved all the rigmarole.'

'Oh I see and did Alan suggest what time you went into the job centre?'

'What do you mean?' His querying look made her realise her meanness.

'Never mind.' She shrugged.

'She's too pretty to want to be just a cleaner.'

'Well even if she stays only a few months it'll help us.' he said missing her point. 'And she doesn't mind staying at Lambing Cottage.'

'Alone with Alan?'

'You have him all wrong you know. He can be a perfect gentleman.'

'There's only one bed.'

'And the sofa. He said it would be all right.'

'I bet he did.'

In the morning Merle turned up at six thirty asking what she would do. When she cheerfully started on the toilets and bathrooms and still had a smile on her face at coffee time Wren had to admit she was good to have around. Anyway she could hardly reveal exactly how she was aware of the secret between Alan and her.

As she placed the kettle on the range shame trickled sweat under her arms.

How could she ever let her know she's seen her making love? She shook her head to dislodge the shame but it clung like mud to boots.

CHAPTER FIFTY TWO

'So do you admit it?" Lintern was closing the payment file after the last guest had turned their car out of the drive leaving the Lodge all of Tuesday, Wednesday and Thursday to recover. He came over to where she was scanning the pantry for her replacement list.

'What? I admit to nothing but my name.'

'Oh', he laughed, 'so much? Do you agree then that Merle is the success we hoped she would be? This last month has been proof.'

'Well, she certainly takes the weight off me.'

'She has learned so quickly. She adores the countryside, smothers the animals with kindness and understanding and has become a good friend to you. She handles Winger beautifully.'

If only he knew how beautifully.

'I must admit that I am less stressed and the trial French menus we worked on together were a surprise hit….and the French wines.'

'And', he pulled her towards him, 'we have had much more time for closeness have we not?'

She accepted his kiss returning the love it brought.

'I want to give them a bonus and some time off, if you agree.'

'Well yes, OK,' Wren replied. 'As long as it isn't a week-end.'

'You know that Granddad and Lillian are coming next week?'

'Yes of course.'

'Well I thought, then. I'd rather have them to ourselves. The place will feel more like a home than a Country Hotel with just family.'

'Wow! Thank you.'

Wren thought Alan looked almost childlike as he stood beside the range and counted the money from the envelope Lintern had just given him.

'I can take you home on this Merle. Mam and Dad will not believe I could have such a beautiful girl.'

Merle looked slightly worried as she slipped her envelope into her pocket. 'I'd really like it.'

Alan pumped Lintern's hand enthusiastically. 'I'll check train times. Can you give us a lift to York station?'

'No.'

'Oh!' Alan looked shocked, all this kindness suddenly burst.

Lintern laughed at his face. 'You can take the Land Rover; don't want to be wasting half your bonus break on draughty platforms.'

'Yes!' Alan punched the air. 'You are a real gent!'

As they reached the door, rushing out to pack, Merle looked anxiously at Wren before beckoning her silently to her.

'I have little secret.'

'Secret?'

'Down at cottage...oh I know I haven't asked and I should have, but I have a pretty cat, he came with me for his home.'

'But you should have said; why should we mind?'

'Well...,' Merle left what she was going to say in favour of an appreciative smile.

'What's its name?'

'He Bob. Well, he was Bob but he have road accident in York, lost one of back legs so now we call him Wobblybob.'

'You want me to feed him?'

'Yes. But not just with food. He special, what we call 'jolie-laide', pretty and ugly. The both laughed in their shared love of animals.

'I know. You want me to cuddle him, talk to him?'

The look of relief made Merle even prettier. 'Oh Wren only you understand this things.'

It wasn't the walk down to Lambing Cottage that set Wren's heart racing, she loved the exercise and the chance to cut wild flowers and foliage for her flower displays on the way back, it was the thought of entering Alan's personal world.

Chummy took the path easily giving the funny little noise he had given that awful day she'd tried to wipe from her memory without the tiniest bit of success. At the end of the dry track that filled lungs with dust in summer and grabbed feet with mud in winter, Chummy became louder. The sound brought a bright tabby face decorated with torn ears and crumpled whiskers to the slightly open kitchen window.

As he jumped she could see he knew he would fall awkwardly but felt it was worth it. Wren watched as the two animals touched noses and smelled each other's adventures. To her hands the tom felt slightly rough and battle scarred but he adored a woman's touch and seemed to have lost no confidence with his leg. After quite a display of welcome, Wren felt for the key in her pocket.

Her hand stopped with her heart beat on the knob, only a defenceless animal in need of care would drag her into Alan's home.

It was garlic that first hit her senses. It seemed to have permeated the walls from both the cooking and the rope of fat bulbs that hung above the old beige Belling oven. Wobblybob went straight to the newspapers where two saucers, licked clean, lay begging.

'Now Chummy, no!' Wren forked the fishy smelling food from one of the tins left on the draining board and filled the other saucer with water. Everything was sparkling. A collection of continental cooking pans hung from hooks on the ceiling just missing the sofa that had come from the Lodge but was now enhanced by tasteful plump cushions and a batik throw. There was only this room and the bedroom. Wren felt guilty that two people lived in this tiny space without even an inside lavatory. The kitchen sink had to be used for everything. They had never even asked to use one of the baths and yet they were both so clean.

Drawn by the photographs displayed on the old sideboard Wren smiled as she saw French family in French clothes smiling amongst trees shading a French garden. There was nothing of Alan's family. All too drunk to hold a camera still she thought. She could resist the urge to search for booze bottles empty or full. There was a little pile of books to the left, all French topped off by a passport Wren had never seen before. The face beaming out from the photo was only young and joy seemed to spring from the eyes. How old was Merle? Wren had never asked. She summoned all her school French to study the date of birth, but it was easy, September six 1948. Only one week younger than herself. She smiled to think of the different welcome this baby would have received.

Guilt made her replace what she knew she should never have touched.

Wobblybob went to his bed and kneaded the old jumper he slept on asking for rubbing to complete his joy of having a full tummy. She picked him up. This was the only bed she'd be going near in this cottage. The thought drew her eyes to the closed bedroom door. The image that could find no way out of her brain played itself again.

'You were here then weren't you Wobblybob? Just as Merle was living here in secret so were you.'

It felt strange being in some-one else's life and yet Merle had made this place so attractive. She had a flair; there was no doubt about it. She seemed to belong to this place and not just Lambing Cottage; the Lodge. She seemed to belong to the Lodge. This was what Wren felt every morning when she arrived to serve breakfast and do chambermaid duties. It wasn't just Wren who had taken to her; Lintern often said he couldn't manage without her. Pudding and Dumpling loved her as if they'd known her all their lives and Chummy took to her in a way he never did with Alan.

Had they met in previous incarnations? She fell back into the sofa with Wobblybob on her knee. It was easy here to send her mind back for recognition of Merle's energies. Nothing came. But there was something, a slight discomfort and a certain feeling that there was a connection but it was too nebulous to find.

She slammed the door and ran all the way home.

The excitement of Sir Saul's first visit in years to Troutbeck Lodge was compounded by the fact that he was bringing Lil. How she'd managed to persuade him into that Wren didn't know but joy lifted her heart as she arranged Foxgloves with purple Sweet Rocket and vibrant fern leaves.

When Lintern heard the car arriving he jumped up, returned to a little boy by excitement.

'They're here! They're here!'

Chummy ran out with him and Wren was only steps behind. Lil had on her good hat as she emerged sweating and travel sore from the Vintage Rolls Royce. She looked florid against the cream bodywork.

'If I'd 'ave known it was this bloody far...' she started but her first glimpse of Wren flooded her words with tears.

'Oh darlin', darlin'!'

Wren finally felt the arms flung around her like a starving octopus relax.

'I can't believe it! You're here Lil; you're really here.'

It took ages to prise Saul away from Lintern but the keenness felt by both parties to enjoy the Lodge and all they had made of it whisked them into the hall.

'What?' Saul's eyes swept around the welcoming woodwork and furnishings. 'I can't believe it. It's not the same place. Where's that throat grabbing smell of damp gone to?' he breathed in the lavender waxy fragrance from the polish. It is just like when Letitia loved it.

Lil, bursting with pride said. 'It's no better than I would expect from my girl. She knows how to make something of nothing does Wren.'

She came over and linked her arm into Wren's pulling her without words for a tour of the place she'd never visited before.

'Well!' Lil sat back still in her hat after a light lunch of salmon with watercress sauce and rosemary buttered vegetables. 'You won't be diving into the cake tin I brought you after that will you?'

Wren started clearing the dishes.

'You are joking aren't you? It's all I've been thinking of for weeks. Why else would

I have emptied my shelves?'

'Well I must say, I baked all day yesterday.'

'I bet Jim ate half of that. How is he Lil? Still driving you mad with all that wheezing?'

Lil's eyes fell to her lap.

A difficult silence settled, smothering all laughter.

'What is it Lil? What!'

Paleness replaced Lil's usual rosiness.' Wren he died just before Christmas.'

'And you didn't tell me...I would have been over like a flash.'

'I know you would pet and that's why I never let you know. Saul told me how full this place was for the festive season and how busy you were.'

'But...'

'But nothing Wren. You were wonderful to 'im when he were alive. He would understand.'

'Oh Lil. You must be so lonely all by yourself.'

She noticed the furtive look between her and Sir Saul before she answered.

'No, not at all. I gave me council house up Wren. A young couple from High Spen jumped at the chance. I live at Amblin now.'

Wren waited for more.

'Well Saul needs me as he is getting' on. It was daft all that travelling when I had nothing to go home for weren't it?'

Saul kept his eyes from Wren's and Lintern's but they both noticed that Lil had used 'Saul' not 'Sir'.

All questions and embarrassment hung like lead in the silence.

'Coffee?' Lintern pushed back his chair. 'We've got some Nescafe just for you Lil.'

'Ooh lovely. I can make that mud but I can't drink it!'

Two days passed in mutual pleasure of showing off and appreciation. It became clearer that Saul and Lil were mixing the soil of the past with the seed of the future and Lintern was happy. Wren copied out several recipes for the woman she loved but the favourite was Rose Pudding from the court of Richard the second. Saul laughed at every quip of Lil's and Lil fussed over her employer in a much more familiar way than she had, taking hairs from his shoulders and crumbs from his moustache with great fondness.

'We love the herb garden and the vegetable plots. You have a fine crop of asparagus promised. I wish you had time to do Amblin garden. Smith doesn't have the touch although things are a lot easier to manage since you sorted it.' Saul guided Lil to the most comfortable sofa in front of the tea tray after the walk they'd taken to allow Wren and Lintern to get ready for the guests arriving the following afternoon.

The energy between the four was heavy with un-asked questions straining silent tongues.

'If you didn't need our beds you'd not be getting rid of us you know.' Lil said watching how Wren gracefully served tea. The whispering liquid stopped tinkling into the thin and pretty cups.

'Oh. I...'

'She's only paying you a compliment Wren. We both are. You have made this place fabulous.

Anyway, we are having a night in Harrogate.'

It was the first time Wren had ever seen Lil blush.

'It seems a shame to come all this way and not show Lillian my old haunts. Besides I want to visit Marshall and Snelgroves for a couple of new suits. Promised Lillian a new hat for Sundays.'

Lil tried to water her embarrassment by searching for words, any words. 'But I'll not be forgetting how to make your Lemon Drop Scones or that hot buttered cinnamon toast Saul can't get enough of.'

When Merle returned next day she brought with her a little box of Rington's tea in a tin caddy with the Tyne Bridge, Holy Island and Dunstanburgh Castle painted on.

'Just a little thank you for looking after Wobblybob, he look so well.'

Lintern had been loading the car ready for Lil and his grandfather to start the drive back to Amblin Hall via Harrogate when Alan and Merle had come up the drive in the land Rover. Alan stopped to help, urging his girlfriend into the house.

'Oh; and who is this?' Saul looked surprised as he came into the kitchen with his morning tea tray.

'This is Merle my second right arm. Merle this is Sir Saul, Lintern's grandfather.'

He stepped forward eyes glowing but not just with the appreciation of meeting a pretty girl.

'How charming,' his senses searched hers, darting in need of recognition. 'I have the distinct feeling we have met before. Where are you from?'

'Charente in South west France Monsieur, a little town called Chalais.'

He looked predictably enchanted by her smile and accent.

'Well, I've never been there and yet...'

Lintern came in then with Alan.

'Grandfather is your suitcase ready.'

'Yes dear boy it is on the bed.' Both men caught the searching look going from Merle to Saul but when Lil flurried in it was nowhere near satisfied.

Lil looked at the pair and then at Wren. No smile altered her face.

'Oh Lil, this is Alan and Merle, the help we told you about.'

'Charmed I'm sure.' she said before walking past them to the car. Wren followed her out to find her dusting the Spirit of Ecstasy with her hanky.

'Lil; are you all right?'

Before she could answer the other three came out carrying luggage. Merle had the plastic containers of the food Lil and Wren had spent the day before experimenting on.

The car was packed, watched by an unusually quiet Lil. When only Lintern and Wren remained outside Saul hugged them both, beaming his admiration.

'It has been a pleasure having you Grandfather. I'm so glad you are looking after him Lillian.'

Saul started the engine but Lil found it hard to leave go of Wren before getting into the car.

'Watch those two Wren.' she whispered as she bussed her cheek. 'It wasn't just Saul that woman couldn't take her eyes off. Too pretty by far.'

'Oh Lil. They are all right. They're hard workers.'

'Doesn't mean they won't be trouble. He looks familiar. You don't like him do you?'

'Not much. He's actually from our council estate, knew him when I was little.'

'What's his name?'

'Alan Taylor.'

'What; those scruffs? 'im and 'is brother used to chalk all over me wall, never knew I knew what those stupid words meant. Chased them with the broom one day, they sent in the parents. Mother's got a gob on her. She's a right one, trouble from all accounts.' Wren's heart fell when she remembered the Christmas abuse from Alan's mother. It had affected Ivy badly.

'Are you coming or not Lillian? White Swan for lunch!' the voice intruded.

'Yes of course.' Lil said pushing her ample bottom onto the leather seats.

'Isn't he supposed to be in the army?' she whispered into Wren's final hug.

'He was.'

'I think you'll find he still is Wren. Have you asked him why he's not there?'

'Come on, break it up you two. We want to get to Harrogate before dark you know.' Saul laughed.

Wren clung to the look between Lil and herself as the car pulled away. Thoughts, dug up, threw bones of dread into the settling dust.

Lintern took advantage of Merle and Alan already being at the Lodge to call a briefing about the expected guests of the following day. Wren was relieved to hear Lintern would be doing the gun activities allocating almost all the fishing to Alan.

When Wren was alone with Lintern she voiced something that had been gathering in her head.

'It's time we put those two on an official footing.'

'What do you mean?'

'National health stamps, income tax.'

Lintern groaned.

'It's important Lintern. If they get caught so do we.'

'OK. We'll sort it. Now have you got everything in hand for the guests?'

It may have been happening before Lil pointed it out but now Wren noticed every smile, each lingering look Merle gave Lintern.

'Don't be silly!' Lintern said when she mentioned that she seemed too familiar with him. 'She's our staff; she has to talk to me.'

'Not with those eyes.'

'What? Don't be silly. She is pretty involved with Alan in case you hadn't noticed.'

'Is that the only reason?'

'The only reason what?'

'That you don't respond?'

'There's nothing to respond to Wren. What's brought this on?' His voice had softened when he realised she was serious.

'Wren you are the one for me. I love you, we work well together and we have a past life link that will always keep us together remember.'

He pulled her to him. 'Silly baby. Why would I want any-one but you?'

'What if you had an even stronger past life link with some-one else? What if I were the wrong person for your love?'

'What? What a silly….Well I'd know now wouldn't I? You are the only one for me.'

His kisses convinced her.

Almost.

The fresh guests were active and demanding. Wren and Merle were making lavender and lemon scones and rosemary jellies for afternoon teas when Merle asked a surprising question.

'Did you know there is new pit owner at Garesfield?'

'What...where?'

'Where your dad used to do the work, Alan's too, there have been some changes.'

'Oh, how do you know?'

'Alan took me. That pit is surrounded by wonderful woods. I walked for hours in between lush ferns and foxgloves. I felt I belonged there, did not want to leave. And the birdsong....it reminds me of my Charente.'

'Don't they kill songbirds for fun in France?'

'Some do, some eat! Not me. My ears need them as much as my soul.'

Wren wasn't sure why she felt shocked and so uncontrollably jealous.

'Did you go to my wood?'

Merle rubbed butter and flour crumbs from her hands and reached for the sugar bag.

'Your wood?'

Suddenly this conversation made Wren's legs shake.

'On the other side. Behind the ducats, the houses the miners live in.'

'No houses now, just piles of the yellow bricks and the rotten wood.'

Wren watched Merle pour lavender infused milk into the scone mixture before she forked it into a ball.

'Rat infested slums Alan's mam said, addled the brains of any-one who lived there.'

Wren turned away and stirred her bowl of hot water and sheets of gelatine fighting to hold back the tears.

Merle picked up the rolling pin and lightly rolled her lemon and lavender mix on a floured board.

'I went to the woods though, on myself walk. Beautiful! Your woods you say?'

'I grew up there. Couldn't get enough.'

'Well this I understand. My father took me to the woods every opportunity he had, when I baby small. I loved them so much he gave them to me.' Merle's face reflected the beauty of her thoughts.

The tension in Wren's throat refused to be swallowed away.

'Your father gave you woods?'

'Yes, silly is it not? Well, they weren't his to give this of course but whilst I was little I believed him. He meant I deserved them, you know, for the spiritual as I knew every plant, animal and bird. He named me after sweet little bird you know. Merle, it French for, what you say? Blackbird? I lived to be in those woods. It was my form of escape.'

'Escape?'

The door opened to allow Alan's head to shoot around.

'They're back early for tea, four full afternoons on the veranda OK? '

Merle rose to shove the scone dotted tray into the oven before filling the big kettle.

'Cucumber sandwiches?' she trilled busily.

But Wren's thoughts were not on tea or guests.

Wren pulled two tea trays out of the cupboard.

'Yes, and rare roast beef with horseradish. Have those orange blossom angel cakes cooled enough for the icing?'

Such deep thoughts would have to be travelled to later and in private.

The mood was lost to work but Merle's words clung to the back of Wren's brain. This girl was so like her. A little songbird. It was strange that her father had given her woods too.

Merle was sitting at Lambing Cottage door between two old enamel pails bursting with red geraniums, Wobblybob on her knee; she was rubbing the cat's ears to eye closing ecstasy. Wren stopped just as she reached the gate and the two women's eyes met.

The mid-summer wind pushed its silky fingers through her hair. Somewhere in the bushes a wren sang its uplifting song clearly into the air. It didn't stop as Wren slipped closer but a second wren, probably its mate, replied in equally delirious tones.

Wren put a finger to her lips when Merle saw her. The women listened together until Chummy, tired of some fascinating smell which had held him up in the lane, caught up and scrabbled to put his nose to the cats.

'Troglodyte Mignon.' Merle whispered with a wink to the dog.

'Trog who?'

'The bird; it French name. It my favourite song. Did you know it is mightier than the eagle when defending its young? They are my special birds. God sends them to be with me.'

Too shocked into deep implications to say anything Wren just listened to the chattering alarm call replacing the song.

Eventually Merle smiled her way back from her reveries.

'Did you want me?'

'I...yes. I thought we might try that lamb and bean dish you told me of but I can't remember what kind of beans you said.'

'Ah oui, Flagelot.'

'Oh. I doubt if my grocery supplier has ever heard of them.'

Merle lifted Wobblybob from her knee much to Chummy's delight.

'I have these in cupboard, enough for a trial anyway.'

Wren followed Merle into the kitchen.

'You are lucky to know all these rustic French recipes. Did your mother teach you to cook?'

'Well sort of.'

'She sort of taught you?' Wren asked.

'No. She was sort of my mother.'

'What do you mean? '

Merle looked pained and Wren was beginning to wish she hadn't pursued the subject.

'I never knew my real mother, she die when I was born. Her mother brought me up. Grandmere never let me forget I killed her daughter.'

Astounded Wren could only utter 'Oh, how odd.'

'Yes it was odd all right. She was resentful of me, had a temper. I left as soon as my Cher Papa died. I couldn't bear to be in that house and not hear him call me his 'Toto' or his Poussin, it mean chicken.'

Implication slammed unmercifully into Wren's memory.

'You left her on her own?'

'Oh no. My sister and brother are there. She could bear to look at them when they entered the room. But not me.'

Cold, damp doubt crept over Wren. Too many similarities. Should she say? Should she ask this happy girl who she really was?

Merle got up to find the beans.

'Here. And,' she smiled taking two bulbs of garlic from the rope, 'you will need this, and thyme.'

Wobblybob followed them to the top gate before deciding that he wouldn't cross his territory boundary even for Chummy. He'd never met the girl cats who ruled the Lodge, but he'd smelled them. Since his visit to the vets he had no interest in females or fighting. Merle and Wren laughed at his predictable behaviour before falling in easy stride together towards the lodge.

'How did you come to York?' Wren asked when her brain seemed to have set in order the first dollop of similarities. Merle smiled showing the lovely teeth that would soon part to allow the charming accent to fill the air.

'English was my best subject at school. I saw picture of York Minster in book. I felt drawn to the place and its history so I asked our man who grew onions how to cross the channel and he told me. I hitch-hiked to York and easily got a job in hotel.'

The similarities were clanging alarm bells but Wren had no control over her mind.

'And Alan? How did you meet him? '

Merle smiled then. 'Well I caught him going through the restaurant bins when I went to them.

I have always loved the red hair.'

'Weren't you afraid of him?'

'At first yes. But one day I noticed he was limping. I dressed awful cut on his foot. That's when I started keeping back the good food so he could grow strong.'

This was too much for Wren.

'One night I let him take a bath in a room just vacated by the guests. I was caught and sacked. Alan felt so guilty but he didn't know where I'd gone.'

'So how did he find you?'

One day he came into the pub on the waterfront where I had begged for a job. He was all clean then, told me he had a job and a cottage. He came in every week for a drink. He knew I missed the countryside and woodland so brought me up here. We became close.'

'You were here before you talked to Lintern about the job weren't you.'

Merle tried to hide the flush that spread over her face.

'I'm sorry. How did you know?'

'Just a feeling.'

'I didn't know you then Wren. As soon as I saw Troutbeck, it big shock, I felt at home. I feel much strongly about the whole place and the people.'

'People?'

'Yes, you and Lintern. He is a wonderful man. I feel as if I have known him for ever.'

If ice could have grabbed her heart it couldn't have frozen any quicker.

CHAPTER FIFTY THREE

The guests rolled in mostly by recommendation now. Some people returned for a second and third time wanting to restore their souls on the North Yorkshire moors, eat wonderful unusual food or take pleasure from the guns and fishing. All were bathed in sweet strains of Mozart or Bach to accompany silver teaspoons tinkling onto china saucers.

Merle and Alan worked hard. Lintern remained his loving self but exhaustion was taking almost all their private time together in sleep.

'We're not taking any bookings for the last few days of August.'

Lintern was massaging the muscles on the back of Wren's neck that had grown tense with a packed weekend full of demanding though appreciative Canadians.

'But we have several letters of enquiry.'

'We don't have to take them.'

'Why? '

'Because I want you to have a rest for your birthday.'

'My birthday?'

'You don't think I would have forgotten do you?'

He moved strong fingers down her back. She relaxed at the massaging love.

'I'd take this for a birthday present any day.'

'You need a break and lovely food you haven't cooked yourself. It's time you replied to those letters from Spain. You are so excited to read of Joyce's plans to become a third world doctor but you don't tell her. George and Joyce will think you have forgotten them.'

'They know how busy we are.'

'Would you like to take a week off so we can visit them in Spain? '

Instead of being pleased, thoughts of the remotest chance of meeting Warwick punched into her stomach. She stood up.

'Hey, I thought you were enjoying that!'

Merle and Alan arrived at seven thirty for the breakfast briefing that had become standard after guests had left. Lintern told them of his planned treat.

'Your birthday! What date exactly?' Alan asked dipping his bread into bacon fat and ketchup.

'Thirtieth of August.'

Alan looked at Merle and winked.

'That's near Merle's birthday. We could have a joint celebration.'

Lintern brought the coffee pot to the table.

'Is it Merle? When?'

Merle blushed knowing that Wren would want a treat to herself.

'It doesn't matter.'

Alan spooned three sugars into his tea then stirred noisily.

'Don't be silly Merle tell them. It's the sixth of September only seven days after yours Wren.'

The voices around her faded into space. What did he say? Only seven days? It was a sentence that had haunted her all her life.

'Wren? Wren? Are you all right?'

Unwillingly she had to let Lintern's concern into her brain.

'Yes... I.'

'See, you need a break more than you'll admit.'

'It's all go go go; Mademoiselle Wren.'

They were polishing the largest bedroom after stripping the beds and allowing the dust to settle.

'It is frantic sometimes, all rush.'

Merle dabbed her cloth into the Lavender smelling polish tin.

'Don't you feel as if you got here in a rush Wren?'

'Where?'

'Here. The world. Your life.'

'What do you mean? '

'Well I have always had a feeling of being born into the wrong place and in a rush.'

Merle mistook Wren's inability to speak for disbelief.

'Oh I know it sounds mad, but I have always felt that. When I was a child at school I felt alone in the schoolyard. I always felt French wasn't the language I should have been speaking. When the school began to teach us English I felt as if my brain had been made for it. I outshone every-one else in the class.'

Merle polished on, withdrawing into her swirling thoughts when Wren's lack of comment suggested disinterest.

'Where do you think you should have been born?' Wren asked knowing yet dreading the answer.

'I didn't know. It wasn't until I arrived in York that I felt happy. Then when I came here my happiness went up. Those woods of yours at Garesfield gave me such a feeling as if I was genetically programmed to roam them. I suppose the answer to your question is England. I should have been born in England. In the middle of a forest like the birds. The songbirds we both are.'

Wren so needed to be alone with her throbbing head to prevent her anxiety smothering her thoughts.

'This polish is so cloying. I need fresh air. Can you finish off do you think?'

Merle looked embarrassed. 'Of course, I sorry...I do silly talk sometimes when I busy!'

Chummy followed at Wren's jogging heels until she reached the little hill from where it was possible to look down to all that was Troutbeck.

She pushed her back to the stone wall where it had been mended by Alan. Before he came it had been impossible to sit here without being attacked by the north wind searching for the smallest chance to chase you off in case you wore out the view it thought its own.

It was possible to see her life from here.

The contentment, the success, the love.
She knew now that it was not hers.

It all belonged to Merle. Even Lintern.
Especially Lintern.

FINAL CHAPTER

'Do you like Merle, Lintern? '

Lintern was just stretching himself awake unknowingly joining the state Wren had been in since two am.

'Mmm? Where's my coffee?'

'Lintern! Answer me. Do you like Merle?'

'Yes, yes you know I do.' he yawned. 'She does an excellent job. But right now I'd rather talk about that smell filling our bedroom. Is it hot?'

'What?'

'The coffee!'

Wren pushed back the covers to pour a second cup, when she left it on his side cupboard she returned to the bed sinking down to snuggle into his back.

'Mmm, now this I like even better.'

He turned to smooch her neck but she eased back so that she could see into his eyes.

They were shut.

'Lintern; please. I need to know. Do you like Merle? Especially like her?'

He groaned. 'Oh for goodness sake, what's this about? You're blinking birthday again? Oh share it if you want but I was looking forward to taking you to Spain.'

'I don't mind sharing my birthday with Merle. She's nice, isn't she? What do you think of her?'

Realising he wasn't going to get what he sought under the covers he pushed himself up to take his second choice of pleasure.

'Yuk?'

'What?'

'It's lukewarm.'

Wren stood up to take the cup from him.

'I'll make fresh. Just tell me first, how much do you like her?'

'I'll love and adore her every inch, as long as it gets you out of here and to the kettle.'

Wren fixed his look.

'How much do you like her Lintern? Just tell me. I won't be cross.'

'I like her enough to have a special meal with her to celebrate both your birthdays. There, are you happy now?'

In the kitchen Chummy had returned from his early morning toilet with a wet curly tummy and sodden paws. She was only half pulled into reality.

'You been gathering dew from the lawn again?' She closed the door so that he wouldn't jump all over Lintern and the bed. He whined when he noticed Dumpling and Pudding still curled up in his basket. He knew he had no chance. The cats would be where the cats wanted to be.

'Never mind.' she rubbed his ears trying to miss the wet bit at the ends. 'Just a few minutes; we'll be out by seven for big walkies.'

She left him to a biscuit and wagging his stumpy tail.

Chummy was off over the moors enjoying the August warmth and the company of the two people he loved most. Wren watched him snuffling in the bracken; occasionally looking back to assure himself they were there. He did that with Merle too when she took him down to Lambing Cottage for the bone she kept especially when she'd cooked a gigot. Even dogs had karma and past life loves.

Wren wondered what Alan and she were doing right now, both of them luxuriating in the late start they had whenever the Lodge was closed to guests. Her mind would only let one image in, the same haunting sight she had hated herself for retrieving.

'Shall we call at Lambing Cottage to make some arrangements?' she spoke too loudly trying to blast torturous thoughts away.

'Goodness! You are keen to get this birthday organised. Don't you want to see George and his girls?'

'Of course, but we can go later, when the Yorkshire cold slaps our ears and bites our bums.'

Lintern laughed. 'Hey, that's the cold I was brought up with you're talking about! You can't miss a single second of your English summer nature can you?'

He aimed his special two toned whistle at the spaniel as he wrapped her shoulders in his left arm to guide her to the two people she knew fate was about to hurl at her.

Merle and Alan were sitting on two pine kitchen chairs at the door of Lambing Cottage. They put cereal bowls to the ground, embarrassed that they'd been caught having such a late breakfast.

Chummy ran to join Wobblybob in lapping the last of the milk and escapee Rice Krispies.

'What no bacon and mushroom sandwiches this morning Winger?' Lintern jibed as he approached the pair shielding their eyes to the sun backed silhouettes.

'Bloody range is blocked, won't light again. Throwing smoke into the room not the chimney.'

Alan yanked his thumb behind him. 'I'll have a look at it later, before September forces us to have it on for heat.'

Merle smiled as she rubbed Chummy's head in welcome. 'None of my French coffee this morning either, can I offer you glass of milk?'

'Thank you, no.' Lintern held his palms towards her and laughed, 'We don't want to intrude on your day off. Just called to ask what you fancy doing for this joint birthday.'

'So you aren't off to Spain to visit your Uncle?' Merle smiled with relief just as she caught Lintern's wink.

Wren hated the way Alan pushed his gaze into her, it was too intimate. He might not mind that their partners were flirting but she did. Didn't she?

'Winger and I might just rustle up a surprise for you two actually. What do you say?'

The men went off behind the kitchen with a conspiratorial punch to each other's chests.

Wren smiled as Merle rolled her eyes skyward. 'I hope it doesn't involve them cooking.'

They both giggled but only Wren knew that something much more important than birthdays was gathering energies around them. Or did she? Her gaze lay on Merle longer than it should have.

Wren's thoughts kept wandering off in so many directions. Different things from her time with Merle burned bright with a new clarity.

The men, acting more like schoolgirls than the macho beings they hoped they were, Merle commented, had banned the women from entering the Lodge for a whole afternoon just a couple of days before Wren's birthday.

Out on the terrace with nothing to do but fight her growing jealousy or admire the view Wren stood up.

'Will you help me gather flowers Merle?'

From the tool-shed, the two women took an enamel bucket each and secateurs.

'There's not much in the way of colour except for second flush roses and a few early dahlias.'

Wren watched Merle throw the rubber ball Chummy had been chewing. His pleasure was palpable. He loved her too. Merle was very loveable. Lintern was very lovable.

She watched the dog retrieve the ball with gravel scattering enthusiasm around the herb garden paths. Finally he walked off with the chewed toy in his mouth and a sunny spot on his mind.

The women, delighted when they reached the bed of forgotten Japanese anemones, stopped.

'Sometimes I think we are like flowers Wren. They have life too. Maybe they think like us. There are not words to describe what it is all about and yet we know it all every second we are here.'

How wise, thought Wren, this simple country girl, speaking in a foreign language, hit such a spot she knew existed but could not vocalise.

'What flower do you think Chummy would be Wren?' They watched his wagging tail disappear into the vegetable plot.

'Oh that's a hard one. Something open and energetic... a Marigold perhaps.'

'Yes that would be him.' she bit her lip thoughtfully. 'I would be a...a French chicory flower quivering on a rubbish tip wasting my bright blue beauty with no one realising I am there.'

Wren felt her heart flip over. She couldn't know what she'd just said; could she?

'And you Wren, let me see. Ah yes, a snowdrop...popping up in a new place, unexpected but brilliant in the dull cold earth.'

'Snowdrops don't last too long.'

'No, but they die down to allow other flowers to flourish in their place, covering their fading leaves with new growth pushing towards the summer. So they are pure and kind?'

Wren knew Merle meant the words to complement but they struck a truth she couldn't have known on anything but the highest level. Immobilised with deepening realisation Wren watched this delightful French girl as she chose pink and white flowers with the best heads carefully avoiding the budding stems.

'What would Lintern be? Can you imagine him as a plant?' she asked.

Merle's back straightened as she looked to her left whilst she searched her imagination. A soft smile came to her. Sheer pleasure, that was what Wren saw in her face. Sheer pleasure.

Eventually Merle said. 'Lintern, now that would have to be some plant. Great to look at, strong, generous, something to treasure. A lucky find on a dull afternoon. Something that brought the sun into an otherwise average day. I know! A sunflower. We have fields of them in France but he would be a rare breed that had grown special. One that every-one sought from far and wide. Well worth the travel.'

She beamed at Wren not realising the significance of what she was saying. Not knowing that she was pushing her friend into a decision that would be the hardest she had ever made.

The morning was light and airy and spoke of excitement of a special day. They brought breakfast paraphernalia in from the veranda, dancing with plates held high as the sniffing cats swirled around their ankles.

'I've got to go into York to pick some things up.' Lintern busied about looking for his keys amongst the breakfast cups.

'Are you taking Alan?' she asked scraping bits of cheesy scrambled eggs into cat dishes.

'No I er...' he turned his back guiltily. 'I've sent him up to the back wood to log that fallen tree. He'll be too busy for firewood next week when those Australians arrive.'

There was an abruptness in his kiss which almost masked the secrecy holding back his smile.

'When will you be back?'

'Don't know?'

She dusted off her hands.

'I'll come with you, could do with a bit of a shop.'

'No!'

Her head shot up at his unusual abruptness.

'I mean...relax here. Tomorrow is your birthday and what I have in store will have you exhausted. Just take it easy.'

'I'll wander down to Lambing Cottage; take some of that fish we have left over for Wobblybob. Dumpling and Pudding are sick of the sight of it.'

She saw his brain ticking.

'I'll drop it off as I pass if you like.'

'No I fancy some company and a walk.'

'Er, well I don't think Merle will be there. Or she'll be busy. Stay here. Put your feet up.'

He gathered the parcel of fish with his keys from the table.

When the door closed Wren felt her heart copy. It had pain to deal with. Thundering, crucifying pain.

Alone on the terrace where they'd had such memories of lavender cream teas and laughter, Wren leaned on the rail to look out over the view that had taken her breath away the first day she had set foot on Troutbeck. Now she had to leave.

Seconds ticked by. Never had she been so alone.

Wren asked the light for help. As ever, none came. She didn't deserve it in this stolen time. It would be wrong. Just like everything she ever did in this life. This wrong life

Chummy, was hurt too. He would have wanted to go in the Land Rover wherever it went just as long as Lintern was driving it. He looked sad when she turned to his whining.

'Come on Chummy. We'll walk some happy endorphins into our brain, shall we?'

He didn't look convinced but it was the best offer he'd had. Heavily they made towards the gate.

Wren felt she had to turn left so that there was no glimpse of Lambing Cottage, empty because she knew for certain that Lintern had taken Merle with him. She was surprised to see the back of the Land Rover as it returned to the road. Lintern must have just left the cottage. Why had he taken so long? Her head turned to see Merle just leaving the gate with the wrapped fish in her hands.

'Merle!' The French girl turned with embarrassment in her smile which she tried to dissolve as she waited for Wren to catch her up.

'What are you doing?' Fury leaked from her brain into her words.

'I...I was taking this to Wobblybob. Lintern has gone to talk to Alan before he....before York.'

Merle looked flushed with the effort of some-one thinking of an alternative to the truth.

'But he left age's ago.' Wren was close enough to smell her 'Jolie Madam' scent freshly applied.

'Yes I met him at the gate. When I asked him what kind of fish is this, he laughed and said not to worry he hadn't caught it.' she gave a diluted, forced giggle. Wren knew her face was stony.

'You know.' Merle's face showed too much and she stuttered at the words. 'Th... That story about when he was six and Saul taught him to fish. He must have told you.' when it was obvious Wren had no clue Merle gabbled on not wanting to upset her employer further.

'For two days he caught nothing. On the third day the stubborn boy he was wouldn't leave the river until he had proved he could be a big, strong fisherman. Everyone went home but he stayed behind. As it was getting dark the grown-ups hatched a plan. Some-one distracted him whilst Saul put a kipper on his hook so that when he returned to his rod after drinking the pop they had brought him, he was triumphant. Lintern said he was eighteen before the penny dropped and he realised a kipper was a smoked herring from the sea.'

Wren fought her tongue into submission. Pushing down thoughts of murderous revenge gagged in her throat. It was here again, that easy need to kill for revenge.

'Oh but you must know that story. I am sorry if I bored you. Did you want to catch Lintern?

He said he'd only be a short while?'

He was coming back for her?

Jealousy and resentment hauled murderous thoughts from where Wren had tried so long to bury them. Lintern had never told her that secret of his childhood yet he had laughingly recounted it to this pretty and enticing girl who all too plainly adored him. When? When had they been so intimate?

'No. Chummy is expecting his walk.' she said abruptly as she turned with her fists clenched to her side. Killing desires clung heavy and damp around her brain. Sometimes they were too hard for her to hold in.

She made her way off the road and along the edge of the wood relieved that the sawing she could hear was deep within it. Alan was the last person she wanted to see. He would only gloat at her unhappiness whilst pretending not to notice. He, plainly, had not sensed the growing closeness between the two people he most loved. Contradictory loyalties came in assaulting gulps.

Her feet were as sore as her mind when two hours later she rounded the top of the hill to smell woodsmoke. Alan would be burning the litter of the fallen tree. Yet; she caught sight of a dense column rushing to find the sky. There was too much smoke, great murky billows lifted upward but it was not coming from the wood. As she scrabbled up the shale for a better view Wren's eyes fell to the source of the blackening plume. It was Lambing Cottage.

Running pounded her fearful heartbeat into her ears as Chummy followed, barking in distress.

The gate flew back on its hinges from frantic hands and the road seemed to have stretched longer and longer.

'Wren!'

The scream came from behind the cottage. Merle had tumbled dirty and terrified out of the bedroom window. Wren ran to her helping her to her feet one of which was twisted.

'What on earth... I thought you'd gone...?'

'It's the stove! I got Alan to fix it so I could make you a special birthday gateaux like my father made me every year. It was so sudden.'

'But Lintern said you were going out!'

'I told him it was a secret, to keep you away. He said when he brought the fish for...Mon dieu!

Wobblybob. He is in there! He was asleep on the sofa!'

Wren watched Merle drag her broken ankle around to the front door.

'No!'

'I must! I'm all he's got.'

If she died in there it would get her out of Lintern's affections and save Wren's conscience from another murder. But that would rob her of her one opportunity. What was she thinking?

She had been told; all those years ago that she had only one. Confusion riveted her to the spot. She became engulfed in such a need for life yet such a desire for death.

Merle pushed the front door open feeding and unleashing a great whoosh of flames. She hesitated, it was almost enough time for Wren to stop her and go in her place but she held a shaking arm over her face and disappeared into the burning house.

Wren felt as if she was halfway to a faint, unable to lift her consciousness enough to take in what her eyes were sending her. Suddenly it was of such monumental importance to save the second body of the spirit whose life she had stolen. New strength shot into her. This was the one chance she had to make up for the terrible crime she had committed. She was on a path too great to stop.

Burning smoke hit the back of her throat stinging her lungs. Blue curtains were being gobbled by the blaze. The old wooden beams were licked in flames; everything above her was on fire.

Wren hit the floor where the air seemed less poisonous. She could see Wobblybob cowering under the dresser. It was too late. His little feline soul had already ascended.

'Merle! He's here!' Wren called to move Merle nearer the door where she could drag her to safety. She heard Merle crawl towards her but just as she reached her back she was pulled away.

'Thank God!'

She heard Alan's desperate voice as he lifted his girlfriend into his arms and out of the house.

Wren tried to stand but the portion of ceiling nearest the fire dropped blocking her exit. Black smoke and heat woofed into her. She heard Merle from outside.

'Wren! Wren!'

Seconds later Alan was moving burning wood with his bare hands. She went towards him but fire fell from above knocking him to the floor.

'Get out Alan! Get out now!'

But he kept crawling towards her. His voice rasped through the suffocating fumes.

'You aren't the only one with Karmic debts to settle Wren!'

'What…do …you…mean?' she half choked, half gasped.

'It was my job to get Merle to Lintern!'

'You can still live! Get out!'

'But there's more. Don't you know Wren?'

He opened his mouth but the smoke he pulled into it felled him. Bits of the cottage burned between them. What was left fell thunderously, crushing the life out of them both.

Wren felt her spirit leave the body she had stolen from Elia, from Merle.

No loved ones came. She had no right to expect Alessandro, but Tot or June? There was no-one.

As her spirit rose above the burning cottage she saw Merle shocked into stillness as she realised there was no hope.

Wren knew Merle belonged to Lintern now. Always did.

The sad thought caused her spirit to go to him. She found herself at the gate she had been offered sixpence to open that very first day she had come here.

Lintern had left his Land Rover door open to pull at the string still used as a fastener.

Driving impatiently almost bumper to bumper was Sir Saul in the Rolls Royce stuffed with Lil, Mr. Foggin and Indira. Beside them was a pretty and very pregnant girl turning a bright new wedding ring as she enjoyed the arm of Jeremy around her.

Lintern was laughing as he climbed back into the Land Rover. Something made him stop mid-step and he turned to where he could have seen her had she been physical. Finding nothing but a feeling, he joined the other people who were laughing. Squashed in the back with luggage weighing down their knees were Betty and Joyce. George was in the front beneath huge string bags of oranges and garlic. He was entertaining them by sticking Tot's pipe into his mouth and doing Popeye impressions.

Wren watched as he returned it lovingly to her painting case beneath the fruit.

'George?' Lintern said as he looked in the rear view mirror. 'I don't know if I need your permission to ask for your niece's hand, but I have a ring in here.' he patted his shirt pocket.

Encouraged by the delighted female passengers he opened the box to show a single diamond ring threaded on the shining strand of Wren's hair that had saved his life.

'It's not just a birthday present. I intend to be with her for the rest of my life. I want to marry her.'

His sheer joy and the pleasure on every-ones faces compounded her need to be with Lintern.

She couldn't leave him now. His heart would crush with sorrow.

She had to re-enter her body.

This had been the surprise Lintern and Alan had prepared for the joint birthday.

She shivered at what the group would discover when they got to Lambing Cottage and Merle.

It took a split second to return.

Her legs, held by a burning beam, had almost disappeared. A stone lintel had crushed her skull to nothing. The hair Lintern so loved was burned away to only an acrid smell.

There was no way she could ever use that body again. It was half destroyed.

'NO...O...O...O!' The wail carried out into the Universe and beyond.

All she could see of Alan was his foot. There was no ascending spirit.

She went to Merle sobbing into Chummy's fur on the grass. He wasn't there. Neither did she sense any guides coming for him.

What a waste, what a ridiculous stupid waste of time, a life and all the anguish and pain. The whole reason she had committed this crime was to find Alessandro and she hadn't even come close.

From her hopelessness she felt something small but great, growing. What? What was it?

'Wren.'

It was a misty, light filled whisper.

But where?

'Wren, my love.'

Not daring to believe what she felt, she oscillated to a splendid violet shimmer.

'Alessandro?'

'My love.'

She felt her energy vibrate with relieved ecstasy but where was he?

'Alessandro! I did it for you, to be with you, but you weren't here.'

'Are you sure?'

'Yes I searched! I examined every place and everyone.'

'I was here.'

'But you weren't. Oh I don't know how I expected you to be when you had such a unique and vital job to do for some-one special. Pain and longing were all I knew without you. I came here to search the world for you. I only got around a tiny portion of it.'

'I have always made my soul an envelope for your soul, my love a grave for your struggles. How could you believe that I would leave you alone to the most important task a spirit has ever taken?'

Confusion muddied her energy.

'But I don't understand. Me? No, that was you!'

His love and light magnified to hold her in safety, wrap her with knowledge.

'Have you never realised. It was you who was needed to be central in this experiment. You were the one pushing human and spiritual boundaries.'

He paused to allow the great new truth seep into her.

'We did not know what was next after we had come countless times into the arena of life and left again, when we had done it all, this was what was next.'

'You are the great one Wren not me.' the energy was thick with love between them.

'It was challenging for me too. I've never had to split my energy like that before. Now we must return together to find out what it is to live above finite things.'

The staggering weight of too many emotions engulfed her.

'But I don't...? Alessandro I searched everywhere life led me. I searched every person I came into contact with. I never found you!'

'I was there. Do you think I would ever leave you?'

'Where? Who were you Alessandro? Who?'

'Wren my love; my soul mate; my heroine of life. How many times have I said that the greatest power in human life is longing.'

'But I longed so much for you, yearned, you never came.'

'Didn't I? It was right that you couldn't know me.'

'Tell me Alessandro. Tell me! Who were you? '

The vital spiritual energy rose to an almost unbearable shimmering brightness. She needed this love to understand his answer. When it came it shot her backwards through each moment, every agony of her wrong life.

Wren, I was every-one.'

Ends.

Wrong Life, Novel by August Smith

Poem 'What is Dying?' Written by Bishop Brent.

Made in the USA
Middletown, DE
16 September 2025

17689021R00337